County Council

Libraries, books and more . . .

11/6/15 2/16 LAD 29/3/19 I		
WITHDRAWN		

Please return/renew this item by the last due date.
Library items may be renewed by phone on
030 33 33 1234 (24 hours) or via our website
www.cumbria.gov.uk/libraries

Cumbria Libraries
CLIC
Interactive Catalogue

Ask for a CLIC password

First published in 2014
by Hansib Publications Limited

P.O. Box 226, Hertford, Hertfordshire, SG14 3WY
United Kingdom

www.hansibpublications.com

Copyright © Donald Hinds, 2014

ISBN 978-1-906190-68-2

A CIP catalogue record for this book
is available from the British Library

Printed in Great Britain

*"England expects! England expects!
No wonder they call her 'The bloody Mother Country'!"*

Attributed to F.S. Trueman
Yorkshire and England's greatest fast bowler

Also by Donald Hinds

Journey to an Illusion: The West Indian in Britain (1966)

Black Peoples of the Americas, 1500-1990s (1992)

Claudia Jones: A Life in Exile (with Marika Sherwood and Colin Prescot, 2000)

At last a novel dedicated to my wife, Dawn, who has had to wait a long time and who patiently shook me back to reality as I stood with shoulders bent and downcast eyes at yet another rejection from literary agents and publishers. The spell is now broken!

I wish to thank my readers, Morag Thompson, "MB", Nilu York, Diane Langford, Jon Newman and Professor Kester Isaac-Henry for their insightful comments. The faults, however, remain mine alone.

PART ONE

In the wake of a dream

So you have seen them
with their cardboard grips,
felt hats, rain-
cloaks, the women
with their plain
or purple-tinted
coats hiding their fatten-
ed hips

The Arrivants: Rites of Passage,
Edward Brathwaite, London, 1967

1

Flight-Lieutenant Melbourne Welch first came to Brixton in the late summer of 1945. He had just won the war; but that was not a lap of honour. He had another year to go before demobilisation. What was uppermost in the young veteran's mind was that he had missed the great black American saxophonist, Bigman Ellis, when his quintet appeared at the Arena, Tottenham Court Road. Now that they were appearing at the Empress Brixton he intended to make up for missed opportunities. He was even prepared to face the wrath of the British military in order to attend, though he did not have to, as he had a weekend pass. A saxophonist himself, Melbourne had to hear and see the great man. He had to see Bigman, from whose every pore sweat would ooze as he blew his horn, his eyes bulging. In the beginning Melbourne and his friend Jimmy had decided they would have time to go to Jimmy's white woman friend in Mostyn Road. If they were lucky, they would get two or three hours' sleep before having to hurry to Kings Cross Station to catch the train to their camp in Yorkshire.

Melbourne was surprised how easy it was for them to join the party backstage after the performance. Eventually they ended up at the Black Star Club, off Farringdon Road. This was the haunt of black GIs and black British colonial servicemen and women. Melbourne and Jimmy knew they could spend only an hour or so but that was enough. They were within walking distance of King's Cross, anyway. They were up close to Bigman and Isaac "Fingers" Bone, the pianist. At around two o'clock, the resident band took a break and Fingers sat down and began tinkling the ivories, or as he called them the "bones". Whether by accident or intent Melbourne had his saxophone with him rather than having left it at Jimmy's place in Mostyn Road; he felt awkward standing there holding onto the instrument case.

"Hi, buddy," said Fingers. "You got a gun in there? Somebody tell this guy that the damn war is over." Melbourne took his saxophone from the case. "OK," said Fingers, "it ain't a Thompson machine-gun. Can you blow that horn?"

Melbourne nodded.

"Now follow you' leader." He started off with:

> *Hi, baby, I know why you are cryin',*
> *I know why you are blue!*

Melbourne held his own, moving in unison with Fingers and reining in all impulses to imitate Bigman's phrasings. Fingers was pleased with him. People moved back from the bar and crowded around the impromptu session. It was not yet a contest; Melbourne was not challenging Fingers. Suddenly, the pianist said, "OK, buddy, your call. Take it away." Melbourne took the solo. The ripple of applause emboldened him. Recalling that Fingers was Jamaican-born and had only recently become an American citizen, Melbourne moved effortlessly into:

> *Sly Mangoose, you name gone abroad.*
> *Mangoose go eena Bedward kitchen*
> *Take out one of him righteous chicken*
> *Put it eena him waistcoat pocket*
> *Sly Mangoose!*

Fingers, who had seemed ready to close the session, turned again to the keyboard. He looked at Melbourne. This cheeky puppy had stolen a march. He would teach him. The contest had begun. The crowd applauded ecstatically as both players raced neck and neck to a breathless finish. The audience would not let them go.

Melbourne led with:

> *Lay down, Janey, lay down 'pon you back!*

"No, you can't play that!" shouted an embarrassed Jimmy. "That is pure rudeness! We have ladies from Jamaica here, man."

Despite the fact that many warriors, men and women from the island were humming the tune Jimmy waved his hands, signalling to Melbourne to stop, but Fingers knew the tune too: *Cock up you foot and take you sago pop.* Eventually they calmed down with, *I went to Sandy Gully...* They closed with, *Gie me back me shilling with the lion 'pon it.*

By this time several of the bandsmen had returned. Eventually it proved irresistible for the great man himself. Bigman joined in, to thunderous applause. The session continued for another half-hour. At the end Bigman gave Melbourne a bear hug, held high his right hand as the referee would a prizefighter who had just won a bruising fifteen rounds.

"Bunny Welch, ladies and gentlemen!" he said.

Since that night, Melbourne found it impossible to separate his moment of triumph from the day he first came to Brixton.

The second time he came to Brixton, he stayed at Jimmy's lady friend, a white middle-aged war widow, who owned a large house in Mostyn Road, off Brixton Road, not far from the Oval. Melbourne did not inquire into the origins of the friendship. He had her down as a shrewd operator, for within three years of the war being over she was running a hostel for black ex-servicemen. It was supply and demand. He never forgot that lesson in economics. When eventually he was demobilised in Jamaica, he quickly returned to London on the *SS Almanzora*, before the cold winter of 1947 had properly started. He remembered his father saying his goodbyes:

> "But, boy, it seems you just come out here to take fire! Them white people not gwine open them arms to you, now the fightin' is over and Mr Hitler is dead. You was never cut out to be a cultivator or... what you call it? Subsistence farmer... so go with me blessing. England no so far away any more. When my generation did go to fight in the First World War it took us six weeks to get to Southampton. Today you fly to New York, then to London, it will take only two days. The world is smaller than when I was your age."

Once in London, Melbourne obtained a long lease on a property in Coldharbour Lane. The basement housed the Colonial Club. The first floor, his flat and a small office and the rest of the house he rented to other ex-servicemen who had been demobilised in various parts of the Empire and had all returned to the Mother Country they had defended from the obscenity of fascism, hoping for and expecting a better life than what awaited them in the colonies.

The immediate post-war years were good for Melbourne. He was on the jazz circuit and his Colonial Club was popular. Apart from his financial security, he enjoyed the atmosphere of London now. True, there were bombed-out sites everywhere, but they served to remind everyone of six years when the Empire and Dominions closed ranks to defend Britain. There had been no pretence that there was not a colour bar. He was one of those who had long supported Learie Constantine's fight against racial discrimination. When racial incidents surfaced many people blamed the sensitivities of a few thin-skinned colonials. He agreed with the local paper, which in 1949 remarked, "... *now the war was passing into history the fascists were back on the streets with their hatred of minorities. They were the crypto-fascists.*" It was they who started the Deptford riots in late summer of 1949. Melbourne was at the trials and later at the conference on Race Relations held at Goldsmith College, supported by the Council of Churches, Civil Liberties and the Trades Council.

Up until then he had been an observer. Then one day in Brixton these "crypto-fascists" propelled him into local and eventually national prominence. It happened quite by chance.

II

As Melbourne came out of the Brixton Tate library he became conscious that something was going on at the corner of Rushworth Street and Effra Road opposite the Orange Luxury Coach Garage. Getting closer, he saw a small group of people gathered around a van that was wrapped in the Union Jack. The British Union of Fascists was back on the streets! As he came into earshot he got the full blast of the speaker's tirade:

"Yet another boatload of these semi-illiterate, semi-savages arrived at Plymouth only last night. Why have they come? I'll tell you. To live off the welfare state. They crowd into rooms like flies round a wound... they are destroying the very fabric of our society... taking our jobs... our houses... They even prey on our women of lesser intelligence, living off immoral earnings. I tell you, no civilised society would put up with this state of affairs except this crypto-Communist government that takes its orders from the Kremlin. The United States of America excludes or severely restricts the entry of these lesser breeds while allowing large quotas of Northern Europeans to enter. Australia does not allow Asians, Negroes or other non-whites to enter their territory; even coloured seamen are not permitted to go ashore on leave when their ships are in port. South Africa, thank God, now has a government dedicated to Separate Development. They recognise that the black man is a million years behind the white race in the evolutionary scheme of things. Yet this government, where ministers give their daughters to blacks in marriage, is hell-bent on an open-door policy that will level the races. There'll be an infusion of Negro blood into the veins of the British working class, which will reduce them racially to the level of Sicilian or Cape Coloured. I say to you that such a racial stew could not have made Britain great."

His colleagues tried to lead the applause, but the crowd showed a lack of enthusiasm. Suddenly above the feeble clapping came the deep booming voice of Melbourne Welch.

"May I remind you it was that same stew of races that smashed the Nazis. Those Aryans, Northern Europeans, the Master Race types you so obviously support, were the enemies a few short years ago. I remember when you would not have been allowed to peddle your cancerous hatred from any street corner of this country. At that time people like me were putting their lives on the line to defend the Mother Country."

The applause was spontaneous and loud, completely throwing the fascist speaker off line.

"Obviously, Britain has an obligation to her coloured colonials," the fascist began lamely. "You, sir, sound like a scholar. We will open our doors to scholars, we must train you for the task of developing the impoverished islands of the West Indies and the dark lands of Africa."

"You are going to train me?" exploded Melbourne. "How dare you assume *you* are my equal, much less of the mettle to instruct me! Tell these good people where you were during the war? Go on. If you were in the same war as me you'd know of Treblinka and Belsen. They were the sum of your philosophy of racial hatred. How could you and I have been in the same war? Here you are standing at the corner of a street in a country I fought to defend, peddling the same obscenities that Hitler engaged in on the street corners of Bavarian towns in the 1920s and 1930s only with less flamboyance."

"I'll have you know that I was on the Normandy beach." The speaker was red-faced and quivering with rage, but he was spared nothing.

"You're a liar and a hypocrite," Melbourne attacked. "If you were on the beaches of Normandy then you must have been fighting against your principles. You must have been a fifth columnist. How many British soldiers did you betray?" The crowd roared its approval of Melbourne. "But this I tell you, and listen well. People like me came to these embattled shores at the invitation of the Mother Country. We were called to put our lives on the line. That we did willingly. Now I have to stand and be insulted by cowards like you. We say wait till there's a Third World War. Hopefully by then we'll be leading our own governments of independent countries. Bases will have to be bargained for, and our young men may not feel disposed to rally around the flag like my generation has just done and my father's generation did in 1914. Think on that..."

The crowd, ever changing, gasped at Melbourne's threat. He tried to regain ground.

"Happily, you're not representative of the great British people." This brought the crowd, which was now about fifty-strong, back to his side. Almost unnoticed the few blacks, who prior to Melbourne's outburst were on the periphery, had been drawn to his side like bodyguards. Blacks and white well-wishers protected him, but with less pretence than the old Fordson van being shielded by the Union Jack. The crowd, which had even attracted a couple of policemen, buzzed with expectancy, awaiting the next statement from either man. What they got was a soprano from the back of the crowd.

"I'm a reporter from the *South London Citizen*. Don't you think this coloured gentleman is more than a match for you? Won't this force you to re-think your attitude to the intelligence of the people you've been deriding?"

"No one here is fooled," said the fascist speaker. "This man is an exception. You can teach a chimp tricks, but a school of monkeys is another thing."

At this unfortunate analogy an agonised cry went up from the small group of coloureds and sympathetic whites. The coloureds surged forward, screams heralding a stampede, and soon battle lines were drawn.

"I believe the wrong type of immigrants are infesting the area. These Jamaicans are mainly ignorant jungle farmers. I was on a troop ship in the West Indies in 1943."

"I'm a Jamaican," shouted Melbourne. "I also have the right, according to the 1948 Act, to say, *'Civis Britannicus Sum.'* Are you aware of the British Nationality Act of two years ago?"

The moment for angry debate had passed. The fascists too had found some supporters, not because of the force of their argument, but in the nature of race relations in Britain anyone claiming to put the interest of whites above all else had to be supported. The police, remembering only too clearly the Deptford Riots of a few months earlier, stepped in and soon dispersed the crowd.

The following week the *Citizen* carried two pictures of Melbourne Welch on its front page. There was a big picture of the uniformed Melbourne at an airbase with planes in the background; the smaller picture was of a studious-looking Melbourne in civilian clothes sitting at a table piled high with books. The headline above both pictures said in Latin, *CIVIS BRITANNICUS SUM.* Bracketed in smaller type was the translation, (I am a British Citizen). The article portrayed the loyal young colonial leaving school and joining the RAF. It was the story of hundreds of thousands of Empire citizens. Men and women, some still in their teenage years, rushing to the beleaguered Mother Country. Many found it difficult to settle down to post-war colonial life. Some returned to help rebuild war-torn Britain and in the process better themselves. The newspaper recalled the arrival of 492 Jamaicans on the *SS Empire Windrush*, two years earlier, seeking a living. The newspaper said that Welch was on the Mayor's list at a reception for some of the *Windrush* men who were housed temporarily at the deep shelter at Clapham. Population shifts were an inevitability of war. Perhaps with colonials coming over here, working and sending money back to their relatives, the colonial economy might improve. This could be a better course than Whitehall's countless Five-Year Plans, which might look good to junior economists in the Colonial Office but went practically unnoticed in the colonies. It pointed out that men like Welch, who was studying Economics, might be showing the way forward. Welch was dedicating his life to better relations between the host community and the newcomers. He was Secretary of the Black Ex-Servicemen and Women and British Citizens Association. He was also owner of the Colonial Club, situated in Coldharbour Lane. The former Flight Lieutenant was also an accomplished jazz saxophonist.

This article led to invitations from the Colonial Office and the Migrants Service Department. They wanted to meet someone who was in touch with immigrants or, as one official at the Colonial Office said, completely oblivious to the fact that his statement was in appallingly bad taste. "People like you who are at the coal face, as it were."

Within a year, Jimmy Fairfax calculated that seven national newspapers had quoted Melbourne on the subject of coloured immigration. It was Jimmy Fairfax who told him that the producer of the BBC Caribbean Programme wanted to speak to him about a broadcast. It was to be a discussion between ex-servicemen and women on Britain now and during the war. Jimmy had shown the producer the article in the *Citizen*. The producer had originally invited Jimmy to speak but the place had now gone to Melbourne. Ever selfless, Jimmy did not mind. Always promoting others, Jimmy would have preferred the position of medieval king-maker to that of a medieval king. Before long Melbourne Welch was a member of the Migrants Advisory Board and for a while was second only to Learie Constantine as the best known black resident in Britain.

2

One Friday evening late in November, about seven years after Melbourne Welch's encounter with the fascists at the corner of Effra Road, two dark figures with slouched shoulders shuffled dejectedly along Acre Lane, moving in opposite directions like two torpedoed hulks on a collision course. Such was the mood of the country at the time towards black migrants that if there was the remotest chance that those two cold-looking figures would sink into oblivion everyone would pretend the collision had never taken place. Muffled against the damp depressing weather they continued to walk toward each other. When scarcely a yard apart, one man swung to his left; the other slowed his pace and swung to his right. As both entered Brixton's main post office, located opposite the Acre Lane entrance of Lambeth Town Hall, they were shoulder to shoulder, like soldiers falling into line, having drilled this routine until each step was perfect.

"Hi, man," said the man, who had turned to his right.

"Ah! co'lad," said the other man. Any bystander listening would be surprised that the second man should address the first by his race. It was some kind of recognition that he was not alone.

Hearing the familiar accent the first speaker needed nothing more to identify the other's country of origin. He was a Jamaican, aged about forty-five, tall and of light complexion. His face was drawn as if he was recovering from a debilitating illness. His moustache was wet. Now that he was in the warmth of the building he pulled his hands out of his coat pockets, held a well-used cotton handkerchief to his nose and blew as if it were a signal of freedom. He examined the handkerchief as though reading an omen of great foreboding.

"Jeesas, man," he said to the first speaker, "Ah tell you, when you blow you nose in this country you 'kerchief turn black." He continued to gaze at the crumpled piece of cloth as if it had incontrovertible evidence that he was in the grip of a terminal malady.

"Been here long?" asked the other man, who wore a London Transport bus driver's uniform with the red fractured circle on his badge signifying that he was a bus driver.

"Five months and three weeks now." He was precise, but spoke with a despondent sigh, uttered over his shoulder. "Them tell me at work that this darkness gwine last till March. True?"

"Yes," said the bus driver. It's winter, you know," he continued in the role of an expert on the vagaries of the British weather. "The days them short now, but come spring and them will start getting long. So you got a job then?"

"Kinda. Doin' labouring on a building site. I was a foreman for the same firm, Biggs, Biggs and Grandy, when they come to Jamaica to build Queen Elizabeth Hospital and the Long Bridge in Portland. Still I suppose it is work. You been here long?"

"Five years." He screwed up his face as his brain raced over the years, "Tell a lie, is eight years." As if to show seniority he added, "I came up in '48, on the *Windrush*."

"Lawdjeesas, you is bornya! Me tell you, me not staying in this country long. Five years will be too long."

"That is what I told meself when I got off at Tilbury 1948, and I'm still here. You better mind that your mouth no catch you out." He bought postal orders and stamps and moved so his new-found friend could get to the counter. Soon both men were outside the post office and facing the Acre Lane entrance to the Town Hall.

"You'll find out that after you put the first winter behind you the others seem to rush past. Wait till winter gone and you will feel alive."

"Alive? Is that what you call it?" He pulled in air through clenched teeth. "Man, is existin' me existin'. You can't call that livin', five big men in a room, three in one bed and two in the other."

"Well, that not too bad comparing with what we used to put up with in '48. Me spent the first six months down in the Clapham underground deep shelter. When we leave there a Pole, he was Jewish, rented us a basement in Aldgate East. Thirty shillings a week he knocked each one for every week. There were eleven of us! Luckily five of us we were on nights so when we got home the other six were at work."

"Well, me not use to it."

"You think me ever got accustomed to it? Me wife said to me later, 'How comes you always write such cheerful letter home 'bout how good things were in London?' Well, you just write home and send the postal orders. You keep hoping that things will get better. We come to the mother country with great expectation! Right?"

"I guesso. By the way my name is Walters, Colonel Walters." He stuck his right hand out, stopping abruptly, so he almost tripped up the other man. Both men shook hands.

"Isaiah Morgan, but everybody call me Ziah. Some of me friends call me Prophet. Hope we will no more be strangers," he said, quickly putting his hand back into his gloves." So what, is Colonel you christening name?"

"Funny, eh? But my mother name me after a' Englishman she was working for around Portland way, a Colonel Edwin Radnor. He must have breed all the young black girls who worked on his estate. I guess that' where I get me brown skin from. So now I got all of that man damn names: Colonel Edwin Radnor Walters. It seems like me mother was trying to show the other girls that she was the Colonel's special. He was a real colonel. Them say he fought in the Boer War. Where I work them call me Nello. I don't mind that too much. Is when they start calling me *Sunshine* and *Curly* that I get vex. If you want to call me Nello, I don't mind."

"There's a place over in Portland call Radnor Valley."

"The same. So you know Portland?"

"Me used to drive bus back home. Remember the Eastern Queen? It was one of the old Greyhound buses the bus company got from America. I was driving it in '48 when I decided to book my passage on the *Windrush* for twenty-eight pounds ten shillings."

"How much! Lawdmegawd, is seventy-five pounds me pay."

"Well, the word for it in this country is inflation."

"Dam' thief me call it. You know what me missed most? Me wife Simmonds Spring bed. Lawd, that woman is fussy about her bedroom. She use to tell me she no care where I rudeness me women them as long it no 'pon her Simmonds Spring." Both men laughed hard, then Nello became serious again. "I made a mistake coming here. I was in a good job paying good money. Boss man liked me; he gave me a letter of recommendation when I told him I was coming to England. That's why the Company Biggs and Biggs took me on without any fuss since I was one of them foreman in their Jamaica business. I still fret, though. But like you say, I can't write home and tell me wife and children that! No, man, I got to say everything is honky-dory, as they say."

"Is like that for everybody when the first winter hit you. To tell the truth, every winter I swear it gwine be the last I spend in this country. Man a got a big toe that never seem to thaw out from the first winter I spent in this country. When it comes to chilblain my feet feel sore, man."

"I shame to say that last week I was so down in the dumps, as they say, that I wonder about committing suicide. You know what stop me? Is that they would bury me in this cold climate, with nobody to bawl over me unmarked grave! I decide I must work and save money so that if I die here some good Christian person would take it 'pon themself to send the body home. Trouble is I don't know personally any Christian person in this country."

"It not that easy to send a body home, you know!" said Ziah, "You mus'n be depress. You getting too down-hearted. You feelin' low because you miss you family them, and because the place where you staying is not too nice. You will soon make friends and everything will look better. I tell you what, come home with me. I think Miss Myrtle, that's me wife, is cooking cowfoot stew and rice."

"Wait a minute," said Nello. "You did say cowfoot stew and rice? I wonder if she cook broad beans in it?"

"Yes, man. There's a place over Aldgate where you can get most of the foodstuff we coloured people eat back home."

"That would make a change from fish and chips, toad-in-the-hole and all that tasteless stuff I been eating for nearly six months," Nello said, trying to fight off another bout of depression. "A well-establish man like you could help a man get a room. If I tell you some of the things that happen in that room, with all five big man them there trying to sleep, you would think I was lying." He paused, looked at Ziah. "Last night two of them bring back one little dutty prostitute and them set 'bout rudenessing off this little white girl. I tell you, she look like a wet chicken. Them 'pon the poor little thing all night. I was so shame, because I always think that sort of business was private. Now you tell me, how you could rudeness a woman with four other man in the same room? I tell you something further, this morning she get up, put on her lipstick, brush her hair, straighten her crush-up skirt and walk out of that room looking like a million dollars. Though I swear is five pounds they give her, you know? And they work that poor girl all night long. One off her, the other 'pon her!"

"Is big money that, you know," said Ziah. "My wife don't take home seven pounds a week after tax. If that girl do that three or four times a week she in big money. When you think that she might be living with somebody in a council flat where the rent only cost fifteen shilling. Of course," Ziah the Prophet said, "if she got a pimp, he'll just take away most of what she earn. A lot of these white girls them go from one coloured man room to another, and these niggers ain't saying no. It seem they feel them manhood is at its best when them climb top a white woman."

"Is revenge, I hear one of the boy say to his mate the other morning."

"Revenge, against who'?"

"Me never ask, but I suppose it got to be against the white man. Is him that start it back in slavery days. And if the man me mother say is me father is true, then it still going on," he said seriously. "I tell you, Ziah, I can't put up with this sort of slack, untidy business. I got to get out of that room. I give anything to be able to lock my own room door and put the key in me pocket."

"Hold on, man, hold on, I might know of something," said Ziah.

"You mean it?" Nello grabbed Ziah's hands. "You really, really mean it?"

"I know of a fellow who is planning to buy a house, but if it go through he won't get his keys until after Christmas. So there won't be any movement until the New Year."

"No mind, man," he was now wringing Ziah's hand. "Put in a good word for me, please, man. I will be in you debt forever and ever, so let it be!"

"OK, OK," said Ziah trying to retrieve his imprisoned left hand as they stepped into the busy road and crossed to the railings outside the Prince of Wales public house.

"I remember when you couldn't get a drink in that pub," said Ziah. "It took a man from Jamaica, an ex-RAF, to cause a whole lot of botheration before we coloured could go in and have a drink. One time this ex-RAF guy, Melbourne is his name, even bring his band and play some mighty blues outside, right here. All the customers come out with them drink to listen. The landlord come and beg Melbourne to come inside and play his music."

"You go to pub?" asked the newcomer, showing little interest in community politics. "You is a real London man."

"Don't tell me you never use to go to the rum bar back home."

"What! Me wife use to say that the Chinee man who owned the bar shoulda charge me rent," they both laughed and slapped each other on the back.

A redheaded boy of about ten stepped up to them, three or four others hung back. "Please, mister, what's the time?"

Nello was about to pull back his sleeve to check his watch when Ziah elbowed him hard, then pointed to the clock above the Town Hall.

"What happen, lads, can't you read the time?" He lowered his voice so that only Nello could hear, "Damn little scallywags! They're teasing you. They only ask coloured people to tell them the time. Them think you have to look up on the sun if you want to know the time."

"I see, I see," said Nello, recalling other times when he had been asked the time. "So where they think I gwine see the sun at this time of the year in this country?"

Suddenly the boys changed tack; they bent their knees and began scratching their ribcages. "Ugh, ugh, Cheetah, Cheetah. Where's Tarzan?" They scuttled off down Coldharbour Lane.

"Back home any little boy do that to big people you fetch him a lick up him backside till him wet him pants."

"Whatever they do," pleaded Ziah, "don't touch them. Pickney and dogs rule this country. Them send you to prison if you so much as kick them dogs."

"No bother me 'bout them and them dogs. A woman got on the bus the other day with this little dog, no bigger than a rat, and it start to lick her face, even her mouth. Hear this other woman, 'He's a friendly little soul, ain't he?' Well, I tell you I feel sick to think of it. Back home dogs live outside. Over here I hear they sleep 'pon their owner's bed!"

As the two men talked, a policeman approached them. "You blokes having a problem?" he asked, not appearing friendly.

"No, officer," Ziah said. "Just trying to tell my friend here that he should come home and eat something before he goes to the picture palace."

"Good idea. So you'll be moving on then," he suggested.

"Yes," said Ziah, towing the puzzled Nello along.

"But we wasn't doing anything," Nello protested in a whisper to Ziah.

"You watch them coppers. Them are no friends of us darkies. Them raid the Coconut Club in Mayhall Road last Saturday and take the name of every man-jack in the club," Ziah's voice sank to a conspiratorial whisper. "If me wife every hear 'bout it, she will kill me. She no know I was at the club last Saturday. You know what happen in these clubs? Music! Drinks! White women! Hardly any black women at all. Our women don't go to pubs and clubs, you know, so is mainly white women there and our white neighbours don't like it one little bit. Police, white neighbours and me wife, no difference between them on that score. I tell you me dead if me wife find out."

Both men started down Coldharbour Lane. At the junction with Atlantic Road they crossed and continued under the railway bridge, past the entrance to Brixton Market on their left. With the Labour Exchange behind them, they faced the tenements of Somerleyton Road and Geneva Road. These black decaying edifices; buildings that had stood for a century or more with their backs to each other as if engaged in a bitter feud for generations, were the refuge of the newcomers. The men waited for a break in the traffic, then ran across the road and turned into Geneva Road. A hundred yards or so along, they went down the basement steps. Ziah opened the door with his Yale key and the smell of highly spiced food simmering on the cooker assaulted the nostrils. Colonel Walters sniffed like a dog gaining on its quarry. A corridor ran the length of the basement. There were two cabinets, perhaps to store kitchen utensils and food, and at the far end a cooker with pots over low fires. Nello had traced the source of the aromatic smell. Ziah squeezed past his bicycle peeled off his coat and hung it against the wall. He knocked timidly at the room door.

"Myrtle, Myrtle, you in there?"

"Is where you expect me to be?" came the reply. "You think me run off with the milkman? Lawd, man, stop you foolishness, you hear."

"Me got company," said Ziah, opening the door only enough for himself to pass through.

"Come in, no! Tcho, Ziah Morgan, you stand 'pon ceremony too much."

On hearing this Ziah pushed the door wide and Colonel Walters followed him into the room. This was the sitting room furnished with two early post-war sofas facing each other separated by a dining table which could seat six. There was a radiogram and Nello recognised the soothing voice of Nat 'King' Cole singing *Love is a Many Splendored Thing*. At the further end of this sitting room was a partition marking the boundary with the bedroom. There was the absence of a door, and stood Mrs Myrtle Morgan. "Sit down nuh!" she waved and smiled.

Nello recalled his manners from back home. "Is stranger visiting Mrs Morgan; and like me grannie would say si'down good me a come."

Behind where the woman stood was a crowded room, but not with bodies as Walter's room in Concannan Road. His eyes took in the double bed, the carefully laid out dressing table and the shine on the polished wardrobes with the suitcases on top of them. Yet it was a tidy room. The counterpane was expensive and decorative, the dressing table uncluttered. A vase with plastic flowers was perched precariously on the mantelpiece, beneath which was a blocked-off fireplace. A paraffin heater in front of the redundant orifice sent out sub-tropical heat.

Myrtle was a black woman denying any suggestion that her ancestors had crossed the paler racial boundaries. She was of medium height, plump and with a pleasant smile. She moved easily towards the visitor, because Ziah had somehow managed to step aside and push his new friend forward so Myrtle could reach the visitor's outstretched right hand.

"Black people aren't strangers in this country, it's just that you no meet them yet." She smiled as she shook hands with Nello.

"Myrtle," Ziah said, "I want you to meet Colonel Walters. We met in the post office. I invited him back for tea."

"For what?"

"For tea."

"Me glad I not gone deaf," she said.

"Please to meet you, Mrs Morgan."

"Same here. Some people call me Miss Myrtle, others call me Aunty. As long as me have the ring 'pon my finger me no particular if people don't call me Mrs Morgan."

"The *Nora Bobb*! Why in Jamaica them call wedding ring Nora Bobb? I must ask Lincoln. I tell who will know, Lonso. These are two clever young coloured boys. You will meet them soon."

"Ziah Morgan, shut you mouth, tcho, man," she scolded her husband, then returned to the visitor. "So you are Colonel? I never know Jamaica got army."

"Me father was a colonel in the English army. Since I come here them call me Nello."

"Don't mind the English, them like shorten everybody name. My name is Isaiah, but from long time people call me Ziah and I don't mind. Still the English call me Zie. Them lazy when it come to call people own name. So, Miss Myrtle, we going to have a cuppa?"

"G'wey, Ziah Morgan. Tea indeed! You too damn English!"

"Me in this country long time. Me is anglicised."

"You is what? Lawd man, don't crack you jawbone with them big word, you hear," she laughed, motioning Nello to a seat at the dining table that was wedged in an alcove to the far right of the room. She opened one of the wardrobes and brought out a bottle of Jamaican white rum, "Ziah, get the glasses. You'll take a little something to wash the smog out of your throat, Colonel?"

"Miss Myrtle, that is the best thing anybody say to me in a long time."

"So," said Ziah Morgan coming in from the passage with the glasses, "is there you choose as the new hiding-place for the rum?"

"Ziah Morgan, stop you foolishness. You think me going to put it back at the same place? If you did have any sense you would shut your mouth and pretend you never know where I got it from, then perhaps I would have made a mistake and put it back," she laughed as she poured the rum.

"What's for dinner?"

"Ziah Morgan, don't give botheration, you hear? Is what you think? Bangers and mash!"

"You want me to beat you, woman?"

"Me going to pretend me never hear what you say. Just one drink and you go wash you' hands in the passage and come and sit down. Nello, I hope you eat cowfoot stew and broad beans."

"Is now I know I dead and gone to heaven. Boy, Gawd good, you see," said Nello. It was difficult to discern whether it was the white rum or sheer emotion brought tears to his eyes. Ziah meanwhile had quaffed his drink and was reaching again for the bottle, but Myrtle grabbed it.

"Tcho, man, no one little spit you spit in me glass? Today is Friday, you know," Ziah protested.

"Eh-eh, what that got to do with the price of anything?"

"I bet me old man and him brother Mass John back home in Zebulon in Portland, Jamaica is drinking right now ena Chin Fat rum bar. Friday is pay-day and I can see them now, sitting around the domino table, laughing and drinking right through till the Chinee man shut up the bar early Sunday morning."

"The old reprobate," snorted Myrtle. "He is preserved in white rum, just like you preserve fruit in rum for the Christmas cake." She stared at her husband. "I hope the money you sent home you got the sense to send it to Gody Madre, because if you' old man Dada Cronji get hold of that money, that's it!" She brushed her hands together as if knocking off dust.

"Now you slandering Dada Cronji," said Ziah in mock petulance. "From I was a little boy Gody Madre always send one of us pickney to the Public Works Depot on pay-day. Ask anybody you please and they'll tell you the same, same thing: as soon as him get paid Dada would take out his drinking money and put the rest away. Him not touching that money till one of us pickney come to collect it."

"You don't get vex with me," she said in a conciliatory tone. "You know I like the old reprobate. How old he be now?"

"Seventy," said Ziah, "and him is as lively as a goat kid."

"You mean an old ram," she said, as she was more than halfway through the door into the passage, so neither man heard her.

Nello shuffled in his chair. Here he was in a well-heated room, with the tantalising aroma of food permeating the place. The banter of his hosts reminded him of his own family and friends back home in Jamaica. Ziah Morgan was like any of the five brothers Nello had left back home: they were loud-mouthed, too talkative and generous to a fault. Myrtle was like four or five of the women he had known when growing up in Radnor Valley. They were the first to be called out when a woman was giving birth or if someone was ill. They would know the right herbs to boil, the right kind of bush-bath to give the sick. When someone died, they would be there to lay out the body. Later they would cook the food, not forgetting the *mannish water* (a soup made from the ram's testicles and penis) for the men who dug the grave and made the coffin. When Miss Myrtle talked of soaking fruit in rum for Christmas cake, she sounded like the women who rallied around at weddings, who made the cake and cooked the curry goat and rice. These women were the heads of their families. Their husbands were usually the men who always had money in their pockets, who wore clean clothes like well turned-out schoolboys but were never henpecked. These were the women men wanted beside them in this country. If he was going to stay here he would have to send for his wife Prudence, although he knew nothing short of a miracle would get Prudence out of her village.

"What happen, man?" said Ziah. "Look like you drop off!"

"No man," said Colonel, "me thoughts was all back home. Me missing me family, bad."

"Never mind. You'll soon be standing on you own two feet. You can send for you wife and really start to make a good life here in London," Myrtle consoled her guest. With equal firmness she turned to both men, "But for the time being you all go wash your hands while a put the food on the table." She gently shooed them out of the door as if they were schoolboys.

They went out into the passage and Ziah took a large bowl from beside one of the cabinets, caught water from the sink near the cooker, topped it up with hot water from the kettle, then propped it on a stool.

"I can't wait to move to somewhere a little more convenient. Never mind," he sighed, then he brightened. "As old-time people always say, 'you got to stand on crooked and cut straight'!"

"You go first," Ziah motioned to Colonel Walters to use the bowl.

"You got a towel out there, Ziah?" asked Miss Myrtle, opening the door and handing a brightly coloured towel to her husband. "Tcho, man, you too forgetful."

Ziah handed the towel to Colonel, who put it to his face and inhaled the camphor.

"Miss Myrtle, if you did want to get rid of me, you going about it the wrong way," he said. Myrtle Morgan smiled and replied encouragingly. "The two of you hurry up, cowfoot get sort of get gooey when it get cold."

There were four dishes on the table, one containing the cowfoot and broad beans stew, another piled high with rice, a third with yam and sweet potato, the fourth with sliced tomato and cucumber.

"Miss Myrtle," began Colonel shaking his head in absolute disbelief, "I never guess that this type food exist in England. Here me was thinking that in England all food were either Fish and Chips or Toad in the Hole!" they laughed, "Is where you get yam and sweet potato from?"

"You can get most things, if you know where to go. There is a stall in Ladbroke Grove Market run by a Greek family. Them sell everything, I think them get them goods from Africa. However, a friend of ours came up last week, so this is real Westmoreland Afu yam."

"Edna is not from Westmoreland," Ziah interjected.

"I know that, but as a Kingston higgler (haggler) I have bought and sold enough Afu yam in my time to know this comes from Westmoreland," said Miss Myrtle, not expecting her expertise to be challenged. It wasn't. "Now grace the table so we can get something to eat."

Isaiah Morgan thanked the Lord for families across the seas, for friendship, and the food on the table. He asked for blessing, then paused and before he thought of anything else Myrtle interjected a loud "Amen".

"You cut me short," he said.

"Well, you didn't have to preach a sermon. The Good Lord is busy. Start helping yourself, Colonel... I mean Nello". Myrtle turned the dish with the stew so that the handle of the serving spoon was pointing towards the visitor. Thus encouraged, Nello tucked in. They ate in silence for a while, then she jumped up, excused herself and went out into the passage, returning with a bottle.

"Carrot juice," she announced. "I had it outside the window in the cold, seeing we don't have a fridge yet. Remind me that I got the jelly outside the window, too."

"I was talking to Nello." he paused uncertain if this was the right time to broach the subject, then he hurled himself forward without any inhibition. "I was saying to Nello that we might know someone who could help him out with a place to live, but it won't be until after Christmas, perhaps early in the New Year."

"Lawd, Isaiah Morgan you mouth can really run way with you, eh! I belong to those people who never feel certain of anything till they have it in their hands signed, sealed and delivered. If you don't put you mouth 'pon people business and it come true, well, there might be something in what you say for true, but let us wait and see."

Colonel was not at all put out by the mysterious reply given by Myrtle. Caution was called for in all instances, whatever the circumstances.

"You is the first coloured people I meet since I come to this country with so much room. How come you get this place?" asked Nello.

"In this country," said Ziah, "is not what you know, but who you know."

" I get the picture," said Colonel, but looking at his host for further explanation.

"This house and two more in Somerleyton Road owned by an old white woman that took a shine to this Jamaican ex-RAF fellow who is a friend of

Ziah's brother and was also in the RAF, so with a little string-pulling he got this place for us."

"As I said," Ziah Morgan began, "is who you know."

"And who they know," intervened his wife.

"All right, all right," Ziah wrestled the conversation from his wife. "Hopeton, that is me brother, he is a big brainist. He just finish studying law, you know."

"Eh, eh, so Hopeton is big brainist? I would not call him that. Everything is due to that wife of his." She leaned over to Nello and spoke in a conspiratorial tone. "Me is not one for this coloured man and white woman coming together, but me have a lot of respect for Mary. One day when we have time I must tell you some of the things that gal had to put up with. For Hopeton to pass his Law examination she would lock him up in his room and drive away all those layabout friends," she looked straight at her husband, "and that include his older brother too."

"Well, you know what they say about all work and no play."

"But you just say Hopeton is a big brainist, that is not being dull." They all laughed.

"So you well established here, then," said Nello.

"I wouldn't call this established. Ziah only got this place after I came up a couple years ago," she caught her husband's eye and quickly the condemnation evaporated from her voice. "It take a man and a wife to make life in this country; I not here four years yet, but we going to make it."

"You know that Hopeton have a really big house in a town in the Midlands call Maudslay and is only him and his wife and two children living there. He was one of the first coloured to own a house in England and not rent out any of it." Ziah was proud of his brother's achievement.

"And all that is Mary's doing. When they was buying that house Hopeton couldn't show him black face at the estate agent, not even when the time come to view the house. Mary always had to go alone, pretending her husband was still in the Air Force in Germany. Of course, because she is a pretty white woman, them all make up their mind her husband was white. A lucky thing Mark was not born yet. Well, I tell you, all hell broke loose when time come for them to move in. A whole pile a bangerwrongs and ructions took place, including shit being pushed down the letter-box."

"You lie!" interrupted Nello, his face betraying his disgust.

"Gawd is me witness," said Myrtle.

"And that is not half of it. Even the estate agent business (I will always remember their name, Bright and Hope) went bust after people started to accuse them of letting in Niggers. They also had shit down their letterbox at their office and even in envelopes. Can you imagine that? Someone took time and effort to put it in an envelope. It's not easy here in England, though if you got a job, you can earn good money compared to Jamaica, but life not easy. I tell you, rain a-fall but dutty tough!"

"We don't know nothing about all this back home," said Nello.

"Nobody would believe us if we write to them back home telling the truth about England, the Mother Country. So you send photos that you pose for with you white fellow workers and everybody back home think we living in paradise," said Myrtle. "But for all that you can get by. You can't pick up yourself and go back home with your tail between your legs. If we manage to get a bigger place we plan to send for our youngest girls. If them have the head for it, education is free. Back home we could not begin to think about sending our twins to secondary school. We had to wait till I come up here and start earning. So since last year they started at a good school."

"The thing about England," said Ziah, "is that the dream no dead yet."

The three talked late into the night. When Colonel Walters at last left he knew he had found two friends. He was invited back for Sunday dinner. It had been revealed that the Morgans were planning to buy their own house. They were in fact the mysterious people who hoped to take possession at the turn of the year. He felt happier than he had been since coming to Britain. There was a new spring in his step as he walked up Coldharbour Lane. He turned up the collar of his coat against the wind, but unlike other times he did not slouch. He seemed to have shaken off that despondent feeling of being an alien. Tonight he felt bold. Warm blood coursed in his veins. He muttered to himself, "Ziah said, the dream no dead yet! Well, boy, Colonel Walters no start dreaming yet, but when I start, it going to be a big one. A real monster of a big one."

3

He dreamt he was in a wide field surrounded by mountains. He was standing in a huge dish that was covered with fine grass. Behind the rim, all around the bowl in which he stood, he heard people shouting but could not make out their words. It was perplexing that he could see no one nor hear distinctly what was being said. He was afraid of being alone and he began shouting, yet could not hear his own voice. He thought he shouted, "Is anybody there? Can you hear me? Can you help me?"

How absurd it was, because there were people out there who were shouting louder than he and so would not be able to hear him. But were they not watching him, seeing his distress? Then he thought that perhaps it all started with everybody in this dish-like valley, and they had escaped, all but him. He alone was left in the valley. Perhaps their shouting was the beacon to light his way out! Was this the valley of the shadow of death? If not, why had he not joined those whose voices he could hear? He was twenty-two years old, agile, yet had not reached even the foothills of the mountains.

Had he chosen to stay because of the beauty of the valley? As he pondered his predicament, the valley began to sway. It was as if someone had lifted a dish by the rim an inch or so off the surface of a table and then let it go; that it clattered drunkenly at first, then trembled to a standstill. At that moment he thought that the valley was volcanic. He was petrified. Would there be an explosion? Would he be blown to atoms or fall into a bottomless pit? He shouted yet louder and this time heard himself say, *"O generation of vipers, who told you to flee the wrath to come?"* His voice did not carry the authority of a religious admonition. He wondered why no one had told him to run. Why had he seen no one running? Where was the prophet in his camel-haired coat? Was he up at the rim sitting in the shade, like Jonah watching from his shaded arbour? It did not matter now. He knew now that he had to run, it did not matter in which direction; he was in the centre and the rim was equidistant from the vortex. But the rim seemed to be moving away, so that it remained the same distance from him however fast he ran. Abruptly the tremors ceased. In front of him stood a white man in white suit and helmet, the figure of colonial history. He handed Alonso a small case and said, "The Ambassador will see you now."

He thought he had died and come to judgment! He knelt to examine the contents of the case. The white man had disappeared as quickly as he had appeared. Alonso took from the case a white shirt, a pair of cricket boots, white socks and some cricketer's flannels. He started to undress out there in the middle. Suddenly, he thought, "I could be undressing in the middle at Lord's or the Oval, the Gabba or Sabina Park."

But there was no applause. He dressed in the pure whiteness of a cricketer. He strode with vigour and pride, as if walking towards the pitch. There was no pitch. Suddenly he was outside a white door which was guarded by two white officers; a third officer on the other side of the door opened it and said over his shoulder to someone further inside, "Call the Ambassador!"

He was hauled into a court where the judge in his sombre stateliness was ready to hear his plea. The judge covered his mouth with the palm of his hand as if to stifle a smile, then throwing caution to the wind flung his head back and burst into the most infectious laughter imaginable. He pointed in the direction of Alonso's groin, and behold he was naked before the judge. Ashamed, he turned on his heel, fled the court. As he ran he tried to cover his lower anatomy, shielding his penis with his hands. He tripped and started tumbling into a bottomless pit.

He woke feeling very frightened. The room was bitterly cold. There was no reason for him to get out of bed before midday so he turned to the wall, covered his head and settled once more in the warmth of the blankets. Before long he was dreaming again. He was walking along a white-marled road that stretched towards the horizon. On both sides of the endless road the grass was covered with powdered marl. He had started out wearing a black suit, but as he walked that interminably long road the continuous showers of fine white marl had settled on his clothes and areas of his uncovered black skin. As he went the unseen host greeted him with peals of laughter. He thought of taking off all his clothes. Allowing his body to be covered all over with the fine white powder, they might stop laughing. Suddenly he was no longer on the white-marled road, nor was he naked. He was driving a bus full of passengers. They were happy because they were singing. He could not turn to look at them but there were many, for their singing was like a choir. How many voices were there, singing, shouting, laughing, yet how few were the people he had seen in his dreams! The bus did not keep to the highway, but hovered across fields like a craft from another world, skimming the surface of lakes, through shrubs and up steep mountains. He was struggling to get it to the top of the peak. In desperation he took some rope, lassoed the peak and was pulling the bus slowly up to the top; and still the passengers sang although they were hanging over a precipice. He could not identify the song, but it did not matter. That dream was the end of a chapter. The page was turned.

He dreamt another dream without waking. He was in a boat drifting down a sluggish stream, and huge alligators hurled themselves into the water and drifted towards the boat. His right hand trailed in the water and he could not pull it back. He was frightened. He tugged and tugged. Ahead he saw a huge alligator with jaws opened like a tunnel. He prayed he would faint, so as not to feel the enormous jaws snap shut. The boat drifted in, the jaws closed and he did not faint. On he drifted past half-digested fish and a cow's hind leg. He hated the smell of carrion in the alligator's stomach. He panicked, seized an oar and smashed it against the wall of the creature's stomach. There was an explosion! Water rushed in and he paddled furiously and escaped the guts of the alligator. He rowed and rowed, hoping to find a city. He thought he had a message but could not find the city. He pushed the boat ashore and there was a number fifty-seven bus going from Victoria to Tooting. He ran and caught it. The conductor, a white man with a waxed moustache, asked where he was going and he said to Brixton, but the conductor said the bus would not be going through Brixton.

"Why not?" he asked.

"Because there are big crocs there, and I ain't got no guns," he said.

He told the conductor that he was lying and was using a double negative. In retaliation the conductor pushed him off the bus. He was a long time falling. When he hit the ground he looked up and he had fallen from a coconut tree. A lizard had run across his hands and he had panicked, let go his hold and fell. As he limped away he looked at the slow-moving greyish lizard; now he knew it was not an alligator that had swallowed him. He was confused and at the same time embarrassed. How could a croaking lizard a mere nine inches long be the monster of his dream? He heard laughter again; he turned. This time it was not the judge.

"Blossom!" he said. She had grown in the three years since he last saw her. "Flowers!" he shouted his pet name for his sister. Even louder he shouted and even then she did not answer. She laughed and ran past. Gradually he realised where he was; they were by the deep hole made by a noisy gully at the bottom of Deacon Charles canefield. She ran ahead, still laughing. As she ran she tore off her clothes, flinging them to the wind. He ran after her but could not catch her. She plunged into the deep hole, disappearing under the ripples. He too plunged in, diving deep, deep, still not reaching the bottom, unable to catch her. He started back to the surface, suddenly felt her arms around him from behind. Her nakedness encircled his body.

"The ambassador," she said close to his ear, "said we must be married."

He reached back, trying to dislodge her so he could see her face, but she clung on tightly. She had her legs around him as if he was giving her a piggyback.

"We must do as the ambassador said," she urged.

He wondered how she could talk under water, and why he could not see her face. They were floating among the reeds. She was still on his back. He tried to twist and face her, but she was fastened to him like a fresh-water mollusc attached to a stone in the river.

"No," she said, "the ambassador won't have that," she said. "Marry me first."

"Yes," he said. "Yes, oh, yes."

Then he awoke and his seed had spilt on to the blanket. He was conscious of lying on his bed in Ostade Road, Brixton Hill. He felt in need of a wash. He lay there trying to make sense of it all. What did his dreams mean? Was it one dream with different scenes? Of one fact he was certain, he was now wide-awake. He recognised the old wardrobe at the foot of his bed; a functional piece of furniture reminiscent of the war years. Why did African landlords inevitably choose the cheapest second-hand furniture they could find? He lay there sticky, uncomfortable and cold. The ticking of the Baby Ben clock began to irritate him. He wondered why he did not get up, then realised he could not move. His vision and hearing were all right; he could see the spider on the wall, and hear the milk float whining outside on the street; yet he was pinned to his bed as if anaesthetised by the fangs of some enormous reptile. He struggled, but could not move. From this position amid old familiar things, he saw a white girl in her underclothes sitting at his dressing table, combing her hair, which was the colour of newly minted copper coins. He watched as she stood with her back to him and stepped into her skirt. He thought he would be able to see her reflection in the mirror, but there was none! Was she a vampire? Perhaps it was because his head was resting on one thin pillow he was unable to see her reflection. Whatever the reason, he was sexually aroused by the vision of a young girl dressing just a few feet from him. As she pulled herself into her blouse, he watched terrified, immobile, speechless and confused, expecting her to turn around. Now he would see her. Who was she? Was she a ghost who had once lived here in this room? Had she died in this room? Her clothes were modern so she was not from centuries gone. Was he still dreaming? When she was fully dressed, she passed quietly towards the door, her face still away from him, her copper-coloured hair hanging to her waist, her profile concealed. She went out, but before the door closed she took two steps backward, as if in reverse gear. Her hair moved gently like a pendulum. Her left hand reached behind the door, from where she took a mackintosh and an umbrella. He heard the sounds her shoes made as she ran down the stairs, and finally the front door slammed shut. He awoke. He was certain of this for now he could move his head and his hands. He could even shout, "Shit!"

He sat up as if a spring had been released. He was sweating profusely, his heart racing. He heard the postman's three rapid knocks. He shot out of bed, threw his dressing gown around his shoulders and started down the stairs, still struggling into his gown. By the time he reached the door, the postman had dropped some letters and moved on up the street. Alonso opened the door to shout after him. The postman turned, walked back and pulled a large envelope from the bottom of his pile.

"Sorry, mate, I couldn't get these through the letterbox. What have you got in these? Saucy photos? It says here 'Do not bend'." He handed the envelopes to Alonso, who quickly withdrew into the passage. He did not tell the postman these were assignments from a correspondence college.

He sorted out the mail and headed back upstairs. He had forgotten to ask the postman if he had seen a girl in a mackintosh. Just as well. The postman would have thought of a black girl. Describing a copper-haired white girl leaving his room at nine o'clock in the morning would arouse such angst that any humour intended would have been lost. He climbed the stairs back to his room. He threw the letters on his bed and proceeded to light the paraffin heater. He examined the letters. There was one from Blossom. He could not read it. He remembered his dream, and felt ashamed. It was as if he had to look in her face after seducing her. The letter terrified him. He felt full of remorse, nauseated. Then as the glow from the paraffin heater began to radiate its warmth around the room, a voice deep within him said, "It was a dream. It didn't happen!" With that assurance, he picked up his sister's letter. Any thought of incest that might have flickered across his mind was always ruthlessly expunged. He opened the letter nervously.

II

Nino,

Rain, rain, rain. It has not stopped for three days. Another thirty-seven to go. I am listening out for the sound of Noah building his Ark. Spare a thought for the poor old man sailing around with all those critters. I think I have an idea, stuck here as I am with five sulking, bawling kids dragging mud all over the place. Since you left home, some six years ago aged fourteen, our mother has managed to produce four more kids, and is making the fifth. It is a habit with her. She is like a spider with that huge pouch with her young ready to burst out and devour her. Is it true that young spiders eat their mother? I am sure I heard it somewhere. Anyway there is a dried out husk of an Anancy spider up there in the rafters, (and don't you dear say anything about my cleaning. I could not reach up there without a ladder) Oh my head! The thought of matricide; plus cannibalism taking place up there above my head, while I sleep frightens me.

Poor Mama! What will come of her and all these children? As if all that was not bad enough, our stepfather has another woman. Guess whom? Susu White! There is nothing we can do. Don't let Mama know I told you.

The trek to England, as Count Lasher would say, is gathering momentum. Surprise of the year saintly Winnie Price has gone to Camberwell, England. You might bump into her one of these days. The story is going around that Elias Carter sent for her. No one can ever recall those two ever talking to each other. He must be old enough to be her father. This England thing is making some strange alliances! Last week Lovie Grey and Daphne Walker from Ma'jilly Gully flew away to Birmingham, England.

People are asking when you are going to send for me. I continue to tell everybody that I am not interested in going to England. Are you not proud of my acting? When I write to you again I will by then know my date of departure. I pray you get that flat or apartment, whatever you Britishers call it, soon.

Mama received your generous postal order yesterday. I will write her dictated letter to you soon. I can not wait to see you.

Su hermana,
Rosita (Flowers, Blossom, Rosie whatever)

He felt close to Blossom after reading her letter. He could almost feel the distance of five thousand miles diminishing. Once again he was embarrassed by his dream. He tried to dispel the sequence of dreams by concentrating on himself. He was born twenty-two years ago in the town of Bocas del Toro in Panama, the grandson of Jamaican grandfather and grandmother an extraction of native Indians and descendants of the conquistadors. So his mother was the daughter of Jamaicans who had moved on; some people said they had migrated to the United States, others say that they had moved south to Colon, and still others say they moved north to Port Limon in Costa Rica. Wherever they were, he had never seen them. Perhaps his grandparents had never heard of him. Sometimes in a philosophical mood he saw life as a moving stairway along a highway with turnings and junctions. He considered the disappearance of his grandparents Campbell as the first great junction where decisions had to be made. His mother exchanged the name of Campbell for that of the young man she married, Alfredo de Campesino. Then the second major junction loomed almost without warning. Alfredo de Campesino worked as a night watchman at a factory and was killed during a robbery. The company paid compensation, and for reasons of safety Inez Campbell de Campesino and her two children Alonso and Rosita (Blossom) went to Jamaica. That was far away enough from the gang that killed her husband. Alonso was three years old and Blossom was still under two when their father was killed. The family had first moved to Kingston. It was bewildering to Inez in custom and language. She was grateful to her cousin Ivorine Lopez, who used to teach English at a school in Bocas. Ivorine had returned to Jamaica before the Campbells did their disappearing act and Inez had corresponded with her for fifteen years. It was this Ivorine who had now established herself as a teacher of the Spanish language at a small private school in Kingston, came to Inez's rescue before the money ran out. She even suggested that she reverted to her parental name of Campbell. Aunty Ivorine or Gody Ivo as she was more widely known, retired to a village in the hills above the Yallahs River. When Inez followed her Ivorine further advised her to buy an old ramshackle house and the land that went with it in the district of Guava Flat. It was hoped that the land would sustain the family when money eventually ran out. That was how they, Alonso and Blossom, acquired a stepfather in Bullah Cameron and Inez a husband. He was at first employed to work the land and over the years worked his way into the family. The marriage took place when Alonso was seven. Both he and Blossom had never got on with Bullah. He recalled Blossom's screams when she was turned out of their mother's bed to make room for Bullah. Things changed. Their mother was now coping with a new husband, no longer the head of her household, no longer three, but with a baby on the way she was to discover that it was not a matter of extending her family, but that she was about to start a new family. Alonso and Blossom took refuge in what was their first language, Spanish. They were known as the *'Panya Pickney, dem'*. They learnt to depend on each other, especially as they were teased mercilessly by other children. Neither could remember their time in Bocas del Toro, but to all they were known as the "Spanish children, them". Their life was an eternal vigil. If one was asleep, it was because the other was awake. Bullah Cameron was resentful of them both. He would beat one and watch the other suffer, but he could not prise them apart. There was a part of his home that was not his, this enclave that he could not capture. They were like fleas down a dog's back, always just outside the reach of its paws. They shared a room, quite often a bed, until Bullah's first child had to make room for his second child. By the time the third child came along, Bullah had succeeded in driving Alonso from his home.

III

Alonso heated water over the paraffin heater, spread newspaper on the floor around a stool on which he had placed a plastic bowl. He poured water in the bowl, stripped to his waist and began his ablutions. As he washed the back of his neck and his shoulders he thought he could still feel the weals of the lashings he had received from Bullah. Anger welled up in him.

Agnes was the huge donkey which Bullah had mated with a horse. The birth of the hybrid was less than a month away. Alonso was fetching home the donkey one evening and as he passed outside the school gate some boys were playing cricket in the road. He could not resist the temptation to join in. Foremost in his mind he recalled that the Three Ws, Worrell, Weekes and Walcott, had each scored centuries against India. He had always imagined himself to be like the flawless Worrell! He tied Agnes to an overhanging branch of a mango tree and joined the boys. In an extraordinary burst of medium-pace bowling he got out Son-son and Boysie, the two best batsmen in the district. He walked back, about to run in to bowl to Chippie. If he could get him out too that would be his personal hat-trick, although neither Son-son nor Boysie had been bowled by consecutive balls. He took a longer run-up to bowl to Chippie. At this point all hell broke loose. Agnes the pregnant donkey had apparently stretched too far over the embankment to get at the elephant grass, had slipped and tumbled over the embankment. The taut tether jerked the pregnant animal to a sudden stop in its tumbling. It was being strangled. In its agony it began giving birth prematurely.

"Cut the rope," somebody yelled, "cut the friggin' rope!"

It was like an explosion. It was birth and it was death also. From what was a few boys playing cricket in the road there was now a crowd. Men vaulted over the embankment to act as midwives to Agnes. Alonso stood watching. There was tragedy and there was wonder. Suddenly he was airborne, then he was falling. He did not fall like a mango from a tree but was suspended in mid-air. Time enough to realise he had been struck a mighty blow on his right cheek. As he hit the ground he rolled like an agile wicket-keeper snatching a catch in front of first slip. He pulled himself to his knees like a boxer refusing to take the count. Instead of the referee he heard the sharp barb of Bullah's voice. "Ah kill you tonight. Ah bus'up you rarse!" Alonso felt the kick against his right ribs.

"Yu gwine kill the boy?" Alonso thought he heard that, but he knew not who said it. He did not know that Bullah had been restrained. He had no clear memory of being helped up, of being half-dragged, half-carried to his mother's house. He was vaguely conscious of the heart-rending scream of both his mother and Blossom. He tried to speak words of comfort, but instead he spat out blood and a couple of teeth. The screams intensified. His head felt heavy. The right side of his face was disproportionately heavier than the left and he could open only one eye, the left. His tongue was too big for his mouth. Among the screams he felt cold water on his head, his sister's hands around his neck, the contrast of hot tears on his cheek. Amid the ache and the screams he thought he heard Son-son say that they were going to ask Buchanan, the police corporal from Abbey Look Out station, to shoot Agnes and end her agony. Suddenly there was a loud crack and then silence.

"He get drunk now. You must go now. Run," his mother was dragging him to his feet. "He kill you if he find you. You must go," but Blossom's arms fastened even tighter around his neck.

He heard the commands. He did not want to disobey, but his aching head could not pass on the command to his feet. In his mind his death would be liberation. His mother and sister Blossom would be free; curiously, he did not think of his younger siblings who were fathered by Bullah. If Bullah should beat him to death, he would be arrested, tried and quite possibly hanged. In Alonso's fevered mind the whole thing would be over in minutes; he comforted himself that being dead he could watch from some peaceful place the drama of Bullah, terrified, being dragged to the place of execution and his soul being sent to hell.

The wailing of his mother and Blossom increased. He heard Perro the dog barking excitedly. All announced Bullah's homecoming. Yet Alonso could not run. His mother went to meet Bullah, who hurled her from him against the hibiscus border and moved relentlessly like some carnivorous beast towards its quarry. The rope in Bullah's hand was wet and heavy, wrapped around his palm like a tight bandage. It was looped so one lash became two. The first lash also caught Blossom on her right arm that forced her to let go of her brother. In truth Bullah did not really care. The death of both would solve a problem. He did not think of the consequences. After the first six lashes Alonso lay as if paralysed. The blows continued to rain down on the inert body. The first break came when the faithful Perro leaped at Bullah's leg. The dog succeeded only at gripping his trouser leg with its powerful canine teeth. Bullah swivelled to hit the dog with the rope. It backed off with a yelp, but quickly regained ground and was barking menacingly.

Inez Campbell had disappeared into the house only for a moment. When she reappeared the crowd that had witnessed the death of the donkey had transferred its attention to the beating Alonso was receiving. Inez gave a blood-curdling scream! Then she was on Bullah, springing on his back like a lion bringing down its prey. Now it was Bullah's scream that focused the villagers' attention.

"She cut me neck! She done kill me! Me wife cut me up. Lawdmegawd! S'medy call the police!"

The attack on Bullah was so sudden, so furious that he had dropped the rope and was grasping his neck with his right hand just at the time the second slash of his own razor made contact on his forearm. Just as the third blow was about to be struck, Bullah leapt from the veranda. At this point Corporal Buchanan arrived. It was the police corporal who prevented what might very well have been two murders by firing his revolver for the second time that evening. The unexpected report of the revolver stopped both husband and wife in pursuit of their murderous intent. Buchanan pushed Bullah against the orange tree. Inez Campbell Cameron in an instant dropped the bloody razor and knelt beside her son's inert body.

"Me a-bleed to deat'. She kill me dead," Bullah sobbed.

"Tcho, man," said Cranje Miller, "you draw more blood from that boy than you wife draw from you."

"Ef it was one a me pickney Bullah beat like that, Ah woulda kill him. See Gawd deh, Ah mean it!" said Geddes, who had ventured in the yard and was comforting Blossom.

35

The Headmaster arrived with his first-aid box. The men lifted the unconscious boy to his bed and the teacher started to clean the wounds on Alonso's back.

"I would feel better if Doctor Cole sees him," said the teacher to the corporal.

The next morning the men from the village carried Alonso on a stretcher to Abbey Look Out, where Dr Cole had his surgery.

No one was ever sure who decided that the sick boy should be taken to the home of Gody Ivo. She owned the big house known as Top House. This was partly because it was on top of the hill overlooking the village of Guava Flat. More importantly it was the biggest house in all the neighbouring villages with the exception of Bloom Hill above Abbey Look Out, where the Simpsons had lived before the end of slavery. Gody Ivo was cousin of Alonso's father, and like him she too was born at Bocas del Toro, but her parents had returned to Jamaica when Ivorine was a child. It was she who had encouraged Inez de Campesino to buy a house in this remote village of Guava Flat.

She had never liked the liaison with Bullah Cameron but had kept her own counsel when Inez married the shiftless one trouser on, one off, almost illiterate man.

Even with the medicine prescribed by Dr Cole it was a week before the fever broke and Alonso began his recovery. During the days of high fever and delirium Inez de Campesino Cameron and Rosita kept watch at Alonso's bedside. The first night that Alonso spent at Top House, past midnight when it was expected that everyone including Inez had gone home to see to her other children, Rosita was found curled up on the veranda outside the window of the bedroom where her brother lay. The faithful Perro was beside her. Gody Ivo lifted the sleeping child and placed her beside her brother. From then on the two *Panya pickneys* came to live at Top House.

The summer of his seventeenth birthday, Alonso passed his Third-Year Jamaica Local Examination, and Blossom passed her First Year. That year he read several novels by Captain Marryat, R.M. Ballantyne and R.L. Stevenson, but it was *Kidnapped* by Stevenson that left the deepest impression. Bullah was his wicked uncle and he knew he had to leave home. He had letters of reference and introduction from the Reverend Carr, Baptist pastor of the church at Grass Piece, the headmaster at Guava Flat and the redoubtable Gody Ivo, who had once been a teacher. She was also well known for collecting the young daughters of her poor relations and turning them into young women capable of finding their way in the world.

The time came for Alonso to leave and that meant leaving Guava Flat. He breakfasted heartily on roasted breadfruit, sussumber and salt mackerel and cups of coffee made from the plants that grew right up to Aunty Ivorine's back door. That made it genuine Blue Mountain coffee. Only the evening before, Blossom and another of the girls had roasted the beans and ground them in a small handheld mill. He looked up towards the Blue Mountains and realised he had tasted the best coffee there is. When he had finished drinking it, he resolved to walk out into the wider world.

A small contingent of friends had gathered to wish him God's speed. It was an emotional farewell. His mother and Aunty Ivorine looked around for Blossom but could not find her. The boys at the gate grinned and slapped him on his shoulder. He knew he would be seeing some of them in Kingston eventually. He looked again for his sister. Why was she not there? Then someone pointed to a figure standing where the road bends above John Crow Gully.

"Go!" said Aunty Ivorine and Inez in unison. "She want you all by herself." He started to walk down the road. Boysie started after him.

"No, Boysie," said Aunty Ivorine, "let them alone."

He made up his mind to walk the two miles to Pretty Turning, then on to Long Wall and some six miles further on to Iron Mango Tree via Surrey Hills. No one was able to convince him that the market lorry the *African Queen* would later that evening carry him with reasonable comfort out of the hills to Kingston. Instead he decided to walk the ten miles to Iron Mango Tree. This was a busy junction where he hoped to get a bus and arrive in Kingston ahead of the *African Queen*. He had left his suitcase with Boysie, who would in turn give it to his aunt who was going to Kingston to sell the ground provision that her land yielded. These were red peas, gungo peas, sweet potatoes and breadfruit. In his mind Alonso recreated the opening paragraph of *Kidnapped*. Alonso raised his hand but did not look back as he waved to the citizens of Guava Flat and walked away. From the hills he could not see the sea, neither did he expect Kingston to smoke like a kiln, but that its streets would consume nearly all who touched them with naked feet.

Half a mile out of the village he caught up with Blossom.

"I don't know how to say goodbye," she said. "I don't want nobody see me crying. That is why I run all the way out here." She walked close to him, her eyes focused on her toes. He noticed she was not wearing her shoes. She walked with him as far as Rhodes Fording, then stopped, as if the Yallahs was the dividing line.

"I never know any time without you," she said. For the first time she looked him in the eyes. "Now you leaving me. You soon forget me."

He assured her that not a moment would go by without her being foremost in his thoughts. He urged her to look towards the next holiday when she could come to stay with him. He was certain she was safe at Gody Ivo. They hugged and kissed. He told her to go and not look back, but if she went quickly to the bend above John Crow Gully, she would be able to see him as he walked up the white marl road at Long Wall. He stood and watched her walk away. He thought of soldiers going off to war. This is what they must have experienced bidding farewell to their relatives.

The parting was no less difficult for him. Indeed he was back at Guava Flat the next weekend to tell of his good fortune in obtaining a job with Parkins Travel Agency. Travel agencies had become a growth industry fuelled by the phenomenon of migration to the Mother Country. Three months into full employment, he bought his first second-hand bicycle. Now he could get out of Kingston every Saturday evening when the agency closed for the week's business, only to ride back Monday morning. It was as if he had never left the village.

Alonso read again his sister's letter, then he sat down and wrote a fulsome reply. At last he was able to tell her that the money for her passage to England had been paid in full. Parkins Travel Agency should be writing to her at Miss Wilson's, the woman with whom she was boarded Mondays to Fridays while attending Wilberforce High School just off Mountain View Avenue in Eastern Kingston. He himself had stayed at Miss Wilson's after Myrtle Morgan had left to join her husband in London. He thought she should have a date in March or April.

He left early so that he could get postal orders at the post office. Suddenly he felt hungry. He went into the little kitchen that was jointly shared by the tenants on the two floors beneath his room. He hated the thought of Blossom coming up before he could find suitable accommodation. He would have to talk to Myrtle Morgan again. In the kitchen he shared a cupboard with the Nigerian brothers who lived on the floor below. The left-hand section of the cupboard was his. Cooked food he stored on the top shelf, groceries on the one below, vegetables on the third one down and pots, pans and plates and cups on the bottom shelf. He heated up yesterday's left-over rice and corned beef, brought it back in his room on a tray. As he ate he thought of the girl at the end of his series of dreams. It bothered him. He wondered what Myrtle Morgan would think of it.

He was early getting to Brixton Bus Garage, Streatham Hill. He was neither hungry nor thirsty, but after collecting his conductor's box and checking his ticket machine he went upstairs to the canteen, where Myrtle Morgan in her white apron and cap was serving food to bus crews. At last there was a lull and he was able to relate his dream of the white girl in his room.

"Keep you voice down," she warned. "Them might think you got white woman in you room, for true. Me just can't stand the tension," she wiped the damp cloth on the counter. "You story is funny enough, but I heard one just like that over Hackney way. A couple moved into a room that had a piece of carpet. Them should a known that something was wrong because black people don't get rooms for rent with carpet. Well, the woman cleaned the room and sweep off the carpet. I hear say that a big bright red spot come up on the carpet. She went out got cleaning material and clean the carpet again and guess what the big red spot come up all the brighter and when she touch it, it felt wet. Them start feeling funny about it, so when the landlord came around again they told him about it. He said, 'Don't tell me that piece of carpet is still there. It was the carpet the last tenant bled on when he slit his own throat. The man who cleaned the room was told to throw it out.' I hear say that man and woman was out of that house so fast, you couldn't see them for dust. I bet you that girl used to live in you room. I bet she took an overdose. These girls kill themself if they are jilted or pregnant. If you talk to any of the neighbours you better ask them. Boy, I wonder where she slept last night. I tell you, boy, if ever she played with you, then you manhood gone." She clapped her hands and brushed them in an act of finality. "Gone, gone!"

He laughed nervously as he recalled the lines of a song, part of a mento tune that the men outside Naipaul rum shop at Abbey Look Out used to sing:

> *Me drink white rum and me tumble down,*
> *Me no want duppy gal come fingle me.*

For the first time the true meaning of the song came to him. Were these men afraid that after they might trip on their way home along those unlit and haunted roads, then as they lay in a drunken stupor the ghost of long-dead women, or duppy women, would interfere with their manhood? Alonso thought of his erotic dreams. Was the ghost of that duppy gal, as they would say in the Yallahs Valley, in bed with him? It was no longer a dream. Are ghosts not prejudiced? Why should a young white woman, ghost or not, want to climb into his bed? Can a ghost cause sexual arousal in a man? Alonso's driver came into the canteen and said their bus had arrived. He would be working from two o'clock to quarter to eleven, with little time to think or even daydream.

He remembered it was a number ninety-five bus running from Tooting Broadway to Cannon Street in the City. In an hour's time it would be the rush hour. At the moment it was quiet enough for him to stand on the platform and notice the names of shops and other businesses. He enjoyed the surprise on passengers' faces when they asked for directions and he could give them clearly and confidently. The driver had pulled into a request stop and Alonso helped a young woman with two small children and a pushchair get on. He stowed the pushchair in the alcove behind the platform and straightened up ready to ring the bell, when he saw her! She was kneeling in the shop window arranging the dress on a model. Her copper-coloured hair hung like a waterfall bathed in the red sunset of a tropic evening. This was the girl in his dream. As far as he could recall she was wearing the same blouse and skirt she had put on in his room. He was again caught in a trance. He stood like some latter-day Sir Bedivere revolving erotic memories of his dream. Then there was a banging from the front of the bus. Bill, his driver, had clasped his hands as if at prayer then leant his head against his hands, indicating that Alonso had fallen asleep. Alonso sprang to life. The woman with the two small children was holding out her fare to him. He rang the bell, the bus jerked away.

On successive days he would make sure he was standing on the platform determined to get another glimpse of the girl. Perhaps this time she would turn around so he would see her face, but weeks dragged by and he never saw her. One day when it rained and old ladies had to be helped on the bus, he turned and there she was! She was standing in front of a model buttoning its jacket, then her arms came up and swept away her hair as if to say, *'enough. Look on my face and worship me!'* He gasped. She was a very beautiful young woman perhaps in her mid-twenties. She had prominent almost oriental cheekbones. She looked at the bus, but not him. He floated throughout the rest of the day. At the end of the shift he took a bus back to the shop. Of course, it had been closed for hours. But he had to go back. He stood close to the glass, staring at the models. Perhaps she was one of them! Perhaps she would come alive. Does that only happen at midnight?

"Some men just like looking at women's clothes," said a woman's voice close by. "It doesn't matter what it is," she was annoyed. This jerked him out of his stupor.

The woman's male companion pulled her away. "He's probably window-shopping, dear."

Alonso turned away, stung by the implication of the woman's statement. He walked through the dark wet night to his room in Ostade Road. That night he willed the girl to reappear. Now he had some idea of what she looked like he was ready to accept the apparition. After nights of expectation he had to come to the conclusion that having seen her face he had succeeded in exorcising the ghost of Ostade Road. A month or so later he actually saw her three times. Twice she looked at him and smiled. On the third occasion she stepped away from the model she was dressing. He read her lips: "Do you like it?" To which he nodded his head. He thought of going in the shop; he could pretend he was buying a dress for his sister. But he could not summon up the courage.

4

The room was quite large but badly in need of redecoration. The ceiling and the walls were covered with the residue of black smoke emitted from paraffin heaters. The smell of food cooked on a small gas ring in a corner of the room mingled with the acrid scent of unwashed bodies and sweaty clothes. Originally there were four ways by which foul air could escape this room. There was the connecting door between this room that was intended to be a front sitting room and the adjacent room that might have been a dining room. Now it was closed and a stout bar was nailed across the double folding doors. A huge wardrobe had been hauled across to reinforce the idea of no entrance. Smoke and foul air once upon a time would have escaped through the chimney, but now the fireplace was boarded up, although occasionally slides of old soot that had accumulated over the years could be heard crashing down behind the hard board. The third means of relieving the room of foulness was the wide bay windows, but the woodwork had been so badly painted and so repeatedly that the frames were stuck fast, and no amount of shaking, pushing and heaving could loosen them. The only other outlet was the door from the passage, but its main purpose seemed to open long enough to admit the inhabitants, and then close to preserve privacy. Indeed all rooms in the house, either by design or coincidence, permitted quick entries and fast exits, these apertures, like sluggish sewers, discharging into the common delta, the passage, with the peculiar scent of the house contained like a dam.

The scent of the house was alive. It invaded everything that came within its domain. It attacked like a malignant disease, ingratiating its debilitating embrace with the body. Winifred Price had smelt it on Elias' clothes when he met her on her arrival at Waterloo Station a fortnight ago. It had clawed at her when she entered the house. As she entered the passage she knew she had tracked the malignancy to its lair. After a day or two, when she had been directed to the Labour Exchange in Rye Lane, Peckham, she realised that she too was carrying around the spoor. She wondered if every house had its own distinctive smell. Was the clerk at the Labour Exchange wearing an artificial smile while she dealt with her able to tell her customers apart merely by the smell of their houses?

Two weeks had dragged slowly by and Winnie still had not unpacked her large suitcase. She was frank with Lias about the smell. She had been a country girl all her life and was used to all smells, but this was different.

You could not walk away from it or expel it from your lungs. It permeated all, followed you like an unseen shadow. She told him she would like to get rid of the smell. It meant cleaning the room, scraping the paint from the window frames and letting the bad air out. Lias guffawed. To his way of thinking people did not come to England to clean white people's property, he told her. He was just interested in earning enough money to buy a piece of land in Jamaica, build a house, employ people to work his land and live out his life drinking ice water under a mango tree. He thought he could accomplish all that within five years, perhaps six, of hard graft. He was not against her cleaning the place, but throwing the windows open was a step too far. Winnie wondered if this was an immigrant scent; would she in time, like Lias and his brother come to accept it? She sat on one of the two beds in the room and listened to the chattering of the pot cover as the potatoes boiled on the gas ring in a corner. She looked at the clock over the mantelpiece and a feeling of great anxiety descended like a pall. Lias and Ivan would be home soon, and she began to accept that there was more to her disillusionment than the rancid smell of the house.

It was the nights she hated most. God! How she hated the nights. The sweaty night creeping closer and eventually covering her with its clammy malodorous body.

She hurriedly got off the bed and started to fold and pack away the washed clothes that were hanging on a line stretched across the room. They dried by the warmth of the paraffin heater. Suddenly she stopped and leaning forward pulled a pair of her panties from the back of the heater. The tiny garment was dry. She climbed on a chair to reach the top of the wardrobe where her still unpacked suitcase was. Swiftly she stuffed the article into the case. She recalled the mounting anger in Lias' voice as he criticised the length of time she spent in the bathroom washing her body and her underwear. To his mind the frequent change of underclothes and the need to bathe were the sole preserve of those involved in regular sexual activity. Since they had only consummated their relationship in two acrimonious encounters, he did not feel obliged to involve himself in the ritual of regular trips to the bathroom. He remained suspicious of Winnie's motives. He was content to wash his hands, face and feet in a huge red plastic bowl in front of the paraffin heater.

She stacked the clothes neatly on the bed. She would iron them far into the night while the men slept. It would afford her less time to fight off Lias. Less time for her to lie face-down, tense, sick and cold as his hands clutched at her. Less time to listen to his entreaties. Less time to smell his peculiar acrid scent, stale with sweat and sperm. Less time for him to try to force her to uncross her legs by wedging a great toe between her ankles. All this with Ivan barely an arm's length away across the room in his own bed. Insomniac and with watchful ears, Ivan turned incessantly and noisily as his brother fought for sexual gratification.

She wiped the tears from her eyes. She went to close the curtains. At the window of the house across the street she could see a couple moving lovingly towards each other. They embraced. Winnie drew the curtains angrily, shutting out the reflection of her own desire. Once before, she had watched a couple commit the sin of fornication in a canefield back home. That was when she realised Sister Winifred Price was backsliding from the strict demands of the Bible Church of God. She had enjoyed the feeling that enveloped her as she watched and listened, although she realised it would soon possess her and drag her down, down, down *destruction's broadway*. The highway to hell opened its vast avenues a week later when she and Son-son were walking back from Abbey Look Out on a rainy night. They sheltered in the old boiling-house where sugar used to be made. She woke from her reverie, her loneliness suddenly deepened with the scraping of keys in the Yale lock.

"Evenin'," said Ivan. He was the older of the two brothers by a few years, in his late forties, and had left a wife and eight children back home, plus three or four others by other women including Winnie's eldest sister, Blacky. He had left Jamaica less than a year ago to join his younger brother, who had migrated the year before. Ivan threw a crumpled evening paper on the bed next to where Winnie had been standing. She was unaccustomed to newspapers, evening or morning. She had grown up knowing that headmasters, the Baptist minister and police officers at Abbey Look Out read newspapers, particularly the *Daily Gleaner*. She never considered a newspaper apart of her own life.

"You been back to the Labour Exchange?" growled Lias, a big man who rarely smiled.

"Yes," said Winnie, "I start tomorrow over at a place call Aldgate East. You know where that is? I going to work in a garment factory there."

"Piecework!" snorted Lias. "You have fe work 'ard, 'cause no money in piecework, you know. Ef you go to work and take-up with the other women them and you all start you *susu susu,* you'd be lucky ef you bring home three pounds a week."

"Sorry!" Winnie apologised. "After the white woman question me, she told me I could either go and wash up plates in a restaurant or I could go to the garment factory. She said that because I was learning dressmaking I might like the factory work..."

"Larnin' dressmaking," Lias was dismissive, "just because say you mother got an old Singer sewing-machine no mean to say she is a dressmaker," he sucked air through clenched teeth.

"I don't know 'bout that," said Ivan. "Miss Lou sew for a lot a people."

" Me no say she can't sew. Me say she is no dressmaker. In this country no matter how good you is at a thing, it no worth a spit less you have a piece of paper, and you, Miss High and Mighty Winifred Price, no got no paper.

You should a take the washing-up job. Sometime them 'low you to take home food."

"No worry," Winnie said, "I go work real 'ard. I'm not going to talk to nobody. I going to pay you back the money you send for me passage." No sooner had she uttered those words than she regretted it. Lias spun around towards her with such anger that she hurled herself across the room and stooped cowering beside Ivan's bed. Lias moved towards her, speechless with rage. He towered over her, a black quivering rock heated with volcanic fury. Anticipating an eruption, Ivan touched his brother's powerful biceps, and although his hand was flung off he repeated his action.

"Me is hungry, man," said Ivan, "and something smell good. Come make we eat. Don't get all steam up over nothing, man. You can't eat food when you vex. After all, the woman was sayin' she gwine work 'ard to pay you back you seventy-five pounds. Is what is wrong with that? Unless a-grind you want fe grind it out of her. Boy, that is a whole lot a pussy..."

Lias spun around to face his older brother. He was frothing with anger. "Me and you gwine have a big bus'-up, you know! You carry on and we gwine draw blood right here tonight."

Ivan raised both his hands. "You too damn thin-skin, man." He moved towards the door, then paused. "By the way, I use to bus' you rarse when we was boys and I reckon I can still bus' you rarse today. So don't come to me with any of you big and mighty self."

"Where you going?" pleaded Winnie. She was terrified of the prospect of being left alone with Lias. "I was just going to serve up the food."

"I going to have a piss and a shit, if it's all right with you," the older brother replied. Ivan was no ally of hers. He pulled the door after him but did not close it. A ferociously aimed kick from Lias completed the job.

"I don't like people puttin' them nose in me business," he said turning to Winnie with menace. "I gwine get me money back, and you gwine gie it to me flat 'pon you back."

She could feel his lascivious eyes rolling around her backside and sliding down her thighs. She continued to dish up the food. He hurled himself on the bed. Winnie froze, hearing the rustle of the newspaper as it came fluttering across the room and hit her in the back. He did not order her to come to him, so she continued serving. Then his voice became threatening. "You think any woman gwine bore me nose and put rope through it to lead me like a damn fool? No, siree. It not gwine happen. Every day you drop a bucket in a well, one day the bottom gwine drop off. Me old gran'mammy use to say it take a patient man fe ride a donkey. I gwine ride you right in this bed. P'rhaps not tonight nor tomorrow, but is ride I gwine ride you."

Ivan's return interrupted Lias' tirade. The two men ate in silence.

When they were done, Winnie cleared the plates away quickly. She spread newspaper on a chair and on the floor, then placed the plastic bowl with lukewarm water on the chair ready for Lias. He began stripping to the waist. The nightly ritual had commenced. Ivan took the hint, threw a towel over his shoulder and went to the bathroom.

II

Winnie sat on the bed, becoming vaguely interested in the newspaper. It was not yet time to start the ironing. She did not like reading and the newspaper could not hold her interest. Since she had left school at fourteen the only book she read was the Bible. Even then, she only read those well-chosen passages so often recited by the fundamentalist evangelists. She could not even be sure whether she was reading or memorising aloud. Her church scarcely ever read passages that portrayed the love of God. Their sermons came exclusively from those passages that foretold coming damnation. She remembered reading another story, only three years ago. She was sitting on a bus going along the Windward Road; suddenly next to her was a brightly coloured American magazine, showing two film stars in an embrace, their lips pressed hard on each other's. Although they were white folks she could still remember the embarrassment that welled up in her. She looked away in moral indignation. Since being received into the Bible Church of God eight years ago she had put away all sinful thoughts. She might never have looked at the offending magazine again had not a large woman decided to heave her massive bulk in the seat next to her. Out of good manners Winnie took up the magazine. Acutely embarrassed, she folded it and stuffed it into her bag. Later that night at Foster Lane Open Market she prayed and rebuked Satan for working so hard to make her fall into temptation. However, towards dawn she picked up the magazine and looked again and again at the pictures of the lovers. The glossy pages portrayed film stars advertising their movies. She could not help comparing their glamorous clothes with the dowdy long-sleeved garment she was wearing. She had never used make-up. At the elders' behest she had given up deodorant. What she did not know, certainly did not want, was that at that moment her soul was in full rebellion.

The All-Island Convention of the Bible Church of God began in Kingston later that week. There were many visiting white elders from Canada and the United States of America. Their wives wore beautifully tailored suits like the models and film stars in the magazine. These white women were elegantly made-up and as fragrant as jasmine, but no elder rose to condemn them as harlots. She watched as the fiery Easton Bogle, the black Superintendent of the East Jamaican churches, stood, eyes trained on his shoes, talking to two of the visiting wives. Because he did not look them straight in their eyes he

45

might be forgiven for not noticing their painted faces. Yet this was the man who shouted Jezebel and harlot at the young girls who had lately returned from Kingston with pencil-slim skirts, straightened hair and make-up. But then they were black. What double standards! With shoulders bent and downcast eyes, Easton Bogle grinned as the white women talked to him. How did he see them? Were they exempted from the doctrine of the church? Would they go to heaven despite their perfume and painted faces? Would black women go to hell because they straightened hair and wore lipstick? Her soul was in torment. Later that day she went into Hidalgo's Drug Store at the corner of East Queen Street and West Parade and looked at the cosmetic counter. In full rebellion she bought a bottle of an exotic mixture called *Kalanga Water,* determined to splash it all over herself when she showered at her cousin's place at Penn Street in Jones Town. The God of the white women was going to be her God. She retrieved the contraband magazine and read the story of Phil and Joan. She wondered what it would feel like to be kissed hard on the lips as the lovers had done in the story. Over the next few weeks she read the story again and again. In her mind the park in which the love story unfolded was transferred to the canefield just outside her village of Bun Dutty Gap. She had selected an area where the road bends like an elbow above Guava Flat, where there was always a smell of jasmine, and the moonlight frightened away all ghosts and shadows. She was now using some of the words from the magazine. She wanted to be Joan, of course, but who would be Phil? Long before Satan had directed her foot onto the ladder of evil, she recalled some wicked men sitting outside the Coolieman shop joking about her physical attributes.

"But look ya, Sister Winnie," said one, "you look sorta round and plump like a chicken!"

"She got a good gas tank. The gal got rhythm," said another, complimenting the roll of her behind, "and them headlights shape as if then straight from a Dodge truck."

She glanced down at her breasts. Were they that big? She angrily increased her speed, which action accentuated her rhythmical movements. The whistling continued until she was out of sight.

Later on, she talked to Sister Beah about those wicked and lascivious men who were undoubtedly bound for hell's fire. Why did they compare her to a car when none of them were ever likely to own a car! Now she wondered what Phil thought of Joan's backside. That magazine had brought Winnie to the highway that is the road leading to hell. It was like a moving staircase, and each day she went for a ride as it moved down, down, down to hell. She was practised in the art of jumping off the stairway. The first day she would ride for a couple of yards and then jump off. The next day she would refuse to ride the moving staircase and the day after that she would ride just a little bit further to show she could get off if she had a mind to. But each day she was conscious of looking for her Phil. After that rainy night in the old boiling house with Son-son, she thought she had met Phil, but he did not kiss her hard on the lips. The search went on, the ride on the staircase became more frequent. Then one-day chimeras turned to reality. Elias Carter had written to her mother asking permission to allow him to send for Winnie. It was a part of God's plan *to punish* her for backsliding. There was no escape.

"Set the clock," barked Elias from the cocoon of his bed, to no one in particular.

Ivan smoked and watched Winnie winding the clock. "What time is it?" he asked.

"Five to ten," she said.

"Gwine take a walk," he said. Winnie noticed he had on his street clothes. "Good time," he grunted again. "I gwine take a walk. Oonu don't lock me out." He stood up.

"So," his brother grunted. "So, you wait till the man gone to work, then you go and grind his wife. Well, take me advice and don't go sleeping the sleep just after, 'cause that man might come back sooner than you think and bus'up you rarse before you can get you trousers up."

"You think me fool?" Ivan said, surprisingly jovial. "Me not falling a sleep in another man's bed. Is what you think me going there for? Me not leaving me bed to go sleep in somebody else bed. Me have something else on me mind." He said it with a knowing smile from the door, which this time he hurriedly slammed behind him. A shudder went through Winnie. She was alone with Lias. She had often said she could not relax with Ivan in the room. Now that obstacle had been removed and cold panic gripped her as she searched for a new excuse.

"You no hear me?" asked Lias.

"Eh?" she pulled the iron off the shirt.

"Is what you think you doing? You burning up me good white shirt? I was saying that since you going out to work tomorrow, you better come to bed."

"Just two more shirts and I finish," she said. The germ of an idea was forming in her mind.

"Well, go ahead and iron ten shirt and me still will be here. I not sleeping tonight." Having made this declaration, he pulled himself up in bed, rested against the pillows and began to browse through the newspaper.

She finished the shirt and folded it away in the drawer at the bottom of the wardrobe. With great care, Winnie climbed onto the chair to reach into her suitcase and took out a toilet bag and a bottle of tablets. She shook the bottle to attract Lias' attention.

"Is what happening to you now?" he asked.

"I got a headache," she said, gathering up her things and headed for the door enroute to the bathroom. Returning half an hour later, she sat before the dressing table and plaited her hair.

"I don't understand you at all," he said wearily.

"What 'bout me don't you understand?" but in all honesty she did not want to know.

"If you no like me, why did you agree to take me money to pay you passage for England?" She could see him in the mirror, staring at her back. His eyes did not catch hers. She looked away quickly. "Answer me, no!" he urged.

"Things look different when you back home, you know that." She was shocked to hear the softness in her voice. "We was once church brethren. I didn't know that you backslide when you come to England. We all thought that you still in grace."

"Is who you fooling? You backslide long, long time before you go to Iron Mango Tree," he said.

"No, I left Gap, but I did not leave the church," she added defensively. She knew there had been whispers that Sister Winnie, having put her hand to the plough, had now withdrawn it. The clue to a woman's backsliding was usually that she got pregnant or left to live with a man. Well, there was no man in her life and Son-son had not got her pregnant that rainy night in the old boiling house.

"True, true. I was living at Mango Tree but I was still in grace. I agreed to come up because everybody round me was leaving for England. When I talk with Sister Beah," she lied, "she say that God in England too. She thought we could wait and see which way the Lord was leading us, and we could eventually get married without yielding to the flesh."

A sharp hissing of air through clinched teeth interrupted her. "Woman, you in England now. All that Church of God stupidness is over and done with. You think me was going to pay nearly one hundred pounds to get you over here and treat you like a virgin princess? From tonight you gwine stop all you stupidness. You better come into this bed, or I swear I jump out and grab you. Hear me?"

She turned her face towards him, a voice whispering, *Now, it has to be now!* "Nothing not gwine happen tonight," she said. "I really sorry," she lied.

"I don't hear you," he said, throwing away the newspaper, then leaping out of bed, he roared, "Get you' rarse into that bed and don't gie me any more bullshit, you hear?"

She intended to scream, but it was aborted as the heavy right hand exploded on her mouth and blood mingled with saliva. "Jus' open you friggin' mouth in-a this room tonight and a ram me fist right down you friggin' throat. I warn you, Miss High and Mighty. You acting like a little schoolgirl virgin. I bet you was no virgin when you was at school. You was hardly out a school when Slim breed you," he held her by the shoulder and shook her. "Is lie me a tell?"

"No," she moaned. The experience of having a stillborn child at fifteen had been the prime reason for her seeking religion and forgiveness. That was a long time ago and most people had forgotten her ill-fated venture into motherhood.

"Is what you saying?" He shook her again.

"Is not lie, Lias; like you say, Slim breed me, just like him breed..." she checked herself, because the girl she was about to name was Lias' own little sister. She climbed into bed like a cowed puppy whimpering into its basket. "No punch me again, Lias, I beg you."

"So is what game you playin' with me?" He stood menacingly over the bed.

"Me not playin' no game, Lias," she whimpered.

"Tcho, man," the big man said in a soft tone. "Woman pickney too contrary. Me can't do all this sweet-talking business. Me sorry me lay a finger 'pon you, but you have fe 'gree that you bring me a lot of crosses. Me is a rough country man, me no understand this love and romance foolishness. C'mon, man, I gwine treat you right, you gwine see." He put his huge hands on her shoulder and pushed her back on the pillow. "No tremble like that, man. You gie me what I want and I no lay a finger 'pon you again," he promised.

She struggled. "You punch me like you would kick a dog, then want me to gie you pleasure..."

"No try me patience, you hear," he held her firm.

"Beat me up if you want, but it say in the Book that you can't touch a woman for seven days when she is the way I be now."

He released her as if he had been electrocuted. "So," he said, "ever since you come here is one thing after the other. First you was tired, then you couldn't do it if Ivan in the room. We is big people and Ivan know what man and woman do when they go a bed. So tonight I make up with Ivan to go to him woman place and we could have some privacy. Now you tell me you have the monthly sickness. Well, I don't gie a damn if you sick like the woman in the Bible with the flux, I gwine rudeness you tonight." He lifted her head from the pillow and slapped her. This time she let out the scream before the other slap cut it short. She was not fighting to defend her honour; she was reacting like a wounded animal struggling for its life. She braced herself against the wall and heaved against the bulk of her attacker. Lias did not expect this, and suddenly they were in a pile on the floor.

"I not going to make you beat me up and rape me when I done got me menses. Before you do that I stab you dead in-a this room."

"Ssh, you gwine wake up the whole house," he counselled, but it was too late. There were the sounds of footsteps on the stairs and anxious voices echoing in the passage, followed by a pounding on the door. The landlord's voice enquired, "What's going on in there? People have to go to work in a few hours' time, you know! Shut up in there or I call the police."

"Call them. Call the police," shouted Winnie. "Him a-beat me up. Him a-murder me. I bleeding all over..."

The landlord pushed the door open and finding the room in darkness switched on the light. Indeed Winnie was bleeding from her mouth and nostrils.

"Right," said the landlord, "I'm calling the police..."

"I beg you, no call the police," Lias snivelled. "I never been trouble with them before. Is her fault. You know how it is. Woman is trouble. Them try the patience of a saint. No call the police...."

"All right," said the landlord, more worried about the police and borough officers discovering the number of tenants he had in the house. They would turn on him. There would be an investigation into his business, the general state of the property, the amount he charged per week. The local press would get wind of it. He could see the headlines: *"BLACK LANDLORD EXORBITANT RENT SCANDAL"*. Those thoughts entered his head before the possibility of Elias being charged with grievous bodily harm.

"No, it is not all right," said a voice from behind the landlord. "Just look at that poor woman's face." It was the landlord's white girlfriend who pushed herself into the middle of the room. "I'm a nurse; come, I will clean you up." She led the bleeding, tearful and trembling Winnie upstairs to the flat she occupied with the landlord.

Lias retreated to his empty bed, comforting himself that it would be just a matter of time before Winnie was back and as submissive to all his wishes. Just you wait and see.

"As me grandmother used to say, *'Whatta sweet granny goat gwine run her belly'*," he whispered through clenched teeth as his anger and frustration merged with the darkness of the room.

5

Lincoln did not know anyone at the party. His invitation was not unusual. The black bus conductor on the 45 bus had pushed a card into his hand, as he was about to get off at Camberwell Green. It was an invitation to 'Aunt Beah's birth night party' at an address in Brixton Hill. Now as he turned in to Josephine Avenue he wondered why he was going. The hostess was unknown to him. He put it down to the loneliness he had experienced since coming to London over four years ago. Did he hope to meet someone he could talk to? Perhaps he would strike it lucky and meet a woman. How many lonely men would be at the party with the same hope and expectation? He stopped and was about to turn on his heel when a black man of indeterminate years crossed the road and came up to him.

"We think we lost," said the man. Lincoln looked across the road where the man had left his lady. "We looking for a party somewhere around here."

"The man too foolish, you hear," the woman had crossed the road to join them. "This damn rushin' here and rushin' there make we left the invitation card 'pon the bureau."

"Was it an invitation like this, to Aunt Beah?" He showed them the card.

"The very same," said the woman. "You goin' there? Make we follow you. Before this fool, fool man lost we again." Lincoln hesitated only for a second or two.

"We are not far from Leander Road. Follow me," he led the way.

As they reached halfway up the street they could hear the Shirley and Lee record declaring eternal love. This Aunt Beah was a woman of modern taste. Then again it might be her many nieces and nephews choosing the music, he mused. An old Morris car pulled up outside Aunt Beah's and five black young men got out.

"You see what a happen?" asked the woman. "All these man them turn up with no woman, then they come and want to push up themselves 'pon other man women them." Lincoln felt embarrassed. He too had no female companion.

Inside, the house was packed. Men sat on the stairs talking and smoking. There were few women by comparison. It was a busy session for them; they were all dancing. Men without women were hanging around in a predatory manner, but those in possession of their females were not letting go. Most of the women looked to be in their late twenties to forties, except for a little girl who was no more than ten years old, who was busily darting in and out of the sweating, writhing mass. Lincoln fought his way to the kitchen, which was also the bar. He bought a plate of curried goat and rice and a rum and coke for a total of ten shillings. As he fought his way back to the foot of the stairs, he wondered who Aunt Beah was. There were between eighteen and twenty women, three of whom were white. He had lost the couple he rescued from the jungles of Brixton Hill. There was definitely no chance of getting near any woman to ask for a dance. The journey to the kitchen was not to be attempted twice. The rhythm and blues was pounding away. He decided to go home. He was close to where Alonso Campbell lived; he would rather be alone by himself than be *alone* with company around him. He headed back to Camberwell.

II

Back in the eerie silence of his room, Lincoln poured himself a large drink from the white rum that his cousin Adlyn had given him when he visited her in Birmingham about six weeks ago. His loneliness had steadily become more unbearable since his return. It was in those terribly empty and companionless days that he had written to Enid. He had been in a fever of daring boldness when he plunged headlong into the folly of writing. True, the deadline he had given her had now passed. She had decided to ignore him. His courtship was crude. How could you send money to a young woman, suggesting she use it to pay part of her fare to London? He heard it had been done before. In nearly every case the women were desperate to get away from the drudgery of country life or to escape a scandal. Enid fitted neither description. Why had he done it? He tried to convince himself he would start to woo her once she was in London. She still had the right to refuse him. He would be gallant enough to tell her that the money should not inhibit her from being straightforward in her dealings with him. She could say no. Pay the money back if she wanted. He would not tell anyone else of their transaction. He had never felt so confused. At times he was certain he was going out of his mind. He had even suggested a deadline by which time if he had not heard from her he would know she did not think much of the idea. It would be well if she had thus ignored him, but each day he expected a letter from Adlyn. Worse yet, Adlyn might visit him. Enid would be writing to her. Adlyn would explode in righteous anger about the stupidity of her cousin. The ultimate insult of proposing to buy her with the price of a fare or part of it to England! She would not consider him innocent in this. Did she talk to her cousin about her predicament? What impression did she create in his mind? Did she give the impression his attentions would be favourably received? How dare he send money before asking? He really did not know Enid! He had never seen her when she was angry, really angry!

He had seen Adlyn in a rage. As children her fierce temper could explode like a hand grenade.

Sometimes Lincoln would have been unjustly accused. This time he would have deliberately courted it. Why had he not talked to Adlyn first? She would have told him there was no way Enid would have been interested in his proposal. Adlyn would know why she had suddenly left her job in Kingston and gone to live in the country with her grandmother. In a second it was as if his mind was bathed in sunlight. Was she pregnant? He flopped on the bed. What a fool he had been. Why had he not thought of that before? Such things did happen, even to nice girls like Enid. If that were the case, at least she would know that Adlyn had not divulged her secret. He reached for his drink. He took a long draught and did not hear the first series of tappings at his door. He only looked up when the hinges of the door began to creak as it opened slowly.

"Lincoln, you in there?" The voice was followed by the plump figure of Vicky, robed in dressing gown buttoned high. "You back from you' party already?" She slid into the room with the grace of an animal emerging from its burrow.

"I just wanted to be on my own," he said.

"What sort of foolishness is that? You go to a party to be on you own?"

"No, I left the party because I wanted to be on my own," he said.

"I been to one a these *birth night* party, the house was full a men, hardly any women. Me not like it at all with all these men, them a haul and pull you to try and get you to dance with them. At one party this man hold me tight, tight that I could feel him stiffening 'pon me. Well, me was so shock and vex that me pull away from him and walk off the floor. Most of these men them suffering from woman starvation. Me don't want anybody rubbing up themself 'pon me."

"Some of them are lonely..."

"That no gie them the right if dry fuck me," she said angrily.

"I didn't mean that," he said shamefacedly.

"I not pickin' on you. England is the loneliest place 'pon God's earth. You know, I been in this country six months now and I never hear nobody laugh. Lawd, back home you hear Mass Dolly bus' some laugh, you hear it all the way down at Rhodes Fording. Them call him Horse because of him loud laugh. Here, I wake up and travel to work pass hundreds a people and all I hear is 'Any more fares, please', 'Ten pence' and 'Thank you'. Them hide behind them newspaper or them jes' sit there staring like the living dead. You don't have to hide in you room to be lonely. Everybody in this country is lonely. The other day the paper say a' old woman was dead in her house for three weeks and nobody knew about it."

"All right," he said irritably, "don't go on. I get the picture." Her touching on his loneliness was intrusive and it hurt. He reached for the bottle and waved it at her. "Want a drink?" Then, "Sorry, I forget, you and your aunts are Christians."

"Them not both me aunts, you know. One of them is me mother. Aunty Vie is my mother and Aunty Eunice is me real aunt." Having put the record straight, she set about instructing Lincoln. "Religion never was designed to make us pleasureless. I will drink with you." She took the bottle, poured a drink. "If you know your Bible, you will recall that on the day of Pentecost when the Holy Ghost was upon the disciples, some did say they were drunk, but Peter said, Look, it is only the third hour of the day. He did not say we is Christians, we don't drink. All things in moderation." She lifted her glass. "I drink to good company".

"Well said," Lincoln raised his glass. "I have to watch you, Vicky. You're very sharp."

"Me not sharp. I don't have any edge. Is all roundness. Look no," she grabbed hold of two handfuls of flesh around her backside. "All meat. Big steak to full you' belly," she laughed.

He looked up at her. She was of average height, but grossly overweight. She had a pleasant face with a permanent smile. She reminded him of one of his teachers at elementary school. The difference was that Miss Wilson had made every effort to look elegant. He thought of Vicky as the stereotype big, fat black Mama, so beloved of Hollywood for the parts of maids. Move over Hattie McDaniel! As she sat on the bed beside him, he saw the talcum powder where the base of her neck disappeared into the dressing gown. The smell of talc and perspiration mixed unpleasantly.

Lincoln shuffled towards the pillows. "I thought you had gone out with your folks," he said.

"I did, but after the meeting, them decided to go on to Willesden with Brother Bogle. You know who Brother Bogle is?" she asked.

"No. Who might this Brother Bogle be?" he asked. The rum was getting to him.

"He is the brother of the Evangelist Easton Bogle. Him is a tall, quiet man about my father age, and the damn fool running after me. Them gone to talk about we getting married," she paused, stared at her drink. "I done tell you, loneliness in this country make people turn really fool, fool."

"A girl should be excited about her wedding," he said, wondering if he was getting drunk.

"Me get excited! Me is no schoolgirl," she drank her glass dry. "He got two houses all rented out. I always say if a girl going to marry a man old enough to be her father, then he must have money to treat her like a daughter. What's the time? Them must be nearly back now. I no want them to come and ketch me in you room. You got any mint to take the smell of rum from me breath?"

"On the table, behind that big book. The room door is still open. They would not suspect a religious girl like you to be up here seducing an innocent boy like me."

"No man is innocent."

"Well, the other day I heard Miss Vie telling Miss Nicey that I was a nice, quiet boy."

She got up as if electrified. Lincoln marvelled at her alacrity.

"Quiet maybe, but not harmless. Snake no make noise, setting fowl make a lot of noise, but is which one you would say is harmless?"

Lincoln smiled at Vicky's witticism.

"You playin' fool to catch wise. Boy, I know some quiet ones. The type that butter would not melt in-a them mouth. Is one of them that gie me my first pickney. I was a good girl, you know. Me and this quiet, respectable man was coming back from choir practice. The night was black, not a light anywhere. I was walking ahead, when suddenly him grab me. I think it was because him was about to fall. Before I could bawl out, him was on top of me in the middle of the road."

"In the middle of the road?"

"That is in the country. Nobody comin' by after nine o'clock. Anyway it was so dark that them would have to stumble over we before they know something a go on."

"Did you not shout out?"

"That come later. Before I could say anything I realise I was liking it! I shock you. Tcho, man, you tease a woman and when she start enjoyin' herself you think that she is a whore. I know you all too well," she said. "I was one of the quiet ones too."

"What happened to the man?"

"What you think? Him was a married man, old enough to be my father. Him had a nice wife, nice house, land and everything. Them all say I was asking for it, even though he had a daughter older than me. You know, it's a funny thing about girl pickney. As soon as you bubby start growin' and you hips start spreadin' is like you turn into something terrible. You own father can't look you in the eye any more and can't touch you. Even you little brother them start look 'pon you as if you doin' something real bad. An' all the man them start whistling after you and thinkin' that you askin' for rudeness. Me is right or wrong? Answer me," she challenged.

"You're right. You are a philosopher." He realised that he was quite drunk.

"Me is a philo what? Boy, don't make me crack me jawbone," she was edging towards the door. "I leaving before you start gettin' any ideas," she reached over, took some more mints and started crunching loudly. "The rum smell strong and I mus' get rid of the smell before them two come back." She closed the door behind her.

He drained his glass, sat back on the bed and then flopped back among the pillows. He was asleep within minutes of Vicky's leaving.

6

After five months (or was it a lifetime?) living with her grandmother in the country at Pretty Turning or as the natives say Pretty *Tunning*, the shame had left Enid, but the anger remained. The old lady, who could neither read nor write, but whose wisdom was as potent as any philosopher's, had warned her that anger could twist itself into knots and in time choke her. Strange that the old lady never inquired what her problems were. She encouraged her granddaughter to read the Bible. That became a nightly ritual. Each night Enid would polish the glass shade on the kerosene lamp with its legend: *Home Sweet Home*. That gave her enough bright light by which to read the old Bible. She did not know how old the Bible was, but her father's date of birth and death were written on the inside cover in two distinct handwritings. Her three aunts' names and their dates of birth were also there, as was the date of her grandfather's death. She decided that this family Bible was over fifty years old. Yet, although read in times of great distress and times of happiness, its pages were in excellent condition. Only the spine showed signs of wear from frequent opening. Enid was never angry when she read aloud to her grandmother. She was surprised how she could purge herself of guilt, rancour and hate when she had the book in her hand. Once she heard the old lady singing, and Enid was able to identify Whittier's words:

> *Breathe through the heats of our desire*
> *Thy coolness and Thy balm;*
> *Let sense be dumb, let flesh retire;*
> *Speak through the earthquake, wind and fire,*
> *O still small voice of calm.*

John Greenleaf Whittier, the nineteenth-century American Quaker, was one of the poets studied at Wilberforce High School. But the Bible and the old puritan could not prevent the anger creeping back towards dawn. It fell from the departing wings of night, and grew stronger with the coming up of the sun.

It was Friday evening, and having nothing else to do she decided to embark on the three-mile walk to the Post Office at Abbey Look Out. She wore a cool cotton dress and flip-flop sandals. The sun was dropping behind the lower hills towards Grass Piece in the west into a fiery bank of clouds, but the heat had not fallen from its midday peak. The years in Kingston where she was sent away to high school, and later where she worked, had nurtured in her a profound dislike of walking long distances. The road from Pretty Tunning to Abbey Look Out was maintained by the parish council, thus called a parochial road. Whatever the road to hell is paved with, this one was paved with sharp ankle-twisting gravel and potholes and occasionally shared the thoroughfare with a gully. It was a far cry from streets with cars, omnibuses, bicycles and paved thoroughfares.

It was that time of the year when mango trees dumped their fruits on the ground. The air reeked of fermenting liquor; flies, bees and wasps flew in the face of all who walked in the heat of the day.

Every now and again someone astride a well laden donkey would shout, "Howdy Miss Enid," or "Cousin Enid, how you do?"

This was a mark of respect. For a young woman of the hills Enid was considered worthy of respect. First, she had been sent away to high school in Kingston. Secondly she worked for a well-established law firm, the senior lawyer being among the six best-known men in the country. But above all, she had reached her late-twenties and was neither a mother nor a wife. No man laid claim to her, although if the truth were known none of the young men in the villages around felt worthy of her. They dismissed her from their lustful minds as being too *"stocious"*, meaning she was stuck-up, but justifiably so. Sometimes as she walked past they would start singing, *"Daphne walking is a stocious walk..."* In response to the banter, she would do a little wiggle, then turn and smile at them. Things were different among her female contemporaries. To them a healthy young woman in her twenties who had not yet borne any children was in either of two categories, or both.

According to Miss Love: "She must be as barren as a mule."

Missus was wickedly forthright. "I wonder how many pickney she *dash whey?* Nowadays them know how to get rid a baby before them born."

"P'rhaps she a save it up for Mr Right," said Seeta, who was about three months pregnant with her second child. This last remark drew peals of laughter from the young women.

"Is what you a-say?" inquired Miss Love. "She's older than me and me have three pickney them. Make her gwone save it up. Blood gwine fly a her head."

"P'rhaps it happening," said Missus, "could be why she left Town and is staying up here."

Bet Deacon, who might have been Enid's grandmother's nephew's daughter, called out to Enid as she came into view. Enid's idea of walking close to the embankment to avoid being seen did not work. Bet was notorious, her sharp tongue so fierce that few would engage her in verbal combat.

"Miss Shine, you goin' to Abbey?" Enid was startled. No one, not even her grandmother called her Shine any more. As a fourteen-year-old she went off to Wilberforce High School in Kingston and she had left the pet name behind.

"Yes, Gody Bet," she recovered her composure. "You want me to ask for your letter?"

Everybody was aware that Bet's son, Monty, had just been recruited to work as a farm labourer in the United States. To Gody Bet he was the elite among emigrants. After all anyone with a passport and the fare could go to England, but to get to America you had to be specially recruited and her one son had been specially recruited and tested and passed medically fit to be a cane-cutter in Florida. Bet was sure that after six months the farmer would realise he could not possibly run his farm without the sterling work that her son was putting in. Monty would be asked to stay on. Even if things were bad and he returned after six months he would come home with nice clothes and money in the bank. No one ever came back from England after six months with money; if they came back at all it was because they could not stand the cold. Bet was careful about whom she asked to post a letter to Monty or to collect her letters from the Post Office at Abbey. Her son's address must be kept secret. She was still seething with vexation. Soon after he left for farm work the half-Coolie gal Seeta started telling everyone she was expecting a child for Monty. When she upbraided the hussy, she brazenly said it was Monty's farewell present to her. When she complained to Seeta's mother, that fat-arse woman told her that if she was so concerned about her son's activities, she should have *penned up her boar* and she would *tie up her sow*! With that, a veil was drawn over the matter and would remain so until Monty's return. In the meantime no one was going get his address, and she certainly was not going to tell her son that Seeta was broadcasting the news that she was carrying his child.

Enid walked up the little track leading up the steep rise to Bet's little house. Bet continued to hang out her clothes. She shook the crease out of her husband's long drawers, which were made from bleached flour sacks and which were still bearing the trademarks of the Toronto Mills that supplied flour to Jamaica. She dried her hands on the skirt she wore hitched high above her knees. She went towards the steps and retrieved a letter that was held down by the foot of a rickety stool on the veranda.

"I was going to Abbey meself, but when I see you coming up the road, I say to meself, 'I bet Miss Shine goin' to Abbey,'" she slowed to a conspiratorial whisper. "Miss Shine, be careful with this letter, you hear. I bet you hear what that slack'ntidy gal Seeta telling everybody, that is Monty breed her. When Monty come back, him can settle the matter by ma'shal law."

Enid smiled at the woman; the way the village was talking, it was Bet Deacon who had declared marshal law around Seeta and her mother.

"I don't know what a-happen to the women pickney them in this district! As them left school all you hear is them a-dey with man or them expectin'. Is a good day when you grandmother Gody Flo sen' you to study in Kingston. You notice how all you companions have pickney like rabbit? Look at Miss

Martha little Madge. She just lef' school, you know. Miss Martha say she say to herself, 'But wait, Madge putting on a little weight.' Heh, heh, no breed the little pickney a-breed. Man over Grass Piece who a work 'pon truck, loading it with box and bags, put her in the family way. Then there's Lally from Bun Dutty Gap, she is due soon, is Chippie Brown gi'e her belly. Yes, missis, them is first cousin. Is dog a nyam dog." She looked Enid straight in the eye. "No disrespect, but you should love that old woman for sending you away. The other night the preacher man up at the Wash Foot church said this district is Nineveh and that judgment day is 'pon us. Miss Shine, you must bless Gody Flo..."

"Gody Bet, Nana know dat me love 'er. But look here, I can't stan' 'ere givin' laugh fe peas soup, as Gody Nana would say." Enid slipped into patois easily. Anything else would be to show off.

She started back down the track towards the road, thinking, *Gody Bet, if only you knew!* As she reached the road she felt anger welling up. She detested gossip and those who spread it. She knew what it was like to be the object of gossip. Was she in Nineveh? She would not have welcomed Bet as Jonah. She started out as if she could reclaim the time lost listening to Gody Bet. But what she was trying to do was to push the last year from her mind, determined to expunge the hurt from her soul.

After three years as a very junior clerk in the chambers of one of the island's best-known barristers, Enid thought she had a bright future. Her job was secure. Her circle of friends was quite prestigious. She was also hoping for reconciliation with her mother, who had been working in the United States for a long time. Her mother had handed her over to Gody Flo Enid's father mother when she was two years old and since then had not had much to do with her. However, they were now in correspondence and she had been hoping of late that her mother would sponsor her to come and join her in New York where she would meet her stepfather and her young siblings. If that had come to pass Enid wanted to study law. She had made a note of all the well-known Black colleges. Howard and Lincoln Universities were high on her list. But she now knew that it was not going to happen. No one knew her secret, apart from Olga and Gloria and they did not know her relatives; her secret was safe with them. "Time is a great healer," Olga had comforted her. In six months, perhaps a year, she would wake up and it would not hurt any more. In the meantime she would remain in the country, then go back to Kingston to find another job. She could not imagine returning to her old job. The boss of the chambers had been recently appointed a senator by the Leader of the Opposition, and everybody said that after the next election he was bound to be appointed Attorney General, or Minister of Finance. If things had not turned out as they did, there might have been good prospects for her either in the chambers or in his new Political Office. She would not be famous, but she would have more responsibilities and they would know her at the Hibiscus Club. She would be "that girl who works in the office of one of the country's leading lawyers and politicians". All that and she could not recall a conversation with the great man beyond. "Thank you, Miss Swaby. Put it on the desk." On other occasions it might have been, "Do you know where Miss Dews is?" Then one day she acted as courier taking some documents over to Spanish Town where he was in court.

"Gosh," he said hours later, "are you still here?"

"Yes, sir," she stammered, "I...I was told to wait in case you wanted to send anything back."

"What time is it? Never mind. I told Wellesley to call for me at five," they were walking down the steps of the courthouse as the huge Buick sedan like a supplicant bowed repeatedly as it came to a stop. A young man in chauffeur's uniform raced around from the driver's seat to open the rear passenger door for the boss. He told the chauffeur, "This is *Ena* from the office. We must drop her off in town." He settled in the deepness of the rear leather upholstery. The chauffeur opened the front passenger door to let her in. Wellesley was about to move away from the kerb when a massive Packard pulled up so close to the Buick that it was impossible for Wellesley to pull out. Suddenly the driver of the Packard was tapping politely at the window of the Buick. The lawyer got out and walked towards the Packard. He bent to look in the car, then straightened and shouted at Wellesley, "Go on without me. I won't need you for the rest of the day. See you in the morning." With that he opened the car door and disappeared in the Packard.

"You know whose car that is, don't you?" asked Wellesley, selecting reverse gear so that the Packard could drive away first. That was the first time she had met him. She used to tell herself that they were introduced by one of the country's brightest and best-known sons. Their friendship did not deepen quickly. It was a year or more when she discovered she was pregnant. She felt no shame then, for she knew that Wellesley would marry her. She would be expected to resign her post or to get married quickly so that those not too subtle with mathematics would not notice she had become pregnant before the wedding. She did not think it out of the ordinary when Wellesley asked for a few days to think it over. Only briefly did she think he might not agree to marry her. Nothing was further from her mind than a delegation made up of a wife and assorted relatives. Wellesley's wife! A year of friendship and he had never once let slip that he had a wife and two children in London. She recalled the delegation, but vaguely. She remembered a thick-set brown man in white short-sleeved shirt and khaki trousers and sandals, his arms impassively folded high on his chest, feet planted firmly apart. It was to him she appealed, touching those powerful forearms and saying, "Please talk to me, somebody. What you all want? What is going on?" In the gloom she could not discern many details about Wellesley's common law wife. The male relatives formed a barricade as she fought to reach the front, bobbing here and straining there to get at Enid, the husband stealer, continuously frustrated by her protecting relatives.

It was the stout middle-aged woman who shouted the loudest. Suddenly she reached out and grabbed Enid by the hand she had stretched out to touch the thickset brown man. From that moment she was a shuttlecock. After ten minutes, or perhaps an hour, it was all over. She crawled back on to the veranda and pulled herself into her room. The next day she miscarried.

Abbey Look Out distinguished itself from the other villages in the Upper Yallahs Valley by having two churches; one Baptist, the other Anglican. There was also a post office, police station and courthouse. There was a store run by a Syrian, or maybe he was Lebanese or even Egyptian. The proprietor himself did not care which Eastern Mediterranean country the locals thought his ancestors came from. His store, selling clothes and fabrics, household goods and ironmongers' goods, was at the top of merchandising hierarchy. The grocery shops and rum bars were run by a Chinese family and the other grocery shop, selling beers but not spirits, was the domain of the Indian family which also operated the only public transport via Morant Bay to Kingston. The village presided over the ruins of a great house that was in its heyday before the 1833 Emancipation Act hammered the final nail in the coffin of King Sugar. In those long-gone days, the Upper Yallahs belonged to an English absentee landlord who grandly named his estate Richmond Abbey, its ruins can still be seen in the valley to the east of Abbey Look Out.

Enid arrived at the post office just before six. Having been closed from four o'clock, it now reopened as the post arrived from Morant Bay. The postmistress was an ancient near-white whose family had obviously crossed the colour line three or four generations ago but were careful not to associate with the majority blacks on any occasion but postal business. Her black assistant was one of Enid's distant cousins who had spent a year at Wilberforce but had to leave, her father having run away with a young woman barely a year older than his daughter, leaving his wife to care for their six children. Enid had wished to start back to Pretty Tunning after concluding her business, but this distant cousin insisted she waited so that they could walk back together. There was no twilight and an inky darkness had fallen over the valley. The road from Abbey Look Out to Pretty Turning, which by daylight had some of the most spectacular scenes in all of the Upper Yallahs, by night was no place to travel alone; especially for the superstitious whose imagination could be left bruised and raw.

"I say, is who in London know you well enough to be sending you registered letter? Them don't know they ought to put their name and address at the back?" She gave Enid a conspiratorial wink. "Secret and mysterious. I hope he put his name inside or how will we return it? Remember the days when we used to burn boys' love letters at the four corners and return them?"

"But this time we didn't have to return the letter," Enid said firmly. Yet she too was curious about who had written to her from London. The document was apparently so important that the sender felt it must be registered, but had neglected to reveal his or her identity on the envelope. She knew half a dozen people in London but was in correspondence with none. Some time ago she had written to the General Nursing Council; she was certain their stationery would be distinctive enough. She would open the letter when she got home. In any case, the darkness of the night made it impossible to see her hands in front of her face, let alone read a letter. The mystery had to be maintained, but in such a matter-of-fact way that her companion on the way back to Pretty Tunning would not dwell on it

When she reached her grandmother's house, she felt tired, but at the same time excited. She read to her grandmother from St John's Gospel, about the Samaritan woman, then she read a psalm before going into her own room. It was not really her room. Her grandmother had a policy of raising poor relations' offspring. Enid recalled sharing a room with an older cousin before she went off to Wilberforce. When she returned months ago she displaced two much younger cousins. For the time being they slept in the old lady's room, so she now had a room to herself. She was curious about the letter but was being spiteful to herself. As a child she would save a special morsel of food for that very last mouthful. She wanted to savour it. At last she sat down on her bed and leaned closer to the kerosene oil lamp on the table. She screwed up the wick to maximum light. Her heart was pounding. Eagerly, she tore the envelope open. Three postal orders and a photograph fluttered down beside her on the bed. She reached first for the photograph and recognised her friend Adlyn and a young man she identified as Adlyn's cousin. He was two years below them at Wilberforce. They were not friends. Adlyn had told her he had gone to London. She had never inquired after him. She was puzzled. Then she heard herself scream, a scream born of confusion and desperation. An animal caught in a trap!

"Lawd! Is what happen now?" the old lady shouted. From the stumbling sounds echoing from her grandmother's room Enid knew that the old woman was coming to investigate.

Enid quickly swept the envelope and its spilt contents under the pillow.

"Something run across me foot. It must be a little micey," she said, regaining her composure.

"Lawd me Gad!" the old lady laughed, pushing the door open, "you been livin' in Kingston too long." She shuffled back to her room, still muttering loud enough for Enid to hear. "My blood run cold, you see! Bawling out like that, enough to wake the dead and bid the sleeper arise. Few years in town and she 'fraid of lizard, she 'fraid little micey. Lawd, girl, you livin' in the country now." From the stillness of her room she heard the old lady's bed creak as she lowered herself onto it.

Enid went to the window to make absolutely sure the jalousies were firmly closed. She was not very fond of moths flying about her room either. She retrieved the envelope and its contents from under the pillow, straightened out the letter, and read it:

Dear Enid,

I am sure this letter will come as a complete surprise to you. Of all the people on this planet I bet you would not be expecting to hear from me. I'll not keep you in suspense any longer, you probably remember me. I am Adlyn's cousin. You and Adlyn were two years above me at Wilberforce. As you know she is living in Birmingham. I went to see her about a month ago. She told me she had heard from you. She said you had left your job in Kingston and were back in the country. She did not say why, and I am not asking. However, you must be wondering why I am writing to you.

If you are tired of Kingston, you must be tired of Jamaica. Have you considered coming to England? Almost everybody is considering it these days. The number of boat trains arriving at Southampton and Plymouth has increased dramatically. There is a stampede on, and sooner or later you are going to be caught up in it. I have enclosed some money to encourage you to book your passage. If you consider me forward, then you will have to come over here to tell me off face to face.

The district where I am living, is Camberwell, not far from Brixton. I work for the Post Office as a sorter and am trying to fit in evening studies when I can. I work shifts.

I hope you will see that this letter is unplanned. I am writing it as it comes into my head. Believe me what I am doing now is as incomprehensible to me as it will be to you. I swear I have never done this before. I know you and Adlyn used to laugh at me because I had this crush on you, and I was so awkward with it. Tell me what has changed!

I am writing this in the Post Office at a place with the name of Elephant and Castle. This is a spur of the moment thing. I know if I were to go home, and think it over, I will never go through with this hare brain scheme. I am not even going to read what I have written less confusion and panic should seize me.

If you consider all this impertinent and you are very vexed with me, I am sure you will let me know in the usual burnt envelope tradition. Be careful the postal orders are made out to Parkins Travel Agency. I urge you to go and do business with them.

*If I don't hear from you in a month's time I will take it
you are still angry with me. I am stopping now, as this is
not the time for a long letter.
Hoping this bombshell does not blow up in my face.*

Lincoln

PS. Adlyn knows nothing of this my folly

For more than a week she swung between anger and shame. Anger because she had contempt for all men, and shame because a man three years her junior had offered to buy her for thirty pounds. Thirty was a number of absolute betrayal, whether it was pieces of silver or postal orders. How could he have missed the symbolism? She knew he was a bright young man; Adlyn had praised him often enough. The anger raged and consumed her. She understood what he meant by the "burnt-envelope tradition". A cruel smile curled her lips, recalling that Beryl had earlier reminded her how schoolgirls responded to receiving a love letter from someone they did not appreciate; they would burn the four corners of the envelope and return it to the sender. It was the ultimate insult. Many a young man had been thus mortified. In fact Lincoln had written to her while they were at school. She had not insulted him, then. He was like a brother to her best friend. She had saluted him as my "ardent admirer", then pointed out that she already had a boyfriend of whom she was fond. It was a lie. Could she now bring herself to such juvenile activity as burning envelopes? But was it a love letter? Indeed he had spoken of his boyish crush on her, which was flattering when she was by herself and very embarrassing when she was with Adlyn and the group of friends who went to the Carib Theatre on Friday evenings.

By the second week she could control her anger when she thought of Lincoln. She even felt compelled to look at the family photograph of Lincoln, Adlyn, Uncle Justice and wife Daphne as Lincoln had identified them on the reverse side. What did Adlyn know of this letter? To be sure she read the letter again. She was surprised that she could not find the source of her anger, instead she found a sort of naiveté. He was still the lovesick sixteen-year-old who had ridden his bicycle from Kingston to Pretty Tunning so his cousin who was spending a week with Enid at her grandmother's could see his new bicycle. His father was also Adlyn's uncle. He had been living in the United States. He had come on a rare visit and had bought Lincoln a brand-new Humber bicycle.

"Unless you are planning to mash up you bike before I get back to Kingston next week, there was no good sense in you riding twenty-odd miles to show it off to me. It would still be new when I get back. You did not have to ride all this long way," she scolded. Then she said wickedly, "Unless is Enid you want to show it off to!"

He was a good cyclist. Both girls took it in turns to sit on the seat while Lincoln stood on the pedals, completely in control as he rode along the country lane. That was about seven years ago. She was calm when replying to Adlyn's last letter. She added a postscript, *Your cousin Lincoln sent me a birthday card. Who told him when my birthday was?* If Adlyn was indeed in on this plot she would inveigle it out of her.

One evening in the third week after receiving the letter, Enid said to her grandmother, "Nana, what would you say if I was to go try my luck in England?"

"Lawd, missis, everybody a-go England. It soon gwine get crowded!" the old woman said without looking up.

"Nana, you no answer me yet, you know," she said.

"Is what answer you a wait fer? All me know is that since you pack up you good, good job and come back here, is sit down me a-sit down, waitin' fer you to talk to me. All you been doing is to shet up the vexation inside you heart so that I think you gwine bus' open like when ripe breadfruit fall off a tree and drop 'pon stone. Go England, no. Them say that is where opportunity is."

"Right," she said, "I going to do just that. I think I'll go to Kingston day after tomorrow. If I shake myself I could be in England early in the New Year." She was alarmed at the speed with which she made up her mind. That night she read Lincoln's letter again. This time she smiled. Her savings at Barclay's Bank, Kings Street branch had enough to pay her fare to London. Now there was birth certificate to be had from Spanish Town, passport to be applied for. She would write to Adlyn. Should she plan to go to Birmingham or London. Perhaps London. That Lincoln needs a good telling off and this time he will not have his cousin Adlyn to shield him!

PART TWO

Of hope and expectation

*... It was unemployment there, and full
employment here, that started the invasion... there
is no reason why the natives should not come here
from the West Indies or Africa as freely as our
own provincials have always come to town, for
we are all equal citizens in the Commonwealth.
But it would be idle to pretend that coloured folk
are as welcome here as the Irish, who are not
even in the Commonwealth...*

South London Press, Editorial, 20th August 1954

*... London is a bad place, and there is so little
good fellowship, that the next-door neighbours
don't know one another...*

Joseph Andrews by Henry Fielding, London, 1742

7

It was a cold rainy evening at the end of September; Alonso was still wearing a summer-issue conductors' jacket. He jumped off the bus before it came to a stop. In his right hand he had the conductor's box and the other was still cradling the Gibson ticket machine that was strapped to his chest. He was running fast to get into the building and the conductors' room when a figure sheltering just inside the door from the cold rain called his name.

"Lonso, Alonso Campbell! Is that you?" She stepped into the bright light of the entrance.

"Jeesus!" he exclaimed. "It's Winnie Price. You working here too?" for he thought she was a new recruit to the canteen staff.

"No," she said. "Long, long story, but gwon and do your business. I'll wait till you finish."

"But how did you know I worked at Brixton Bus Garage?" he asked. They did not know each other well although she was from the neighbouring village of Bun Dutty Gap. He rapidly recalled that Winnie had been for a time a leading *saint* of the Bible Church of God and was well known in all the villages of the Upper Yallahs. However, Alonso could not remember talking to her beyond wishing her good morning or good evening, as country people do. He recalled the young men making lustful suggestion at the rhythmic movements of her backside as she walked by. Secretly he found their suggestions stimulating, but he had never dared voice aloud an opinion. He had been so careful with his address that he wrote to his mother care of Aunty Ivorine. He was determined to have nothing to do with his stepfather, so he did not write directly to his mother. Aunty Ivorine got all the letters but neither she nor his mother was likely to engage Winnie in conversation.

After he paid in the day's taking and handed in his equipment, he returned to where he had left Winnie near the door. She was wearing a brown coat that was too small for her. He had never been this close to her and was surprised that she was shorter than he had thought. They stood facing each other, then she dropped her chin onto her large bosom. He could tell she had been crying.

"Hey, what's up?"

"I'm in big, big trouble," she said, her eyes still downcast.

"Look, people are watching. You better come with me. I have a room not far. We'll talk there."

"I was hoping you'd say something like that, because I'm in a whole lot of trouble. Maybe you can't help me, but I have to talk to s'mebody or else my heart gwine burse."

The sharp wind and steady drizzle did not encourage conversation in the twenty-minute walk to Ostade Road, but Alonso's mind wrote scenarios of this woman having come up to join Lias Carter now throwing herself on his mercy. He had known Lias mainly as a relative of Bullah Cameron, who was married to his mother. Thinking a meeting with Lias was inevitable, Alonso experienced deep foreboding. At last they reached Ostade Road. Panic seized him as he led her upstairs. The landlord had a rule against taking women to the rooms late at night. Was half-past nine considered late?

"You not change one little bit," she said, settling herself on the only chair in Lonso's small attic room. She stretched her palms towards the paraffin heater.

"It's not really cold enough for heaters, but I discovered I can also use it to boil a kettle of water for a cup of coffee," he explained. "You still haven't said how you know where I work."

"What you'd think if I say you' sister tell me?" She seemed to enjoy his look of incredulity. "No, don't worry. I never said nothing more than 'Morning' to her. What happened was I saw you on a number 95 bus at the Elephant and Castle. But before I could get on it you ring the bell, and off it went. I ask a bus inspector where that bus was going. He told me, Tooting Broadway. Boy." She broke off to follow another thread of thought. "England have some funny names, worse than in Jamaica, where we have places call 'Me No Call You No Come', 'Alligator Pond' and 'Runaway Bay'..."

"Don't forget you're from Bun Dutty Gap and not far away are Abbey Look Out and John Crow Gully..."

"Yes," she said. Neither of them was comfortable with the conversation. She tried to pick up where she had left off. "I... I told him, the inspector you is my cousin. I asked suppose I want to get in touch how I was to go about it? He said I could go to Brixton Garage. So I get on to the next 95 bus. When I got to the garage, they told me I would have to wait about a' hour before you finish your shift. So I just hang around. I hope I don't embarrass you. After all it's not like we been friends or even cousins, as I told the inspector." She slowed down her story until she came to a stop. Both were quiet. It was obvious that an explanation was required, that he ought to ask some questions. He recalled that Warren Hall in one of his more philosophical moods had pontificated that the black Commonwealth countries are too far-flung for the sun to set on but those black colonials who arrive in the Mother Country are not strangers any more.

"Look, I don't want to make things bad for you, but could I stay the night?" She gave the impression that if she did not say it quickly and she would not be able to get it all out. She paused. It was not enough, she knew it and he knew it. "I guess you've probably heard about me and Lias? I agree to take his money and come to England." She broke down, tears welling up in her big eyes. "I just can't stand him. I come close to taking me own life. Is run me running away from him." She looked towards him. "I not gwine to cause you any trouble. I got the address of an old church sister, but she's living in a place call Maudslay. You ever hear of it?"

"Yes," he said, watching her. "Maudslay is the George Cross town."

"What sort of town?"

"It was something to do with the war. Maudslay has always been an industrial town. They called it the armament capital of the Midlands because it makes guns and equipment for the armed forces. Well, the Germans bombed it on a Friday night and on the Sunday morning the people gathered outside their half-destroyed cathedral and the Bishop preached to a huge congregation from the steps of the Cathedral. Everybody turned up at the factories on Monday and before two weeks had passed they were back to full production. The King gave the town the George Cross."

"What's that?"

"It's a honour, but instead of one person getting it, the whole town got it. It was like giving Hitler the two fingers. You know, like this." He demonstrated.

"But that is rude," she said, looking away.

"Well, nobody complained about being rude to Hitler during the war. That's for sure."

"You know a lot of things. You're very bright. Funny how things happen, eh? Here's me and you alone in a room in Brixton, yet all the time I've known you we never pass two words except mornin' and good evenin'."

He wondered too. It must be six years since he last saw her. He remembered her as one of the righteous sisters in the Pentecostal Bible Church of God. The members literally washed each other's feet and spoke in *tongues of men and angels*! He once overheard the head teacher telling the Baptist parson that he had never met anyone who could understand the language spoken by the brothers and sisters of the Pentecostal Bible Church of God when they were *in the spirit*.

All the young men had fantasies about Winnie, but in an untouchable sort of way. None of the men would have dared slap her backside or put their arms around her waist. Alonso remembered Son-son, the local womaniser (who was nicknamed Errol Flynn), once saying that he would like to be *Sly Mangoose* so he could get into the *brethren's kitchen and snatch this righteous chicken*. A year or so later he heard that Winnie had become a *backslider* while Son-son had joined the church and was now an elder. Son-son had missed his chance, or did he? Alonso looked at her now sitting close to his paraffin heater, in her ill-fitting brown coat, looking dumpy and unattractive. This woman was not at all like the cuddly light-complexioned, attractive young woman every boy had lusted after. The men who sat on the wall beside the Coolieman's shop would call out *"Ma Mud"* when she moved rhythmically down the road.

"I guess we were all a bit scared of you after hearing you speak in tongues of *men and angels*."

She lowered her gaze to the linoleum floor. "My sister sends me all the gossip about 'the trek to England', as Count Lashser said in his calypso. I got a letter from her this morning."

"I just have to get away. You know what I mean?" she was still pleading.

"I think so, but I don't want any botheration from Lias. I don't think I've ever spoken to the man. Apart from that I think he's a cousin of Bullah Cameron, my stepfather."

"Tcho, that no signify. Everybody from them hills say they be cousin, but I promise you won't get into trouble over me problems." She looked up at him as if taking an oath, then dropped her head again. "God is punishing me. I left the church and now like Jonah I'm running away."

"You people always see the God of everlasting punishment. I think God is more willing to love than he is ready and willing to chastise. I remember you used to call down fire and brimstone on us when you saw us chatting up the girls."

"I left all of that when I turned my back on God's work and started down Hell's broadway," She covered her face with her hands. The room was quiet save for the ticking of the clock. "Oh, Lord, don't turn against me in my hour of need." She lifted her head. "Help me, Lonso. I'm sorry to burden you with my problems, but you the second friendly face I seen in this country since I left Jamaica. The first one was a white woman who clean my face when Lias mash up me mouth..."

"You mean he beat you up?" he asked feeling the anger rising in his chest.

"I no want to burden you. Just say you will put me up for the night, and lend me some money to get me to my church sister in Maudslay. You see, I can't take the chance to go back to Peckham to get me clothes. Is the white woman coat me wearing. I stay in her flat for two days, then when I go to the job they promise me over in Aldgate, they told me they could not hold the job since I did not show up last Thursday like a should. Anyway when I was leaving this morning I tried the door and Lias lock me out. Well, him can keep me clothes because I not going back there."

"To tell you the truth I know very little about Lias, but I didn't know he was such a bad man. Didn't he join the church at one time?"

"He join the church fe get in with people. He was never *sanctified*. Old-time people have a saying, *'See me* and *come live with me* a two different something'. You gwine to help me?"

"I don't see how I can refuse. I can lend you some money to buy a change of clothes and pay your fare to your church sister in Maudslay. Don't worry about that. You said he beat you up?"

"Him bus' up me mouth. Tell me, Lonso, is why men like beat up women so? Is it because we not strong enough to fight them?"

"Some women fight back. My mother cut Bullah with his own razor when he beat me."

"I hear about that. When I heard of your situation I did pray for you."

"Thanks," he said. The silence deepened once more.

"You won't let me down, Lonso would you?" she said after an age of them listening to the ticking of the clock.

"I won't let you down, Winnie," he said. "I been working on the buses gone a year now and I never met anybody I knew back in Jamaica. Sometime I would work all of two weeks and not have a black passenger. There is no way Lias going to know that I helped you."

She grabbed his right hand held it tightly then she solemnly kissed it as if he was the Pope offering the ring of the Big Fisherman. "As soon as my friend settle me in Maudslay I gwine pay you back. One hundred-fold."

She closed her eyes then, releasing his hands, spoke quietly as if at prayer:

Almighty God, I do believe. I believe always. I prayed, but, God, it was like you never there, as Job said in the Bible. Sometimes it would be like shouting across a gully and all you get was you own voice coming back. O God, is why you never give me a sign when I was so in need? It is true what is written in the Good Book, 'My spirit shall not thrive with you always.' When you turned your face away from me, I did run away and hide. But I cannot hide from thee, for behold, should I take the wings of the morning and dwell in the bottomless depths of the sea you will still be there. Whither can I hide?

The prayer stopped. She still had her face covered with her hands. There was a long pause, then the sobbing began in powerful spasms and the tears escaped between the fingers. He stood in confusion watching the woman cry. Secretly he was glad he was in the attic room, otherwise his landlord would have been hammering on his door. Without clearly thinking, he dropped to his knees and put his arms around the great shoulders of the woman. She leaned her head against him.

"Don't cry. Don't cry, man," he said to her. Suddenly she turned around and threw her arms around him, her wet cheeks against his face. Then just as quickly she released him.

"I don't know what come over me. I'm sorry, very sorry. I'm all right now." She sniffled.

"I'm sure if the shoe was on the other foot you would help me. We all feel like running away sometime. I ought to know about that."

She gave another great sob and then several smaller ones as if a powerful engine fired her emotions and dragged on minutes after the brakes had been applied.

"What about Jonah?"

"Hey, what was that? "

"Jonah," she said, "He ran away from God. 'But Jonah rose up to flee unto Tarshish from the presence of the Lord.' I am frightened, Lonso. I believe that everything that happen is for a purpose. I feel like Jonah and don't want to bring a storm into you life. I can't work out why it should be you of all the people on God's earth that I should meet. Why you? Whatever happens, remember that the sailors threw Jonah overboard to save their ship. I tell you now, if the time ever come, don't you hesitate to throw me overboard."

He looked at the size of her and mused that he would have great difficulty in lifting her, quite apart from tossing her over board.

"Well, I'm not going to quote the Bible to you, but I don't think that whenever you get to work on time it was God's work and if you're late it was the Devil's work. I wonder what Lias would think if he could see you in my room? I bet he would say it is the Devil's work. You, on the other hand think, it is heaven's doing. You're here now and I promise we are going to sort something out. It's getting late. I didn't ask before, but are you hungry?"

"I'm too upset to feel hungry," she said.

"My room is very small. Two people on my bed would be so squashed that you'd have to separate them with a shovel. I tell you what, if I take off the mattress and put it on the floor, you can sleep there. I'll make up a bed on the base. We better make sure the Devil is locked out. OK."

"Thanks," she said.

The next day he wanted to take Winnie to Brixton. There he intended to withdraw money and let her shop. She was afraid that the first place Lias would look for her would be Brixton. He assured her that although many immigrants had come to live in Brixton, people did not stand at the corner of Coldharbour Lane and Brixton Road looking for runaway girlfriends.

"Me is not his woman," she said vehemently.

"OK," he said. "I'll have to go to Brixton to get the money. When I come back we will go to Streatham or Croydon. I doubt if Lias goes that far from Peckham. I will tell you how to get back."

Two evenings later, when he got home, the landlord was waiting for him in the corridor.

"I waited up for you," the landlord went straight into attack mode. "I noticed a young woman going up the stairs this afternoon. She had a key to my front door!" he exclaimed in total outrage, as if Winnie had somehow been given the combination to his safe. "Naturally, I stopped her. I was about to get the key off her and turn her out, but she pleaded with me that you are her cousin, and that she is only spending a few days and will have gone before the weekend. Is that so?"

"Yes, only a few days. She'll be in Maudslay before the end of the week."

"You should have told me before you invited her to stay," he said in a manner that said *I know she is not your cousin*. "I rented you that room against the advice of my friends who don't rent to West Indians. You people are too rowdy. Apart from that, you all want expensive furniture. You are not like us Africans. We are here to study and then go back home to build up our country. You Jamaicans are here to stay!" It was as if he had wanted to say it for a long time. Now the opportunity had presented itself it was not to be missed. His speech had been carefully rehearsed. "I furnished your room for a single student. If you are going to be living here with a companion..."

"My cousin," he interjected quickly.

"I will have to raise your rent."

"My cousin will be leaving before the end of the week," at last the landlord moved out of the way and he continued upstairs to his room. Winnie, who was listening from her vantage point standing half-in, half-out of the of room door, had heard all that the landlord had said.

"Sorry," she said when he joined her. "I carry trouble round with me like Cain carrying the mark of a murderer. The landlord doesn't like Jamaicans. It's the same all over. Lias landlord is Nigerian and 'im don't like Jamaicans. Him make it plain that him don't like us. Is it because Jamaicans too nuh like Africans?"

"The irony is we are all Africans to the English. After over three hundred years of colonial history most of the English still think Jamaica is a little island off the African coast," he said.

"You think him will ask you to leave?"

"No, but he will be putting up the rent by at least ten shillings if you're not out of here by weekend." He paused as he observed a strange look on her face.

"I really didn't want to cause all this botheration. I'm grateful for all you done. Thanks."

He knew instinctively there was more to come.

"Don't keep thinking about me. I'm thinking of starting a hostel for homeless immigrant women."

"You mockin' me?"

"No, but I don't want you to embarrass me with so many thank yous. I just want to see you straightened out, OK?"

"OK, man. I'm not goin' to embarrass you. I just want you to know what is in my heart. I still wonder what would a happen to me if I didn't see you working on that bus yesterday evening. S'pose you was just sitting on that bus, a passenger like. I would not have a clue where to find you."

"But you weren't looking for me. You just wanted help, and I was the first person you know who came along. If I was a passenger, you would probably have called a taxi and said, 'Follow that bus!'"

"Is now I sure you mockin' me," she said. One arm was folded across her ample chest, the other was pinching and pulling at her lip. "I been worried all day. You a young man. Back home, we not in the same bracket. Anyway I going on thirty-four; that must make me maybe ten years older than you. What happen if all this reach back home? Your sister, your mother and Gody Ivo all in high society compared to me. The way people will tell it will cause a lot a botheration and scandal."

"Wait a minute. Not so fast, Winnie. You leaving soon, right? Who's going to know you spend a few days sleeping on my floor? You posted the letter to your friend in Maudslay, didn't you?"

"That's it, Lonso. I'm not sure of the address. I tried to remember it, but I can't be sure. I know it is in my suitcase back in Lias' room. I swear to you if I was to drop dead my ghost would not go haunt that stinking place. Lawd, did I ever tell you how that room frowzy?"

"Never mind that now," he said, a little irritably. "You were sure last night it was Warwick Road. Is it the number you can't remember?"

"No get vex, please, Lonso. I sure it is 28, but I think it could be Marwick Road. She kinda make her 'W' and her 'M' the same."

"Don't worry," he said, softening his voice to placate for his earlier irritation. "We could write both addresses; I guess the post office will try one, then the other. It will just take more time."

When the landlord realised Winnie was staying with Alonso he increased the rent by one pound. Alonso protested, but the landlord made it plain he must pay up or leave. Alonso had plans to leave before the New Year and was hoping to stay until then. The swingeing increase in rent brought pledges of gratitude from Winnie and promises that she would be out before long. She was aware that Alonso's sister, Blossom, was expected early in the New Year. By then, she would be long gone. This secret was safe. They imagined that neither brother nor sister would willingly talk about Winnie running away from Elias. They too had appearances to keep up. The secrecy suited Alonso, who was beginning to feel his room was no longer his haven. He had spent the first eight months in London sharing with as many as nine men of various nationalities, and he hated it. It was hardly better when he and Lincoln went on to share with two other men. He had promised himself that never again would he share until Rosita arrived. He would always share with her. But then she was hoping to be a nurse; she might be at a hospital hundreds of miles from London and he would only see her during her days off and holidays. During the last six months he liked coming home to his books, his paraffin heater, his little bed, his little radiogram, dressing table, wardrobe and single chair. He did not want to share it with a woman who was not a close relative.

II

He wanted to continue educating himself by listening to BBC Third Programme. He liked listening to talks on literature, music, politics and people. He did not understand all of it, but his radio was still the best friend he had. He had listened not long ago to Beethoven's sixth symphony. He now knew it was called the *Pastoral*, it was written in 'F', opus 68, and had five movements. He was not sure what all that meant, nor how it would help his education. But he now was in possession of all those facts, and they had not been available to him before. None of those things would have been of the slightest interest to Winnie. Instead he found himself listening to Radio Luxembourg! She had once observed that he had a lot of books, and asked whether he had read all of them. Now and then he tried reading, but he could not study. He wanted her out, yet he was aware that for once the empty loneliness of London was no longer lying in ambush in his little attic. Each night he would return to a room that smelt of furniture polish. There would be washing hanging from a makeshift clothes line stretched diagonally across the little room. The smell of drying clothes was masked with fresh air sprayed from a tin. He wondered if the pungent smell of Lias' room had turned Winnie into a compulsive washer and scrubber. Each night when she returned from the bathroom Lonso would bury his head in his book and pretend not to see her folding her panties into a towel and arranging them close to the back of the heater where they would dry without being seen. Lonso had a day off in the middle of the first full week Winnie spent in his room. That evening he prepared to go out.

"I driving you from you room, eh?" He recognised the tone of guilt. "I think I'll be hearing from Maudslay soon. If not, I will just buy a ticket and go there."

"Look, if you're going to stay here and feel sorry for yourself, how about coming with me? I'm going to the pictures. I go to the cinema often. It helps to drive the loneliness away."

"So me is no company for you?" she asked.

"Well, you are here, but we don't talk about the things I'm interested in." As soon as the words escaped his lips he regretted them.

"I see," she said and a deafening silence fell between. He realised he had to act quickly before the silence grew into a high wall with barbed wire and machine guns. He took her coat from behind the door. The same door the white apparition had taken her coat in his dream.

"Come with me to the cinema. They are showing *The Outlaw*. The star is my favourite actress, Jane Russell."

She stood up. A sign, he thought, that peace was about to be restored.

"I never been to the pictures," she said, turning and stepping backwards into the coat as he held it for her. He laughed.

"You're joking. Even in the back of beyond where we are from there were the occasional films shown at Abbey Look Out schoolhouse. We used to pay sixpence. It was there I first fell in love with Jane Russell. She was in a film called *Pale Face.*"

"I know all that film show at the schoolhouse, but I was in the church from I was sixteen. My mother was high in the church before that and wouldn't allow me to go to picture palace."

"But you have been a backslider for a couple years now," he said as they started downstairs.

"When I was living at Iron Mango Tree, I was going to go, but it did not happen. We was planning to go to the Palace cinema but it rained hard that evening. So even if I did go they would call it off because as you know Palace is a' open-air picture house."

They went to the Clifton, a small cinema in Raleigh Gardens, Brixton Hill, built in the pre-war years when cinema was the main medium of international news through its newsreel.

They came back in the dark with a cold rain that attacked the face and other exposed parts of the body. Had they been of pale skin colour their cheeks would have been red. They hurried up the stairs, making as little noise as possible so as not to attract the anger of the landlord or any of his student lodgers. The heater had been left on and Winnie stood close, opening her coat to receive the heat as if it was a lover. Slowly she went down on her knees.

"Boy," she said, "is what I'm doing in this cold, cold country?"

"Well, how did you like your first film?" He was standing behind her. He reached forward to help her from her coat. She pulled the collar of the coat tightly around her.

"Not yet, man," she said, still in posture of prayer to the heater. "I feeling the cold bad, bad."

"So was the cinema the den of iniquity you thought it would be?"

"I don't think anybody bothering about me soul any more. They all know me leave Jamaica to come and live with Lias. They all know I am a fornicator."

"Don't say that," he was not sure why he was so angry at the mention of Lias' name. Until Winnie walked into his life a week ago he had never thought of Lias. "He is an animal," he blurted out. Once again the silence was building up like the parted waters of the Red Sea. She rose slowly to her feet, and accepted his help to remove her coat.

"No bother you'self about Lias. His day will come, just like how God a punish me."

"Just wait a minute," holding her by her shoulders and turning her around to face him. He was surprised how easily she spun around. "I thought you felt safe here," he said. "I never thought you would see living here as a punishment. I certainly won't."

"Hold me down and force me like Lias?" she said. He recoiled, stepped back. It was sudden, harsh and hurtful. "Don't get vex with me. You is the only person in this wide world that I have respect for. I get nothing but kindness and respect from you," she stretched out her hand to touch his face. "I would die for you. Know why? You give but you don't take." She moved towards the chair and sat down. He sat on the bed.

"How comes such a nice and decent person like you left the church?"

"Well," she began, "it wasn't like most of the other young girls, like say Sophie or Miss Love. I didn't leave it for any man. No, sir, no serpent deceive me with a' apple. I started to question certain things. How comes if I straightened my hair, then I committed a sin that is going to take me right down to hell, but the white evangelists them wives could wear lipstick and perfume and yet them still would go to heaven? Once you mind start wandering, you start down Hell's Highway. Soon I find myself watching boy and girl doing rude things in the bush. Before you know it, you start having feelings."

"You watched whom?" He inquired, knowing he would recognise anyone she named there.

"I watch Coolieman and Miss Gee. I was taking the short cut through Dog Bite when I see them go in the cane piece. Miss Gee take off her drawers and heng it 'pon a bush, an' Coolieman jump down between her legs. I did not want to watch but I couldn't move. Then I start feeling nice."

"You were enjoying it?" he teased.

"If it was the Devil that cause such feeling in me, then a lot of us going to hell. I know it was bad of me but remember it was a long, long time since I did it. I was now a big woman and experiencing all them feelings. I tell you I don't know what I would have done if a man or boy had come up behind me."

"You never got married," he said, "yet there were some eligible bachelors in the Church." He watched her as she shook her massive shoulders. "Then of course there were all those fellows in the Upper Yallahs who lusted after you. We used to call you *Ma Mud.*"

"I use to pretend I didn't hear you men. Not you, you was just a little boy then. I did know they call me *Ma Mud* and talk 'bout me gas tank and me headlight, like me was a car. Well, I never find a man I want to put me trust in. Look what Adam say when he and Eve done disobey the Lord: *'The woman whom thou gavest to be with me, she gave me of the tree and I did eat.'* From that time it was always the woman them fault." She rose, but there was not enough room to pace so she sat down again. She shook her head and a look of remorse flashed across her face. "I guess when all this come out in Bun Dutty Gap and even at Guava Flat everybody gwine take Lias' side. I can hear all the man them saying, 'Me, sah! Me not paying all that money and then have fe fight for a bit of rudeness.'" She stood up and looked down at Alonso. "Talk the truth and shame the Devil. Would you pay a woman's passage to England and spend two weeks fighting for a *little bit*?"

"I'm paying my sister's passage. But you mean something different," he said defensively.

"'Course that different," she said. "I mean a stranger woman. Let's say one of those other girls at Gody Ivo, Georgia, Virginia or that little brown-skin' one," she paused and before Alonso could supply the name, she said, "Atlanta."

"You know," he said looking up at her, "Atlanta is not a bad choice. I wonder if it's too late to change my sister's ticket? But Gody Ivo wouldn't agree..."

"Don't joke. Would you spend all that money on a woman then have to fight for a bit of 'rudeness'?"

"I spent a lot of money on you this last week," he realised too late, and tried to make amends, "but that's a loan."

"That's right. So don't expect anything on account," she said seriously. "You gwine get back every penny. You better go to sleep, you 'pon early shift, remember?"

He pulled the mattress to the floor, and wrapping himself in a blanket flopped on the base of the bed. She turned off the light and he could hear her fumbling in the dark before settling down on the mattress on the floor. For an hour, they seemed to take it in turn to be restless.

"Lonso," she whispered softly, as if she really didn't want to wake him.

"I'm not sleeping." Silence fell.

"You should be." There was another pause. He could hear her turn again, and when she spoke it was as if a streak of lightning flashed in the darkness. "You know when people kiss mouth to mouth like in the film we see tonight; what it feel like?"

He rose to his elbow. "You want me to illustrate?"

"No." It was like a strangled scream. There was sufficient shuffling to let him believe the sheet had been drawn over her head.

"You mean you've never been kissed on your lips?" She did not reply. Silence had returned.

"Go to sleep," she said after the longest pause.

His restlessness was increasing. He had got his blanket so twisted that his feet were uncovered. He sat up and managed to straighten the blanket. He covered himself properly and settled down. Then he pounded his pillow with his right fist and settle down again.

"We keepin' wake tonight?" she said from the floor. "You must have a bad conscience. How come a nice little boy like you have such a bad conscience? Is what you have 'pon you mind?"

"You can't sleep either. It must be that scene in the hay loft that bring back all that stuff about Coolieman and Miss Gee to your mind."

"Boy, you feacy, you know. If it was not that the landlord might come to investigate, I'd pull you down to me and really beat you backside."

"You don't have to drag me down to you. I'll come quietly."

"No," she giggled. "You stay up there, you hear? Lawd, boy, you hard of hearing or what?"

He found the edge of her sheet and burrowed under it. He could feel she was naked. The warmth of her body excited him. He nestled up to her until their faces met. He moved his hands along her body and slowly stroked her hips, feeling the velvet smoothness of her skin.

"Me gas tank," the voice was muffled. Her breath was hot on his face. His left hands wandered back to her shoulders and then down to her breasts. He heard the urgent intake of breath and slowly she moved a leg across his body. Then she held him tightly.

"Show me now," she demanded. "Show me what you do when you kiss." She had brought her lips to his lips. He prised her lips apart, even as his body was prising her legs apart. His probing tongue found hers. Again that urgent intake of breath accompanied by a long moan.

"Ma Mud," he said. *"Ma Mud."*

Early in the second week Winnie raised the question of her getting a job. "I got to find a job. I can't go on sponging off you. I will feel better if when I hear from Maudslay I can afford to pay me fare. If I don't hear anything then it's time I launch out on me own. Find a room somewhere and start saving to pay you and Lias back too."

"You don't owe me anything," he said, putting his arms around her.

"You too bad," she said, kissing him on the lips.

"For someone who until last week had never been kissed, you have become quite an expert."

"I got the best teacher in the world," she said, encircling him with her arms. "Silent water run deep. I never know I could ever feel this way. I don't think this is a sin. I want to know who learn you all these things that make me feel so good."

"No one taught me. You just know what to do. Who teaches a cat to catch mouse?"

"Well," she said, "I must be ten years or more older than you. I first did it when I was twelve, so is how come you know more about it than me?"

"I only responded to you."

"So is me is the teacher?"

"You better believe it." He said.

"In that case," she said, pushing him down on the bed and lying on top of him, "boy, you want me squeeze *ducunoo* outa you?"

He felt her full weight but did not mind, for he noticed that she was not wearing a brassiere. He pushed his face between her breasts. He could feel her shudder.

"You bad, really bad," she said.

III

She went to the Labour Exchange in Coldharbour Lane. She was given the choice of two jobs. One was at the Instrument Manufacturing Company in Effra Road, the other at P. B. Moo Rubber Goods Manufacturers, in Streatham Common. They discussed it and she decided that Streatham Common was further from Peckham; she would be safer from bumping into either Lias or his brother Ivan.

Every now and then Alonso would have a brief stab of regret about his changing lifestyle. He did not come home to study any longer, but to be with Winnie. He did not think deeply about their relationship. He would hurry home to her. He wanted to bury himself close to her, to hold her close. The loneliness of the past year had disappeared. It was not like riding from Kingston to see his sister. He knew that people had gossiped about the closeness of the two *Panya Pickney*. "All that hugging and kissing it not healthy at all," somebody had once said. "It like dog a nyam dog." But there had been pure unselfish love between them. He wondered briefly if he would have to choose between Winnie and Rosita. Suddenly he became anxious and angry.

"Is when you going to start studying again?" Winnie asked.

"Man cannot live by books alone," he countered.

"That is no answer, man," she scolded. "I come into you life and start spoilin' you. You' books was you' companion before I come. Now look 'pon you sprawl pon you back listen to Radio Luxembourg. Remember what the poet said? *'The heights of great men reach and kept. Were not attained by sudden flight but they while their companions slept were toiling upward in the night.'*

"The Ladder of Saint Augustine, by Henry Wadsworth Longfellow, which is in the Royal Crown Readers, Book six," he said recalling the main reader for fourteen-year-old elementary schools. "I didn't know you stayed on at school into the Sixth Form".

"Teacher Cousins used to write out these gem of thoughts as he called them and stick them all over the school wall. Funny how you remember these things twenty years after leaving school. This one was my favourite... *Was toiling upward in the night...* "

"But I toil in the night," he said, sitting up and holding her tightly around the waist, resting his head just above her navel. She pushed him away firmly.

"All you men a the same. I ran away from one sex starve *nigger* man, but it look like I jump out a the frying-pan and land right in the fire."

"You comparing me with Lias." He was always hurt and jealous when she mentioned Lias. She went over to where he lay face down on the bed, pushed her hand under his shirt and massaged his back up to his shoulders. He began to relax then slowly he turned over to look at her. She unbuttoned his shirt and lowered her head to kiss his chest, then she blew hard so that her breath coming out of her mouth against his navel made a sound that reduced him to fits of giggles. She lifted her head and smiled, still massaging the area around his navel and expanding towards his pubic area.

"I not comparing you to Lias. I just warning you that too much *night food* gwine turn you worthless. I will have to start rationing you. I sometimes think I leading you astray. You not studying any more and what about this place you have to get before you sister come up. Lawd, what a scandal if little *miss nice sister* come up and find me and you still living together."

That hit him like a bolt. It was four months before Rosita was due. Was Winnie still going to be living with him? Surely she would not move with him to the basement room that he would be taking over from the Morgans when they moved to their new home. Occasionally he had thought of his relationship with Winnie as part of the dream he had the night before he met her outside Brixton Bus Garage. He felt he was not in charge of anything except when making love to her. He was tumbling down the side of a steep mountain towards a chasm. He had neither the energy nor the inclination to prevent the inevitable disaster. He was now divorced from *Network Three*. Of late he would come home from work to Winnie. He talked to her. He held her and made love to her while Ella Fitzgerald or Sarah Vaughan sang quietly from the radiogram in the corner of the room. He did not care about her hearing from Maudslay. He had no more need for erotic dreams.

"Did you know that I too used to call you *Ma Mud* on account of how luscious you looked?"

"I knew the men used to tease me like that, but you was a little boy then. You couldn't be more than fourteen." She shook her head at him. "I'm robbing the cradle. How you say me look?"

"Luscious, tasty, exquisite, delectable, ambrosial..."

"Stop. You make me sound like me is something to eat. At thirty-four me meat too rough fe cook," she moved away, but the room was too small for either of them to be more than two arms length away. "You ever heard them call me mule?" she asked seriously.

"Mule?" he was genuinely surprised. "Because you haven't got children? I never heard that."

"Well, you spend a lot of time in Kingston and when you was up-country, that little stuck-up sister of yours wouldn't let go off you. She used to follow you everywhere."

"I never knew you noticed me, Winnie. If I did, I would have given my little stuck-up sister the slip and wait for you in case you used that short cut through Dog Bite one rainy and dark evening."

"You think you would be lucky with me the way Coolieman was lucky with Miss Gee?" she sighed. "That woman was one of the main people who called me mule because I past thirty and not have a baby. Do you think I'm a mule?"

He was frightened. Did Winnie want to get pregnant? "You were in the church for a long time," he heard himself saying. "I'm sure that if you were not, you would be like all the young women around our area, obeying the command to be *fruitful and multiply*. Some lucky man would have married you long time."

"Most likely I would be living with some man who would give me ten pickneys already."

"But not Lias, though."

"God forbid," she came over and rested her knees on the bed beside him. "Things have a funny way of panning out," she said. "Is who would think that me and you, Alonso Campbell, the little Cuban boy, would be living like man and wife in a room in Brixton Hill, London?"

"I was born in Panama, like George Headley and Andrew Salkey. We're not Cubans," he corrected.

"Same thing, you all speak Spanish. I heard of Headley, but not the other one."

"He's a writer who has a book coming out soon."

"But Lawdy Lawd," she said. For a moment Alonso was not sure whether she was contesting the statement that he knew a writer. It became clearer after she had shaken her head ruefully. "If some people back home could see we now! I know it would kill you' mother dead. As to that little princess sister of your'. She would have a fit just to see me with her precious brother."

"You don't like Rosita. What has she done to you?"

"To tell the truth, a lot of people wonder about you two. You hold hands and even hug you one another in public. None of my men folk ever touch me after I turn' ten. Come to think of it, me mother only used to touch me when she measuring me up for a dress. Yet I see you two running down the road laughing and holding hands."

"If what you are trying to find out is if I have seduced my sister, the answer is no. There's a kind of love that does not need sex to hold it together."

"Don't get vex, man. Ah old enough to remember when you three come to Guava Flat. None of you could speak English. You bound to be close." She went silent for a minute. "That is why we must do something before we end up hurting a lot of people. Listen to me, Lonso, after I get this job you got to help me to find a place. We will have to separate. We can be friends still. I not going to be responsible for coming between you and you' people."

"Why are you talking like this?"

"Because you not thinking. You living with a woman now. We are enjoying ourself. I never live with a man before. We living life as if we people in a book. But I tell you, unless we do something sensible fast it could blow up in we face. One of we got to be strong," she got hold of his throat with her powerful hands. "You enjoying you'self so much that you is not going to do anything about it." She began shaking him. He went limp.

She pushed him back on the bed. "You ever hear the saying, 'You got to be cruel to be kind'?"

"Like night before last when you said no and meant it?"

"Something like that," she said lying down beside him. "I did feel sorry the other night, you know? I was just about to give in when you fell asleep."

"I have not forgiven you. I cried myself to sleep."

"That make two of us," she said. "But that is not what I want to talk about. We talking about life and this is not a film or a book. The film and you' book can be finished and that is that, but this is life and it last a long time. People live long in real life and there can be real pain and hate. So we better get wise or else we gwine to end up with a lot of hurt. I want to remember these weeks with you as the happiest of my life. Somehow I don't think I gwine to see any better days."

He rose to his elbow. Looked down on her sad, brooding face. He lowered his face gently and kissed her on the lips. She no longer giggled when he kissed her. She did not only enjoy the tenderness in love play, but had begun to expect it. Later they made love far into the night. She pulled up her knees under her armpits and enjoyed the rhythmic thrust as Lonso endeavoured to nail her to the mattress. She lifted her back so that only her shoulders and heels were on the mattress. The unison in love making, is like the instrument, the instrumentalist, and the music of a concerto, when the soloist is thrown against the might of the orchestra.

It was early November and it was dry and cold. There was an expectation of snow. Everyone seemed to think there would be a "white Christmas". The sky was clear and there were stars. It was just past eleven. Winnie would be in bed pretending to be asleep. He would be quiet. She would have put a large saucepan over the paraffin heater and placed a dish in it perhaps with rice and peas and spare ribs. He had a keen appetite probably brought on by the good news about the Morgans' new house. They would be in possession before Christmas. That meant that Alonso would be able to get their old flat on Geneva Road. He planned to eat quickly and as quickly use the bathroom so he could climb into bed without waking her, Of course, she would not be asleep. He liked the warmth of her body. He began to think of her as a comfortable nest from which he did not want to fly.

IV

As soon as he opened the front door a feeling of great foreboding came over him like an incoming tide. There was agitated whispering from every floor and room doors began closing noisily as he started up the stairs. The Nigerian woman with the outsized backside who lived on the floor below Lonso's attic room was the last to close her door. She waddled into her room, muttering, "But these West Indians, Lawd. They are trouble makers, ahoo."

There was something wrong. Whatever it was, it was in his room. He hastened up the last flight of stairs. His shoes echoed on the linoleum-covered floor. From outside his door he could hear voices, men's voices, the landlord and Winnie's voices. Suddenly he was in the middle of the *milieu*. In the Babel of sounds and the waving of hands and general jostling for position, he could see Winnie hemmed in by the landlord who was facing Ivan and Elias. He briefly wondered if the landlord had tried to separate Winnie from Elias.

"I will have no more brawling in my house." He was looking at Alonso, but appealing to all the combatants. "The neighbours are sure to call the police. I should have done so myself."

"Gwon no," said Lias squaring up to the landlord. "I tell you blood a-go flow like water tonight. Call the police. Gwon call the police." To reinforce his threat be pulled from under his coat a cutlass, such as Alonso had not seen since leaving Jamaica. They all froze. Slowly Winnie slid to her knees her head bowed showing the back of her strong neck. In the confusion and danger of the moment, Alonso thought of an execution. The blade by itself was intimidating enough. There was hatred, insanity and murder in Lias' eyes.

"Lias!" shouted Ivan. "Man, me didn't know you bring that with you! A prison you a go if police catch you with that, you know." He tried to restrain his brother, but Lias' huge shoulders heaved and shrugged off Ivan's hand.

"Gie me the machete. Is you' woman you come for. You no gwine chop up nobody 'ere tonight. Take the woman an' make we go. Me no want no trouble with the police, you hear me."

Lias turned and pushed his brother out of the way so he was now facing Alonso. "Right, so you consider you'self a big enough man, to climb in a bed with another man woman?" He demanded taking a step close to Alonso, pointing his left fore finger a hair's breadth from Lonso's face. "Well, no *rarse clawt* man, no gwine take me woman from me, hear me? Before that 'appen, me heng for him. Me mean it. Me and Winnie a big people. You is just one *piss'n-tail* boy. We no you companion, so is how you take me woman from me? What happen? Dog nyam you tongue?"

It was not fear that stopped Alonso from speaking. He looked at the illiterate Lias fighting, not for love, but for his possession. It was a primitive emotion. He had taken away Winnie's right to freedom with the price of a ticket to London. She might have considered that Lias' offer was the only way to freedom, but it was the loss of her freedom. She did not escape. Her time with Alonso had only briefly lifted her up to see the green pastures beyond. She too had expectations.

"OK, put away the cutlass," he said. He was pleased that his voice was steady. "Sure, you can kill me, but that would not solve anything. They will hang you. There would be no satisfaction."

"Satisfaction, me *blood clawt!*" he screamed. "I get me satisfaction from the fact that I kill you and that whore in the corner dey. It no more than any man who wears trousers would do. You is a little *piss 'n tail* boy. How come you a rudeness me woman? Suppossen sey people back home hear 'bout this carry-on? Them gwine laugh at me. You see me disgrace? Winnie, come meck we go. You and he and me not companion', you know. If the baby that Coolieman Slim gie you did live it could be Lonso' age!" He stared at Alonso. "But ah what a gwon 'ere? How come she is all airs and graces with me, all laudy-dah madam mucks with me, but she open her leg for you?"

"You filthy bastard," Alonso's fists were clenched. He was not afraid of the cutlass. The space was so restricted there was hardly enough room to wield one. Lias' swung his right hand over the table, and that gave Ivan time to grab his brother's hand. The landlord seized the chance to push Lias. He went straight into Lonso and before anyone had a chance both men were in a pile on the floor on the narrow landing outside the attic room. A twist and a shove and both rolled, bumping down the stairs to the next landing. Lonso was the first to scramble to his feet. Ivan ran down quickly and assisted his brother.

"Make we leave before the police come. I don't want you to go to prison over this no-good harlot. Lias, listen. Make the boy pay you back you money. If he want her, he can have her. I never know why you send fe woman back home, 'pecially one that was'n you woman from time gone. You want woman, come with me down Brixton Market, I show you some women, black or white."

"Me send for this one, and me not giving her up to no *piss 'n tail* boy," he said, looking up the stairs to where Winnie stood. "Gawd Almighty, the police or no African gettin' me out a 'ere till she pack her things. You hear? Pack you things and come.

"Yes," said the landlord. "Go and pack your things and leave my house. I want you all out of here. I don't want any murder in my house. We are respectable people in this house."

Alonso looked up and saw Winnie had on the ill-fitting coat that Lias' landlady had lent her. She had taken none of the clothes she had bought during her stay with Lonso. She hurried down the stairs, as she passed Lias she said, "Me ready!" She went on past Alonso without looking at him and continued to the ground floor. The door opened and she stepped out into the cold November night.

The police did come but they were fifteen minutes late. The landlord told them the noise was the result of a domestic matter but calm had now been restored. Tempers had cooled. Two or three of the student lodgers supported him and the police were sufficiently satisfied to issue a cautionary word. They left without speaking to Alonso, who, like Sir Bedevere in the selection of Tennyson's poem that he had studied for his Jamaica Local Examinations, stood revolving many memories.

8

It was a Sunday afternoon in early December and Nello and Ziah Morgan were seated comfortably in the sub-tropical warmth of Myrtle Morgan's sitting-room-cum-dining-room in Geneva Road. Both men were smoking and helping themselves liberally to the white rum left over from what Myrtle had used to soak the fruits for not only the Christmas cake but also for Vicky's wedding cake. They had both had a sniff of the cake mixture and passed it as food fit for the gods. Myrtle handed the men the mixing bowl after she had put the mixture into the baking tins. She stood hands akimbo and watched the men use their fingers to wipe out the mixing bowls. She shook her head.

"You put me in mind of me twins licking out the bowls when I was baking back home. You want a nice cuppa to wash it down?"

"What? So you think the gods take a cuppa when them eat ambrosia? Give us a real drink. We can smell the J. Wray and Nephew product," said Ziah.

"I hope is not my God you talking about, Isaiah Morgan, you old blasphemer," said Myrtle.

"No, man," he redeemed himself quickly. "All the same when His time did come at the wedding feast at Cana, He did turn the water into wine and everybody did marvel at the quality. I bet you it was not Rich Ruby red wine!"

"The pub them no open yet?" asked Nello. Both men laughed loudly.

"Me no know what you two find so funny." Myrtle hissed.

"So, Miss Myrtle, you head cook and bottle-washer at this wedding? Them is relatives?"

"No, them is not relatives, but I know them from the time I use to have a cold supper shop in Price Street in Jones Town. Vie and Miss Nicey used to buy and sell things down a Coronation Market that was before them started doing dressmaking at a little place on Orange Street. "

"Dem was higgler ... dem know how to haggle. They turn dem hand to anything, Nello," said Ziah.

"Them is nice Christian women," she said. "Is one of them daughter getting married..."

"You know," interrupted Ziah, "I still don't know which one of them is Vicky's mother!"

"You too dam' fast," his wife said quickly. "Vicky getting married to a preacher man from over Willesden way. He has a brother who is high up the

Pentecostal Church of God back home. His title is All-Island Evangelist. Maybe you heard about him? His name is Easton Bogle? Vicky's intended is called Zephaniah Bogle. The wedding is going to be a big affair. Church people from Birmingham, Maudslay, Manchester, Rugby, Bristol all them places coming."

"And you think is all right for me to come?"

"Yes, man," said Ziah.

"I know they say in Jamaica you no need a invitation for funeral or christening but you need one for wedding. Well, here in England black people no stand 'pon ceremony. We turn up to support we one another. So you invited," she paused. "But, Nello, you no say anything 'bout the house."

"I done tell you' husband that I like it. You know I was a foreman carpenter back home, so I can fix and change anything you people want done. Somebody said to me last week that if you doing any serious changes the Council will want to know 'bout it. I don't think what we have in mind, which is fixing up the cellar for child minding, is going to bother them. The cellar is just like this one. It have its own entrance and big windows letting in the light. Your nephew Lincoln was there with us. He agreed with me."

"Him is not me nephew, you know. Him was one of the young boarders I used to look after when them were going to High School in Kingston. He never forgotten me," she said with pride. "Him is like one of me own."

"Not like that other one, Alonso, eh?"

"I don't know that one personally, 'though I hear he is after the women."

"Is what that big mouth, Ziah been telling you?" asked Myrtle Morgan.

"Tcho, man, Nello is like family now," he assured her and then went on heedless of her winks. "She used to look after this one from Monday to Friday. Nice boy, I like him. Him is working on the buses too, but at different garage from me. The other day him got himself into a bit of scrape. It seems that this man sent back home for a woman. Him didn't treat her right, so she run away and Lonso put her up. When the man find out he went there with him machete and cause a lot of bangerwrongs at the place where Lonso was living."

"Lonso put her up like any decent person would do. Thank God it all sorted out now and this woman gone to live with her friends in Maudslay. Lonso was only being kind."

"The boy got Spanish blood in him and for three weeks this woman was in his little room and you gwine tell me that nothing no gwon?" He sucked air through clenched teeth, very loudly.

"Is that all you have in you mind Isaiah Morgan? You' dirty niggerman mind can only think on one thing." She went out into the corridor to attend to her pots.

"Well," Nello said, "people have a duty to give a helping hand. Thank God they do, or else I would not be sitting here drinking white rum and expecting Sunday dinner. Anyway I can't throw any stones seeing that me living in glass house meself." The men nudged each other.

"I guess we make our mind' run away with us too fast sometime. Anywise when we leave here is Lonso going to take over this place. Him sending for his younger sister. I guess she is coming up to study nursing. All the nice black gal them a study nursing."

"You notice?"

"I tell you what though, if I was young and fancy free, I woulda never send for a woman I hardly know nothing 'bout. Before that," he leaned towards Nello and said in a conspiratorial whisper, "I rather find meself one of these white women."

"Who getting a white woman?" asked Myrtle coming back into the room. "So you fancy you chance with that young conductress they put with you the other day."

"Tcho, woman," he said, "When I ready to change you for a new model, she will have to know how to cook rice and peas, curry goat meat and make cake that have so much rum in it you could get arrested for driving under the influence." They all laughed.

"No joke," said Nello, "this black man and white woman business is causing a lot a ruction. The other day I hear two white women talking about someone they know. One said the girl was turned out of the family home. The other woman wondered what's going to happen to her, and the first woman said, 'Oh, don't you mind, some of these darkies will take her in. That's all she's good for now.' These white people treat white girls who go out with black men like shit, you know?"

9

My dear Lonso,

*I am writing this sitting in the toilet at work, because there is
a woman here that know Lias and she is watching and peeping
me and taking everything back to Lias. So it was a good
thing that when you bring the letter from Maudslay you did
not see me but leave it in the manager's office. I do not know
where to begin to say what is in my heart. I guess I am a very
bad person and do not deserve forgiveness. I say it before. I
was fleeing like Jonah and it was not your fault we ended up
in the same ship. You remember I talking to you, telling you
that the time will come when I was to be thrown over board,
for I cannot run from God. Now I am in the belly of the fish
that swallowed Jonah. I do not care any more what going to
happen to me.*
*I love you once I love you twice I love you next to Jesus
Christ.*

Yours in everlasting torment
Winifred Bathsheba Price

Alonso sat staring at the letter unconscious of the fact that he was crying
until the first splash of tears fell on the letter. The wound would never heal.
Gangrene had set in. She was in the belly of the fish in the same way as he
was in the belly of the crocodile in his dreams. In some strange way their
lives were so intricately interwoven that he could feel her pain although
miles separated them.

In mid-January, Myrtle Morgan called him to one side when he came into
the canteen at Brixton Bus garage. She took from the wide pocket of her
apron a copy of the *South London Citizen*. She already had it folded at
pages 4 and 5. The main heading was stark:

VIOLENT COMMON-LAW HUSBAND STABBED
Lover bound over to keep the Peace

His Honour Mr Pryce-Binns was told that Elias Carter, aged 49, of Desmond Road, Peckham was stabbed by his fellow co-habitant Winifred Bathsheba Price, aged 34.

Carter, who came to London from his native Jamaica two years ago, sent money back to Price on the understanding that she would come and live with him and eventually they would marry. To Price the chance of leaving her impoverished rural village must have been irresistible, despite the fact that she did not know Carter well. Her counsel explained that with the flood of migrants leaving Jamaica, the majority of them being men, it was not unusual for men to send for women desperate to escape the poverty trap. In many cases these arrangements worked to the benefit of all. In other cases the partners would come to an amicable agreement where the woman would repay the cost of the fare and then go her own away. In the present case it did not work out well. Mr Carter turned out to be a violent and possessive man, who caused Price grievous bodily harm on a number of occasions. Once when Price tried to escape, Carter pursued her to the house were she had sought refuge and threatened the other tenants with a sword. He had on many other occasions locked her out or locked her in as the occasion caught his fancy.

Fellow tenants will testify that they heard Price's screams for about half an hour before Carter staggered out of his room and collapsed outside another tenant's door. This was a plain case of self-defence. In any case the wound was superficial.

His Honour, summing up, called on the Colonial Office to supervise more vigorously the flow of immigrants to this country. He was in no doubt that Elias Carter was a thoroughly wicked person, but he equally deplored Price's action. He wished he had it in his power to deport both to their country of origin. However, he had been persuaded that Price was erstwhile of good character. He hoped that now she was among friends she would settle down to a useful life in this country. Whether she repays Carter was a matter for private arrangement, or indeed another court.

10

Lincoln had by now become acutely aware that the deadline he had so rashly imposed on Enid had expired. She was not interested. He was sure she would now write a letter demanding that her friend and Lincoln's cousin Adlyn should confront him and tell that love sick puppy to stop, desist and forever more stop send her love letters. He was now resigned to getting a visit from an irate Cousin Adlyn. He was beginning to understand that he had been foisting his unwanted attentions on Enid for the last six years or so. He had been a rash teenager completely enamoured by Enid one of the most popular Seniors in the school. Adlyn had cautioned him that Enid had let him off lightly because both girls were best friends. Enid had said to her she ought to be flattered by the compliments he had paid her but since she was soon to be engaged to another she did not think she should reply in writing or give a personal interview so she is asking her friend and his cousin Adlyn to ask him not to write to her any more.

It had hurt then and now he expected the wounds will be deeper. Lincoln knew that Adlyn would surely come to London to read the riot act. She would try to make him understand that Enid was not interested in him. Adlyn would come to London because this business was not something she would trust to correspondence. She knew Lincoln too well; once he got the essence of the letter he would toss it aside and probably never finish reading it. She would come and pin him down, forcing him to look at her while she laid heavily into him. As a concession she would invite him to come to Birmingham and she would introduce him to some young trainee nurses who had recently come up from the Caribbean.

For the time being he would throw himself wholeheartedly into his other activities. He was up-to-date with his part-time course in accountancy at the polytechnic at the Elephant and Castle. He was determined to be a successful businessman. He hoped to exchange contracts for his first house in Northlands Street, off Coldharbour Lane. With so many blacks stopping him and he supposed every other black person, in the street asking if anyone knows of any rooms for rent, that was a good omen. There was a demand for accommodation. Anyone even without Ordinary-Level economics could see that. Well, he had Advanced-Level economics and was well placed to get part one of his accountancy examination at its next sitting. As he mused, the loneliness returned like a bout of malaria. It was the same malady that had driven him almost racking in pain to Aunty Beah's birthnight party. He was thankful for the respite that brought him back to sanity and saved him from that noisy, sweltering mass of humanity. Despite his love of the vibrancy of rhythm and blues and the calypsos, he was glad he did not stay. The loneliness was feverish in its intensity, draining his body and forcing him into the reclusiveness of his room, a packet of cigarettes and a quarter bottle of white rum, neither of which he particularly liked. He could do without both, but heroes in films and books generally retreat into drink and cigarettes. Why shouldn't he?

He recalled Vicky's visit, a cheerful face in his fevered mind. Now begins the fight back. To hell with Enid! What was thirty pounds? Melbourne had said he had lost fifty pounds at Catford Dog Track last week. Lincoln undressed for bed. On the BBC Light Programme he could hear Jo Stafford singing, *"Suddenly There Is A Valley"*. He stubbed out his cigarette, switched off the light and dropped back among the pillows. The room radiated a glow from the radiogram. The malarial symptom of loneliness began to permeate his body again. Damn Miss High and Mighty Enid Swaby!

Despite it all he slept late. It was now Monday morning. He awoke to the peculiar feeling of being in an empty house. From his bed he could see through the badly closed curtains that the sun was brilliant but without much warmth. There was a stiff breeze that drove the cold through to the bone. It was a good day not to go to work. He would make a cup of coffee and uncoil slowly. He had to go and see the estate agent, Cass & Cass. After that, he might walk on to the Colonial Club. But first he must have that cup of coffee. It was then he heard Vicky's voice outside his door.

"Lincoln, you awake?"

"No, I'm sound asleep." He grasps air loudly through his open mouth to imitate a loud raucous snoring.

"What happening, you talking in you sleep? Open the door. But is what you lockin' the door for? You safe, you know. You ever hear say man get rape though?"

"You not reading the right newspaper," he said opening the door.

"I read the *Sketch* and *Tit-Bits* and Aunt Vie get the *News of the World* on Sundays. There's a lot of big bosoms and long legs, but nothing 'bout a man getting rape in any of the papers."

"It is the bosom that does it every time, baby." He sniffed the air. "Is that coffee? You bring me coffee? You're an angel," he said.

"You lockin' you door from angel? Even though she have big bosom?" She handed him a cup of coffee.

"I've been having some strange visitors of late, you know. One was telling me about how she got pregnant at fourteen."

"Well, as you say, is 'bout the bosom that done it every time. Anyway is 'bout time you get outa bed. You know what time it be? Look, I bring back that form you gie Aunty Vie to sign."

"Well, has she signed it? Good."

"I think so. You get plenty people to join you building society?"

"A few. I send the papers to head office in Jamaica and they write to the savers. If I collected the money people would wonder if I'm running a scam. You know what Jamaican people are like."

"Forgive me prying, but what in it for you then?"

"I used to work for Island Shield Life Insurance before I came to England. It wasn't too difficult to convince them that our people over here want to save in a reliable savings bank back home. It's in ISLI best interest to get in quickly. It would be even better if they have an active agent over here. I told them I didn't want to collect the payments but preferred that our savers sent their money straight to them. I think they liked that. But some day, I hope soon they'll open an office here in London, and guess who's going to be their General Manager in England?"

"You like money too much. I hear you buying a house."

"My first house."

"So you gwine become a property tycoon here in England?"

"I see it as providing a service for coloured people here in Britain. We entrepreneurs call it supply and demand."

"You know a lot of big words."

"Hi, this is good coffee," he did not want to start a debate on Jamaican social class. "Why aren't you at work? Today is Monday, isn't it?"

" I feel sick, boy. When them call me this morning I couldn't even lift me head off the pillow. I real sick, man" she smiled broadly. "Tell me something. How come I been here three months now an' me never see any woman coming to look for you?"

"You got a sister?" Before she could answer he rushed on, "You're dressed for the street." She grinned broadly, opening her coat to reveal her long-sleeved blouse, thick plaid skirt. He did not like the hat she pretended to be peeved, took it off and threw it on the table. He had to admit that, although overweight, she was an attractive woman, with her round smiling face and large mischievous eyes.

"No, but I have a daughter," she responded to his earlier question at last.

"Thanks but no thanks. I don't think I would like you for my mother-in-law."

"Cheek!" she hissed. "My daughter coming up for nineteen in January, the right age for somebody like you."

"That will make you 33. I will be 24 in July. You're too young to be my mother-in-law."

"Lucky thing Irone is not as rude as me, or I would be a grandmother long, long time."

"So what happen about her bosom? Are they sidelights and not headlights? It is you who said that the bosom would do it every time."

"Hi, you better watch it, mister, you talking about me daughter, you know? Nothing is wrong with Irone chassis. She is pretty. She feacy and she got brains. She finish her secondary education at your old school. What them call it? Wilberforce? Him is the man who let the slaves go, right?"

"Well, it's not exactly like that."

"Whatever. She want to come up to London to study nursing. Did you leave Wilberforce before she started there?"

"My *alma mater.*"

"You Alma Cogan?"

"No, that's Latin for my old college. Nothing about the singer."

"Anyway, she said she want to come up to study nursing. You notice it is all black nurses in hospital these days? We Coloureds still a-wipe white people backside."

"That's not all nurses do, you know. It's a very skilled, and caring profession and I'm glad your daughter... what's her name?

"Irone. Her name should be Irene, but me Uncle John spelt it wrong when he went to register the baby."

"She has ambition."

"Is what you a-tell me? I don't have ambition? Make me tell you something, the man who gwine married me have ambition for the two of us. He is a preacher, you know. A lot of coloured people over here belong to Church of God."

"Hey," he interrupted, "I was not cussing. You were fourteen you said when that man raped and gave you a baby."

"Is who say him rape me? P'rhaps that was what him was gwine to do, but me never did fight him, and him never threaten me. I coulda bawl out, but instead I was enjoying it. P'rhaps everybody was right when them say I was asking for it and Deacon *learn* me a lesson. Well, it was not like what we use to get up to in the cane piece with we age group. Him did know what him want an' him never abuse me."

"Abuse! The law in Jamaica is the same as over here. Sex under sixteen is not legal. He did abuse you. It was rape."

"Seyz who?"

"The law. You call him Deacon, I hope he was not a deacon of the church."

" No man, the last time that bugger went to church was when they christen him. Any way the law fool, fool. I was not the youngest in our family to get in the family way, you know. Miss Teasy got her first baby when she was thirteen. Lawd, life hard fe some people you know? By the time she was going on thirty, three different man them gie her four more. How come some of we so bad lucky?"

"Luck doesn't come into it. Is it good luck because your daughter hasn't had a baby yet?"

"I don't know. I think she still thinking you find baby under sussumber tree bush. Or perhaps she is a lot more sensible than I was. Even in Jamaica young people know 'bout French letter. Perhaps she's shame of me. Anyway she didn't grow up with me. Is her father sister she call mother. When she see me, she call me Sister Vicky."

"You are probably right," he said. "I'm sure she knows how to get herself a baby if she wants one, and that knowledge is perhaps why she hasn't got one yet."

"You is right. After Deacon rudeness me that night, I did think that if I go home and wash meself really clean I would not get a baby."

"You are joking!" Lincoln looked at her in astonishment.

"Yeah, man, I was sure nothing could grow inside of me if I was that clean. It must have been four months later when I was at somebody funeral, can't remember who they were burying. I got on this white frock, and me Aunty say to me mother, 'You no see a breed Vicky a breed?' 'B'have you'self, is fat she fat!' When I hear what me Aunty Nicey said, I ran all the way back to where we was living. I jumped over every pothole I could find. I say to meself if you a carrying you can't do that, and me just done it. That evening when me mother, that is Aunt Vie, come home, she call me and rip the dress off me. I was four months gone!"

"I've never met anyone like you," he said, thinking of his own strict upbringing. The aunt who raised him was an elementary school headmistress, married to a police inspector. It was a respectable home. Social mobility had brought it into the lower middle class. Everyone wore shoes to school and was expected to do well. If they were not to leave for studying in the United States or Canada, then at least they would be expected to sit the prestigious Civil Service Examinations. Even though he was a nephew, his aunt's brother's child much was expected of him. It was hoped his father would send for him to join him in New York, where Lincoln had hoped to major in Commerce.

"Words squeeze outa you mouth like egg out a fowl backside," she taunted him. "I can guess what gwone in you house. You all got you own bed and you own room? Well, where we come from all us pickney sleep in the same bed. Sometimes we hand touch-up each other like it was accident. Other time it done 'pon purpose, and when we wake just before daybreak and the little ones dead to the world and rain a fall loud 'pon the zinc roof boy, it nice when rain a fall, you see!" She looked at him. She was pleased the way he hung on to every word she was saying. "You no do it to make baby, you know. Is only the animal of the fields do it all the time to make baby." She kept watching him, knowing his silence was testimony of his vulnerability. She sensed his helplessness and rejoiced in it. She moved closer to where he was. "'Course," she said, "you would run and tell Mummy or Aunty 'bout all them naughty things I talkin' 'bout."

"You are right. Nothing like that ever happened in our house. Still I was never a snitch, or as you would say '*carrygo bringcome*'."

"You too high up for me," she accused. "You is the type a man who got to married the right complexion woman. I bet when you ready you gwine to get you'self a white woman. In Jamaica you is the type to married mulatto women. Over here you go for the real thing. I bet that is the reason why I not seen any woman coming and goin' to you room. You got a white woman somewhere and you think this place not good enough for her." She paused. "Although to tell you the truth the white women them I see you coloured men going with don't look the same like the white women that the white men married. Them look so wash-out! What happen, them breed them specially for you?"

He had heard enough. Acting on impulse he reached up and pulled her down on top of him. His recklessness could not be checked. He pushed the coat aside and began to beat her backside with his left hand. It was awkward, but the strokes were firm. She squealed and, fighting back, used her superior weight to push him back against the pillows. She rolled on top of him and succeeded in pinning down his hands. As the smiling round face hovered above his, he countered by raising his head and planting a kiss firmly on her parted lips as she continued to taunt. She did not expect it. She might have been sexually active for more than twenty of her thirty-three years, but kissing was not part of her repertoire. She tried to pull away, but her huge frame went limp. She crumbled on top of him and then rolled over on her back, although she was still lying across his knees. They did not speak again. She rose to her feet and began to undress. He divested himself of his dressing gown and they lowered themselves among the pillows.

II

Adlyn's letter came in the afternoon post. It was an hour after picking it up that he was able to open it. An hour later he was still too terrified to open it let alone read its contents:

> Enid said you sent her a birthday card. Did I mention she was born in October? I suppose you saw my card before I posted it. It was on the table. Surely you could not have remembered her birthday. I thought you'd grown out of that puppy love you had for her. Be that as if may, at last she has agreed to come to England, though she wants to come to London instead of Birmingham. I wonder why?
> Do you know anyone who might be able to find her proper accommodation? What about asking your friends Melbourne or Mrs Morgan? Come to think of it, what about your grandiose scheme to buy half of South London? If you have any luck call me at the hospital nurses home after eight. I finish at seven all this week. Enid's letter requires an urgent reply.

Well, Enid, he thought to himself, which one of us is going to tell Adlyn the truth? And what is the truth anyway?

III

From as early as 1955 it was being said that the firm of Cass and Cass was the Coloured People' Estate Agent. In the public houses in Lambeth and Camberwell the principal conversation was about the growing frequency of 'For Sale' signs being put up by the estate Agency Cass and Cass outside houses along run down streets in Camberwell and Lambeth. This had grown to mean one thing: *the Coloureds were moving in.* Cass and Cass, Estate Agents, Surveyors and Valuers, at the corner of Burton Road and Brixton Road, SW9; with its awful brown exterior, was known as the Agent of Coloured Peoples. Jimmy Fairfax once said he heard the following story in the Columbus public house along Atlantic Road explaining it all:

> "The British Nationality Act of 1948 allowed the Italian owners of the Grimaldi Siosa Shipping Line to bring the Niggers here so that the Jews, who ran Cass and Cass and the Clapham and South London Building Society, could move them into the house next door. It was part of a gigantic plot to mongrelise Britain..."

But for what purpose? That was never made clear. Indeed it was not only in the public houses that the relationship between Cass and Cass and the Coloured community was being discussed. Soon local councillors seeking re-election to Borough Councils, writers of letters to the local newspapers and street corner politicians were talking about this firm and soon it had earned the nickname of being the Coloured people's house-finder. Alonso, whose bus routes passed along Brixton Road, had over several months showed countless Coloured couples the brown painted Victorian building which housed the offices of the much maligned Cass and Cass. Isaiah and Myrtle Morgan relied on Cass and Cass for their expert knowledge of the area to find them their house in Lilford Road.

Now Lincoln was about to buy his first house, subject to contract, through the good offices of Cass and Cass. Lincoln Grant sat in the small reception room and watched the middle-aged receptionist go about her business. She had a mouth, but no lips. He mused about the saying *pursed lips*, for indeed her lips could be shut as tight as a purse. He detected a lack of friendliness in the receptionist's attitude. Despite what the opponents and rivals of Cass and Cass might think, this lady was not Coloured People-friendly. He got up and started to trace the origins and pedigree of the firm by following the diagram and the photographs displayed on the wall.

C. James Cass had founded the firm in 1898. There was a bracket besides the initial "C" with the name Clement in it. C. James Cass was joined by his brother Oswald R. Cass in 1910 and by O. Roland Cass in 1926 on the death of his father Oswald. In 1930 C. James Cass died and stewardship passed to Clement J. Cass. Since 1948 the founder's grandson had been managing director, Wing-Commander C. James Cass, DSO, who was distinguished by being presented in the uniform of the Royal Air Force.

Lincoln had spoken to him when he wanted to buy the property at 90 Northland Street.

"So you're from Jamaica?" Wing Commander Cass inquired.

"Yes, sir." Immediately he wondered why he had said "sir". He tried to introduce some haughtiness by countering with, "Have you been to Jamaica?"

"I will one of these days. I have a good friend, Dudley Elkinson. He was in my squadron. An excellent fellow was Flight-Lieutenant D.O. Elkinson. DSO, as he was then. Do you know of him?"

Lincoln was aware of his *"Do you know of him"* not *"Do you know him"*. Wing-Commander Cass did not expect Lincoln to know Flight-Lieutenant Elkinson socially. The Elkinsons were white, or near white, and although they owned the Island Shield Life Insurance, for which he had worked after leaving school and for whom he hoped to be an agent in London, he could not presume to know *them*. He thought of the additional link, that Enid had been a clerk in Barrister Elkinson's Chambers.

"I've heard of him. I think everyone in Jamaica must have heard of him," he added. "Apart from being a popular lawyer, he's also a rising star in the political firmament."

"I knew all along that he'd go far," he said, then turning back to Lincoln he looked at him gravely. "Aren't you a bit young to be thinking of buying your own house?"

"One of my heroes is William Pitt, the Younger. When he was made Chancellor of the Exchequer at twenty-two and was teased about his age he replied, 'I answer that I am doing something about it day by day.'" Lincoln said it with a broad grin to blunt any barb that the estate agent might have felt.

Wing-Commander Cass DSO leaned back in his chair and looked across at the twenty-four-year-old who could quite easily pass for a teenager. Suppressing anger at the cleverly disguised rudeness, instead he experienced a glow of admiration.

"I asked because at your age most working-class Englishmen would have their names down for a council house while they and their bride-to-be are busy saving for the big day and the furniture."

"If I put my name down," he said, "it could be ten years before I get one."

"Quite so," the man said. "I am here to sell houses, not to promote the council."

He rose from his chair and shook hands across the table. Before Lincoln could reach the door, he came around his desk and followed him and somehow managed to open the door to usher the client out. He was pleased and yet disturbed to have met Lincoln. The coloured people he had met before were usually older and of the type who were used to meeting white people in authority. They were always grateful. They were in the main barely literate country people who could not get over the fact that you took a personal interest in their own affairs. He had seen young coloureds like Lincoln in the services, but the harshness of wartime discipline always brought them to heel. This young man was showing what he termed the *colonial dilemma*. Should Britain educate them and withstand their arrogance as they demand more and more responsibility? Even though this would inevitably lead to the demand for independence and the complete dissipation of the Empire, or did you keep them as good *colonial subjects?* Perhaps one day he would take that holiday in Jamaica and *chew the cud* with Dudley Elkinson.

As Lincoln pulled the heavy outer door of the firm of Cass and Cass to let himself out he almost collided with a middle-aged coloured couple who were on the steps leading from the pavement. The woman was carrying a large handbag that she clutched as if her very life depended on it being kept safe. Well she might, he thought, familiar with the scenario. They had just been to Barclays Bank. All Jamaicans were familiar with Barclays, Dominion and Colonial, for there was a branch in all principal towns of the island, so it was natural that when they came to Britain the bank they would use would be Barclays. The wife might have had up to five hundred pounds in her handbag. They either did not believe in cheques or maybe did not understand them. Lincoln smiled at the couple. They were about to send Cass and Cass on another mission to find them a house in South London.

Lincoln walked along Brixton Road, passing the White Horse public house on his left and Theo Campbell's Record Shop on his right. There was the last reminder of summer in the afternoon as he headed towards the Colonial Club. The club was closed during the day; however, there was a man on the second floor of the building who cut black men's hair in the passageway some evenings and at weekends. The three or four customers sat on chairs from the barber's room, or leaned against the wall. This week the man had annual holidays forced on him, so he was plying his trade all week. White barbers had on occasions refused to cut coloured men's hair, so a barbershop and a ladies' hairdressing salon were services Lincoln Enterprises would offer once he got things up and running.

"We need to acquire premises and open up businesses," Lincoln said to the barber as he stood glancing around and counting the waiting customers. There were four men before Lincoln arrived, but only two seemed to be customers.

"Is what you mean?" asked the barber testily.

"I mean we have to open barbershops, hair salons, restaurants, like black people in America."

"You come home, man," said a short, plump red-skinned man.

"Seems so," said a skinny black man. "This is not black man country, you know!" He shook his head. "Black people in America no have anywhere else to go, so they have to make the best of what come their way. Me," he emphasised, "is a Jamaican and as soon as me earn enough ah gone me gone. Right back home to the sunshine an' a glass of ice water under the shade of a guinep tree."

Everybody laughed, applauding the man who voiced their shared dream. "Too true," said the plump man. "I in England fe make *money,* no fe make *life.*" They all laughed again in absolute agreement.

"Well," said the barber, "if you blokes don't want to have you natty, natty hair cut 'pon this landin' you can all go out on the High Street. Plenty a barber out there with them red stripe and white stripe sign..."

"I hear 'bout a black man who go an' sit down in a white barbershop. When it was his turn, the barber went out the back an' come back with one a them garden shear an' a milk bottle. He explain that only the shear will cut black man hair and he would have to break up the bottle fe shave him."

They all laughed. Lincoln knew that all this was an enormous put-down of his ideas. He was accustomed to this sort of talk.

"I tell you what, Coolieman," said the skinny man, laughing raucously, "if you open a proper barbershop, you could sell this French letter thingybob."

Again there were loud peals of laughter.

"Who'd like to bet that in ten fifteen years I'll be bumping into you blokes outside the Prince of Wales? You guys not going anywhere." Jimmy Fairfax had come up the stairs without anyone seeing him. "I came here as a teenager in 1943 to fight a war. Here I am, fifteen years later. You know what is the first marker you going to put down? Let me tell you. First you get a woman and before you realise what's happening she is having your children. You need a bigger place. Work it out for yourselves. You can't bring up children if you are sharing a room with another bloke. Women and children need space. Where are you going to get the space? The Council? I went with a cousin to the Council Office this morning and you know what the waiting list is? Fifteen years! That will take you into the early 1970s. I agree with Lincoln, here. Whether you know it or not, you blokes start putting down roots in England already."

"Bossman," said the skinny man again, "that might be OK fe some people. I tell you I was up in America for farm work and there's nowhere like home and that is Jamaica. Me not settling down in this country. Me wife write tellin' me is 'bout time I send for her so we can make life together. Me write and tell her that if she want to come to England, she better wait till I come home, then she can come up. I beg God that I don't dead in this country for me want them to bury me under the pear tree just like them did for me father and grandfather."

"I say, if Rupert Brooke will forgive me, there'll be many corners of this cold, wet and foggy country that will be forever Jamaica," said Jimmy." By that I mean the grave yards in Norwood and Streatham for starters."

"Bossman, you full of big words today," said the plumb man complimenting Jimmy and at the same time wanting to change the conversation. "Is when you going to open the club?"

"Silvester, you know very well this is not the time," Jimmy shrugged off the plea. He also knew when a conversation had been taken as far as it could go. "Call in the office on your way down," he said, touching Lincoln on the shoulder. With that, Jimmy started down the stairs to the club's office.

11

"I want a word with you," said Warren Hall.

Alonso stepped back more in surprise than to let Asquith Kelly and Wellesley Young through the door ahead of him. It had been nearly a month since they all registered at Kennington College of Law and Commerce and he had noticed that this trio was very exclusive. At first he wondered if it was because he had worn the trousers of his bus conductor's uniform, while the trio was dressed in fashionable suits. The truth was their sartorial elegance was more appropriate to the style current to Coloured Americans than to the British scene. That evening Alonso was wearing a blazer and grey straight trousers. He wondered if that meant he was now acceptable to the trio's august company.

"See you at the Horns," said Asquith in his heavy Barbadian accent. "Hurry up. It's your round." He and Wellesley moved on ahead.

"Come and have a drink with us," said Warren, trying to reduce the space between the two who were walking ahead. The Horns public house was at the corner of Kennington Park Road and Kennington Road making it the nearest public house to the college. Wellesley and Asquith strode on with an air of defiance bordering on the pompous, as if their names were enough to link them to the aristocratic personages after whom they were undoubtedly named. The door of the public house was open to catch the last warmth of the fading summer. The two young men paused for an instant to take in the composition of the regulars. Alonso was familiar with this. He had often watched coloured passengers when they got on a bus with nearly all the seats taken, they would pause and survey the available seats, weighing up the white passengers and working out who would not mind a black person sitting beside them. Sometimes they got it wrong. Some white females would shoot bolt upright and with a bad-tempered "excuse me" would move to a seat beside another white person. Others would shrink to the side of the bus to ensure their clothes did not touch. He recalled a large coloured woman saying one day, "T'anks me dear. Now I get the whole seat to meself. T'ank you."

She had sat sideways to give room to the young white girl who had flounced out of her seat to perch next to a large white man.

Now in the public house, the young men were practising their craft. It was Wellesley who spotted the table in a corner close to where three women in lightweight coats were seated. Warren went to the bar. They were accustomed to the sudden hush on their entry, followed by stares. They brazened it out and moved to the corner table. Alonso dropped his briefcase on the floor and went to the bar to assist Warren. It was a long wait. From where they were leaning against the bar they could see the women and hear their attempt at conversation. One had turned to Wellesley and Asquith to inquire their country of origin without any real interest.

"Jamaica?" In her Cockney accent it sounded like *Jim mike 'er.*

"No," said the Barbadian. "She was willing!" the women did not get the joke; perhaps they were not listening, or they were not expecting an answer anyway.

"Girl down our turning going out with a Jamaican," said another of the women. She sat up straight holding her large handbag on her knees as if the very thought of a coloured man instinctively made her want to guard all that belonged to her.

"Related to you, is she?" asked her companion with a dash of mischief, perhaps malice.

"No flippin' fear!" she said. "Rita, look 'ere, there's no need to be sarkey," then she took a long drink of her stout. "Real little tramp she is an' all. She broke off with one of her kind, a nice enough bloke, and took up with this darkie. He's got a car. I don't know how they do it. Just come to this country and, before you know it, going around in cars, buying up houses. Most of them never done a day's work in their life. Living off the social, I shouldn't wonder. It shouldn't be allowed, that's what I think."

"The social giving them cars now, are they?" asked a younger woman who was sitting close by. Her male companion touched her hand and, having got her attention, shook his head in discouragement.

"Well, when I was a little girl I used to be afraid of darkies. Used to see them down the docks where me Dad worked," said the third of the trio of women, who had identified the young black men as Jamaicans. "Me old mum used to tell me and me sister Dot that if we didn't behave the darkies would come and get us. That use to put the wind up us."

"This girl down our turning is going to marry one," the speaker was anxious to get back to her story.

The young white woman at the neighbouring table was bristling with curiosity.

"Get married!" a member of the trio spluttered into her drink. "It shouldn't be allowed. There ought to be a law."

"In some countries there are laws 'gainst that sort of thing," another said.

"It's the children I'm sorry for. Not white, not black even. Whatever's to become o'them?"

The young couple at the neighbouring table got up noisily and walked out.

"Pardon me for breathing," said the speaker, who found her story being continually interrupted. The exit of the young couple sent her down another avenue. "I blame Labour. They let them in. I bet if old Winston was in power he wouldn't have any of it."

"They belong to us, see," said a man who had managed to carry four pints without a tray from the bar to the table where the three older women were sitting. "We're responsible for them. They got nothing, you see. We got to educate them. They want doctors and such like. I know; during the war I was out there." He was interrupted as Warren and Alonso tried to squeeze by to their table.

"Should we join our neighbours?" asked the sarcastic Asquith.

"Who is my neighbour?" inquired Wellesley.

"I hope none of you are in the least bit worried by what you've just heard. This is mild, even good-humoured," said Warren. "If I was to take umbrage every time I hear a conversation like this I would have left these shores ages ago, even if I had to swim all the way back to Kingston Town. In a way I'm grateful that we have been able to eavesdrop on our neighbour's conversation," Warren concluded.

"I don't think we were eavesdropping," said Alonso. "The conversation was aimed at us."

"I agree," said Wellesley.

"What are we going to do about it?" asked Warren.

"Do about what? Tell them they no longer own us. That slavery ended two hundred years ago. That old Winnie came back to power in 1951 and didn't stop the *Auriga*, the *Begona et al* bringing more and more colonials to these shores," Alonso explained.

"Forget it, man," said Asquith. "Even if you jump up on the bar and shout, *'Civis Britannicus Sum'* you wouldn't convince this lot. Change the record, man. Talking about record, I know where there's going to be a good party this weekend. Anybody interested?" he asked. "You two?"

Warren ignored Asquith's question and at the same time addressed him and Wellesley. "Do you know that this guy is a budding author?"

"A what?" asked Asquith, sceptically.

"What has he written?" asked Wellesley, thumbing his cigarette lighter into flame.

"Look, guys," began Alonso, "I haven't published anything. Warren, it seems, like to tell everything on cinemascope-size screen."

"I was in the Principal's office when the secretary handed the phone to Miss Hine. I overheard her saying that her student Alonso Campbell's script had been accepted. To add to that I saw you and Miss Hine talking for a long time. Don't tell me you were setting up a date."

" With my teacher? Don't let the neighbours hear any of this, Alonso looked at his companions and made as if to get up." So on that flimsy evidence you decided I was worthy to join the famous trio?" Alonso rose half out of his seat, and was feeling for the handle of his briefcase.

"Man, sit down," Warren pulled at his elbow. "You ever considered the possibility that you were the snob among the four of us? Anyway what would the *Three Musketeers* be without D'Artagnan? So why don't you tell us the real story?"

"Do I start with my life in Gascony?" Alonso could not work out if the look on Asquith's face was because he could not tell what Gascony had to do with the story of the *Three Musketeers.*

"You see he has a sense of humour," continued Warren.

"OK. I showed Miss Hine a few pages of a story I had written about sharing a room with eight other blokes in a basement off Drury Lane when I just came up. She showed it to a friend of hers who thinks that with some refinement it could be read on the BBC Caribbean programme. That's all."

"That's all," said Warren. "I've been trying to write a story of how I stowed away from Kingston. How I earned my keep as a coalman around the streets of South-East London. Then there was my life as a conscript in the army. And then facing up to the full force of racism because I married a white woman. I can't seem to make it sound interesting."

"You have one hell of a story there, boy. The *News of the World* would snap it up. All human life is there!" said Wellesley, blowing smoke towards the ceiling and following it with his eyes.

"Well, there is humour," said Asquith. "A black man selling coal on the streets of London. I don't know if the part about marrying an English rose would endear you to the public, though."

Warren snapped his fingers. "There's something else I want to talk to you guys about. Thanks, Asquith, for mentioning a newspaper, for that's exactly what some people are planning. How does a monthly newspaper for coloured people in this country sound?"

"Like *Ebony* for coloured Americans?"

"Well, that's the intention but it will take time to build up to what Johnson's Publishing has at the moment. This paper will lead the fight against racial discrimination. We'll at last have a voice."

"Coloured people have been in this country for centuries," said Wellesley, "you think a newspaper is something new? Believe me, that is not original. I came up in 1944 as a teenage recruit in the armed forces. I've seen much more than you guys. Racial prejudice is a strange phenomenon to the British. They don't think it exists. To some you over-react when someone calls you Darkie, or Sunshine. When you go to rent a room it's not that the landlady who is prejudiced in a malicious way. It's just that she's used to having white people around her. This makes it impossible to fight what we know is racism but what the British will not accept. During the war a black serviceman standing at the corner waiting for one of his buddies quite often would have to chose which war widow he accepted an invitation from for tea, and sometimes *something* else. Yet by 1946 there were those who would have us gone. 'The bloody war you came to fight is over. Why don't you go back to your bleeding jungle?' If you don't believe me, ask any ex-serviceman you meet. You want to drop by the Colonial club and talk to men like Melbourne Welch and Jimmy Fairfax. They've been in the thick of things. They even started associations immediately after the war. They tried to educate and to agitate, even to integrate, but not much has happened to wipe out something that the people say don't exist."

"I saw some of the minutes of the *Caribbean Labour Congress*. People like Forbes Burnham and Michael Manley were members," interrupted Asquith.

"Those guys were not after integration in British society. They were after colonial freedom," said Warren. "Anyway I don't think that organisation had much to do with the ordinary plebs. I want to interest you guys in a new organisation some people have just founded. It's aimed at the ordinary migrants and students. It's called the West Indian Workers and Students Association. It's one of the groups behind the newspaper project I mentioned earlier."

"I bet there'll be more students than workers," said Alonso with a thick coating of cynicism.

"Few movements have been started by the people at the bottom," Warren began grandly.

"What about the Chartists and the Labour Party?" Alonso offered.

"They were all middle-class-led, they even called themselves '*Labour Aristocrats*'. If you examine all these organisations you'll find at the head articulate and literate men. Education lifts and pushes the working class on the road to social mobilisation. You ought to know that from your studies," he said reprovingly. "I don't care where you look. It's the same. Forget the *sans-culottes*, it was men of intellect like Danton and Robespierre."

"Skip the lecture; you passed A-Level History, you don't have a degree in it," interrupted Wellesley.

"What about the Peasant Revolt and the Haitian Revolution?" asked Alonso, as if he had just woken up.

"Don't start him off," said Asquith. "Tell us about this workers and students collective."

"I'm in dead earnest. This association has just been formed and some really interesting people are in it. Marcus Garvey's widow, Amy Ashwood Garvey, and Claudia Jones, who has come from the USA after a year in prison. You must read the speech she made to the US Supreme Court in 1953. There are other people, including some heavyweight trade unionists who are over here on scholarship from some Caribbean islands."

"Yeah, yeah, but where are the workers?" asked Alonso.

"I am one," said Warren. "I have the grease under my nails to prove it," he examined his nails for the evidence.

"I'm not," said Asquith confidently. "Even the Conscription Board has accepted my *bona fides* that I'm a student."

"Me too, and I don't need my military record to reassure me, either" said Wellesley. He turned to Alonso, whom he had ignored so far. "They'll be calling you up soon," and there was a hint of spite in his voice. "Now, that is where you are going to come up against racism."

"Tell me about it. I was in the army from 1951 to 1954," said Warren with a curious mixture of pride and relief. "How long have you been here in London?" he asked Alonso.

"How old are you?" asked Asquith.

"I'm here just over three years now, and I'll be twenty-two soon."

"They'll be calling you up within the next six months, I bet," said Wellesley with authority.

"Get one of the lecturers to write a letter saying you are a student. Try your number-one fan, Miss Hine," said Asquith.

"It won't work," said Warren. "I know a bloke who tried that. At his interview the officer told him that the military was the ideal place to study and it wouldn't cost him a penny. My friend didn't study, but when he left the army three years later he had a HGV licence. Don't laugh. A HGV licence is good if you want to drive a long-distance lorry."

"You must be the best informed stowaway in the country," said Wellesley.

"I might have started out as a stowaway," said Warren, pausing for a draught of his beer, "but I didn't arrive in this country as one."

"That might be," said Wellesley, "but the fact of the matter is you started out defrauding the shipping company of the fare to London," he spoke with the judicious malice of a wise old judge summing up in a case of immense historical importance.

"You'd better tell us your story before Judge Jeffreys here have you transported to the colonies," said Asquith.

"I stowed away back in forty-seven. I was working down on the wharf and it was easy to get aboard. I knew a couple of blokes who were sailing to England and arranged to share their cabin. As it turned out, they were in a huge dormitory for thirty-two men. Nobody knew who belonged where. After a week out at sea I was discovered. One of the blokes in the dormitory did a count and his figure for the men staying there didn't match the number of beds. It happened because so many of them came down with seasickness, including my two friends. They had taken to their bunks and I was left wandering around. Anyway by then we had passed the Bahamas, heading out into the Atlantic; it wasn't worth turning back to hand me over to the Jamaican authorities. The spirit of comradeship was such among the emigrants that as soon as the news got around the ship that there was a stowaway they had a whip-round and before long came up with the forty pounds to pay my fare. I didn't have to contribute the twelve pounds I had on me. So I arrived at Southampton as just another immigrant coming to seek a living."

"That's it?" asked Asquith, as if expecting tales of being thrown in the brig, or lashed to the mast, or even walking the plank. "How did you get your travel documents?"

"The first rule of the stowaway is to get a valid passport," said Warren. "With that you can shout, *'Civis Britannicus Sum'*. My friend John Huggins, governor of Jamaica, *requested and demanded that I be accorded all help I may need.*" He drank deeply. *"Without let or hindrance."*

"So," said Alonso, "you and I are two of the workers who'll be joining this organisation, Students and Workers."

"It looks like it. These two will join as students, I suppose. Anyway, thanks for bringing us back to basics. The West Indian Students and Workers Association will be holding a series of meetings to drum up support in different places. You know what I mean? Places where they are bound to meet workers and other places you might call students' strongholds.

"Like college bars with subsidised beer," interrupted Asquith.

"I think," Warren ignored the interruption, "some of the elected officers went to Liverpool and Manchester last week. This Friday they are having a meeting at the Colonial Club in Coldharbour Lane. I'd like you boys to come. You must meet some of the important people of our community."

"Who made them rulers over us? Exodus, chapter two, verse eleven," Wellesley quoted.

"Tcho, man," said Warren, beginning to be irritated by his friend's attitude. "Just come and listen. Who knows, you could find like-minded cynics. You might even be able to form a breakaway branch and emerge as *their* leader. After all that's how leadership begins and democracy was born."

"As a democrat I have a healthy scepticism of those who propose themselves as our leaders," Wellesley said doggedly.

"You blokes are full of book learning. You piss me off, man," said Warren heatedly. "You read about men in history and praise them because they are long removed from your time. Who called Toussaint L'Ouverture and Henri Christophe to be leaders of the Haitian revolution? Whether you blokes want to join or not, I'm telling you there are movements afoot. I too have seen some of the minutes of the *Caribbean Labour Congress* going back ten years. Some of the guys who were running it are back in the West Indies working towards independence. We have always got a voice and will continue to have a voice. We're not plotting a revolution. The newspaper they are planning to publish will amplify that voice."

"My natural scepticism makes me a little cynical," said Wellesley, perhaps disappointed that so far he had not succeeded in getting the better of Warren. "Like the rest of you I've read in the papers what's happening at Little Rock, Arkansas. Then there was that business at Montgomery, Alabama. Suddenly over here people want to be leaders. There is a difference between the USA with its institutional racism and Anglo-colonial problems."

"Anglo-colonial problems!" said Warren. "A Jamaican bloke I know just bought a place in Streatham and some bastard from the neighbourhood pushed dog shit in an envelope down his door, and you call it an Anglo-colonial problem!"

"I meant to say..." Wellesley was interrupted.

"I know a bloke from Grenada, a bit lighter in complexion than Lonso here. This man's sister, who has a different father, looks almost white. He was travelling with her to Liverpool Street for her to get her train back to the town in Suffolk where she's training to be a nurse. Some Teddy Boys beat the crap out of him because they thought he was dating a white girl. Of course, to you that's only an Anglo-Colonial problem."

"Sit down, man," said Asquith, tugging at Wellesley's sleeve. "Racial discrimination exists in this country and we got to stand up and be counted. I think I'll be at this meeting. Wellesley would be there too, but he's returning to Jamaica. He's been promised safe seat for the Federal election or is it because his wife doesn't trust him any more. Then again, it could be a mixture of both."

"You are joking about running for the West Indies Federal Parliament?" asked Alonso.

"What do you think?" asked Asquith.

"Forget this federation business. It won't last. It's my experience that to bring long, well-established colonial countries together as a federation will never never work. Don't cite the United States. The states didn't have three hundred years of separate existence. I say this although I have no intention of returning to live in the West Indies. I been here nearly ten years now, and the truth is I'm not going back to Jamaica. I got kids who know nothing about Jamaica. I owe it to them to make this place better. When it's time for them to go to school nobody is going to stand outside the school gate to prevent them taking their place in the classroom," said Warren.

"See what I mean," began Wellesley, "everything's got to be compared with what's going on in the USA. The British see the problem of race differently from how the Americans see it."

"To the extent that Britain has the largest collection of house-trained Niggers," stormed Warren. "Look, I only wanted to have a little drink and a friendly conversation with you fellows. Now I see you're no different from the Jamaicans from the bush country who said all they are here for is to save up enough to buy some land in St Thomas, Westmoreland or whichever parish that they will go home to. Bullshit! They'll be here in twenty, thirty years' time. We got to do something so that when our children ask, 'What did you do in those days?' we can proudly say we fought back. I don't rightly care if we resurrect Marcus Garvey's United Negro Improvement Association, or the National Association for the Advancement of Coloured People, so long as we do something. Just get your fat black arses to the Colonial Club on Friday. Bring your ideas and questions. Forget the milk and water suggestion that the West Indies has never shown any aggression towards Britain except on the cricket pitch. I promise you that before this decade is over we black people will have cause to stand up and give account of ourselves. Drink up! It's near chucking-out time."

"You said thirty years. That brings us to the middle of 1980s. Boy, you're spending my life with great profligacy. Make it forty years and I'll be ready for my pension," said Asquith.

"I don't care how you wrap up the package," said Wellesley. "The thought of me going round the corner to the little post office to collect my old-age pension fills me with terror. That little old lady positively dislikes me. Maybe she's scared of me."

"But it won't be that little old lady in thirty years' time," said Alonso.

"That's right," said Warren. "She'd be pushing up daisies long time. It could be my daughter, who is six, who'll be serving you then. That makes what we do now very relevant. Don't you see?"

They left the public house under a searchlight of staring eyes. Their conversation had attracted notice. Occasionally, drinkers perched on stools, watching the gesticulations and apparently heated discussion, had caught the landlord's eyes and nodded in a conspiratorial way towards where the four black men sat. But the landlord had spent his working life ignoring family rows and friendly confrontations as customers drank their beers and his forbearance was no less resolved now.

"Tell me," said Asquith, "do they smash our glasses or just disinfect them?"

"Probably both, in reverse order," said Warren. "Several pubs operate a colour bar. Don't you know that? I repeat, now is the time we must organise and start to agitate. Me old grandmother, God rest her soul, used to say, 'Snake say "ef Ah don't twist and hiss old woman would use me to tie up brushwood for fire."' Well, I'm telling you, if we don't organise to combat racial discrimination we'll forever be tied to the lowest paid jobs, the worst housing, and carry the blame for everything that goes wrong in society. You lot better be there on Friday. We want a good turn-out."

When they left the Horns they walked together to Oval Underground Station, where Asquith and Warren got the tube to Clapham. Wellesley was getting a 36 bus to Vauxhall. They talked together for another fifteen minutes or so, then Alonso crossed to St Mark's Church and walked besides the gravestones to Brixton Road. He crossed the wide, busy road and caught a 59A bus heading for Brixton Hill.

II

Alonso had never considered staying in London for thirty years. He did not have a plan beyond wanting a university degree. Even then he was not certain what to study. Sometimes he thought of Sociology, Economics, History or

Languages. Returning to Jamaica with a degree in Languages, majoring in Spanish and French, would guarantee him a good job. He might get a post with the government or end up teaching in one of the prestigious high schools or colleges, or even at the new University College of the West Indies. Perhaps Rosita would come up and graduate as a nurse before he was able to graduate. What would happen then? He had not given it much thought, but it was possible that as he and his sister approached the end of their twenties one of them or both might get married, most likely to people they had not yet met; then they would grow away from each other. He did not like to consider that possibility. He had never had a girlfriend, no one he had felt passionately about. There was Anh, but they were hardly more than pen pals, writing to each other about the latest books they had read. He remembered a lively discussion with Anh Hosang in his seventeenth year. It was a Friday morning in late June and pupils from five schools with their teachers had come to the school at Riverbank to sit their Jamaica Local Examinations. Ahn was the second eldest daughter of the Chinese family who ran the grocery and rum bar at Abbey Look Out. They were discussing the method of analysing complex sentences according to the *Outline of English Grammar* by J.C. Nesfield. She had chosen a familiar example: "Whom the gods love die young." She sounded as if she had been well rehearsed. "*Whom the gods love* – subject nominative," she looked around, as if receiving a round of applause, "Predicate, *die* and compliment *young*." He recalled her air of satisfaction that challenged him to compete with her.

"*The second master of the school has been teaching my sons Euclid since Thursday last,*" he began, "Subject nominative, *Master.* Enlargement of nominative; *the second... of the school.* Finite Verb; *has been teaching.* Predicate Direct; *Euclid,* indirect; *my sons.* Extension of Finite Verb; *since Thursday last.*"

The teachers who had accompanied them displayed collective satisfaction. They came from districts as far apart as Guava Flat, Carrato Gully, Bethel, Wild Cane River and Abbey Look Out. Riverbank was the principal centre where the local examinations were held for candidates from the Upper Yallahs and Wild Cane River. These two students were considered exceptional. Anh was already well known as she had won the coveted Gordon-Bogle scholarship and would start at the prestigious High School of Our Lady The Virgin Mother come next September.

Alonso, ever after that encounter, treasured that day in late June 1953. He remembered the small group of senior candidates who had gathered around where he and Ahn were sitting. Some candidates were in utter dismay at what they could not remember; others found the discussion between Anh and Alonso the grossest act of exhibitionism. No one criticised openly; two or three merely sucked their teeth loudly and went to another part of the schoolyard, resigning themselves to failure. English Language was traditionally the first subject on the first day, a Friday. The first question, which was compulsory, would be the analysis of a sentence. Those were the known facts. However, nothing could have prepared them completely for what was presented to them on opening the question booklet. Randolph Clough, headmaster of Wild Cane River blamed the faceless British Civil Servant on loan to the Jamaica Department of Education who was pretending that these one-room wooden elementary schoolhouses were *colonial public schools*. They must have trawled the files of the Cambridge, Senior and Junior Examination question papers to come up with: '*A merchant, having much goods to sell, caused all his belongings to be conveyed on camels, there being no railway in that country.*' The successful candidates had to pass all eight subjects. By lunchtime, just after the Scripture exam, many had begun to revise the path to their future.

A candidate like Anh had her future already mapped out and was still on course. After three years at Our Lady High School, her wealthy parents would be able to afford for their daughter to fulfil her dream; which was to study medicine. She would leave for a university abroad, probably McGill in Canada, Columbia in the USA or perhaps London University. Alonso knew that after passing his Third-Year Local Examinations he would have to find employment and assume the role of breadwinner for his family: his mother, his sister Rosita and the other children. Despite the different social standing between Ahn and Alonso both students had in common the fact that they were in a way strangers in the world of the Upper Yallahs. She was the *Chinee* girl and he was the *Panya* boy. However, that day they struck up a friendship, the way two contestants who mutually respected one another would find that bond. They spent much time in each other's company that day. At the end of the fourth subject that day, pupils from Guava Flat, Carrato Gully and Abbey Look Out faced the steep climb of three miles back to Abbey, and from there four miles to Carrato Gully, where the Wild Cane River parted company from the Yallahs; one heading eastward and the other southward. On a parallel ridge two miles south of Abbey was Alonso's district of Guava Flat. He had chatted to Anh all the way to Abbey, to the chagrin of little sister Rosita, who was sitting her First-Year examination. She sulked for a week. He felt it best not to show or tell her about the letter Anh had slipped him the next time he went to Abbey, nor did she know he had replied. Many letters were exchanged over the next two years while Anh was at *Our Lady* and he was working for Parkin's Travel Agency in Kingston. Once they had planned a tryst, they were to meet at the Carib Theatre. When she turned up twenty minutes late she was in the company of a much older Chinese woman, a cousin perhaps, daughter of the aunt at whose home she was now boarded. He caught on quickly as she fell briefly out of step with her chaperone and signalled frantically to Alonso that he should not acknowledge her. He continued sending letters through her sister, who worked in a store in downtown Kingston. Some nights he dreamt that they held hands and walked along the secluded paths of the Upper Yallahs.

Now those dreams were rare. Anh should by now have finished at Our Lady and would no doubt be at her selected university. He wondered if Rosita would have any up-to-date news about Ahn. He would ask her when she comes to London in March.

12

Alonso had been to the Colonial Club on a few occasions, when he had gone to have his hair cut. Coolieman, who worked somewhere from early morning until noon was also the caretaker and bouncer of the Colonial club. In the afternoons he also cut men's hair outside his room two floors above the club. It was there that Alonso first heard how easy it was to pick up a white girl in the Colonial Club. He tried to convince another part of his mind that was not the prime reason he went there. Anyway he had not succeeded in picking up a girl of any colour. Was it because he was not attracted to any of the women who frequented the club on their own, or was the competition among men without women so fierce? During the bus strike in May, he had spent some time there with other striking black busmen. They had passed the time playing pool and listening to Fats Domino's "*Blueberry Hill*". On one occasion there was a white girl who said she was nineteen years old. She had a voice so hoarse that the black bus driver (who wore his uniform although the strike was into its third week) suggested she had left her voice out in the damp night air. She said she had run away from her home in Northampton, or maybe it was Nottingham, he could not recall. She had been on the streets since she was fifteen. She claimed her older brother had been sexually abusing her since she was ten. When her father decided to get in on the act she took off at the first available chance. She explained that since her relatives were getting what she had for free, she would rather let strangers have it for a price. Later that day she left the club with the only man in London still in a bus driver's uniform.

Ziah Morgan was a regular patron of the Colonial Club. He had been heard to bemoan the club's decline. In the late '40s it was more exclusive. "The thing with England is that we don't separate the grain from the dross. England is too much of a leveller. We all were thrown together and mixed up. I tell you, there are people rubbing shoulders with me that I wouldn't bother to say 'good morning' to in Jamaica."

It had long been remembered that some of the Windrush immigrants of the summer of 1948 were accommodated in the air-raid shelter at Clapham. Few recall that many more were given good counselling at the Colonial Club. Through its network of contacts many got accommodation and jobs. Fewer still recall with more than a touch of romance the celebration the club hosted the day the West Indies beat England in the second test at Lords in 1950. Now, in this year when England took its revenge on the West Indies cricket team, which was in transition, there was nothing to celebrate.

Alonso was surprised that there was an attendance register to be signed. Dell, the attractive receptionist, explained that tonight was a special night, and it was the intention of the club to write to people about future programmes. He noticed that Warren Hall had already signed in, as had Lincoln Grant. Inside the club he could hear someone imitating Gene Krupa on drums. It was Warren Hall! Lincoln was sitting at a table with Ziah Morgan and Jimmy Fairfax. Lincoln had made it his business to ingratiate with those who were considered leaders in the black community.

Alonso had never seen Jimmy without a pleasant smile so was not surprised by how amiable he was at what was his place of business. They were engaged in what Jimmy assured them was to be the requiem for the West Indian cricket team, which he predicted would rise from the ashes like the legendary phoenix. Lincoln teased him that a requiem was not needed if the team would rise again. He also reminded him that the West Indies and England did not play for the Ashes, at which Jimmy laughed, saying he would remember that *one*. He had to leave the table as the guest speakers were coming in.

When Warren had finished his Kruppa pastiche he came over to where Alonso was sitting. He already knew Ziah Morgan, who was apparently more of a regular at the club than either Lincoln or Alonso had thought. They wondered if Myrtle Morgan was aware of her husband's frequent visits to the club.

"Let's go and get the drinks," Warren said to Alonso. "I hope this place will be full to busting. If so reaching the bar will be tricky once the speeches begin. What you say?"

Alonso agreed for even then they had to fight their way to the bar.

"Let's see," said Alonso, "it's two lager and lime and..."

"And two bitter," interrupted Warren, looking at the girl behind the bar.

"I'll get them," said Alonso. "You two have been away from Jamaica too long, with your mild and bitter."

"Perhaps we're just more mature," Warren said with a nudge and a grin.

They carried two glasses each back to the table. Jimmy came over and spoke quietly to Warren, who nodded and then moved back to the raised platform. Warren sat at the drums again and began his Gene Krupa routine, attacking the cymbals with gusto, on to the kettledrums and back to the cymbals to finish with a flourish. The audience roared its approval, but before they could get back to their drinks and their conversations Jimmy was in front waving his hands. They noticed! They listened!

"I'm so pleased to see so many of you here tonight, brothers and sisters. I really am, but before I hand you over to Melbourne who will be compeering the main event of the evening I have the Reverend R. Locksley Hood who would like to bring you some good news. The Reverend Hood, ladies and gentlemen. Put your hands together."

There was a polite round of applause as a thin sun burnt white man, in a dark suit and wearing a clerical collar, negotiated his way around the tables to the front and shook Jimmy's hand.

II

"Don't worry," he started, "I'm not going to preach a sermon. And in case you're wondering, I'm on orange juice." Louder applause greeted him.

"Many of you from Jamaica will have heard of my father, R. L. Hood." He paused, then continued, "Few in Jamaica bothered to find out what his initials stood for, which in case you are wondering are the same as mine, Robin Locksley Hood. OK, OK, we've heard all the jokes by now. Do I rob the rich and give it to the poor? I'd be that lucky! Anyway my father was briefly at St Luke's in affluent Lower St Andrew before he was moved to poorer St Matthew's, Allman Town, for those of you who know Kingston. He's been there for the last forty-three years and that's where I spent ten of my first sixteen years. But to cut a long story short, my reason for coming to talk to you tonight is to provide something that I am reliably told you don't get easily. I've been told people find it difficult to get services that I think are the bounden duty of the Christian church to provide. It's difficult for migrants to find a church where they can get married or to christen their children and (although I don't look forward to conducting many) have funeral services. I'm pleased to tell you that the Diocese of the West Indies has conferred on me the role of Chaplain to its migrant citizens, and I've further taken it on myself as a Christian minister to include all Commonwealth and Colonial citizens of whatever race or creed from whichever continent. So in future if you have a religious problem, come to see me at St James', just off Loughborough Junction. But wherever you're living I'll be able to find a church near you. I'll perform whatever service you require or arrange for another minister to do it. For instance, tomorrow I have two weddings in Willesden and a third in Leicester. I can't be in Leicester at the same time I'm due to take the second wedding in Willesden, that is obvious. So I have, therefore, arranged for the vicar of a local church in Leicester to do the honours for my parishioners in the East Midlands. So treat St James' as your parish church, wherever you're from and whatever your religious affiliation. Please take a card before you leave tonight. It has all my details. God bless you all."

There was a thunderous round of applause, so much so that Jimmy felt moved to detain the Minister, and held up his right hand like a referee announcing the victorious prizefighter. "As our newly appointed

Chaplain, perhaps you wouldn't mind blessing this evening's proceedings, Canon Hood."

"If you promise not to sip your rum and coke for a while. I'll paraphrase Jeremiah 29:

> "Buy your houses, work hard, get married and plan to have your children grow up in this land believing that they have a right to be here. As you grow, not separately but in the spirit of true integration, so will you build each other up, establishing shops, clubs, newspapers and a community that will contribute and be a mighty force in this land. God will work his purpose out as he did to the captives taken to Babylon. The Lord bless you all and keep you in his grace. Amen."

"Now," said Lincoln, "I'd like to see the Reverend Burchell Knib of the Paradise Road, Baptist Church, Kingston, in a joint like this. This is definitely not a Baptist scene."

"Nor a Pentecostal scene either. Can you imagine Elder Easton Bogle of the Bible Church of God at Bun Dutty Gap in this den of iniquity?"

"I beg you pardon," interjected Warren, rejoining the table, which had been enlarged to accommodate Wellesley and Asquith. "Just because your Bible-thumping prelates choose to use fruit juice for the sacrament doesn't mean the consumption of alcohol is a sin."

"'Wine is a mocker and strong drink is raging and those who are deceived thereby is not wise'. I've never been able to understand what that mean," said Ziah.

"Remember that on the Day of Pentecost," said Warren, as if he had not been interrupted, "Peter did not say, when he was challenged as being drunk, 'How dare you! I do not drink.' He said, 'Look, it is only the third hour of the day.' In other words the pubs were not open yet."

"Catholics and Anglican priests like a little of the hard stuff, you know," began Ziah, but Jimmy interrupted him from the platform. All eyes were on Melbourne Welch, the compere for the evening. Behind him was the group of distinguished guests, whom Warren began to identify. "Amy Ashwood Garvey is the big lady in the African *kente cloth* robe. She was born in Jamaica but traced her roots back to the Gold Coast."

"Me think her name was Amy Jacques Garvey," suggested Ziah Morgan. "I marched with Garveyites back in the thirties."

"The lady you're thinking of was his second wife," said Warren, wanting to finish his introductions before Melbourne Welch began to speak.

"Two wives called Amy?" Ziah was intrigued.

"Claudia is standing next to Melbourne, that tall guy talking to Mrs Garvey is the writer Jan Carew, then Manchanda, Roy Henry and I can see at least three Labour Members of Parliament."

"Once again, ladies and gentlemen, very distinguished guests, the Colonial Club is proud to host an event of great significance to every migrant from the non-white Commonwealth living in these islands. On the platform with me are some of the people who have been speaking for us when the barrage of abuses, of insults rain down on us. This torrent comes from the fascist right, the anti-black press, which means almost all of Fleet Street, our numerous detractors, and the Negrophobic politicians, present company excepted. We've always had a voice, be it *The Keys* published by the legendary Dr Harold Moody or the more recent *Caribbean Congress News* from the Caribbean Labour Congress. Those were in-house journals scarcely reaching beyond the membership of those organisations. I've always thought we need a journal like the *Chicago Defender*, fearless in defence of its people, yet erudite and with the capacity to encourage young writers. But it must above all be truly a people's paper. I know one person who is supremely qualified to edit such a paper. A woman who has been fashioned on the anvil of race relations, a woman who declared before the USA Federal Court held at Foley Square, New York, the 23rd February 1953: '*Limits of Tyranny are the measure of our Resistance*'. Ladies and gentlemen, I give you Miss Claudia Vera Jones."

The woman who stepped forward was taller than Alonso expected, and elegantly dressed, but not expensively so. Alonso decided that she looked like a professional woman, a doctor, lawyer or the head of a successful girl's school. Certainly she did not seem like someone wearing her Sunday best. She had a pleasant smile, not unlike that of a singer waiting to charm the audience. She had a folder in her left hand. When she spoke, her accent was American, not West Indian.

III

"The case for a newspaper dedicated to the interests of Coloured People residing in this country from the Commonwealth and colonial countries has been made by Melbourne Welch and others. I shall reinforce what has been said. With the increasing migration of West Indians and other coloured peoples from the Commonwealth to Britain, the monster of racialism has raised its head, in the same Mother Country that many of you present here tonight fought bravely to defend against the fascism and intolerance. A dozen or so years ago you might have thought that with the defeat of Nazi Germany and the extraction of the poison of the Aryan code we were at the beginning of a New World Order. Recall the racist crowds outside the Central High School in Little Rock, Arkansas. Much closer to home is the colour bar practised by some publicans, as in the case of the Lord Nelson, not far from where we are tonight. How can we ignore that infamous article in an otherwise respectable weekly journal in which a headmaster declared that black pupils are educationally sub-normal? We need to refute these scurrilous remarks. We need to attack racial injustice from whichever quarter. Our watchword must be racial harmony with dignity.

"Scarcely ten years ago an act that some might have seen as acknowledging with gratitude, the sacrifices of the far-flung empire was passed, boldly proclaiming to the world that each of its subjects should say with pride, *Civis Britannicus Sum!* The situation has been further influenced by the rising tide of the African liberation movements, with the former Gold Coast, now Ghana, leading the way under Kwame Nkrumah. Hence in order to meet the economic and social needs and demands of the immigrants, as well as to channel their political consciousness in the right direction, the *West Indian Gazette* is being planned with a possible launch date in February next year. The paper is provisionally called the *West Indian Gazette* for two reasons; one, the idea was first floated by the West Indian Students and Workers Organisation; and secondly the majority of immigrants arriving here are West Indians. It's quite possible that in the near future there could be a change of title, or at least a subtitle could be appended.

"We envisage that from its inception the paper will be broad, democratic, fighting for independence for oppressed colonial peoples; for Afro-Caribbean-Asian solidarity; for peace, and against racialism in the United Kingdom, South Africa and the USA, with a socialist approach. With this broad approach we hope the paper will win wide support among West Indians and Africans in particular, and the broader Labour movement in general in this country will give its support. The paper will educate, not least some editors of Fleet Street, who apparently think that Ancient Ghana was a Muslim state in the Sudan, and those who think that being black is synonymous with being a Jamaican. Those who think that migrants are here to be housed and be a charge on the state at the expense of working-class white people.

"With over a quarter of a million Coloured migrants already settled here, we're proposing a modest print run of 20,000, with a readership of between 30,000 and 40,000. The paper will start as a monthly with expectations of it becoming a weekly. We hope to have agents in all cities and towns where our brothers and sisters live. We will be depending on you to give us contacts the length and breadth of the country. We aim to make this a peoples' paper. We will be bringing you the news from back home. Wherever that is. Of course we will be publishing the news about ourselves. Besides these we'll be promoting social, political and cultural functions.

"Although it's not my intention to monopolise your time, I think I'll read to you part of my presentation to the Committee that appointed me to conduct research into the feasibility of a West Indian paper." She looked quickly in the folder she had been holding, and extracted a typescript.

"In considering this talk to you it was difficult to separate the current ideological, political, economic and social trends manifesting themselves among the quarter of a million West Indians resident in Britain from the logical importance of a West Indian press.

"An urgency attaches itself to such a talk since, we would be failing in our political duty were we to continue to ignore the problem, and if the word ignore is too harsh a characterisation to apply ourselves to its solution. I have sought therefore in preparing this report to divide my subject matter under five headings:

(1) The West Indian Community and the extent of its social organisation
(2) Concerns and issues which they are raising
(3) Perspectives, i.e. the permanence of this community in the UK.
(4) The West Indian Press, its role, organisation and measure of its support.
(5) Some recommendations

"There are many West Indian Organisations. Foremost are the Ex-Servicemen and Women Association and the Caribbean Congress. By their very nature these organisations are not easily accessible to the average migrant. Some people have suggested a British branch of the National Association for the Advancement of Coloured People. In its favour, one could say that it has had a good pedigree going back to the Niagara Falls Conference in the early years of this century. Spearheading its thrust were such distinguished people such as W.E.B. DuBois, Thurgood Marshall, Spottswood W. Robinson and Roy Wilkins. But a successful organisation must grow out of the experiences of its members. Here in Britain our communities cry out for a national organisation born out of our struggles and experiences.

"The principal concerns among the migrants are manifold. Foremost is the right to jobs. We have the right to proper housing. We have a right not to be scapegoated as agents of instant slums. The fact is that West Indians and other peoples of colour have been caught up in the smoking-gun theory. It's easier for West Indians to find accommodation in the decaying city centre where landlords triple the rent, but a roof over one's head demands that you pay whatever the landlord asks. There's nothing peculiar about the West Indian wanting to live with friends and neighbours who share a common culture. On the other hand the white working class is more mobile. Whether it is through blind prejudice or through social mobilisation or inducement of New Towns, with its 'no coloured' tag, is a matter for conjecture. How can one blame West Indians for the unsalubriousness of Geneva and Somerleyton Roads?

"On the permanence of West Indians in Britain, it has been pointed out that no migrant intends to stay for more than five years. I understand that's true even among those who have spent more than ten years already. I daresay even our ex-service men and women who came here to win a war now have quite another war on their hands." Loud applause interrupted her flow.

"I was intrigued by something the Rev Mr Hood said earlier, people are getting married and having children, now that does not strike me as if that is a short-term policy. Children in reality mean expansion, bigger and better accommodations, training for better jobs, the right schools for one's children, careful planning for the future. Sending for one's relatives gives a whole new meaning to the saying that by giving a man a fish you save him from today's hunger, but if you teach him to fish his future is secured. That to me does not look as if it can be done in five years. I daresay those who eventually settled at the docks in Liverpool, Cardiff and the Thames Docklands didn't think about permanence either. Let us think about the homelands by all means. Some of us may retire there. Others may return to hasten independence and the future of this world. But we should not strike too much of a pose over the unleavened bread, with our staffs in our hands and already standing up as if to depart in a hurry.

"Melbourne Welch has already told you that the *West Indian Gazette* does not claim to be the first black journal to be published in this country. Although it is in a way the child of the West Indian Students and Workers Organisation, the *Gazette* aims to be the people's paper of the migrants from the black Commonwealth and Colonies. From its London base it hopes to reach out like a spider's web to all the areas where black migrants reside. This paper will inform, defend and educate the people of their right to live in harmony with their neighbours in a dignified way. The politics of the paper will be socialist. It will support the struggles in Africa, in Asia, in South and Central America, and also of the Coloured people of the United States of America to achieve their civil rights as guaranteed under the Constitution, in true dignity.

"I recommend that you support this venture. You must disseminate the paper to all corners of the country, making it a web of activity. You must become its reporters by sending in your news. Make it a true newspaper, reaching out to North, East, West and South. As a democratic paper, we will publish what you say. But a warning: the Laws of Libel in this country are quite punitive, so be careful. It doesn't mean the *Gazette* will replace your daily paper, but you'll see in the *Gazette* a paper written, produced and published by people who are familiar with the problems, the tribulations, which are peculiar to your sojourn in this country. You can make a start tonight by giving us your name and address as the nucleus of our subscription list. The paper will be selling for sixpence per copy. Should you feel like taking out a year's subscription or more even, our charming hostesses Carmen and Della would be only too pleased to take your money and give you a receipt. It is possible to buy shares in the paper, if you are interested, please indicate when you give your name and we will contact you later.

"Finally may I introduce some of the people who will be managing your paper. On my right is Mrs Amy Ashwood Garvey, Chairman of the Editorial Board; on my left, Mr A Manchanda, our General Manager; and Mr Jimmy Fairfax our Advertising Manager; and Mr Warren Hall our Sports Correspondent. I assure you that all these people on the platform here tonight are fervent supporters of this project, so please don't be afraid to engage any of us in discussion about the paper. I know that many of you don't like a public debate, so don't be slow in having a one-to-one."

There was a standing ovation and a wave of humanity surged towards the platform and the bar. Out of this chaos appeared five or six attractive Coloured hostesses. None seemed to be much above twenty. They handed out cards on which were places for names and addresses and a line stating: "I wish to take out a subscription for six/twelve months."

IV

Warren fought his way from the platform to the table where his friends were sitting.

"Didn't I tell you she was quite some woman?"

"Impressive," said Lincoln. "She comes highly recommended, being a close friend of Paul and Essie Robeson and a protégé of DuBois. My dad was at her farewell party at Hotel Theresa New York..."

"You know that she's a Communist?" Wellesley interjected.

"So?" Lincoln asked irritably.

"Well, as an entrepreneur you may be political opponents..."

"Never mind that," said Asquith. "What will give me nightmares is the thought of Warren here as sports correspondent. This man doesn't know his square leg from his silly mid-on."

"True, true," said Warren, "but I'll have you know that although I wasn't at Lord's June 1950, I was at the Oval two months later and saw every one of the 503 runs the West Indies piled on. I even watched Len Hutton carry his bat for 202... Leave that aside, this is a night for caucusing. Get up, you guys, and start mixing."

"Another damn American term!" grumbled Asquith.

13

Alonso's position became untenable after Elias and his brother had stormed his room in Ostade Road. A week later he moved to an address in Lancer Avenue, off Stockwell Road. The tiny room overlooked an overgrown back yard where the previous occupant had dumped all they did not wish to take with them. Alonso's new landlord was a thin and very black man who reminded him of an upturned broom. He had an enormous head, a thin face with a bulbous nose, thin lips that had forgotten how to smile, or maybe had never learned how. On accepting Alonso as a tenant, he reeled off a list of things he did not want tenants to do. He did not accept tenants who owned television sets; tenants whose female visitors gave the intention of wanting to stay overnight; tenants on very late shifts coming in after midnight. No light bulbs should be over forty watts. He did not like students; they used up too much electricity studying far into the night. He did not like the windows opened lest the curtains get blown outside and become dirty. Alonso found that last statement was reinforced in a practical way when he discovered that the window in the toilet had been nailed shut. When he went to pay his first week's rent he knocked on the landlord's door and as it slowly opened he could see behind the man. There was a bed with an opened Bible on the pillow. The open pages were black. Alonso wondered if the man had been sleeping with his head on the pages of the Holy Book! It had been known that there were some people whose superstition led them to believe that the open Bible is protection from evil. To them Satan often appeared as the malevolent spirits of the dead and only the Holy Writ could protect any poor mortal they encountered. The landlord's black face was ashen with the aid of some white substance. This led Alonso to muse that the man's sins as black as night had been transferred literally to the pages of the Bible, leaving his face like a death mask.

Alonso stopped in the kitchen on his way to his room. Two women greeted him with smiles.

"Welcome to Castle Folly," the younger one said.

"Castle what?"

"No listen to her," said the other, "she too fool, fool. By the way my name is Lurline and this is my sister Puncie."

"Mine is Alonso."

"Well, I hope we won't be strangers any more," said Lurline, while Puncie nodded.

"His name... him upstairs, that is, his name is Foley and this is his castle with all his rules and regulations. I call it Folly Castle. Did he tell you he creeps downstairs and put the night latch on sometimes?" said Puncie.

"No, but I told him that I work on the buses and sometimes get home after one o'clock."

"I work on the underground. I also get in late sometimes," said Puncie.

"I think he did it because he thought you were bringing in a man," said Lurline, "even though we share a room."

"I'd be that lucky," said her sister. "To find a man, that is. By the way, you don't have an older brother, even if he's not as good-looking like you?"

"Puncie!" her sister reprimanded.

"Well, he is kinda cute, but him is too young for me. Now-a-days them coming to England straight from out of school, tcho, man!"

"No pay her no mind," said Lurline. "She talks brazen-like, but she's a good girl. Says her prayers every night," They all laughed.

"Did you see the bible on the pillow?" asked Puncie. "He sleep with his head right in the book of Psalms. You never see how the grease from his head blackened up the pages? All that white stuff 'pon his face is to ward off duppy, you know!"

"Nobody believe in ghosts in London," said Alonso.

"You want to bet?" Puncie looked at her sister. "Should we tell him?"

"Tell me what?"

"About the duppy girl in his room."

"You mouth big, eh," shouted Lurline, "you no see the pot boiling over?"

"A young white girl killed herself in your room."

"Big mouth, Puncie!"

"My mouth might be big, but my lips are kissable."

"Is who tell you that?" asked her sister.

"Never you mind," Puncie continued. "She was fifteen and in the family way as white people delicately put it, so she close the door, stuff clothes under it and turn on the gas. The English funny that way. Sex belongs to big people and is only for having children, continuation of the species. You play with it and start breeding when you under age and you have to do the honourable thing. Poor kid. Any girl back home at Red Wattle Gap, St Mary where we from, who never had a little bit of the other by the time she was fifteen..."

"Speak for yourself," interrupted Lurline sternly.

"Anyway," said Puncie "watch out for the smell of gas in your room. Tenants nuh stay long in that room once dem hear the story and smell the gas."

The conversation in the kitchen did not prejudice Alonso. He had known for some time that the Morgans were leaving Geneva Road for a new home in Lilford Road, and arrangements were made for the tenancy of their former flat to pass to him. The location did not appeal to him. He was more taken in by the space and with his sister (Flowers was his familiar term of endearment for her but she answered to Blossom from people outside her family; Rosita was on all legal documents) she was due to arrive in London soon. This basement apartment was about the right size for a brother and a sister.

For the short time he was at Folly Castle, he did not smell gas. He told Puncie a few days after the encounter in the kitchen that he had a dream when he was living at Ostade Road. He told her about the young white girl who dressed in his room while he lay on his bed paralysed with fright or maybe it was really a dream. Puncie thought that all old houses had their stories. She reminded him that his dream of six months or so ago might have been just a prediction about Folly's Castle. He told her that the girl in his dream was much older than fifteen, but Puncie told him that dreams were always confusing when it came to details. She hated being alone in houses, this one in particular. She worked shifts on the Underground and invariably she was on her own from morning until early noon. He reassured her that at least for that week they could keep each other company as he was on early afternoon shift at his bus garage.

II

The next day he was having a cup of coffee and a bacon sandwich. He had grown out of the habit of a regular breakfast. It had gone eleven o'clock and he was hungry. He was due to start working after two o'clock with a break between five-thirty and six o'clock, at which time he would have his main meal of the day at the canteen at the bus garage where Myrtle Morgan still worked in the kitchen. He looked up as Puncie came into the kitchen wearing baby-doll pyjamas.

"Carroll Baker has a lot to answer for," he said, looking away quickly. He followed his remarks with a slow whistle.

"Look, boy, you behave yourself, you hear? I'm a big woman, and I wear what I like." She paused. "But wait, you think this is for your eyes? Let me tell you something. I'm a big woman. I have a thirteen-year-old daughter in Jamaica, so just mind what you saying to me." She flounced out of the kitchen. He could hear her climbing downstairs to her room. She returned shortly, wearing a dressing gown. "I hope this cool your temperature." He rose to go, but she stood in his way. "Look," she said, "I don't want to hurt your feelings. It's that I'm thirty-two going on thirty-three, I don't know your age, but you is too young to be making a pass at me. Or as me grandmother used to say, 'Boy, you no old enough to be putting question to woman'!"

"Drop dead!" he said lifting himself half-out of the chair

"Sit down and have your breakfast," she ordered. "I think we ought to understand each other. What you doing is what they call window-shopping, but the next thing to happen is you start putting question to me. Right?"

Had Alonso dared to look at her he would have seen that her visage was not as severe as her voice.

"I didn't mean to be impertinent," he said contritely. "I was just running joke..."

"OK, let's forget it. Anyway you could not be seriously paying me a compliment, when me legs big like tree trunk. Look 'pon them. Look no," she encouraged.

"I disagree..." he broke off and slapped his open mouth two or three times. He kept his eyes averted from the legs he knew to be quite shapely. "I'm heading for trouble again," he said.

"I say forget it," she snapped, dropping the hem of her dressing gown, which she had pulled halfway up her thighs for Alonso to inspect them. He did not. She turned her back to him and switched on the toaster. She loaded two slices cut from a crusty loaf. "So you still haven't smelt any gas in your room?"

"No. Not a whiff," he said, thinking that this woman could change mood as quickly as the chameleon can change its colour. "I do hope, however, I could open that window, just to let in come fresh air."

"Fresh air? In London? Last night I tied a handkerchief over my nose because of the smog, and this morning the handkerchief was blacker than me hand. I wonder what this London air is doing to my lungs," she looked at Alonso. "Young boy, you should worry a lot, seeing that you smoke. Why don't you give it up, before it's too late?"

"To tell you the truth, I'm not a real smoker. I can stop any time I want."

"That is what them all say."

"I tell you, I can do without smoking. If I have company I don't need a cigarette."

"OK," she said. "Gie me your cigarettes and when you want one come to me for it."

"They are in my room."

"Go get them, then," she challenged. The toast popped up. She took the slices out and proceeded to spread an inordinate amount of margarine on them. Meanwhile Alonso, having finished his sandwich, washed his cup and plate, returned them to his allocated cupboard and went to his room. The packet of Senior Service he bought the previous weekend still contained seven cigarettes. He was hovering over the table when Puncie came in, balancing in one hand a plate of toasts, a knife and a jar of marmalade and in the other two full mugs of coffee.

"Used to like jam on me toast, but I gave it up, because I can't stand looking at that *damn golliwog* on the bottle. Any of them white people ever call you golliwog?" She placed the mugs of coffee on the table; with one continuous action she snatched the packet of cigarettes and stuffed it in the pocket of her dressing gown. "Of course," she said, "this no say nothing, because as soon as you go outside you gwine buy yourself another packet."

"You don't trust anybody, do you?"

"Me? You damn right, me no trust any man."

"I thought I was a boy. What happen? Have I suddenly grown up?"

"Perhaps all this reading," her eyes surveyed his books, "and book learning and the way you speak make you into a man before you' time. You know like force-ripe mango."

"Eh, eh," he said, drawing out the last syllable, "you really don't like me, eh? What me do to upset you so? If it's the pass I made earlier, then I'm sorry, but even if you throw your cup of coffee over me, I still think you have shapely legs," he quickly dropped to his haunches, hiding at the other side of the table. She continued to eat her toast and marmalade, apparently oblivious of his comment and his comic action. The dressing gown had fallen away from her knees, revealing her lower thighs. She crossed her knees and pulled the dressing gown across them. It fell away again. This time she ignored it and continued eating. When she finished she placed the plate on the table and, taking up the coffee, went to the window.

"It is raining. I used to like being in bed when it is raining," she turned to look at him and, as if to make it clear beyond any misunderstanding, she continued, "That was when I was a little girl. Boy, it could rain in St Mary with the rain beating down on the zinc roof." She remained silent, drinking her coffee and looking out of the window. "Well," she said, moving away from the window, "that was a long time ago. We all have to grow up, but take me advice and don't do it too quick. Enjoy your youth..."

"Look," he said sharply, "I am past twenty-one. I can vote. I can get married without parental consent." When he saw that he was not impressing her, he said, "A companion of mine got a woman pregnant when he was only seventeen."

"All right, all right!" she put down the mug and held up her arms in surrender. "So you have a four-year-old pickney! I hope you supporting it."

"I wasn't talking about myself," he said, feeling quite annoyed, "you better go before the landlord return and find you in my room." He turned and opened the door slightly.

"You're right," she said. "You would get thrown out. Remember, coloured people no have protection over here. No rent book, no security."

"Me? Why me? You are the one in my room!"

"True, but Uncle Cyrus won't see it that way."

"Your uncle?"

"Oops, I'm sorry. The old fool is married to our mother. Oh, about twenty years now. Why do you think we let him watch and peep 'pon us so?"

"He is your father?

"The wicked step-father more likely! Him went to live with my mother when I just started school."

"So where is your mother now?"

"In Jamaica looking after her grandchildren and keeping out of the way of this miserable old bastard. She was up here, but she went back home for a bit of peace and quiet. Lurline and me are planning to buy our own house. We put up with enough of his foolishness. You would think that we are little pickney. The house is coming through soon."

"Í have friends who are buying their own houses," he said.

"You must introduce me. I want a rich man. You can make money if you own a house in London, you know. I reckon the old bastard make twelve pounds a week off this house and he don't pay any taxes on it. I tell you, there is money in property. So introduce me to your friend them."

"One is married to a very nice lady, and the other is only two years older than me."

"So what? Him is twenty-three and him buying property. Give him my name and address if ever him want an adviser in the shape of a loving cuddly big sister."

"Is that what they are calling it these days?"

"Is what you mean?"

"I'm just a little boy," he said, pretending to sulk, "I don't understand big people's argument. I just wonder what you mean by cuddly sister."

"Playing fool to catch wise, eh? I had a child when I was your age. It could have happened much earlier if I was not careful or perhaps lucky."

"So is what you telling me? You were somebody's cuddly sister? Well, as they say, if you cannot be good then be careful. They never said anything about being cuddly. Although they have this black performer call 'Cuddly' Dudley. I wonder what they mean?"

"Is what you after? You want me to call you 'Cuddly' Lonso?"

"It doesn't rhyme. You better stick to good little boy."

"I was not good and I was not very careful either." She looked at him. "So what you do? If you're good, you don't have to be careful?"

"You only have to be careful if you get the opportunity, and when you happen to be a little boy you don't get the opportunity, do you?"

"You putting question to me?" she asked moving closer to him.

"Which question is that?" he removed his hand from the door, pushed it shut. He leaned against it. "What is the question you want me to ask you?"

"Something that will make me stop calling you a little boy."

"Promise me you won't get vex with me."

"Promise."

"I still think your legs are lovely. They are so shapely and smooth."

"Smooth! How you know that? Anyway that's not a question. Don't look so surprise. I went to school too, you know. I even pass' the Jamaica Local, first Year. So you like me legs?"

"Errol Flynn said he likes a woman's leg because they have to get close to his."

"Never mind him. What you telling me? You want my legs next to yours?"

"That is one of my questions."

"You still not asking. You like all men, you suggesting, and I'm a poor defenceless woman alone in your room..."

He moved closer. She stood still. He reached for the dressing-gown belt and pulled it loose. She watched him as if she was indeed defenceless. When he reached to unbutton her pyjama jacket her hands came up and held his, as if to prevent whatever he had in mind; suddenly she released his hands. He continued to unbutton the jacket. Her face had become soft and beautiful. He began to push the jacket and the dressing gown from her shoulders, revealing two large breasts. With an almost child-like action she extricated herself from her night apparel. He stroked her shoulders, drew invisible lines around her huge breasts, then slowly began to stroke them. He felt her shiver.

"Cold?"

"Hot," she gasped. She clasped her hands behind his neck and pulled him against her breasts. "You never say anything about me bubby. Is me leg you after from the start."

He let his right hand wander past her behind and began stroking her exposed thighs. Moving his face over the contours of her chest, he suddenly parted his lips and kissed a nipple. There was a wild flutter that unbalanced her. He held her firmly as she swayed. A moment later and she cradled his face in the palm of her hands and lifted his head to the level of her face, focused her eyes on his.

"Only one other human being ever did that," she said, "and that was my baby daughter, and that was a long time ago. A very long time ago," her voice trailed off into a whisper.

"She did it for food. I'm doing it for pleasure."

"It is pleasurable!" She said, lifting her breast to his lips. "Pleasurable..." and her voice trailed off into rhythmic grunting. They dragged themselves across the room until they felt the bed against their thighs and collapsed onto it.

III

"Puncie! Puncie! Girl, you in there?" It was Lurline. Alonso struggled to disentangle his limbs from Puncie. His actions were that of a cornered untamed animal, desperate to escape.

"Is what you doing? Why you getting up?" Puncie held him firmly by lying across his chest, her elbows resting on his shoulders. Above his head her breasts hung like carefully sculptured aubergines. Turning her face towards the door she answered her sister. "Yes, me in here, and the door no lock. Come in, no?"

Thus invited, Lurline entered the room. Alonso turned his face towards the wall.

"You shameless hussy!" Lurline said without malice. "Is what you doing to the young boy? They have laws, you know? You gwine get you black arse in prison for seducing a minor."

"Him might look young but him certainly not a minor, as you very well know already. Now suppose you say exactly what you want."

"What me want?"

"Yes," she said, dropping her head on Alonso's shoulders, as if claiming her possession. "Remember that there's nobody in this whole wide world that know you like me know you."

"So is what you think me want?"

"You'd like to do what we just done, if you get the chance," she sat up and swung her legs to the floor. Reaching for the dressing gown she threw it across her shoulders and struggled to get her hands in the sleeves. "Him might only be young to you, but him no little."

"I could tell, missus. I could tell from all that grunting noise you were making. Girl, you must discipline yourself. You is in England now, and you must do like the English."

"How comes you know how the English do it?"

" It is in books, if you know what to read, missus. Them lay back, shut their eyes and think of England. No shouting and groaning like you, who sound like you at a football match."

"So what happen, you was outside all this time counting bars?" She glanced to where he lay with the sheet drawn over his head. "Look, you making Lonso shy."

"Shy!" exclaimed Lurline. "With all your noise I come up here to see if he was killing you."

"Leave my room. Both of you!" It came out in a muffled voice from the rumpled bedclothes.

"All men is the same," said Lurline, reaching over and pulling the sheet, "when them belly full them don't want to know... Gees," she said, "the boy in the altogether."

"Leave him alone," said Puncie.

"You the same," Lurline said, a little sadly, "you belly full. Go wash yourself." She spread the sheet over Alonso and turned to leave the room.

"Is vex you vex?" the younger sister asked.

"Is a long time since I fight over a man. Anyway you half-kill him already."

"Don't talk about me as if I'm not here," Alonso said. Uncovering his head and lifting himself to his elbow, he looked at Lurline and for the first time realised that the older sister was the prettier, smaller of stature, although heavier at the hips. "Now if you two women will kindly leave my room, I have to get washed, dressed and get to work."

"Oh, shit," shouted Puncie. "Work! This no gwine pay red-herring taxes!" and she ran downstairs to the bathroom.

Lurline reached the door, then she turned. "You like her?" she asked.

"You not getting ready to marry me off to your sister, are you?"

"Only if you like her, or I should say love."

"Look," said Alonso, getting up and wrapping the sheet around his middle. "What happen, just happened. She had a need. I had a need. We are adults."

"All I ask was if you like her."

"I liked what we did. Is that what you want to hear? Or are you jealous?"

"I don't think you have anything me should be jealous of," she slammed the door. Alonso could hear her footsteps going down the stairs.

IV

The next day was Alonso's day off. He slept late that morning. He could hear the sisters in the kitchen. He decided that he would read. He had bought an old copy of *Joseph Andrews* by Henry Fielding in a second-hand bookshop in South Croydon for one shilling. He picked up the book and started to read the chapter heading. He smiled at the names he came across: *Sir Thomas Booby, Mrs Slipslop* and *Mrs Tow-wouse.* Were the names meant to be descriptive? An hour and a half was not enough time to engage Miss Hine in a discussion on Fielding; anyway his books were not among the prescribed books. He wanted to start the book, but he could not concentrate. He had read *Tom Jones* by the same author, of course, there were Squire Allworthy and Messrs Thwackum and Squares, this time the author seemed to have out done himself. His Literature teacher Miss Hine encouraged him to read Richardson's *Pamela*, but he did not like the epistolary style. Instead he returned to the twentieth century and read Hemingway's *The Old Man and the Sea* and Françoise Sagan's *Bonjour Tristesse,* during the last week. He made a promise to read Sagan in French within a year. His thoughts were interrupted by the women talking loudly as if determined that no one should sleep after ten-thirty in the morning. Suddenly there was a knock at the door.

"It's not locked," he said. He sat up in bed and watched the door swing open and Lurline entered bearing a cup in one hand and a plate of toast in the other. She was followed closely by her sister with two steaming mugs of liquid.

"Breakfast is served," said Lurline.

"And we mean breakfast," said Puncie. Both women were dressed for the street. Puncie was wearing her Underground uniform. "You still on late turn, or is it your day off?"

"So you do wear pyjamas after all," observed Lurline, before Alonso could answer Puncie.

"When I sleep alone. You never hear that the angels don't like to pass and see you naked?"

"But they don't mind two people being naked?" And before he could reply, "Now answer that."

"We sharing our breakfast with you because we want to ask a favour of you," began Puncie.

"No," Lurline looked at him with a smile, "you not that lucky. Boy, I hearsay you good, but not good enough to take on both of us!"

"Whatever do you mean?" asked Alonso shyly while accepting one of the cups Puncie was still holding.

"Lightning no strike twice." Puncie said.

"Specially two bolts in one place, or should I say one bolt in two places?" when no one laughed, Lurline offered him a slice of toast which was heavily covered with marmalade, and continued the conversation. "The favour is, we want to find a place in Camberwell."

"Caspian Road," said Puncie.

"I know it. Are you sure that is not Caspian Street you want?"

"You sound like the English. They never think you could be right," said Puncie, wearily.

"You will come with us, then?" asked Lurline. "You talk well and if anything happen, they will listen to you?"

"You lost me!" he said, looking from one sister to the other. "You better tell me what's going on. Today is my day off. My plan was to do some reading and write an essay before evening class."

"You got the whole day," said Puncie, who seemed to be watching his every action, even to his dusting the crumbs of toast off his fingers onto yesterday's *Evening Star* and picking up the copy of *Joseph Andrews*. "I guess we still nervous about what happened to Uncle Cyrus and our mother, Miss Maude, when they came to view this house."

"That was back in 1953. Cass and Cass told them that one of their people would meet them outside the house..." Lurline was interrupted by her sister.

"They got here before the estate agent, but so many people were watching them that they decided to knock and see if the people living in the house would let them wait inside. A woman opened the door, and... and when she see..." Puncie dissolved into laughter.

"When she see the two black faces looking at her," Lurline took over, "the woman fainted."

"She knocked her head as she fell. Blood started flowing down her face. The little girl behind her started to bawl. Uncle Cyrus turned to run. Miss Maude heng on 'pon him. The neighbours rang the police and the ambulance," Puncie had become sober again. "Lucky the estate agent turn up when all this was going on. He was able to smooth things out."

"Did this really happen? After all there were a lot of black Empire Service people here during the war," said Alonso.

"You think that matter?" asked Puncie. "Jesus was a Jew, but that never stop Hitler from killing Jews, to protect white Christian people."

"I must introduce you to Warren. It sounds as if you studied at the same school," he said.

"I tell you, when that woman realised these black people were going to move in and be her landlord, she forget about being a sitting tenant and cleared out," said Lurline. "Is so it go, Puncie?"

"Is who give you that fool-fool name, Puncie?" he asked.

Puncie jerked her head towards her sister. "She could not say Prudence. No ask me how she made it out to be 'Puncie', but ever since, that is what people call me. I don't mind it. It suit me."

"It kinda rude," he said. "You want to hear the language of some of the Cockney bus drivers and conductors. A passenger called me a 'ponce' the other day. Do I look like a pimp? But of course, in Spanish P-o-n-c-e is a proper name. Ponce de Leon sailed with Columbus in 1493. There's a town in Puerto Rico named after him."

"You know that I work in a hospital, St Peter's? Well, there's a nurse there from Malaya, her name is F.U.C.K, and nobody will call her by her surname. Sister calls her 'Nurse Fuchs' and she refuses to answer. 'My name is Fuck,' she would shout back. All the other nurses call her My Lien, that's her Christian or first name." said Lurline.

"The other day when they were playing cricket, the man on the radio said the batsman was caught in the slips, and this fool-fool cleaning woman said, 'Why was he wearing a slip?'" said Puncie.

"That's an old one," said Alonso. "What's happening at Caspian Road?"

"We want to look over a property there," said Puncie.

"Big mouth," said Lurline.

"Tcho, man, it like being pregnant; you can't hide it for long. Anyway we have to go up to Cass and Cass to pick up the keys. So where is the secret?"

"You people mean business! How long have you been in this country? Eighteen months? And you're buying your own house already!"

"We are both working, then there's our moonlighting as hairdressers and we throw partners," Lurline ticked off their means of earning and saving since their arrival in Britain.

"If we like the house," said her sister, "you could rent a room, that is if big sister no object."

"How the song go? 'God help the man that come between me and my sister...'"

"'And God help the sister that come between me and my man,'" Puncie continued with a poor rendition of the Beverley Sisters' song.

"All this bantering is very flattering, but I'm not your man."

134

"I glad to hear it," shot back Puncie, "because I'm sending for my daughter. She's going on fourteen, and I tell you she is pretty. Me not into having a man that will be casting his eye 'pon me girl pickney. You a little old for her now but by the time she turn twenty you still won't be thirty yet."

"And you'll be knocking on forty. Anyway is who tell you that these brown-skin educated guys want black women? It's white women they want. They call it improving the colour," said Lurline.

"Am I the only subject of your conversation? For the last time, I'm not your man. I'm not anybody's man. I'm not after your thirteen-year-old girl either. I don't care how pretty she is. I have a lot to do with my life and a steady relationship with any woman, white or black, does not figure in it at the moment and for a long, long time in the future."

"Did he tell you that yesterday?" Lurline asked her sister.

"No, missus," came the reply, "him was too busy enjoying what I was giving him."

"What you think would happen if I was to go and tell Uncle Cyrus that him get you in the family way and is denying it..."

"What!"

"Is joke me a joke," laughed Lurline, holding on to her sister as if to transfer the mirth into her. They laughed loudly while embarrassment mixed with anger swelled up in Alonso.

"No go have a heart attack, whatever you do. Oh, God, boy you should see your face. You can't breed that one, boy. Her luck good, you see. With me, a man just has to say 'Hello, nice chile,' and me pregnant. It happened three times."

Alonso regained his composure. He looked at Lurline and said, "Hello, nice chile!"

"I already got two boys and a girl. What would you like it to be? I want another girl."

"If I promise to come with you to Caspian Road, would you two obeah women get out of my room so I can get dressed?"

"Is what him have to hide?" asked Lurline, looking at her sister in mock bewilderment.

"Me don't know. Is two of us, we could hold him down and have a look."

"Out," he said sternly, jumping up as both women moved towards him. "You lay a hand on me and I'll scream till the neighbours call the police..."

Puncie held him while Lurline tickled him. "Tcho, him not ticklish," she said disappointedly. They released him, gathered up the mugs and plate and went out of the room laughing.

V

They collected the keys from the Estate Agent, Cass and Cass. Then they walked along Brixton Road to the junction with Gresham Road. There they caught a thirty-five bus going to Chingford Hatch in Essex. However, their journey to Camberwell took twenty minutes. They alighted at the Camberwell Green end of Walworth Road and walked for about five minutes then turned right, another five minutes and another right turn brought them to Caspian Road. The road started with shops on either side and then became residential. Halfway down the road two fair-haired boys, about ten years old, who bore a remarkable resemblance to the urchins in the Bisto gravy advertisement, approached them and asked what time it was. Puncie was about to say something rude when Alonso stepped forward, pulled back his cuff and showed a rather expensive watch.

"Go on," he said, "you can read the time for yourself." The boys, who wanted to see if this black man would look up at the sun to try and read the time. The boys did not look at the watch. Instead they ran off, shouting, "Bye, bye blackbirds!"

"When I was growing up, if I was rude to any big person they would go straight to me mother and she would give me backside hell."

"Worst of all, if that big person was a relative them would take it 'pon themself to slap you. But over here you dare not touch children or dogs," said Puncie. "If we buy this house, I'll be watching out for those scallywags."

"The one with the for sale sign, must be number forty-nine. And look, a black woman is going into the house next door, that must be forty-seven," said Lurline.

"Make sense," said Alonso, "a black family moved into forty-seven, so number forty-nine has cleared out. Next will be number fifty-one. Nobody wants a Nigger for a neighbour."

"That's why them don't vote fi Labour."

They reached the house. While Lurline was unlocking the door, Alonso saw the curtains move in several houses opposite.

"The natives are getting a bit restless," he said.

They spent about half an hour inspecting the property. All the furniture and floor coverings had been removed. The rooms were in need of redecorating. There was no sign of dampness.

"What you think?" asked Lurline of Puncie.

"What do you think?" asked Puncie of Lurline.

"It all right." They said both at once.

"I agree. Make we go for it," announced Lurline.

"Agreed. What you think, Lonso?" Asked Puncie

"Have I a vote?"

"No, but that shouldn't stop you," said Lurline.

"We just asking," said Puncie.

"Since you asked, I prefer it to Lancer Road or Castle Folly, as you call it."

"I think I prefer upstairs," said Puncie. "We can rent out downstairs."

"You crazy, there are four rooms upstairs to rent out. Downstairs we each have a room and there's a big front room that we can furnish real well. Anyway we want the benefit of the garden. I fancy myself a gardener," announced Lurline.

"In England? Is what you know about English flowers and all that? But see me crosses with this woman. The toilet down here is outside. What we gwine do during the winter? You see the downstairs bath? It is what them call a hip-bath, and it in the Kitchen!" observed Puncie.

"Two things," said Lurline. We can't offer tenants outside toilet. Second thing is when our children come up, this is gwine to be a family house except we want room to do our hairdressing. We won't be having tenants then. So before long we will have the whole house to ourselves."

"Some of what you said make sense. Perhaps we can put up an extension to enclose the toilet," suggested Puncie.

"You will need planning permission from the council. If they grant it, you will be looking at a huge bill." Alonso said.

"How come you know so much about it?" demanded Puncie.

"I have friends who are just waiting to get their keys for their new properties."

"We can discuss it some more," said Puncie, "but it's time for me to leave for work. Where is the nearest tube station?"

"I thought you are the Underground expert," teased Alonso. "You can either get a thirty-six up to the Oval for the Northern Line, or get a bus going to the Elephant and Castle and get the Northern Line and the Bakerloo Line. There are lots of buses going to the Elephant."

"I will go to the Elephant," she said. "What you two going to do with you'self?" She looked at them. "Oh, no, you not christening the house before we buy it. Lonso, you got an essay to write, and evening school later. Now lock up this house and take the keys back to Cass and Cass."

She snatched the key from Lurline and somehow manipulated both Alonso and her sister out of the house.

"Puncie, you ever think of anything else?" Alonso said disapprovingly.

"You don't know the half of it. I tell so much lies to cover for her since she was fourteen that even now I can't stop. I have enough to blackmail her and bleed her dry," said Lurline.

They walked back to Walworth Road and crossed over. They stayed with Puncie until her bus came. Lurline and Alonso walked back to the corner of Camberwell New Road, and waited outside Camberwell Bus Garage for a bus going to the Oval.

"Look!" said Lurline pointing across the road to the Grand Cinema, "they're showing *Mom and Dad*. When that film was out in Jamaica, we

queued up outside the Palace Theatre to see it. The queue could almost
have reach back to the Parade Grounds. We could not get in. The next time
I tried to see it, rain start falling, and as you know the Palace was open-air."

"If you really want to see it we can get to Cass and Cass and still make
the early show."

"You got evening school. I don't want to come between you and you'
studies."

"Let me worry about that. Why do you want to see it? They said it's
about two youngsters playing with sex. That won't do anything for you."

"If you put it like that. But then again some of the books you have in
your room got nothing to do with any examination I ever heard about. But
you're right. Let's go home and I will cook oxtail and butter beans, and
steam rice. How that sound?"

"Better than watching actors doing what they do best, pretending."

"OK, that's settle' then."

VI

On their return to Castle Folly, Alonso was surprised at how big the front
room shared by the two sisters really was. Even with the two single beds and
two large wardrobes there was still plenty of space, with a very expensive-
looking dressing table adorned with crochet-work and make-up articles.

"Most of what's in this room belong to us. We saw them and liked them
and bought them. We used to have a hairdressing business on Price Street in
Jones Town. When our mother returned to Jamaica and said we should try
our luck in London we sold everything lock, stock and barrel. That's why
we have a little money left to go towards buying that house," she explained.
"We do a bit of hairdressing on the side, and people are getting to know
about us. This Saturday we're doing a young bride's hair and her bridesmaid
too. She getting married in the afternoon in Stamford Hill. We have to go
over North London early, you know. There's a lot to do."

"I have a friend who is branching out in business. I ought to introduce
you. He's thinking of opening a hairdressing salon for black people. The
majority of coloured women have to get their hair done in corridors of
people's homes or in the hairdresser's bedroom, that is if they can find a
black hairdresser of quality. It's the same for us men. There are no black
barbershops."

"We have plans," she said. "Is your friend the one who's just two years
older than you? He seems to be going places. You must introduce us. He
got a girlfriend? I bet she's white!" she laughed. "The problem for us women
in our mid-thirties is that the men of our age most likely have a whole tribe
of children back home and two or three women waiting for support money.
I can't get involved with that, you know, 'specially when I have three pickney

of me own to support. The other problem is that people like you're too young. I go to a party with you and everybody will think you is my little brother. In a few years' time them start wondering if me is your mother. Ten years down the road and you off to a new model, most likely a white woman. When it comes to white women, you all don't care how old she be or what she look like, as long as she's white! Sometimes I think you all just want to get back at the white man for what him did to black people during slavery time."

"The problem facing young ones like me is that girls of our age are few and far between. There are six blokes after each girl at a party and, believe me, these girls know it. I heard that a guy went over and asked a girl for a dance at a party. She looked him up and down like a washerwoman looking at dirty clothes. She asked him to pay her back the money her father spent on her fare to get her over here to study nursing. Seventy pounds! That is what I call a very expensive dance!"

"I don't blame her. You dance with these blokes and them start to rub themselves 'pon you. What they start doing to you, you would think that them in bed with you, and you willing for it to happen. I told one of them the other week that the Sunday papers is full of pictures and writings about whores round Hyde Park Corner and Clapham Common. He ought to go there and try his luck. I just push him away and walk off, leaving him in the middle of the dance-floor with an erection like Nelson column. I have not had a man in my life since before my mother come back and tell me that I should go to England," she paused and looked at Alonso, "but I'm not that desperate."

"You left him on the dance floor?"

"What else you want me to do? Him walk off with both him hands in his trousers pockets to disguise his bulge. It shame him so bad that him leave the party right away."

"Gee!" said Alonso. "Oh, boy. Say what you will about rock 'n' roll, but it's so fast-moving that you don't have time to feel sexy."

"Hi, tell you what," her face lit up, as if a brilliant idea had just sprung into her head. The light bulb effect. "Sit 'pon that chair. Gwon sit down, man, quick," she guided him to a chair. "I got an idea. I gwine give you a crew cut like the black GIs them. Flat on the top and short back and sides," she spread a towel over his shoulders, then she fetched a little case and extracted from it scissors, combs, shears, and several bottles of oils. She sprinkled a sweet-smelling liquid on his overgrown head of thick hair and started cutting with the shears.

"Good hair," she said. "P'rhaps mixed with Indian."

"My maternal grandfather was half-Spanish while my grandmother's parents were native Mexican Indians and Jamaican."

"Quite a mixture. The whiteman' race hardly show anywhere else in you," she paused, stepped in front of him and raised his chin with a crooked right forefinger. "'Course, some people I know and Ah not calling any name might say you have more than a little of the Latin lover in you, but me know nothing about that."

"That can be soon rectified," he reached out with both hands for her hips.

"Boy, behave you'self," she said. She dropped both her hands and swept them wide, disengaging his hands from her hips. "Don't bother the artist when she's working. Or as they say, 'let sleeping dogs lie'. This old dog wouldn't go just for your fingers, boy. Is the whole hand it would go for," she said without a break in her work. When she had finished giving him the crew cut, she again lifted his chin. "You ain't got much moustache, but I will shape it up for you. Done!" she said, carefully removing the towel from his shoulders. "I will shake it off outside later. Now Mister What-ever-you-last-name-is, go and look over there in the dressing-table mirror. What you think?"

"All I need now is an American accent," he was pleased with what he saw. He was wondering whether it would be appropriate to offer her what it cost him the last time he had his hair cut. Suddenly there was a loud knock at the door.

"Lurline?" He recognised the voice of the landlord. "You got that boy in there?"

"Is checkin' you checkin' up 'pon me, Uncle Cyrus?" Alonso could see from her posture that she was getting irritable.

"I just want to know if you have a man in me house." She flew to the door with the agility of a charging bitch. She yanked the door open so that it banged against a wardrobe.

"I ain't a schoolgirl," she spat out.

The fury of her charge had sent him back against the opposite wall of the corridor. Alonso saw with sudden fear that she still had a pair of scissors in her hand. "I ain't you' pickney. And if I was, I'm a grown woman with three children of my own. Is what you a-watch and peep me for? Listen, now, you better get you maga rarse up them steps before you have an accident." The man backed slowly up the stairs. Lurline turned and kicked the door shut.

"Mind me door," he said halfway up the stairs. She stood with her back to the door trembling with fury. The voice of Cyrus Foley could still be heard. "Watch and peep you! If you mother did watch and peep you properly you would not breed for three different men." She had the door open in a flash while Foley was still in mid-sentence. "You all the same. Money a hand, back a ground..."

"You calling me a whore?" she flew out of the room and took the stairs two at a time. Alonso feared she would reach Foley (who having a head start was near the top of the second stairs and almost within reach of his sanctuary) and plunge the scissors into him. Alonso caught up with her outside the kitchen and, locking his arms around her waist, struggled to pull and drag her into the kitchen. He pushed the door shut with his right heel. He continued to hold her until she calmed down and her breath became more regular. He could feel that her heart was no longer racing.

"OK, OK," she said. "If I don't get out of this house, I gwine kill him."

"They hang women in this country," he said, loosening his grip around her waist. "It's not worth throwing away your life or your freedom because of this man. Besides, you have three children who need you."

"You right," she said. She dropped the scissors on the table as a sign of surrender. "I never could find out what me mother saw in him. You know, the only time she really feel good is when he's not around. She told me she would be happy if him was to find another woman. Believe me, when a woman starts wishing her man find another woman, then what they had in the first place is over. She would give him a divorce if only him would ask for it. Is not lie me telling." She put her hands on his and was about to push them apart, but she pulled them tightly around her waist. "Thanks," she said. "If you didn't hold on to me, and I did catch him, I might have stabbed him."

She began trembling. She buried her head on his shoulders and cried uncontrollably. He held her tighter. He began softly to massage her shoulders, which were rigid with tension. After a while she eased herself out of his embrace.

"He shouldn't call me a whore. This time he went too far. It's true that my children all have different fathers, but it not because my behaviour was *slack'n'tidy* like. I was twenty-five years old when I had my first chile. Puncie had her chile when she was nineteen. I thought I was barren, though I didn't set out to get pregnant. Anyway it is me who break up with me baby-father. This man was in the police force and think even to this day that he should have a woman in every district! It was a good four years before my other baby and that time the guy sound really good; he was waiting to go up to his father in the States and he was going to send for me. After three years and I never heard gunfire after him, I finally got the message that he gone for good. I did promise myself no more, but things happen, and when I realise I was pregnant I never even bother to tell this one that I was carrying his chile. You know what? He must have guessed, because I haven't seen him since." She looked into Alonso's eyes. "I never take money from any man. I never even bother to harass them for maintenance. Tcho, man, me never run after anybody. So why is he calling me a whore? '*Money a hand, back a ground*!' That is what whores say! That is what they do! This man is out of order. I not putting up with it," she shook her head defiantly.

"You'll be moving out soon. You don't have to see him again. Let me make you a nice cup of tea. The English swear by tea. It's the great restorative. Any time they're upset, like when Napoleon was causing them a spot of bother, they just dropped everything and made a nice cup of tea, then they met him at Waterloo and the rest is history. The same thing happened when Herr Hitler tried their patience..."

"All right," she said, holding up her arms in surrender, "so long as that man in that room upstairs don't start saying, 'Me get a mug of tea in hand so me put me back a-ground."

"Perish the thought. You would spill it!"

She pushed him away playfully. "Don't make me laugh," she said, laughing. "Me head hurt. I have to go to my room for a pill."

He reached out and touched her face. "Anybody ever tell you that when you smile you are quite handsome."

"Only when I smile?" She took hold of his hands and examined them. "It's soft like a baby' bottom. I bet you never did a day's hard work in your life." She let his hand go. "Is what me a-do? If that man come in here and find us holding hands, him going to start his nonsense again, and this time I will hurt him. Oh, me head. I get headaches when I get upset. I must take that pill. Bring the tea when you make it."

When he got to her room she was sitting on her bed in a dressing gown, head in hands.

"My head is still thumping," she said. "I just took a pill. It will go in a minute. Put the tea down on the table there." She said, without looking up.

"Do you get them often?" he said, feeling anxious. "Why don't you lie down? It's too late for me to go to my evening class, but I can go up and make a start on that essay. I'm on early for the next six days starting in the morning. I'll see you tomorrow evening."

"I'll lie down, but don't you go. You could start writing you essay here. There is pen and paper right on the table there. Like the eunuch said of old, what is to prevent you?"

"Somehow I don't think this is the right atmosphere to begin to write an essay on, *The Upheavals in England from 1641 to 1660 was only a Civil War, not a Revolution!*"

"You dead right. Is what that all about? Just listening to all that make me head hurt more. No, don't go. When we was up in the kitchen you was rubbing my shoulder blade and it felt good. Perhaps if you do it again, the headache would go. In the TV advertisement they say headache is caused from tension and sometimes it is in the shoulder."

"And of course, you being a ward maid would know all about that," he said, smiling at her. She rose from the pillows and turned so that Alonso could reach the back of her neck. He held her shoulders and using his thumbs began to massage.

"Ooh," she said, "that feels good. She lifted her shoulders and rolled them back. "Yes, that's good. Real good." He continued his massage and became aware that she had nothing on under her dressing gown. As he was massaging her collarbone his fingers moved imperceptibly down, down,

down towards her breasts. Her head jerked upwards. He lowered his head and pressed his lips against hers. She lifted her hands clasped them behind his head and pulled him down on top of her.

"How is your headache?" he asked.

"Gone," she said. "Touch bubby, kiss 'pon lips and back 'pon bed," she giggled. "You better go lock that door. I would not but it pass him upstairs to barge into my room just when things..."

VII

The sisters moved out towards the end of November and Alonso moved with them. They knew his coming with them was going to be temporary until the Morgans moved from Geneva Road to their new home in Lilford Road. The tenancy of the basement in Geneva Road would provide Alonso and his sister with sufficient room in accordance with the expectations of a brother and sister sharing a small flat. Lurline and Puncie had both declared that they could not conceive any possibility of falling out with Alonso which would require him to leave.

Puncie, ever the forward one, had voiced the possibility that Rosita might be a stuck-up little cow, having had all that high-school learning, and her being "high-colour" she might want to be the only female in the castle however humble it might be. So Geneva Road it must be and not Caspian Road. Once when they were alone, Lurline told Alonso she would miss him, but she had come to accept that his staying at Caspian Road might drive a wedge between she and her sister. Although she had warned Alonso not to fall in love with either her or Puncie, she was beginning to entertain feelings for the young man that she had never before experienced. She had grown to like his caresses. She loved his hands gently stroking her body, the poetry he sometimes read to her. One day as he revised French for his evening class he was reading Baudelaire. She felt excited by his voice and the sound of the language she did not understand. He asked her if she would like a translation. She said no, although she wanted to know what it was called in English. He told her it was "Autumn Sonnet" and there was a line that went: *'Strange lover, what merit do you find in me?'* She had found merit in him, but it was more a feeling, not something she could describe. She could not see it the way Puncie saw her relationship with him. She had once said that what was between her and Alonso was like the fruits of summer. The birds descend and gorge themselves and when summer is over move on. Lurline considered Alonso like a favourite doll to her sister. Customs change and new playthings come into vogue. Lurline knew if she accepted what was passing between her and Alonso as love, she and her sister would quarrel. Sharing the same man was a time bomb that was bound to explode in their faces. She was glad he was going.

She raised her head above his, one day when they where in bed, and asked him, "Why are you not forty-one? I could love you if you were six years older than me. That would be all right. Why are you grinning?"

"It wouldn't be me. My mother is forty-two!"

"What!" she sat up. "She's just nine years older than me. We could have been to school at the same time. What would she think of me?"

"She would say you are corrupting her boy. Little does she know that Miss Flo did that seven years ago, when I was fourteen."

"You rudeness a woman when you was fourteen? "

"I mean a big woman. She must have been about thirty at the time."

"But that's against the law!"

"She told me the self-same thing. She said she'd go to prison if anyone should hear about it. If I kept quiet she would do it again with me. That's why you are the first to hear of it."

"Me interested. Tell me did she keep her promise?"

"One more time, then she went to live over at Caratto Gully and I never saw her again," he said, then he started to reminisce. "It was pimento season. I was trying to earn some pocket money breaking pimento. You know what I mean? I was up the pimento tree breaking the clusters of pimento and dropping them to the ground and she was picking them up and stuffing them in a big crocus bag. Later on she and her children would pick off the berries for drying."

"I grew up in the country, you know. My district is called Red Wattle Gap, St Mary parish. I know about bruking pimento," she said impatiently. "Go'n."

"Suddenly the sky was dark and a thunderstorm burst on us. We had to run through the cane piece to reach the old hut. By the time we got there we were drenching wet. To my surprise Miss Flo pull off her dress and start wringing the water from it. 'Boy', she said, 'you better tek you clothes off before you ketch relapse.' What do you think country people mean when they said relapse?"

"Pneumonia, I think. Go'n."

"I turned my back and took my shirt and trousers off, standing there in my underpants, which too was soaked through and through. When I turned around Miss Flo was lighting a fire and spreading her frock and her drawers to dry. 'Gie me you things,' she said and proceeded to wring the water from them and hang them to dry. I was trembling, perhaps from the change in temperature, perhaps from fear of standing next to this naked woman. Then she picked up a crocus bag, threw it around her shoulders. She saw I was trembling and still had my underpants on. 'A tell you, you gwine ketch relapse, come, yeah.' Whether I moved or she pulled me I can't remember. I remember that she yanked off my underpants, saying they were wet. She put them on a stone near the fire and then threw the crocus bag around my shoulders and pulled me close. I remember the warmth of her enormous body, but the trembling wouldn't stop. I also recalled her voice, half-mocking but soft and soothing. 'Boy, you a-stiffen up 'pon me... But see, yeah, the boy is big like a man, a real big man. Nung I know what dem mean 'bout you havin' *Panya* blood' You can guess what happened next."

"Yes," she said, "I can guess. You have that effect on older women."

"I've never made love to a woman my own age, or younger."

"So your first experience was with a woman just three or four years younger than your mother. That no healthy at all!"

"All that rubbish that boys are in love with their mothers and girls in love with their fathers!"

"Don't knock it. There are lots of stories about incest among people who sent for their children, or as we say in Jamaica, *dawg a nyam dawg*."

"That's not love. That is an abuse of power."

"Maybe, maybe not. Back to you and me. I don't know how we going to pull our neck out of this chokey. Your sister must not know about any of this. I couldn't stand her scorn. Would she write home and tell your mother? It would kill her. Lord, the disgrace."

"What about my feelings? Don't they count for anything?"

"I seem to remember you reading me a poem that go, '*It is better to have love and lost than never to have loved at all'.*"

"Tennyson.*"

"In all this nastiness is the women who always get the shit in her face. A man just get up and pull on his trousers and go off and boast how many times he did it and with who', whether it is somebody as old as his mother or young as his daughter it no matter. He's a stallion and all his friends slap him on the back and he is a' Errol Flynn. When a woman have a fling with a young man she is a whore. We never seem to screw anybody. You all screw us!"

"That's not fair," he said defensively. "We make love. It's a joint effort. A partnership."

"That no what Adam said about Eve. He said '*The woman, whom you gave me, did deceive me'.* Perhaps we can't stop sudden like, but nobody must know."

"What about Puncie?"

"'Specially Puncie. Anyway, she can step away like a man. You just a little adventure to her. Me not being jealous of me sister, but be warned: if you fall for her, you going to get hurt real bad. I don't think I would like that. I don't want anything to happen that will bring bad feelings between me and me sister. You know the song, *Gawd help the man who come between me and me sister...*"

"*And God help the sister who comes between me and my man,*" he finished the signature tune of the Beverley Sisters.

VIII

The first time Alonso presented himself at the Morgans' with his crew cut, he was met with silence. Then those assembled started laughing. His head was twisted this way and that, and there were many exclamations in imitation American accents. When everyone had had their fun, the general consensus was that the style had been executed with great professionalism. Alonso was surprised that the two great conservatives, Lincoln and Asquith, insisted on introductions in the hope that the artist would practise his craft on them. They were briefly taken aback that the artist was a woman. Immediately they could see the delicacy of the cut, then they began to praise the artistry. Alonso had little choice and duly introduced the sisters a week later. After all, they had wanted to meet the budding entrepreneur, Lincoln. The idea of operating a hairdressing salon in Brixton appealed to them. Alonso brought the sisters to his circle of acquaintances at the Morgans' the next Sunday evening. Lurline he introduced as his Tonsorial Artist; Puncie he called the *facy* one.

"You mean feisty," corrected Asquith

"We probably mean that, but in Jamaica that's how we say it," Warren pointed out.

Myrtle Morgan was particularly happy to meet the two hairdressers. This would save her the journey to Willesden on the Bakerloo Line to the only professional black hairdresser she trusted. Myrtle was quick to point out that the woman in Willesden did her clients' hair in her kitchen.

Lincoln was involved right from the start. He had already been negotiating for premises in Railton Road, Brixton. He thought the place would be ideal for a barber's shop too. He changed his plans after meeting Lurline and Puncie. He would now have a hairdressing salon on the ground floor and the barber's shop on the first floor. The sisters, however, would not agree to be employees and Lincoln found that it was necessary to go into partnership with them. Coolieman, the barber who erstwhile plied his trade in a haphazard fashion above the Colonial Club, changed his mind about cutting hair only at weekends while working as handyman and bouncer at the Colonial Club. His only problem was that since many working men only had Sunday as a rest day He worried about loosing trade so he planned to let the men come to the shop through a side door and continued his business.

He accepted that the status of a barber employed in the room above CURLS to be very glamorous. Certainly to be involved in Brixton's first black hairdressing business would not compromise his plan of spending only five years in Britain. His new status of being Brixton's first black professional barber should not mean permanency in Britain, but might very well increase his efforts to make enough money to enable him to retire to a place in the sun.

The salon was opened early in December to great fanfare. In attendance were liberal members of the local borough council and a representative from the West Indian High Commission. Some Caribbean personalities from the field of entertainment were there to add glamour and lend support. Also present was the local Member of Parliament for the Brixton area, the sympathetic Colonel Lipton. It was all recorded for posterity in the local press and the *West Indian Gazette,* whose editor was asked to cut the ribbon that symbolically opened the doors of the salon. Lincoln was awarded the kudos of being Black Britain's dynamic young entrepreneur. He was pressed to make a speech and obliged reluctantly. He pointed out that over the centuries many peoples of different cultures had been to this country, some because they had knelt at the feet of the conquering British army. They had added to the richness of the language, the wealth of the nation and the character of the people. The West Indian migrant would continue in that vein and in doing so must show a degree of independence, not living down to being associated with slums and deprivation, but living up to the vibrancy of Caribbean society, including demanding all amenities associated with the second half of the twentieth century. Today's event was just one small step on the way.

14

It was all too much for Myrtle Morgan. It really did not bother her that it was odds-on that it would snow for Christmas. She had told a Jamaican woman who huddled under her umbrella as they waited for a bus to Brixton Market, "The thing to do in this country is to dress as if you are expecting the worst."

It was a mild rebuke to the woman who had taken shelter under Myrtle's umbrella, as if the fact that they were both Jamaicans gave her the right to share. Myrtle did not like the smog either, but she usually arranged her scarf so that it covered her mouth and nostrils, and she spoke little until she was indoors. British winters were harsh and not at all to her liking, but she had survived three and was now into her fourth year. Winters were not too much for her.

"You' ears too damn hard," she shouted at her husband. "You never listen, when I talk to you. I done tell you that with Vicky getting married the Saturday afore Christmas, it madness to move to the new house."

"No blame me. Is you' choice to make you'self head cook and bottle-washer at people weddings," he said defensively. "It not like them is family."

"This is family," she shouted.

"Family?" he enquired. "It is the first time me hearing that. I think we was just friends".

"Yes, we family," she affirmed. "Everybody from Guinea Fowl Walk is family. I grow up with Vicky's mother and aunty. Them will all be dressed for church; you can't expect them to hurry back and get in the kitchen. Them need me, Ziah Morgan. Is blind you blind that you can't see that?"

"But you going to church too. You gwine dress-up too."

"Sometimes I just can't take you' foolishness. Vicky going to need her mother and her aunt by her when them taking the pictures. I will go straight to the hall to see that things a move OK."

"You bake the cake and iced it, and it look good, and a bet it taste even better," he meant to smooth-talk his wife. "So what happen, the groom don't have anybody to help out?"

"Ziah Morgan," she scolded, "always asking damn foolish questions that you 'ready know the answer. Zephaniah Bogle has a sister who is a nurse in Maudslay, but you don't think she's going to come and work in the kitchen cooking curried goat and rice, fried plantain and cutting up alligator bread and serving like a maid, do you? She said she is a Sister in her hospital, and God knows there are not many black hospital Sisters around. She wants to be the first black Matron, you know? Black people a begin to have ambition in this country."

"You talking to a man whose brother is a practising barrister. Him say he going to be a QC one day. Look at Lincoln, him not yet twenty-five and buying his first house and running a business as an agent for a insurance company back home."

"Ziah, you not fifty-five yet. Is what happen, ambition dead at thirty? Well, make me tell you something, come next year and me going to shake meself and show you what ambition is."

"And do what? Woman, we'll be grandparents soon. You was complaining that moving house afore Christmas too much for you, now you want to be one of them ladies in the House o' Lords them talkin' 'bout?"

"I've been thinking of doing some child-minding. Don't look so surprised. I haven't work things out yet, so you can close you mouth," she placed her fingers under her husband's chin as if to force his mouth closed. She sighed, "All the same, time is short. I don't want Christmas to find me still sewing curtains, choosing carpets and furniture. It gwine to be a rush, man."

"Me and Colonel have things under control. We talk to the furniture people and them going to deliver everything before eleven o'clock on Saturday. Friday night we will lay the linoleum. Lonso said that he's coming to give a hand. Sunday is his day off, so we will be able to arrange the rooms. Then we move all our belongings from here on Tuesday."

"Me not moving anywhere on Christmas Eve. Lawd me God, Ziah Morgan. It means that I won't know where anything is on Christmas Day. Me just can't stand all this botheration. I was looking forward to going to Christmas Morning service now that we have a church where we are welcome. God bless the Reverend Mr Hood."

"Is the Reverend Hood welcoming you, not the church members. I bet the congregation will just be as cold as the English weather. I never know a people who is just like their climate more than the English."

"Is God who welcome us," she said.

"Is true," he agreed. "Look, man," he said soothingly to his wife, "things going to work out, even if Sunday we have to work through the night. I know the removal man, his name is Warren Hall, I think he and a white man run their moving business. He will move us when we say. All we taking from here are what is in the kitchen the sitting room and the bedroom and we clothes. It won't be a problem, man. I'm sure Lincoln and Lonso will be around to lend a hand. You wait and see, everything will be OK. Tuesday night you will be stuffing the bird in your own kitchen. Who we having round for Christmas besides Colonel, Lonso and Lincoln?"

"Only Vie and her sister."

"So that make me and you, that's two and three, that's five and two that make seven. I was thinking we ought to have a house-warming party. What if we have a New Year's party," he was watching his wife intently. "You know, just a few friends a little music and a few drinks..."

"Ziah," Myrtle said, as if to a demanding child, "we buying a house, we no win the pools."

"I know, Miss Myrt, but we got to have a little party," Isaiah glanced at his wife then decided to prey on his wife's superstition. The estate agent did say somebody had died in the house a few months back. I think it would be a good thing to give the duppy a little white rum."

"Is who they said dead in the house?" She was suddenly very interested.

"Some old dear. What you say we give her a little white rum instead of her gin and tonic."

"I don't know, Ziah. All the debt we take up over the last few weeks make me head hurt. I really don't know. We will just have to see."

"It don't have to cost the earth," he re-assured her. "All the people we ask we'll tell them to bring a bottle. All we have to do is to cook some goat meat. You do a good curry."

"I still not so sure, Ziah. I know that all our real friends will bring a bottle. That's not what bothering me. You know how them young black boys with cars just cruise around and invite themselves into decent people's parties? That is where the trouble starts. That's why the police raiding people's houses. The papers them full of it."

"Me and Colonel will be at the door turning away people we don't know," he said.

"That is when all the fuss start. Me cannot stand the botheration."

"I never hear anybody moving into a house without a house warming party. We just have to make the white duppy know that black people take over the house. Listen, I tell you a story. Them bury this black man in Streatham cemetery besides this old white couple. You know what, them go dream to them daughter that since this black man in the grave next to them all them hearing is jungle music. Their eternal peace turn into a Saturday night 'jump-up'." He laughed, but on looking up he saw that his wife was not the least bit amused. "What happen, you no think it funny?"

"No!" she said firmly. "I bet is some white man make up that. Never mind 'bout the dead. We better watch out for the living; like day follow night they'll be saying the same 'bout us if we turn up the volume a little. I don't think your mate was talking about the dead, God rest them soul."

"Tcho, man, you spoil the joke," he said.

"Ziah Morgan," she said firmly, "there was no joke there in the first place," she watched her husband pretending to be reading the paper. "Suck you' teeth all you want, I don't see anything funny in it. What did the boys think when you tell it to them?"

"Lonso laughed, but Lincoln just suck him teeth. You sure that him not you son? I swear sometimes I think you got to tickle that boy to get him to laugh."

"Well, if him is me pickney, I want to know where you was when I was carrying him. Now, it is different if I was to say you is Lonso father."

"What you mean? The boy was not even born in Jamaica," Ziah sounded very defensive.

"All that time when you was away driving Wray and Nephew rum truck sometime me never see you for weeks on end. You could have gone to Panama."

"Me going to bed," Ziah announced abruptly. "I'm early turn tomorrow."

"Me father and me uncle them went to Bocas, you know," she said.

"That no news," her husband said. "Why do you think them call him Paco when his real name is Earnest? The generation born before us travelled abroad too, you know. Lonso said they built the Panama Canal and planted the banana and the sugarcane for the United Fruit Company. Me uncle went to place him call *Kama Why*. Is the other day Lonso tell me that is not how it pronounce and that it is a real place in Cuba, but I still can't say it the way he say. I wrote it down on a piece of paper. Here it is... C-a-m-a-g-u-e-y."

"Him was born speaking Spanish. What happening, you gwine start learning Spanish too?"

"Him was a child when his mother took him to Jamaica," he said.

"I know that, but the mother did not speak any English so she always speak to them in Spanish. So what you think about Lonso taking over this place?"

"Is why you have to go over that time and time again. This place is big enough for him to share with his sister. Anyway as long as I get rent money every week me is a happy bunny," he looked at his wife. "Is what the matter now?"

"I wish that Lonso was as careful with his money as Lincoln. I know that he's older than Lonso, but there must be just two or three years between them. Lincoln is buying his first house and Lonso moving into Geneva Road. It seems funny to me. He could get a room here with us. We know him long before we met Colonel."

"Ask him. You know him well enough. If Lonso don't want this place, I would still have to find a tenant. I still own it until 1959."

"The council might have knocked it down by then."

"I don't know. These buildings should be preserved. They could rip out the inside and fix it up real good," Ziah had read about a group of people who were leading a protest campaign to preserve some old building. He liked the towering buildings of Somerleyton and Geneva Roads. He liked their nearness to the Colonial Club and the Nelson Public House. His new house in Lilford Road was going to involve a good twenty minutes' walk to the centre of Brixton. He had better not raise the subject of getting a car until they were well settled into the new house.

"Well, me is glad to be shot of this place," she said in her mixture of Jamaica and English colloquialism. "Anyway you just thinking 'bout how far you will be from your cronies."

"Tell me something," he said and he actually scratched his head. "Lincoln is buying his own house, yet he is asking you to rent this woman a room. What is going on here?"

"I don't know what's going on. All I know is what Lincoln tell me. His cousin in Birmingham wrote to him asking him to find a room for her friend who is coming to London. Lincoln asked me, and we said yes. I know no more, but I bet you got some ideas."

"Lincoln full of big talk. Colonel and me went with him the other day to look over the place him buying. The family had just moved out. You know that him is not planning to live there, well, not right away. So that will give him five rooms to rent out. That is going to bring him more than fifteen pounds rent every week, and his mortgage is only sixteen pounds per month. No wonder him already talking about buying another house. He said him want to start a company call Ebony Accommodation. Watch my words, that boy going to milk black people dry."

"Black people want room for rent and if him can supply them, good luck to him I say."

"That is it," Ziah interrupted sharply. "That is what him said when Colonel tell him that him was taking advantage of black people. Lincoln calls it supply and demand. So he was talking to you. That boy is going to be rich, very rich before he reach thirty."

"Is you used to tell me about those Hungarians who used to rent black people room over Ladbroke Grove way. You think that them use to rent them property because them like black people? Them rent those slums because black people wanted place to live and they know that they could make money off black people because of the demand."

"I see that Bigshot Mr Lincoln winning you over. I suppose him ask you to join his company?"

"No, but him give me a good idea, which I have been sleeping on."

"So you not going to tell me till this dream turn into a nightmare?" he asked.

"Wait and see Isaiah Morgan, wait and see," she looked at her husband. "Tcho, man, don't look so crestfallen. I not going to spend the furniture money on a holiday. I'm planning to fix up the basement and do some child-mindin'. These young black women having lots of kids and them still have to go to work. So what you think?"

"Why bother ask me now when you mind done make up long time? I bet your business advisor Lincoln did... what is the word I want? ... yes, them call it research. As to me, I'm just you husband."

"Is what you mean by that?"

"Nuthin. You could make money from that scheme. Did you think it up or is Lincoln put the idea in your head?"

"What happen, you no think I can think things out for meself?"

"I always knew you were not just a pretty face."

II

Ziah Morgan was at the new house before any delivery was made. He had a bottle of white rum in his toolbox. As soon as he had got in the empty house and closed the door behind him he uncorked the bottle and with the solemnity of a priest at High Mass he sprinkled a few drops in the passage with the exhortation "*to absent friends*". He continued throughout the house sprinkling the potent liquid, offering libation to any spirit who might have been ill-disposed to blacks taking up residence in a house where they had lived.

"You think it safe to strike a match?" asked Lonso taking out a packet of cigarette and offering them to Ziah and Colonel.

"Yes, man," said the host. "I got the kettle going. You want a cuppa?"

"Don't insult me," said Colonel, "you got any more of the real stuff?"

The only utensils available in the kitchen were a kettle which whistled like a demented nineteenth century steam train; two cups and three plastic cups deformed by the hot liquid they had contained at frequent intervals. Ziah ran the tap water over and into the containers, rather than washing them. He tipped white rum into the plastic containers and nodded to his guests, as he corked the bottle. Colonel took up his drink with true reverence like a sacrament.

"I remember when me grandmother died, long, long time ago when I was a boy. Me uncle sent me to go and buy rum from the coolieman shop for the men that was digging the grave and those that was making the coffin. Well, when I come back the first thing that Old Mass Charles did was to tip some of the rum 'pon piece of wood, then he light a match and tried to burn the wood. Well, boy, you think the wood would burn? It just went *pip... pip... pip*. You know what? Them send me back to the shop to tell the coolieman that him was a damn thief for watering down the rum and he must send two bottles a the real stuff or else them not going to pay a red cent."

"Did you tell the coolieman that he was a damn thief?" asked Lonso.

"No, man, I was a little boy, I could not talk to big people like that. I just told him what Mass Charles had done and said that them want two more bottles of the real stuff. He knew what was going on, for he went into his store room and come back with two bottles. Mass Charles burn these too, and boy they set alight so quick I was frighten in case the whole place was going to burn down."

"This is over proof," said Ziah, "but the place won't catch fire unless Myrtle come down and find us standing around. I done promise her she will be able to move into her new house Christmas Eve, and we going to keep that promise, right, boys? So drink up and let's get to work," said Ziah, leading the way by drinking his rum in one long draught. "Lincoln will join us later. Hope him remember that I ask him to buy some grub."

It had been decided that apart from landlords Isaiah and his lady, Myrtle, the only other person who would move in before Christmas would be Colonel.

Myrtle Morgan paused briefly outside her new home. She looked up with pride then, taking a fresh hold on the bags she was carrying, she started up the steps. Once inside the house she put down the bags again and breathed heavily.

"There's just one thing wrong here," she said aloud to herself, "I should have taken the rooms on the ground floor. But that would mean that all the tenants would be treading all over me nice clean floor. No, if them have to come through here to go up to their room it would be too much of an invasion. Well, as long as I can go out in the garden to heng out my clothes and can sit there in the summer, the tenants can have the rooms below me. Anyway there's a big cellar. Colonel going to fix it up so I can have space for the children I intend to look after when their parents are at work."

She took a deep breath, picked up her bags and started the climb up to the third floor. Two minutes later she stopped outside the door of her kitchen. She opened it and, pushing a couple of the bags with her feet and dragging the others, she was in the middle of the kitchen, standing on the new linoleum floor. She looked around like a conqueror examining her new territory. There was a new cooker, new refrigerator, cupboards, table and chairs. It would be her capitol. She had not forgotten the early days when she shared the cooker on a landing in the house in Leander Road, Brixton Hill. Other women were always opening her pots. Although they had an arrangement that one woman or at most two would use the cooker at any one time there was always this invasion of privacy. She had soon learnt that although the landlord had provided a cupboard beside the cooker that the women shared, each shelf belonging to a different woman, things had a way of disappearing and complaints led to frequent unpleasant rows.

"Well," she said to herself, "nobody is going to cook on the landing of this here house." She might not have seen it as a general improvement in the lives of immigrants. She knew full well that it continued in many houses where migrants live. At Geneva Road she cooked in the passage of her basement flat. But it was she alone, and being the person she was, she had often scrubbed down the walls and opened the door and windows in an effort to get rid of the smell of spiced food. She recalled attempting to do the same at Leander Road only to be met with the sarcasm of one woman.

"Missus, you have time! You think me leaving Jamaica come to England to clean backra people wall and ceiling? When me go back to Jamaica, me just send back to the country for a poor cousin and get them to do me cleaning. Me finish with scrubbing and washing down."

When she heard that, Myrtle had fled to the small and very congested room, flung herself on her bed and cried. Then she thought that back to her days in Kingston. She had sent for a poor cousin from the country to come and do her scrubbing, washing and cleaning. Amid her tears he paused and then was convulsed with a giggling fit. She remembered the poor girl, fifteen or sixteen years of age, was caught staring at the clothes she was given to wash and turning to her said, "Gody Myrtle, a what them call this?" The poor girl had been looking at a brassiere belonging to Myrtle's oldest daughter. This had prompted Myrtle to buy the girl a pair. When asked later how it was, the girl said she felt tied up.

As she sorted through the bags she wondered whatever happened to Cooliegal. She had stayed with her for about three years then she had got pregnant and had gone to live with her boyfriend, a young man who made his living selling charcoal. He would push his handcart from street to street all over Kingston, shouting "coo-al, coo-al". Well, with England open wide these days you never can tell. The next time she sat on a bus the black woman next to her might be Cooliegal.

She remembered somebody had said that England was a leveller! As far as the English were concerned all blacks were the same. They had all come from somewhere in Africa, which was synonymous with Jamaica. Myrtle knew that migrants were individuals. Look at a man like Colonel and the people that he was sharing with. Back home he would not play dominoes with them. Her grandmother used to say that the bones the dogs were fighting over in the street were all different, as some fell off good tables. As the dogs yelped and snarled over the bones their canine minds could not comprehend the quality of the linen or the lack of it on the tables from which the bones came. Some bones were never touched by human hands; after they were cooked the meat was very carefully carved from them. In other cases strong human teeth had bitten, chewed and slurped over the bones. Coming out of her reverie Myrtle Morgan picked up the bags, the contents of which were not intended for the kitchen, and went out. She felt a surge of excitement as she opened the next door, which led to her bedroom. The double bed reminded her of pictures she had seen in books of horses in the old days, covered from back to fetlock in one gigantic spread. She had bought the beautiful counterpane in Ridley Road Market and had steadfastly refused to use it at Geneva Road. Now here it was in all its medieval glory. This was the coat of arms of the mistress of this house. Everything matched, the wardrobes, the dressing table and the bedside tables. Thank God there was no longer any need to balance suitcases on top of the wardrobes. It had always reminded her that there was no permanence in her sojourn in England. You had to be ready to go at a moment's notice. Now she was settled. The coming year she would send for their twin daughters. Ziah could forget about buying a car. She wanted the girls here before they passed the age to attend secondary school. She went over to the dressing table and sat down. She still had the scarf, which was colourful indeed, but its main purpose was to hide the rollers that Gladys had put in her hair when she straightened it this morning. They would have to stay a bit longer now there was a church where she could attend Christmas morning service; she wanted to look her best. She would wear a hat, although the English seemed to have given up that practice. She re-adjusted the ornaments, which were nestling in the crochet doilies, checked the combs and brushes, the jewellery box, the ring tree and flicked away an imagined speck of dust. She stood up and looked around the room and was pleased. She crept out as reverentially as one would leave a sanctuary. In Front of her, at the far side of top of the stairs, was the door to the front room. She pushed the door open and walked over to the window. She regretted that people would not be able to see the splendour of the place as they walked past, but her front room was three floors above the pavement. She had been more than a bit nervous at choosing the suite because of the cost, but as the salesman Mr Collier had asked, "How often are you going to choose another suite?" It was the best she had seen, and it was very expensive. Little wonder the salesman had given them the coffee table free of charge. She did not want the bar, but the salesman sided with Ziah. Finally she had to agree that it matched the display cabinet quite well. This front room was worth waiting for. She made up her mind that Ziah could have a New Year's party after all. She was adamant there would be no dancing. She would have a few people in for a drink and something to eat. A room like this had to be shown off. She sat in the chair that Ziah presumptuously called *his* chair. She was directly opposite the television set. It was her first, and she had not yet summoned up the courage to switch it on. She was more familiar with the radiogram, which Ziah had said was a *'blue spot'*, whatever that meant. She got up, went over to it and tried to find Radio Luxembourg, but found the BBC Light programme instead. There was a comedy that did not make her laugh, but the audience response was enough to cheer her up. She felt the urge to be childlike so she went to the bar. Ziah had already opened a bottle of Rich Ruby wine. She poured herself a glass and went back to the chair. She pushed the stool in place, sat down and put her feet up. She wished Ziah and Colonel would not come for another two hours. This, she thought, was not too much for a hard-working woman to ask. She smiled as she drank. The audience in the radio sketch laughed at something the comedian said. She wondered why she could not understand the accent. She was still slow in understanding the English humour. She resisted the urge to go to the kitchen to start the preparations for Christmas. She would get up when she had finished her wine. She would have to wash the glass. There was no way she would tolerate dirty glasses in her front room.

III

When Ziah Morgan told Colonel and Lonso of his plan to remove the furniture from the front room, they were petrified. The thought of dismantling the arrangement and piling the furniture as best as they could into any other room was treasonable. Alonso had long ago cast Myrtle Morgan as a Lady of the Wardrobe of the seventeenth- and eighteenth-century England. She could be as fierce, domineering and single-minded as Sarah Churchill and as indomitable as Abigail Marsham.

As Ziah explained what he had in mind, Colonel began shaking his head. The more Ziah explained the faster Colonel shook his head.

"You better mind you' head don't fall off you'neck," Ziah cautioned.

"It's not my head you should be worrying 'bout," Colonel said. "I tell you, if you go through with this foolishness, is you and anybody who help you gwine lose your heads."

"Prophet," Alonso began, his hands going instinctively to his throat, "Gody Myrtle would have us hanged, drawn and quartered. You know what that means?"

"I don't want a history lesson," said Ziah. "I got people coming round. You blokes helping?"

"Not to dismantle Gody Myrtle front room," said Alonso. "That would be a felony, a hanging offence."

"I tell you what," said Colonel, "let's go and clear out the basement. I had a good look at it yesterday. We only have to move a few bits and pieces, and hang up a few balloons and some Christmas paper and, bingo, we ready to rock and roll. Come, let us start working."

"Wait a minute," Ziah began to laugh. "You blokes think I was talking about Miss Myrtle front room, *the front room?* The white rum gone to you head. It is the room on the first floor I talking about. It got furniture but no carpet. Come, guys, we got work to do."

"I done tell you," Myrtle Morgan said angrily to all three, but to her husband in particular, "I don't want no jump-up in this house. You don't know that police raiding coloured people's house because neighbours ringing them to say 'them Niggers are at it again with them loud music and wild drinking'? I don't want to start off bad with my neighbours."

"Tcho, man," said Ziah, "Me take care of things. Me done invite them at number 138."

"You done what?"

"Invite."

"Me heard you, the first time," she said. "Is what you done that for?"

"He been talking to me all last week quite friendly like."

"I bet now he know how many pickneys we got, how much money we got in Barclays Bank."

"Is what you telling people? Myrtle Morgan, me is no gossip. And this fellow Alf didn't ask me any question. All we do is to talk about the weather and that England whip the West Indies tail. Him seem nice enough."

"Anyway," said Alonso, "if things follow the usual pattern, they will soon move away to some new town where blacks never darken the streets."

"Lonso," said she, "shut up! I don't want any usual wisecrack. I don't want to give these people an excuse. Anyway, you not moving that radiogram from my front room. No siree bob!"

"No, man, you think them mad?" said Colonel. "I lending mine. It smaller, but it got a good sound."

"I never know you got a radiogram, Colonel?"

"I couldn't resist it. I will be living on my own now. I guess I need a little company. This kinda life can be lonely, you see. Anyway I was looking in this store along Atlantic Road and a see this little radiogram and it look at me and say take we home. I just could not resist that plea..."

"The radiogram begged you to take it home?" asked Alonso and Ziah in unison." The party burst into laughter.

"Me not 'gainst you getting a radiogram, especially when you got such a seductive plea. I heard of landlords charging tenants extra for radiogram and television and even young people who studying late in the night got to pay more. Them say it's to help out with the extra electricity. Me, I call it daylight robbery. So what's going to happen, you gwine to be the disc jockey?"

"Yes, man," said Colonel, "I called in at Theo's Record Shop. I got me the Platters, Frankie Lymon, some rhythm and blues and Fats Domino. I ain't going to be lonely no more."

"So you all line up 'gainst me? All you men stick together, right? Well, I tell you, if there's any bangerwrongs and botheration all three of you spending New Year's Day out on the street."

"We not 'gainst you, Miss Myrtle," said Nello. "We just feel that if anybody want to shake them leg, them not gwine to do it upstairs in you front room. Them can come down here. Anyway nobody coming in this house unless one of the three o' us know him or her. None of those boys who cruise round in their Austin Cambridge and Morris Oxford looking for parties gwine come in here."

"Anyway the Colonial will be bogeying until dog 'fraid," said her husband.

"That's what all the birds will be doing," said Alonso.

"Birds!" exclaimed Myrtle. "Well," she said moving away, "these young women nowadays are so flighty, no wonder they call them birds."

If Myrtle Morgan's first wish of 1958 was that her guests would take their leave by one o'clock, and if that was a precursor of all her wishes for the New Year, then the omens were not good. By ten o'clock on the evening before the New Year, she was presiding over a lively but reverential group in her upstairs front room.

Alf and Elsie their new next-door neighbours had arrived just before ten. Alf wore a suit which was evidence that the first and paramount duty of post-war styles was to cover the individual and to last as a monument to British craftsmanship. Elsie's suit was of the same vintage. Alonso was convinced that this couple had worn these outfits at every occasion that demanded their dressing up since the end of the war. Alf was very talkative and chain-smoked Woodbine cigarettes, refusing to accept Alonso's Senior Service or Colonel's Capstan; only when Ziah got out the Jamaican cigars as a part of the ritual of toasting the New Year did Alf forgo his Woodbines. Elsie was a large quiet woman whose eyes swept around the room like a searchlight. She was tense as the wife a missionary might have been on first encountering the natives of a nineteenth-century African village. She sat on a chair with her handbag held firmly on her knees like a child on best behaviour. Elsie as did her husband drank very slowly the bottled stout that their host offered.

Myrtle had invited Dora, a young white woman with whom she worked before going to the Bus Garage canteen. Dora had arrived with a baby in a carry-cot. The baby continued to sleep peacefully in Myrtle's bedroom. This young woman was the only person who would speak to her at her first job, a leather factory in Bermondsey. Dora herself had become a sort of exile because she had shown tendencies of becoming a "nigger lover". Myrtle remembered vividly the graffiti on street walls exhorting the nation to "KEEP BRITAIN WHITE". Such an exhortation had been freshly chalked up outside the factory one Monday morning. That was also the week that Dora told her she was going to get married and wanted Myrtle to be a witness. No one else at the factory was told. The ceremony was at Camberwell Register Office. Apart from the bride and groom there were the bride's widowed mother, an uncle and, of course, Myrtle. After the ceremony the wedding party took a bus to the Sir William Walworth public house where the bride's uncle was a barman. Lunch was provided in a little room. This was in striking contrast to any wedding that Myrtle had ever attended. She wished she had baked a cake. Later on Myrtle was to find out that it was not only because of poverty, but that the groom was a political refugee newly exiled in 1956 from Hungary. When Dora returned to work she practised the art of taking off her gloves with her wedding ring embedded in it. Great consternation swept through the factory when, in the spring of 1957, it was obvious that Dora was pregnant. Mavis, the forelady, was overheard reminding, "You lie down with dogs you get up with fleas." Myrtle and Dora were convinced Mavis was hinting that, because Dora was a friend of Myrtle's, it was obvious her mysterious boyfriend was Coloured. The deception, as it was discerned by her erstwhile fellow workers, was kept going until Dora went on maternity leave. She returned to the factory some months later with her blond infant son and her husband Imre. Myrtle had often told Dora she reserved a special place in her heart for her. Alonso guessed that Dora was about twenty-five.

He considered her to be two stones too heavy. She struck him as a woman who would dedicate her life to being a loving daughter, a dutiful wife, an ever-present and adoring mother and sad widow locked into decades of mourning.

Right now she was playing the daughter of the house, collecting coats and disappearing with them into Myrtle's bedroom, returning to make sure everyone had drinks. She never missed an opportunity to speak about Myrtle's friendship and to put her arms around her. She led the chorus of approval about the smartness of the front room. She also talked incessantly about how wonderful her baby was, sleeping right through the night, which was a good thing since she, Dora, slept like a log and Imre was studying most nights. She recalled how prejudiced the women at the factory were; she would not mention some of the things they said about Coloured people.

"It would make you all blush, not that you could see Myrtle blushes anyway." She hugged Myrtle and pinched her cheeks.

Isaiah Morgan had invited his mate, Sid, a short fat man with a bald head with a fender of hair around his ears. He had been a bus conductor since being demobilised. He apologised that his wife could not be with him, but she was with the children. Apart from that she had an idea that the New Year should come and find her in her own house. Sid was the garage's union representative. He was a highly respected man, and a senior conductor who would frequently take new bus conductors out on their *on the job training*. He had refused the chance of becoming a bus inspector. Cynics said that with overtime and the honorarium from his union activities he was better off financially anyway. He was also a local councillor, who behaved as if he was a Member of Parliament. He once told Ziah that if all that happened to him since the war had happened in the 1920s or 1930s he would be on track to becoming an MP, but since the war new Labour Members of Parliament were from the red-brick universities. Realising that Ziah did not have a clue what a red-brick university was he set about educating him. Ziah nodded, hawed and ooed for half an hour until mercifully the topic changed. He said he was an implacable enemy of prejudice. He would have no objection to his daughter (she was only nine, bless her) marrying a coloured man, but they should not have children. It was the children of mixed marriages he was sorry for. He did not volunteer why he pitied these offspring, which would have revealed the reason for his prejudice. For Alonso considered that Sid was prejudiced, despite his willingness to sacrifice his daughter at the altar to a mixed marriage. Of course, he was politician enough to kiss babies and pat dogs before going home and kicking the cat. Sid said that one of his Jamaican friends had initiated him into drinking lager and lime. So he was prepared to finish 1957 with lager and lime and would welcome 1958 with a glass of the same.

At some time during the evening Myrtle referred to Colonel, Lincoln and Alonso as the three bachelors. She was quick to correct herself that

Nello had a wife in Jamaica. The two younger men were like the sons she never had. She had four daughters, two grown women with good jobs in Jamaica. She considered them to be too choosy. Perhaps that was why neither of them was married. She had twin girls, the last fruits of her womb, at Wilberforce High School. Born at a time when she thought she was beyond childbearing, such children were known as "washbelly". Her great wish was for them to finish their education in England. Her next project was to bring them to London.

Dora had launched into a long story about her family. She recalled an aunt, who must have been about sixteen at the end of the war, because she Dora was twelve at the time. Her teenage aunt had struck up a relationship with a coloured American soldier. For that she was arrested and as far as anyone knew was still in a mental institution. A chorus of denial went up, but Dora insisted her story was true. She had an idea that someone in the family had stitched her up. Some of them had marched with Mosley before the war, and she thought somebody had testified that the sixteen-year-old was mentally unstable. Alf was embarrassed and quickly mentioned how splendid the coloured troops had looked during the war, when not many people bothered about racial differences, apart from the Americans, of course. He remembered his mother telling him that an old lady along the street where they lived invited a white GI to her house for tea and later invited a Jamaican from the West Indian Regiment, and how the white GI made his apologies and walked out. Alf tried to imitate an American accent. "Ma'am, you're very kind, but I ain't never eat with a Nigger, and I ain't going to start now."

"Well," said Sid, "Althea Gibson won Wimbledon fair and square. Good luck to her, I say." Looking at Ziah he said, "And I took a fiver off Zi here. He bet me the West Indies would take all five tests. When are they coming back, Zi?"

"They'll be back in 1963. Watch out!"

"You a betting man, Lincoln?"

"I'm a businessman," he said, "I'll take you on."

"Sid," said Myrtle, "did I hear you right? Ziah bet you five pounds that the West Indies would win? But, Lord me God, that is nearly a week's wages for me!"

"That's it, Zi," said Alf, "no pocket money for the next two weeks." They all laughed.

"That was a long time ago," said the chastened Ziah. "I didn't lose on the 1950 tour."

"I see," Myrtle said, like someone who had a revelation. "So you been gambling long, long time. I bet you can't go into the kitchen and see if those patties I put in the oven are ready."

"A shilling say you can't," Alf offered.

At about five minutes to midnight Dora and Myrtle started to replenish the glasses. Everybody stood up, glass in hand, as Isaiah went over to the radiogram and turned up the volume so the mighty sound of Big Ben could chime in the New Year. In the direction of Brixton Road someone had let off a firecracker and nearer there were shouts. In Myrtle Morgan's front room they raised their glasses and wished each other a happy New Year, 1958. They went around kissing one another on the cheeks. Within half an hour of the New Year, there was knocking at the door. Miss Vie and Miss Nicey had arrived. They explained that they had for years welcomed the New Year in church and although they loved Miss Myrtle as their other sister they had not the slightest intention of breaking the habit. They were fulsome in their praise of Sister Myrtle's front room. They promised that now they had managed to get Vicky off their hands, it was time they set about improving their place. It seemed Vicky had been a great burden to them. Now she was married they had drawn a line under those thirty-three years. They accepted Myrtle Morgan's praise of the beauty of Vicky in her bridal dress, how Reverend Locksley Hood had performed a service so divine that no one bothered that it was bitterly cold. Miss Vie went and stood beside Lincoln. She extolled his brilliance as Master of Ceremony. To this all who were present at the reception agreed. Say what you will, Miss Vie declared, you could have mountains of food and a bottomless well of drinks, but at a wedding you need above all a good Master of Ceremony to keep things rolling. Miss Nicey thought Lincoln had brought a lot of jollification to the role of Master of Ceremonies. She thought the whole thing was very gladsome.

"Boy, you was so good that I feel like going out and getting a man to be married to, so I can hear you talk all those flattering things about me," said Miss Nicey.

"I tell you what," began Alonso, "I'm his agent. From now on you come to me and I'll arrange his engagements for ten percent of the fee."

"You not trying to muscle in, are you, Lonso?" asked Nello.

"No, man, just trying to preserve my client's talent. Master of Ceremonies, after-dinner speaker, all functions catered for, we also do bar mitzvahs."

"You could make a packet there," said Sid, "really good after-dinner speakers can clear one hundred knicker a night. This bloke I know is on the circuit in the United States. Imagine what someone like Vincent Price demands!"

"Thousands!" said Alf.

"But he is a film star!" said Nello and they all laughed loudly.

"I'll go," said Alonso responding to the doorbell. "Want to bet it's Warren? He said he'd come as soon as they ring in the New Year at the Colonial."

He found Asquith and Wellesley and two women waiting on the steps. Peering up the street, he could see the brake lights of Warren's Morris Oxford as he negotiated the intersection and turned left into Loughborough Road.

"He's gone to collect some friends," said Asquith. Seeing the look on Alonso face and recalling an early conversation when he voiced their hostess's anxiety about unknown people coming to her place, he added quickly, "Don't worry, Warren will personally vouch for these two elegant ladies. This is Warren's lady Sue and Wellesley's wife, Iris."

Warren's wife was white, with an abundance of very black hair that did not seem to compliment her pale features. She was tall and smartly dressed, wearing bangles that threatened to fall into the palms of her hands. She raised her hands frequently so the bangles jangled back towards her elbow. This action she performed in unison with a toss of her head, as if she had to shake her hair into place. She did not speak, but pointed up the stairs as she continued to look at Alonso. He nodded and she started up the stairs, followed by Wellesley's wife, Iris. She too was tall, but thinner than Sue. Her complexion was which was generally known in Jamaica as "St Elizabeth red-skinned woman". Somewhere towards the end of the bad old days of slavery a slave owner had left the matrimonial bed for the hut of a slave woman and produced a race bridging the black and the white divide. Being elevated above their mothers' status to become a part of the supervisory race was the benefit bestowed on such offspring. A hundred and fifty years after slavery was abolished descendants of this race were still the preferred office staff and bedfellows of the emerging black professional class. Alonso was not surprised at Wellesley's choice. Iris had a frown on her face as if she had come to something quite disagreeable; as Miss Myrtle was later to put it, "She skin-up her face like she stepped into something quite unpleasant."

Iris walked ahead of her husband. Wellesley adjusted his glasses frequently, as if focusing at a different angle while he approached the steps. Asquith brought up the rear of the party, jacket flung wide and trying to get into the rhythm of the music, which permeated the whole house. Alonso could see that Ziah had met them on the first floor and was accompanying them into the heart of Miss Myrtle's territory. Alonso went back to the front door. He lit another cigarette and began to mime Fats Domino's "*Blueberry Hill*". Before long he heard Warren's car. He opened the door. Warren was leading his party of four young women up the steps. Warren turned from the second rung of the stairs; looking over the heads of the young women, he said, "Della and Carmen you already know, the blonde is Betty and the one with those crazy eyes is Ezinma."

"What is crazy about my eyes?" she demanded. Alonso guessed she was Nigerian. He had heard the accent often enough when he lived at Ostade Road.

"Don't pay him any attention. You have gorgeous eyes. He is flirting," said Betty.

"The commissionaire," said Warren, "is Alonso. He's a Latino masquerading as a Jamaican. You have been warned."

"He doesn't look too dangerous to me," said Betty.

"He is the proverbial still waters," said Ezinma. "He has a reputation, and I have proof of it."

"Ooh," said Betty, looking back down the stairs at Alonso.

"Have we met?" asked Alonso of Ezinma.

"No," she said, without looking back at him. "But neither have I met Errol Flynn."

They were now outside the great front room. They entered, divested themselves of their coats onto the waiting arms of Dora, who dutifully put them in the bedroom. Myrtle watched the newcomers' look of admiration of her sitting room, then announced that she had curried goat and rice. This delicacy had been prepared in advance of New Year's Day; it was Myrtle's tradition that cooked food be available in abundance just in case a starving horde of friends and relatives should descend on her for no other purpose than to test the extent of her hospitality and generosity.

Alf, Elsie and Sid declined the offer of curried goat and rice. Elsie because her stomach had an aversion to spicy food. She knew that she could not survive in foreign countries where people were in the habit of cooking foreign food that was always richly spiced. She was anxious no one should misunderstand her. She had no prejudice against foreigners. She saw enough of them during the war, even worked with them. If she ever had any observation against people coming to this country it was on account of the smell of their spicy foods. She was quick to admit that she had never smelt Miss Myrtle's cooking. Her husband begged his host to forgive him, but he had always thought that goats were pets and should not be eaten.

On hearing that Alonso began to hum "*Mary had a little lamb*".

Myrtle, determined to play the ideal hostess, brought in what Warren considered the '*peas de resistance*': the Christmas cake, the one she had hidden away for such an eventuality as this. The ingredients had been soaking in Jamaican over-proof rum since early October. The finished product was dark and moist. Myrtle cut generous slices and the indefatigable Dora, now aided by Miss Nicey, provided an excellent waitress service, while Miss Vie assisted Myrtle in heating up the curried goat and the rice. Elsie's delicate stomach did not rebel against the cake, despite Warren's warning that there was enough white rum in each slice to start a fire if one should breathe on a naked flame. It might have been the smell of the rum, but no one seemed perturbed by the aroma of the curried goat and rice when it arrived. The combination of the alcohol and the obvious relish with which the other guests were enjoying the plates of curried goat tempted Alf to try it, just a little and then a little more. He could not entice his spouse but did succeed in tempting Sid to try it. He thought it had too much pepper but he served in the Far East during the war and was determined to show his British mettle.

He knew a thing or two about curry. He announced that the Indians in the Caribbean had taught the trade well to the people of the West Indian colonies. He pointed out that Sonny Ramadhin was an Indian from Trinidad. All well and good, thought Alonso, if his cooking of curry was as good as his prowess at bowling spinners. To have one hundred and seventy-nine runs taken off his bowling from ninety-eight overs was less than two per over.

IV

After the company had been fed, Ziah Morgan invited those who wanted to dance to adjourn to the front room on the first floor.

Betty and Ezinma were dancing to Bill Haley's 'Rock Around The Clock'. Ezinma was jiving; when she let go of her hand Betty would go into a spin. Ezinma was clicking her fingers in rhythm; she held out her hands waiting for her partner to move with the beat towards her, Betty was making three steps and then spinning. Alonso waited until she had spun far enough away, then he stepped in and held the one with the gorgeous eyes by the hand and started to jive. Released from Betty, Ezinma stepped up her movements to the rhythm and suddenly everyone stopped to watch. It was now a competition. Woman versus man, or perhaps Africa versus the Caribbean. As with many cultures, it was to be a dance to the death. But this music had an end, and they both knew it. One last push, a pull and push and a spin, Alonso half-turned as he pulled Ezinma, so as the music ended she was across his back. It gave the impression of being carefully choreographed, but it was an impromptu action that would most certainly have failed if attempted again. They enjoyed the applause, and politely embraced one other.

"I see what you mean," said Betty. "These silent waters not only run deep but they splash and cascade over some rocky ground".

"Yes," said Alonso to Ezinma, "what have you got on me?"

"I was at Ostade Road that night," she said. "Must I say more?"

"Yes," said Betty, "what happened that night? You must tell."

"He had a woman in his room," Ezinma said quickly.

"Is that all?"

"What were you expecting to hear, Betty?" asked Ezinma.

"The bit that the *News of the World* would pay real money for," said Betty.

"Well, that didn't happen at Uncle Josh's house." Ezinma was looking at Alonso; she knew that he thanked her. The next record was Fats Domino's 'Blueberry Hill'. She clicked the thumbs and first fingers of both hands as she danced. Alonso could only click the thumb and forefinger of his right hand. They were dancing close, doing what was known as the *yank*.

"Are you from the Lagos?" he asked.

"Do you come here often?" she asked.

"This is really a house-warming party," he said, not wanting to quarrel with her.

"I am from the Eastern Region of Nigeria. I am an Ibo," she volunteered, "from Calabar."

"Calabar is a college for training Baptist parsons in Jamaica," he said.

"An inevitability of colonialism," she said. "They say that there's a Trinidad in every Spanish-speaking country."

"That might have been the spreading of Christianity rather than the spreading of Colonialism," he said. "Columbus sailed into the Gulf of Paria, which was not called that yet, he saw three peaks raised high above the island. He thought it reminded him of the Trinity."

"You're an inexhaustible fount of information. I can't recall ever having a lesson in rock and roll, history and geography while being flirted with."

"If I was really flirting I would have mentioned your gorgeous eyes, beautiful cheekbones, wonderful figure and superb sense of rhythm."

"Remember," she said as a warning, "I do have your secret and I can't recall that Winnie... that's her name, isn't it? I can't recall that she was outstanding in any of those departments."

"Wow!" he exclaimed. "You really don't like to dance and talk at the same time, do you?"

"I'm weary of the West Indian male declaring open season on all black women. They say it's because there aren't many of us around. Still I don't want to have my guard up all the time."

"Would it make any difference if I told you that Winnie was someone I knew from back home and that she was running away from a violent boyfriend."

"I heard that story before," she said in a voice that meant *and I like better the other version; I'm not likely to change my mind.*

The dance came to an end she walked over to Betty. In a moment she came towards him with Betty in tow. "Elizabeth thinks I'm monopolising you. Happy times," she placed Betty's hand in Alonso's and went off to dance with Nello.

"You rotter," said Betty, sticking out her tongue at her friend. Alonso pulled her closer and she responded by leaning into his arms as Nat King Cole affirmed *"Because You're Mine"*. "You are a good dancer. Did you have some training, or did it just come naturally?"

"I hear the music and just move to the rhythm. Has it strikes me it's only us humans who have to formally learn anything vital to our social well-being? Cats, dogs, snakes, know it all from birth."

"Let's dance," she said "I don't think I could take in anything so heavy at this time of the first morning of a New Year. We worked until seven o'clock yesterday morning, then got the train to London. We've been partying since midday yesterday. If I slump, just prop me up in that chair over there and let me sleep until next year, since that brother-in-law of mine is oblivious to the time. Apparently all Jamaicans learn to ignore time instinctively, the way cats learn to arch their backs."

"Ouch! that hurts," he said into her ears. Her chin was on his shoulder. "By the way it is now *the next year*," he reminded her. "Is Warren your brother-in-law?"

"Didn't you know? Sue is my sister."

It occurred to Alonso that Warren was like a life told in serial. He already knew he had been a stowaway, he had been in the army, he played the drums rather well and that he was studying several subjects at evening college, but there was more to be learnt about this man. He looked around the room, if only he could get them to tell him their stories. It could be like *Canterbury Tales*. He could write them down. What a book that would make! He might even try and get it published as a follow up to *Nine in a Basement*. He still could not think of himself as a writer. After all, he could pick out several tunes on a guitar but that did not make him a guitarist worthy of playing in any band, let alone being a soloist. The record finished and he went over to the punch bowl; when he got back Betty was talking to Warren and Sue. He could not help wanting to know more about their relationship.

15

In the bitter winter of 1947, Warren went to the Labour Exchange again. It was to have been one final, desperate plea to find a job. He was sent to what he thought was a small removal company for a job as a van driver's mate. It turned out that his prospective employer was a man with a lorry who had a contract to deliver coal in South London. Warren had little time to think about the incongruity of the job. A black man delivering coal and becoming so black that many of his customers must have thought that when he went home and washed himself a white man would appear.

The lorry was an old Fordson that might have seen action during the war. Its owner and driver certainly saw action with the Eighth Army and had been sent home in the middle of the Italian campaign with a bullet in his leg. Warren got on well with his employer to the extent that he was rented the basement room of his house.

Warren was washing himself one evening when he became conscious of a face pressed hard against the window, a pair of eyes peering through the hurriedly drawn curtains. Luckily, he thought as he went to adjust the curtains, he was naked only from the waist up. He wondered if those eyes were ever there when he was stripped from head to toe. It did not help when he overheard the person to whom the peering eyes belonged, Betty Ashby, telling one of her companions on another occasion that *he was black all over*, as black as the coal that he and her dad delivered throughout the boroughs of Camberwell and Lambeth. When the other girl asked if she was not scared of the *blacky*, ten-year-old Betty had boastfully said no. She had seen coloured men before; during the war one had given her a bar of chocolate. Her mother had been very angry and had told her that Blacks would take her to a place called *Dixonline*, where there were countries like Jamaica and Africa and she would never be seen again. She said she was not afraid and her mother had boxed her ears and insisted that they would do very bad things to her, that little white girls who did not behave and continued to accept sweets from the Blackies would be put in homes from which their parents would never be able to get them back. Betty did not like that, but still she was not afraid, though she was careful. She did not think the blackies would harm her. Now the war was over and there was a blacky living in her parent's basement, she wondered if he was from the *Dixonline*. She insisted that she was still not afraid of this blacky, and she did not think her parents would hand her over to the authorities to be put away. She was nearly eleven then, or, as her mother said, eleven going on forty. One day, she felt bold enough to unlock the door and descend the steps to the basement. It was afternoon, her father had just returned and was asleep on the settee, and his tenant was in the basement. Her mother was still at work, so were her older brother was in the army and her sister Sue was with her husband living in Yorkshire where her husband was stationed.

Betty paused on the bottom step, her heart pounding, and wondered if she dared knock at the door. As it happened, she did not have to because the tenant was not in his room. He was at that very moment returning, having been dropped off by her father at Warren's request in Brixton to visit a friend.

"What have we here?" he asked, smiling at the overweight schoolgirl.

"You touch me and I scream," she said, at the same time holding an apple. "I brung you this."

"Why, thank you, Miss Eve," he said grinning.

"Me name ain't Eve," she said, and threw the apple at him as she fled back upstairs shouting, "it's Betty, as you done know already."

"And mine isn't Adam, either," he said, biting into the apple, as he closed his door behind her.

Their next encounter was a fortnight later. There was a knock on his door. Betty was standing there with a cup of tea. "Me dad said to brung you this," she thrust the cup so that it shook and some tea spilt in the saucer. "And I still ain't afraid of yer." She turned and ran back up the steps.

II

A year and half later he was conscripted into the army. He did return to see his old employer three or four times over the next three years. A few months before he was due to leave the army he went to look for John Ashby. That was shortly after the death of his wife Elizabeth. That was the first time he met the elder daughter, Sue. She was married to a sergeant in the same regiment as Warren. They had never spoken to one another on a personal level and did not know of their connection. Even when the relationship was revealed they never became friends but they at least began to talk. Peter left the army before Warren and went back to Germany to live with his German lover in Hamburg. Sue and her two young children returned to live at the family home. John Ashby had become aged in a short period and the old wound in his leg was threatening to cripple him. When Warren left the army, John was pleased to give him his job back. He had lost the contract with the coal company as a result of nationalisation and was now moving into the removal business. Failing health forced John to depend more and more on Warren. After a few months, with a good deal of pressure from other relatives, Johnny, a nephew of John, joined the firm.

In the meantime Betty, was working as a ward maid at Camberwell General Hospital. She was encouraged by a kindly Ward Sister to train as a State Enrolled Nurse. At the end of three years she began to train for the higher grade of State Registered Nurse at a Midland Town. Warren saw little of her, and had heard at one time that she was engaged to be married. Of Sue he did see a great deal, particularly after Johnny left the business to become an underground train driver.

Sue worked as secretary of the business, which needed more jobs to support three members on full-time salaries, so Sue left and found employment in a high-street department store. Eventually she became a departmental manager. She and Warren were quietly married at Camberwell Registry Office three years after he left the army. It was a small affair attended by her now crippled father, her older brother, his wife and Betty. Sue pointedly did not invite any of her fellow workers from the store, neither did she think it necessary to mention that her husband was black. Her children never called him "Dad". They continued calling him "Uncle When", which was the closest the older boy could come to saying "Uncle Warren". John had watched the friendship between his older daughter and Warren deepen into a relation that could support marriage. Although he had deep respect and perhaps affection for Warren he did not particularly want him as a son-in-law. Once the old man had let slip that although he would not like to see a law passed forbidding black to marry white, he was worried about any offspring there might be. However, he assured himself that now that Sue had two little blond boys, she would not want any more children. He tried to hide his disapproval when a few months after what was in fact Sue's second marriage she was pregnant.

For some time John Ashby had been worried that his younger daughter was getting too fond of the Jamaican. Betty had been born after he had passed fifty. This evidence of his virility was the toast of many nights in his favourite pub, the Admiral Rodney. Many glasses were drunk in honour of "the best job he ever did"! If this black man was going to be a part of his family, it was better that he married Sue. Johnny, Sue's cousin, had a point of view not far from her father's. Warren was a nice enough bloke, but their friendship was in no way enhanced by becoming his cousin-in-law. Then again, he told his Cousin Sue, if Warren was white, she would be very fortunate to have caught him. Did that mean that, despite being black, Warren was a better catch than her first husband Peter?

If Betty had a problem, it was the same one that her father imagined he saw. She repeated what as a determined but frightened little girl she had said all those years ago, *"I ain't afraid of yer, see."* Despite the fifteen or so years' difference, she was very fond of Warren. When asked to suggest a name for her new niece she had no hesitation in giving the name Elizabeth, and the familiar Beth. She at once wrote a letter to the day-old infant:

My Dearest Beth,

You won't remember any of this so I am writing it down. I was present at your birth. I was as eager to welcome you into this world as either of your parents. Your Dad said he would only be in the way so he sat in the waiting room having cups of tea. I think he was only hanging around until he was told all's well before slinking off to the Victory, a nearby public house. Somehow fathers think that a public house is the place to go after the safe delivery of their offspring. The real work is done by mothers. We will talk about that later. I was there and I can say with honesty that I was the first member of your family to take a good look at you. Your Mum could hardly summon up any more energy than it took to inquire after your health and whether you were a boy or a girl. She was pleased you were not a boy, and if you promise not to tell anyone, so was I.

Now down to the nitty-gritty of life. I have taken my pen in hand; that is silly for a start, how else would I take it? You see, you are going to be coming up against these silly sayings as you get older. You might as well get used to it. Quite soon your parents will want to have you all to themselves. This is called bonding, or quality time. I think these are American terms. You see they did not only help us to win the War, but they injected more than a little jazz into our language. That is another thing you will have to understand. The English language, your language and mine, seems to be growing only in America. We will have lots of arguments about that in the future. Back to this quality time thing. Your parents will demand more and more of it. It is pathetic but it makes them happy. Parents do lots of dumb things. Adults just can't think logically as children can because people's brains start to rot when they're teenagers or something and by the time they get into their thirties most of it has gone. They just make things up as they go along and can't form coherent arguments any more (which means you'll be hearing the words 'because I say so' an awful lot). Just remember there's always a funny answer to every stupid thing they say (even if they don't think it's funny).

This is just a quick run-through of everything you need to know. Don't puke on your mother, do it on your father (she'll remember forever, he'll forget in a week). Chocolate tastes excellent; mud isn't so good. Cats are for shouting at, not for grabbing by the tail. The universe is finite but without boundaries, a beginning or an end. Atoms are made of quantum particles, such as quarks, gluons, neutrinos, etc (I read that somewhere, don't worry, I don't understand it either, but it may have some bearing on the thousands of atomic bombs that the West and the East use to terrorise the world). Let us hope they will grow out of that habit. While we are on education, school is quite good once you resign yourself to it. Work is always a drag. Females (that's the gang us girls belong to) are far superior to males, that's the union to which your Daddy, Granddad and your uncles belong. Grandparents are a soft touch, and most of the time so are aunts. The latter must be handled with more subtlety. Smoking is cool except when you become addicted you feel really unhealthy and everything you own stinks badly. Some people think it's bad, some say that's rubbish, and perhaps by the time you are my age we will know the truth. Drinking is fun, fun, fun. The sky is blue because it goes well with the yellow sun. Watch as many cartoons as you can. Don't draw on walls, find weird places to do it where it'll take ages for anyone to notice (try the underside of drawers, the bottom of shoes). The sun is yellow because it looks nice with the blue sky. If you ever plan on running away, call a cab and get your parents to pay for it. Finally, if in doubt give me a ring, we can go to the zoo and have a chat. Always have a shilling tucked away on your person so you can get the bus home or to my place. I promise you some fun times.

Your loving Aunt
Betty

III

Sue had always been aware of her younger sister's crush on her husband. Sometimes it irritated her. At times she was jealous, but she knew Betty was one member of her family who had truly accepted Warren. Betty was always taking Beth out in her pram. At first people would see a young blonde girl pushing a pram, and they would get a fleeting look at a pink face and smile their approval. But when the summer approached and Beth had grown to the extent that she could sit up and show off her curly hair, the smiles became frozen, and some people voiced their disapproval.

"It's disgusting, I say. What chance has it got? Not white, not black. It shouldn't be allowed."

Sometimes Betty took up the challenge. "Her chance would be excellent if there weren't people like you about."

At other times: "How could she have done it? And with a black man too. How could she?"

"I closed my eyes and thought of England. It was so good it must have been love." That had sent the two middle-aged gossips summoning up more energy than their weary, unwilling and arthritic legs could carry them. Sue was present on that occasion. She pushed Betty's shoulders so violently that Betty had to grasp the pram firmly to correct its balance.

"Don't pay them any mind. You'll soon get used to it."

"That's where we differ," the younger sister said. "It won't go away. Beth will be getting that sort of crap for the rest of her life. We must show her we love her and that she is wanted."

"You're talking about my child," said Sue. "I love my husband, that's why I have borne him our child. I'm not going to have a row with these people on the street."

"Sometimes, Sue, I think you are a closest lover."

"Whatever do you mean?" said Sue wrestling the pram from her sister. "Give me my child," and with Betty neatly elbowed out of the way, she stopped the pram, lifted the baby onto her shoulder, then released the pram to her younger sister. "How dare you? I'm her Mum, indoors and out of doors. The same goes for my black husband. I'm his wife in bed and out here on the streets. And you better believe it. I know you, my little sister. You would wear a sign on your forehead saying, 'Look, I'm married to a black man.' Well, I didn't wear one for Peter saying, 'I'm married to a fair-haired six-foot-one white boy from County Durham,' so at least I'm consistent. I'll fight for my man and my child against all-comers and, baby sister, that includes you."

Betty rested the handle of the pram against her hips and gave her sister a round of applause.

16

Wellesley met Iris at one of the frequent BBC wartime broadcasts presented by the legendary Miss Una Marson. That was towards the end of the Second World War when the *Caribbean Calling* programmes were grateful acknowledgement of the contribution that contingents from all parts of the West Indies were making to the war effort. Wellesley, still a teenager, arrived after the D-Day landing and did not see active service. Iris had been a member of the ATS for two years before she met him. They married in 1946. A picture of their wedding was published in the Jamaican papers. They both returned to Jamaica in 1947; Wellesley joined the constabulary and Iris trained as a teacher at Short Woods Teacher Training College for Women. She gave up her training before their first child was born. Shortly after that Wellesley left the police force to be a contracted agricultural labourer in the United States of America. His first contract was for only six months; the second for nine months and the third went on for eighteen months. On his return he tried his luck as a taxi driver and finally became driver for Dudley Henkelson. Although they had never met during the war, they were both in the armed forces in England. Henkelson became a Wing-Commander and Wellesley was a private. It was during Wellesley's contracts to the United States that Iris decided to return to London and train as a nurse. She was now a Sister at an East London hospital. Wellesley had rejoined her and their two children. She was determined that he ought to improve himself, so now he was studying Law. She had heard rumours of her husband philandering in the years they had been apart. She was not naive enough to believe in his professed fidelity but dismissed much of the gossip as coming from people with whom she would not lower herself to discuss anything of such delicacy as the relationship between a woman and her husband. Iris still remembered Wellesley's frequent telephone calls, his protestation of love, his aching loneliness for her. He had decided to fly to London and work hard on his degree. The driving of a prominent lawyer to and from the courts in Jamaica had rekindled his interest in the Law.

17

Melbourne Welch ignored the advice given by well wishers and agreed to meet Birbeck Samms head-on in one of Reverend Locksley Hood's well-attended "Peoples of the Empire" debates. This one promised to be special; first of all Melbourne had previously taken part in a television discussion and, secondly, the journalist Birbeck Samms was to take part. Samms had used his connections to get a television producer to record the debate with the aim of using it sometime in the future.

However, some weeks before the debate in St James' Church Hall at Loughborough Junction, Melbourne had taken part in *Meditation*, a Sunday evening religious discussion programme on television. Although Religious Correspondents were not in the same league as Political and Sports Correspondents, their review of Melbourne's experience as a black Christian had brought them to the forefront of the debate on immigration. They were at once outraged and condescending. Their comments brought a plethora of viewers' letters as the nation again awoke to the spectre of immigration.

Melbourne had spoken to the camera about being a black man and a Christian in a predominantly white country. He touched on the incongruity of the hope of spending eternity in the company of the rector of St Swithin, Rotherstone, who had recently preached a sermon based on Genesis 9 verse 25: *"cursed be Canaan; a servant of servants shall he be unto his brethren"*. The sermon also appeared in the parish magazine that was run off on a Roneo machine and intended for the two hundred or so parishioners. However, it formed part of a question to the Home Secretary in the House of Commons and the core of an article by Birbeck Samms. The rector of Rotherstone was convinced that what he said could not be the catalyst for stirring up hostility against the black immigrants, whom the white man had a bounden duty to guide and protect. It was a sacred duty as was being promulgated by the Apartheid policies of the government of South Africa. He warned against people using the role of masters over the blacks to encourage and condone lynching, as some over-zealous people in the Southern States of America had been known to do. The servitude ordained for blacks, as he saw it, did not mean they were any less human. After all Ham, whose action precipitated the curse, was Noah's second son. The rector generously pointed out that some descendants of Ham did become mighty in their own country, although they were subjected to the Nations of the Shemites from whom Europeans descended. He produced no evidence of this. No doubt the fact that he had identified Nimrod as being black was evidence enough of a balanced argument. He, however, insisted that the mighty empires of the Greeks, the Romans and, mightiest of them all, the British were in accordance with the curse of Noah. The cost of seeing the nakedness of his father was not to be visited upon the third, the fourth, the seventh or even the tenth generation, but in perpetuity. That heinous sin of seeing his father's penis was still being perpetuated in the obscene liaison between white women and black men. As the uncovering of the nakedness of the daughters of Shem, Noah's true heir, continued, so must the punishment

It was against this background that Melbourne Welch, businessman and ex-RAF spokesman for black migrants in Britain, faced the camera to meditate on being a black Christian.

A friend had suggested last Christmas that at last he understood why Mary was unable to find a room in the City of David. It was true that Bethlehem was crowded and accommodation scarce, but so scarce that a heavily pregnant young woman could not be lodged, even in a storeroom? What if she was black? Well, let's admit it, the Holy family were black enough to have taken refuge in Egypt, in Africa.

In Little Rock, Arkansas, nine black children were turned away from the Central High School, despite the fact that their academic achievements were among the best in the State. Christianity has yet to come to grips with death and the brotherhood of man. Very few Christians are willing to die in an effort to shorten the journey to that celestial city. On the second point, if we practise hatred of our fellow men and women, then in various ways we are practising jealousy and covetousness. These are sinful habits and if we die in sin, then we are unredeemed. Can redemption take place in the grave? A black Christian who has endured all the slings and arrows of discrimination certainly has earned the right to stand in the presence of God as a black saint. Will the Rector of Rotherstone accept that? Does he see some purification that the grave affords what the holy sacrament of baptism cannot accomplish here on earth? As the camera pulled away, the music rose... This time it was not Mozart's *Ave Verum Corpus* but Elgar's *Variations number nine, Nimrod.*

A month later the "God Slot", the twenty-minute Sunday evening religious programme on television, invited Melbourne to discuss Christian racial views with the journalist Birbeck Samms. The latter had written much about Black Immigration to Britain.

Samms was described by papers of the left as a piece of newspaper driftwood in the sluggish waters of the conservative right. He had worked his way through most of the publications of any worthwhile reputation and had now been washed up on the pages of a Sunday paper that boasted of employing Britain's most feared journalist. Samms was *"the man who dared to ask the questions you wanted answered. It had taken the gag off the man that other papers would want to silence..."* In fact, some other journalists hinted that Samms was bloated by drink, and had permanent gravy stains on his tie, with his best days behind him. The *enfant terrible* of Fleet Street was now *the purveyor of popular sentiment; the next man to hurl a brick during a riot; the leader of the second wave of laughter at a comedian's joke.*

He supported capital punishment, conscription to the armed forces, the stockpiling of nuclear weapons, a crackdown on all movements for colonial freedom; a white dominion consisting of Australia, Canada, New Zealand, South Africa and the Central African Federation. He was against black migration to the United Kingdom, except for *bona fide* students, who must return to their native land on completion of their period of study. He wrote against homosexuality, though it was rumoured that he lived with a pretty young African, whom he swore he was helping through university, and that the young man would very soon be returning to his own country.

Samms' thesis was that the black man had no history, no inventors, no leaders of note, which was not surprising since he was half a million years behind the white man. Being made hewers of wood and drawers of water was like being an apprentice, a system devised by wise men in the 1830s, which would have benefited the West Indian ex-slaves and their descendants had not the usual folly of so-called liberals prevailed and got the scheme cancelled in 1838 in favour of emancipation. He thought the apprentice system offered to the slaves in the West Indies provided more than what was being offered to the white slaves of the mills in Yorkshire at the time, and he recalled the words and activities of Richard Ostler into evidence.

The infusion of Negro blood into the veins of the English working class was a corollary of immigration from the West Indies. Britain was fast becoming a Creole society. Think of the people who ruled a third of the planet since the eighteenth century. Think of the people who fired the industrial revolution, which laid the foundation of the modern world. Think of the people whose tongue is the first language of this planet, people who stand as a bulwark against tyranny, be it fascism or communism. The British are a people on whose shoulders rest freedom and democracy. An Englishman has the freedom to invite any man into his home, but that man is not wise if he allows the guest to proceed to violate his women and destroy his house. If that man had acted like the good Samaritan who bound the victim's wounds and left him at an inn, promising to pay the cost on his return, it would be charitable enough and downright neighbourly, anything else would be a burden and an unfair imposition.

The question plaguing every Englishman is one that the papers will not print, that radio will not broadcast. Yet that question hangs heavily over the breakfast table and at every family gathering: *What if our blonde-haired, blue-eyed daughter should come home with a Negro and say she wants to marry him?*

When calm was restored Melbourne began slowly. He had been in earlier years a cricketer of some note. He was a batsman playing himself in. He pointed out that Europe ended at the Bosphorus; that the Asian land mass begins on the eastern shores of the Strait. It seems significant that none of the great world religions have their origins in Europe. Christianity came West and became white, replacing the gods of Valhalla and Mount Olympus. Islam went east and maintained its roots. The shaky tolerance within Christianity shows without a doubt that had Christ been born somewhere in Europe, in Bonn, Birmingham or Oslo, it would have been an exclusive religion.

The foundations of the modern world were laid in Africa and Asia Minor, not in the Midlands of Britain. If the curse of Ham is to be sustained we cannot ignore that he was Noah's second son, exposed to all the experiences of the time, although perhaps not to his brothers' sense of shame, and to their liberal acceptance of drunkenness. It is difficult to work out the distance of half a million years between brothers. Incidentally it is debatable what Shem and Japheth covered up, since they walked backward to where their naked, drunken father was sleeping. But what is most telling is that generations of theologians have ignored the fact that it was not Ham who was cursed, but, but his fourth son Canaan whose descendants did not dwell in Africa but in that region of Asia Minor which bore his name, Canaan the Promised Land.

An apprentice system raises the expectation of becoming masters. That can be seen in the white Dominions, but India and Ghana according to Samms should not have aspired to that state. The system is fatally flawed. Three hundred years of being masters in other people's homes, as Gandhi famously put it, has not made Britain a credible adviser to South Africa in its practice of *apartheid,* or the United States of America in its racial policies. Look at the stand that the United Kingdom of Great Britain and Northern Ireland, head of the largest empire the world has ever seen, took during the war when the GI arrived. Let me read from a wartime document:

Notes on Relations with Coloured Troops:

Be sympathetic in your mind towards the coloured man, basing your sympathy on knowledge of his problem, of his good qualities and his weaker ones. White women should not associate with coloured men. It follows then they should not walk out, dance, or drink with them. Do not think such action hard or unsociable. They do not expect your companionship and such relations would in the end only result in strife. Try and find out from American troops how they treat them (coloured troops). Avoid such actions as would tend to antagonise the white American soldier ... enemy propaganda will make every effort to use the colour question to stir up bad feeling between people in this country and the coloured troops and between American white and coloured

*troops. Never pass on a story that would tend to create
disaffection and do all you can to scotch such rumours when
they come to your notice.*

There was a war on. There were black troops here from the West Indies,
Africa and Asia. We were fighting for freedom, for dignity of the human
race with men who did not believe any of it.

If the daughters of Shem and of Japheth must be protected from the
sons of Ham, then it follows that the daughters of Ham should also be
protected from the sons of Shem and Japheth. Anglo-Saxon means
descendants of people from North-west Europe. If it is possible to trace the
Reverend Gentleman from Rotherstone's lineage back to Noah, then it must
be equally possible to stretch my ancestry to the same patriarch. It is a fair
assumption that the blue-eyed blonde and her lover are moving along the
same evolutionary path and we are not yet at the noon of our human race
ultimate state. On the other hand, Mr Samms might want to consider the
fact that *Neanderthal Man*, who some say was the original European, did
not make it far down the evolutionary road. It was *Homo Erectus* the African
who is the father of us all.

One local paper carried the headline: DAUGHTERS OF SHEM,
SONS OF HAM. The Fascist newspaper carried the headline
DAUGHTERS OF SHAME!

II

It was generally considered that Melbourne had acquitted himself rather
well. Most immigrants and those liberals who were impetuous enough to
lift their heads above the parapet were satisfied with his performance. But
there were many well-known voices that were raised against the modern
phenomenon of discussing racial matters in public. In the noonday hours
before opening at the Colonial Club, Warren Hall, Jimmy Fairfax, Alonso
Campesino Campbell and Betty Ashby were reviewing some of these
statements, the afternoon of the Tuesday after the televising of the Meditation
episode in which Melbourne had taken part.

"One thing is certain," said Warren, "Robin Locksley Hood has scuppered
his chances of ever becoming Archbishop of Canterbury. If he's ambitious
he could be pastor of a thriving church, providing he doesn't mind being
dubbed Bishop of the Black See, or Dean of the Immigrants..."

"Pity," said Jimmy, "Robin Cantaur has a certain ring to it."

"Especially when you read that one of his parishioners had said, what
Locksley Hood had done was tantamount to robbing the ordinary white
parishioners of their birthright and handing it over to the newly arrived
blacks," Alonso pointed out.

"Does anyone know what Mark 7, verse 27 is about?" asked Betty, looking up from the paper she was sharing with Alonso.

"'Let the children first be fed: for it is not meet to take the children's bread, and cast it to the dogs'," said Jimmy, without looking up from his paper.

Betty let go of her section of the paper and Alonso had to retrieve pages of the broadsheet, which fluttered to the floor.

"I think Melbourne was right when he said that Christianity came West and became white," she said. "These people really believed the portrait of the blue-eyed and red-haired painting is a true likeness of Jesus Christ. I don't think they even realise that Jesus was born a Jew in Asia Minor, nearly two thousand years ago."

"And was not a Christian," interjected Warren.

"Don't get philosophical," said his sister in law. "How do you see me? The daughter of Shem, the daughter of Shame or plain Betty Ashby from Camberwell?"

"How do you see yourself?" asked Jimmy.

"The latter," she said. "But it's how people see you that really matters."

"I vote for daughter of Shame," her brother-in-law laughed loudly. "Look at how the tabloids would see it. 'Blonde found with three black men.'"

"Is that all I am? A blonde?"

"Even if they drop the colour of your hair, the headline would be still very revealing," said Jimmy. 'Woman found with three black men', would still identify you as the daughter of Shem, according to the Vicar of Rotherstone and all of Fleet Street editors."

"I guess all this was intended to make me feel important. It doesn't. If anything it makes me feel very angry."

"I think the British have added race to the list of things like the sex act that must not be discussed in public," said Alonso.

"Anywhere!" said Warren. "Heard one woman telling another the other day that she went around to her son's and nearly died of shame. He and his wife were in their bedroom making funny sounds. *Two o'clock in the afternoon, I ask you.* In my day that sort of thing was done between ten and twelve at night, and you didn't make any sound. Disgusting, I call it. I don't care whether they are trying for a baby or not. I was so embarrassed that I got out of that flat fast. I still can't look that Madam, my so-called daughter-in-law, in the eye.'"

"Boy," said Alonso, "you were listening very closely. You haven't missed out anything!"

"Most likely, he made it up. He writes short stories, you know," said Betty without looking up from the paper. Changing the subject, she asked, "Can somebody tell me how many Adams there were? One for every race or was there only one as in the Bible. Did we become many races as we wandered over the planet adapting to climate and other circumstances?

Melbourne did suggest that we might evolve into a single race. Do you believe that? Come to think of it, in books and the cinema creatures from outer space all seem to be of one kind from whichever planet they are from. It seems that it is only on planet earth that we have several different races. Don't you all notice that?"

" *'If twenty millions of summers are stored in the sunlight still. We are far from the noon of man. There is time for the race to grow'*. I don't know if that is what Tennyson had in mind, but there is much to debate in those lines," quoted Alonso.

Warren said, "Perhaps our space-exploring days will be after we've evolved into a kind of oneness."

"You two ought to be in partnership; a quotation for every eventuality. The peasant and the stowaway," said Betty.

"Maybe I'm a stowaway, but I want to be a well-read stowaway. Did I ever tell you...?"

"Here it comes," warned Alonso. "Go on. Did you all get the play on Campesino? Which is the Spanish for peasant?"

"I was in a bookshop in Kings Street, Kingston Jamaica one day. I was at school, or I should have been at school in Greenwich Farm, Kingston, but there I was in this bookshop. I was looking in a Latin book 'Tacitus Agricola' when two high-coloured boys came in the shop and came round to the Latin section. They took one look at me and decided that I did not belong to that section. I could tell that they were thinking I might find the Superman comic too difficult. They wanted to know if I had studied any Latin grammar. Believe me, it was not kindly meant. From that day I decided to educate myself. I read everything I could lay my hands on. I even went back to the bookshop and bought the book. I still can't read it but one day I will. At last I've found a college where I can start learning Latin. I'll show those bastards."

"But you don't know who they were," said Alonso.

"Can't be certain but I think they belong to the Henkelson family."

"They owned the Travel agency that I used to work for. They also owned the Island Shield from which Lincoln expects to make millions. All their sons were educated either in Canada or here in Britain. You're putting yourself up against some formidable opponents."

"I know, but tilting at windmills in the absence of giants is not as daft as it sounds. There were many who said that Melbourne by taking on Birbeck was tilting at a windmill."

"He looked like one, especially when standing and waving his arms around," said Alonso."

"I have a feeling of deep foreboding this is going to be the year when race comes out of the closet. You mark my words," said Jimmy Fairfax. "The migration figures from the West Indies for 1957 have already reached new heights and a lot of once-supportive MPs are now running for cover. In the Labour Party the natives are getting restless. It's not difficult to see why. Traditionally Labour had the run-down urban areas, and that's where the new migrants find accommodation. This doesn't suit the Labour voters so they move out to the new towns or, as they usually put it: 'A nice quiet area where we can bring up our kids'. If you look around the West Indies, the picture you get is that we're very conservative. Apart from Cheddi Jagan there hasn't been anybody who raised the blood pressure of the Colonial Office. So Labour is worried. They are asking whether the Coloured migrants will join the trade unions. Will they vote Labour? Will they vote at all? At the next election we may see the Conservatives challenging hard for Clapham and Brixton, you wait and see."

"I miss the passing of the old patronising Tories," said Warren. "In the days just after the war they were appalled that anyone should want to stop colonial citizens travelling to the 'Mother Country'. They thought they had a paternal duty to look after their colonial subjects. Now the new Tories are as worried about Coloured people as the Labour Party."

"You've lost me," said Alonso. "I thought the Labour Party was the colonials' friend. You know the score: Sir Stafford Cripps going to Jamaica in 1937 to be in at the birth of the People's National Party, and then going to India promising independence for India's supporting Britain during the war."

"As I said," stressed Jimmy, "it was Labour who started rocking the boat, when they found the first hundred... then thousands of blacks in their constituencies upsetting their traditional supporters by rivalling them for jobs, houses and women. The Tories from the shires were safe, so were their daughters in the quieter middle-class enclave of towns. It will only affect them when blacks start to move out of Somerleyton, Geneva, Mayhall Roads for the more salubrious sections of Streatham, Norbury, and so on."

"Well, things are coming to a head in Little Rock, Arkansas," said Alonso, "and you know what they say: 'if America sneezes, England is bound to catch a cold'. So far, Birbeck Samms has been on radio and television since his encounter with Melbourne. Is he ascending or descending."

"He could become the hack journalist of the far right," said Jimmy.

"You mean that they could offer him a safe seat?" asked Alonso.

"No," said Jimmy, "the Tories wouldn't touch him. He's too vulgar. And he'd be stupid to throw in his lot with the Mosley crowd. They're not going anywhere. They are a pain in the backside, but they don't win seats."

"They can cause Labour to lose seats; that's near as damn it to winning seats," said Warren.

"Well, as I said, this will be the year race comes out of the closet. Mark my words." Jimmy slid from his stool and walked towards the club's office to answer the telephone.

18

Myrtle Morgan liked Enid from the first time they met. She used an old saying of her mother's to explain her feelings about Enid to her husband. "The moment that I see her me spirit take to her."

Indeed Enid had quickly put her stamp on the room. The bed was always immaculately made up, her dressing table tidy. The two chairs were always placed out of the way. The rugs were laid out as if in a showroom. For all that, Myrtle could not convince her husband exactly what she meant. After all she liked Dora, whose flat was the most untidy place they had visited. On one visit Myrtle was given a cup of tea and to avoid putting her lips to the rim where someone with a bright lipstick had drunk before her, Myrtle picked up the cup with her left hand. She told Ziah that the day Dora gets a dog would be the last day she would visit her flat. She had Dora down as a person who would let the dog eat off her plate and sleep curled up at the foot of her bed. She was sure that Enid was a Jamaican woman who would insist that for dogs to come onto the veranda was a step too far. She had heard stories of people allowing their dogs into their houses although the tropical nights were warm enough for dogs to curl up in their baskets under the verandas.

Ziah Morgan, like most men, felt deeply with his eyes. He saw Enid as being an attractive black woman who spoke with an educated voice. He knew she had attended the same popular high school in Kingston all his two eldest daughters had attended and the two younger girls were currently there. These young people are becoming part of a class above that to which he and his wife belonged. He too had moved away from the life his mother and father had lived. It was what was called progress.

"So, we expecting a another wedding, then?" asked Ziah.

"But see here!" Myrtle was caught off guard by her husband's question. "Me is not Lincoln's mother, you know."

"What me see is, that since she come the two of you as thick as thieves. First thing you rent Lincoln a room here for her, when him done buy his own place and could find room for her there."

"Look at it this way. Enid has a friend in Birmingham who happens to be Lincoln's cousin, Adlyn. She asked Adlyn to help her find accommodation in London. Since Adlyn doesn't live in London, she asked her cousin Lincoln to find Enid a room. I think Lincoln likes Enid. I think he feels that if he rented her a room at his own house it would look like he was moving too fast. What you think about that?"

"You may be right. As it happens we got a room so he rent from us and give the young woman a little space. You could be right. It's the sort of thinking that would come into him head. But if I know you, you already start soaking fruit in white rum getting ready for the wedding cake..."

"Isaiah Morgan, shut you big mouth," and she giggled like a schoolgirl.

Enid stood at the window of her room and looked out on a cold wet January London day. She had been crying for most of the morning. She had hoped that coming to London would be a liberating experience. Instead she felt shut in and lonely. She had awoken early when someone slammed the front door, presumably leaving for work. She had the distinct feeling that she was alone in a large empty house. Silence had descended all around her. She could have been the only person on the planet. Now as she stood by the window she could see people shuffling along the pavement. It was not like the proverbial ships in the night; ships might have hooted in recognition of one another as they passed safely by. No one seemed to know anyone else in London; even those who lived on the same street did not seem to recognise each other, and if they did it was not enough for them to stop and pass the time of day. How she longed to hear raucous voices, the animal noises of the Jamaican countryside she had left only three days previously!

She had learnt the words "hawker" and "haggler" from her school textbook and had thought that in London there might be one or the other shouting out their wares. What she saw were figures bundled in winter coats or mackintoshes hurrying along. She moved closer to the window and placed her palms on the wooden frame, alarmed at how cold it really was. She felt the draught like a thin blade slicing her fingertips. There was a slight rattling of the lower pane. Suddenly she recalled the opening lines of *Jane Eyre,* one of the prescribed novels for the Third-Year Jamaica Local Examination Literature Paper: *"...the cold winter wind had brought with it clouds so sombre, and rain so penetrating that further outdoor exercise was out of the question..."* The idea of a black woman standing by a window in the middle of a London winter quoting lines from an English novel compounded the riot of feelings crowding her mind. Did English people wake up quoting Shakespeare? *"Blow, blow thou winter wind."* Well, as her headmaster the redoubtable T. Wilberforce Clarkson used to say, European colonialism had a lot to answer for.

It was not yet three o'clock, but it was dark enough to have the lights on as she sat at the dressing table getting rid of the telltale tears. She missed the bright light of the tropics. She missed the heat of the sun. She missed the loud cries and even the vulgarity of the young men in their torn work clothes as they saluted each other. She missed the barking of dogs, the braying of donkeys, the smell of freshly brewed real Blue Mountain coffee wafting on the morning air. She even missed Kingston, that sprawling, noisy, vulgar city devoid of beauty. She had always been comfortable with her own company, now she feared that she might not like the loneliness of a room in London.

Once again pressed against the window, she could see some distance up the street. It was almost empty and so quiet. So graveyard quiet. Occasionally bundles with head, arms and legs reminding her that there were people about. She could see a woman pushing a pram, a man was riding a bicycle; although she designated sex to them she could not be certain. No one seemed perturbed by the rain or the cold. She felt a shiver as she thought of joining the workforce in a week or two. The weather could not be used as an excuse for not going to work. That phrase had been used so often since her arrival in London that she thought it was not merely good advice, it assumed the proportion of a threat. She did not need harsh reminders. She was beholden to Lincoln. There would be rent to pay, food and more suitable clothes to be bought. "Oh, God," she said involuntarily, "what have I let myself into?" At times like this she questioned her reason for coming to London and not going to Birmingham where Adlyn was. As she stared at the action or lack of it on the street, she became conscious of a figure in a brown coat holding high an umbrella coming down the street. The figure had her head bowed and the umbrella tilted at an angle to keep the rain out of her face. She seemed skilled in avoiding puddles on the pavement with deft footwork. When the woman reached opposite the Morgans' house she paused and lifted the umbrella, and Enid recognised Myrtle Morgan. A minute or two later Enid heard her steps on the stairs. She went out on the landing.

"Miss Myrtle, you wet and look cold."

"It wet and cold out there, you see," Myrtle Morgan threw breath sharply through clenched teeth. "Girl, this is England. The winter getting into gear. Missus, no make duppy fool you, there's worst to come."

"Miss Myrtle, don't frighten me, you hear?" pleaded Enid. "I was standing at the window and fretting because Lincoln said that tomorrow he's coming to take me to the Labour Exchange. I hope all this rain and cold change by tomorrow."

"You'd be lucky, girl! This weather not changing for the better before April."

"April!"

"And even then you can have some wicked days right into May."

"You joking, Miss Myrtle," she looked pleadingly at the older woman. "You happen to know when the next boat leaving for Jamaica?" They both laughed, holding on to each other for support.

"Girl, we all feel like that when we just come up. Then it dawn on us that even if you don't like it, you still have to work and save up for the passage home. That will take time. Then you tell yourself you will need a little money to get started again back home. So if you is a man the next move is to send for your wife to help you earn and save more. Next thing he is buying a house and now them start thinking of sending for their children.

It grow 'pon you slowly. It is like you are in the middle of a river; whichever way you look the river bank is the same distance away."

"Thanks for your encouragement."

"Anyway I got to go back out in the cold. I forgot to take the paying-in book for the furniture store, and I want to look around Brixton market. There's a stall in the market that sells good curtain material. You fancy coming out with me?"

"Lord, Miss Myrtle, I feel like diving under the blanket and staying there until April or May."

"Me dear," said Myrtle Morgan patiently but firmly, "that no how it goes. This is England! The weather no stop you from going anywhere. I always say that if a person work in England and sen' money back to people in Jamaica, those people should be grateful. Nello was telling me the other day that he sen' ten pounds to his mother-in-law before Christmas. She wrote to say thanks, but it not 'nough. Ten pounds! I don't take home ten pounds a week in my pay packet! Them people back home don't know what it's like to live and work in England. But never mind, girl. Stay warm. Another time, eh? I going to make meself a cup of Bovril to warm me up, then I'm out again."

Enid followed Myrtle Morgan up the next flight of stairs to her kitchen. She watched the landlady lit the gas fire under the kettle, before slipping out of her coat. The discussion on the weather continued.

"You know," said Enid, "in 1951, during the night of Hurricane Charlie, I was on my way home from School in Kingston when the Anglican Church at Pretty Tunning was wrecked, and came crashing down on twenty-three of us..."

"Lord Jesus Christ!" Myrtle exclaimed, then piously, "Lord, I didn't mean to take your name in vain." She placed her palm over her mouth as if to prevent any further digression.

"All my young life I always thought the Anglican Church at Pretty Tunning was the biggest and safest building in all the Upper Yallahs. My grandmother used to say that when the church was built she was a girl not courting yet. Don't ask me how old you have to be to start courting in those days. She used to fetch sand from the river for the men to mix the cement. That church was made out of stone and it was strong. Well, that night Hurricane Charlie just tore down one of the two palm trees outside the front door and sent it crashing down the right-hand side of the aisle as you look towards the altar. Lucky for us, we were all sitting down on the left-hand side. God did look after us, for only Miss Matty was injured; her leg was broken. My grandmother said it was God's judgement because Matty Brown was always putting her mouth in everybody's business... Anyway, what I'm saying is that was the worst elemental catastrophe I ever had to face. A bit of cold weather and rain in London can't measure up to that night of Seventeenth of August 1951. I will wrap up warm in another of the cardigans that my friend Adlyn sent to me. I going to come with you, Miss Myrtle."

"That is the spirit, girl," Myrtle said handing her a mug of Bovril. "I hear so much about Adlyn from Lincoln and now you, I can't wait to meet her. To tell the truth, I used to think Adlyn was his girlfriend..." She broke off, as Enid appeared to choke at the very thought.

"His girlfriend! No, man, Adlyn is his first cousin, his aunt's daughter, but she is like a big sister to him. We've been friends since high school. Do you mean he has not shown you her photo?"

"I believe him now. Lincoln is a nice young man, but he does put up the barriers when he feel like it. He could do with a good woman behind him, or beside him," she paused and looked up at Enid, who immediately recognised what Myrtle meant.

"I guess Lincoln take me for another sister, even if I'm not the favourite," she said and turned to glance at the gathering gloom outside the kitchen window. She could still feel Myrtle's eyes burning into her cheeks. She had to say something else. "So many of our black boys turning to white girls, I suppose he will soon find one..."

"I wonder what Adlyn would say to him 'bout that?"

"I know exactly what she would say," Enid quickly regained her composure. "'So what, you stop eating rice and peas and gone over to fish and chips?'" The two women started laughing again. Myrtle slapped her thighs and laughed until the tears ran down her cheeks.

"Girl, you will do, you will do!"

II

Another half-hour and the two women, suitably padded, wrapped and overcoated and sharing an umbrella, left the house. They were walking in the cold drizzling rain towards Brixton Road.

"It's the start of the rush hour; we'll have to wait if we is to get on a bus that isn't too crowded," explained Myrtle. Looking at her companion she said, "I hope it's not too cold for you?"

"All of my body is warm, except... well...my breast, my nipples seem to be the only part of my body the cold seem to get to."

Myrtle looked at Enid. "Girl, you not alone in that. Every woman I talk to say the same thing. The cold get to the nipples."

"I wonder how these nursing mothers manage? Especially seeing that some of them only got their brassiere under their blouse and coat. If ever you find out, tell me."

"I wonder how that would come about, Miss Myrtle?"

"You young," Myrtle pushed her elbow against Enid's ribcage, "me is old fowl."

It did not take them long to get a bus, as three came along at the same time. It was a short journey and soon they were getting off the bus in front of Woolworth's. They walked back to Collier's Furniture Store. The store was warm and the women released their fingers from their gloves. The manger recognised Myrtle.

"Mrs Morgan! Mrs Morgan," his right hand was held out in greeting. He turned to a younger man. "This is one of my best customers. If I was run over by a 109 bus tomorrow, and Mrs Morgan comes in and want anything in the shop, give it to her." He considered his voluble promise and quickly added, "For a reasonable price, of course. Now, have I not treated you right? Tell my nephew how I treat you...and who's this gorgeous young woman? Don't tell me she's your daughter. You're too young to have such a grown-up daughter..."

"Murray, stop the salesman pitch. I not buying anything today. I just want to pay you some money before you take me house away from me for not paying..."

"Don't ever say things like that. I'm shocked. I'm hurt. Come into the office." He led the way. "Your nephew was here yesterday. What a clever young man! No flies on him, I can tell. He has brains, that one!"

"Murray, I hope you treated Lincoln right, you now..."

"Mrs Morgan," the furniture salesman interrupted, "don't worry about him; feel sorry for me. I was thinking of offering him a job..." They laughed. Enid felt there was a conspiracy to raise Lincoln in her esteem. They finished their transaction in Colliers and headed towards the market.

Enid was not surprised at how crowded it was, after all she had the experience of the markets of Kingston's Coronation Market, Redemption, and Constant Spring Road Markets. What surprised her was how orderly people were. If Myrtle stopped to look at a stall and Enid stood behind her, soon a queue would form behind her. To avoid this she stood beside Myrtle. They were examining curtain materials when a very large black woman nudged Myrtle Morgan and in a foghorn voice announced, "You is the last person I 'spec' to see in Englan'!"

Myrtle turned, with a mixture of annoyance and surprise. "I could say the same about you."

"Well, Missus, since everybody seem to be headin' for the Mother Country, I say to meself, girl, you better go see what a-happen. Me sharin' a room in Arlington Road. It no home, but it will do for the present. Stay 'pon crooked and cut straight, as me mother, God rest her soul, used to say."

After ten minutes or so, Myrtle, still somewhat irritated and impatient, said, "We'll run into each other again. Arlington Road, you say? You know how it is, I got to get home and start the cooking before the man get home."

"Yes, number 101. I would write it down, but I don't have pen and paper. So where you living? Dis is one of you daughter?"

"Where we living is not too grand either. We leaving, as soon as me husband get a promise of a place in Stamford Hill. I hope it come through. We daughter just come up last week," Myrtle nudged Enid, who nodded in agreement to Myrtle's deceitfulness. Both women started edging away.

"Mind how you go. You never can tell, we might bump into each other again." She spoke to the back of the retreating women.

"I won't bother asking you if she's a friend," Enid said as Myrtle stopped at a fruit and vegetable stall. Myrtle took a deep breath before turning to her young companion.

"Friend! I think the government should start checking up on who they're allowing to come into this country. If they give me the job checking on people, somebody like that woman would never leave Beeston Street."

"Why Beeston Street? It not too bad there."

"That woman used to live there. Not that I ever gone visiting her, you understand. To tell you the truth I don't even know her real name."

"But she know you."

"Yes, yes, that's because..." Myrtle paused, paid for her fruits and vegetables, then continued, "She used to sell fish. You lived in Kingston. You know the type. She had a big basin of fish on her head, walking from street to street shouting, 'Buy you fish, fresh fish'. The ice that was to stop the fish going off would melt and drip on her clothes. The woman still smells of fish. Didn't you smell her? There was this woman a tenant of mine living in my yard that trust fish from her and would not pay her. That fish woman (we used to call her Crawfish, because she also used to sell lobster), she would come outside my yard and start carrying on. One day I heard her say, 'You wait till I go down to me yard in Beeston Street and change out of these clothes, and put on me empire-line dress, when I come back all hell gwine bus' in this yard in Penn Street. Well! I never could work out why she had to dress up and look nice just to come and disgrace herself with all that cussing. For although she did change, she still stink of fish! She turned up with a man. Girl, them start one piece of something! I treat you like me own daughter so I wouldn't tell you some of the words them use. The woman them want, my tenant, was not even back from work yet, so me went out and paid what my tenant owed her. I was not going to have this crawfish woman declaring Marshall Law outside my yard. Don't forget I had a little cold supper shop out at the front with some decent regular customers."

Myrtle continued to complain for another half-hour about the indiscriminate way the government was letting in immigrants.

"But isn't that the same thing the white people saying about us, Miss Myrtle?"

"I know, girl, but some of us give them good reason. Just you wait till you go to a party and see the riffraff that come pushing themselves 'pon you asking for a dance. They do it to me too, you know. Big old woman like me," she laughed and seemed to be returning to good humour. They left the market without buying the materials for the curtains. Myrtle Morgan told Enid that there was another market at a place called East Lane. They could go there.

"Today?" asked Enid, depressed at having to spend another hour or two in the cold and the rain.

"No, man," said Myrtle, "you no see the time? In this country everything close down by five-thirty. We leave it until the weekend." They crossed the busy Brixton Road to the pavement outside Morley's Department Store where they caught a bus for the return journey.

III

The Ministry of Labour, Brixton Office was near the Coldharbour Lane entrance to the market. The office was crowded and a feeling of despondency came over Enid as she realised that the majority of those waiting to be served were coloured, with a variety of accents signifying the polyglot Empire and Commonwealth.

When it was her turn to be interviewed the clerk began using a mechanical voice. Enid could read her thoughts. This interviewer had seen hundreds of immigrants who possessed no more than a British passport and the price of a ticket to England. *It ought not to be allowed. This one probably wants to be a nurse. They all want to be nurses, even if they can't spell the word hospital.* Enid watched with growing interest the bored features of the middle-aged woman lighten when she was presented with Enid's Senior Cambridge Certificate and a reference from the Chambers of a Queen's Counsel. With a pleasant smile the woman excused herself and, taking the certificates and reference, went to a desk further in the office to someone seemingly to be in authority, who was shown the papers. Soon four people were grouped around the desk talking and glancing in Enid's direction.

Enid looked up at Lincoln, who was behind her chair. "Do they think I forged them?"

"I went to the Rye Lane office three years ago, and it cause quite a stir when I presented my Jamaica Third-Year Local Examination and my Senior Cambridge. After that, I hear, they started asking young people for certificates of education. It seems Brixton has caught up with Rye Lane."

"Don't they know anything about the Empire?" asked Enid. "The Director of Education in Jamaica is an Englishman called H.H. Broughton. That must have been a top job in the Colonial Service, I think Mr Broughton is rated third or fourth after the governor."

"One thing you'll learn very fast is that the English people you and I are likely to meet don't know anything about the Empire and what's more they don't give a damn! Jamaica to you and me might have been the first British colony to give the Mother Country a bombing plane in her hour of direst and need, but that was a long time ago. Today Jamaica is somewhere in Africa and the natives share the trees with their cousins the monkeys... Look out, she's coming back. You've confused them. You've probably been down from the trees long enough for the missionaries to have taught you to read and write." Enid pushed him away and sat up right in her chair.

"Well, Miss Swaby," the woman said with a surprised look, "you seem very well qualified. I apologise for that little conference, but we don't see much evidence of educational qualification and work references from you people. My colleagues think that perhaps you'd like to try for the Civil Service as a typist. What is your speed?"

"Just over forty," Enid said.

"What do you think about sitting a test? The Civil Service sets its own tests. They are currently recruiting people for the typing-pool. Or you could consider testing for a clerical assistant's post. Your duties would be mostly filing and messages," she could read nothing in Enid's face. "Both positions have a career structure; it's not like being a bus conductress," she was still trying to read Enid's expression, so she looked at Lincoln with a frustration fast turning into anger. "It's the best advice I can offer," she looked at Enid once more, just as one of her colleagues approached her desk and handed her a piece of paper. She glanced at it. "I could arrange it for next Monday. I'll write down the address and how to get there."

When they left the Labour Exchange Office the winter's sun was shining brightly. Enid was surprised at the change in the weather in the space of a day. As they walked up Coldharbour Lane, Lincoln said, "Well, what do you feel about becoming an English Civil Servant even though it will be lowest rung?"

"Does it pay well? I have debts to repay," she glanced sideways at him. "Well, I can't let you go on looking after me."

"You owe me nothing."

"Yes, I do," she had her hands on his shoulder and was shaking him. "Yes, I do. Don't tell me that you would do this for every girl?"

"I couldn't afford to do it for every girl, but for any other girl it would be a loan and I would expect her to repay."

"What makes me so special?"

"I love you and want to marry you."

"You proposing to me in the middle of the road?"

"I will go down on my knees if it would help."

She stopped abruptly and looked at him. "Don't you dare! You attempt any such foolishness and I will run away! Jesus! Boy, you don't waste time. I was hoping you had outgrown that puppy-love business." She realised that her voice was harsher than it should be. She glanced sideways at Lincoln and smiled. He deserved better than this, much better, she thought. "Anyway," she began, at the same time elbowing the man who had come to her aid at the darkest period of her life; this man who was providing for all her needs until she could fend for herself. "Promise me you will not mention love or anything like that until we see how things turning out. Promise me!" She tried to tinge her voice with hope, which she could see pleased Lincoln, "Let's be friends, eh?" and they walked on.

"I propose..."

"Lincoln!" she stopped in her tracks, fists raised threateningly.

"I meant to say that we could either go the cinema or go for a ride up to the West End, or I could take you home, light the heater to warm up the place and talk."

She thought for a moment. She had enough fresh air, walking all the way from Lilford Road, and although the warmth of her room was inviting, she thought it might send the wrong signals to Lincoln. Even though it was not his fault, her confidence had taken a great blow over the last year. What she had heard from Myrtle Morgan, what she knew of him and what she had observed in the last few days, she was hoping that Lincoln could restore in her the trust she had lost in her fellow human beings. She walked closer to him, linking her arm through his. He turned to look at her, smiled and a billowing tide of warmth seemed to radiate from his face.

"Oh, the cinema," she said hastily. "It must be two years or more since I went to the Carib Theatre. I think we saw...well, it doesn't matter, anyway...."

"What doesn't matter, the party, or what you saw?"

"Don't cross-question me," there was a flash of irritation in her voice. "Why don't you take me back to Lilford Road, then you can go on to where you're living?"

"Look, let's start again," he said contritely. "We go to the pictures. There's a musical at the Odeon. Rodgers and Hart, I think."

"The people I know talk about the stars in a film, you mention the writers," she chided.

"I know Frank Sinatra is a favourite of yours. I didn't mention his name, because I didn't want to be accused of another attempt at bribing you."

"OK," she said, "to the cinema then."

IV

A month in London and Enid was quickly adapting to living in London. She took Myrtle Morgan's advice seriously and never left the house without her umbrella and a mackintosh. She had learnt to treat the English weather like a cunning animal. A bright March morning with sunshine streaming through the windows was neither guarantee of a mild winter's day nor a rainless afternoon.

"Treat every day as if you expecting the worst," Myrtle had told her, "then if it no snow or it no rain and it no cold, you get a bonus."

She was looking forward to having Adlyn spend a week with her. It was over three years since she left Jamaica to study nursing in Birmingham. Enid had concealed much from her old friend, and was still uncertain how much she should disclose. Yet she could not avoid the excitement and the fun that was in store. She worried slightly about Lincoln's role. She knew he would be at his cousin's side. Enid had not confided to Adlyn what part Lincoln had played in her coming to England, but Adlyn was a perceptive person. Two and two would always make four, no more no less. There was little doubt that she liked having Lincoln around. She admitted to herself that if she was playing things to her own agenda, so was he. He did not come every day now, as in the beginning, and even when he did come, he would spend half the time with the Morgans. Sometimes she could hear them laughing. Other times he would call in to see Nello Walters, with whom he was planning some business deal. On these occasions she would be angry with him, knowing that he was doing this deliberately. Once he had come to her room just before he was about to leave.

"So you were here?" she had asked, not hiding the sarcasm.

"Missed me?" he asked, enjoying the annoyance in her voice.

"No," she said hastily, "I guess you know these people better than you know me."

"Whose fault is that?" there was more than a hint of accusation in his voice.

"You start being mannish with me and I'll get Adlyn to straighten you out," she said.

"The last thing I want is to have the two of you ganging up on me. I still have the scars."

"A warrior's trophy," she said smiling.

"I guess," he said.

V

The Sunday before Adlyn's arrival, Enid spent the afternoon with Lincoln in Lothian Road. They had lunch with his landladies, Miss Nicey and Miss Vie. It was traditional Jamaican Sunday lunch: escovitched fish, rice and peas, with a side dish of salad made up of cucumber and tomatoes, with carrot juice to wash it all down. When they returned to Lilford Road, the Morgans were entertaining. Myrtle Morgan heard them come in and, leaning over the banister of the landing, she invited them to come up to meet her visitors. Enid asked Lincoln to go on ahead while she went into her room to divest herself of her coat, umbrella and mackintosh, and no doubt to check her appearance in the mirror. When Lincoln entered the Morgan's front room, he recognised everyone. He was still standing by the door when Enid caught up with him. She tapped at the door while poking her head above

Lincoln's left shoulder. Myrtle Morgan moved towards them and half-turned to her guests with one hand sweeping an arc while the other beckoning to the new arrivals. "Meet two of my favourite people. Them is like my own flesh and blood. I tell you what, do me a favour go in the kitchen and bring a tray of things I got prepared there. By now the kettle must be boiling. Make some tea..."

She broke off as Enid pushed Lincoln out of the way and took three steps into the room. With some distance still between her and where Wellesley and Iris Young were seated, Wellesley half-raised himself from his seat, a look of wild panic on his face. Enid turned to Myrtle Morgan.

"No, Miss Myrtle!" there was a deafening silence when even the ticking of the clock on the mantelpiece seemed suspended. "If I was to make tea for somebody in this room I would have to get the water from the toilet. And your toilet is far too clean..." Her frame shook three or four times, she swayed unsteadily and fell against Myrtle. For more than a year her anger like a torrent in its October fury was swirling and lashing against the obstacles of landslides and uprooted trees and dislodged boulders. Now hurling itself with renewed strength gathered from a myriad contributory gullies, it heaved like a mighty tidal wave and crashed over its banks, dashing headlong, sweeping all in its path. Enid was sobbing and beating her fists against Myrtle's chest. Lincoln eventually managed to pull her away from Myrtle, who despite the blows still had her arms around the hysterical Enid.

"You poor chile," she comforted Enid, "is what bothering you so? I never see you like this. You trembling like a leaf."

Lincoln although supporting Enid, did not take his eyes off Wellesley Young and his wife. The latter's face displayed surprise, confusion and now anger. Wellesley rose, pulling his wife out of her chair. He looked towards the door as if plotting the fastest exit without encountering Enid.

"No, man," said Lincoln, somehow manipulating himself, Enid and Myrtle who was still clinging to the sobbing woman. "You're not going anywhere. Some explanation is called for and I think we'd all like to hear it from you."

"I won't be insulted in front my wife. Move from the door before I..." Wellesley said, moving deliberately towards the door.

"I'm not going anywhere," said Iris Young, disengaging her hand from her husband's with a shrug and a push, and returning to her seat. "Whether the insult is in front or behind me I want to hear what this woman has to say. I suggest you stay and listen." She looked with suspicion on her husband. "After all, you're the lawyer," she said. "You can defend yourself, and if it's slander, then sue her." She indicated with an authoritative jerk of her head that she wanted him to resume his seat.

"You poor chile. I never see you like this," said Myrtle as she helped Lincoln to lower Enid onto a chair. The fact that she had known Enid for less than two months did not enter her reckoning. She liked Enid, trusted her and that was enough. She had her arms around her shoulders. Enid was still sobbing, her head slipping down to rest on Myrtle's ample hips as Lincoln directed her to the chair. She now cried into Myrtle's skirt. Lincoln knelt attentively beside Enid's chair.

After an eternity when time itself was suspended, Enid lifted her head and began wiping the tears from her cheeks with her knuckles before Lincoln handed her his handkerchief.

"Look at me...I'm making a fool of myself... I promise myself that this is one thing I would never do again. I'm sorry. I think I'd better leave... sorry."

"Nobody leaving this room till I get some sort of explanation. You came into this room, look at my husband and start hurling insults. I want to know..."

"Take your time. Chile, take your time," Myrtle cut in, simultaneously comforting Enid and appealing to Iris Young for tolerance.

"Your husband?" Enid lifted her head looked at Iris, then buried her face once more in Myrtle Morgan's skirt.

"I didn't know he had another woman," she raised her head to look Myrtle in the face. "Married! I wouldn't go with a married man, Miss Myrtle. I beg you to believe me. See God dey."

"I believe you, chile," Myrtle Morgan said convincingly, as if Enid's calling on the Divine to support her case had put moral scruples beyond dispute.

"You know what churned up me inside, Miss Myrtle? It wasn't that him got me pregnant. No, it wasn't even that him disappeared as soon as I told him I was expecting. Lots of young girls get fooled by men and end up having to bring up babies on their own. What bother me, and, Miss Myrtle, it hurts me in more ways than one, was that he had to go and tell that woman, the one he had a child with, and she was big, big pregnant again. He had to go and tell her about me. She and her family came to where I was living and them beat me up really bad. Some people rescued me and took me to the Lying-In Hospital in North Street. I nearly died... I lost the baby."

"Which woman was that?" asked Iris Young as if she had just woken up.

Enid lifted her head and looked at Iris, she shook her head. "It sure wasn't you. She was a big brown-skinned woman. St Elizabeth red skin..."

"Beryl Geddes!" shrieked Iris and turning to her husband she leapt on him with unreserved fury. It took Isaiah Morgan and Nello Walters, who had run post haste from Nello's room on hearing the commotion, to pull the angry wife off Wellesley. "You dirty bastard. You went back to her. The pig went back to the wallow and the swine to its vomit..." she was incandescent with rage.

"Look, man," said Isaiah, holding on to Iris but speaking directly to Wellesley, "I think you better leave. I don't know how much longer I can hold on to this woman." Then appealing to Nello, who had released his grip on Iris, "She's strong, you see! Help me no, man!"

Seizing his opportunity, Wellesley bolted for the door.

"And..." shouted Iris still struggling to free herself, "you better not be in the flat when I get back. I don't want to see a book or a hanky belonging to you when I get home. It's OK now, Mass Ziah. It OK now, you can let me go now." Isaiah Morgan released her, but along with Nello Walters they stood close, ready to grab her again should she bolt for the door or approach Enid, who was still crying. Iris straightened her blouse and skirt before collapsing in her chair, head in hands, tears streaming like rapids. Colonel Nello Walters hung his handkerchief before her. She lifted her head saw it and took it. She dabbed her eyes and wiped her nose. "Iron Front Geddes they used to call her. When she was fifteen, just out of school, her father found her in the Old Boiling House among the cane trash with five boys, and Wellesley was one of them! I don't know what she got that sweet him so. Over the last twenty years him keep going back to her. Miss Myrtle, I'm fed up. I know she said that her first child was Wellesley's, but him promised me he wouldn't go anywhere near her again. The first sign that he was breaking his promise I light out for England, though I know I was three months gone." She shook her head and looked to the men for sympathy. "Is what the matter with you men? Why is it that one woman can't satisfy you all?"

Both of the older men stepped back as if scalded with hot water. They glanced at each other, then spoke without much conviction. "We not all alike," said Nello.

"Is thirty-odd years me married," said Isaiah, "and never so much as look 'pon another woman."

"Shet you mouth," said Myrtle, "is twenty-seven years we married. That shows how much you know. Apart from what I would do to you if you come in my bed smelling of another woman, I would make our four daughters have a go at you first."

At another time that might have sparked laughter, but not now.

"I mean it this time. I want him out of my flat! Out of my life, my children's life," said Iris to nobody in particular, "I'm not putting up with this any more. If what Geddes got a-sweet him so, he can get a room somewhere else and send for her. If him don't clear out his things the rag and bone man get every piece of clothes and every book I find belonging to that low-down bastard. You think I'm joking. Just you wait and see. Bastard!"

"I'm sorry," said Enid, lifting her head.

"Sorry for what? Our marriage reminds me of a man who used to live in our district. He had one pair of trousers. My mother used to say it was patched in so many places that you couldn't tell the original material from the patches. That is my marriage! Girl, if it wasn't you, it would be some other woman. As far as we know you weren't the only one. Wellesley was three times in the States on farm work contract. Well, the second time he was there, he caught the *clap*. Girl, count yourself lucky. He can be a charmer at times, and that's what makes us women so forgiving. The other day my aunt in Birmingham was having a real go at her husband. 'Every place me turn you under me foot. Turn off the damn television and go to the club and play domino with the other men, them. Go and have a drink and stop getting under my foot, tcho.' I thought to myself, Aunty, you don't know how lucky you are. You know where your man is every minute of the day."

"I don't know about all of you but I could do with a stiff drink," said Isaiah. "We still have a little white rum left...Wait, was that the bell? You don't think the neighbours called the police?"

"I'll go and see," said Nello. "Stay calm," he counselled as tears welled up in Enid's eyes.

"I bet is Lonso," Myrtle said. "He said he might drop by."

It was indeed Alonso.

PART THREE

On a turning wicket

Since I come 'ere I never met a single English person who 'ad any colour prejudice. Once, I walked the whole length of a street looking for a room, and everyone told me that he or she 'ad no prejudice against coloured people. It was the neighbour who was stupid. If we could only find the 'neighbour' we could solve the entire problem. But to find 'im is the trouble! Neighbours are the worst people to live beside in this country.

Because They Know Not, A.G. Bennett, London 1959

19

It was the morning of the day that Rosita Maria de Campesino Campbell was due to arrive at London's Heathrow Airport that the Colonial Club was burnt down. Alonso awoke to the sound of the emergency vehicles racing to the scene with their bells clanging. In the light of day the basement and the ground floor were blackened and charred, giving added meaning to its nickname The Black House. The name stuck because it housed the Colonial Club in the basement, a black-run travel agent and a tailoring establishment on the ground floor. On the first floor was a small flat where Melbourne Welch once lived, but since he had been spending more time with his white woman in Ladbroke Grove it had been rented. This was where Coolieman had a room. Until he moved to Mayhall Road this was where he cut hair at weekends and occasionally at evenings during weekdays. The second and third floors were occupied by a firm of solicitors that had a black law clerk and drew most of their clients from the black community.

The fire had been caused by faulty electrical wiring in the club, according to the preliminary report from the Emergency Services. It was pointed out that a number of electrical instruments were used in the club. However, by mid-morning rumour was rife that some Teddy boys were seen running away from the area before the fire. The eyewitness was said to be a white woman of easy virtue who slept with black men, so no one expected the police to take her story seriously. Others said that once Melbourne had his now famous confrontation with Birbeck Samms, it was inevitable that something would happen, if not to Melbourne himself then his premises. The national press and TV came down to record the end of an era.

Alonso tore himself away from the milling crowd. His sister would be landing at Heathrow soon and from there would go by coach to the Victoria Terminal. He wanted to be there before she arrived. It was winter and he had bought a coat that he hoped she would like. She had sent her size, but he wondered what her taste in clothes might be. He went to the store where Sue Hall, Warren's wife, worked. Sue assured him that the colour and the style would appeal to a fashion-conscious nineteen-year-old; however, she was prepared to exchange it, but only after one wear. He folded the coat over his arm and took a taxi to Victoria.

He had to wait about an hour before the coach arrived. The first of the arrivals to come into view was a middle-aged woman in a bright print dress and an ill-fitting cardigan. She was trying to control three little boys in suits, each tugging at bags that looked too big and heavy for their seizes. The woman was struggling with a large suitcase that had been battered out of shape. Alonso was lost in wild malicious guesses as to which country district some of the passengers might have escaped from when he saw her. Rosita was wearing the suit he had sent. He was surprised how tall she had grown in the three years since he had last seen her. The man beside him, who had sucked his teeth every time a group of passengers came into view and his wife was not in it, stared at Rosita and said, "What a good-looking gal! I wonder who she looking for?"

"Me!" said Alonso, waving his hands high. She saw him. She had a bag over her shoulder and was tugging an extra-large suitcase on wheels.

"That grip look heavy," said the impatient man to Alonso. "Wonder what she got in there - white rum for the wedding?" the man laughed loudly, pushing his elbow hard into Alonso's ribcage.

Alonso did not reply. She had dropped the case and was about to run towards him when she remembered there were other passengers behind her. She regained her hold on the case and struggled on. At last she reached the barrier. Letting go of the case, she leapt on her brother, laughing and crying at once. There was much hissing of teeth from those who thought that showing affection in public was embarrassing.

"Welcome to London," he said as they released each other. "Put this on. Aren't you cold?"

"Freezing," she said, struggling into the coat. She held on to him while they waited for a taxi. She clung to him in the taxi.

"Do I hear wedding bells?" asked the cab driver. "You people have big wedding parties. There was one at St Matthew's last week. Holy mackerel, must have been a hundred guests. How can anyone afford to feed a hundred people? Me daughter got married two years ago and I won't recover for years, and that was only family and friends. I'm for changing the custom that the father of the bride pays, what about the groom's dad? I would like to see the inside of his wallet. I got another four daughters, you see. Young still, but they grow up fast these days. Go to the Register Office, then take your mates down to the pub for a drink, I told them. No, Dad, they say. We want the whole shooting match. White dress, Rolls Royce, church, the lot," he rattled on.

They squeezed hands, looked at each other and giggled. When they reached Geneva Road, Alonso paid and tipped the driver. The taxi swung into a U-turn and the driver hung his head out of the window and shouted to Rosita, "No nonsense, let him make a honest woman outa you," he eased the cab into gear and roared towards Coldharbour Lane.

"You didn't tell him I'm your sister!"

"You didn't tell him I'm you brother! Let's get in. I left the heater on. Dangerous, but it should be safe enough. Anyway there's no smoke and no fire." He hoisted the case onto his shoulders. "What have you got in here? You didn't pack a couple of our siblings in here, did you?"

"It's all I've accumulated on this planet in my nineteen years. There are letters from all your siblings and Gody Ivo. Mama wrote to you in Spanish. It's a long letter; she wouldn't let me read it."

"They must have written on tablets of stone."

He led the way down to the basement. She followed carefully, so that her new coat did not touch the sides of the steps. He went through the front room, weaving his way between the furniture. The bedroom now had a partition. His portion of the room adjoined the sitting room. He heaved the case onto his bed.

"This one is mine," he said, sitting on the bed. "Yours is in there," pointing to the other side of the partition. "It has a dressing-table."

He went towards her and embraced her again. "This is going to be our home for some time. Welcome to London, little Flowers."

"Never leave me again," she said, clinging to him, then stepped back as if to continue an inspection. "What am I saying? Of course, you'll leave me. Brothers always do."

"The taxi driver didn't think so," he laughed. "You know, he was right."

"What are you talking about?"

"The man who was next to me at the barrier when I was waiting for you said you're a good-looking gal. I'd forgotten how pretty you are. Come, let me help you out of your coat."

"No; this room might be warm to you Londoners, but a couple of days ago I was trying to find somewhere cooler than 80 degrees in the shade." She pulled the coat around her, stuffing her hands deep in the pockets and standing over the heater.

"You have a long wait for that kind of heat. If you're lucky this July we might have some hot days. Do you like the coat?"

"Love it, and the suit. Mama said it was chosen by a woman," she turned to face him. "You have a woman?"

"No," he said, blotting out the picture of Lurline who was in this very bed two days previously, "but I do have friends who are married or live with women."

"So Mama was right, you had help in choosing this suit?"

"Only to confirm my choice. Let me make you a hot drink. What do you want, coffee, tea, chocolate? Are you hungry?"

"I must learn the language of London. In Jamaica we say coffee-tea, chocolate-tea and green tea. Just a couple of years and you've forgotten your language," she teased. "I don't want a drink, thank you. I'm tired," she stifled a yawn, "but I'm so pleased to see you I couldn't sleep right now. Do you remember Ransford Carr?"

"The Baptist parson at Grasspiece younger son is called Ransford. He was named after a governor who took up his duties the year that son was born, I guess. I have not been in London all that long you know."

"We sat in neighbouring seats He is going on to see his brother Burchell in Boston before going on to Canada and university. When we got to New York, do you know where they put us up?"

"No, where?"

"At the Hotel Theresa in Harlem. It was nice, and I mean super-nice. I shared a room with a girl called Mavis, she's going to Birmingham to her boyfriend. She left her baby with her aunt back in Jamaica. I got some picture postcards from the Theresa. I'll show them to you when I unpack."

"Leave that until you've rested. Stay near the heater. Well, did Burchell remember me? I'll get you a hot chocolate."

"Yes, sir. Of course Burchell remembers you. Everybody know about the *Panya pickney dem* from Guava Flat," she said, then as quickly changed the subject. "You're my big brother. Mama said I must do what you say."

"I hope you remember that a couple of months down the line?"

"Or else?"

"It's very cold outside, little sister." He pointed towards the door.

"In here too. Oh, *hijo*", she called after him, "you wouldn't put me outside, would you?"

He returned with two mugs of chocolate and handed her one. She motioned for him to sit beside her on the bed. She held the mug in one hand and rubbed the other against it to warm her fingers. She leaned against him.

"At last. How I longed for this moment. It's going to be like old times. Just the two of us again. Two little kids whose mother couldn't protect them from her man. The other children of the district didn't like us. We were brown-skinned foreigners who spoke another language. We wore shoes all the time. Remember? Only the old man they called Coachie would speak to us."

"Papa Coachie. He drove a horse-drawn taxi in Colon during the building of the canal. He was a distant cousin of our grandfather. As young men they went off to Panama Canal Zone and worked in Colon. To us children his old house was one of our few places of refuge. It was he started calling us *Panya hijos*, which eventually became *Panya Pickneys*. He called you *hija* and me *hijo*. You called me *hijo* a minute ago. Do you remember that?"

"I remember. The old house had a veranda where he had his rocking chair. Well, he's dead now, though people still say that they can hear the creaking of his chair when they pass where his house used to be. The usual improbable duppy story," she said, hiding under his armpit.

"Mind the hot drinks!" They put the cups on the coffee table, so they could cuddle again.

"Papa Coachie wouldn't harm us in life or death," he said, releasing her. It was as if those years had been deep-frozen to be taken out now and defrosted against the fender of nostalgia.

"Over here migrants stay together because the English claim we're different. There is a difference, though. When we were kids the other children didn't dislike us but they couldn't speak our language. I think they found us strange; they wanted to be friends but we didn't trust them."

"It brought us closer. I want us to be close again. I know it sounds corny for a sister to say that. After all, many girls my age have babies to care for and here I am still clinging to you. *Hijo*, you play so many male roles in my life." She paused and looked at him. "Would I be saying that to my father if he was with us?"

"Perhaps. Fathers ought to be role models for their sons and daughters. I can't remember what he looked like. Not surprising, I was only four years old when he died. Come on, Flowers, let's not be sad. Let's laugh for we are together again. Me and my beautiful *hermana.*"

"I showed your picture to a girl at Wilberforce. You know what she said? 'It's not healthy for a girl to have such a good-looking brother.' I told her it's a good thing you're my brother since I'd be crushed in the line of girls who are after you. As your sister, I can have a private audience with you whenever I like."

"Where are all these girls lining up to reach me? Stand back," he pushed back to arm's length so he could better examine her, "if you weren't my sister you'd be ahead of Dorothy Dandridge, Eartha Kitt, Ava Gardner, Jane Russell and Brigitte..."

"If you know Dorothy that well, can you ask her if she'd bring Harry Belafonte to my next party? Or that beefy William Marshall?"

They laughed, playfully pushing and hitting each other.

"Mama said I should try my best to get on with your girlfriend. When do I meet her?"

"I haven't got a girlfriend."

"I'm nineteen," she said, as if that meant she had the key to all knowledge. "I wouldn't be surprised if some woman helped you fix up this room. Irone, the girl I told you about at Wilberforce, got vex with me because I didn't give her your address."

"Why didn't you?"

"She's not right for you."

"What type is right for me?"

"I'll know when I meet her. By the way, Irone is coming to London soon and her people know Gody Myrtle. She doesn't know that I know that for a fact. But then I didn't tell her I was coming to England either. She is out as far as you are concerned."

"Have I the right to censor your lovers, then?"

"You won't have to do that for a long, long time yet."

"Am I to believe that a pretty girl like you hasn't had boys swooning at your feet?"

"I've had my share of love letters. A girl has to put a price on her own head if she's to get anywhere in this world. What most boys want is for girls to lower the price. I'm not prepared to barter. As the taxi man said, *you* will have to make a honest woman out of me."

"That's illegal everywhere."

"Abraham married his sister, Sarah."

"But she wasn't his mother's daughter."

"So it's OK to marry your father's bastard daughter?"

"That was Abraham's excuse."

"Why are we having this conversation?" she yawned. "Oh..." she stopped.

"What?"

"You are only going to tease me about something which does not matter?"

"It does matter if you want to talk about it."

"Okay then," she said. You would never guess who sat in the seat next to me from Palisados to New York."

"Give me a million and half guesses and I bound to come up with some one from the entire Jamaican population."

"That will take weeks and I am tired."

"Well?"

"Ransford Carr," she hid her face.

"Flowers! Ransford Carr has been mentioned all ready... and you are blushing!"

"I'm not. I do not blush."

"You are having a good try," he teased. "Does that mean that he has finished at the University College, then?"

"It would have appeared so. He is off to Canada for further studies in Toronto, I think?"

"Theological college, I suppose?"

"No that is his older brother Burchell, but he is studying at Boston and Ransford is meeting up with him, spend sometime before going on to Toronto. He ask for my address and I gave it to him. I hope you don't mind."

"Why should I? You are my sister and not as the taxi driver seemed to think, my girl friend."

"You sound a little jealous," she accused, "now who is blushing or a little embarrassed."

"Not me. Why should I? I always know this would happen. Attractive girl like you is bound to meet a nice bloke and if he is as well connected as Ransford all the better. We will talk some more but you're tired. Go through to your bedroom and pull back the bedclothes and just slip under."

"In my coat and suit?"

"Why not?"

"Only a man would say that. Now I'll go into my part of the room, I'll call you when I'm ready to be tucked in."

"I have a dressing-gown wrapped around a hot-water bottle in your bed."
He followed to the partition and dropped the screen. He gathered up the
cups and went out into the corridor to the far end that served as kitchen.
Alonso washed the dishes that had accumulated since the day before. When
he returned to his side of the bedroom she was standing in the screen door.
"Is this contraption for me?" She meant the screen. "We didn't need one
the last time we shared a room."

"Changes, little sister. I thought you might need some privacy. A man I
know called Colonel Walters (Nello for short) put up the shelves and made
the screen. Back in Jamaica he used to work for that big British firm Biggs,
Biggs and Grandy who built the long bridge in Portland and the Governor's
Tower Hotel and the Hibiscus Lodge on the North Coast. They are probably
still out there building other projects."

"Who hasn't heard of them? I think they are the people building the new
deep-water port for the Bauxite Company." She emerged from behind the
screen, tying the dressing-gown belt. "It was considerate of you to buy me
this lovely dressing-gown. You're going to make some girl a great husband.
I only hope she'll be a great sister-in-law too."

"Like I said, Nello (that's Colonel's nickname) works for the London
branch of the firm as a carpenter or joiner. He built the screen and put up
the shelves," he waved towards the books. "He came with references from
the Jamaican branch hoping that Biggs over here would hire him, but he's
scared of the cold, so he managed to get transferred to the factory where
they build windows, doors and frames. In the meantime he does odd jobs in
the evenings and at weekends."

"Thanks for my dressing-gown," she said, spinning around until the hem
billowed out.

"It's not yours. That's mine!"

"Was yours," she flopped on his bed. "I should have a bath."

"Have one when you wake up. The bath and the toilet are outside..."

"What? Like outside of this building?"

"The very same. However, the tenant before the Morgans made and
adoption. The kitchen table cleverly disguise a bath. Lift up the tabletop
and there is a good size bath which takes hot water from the taps at the sink.
That is as good as it gets for the toilet is still out there."

"Please tell me that you are joking."

"I am not joking."

"What happens in the dead cold of the night?"

There is a pale."

"A pale? As in a chamber pot?"

"The same."

"That is gross."

"There is one next to your bed."

"You can take it away."

"Why don't you get some rest? We can go over the domestic arrangements later."

She folded her arms and tried to look disappointed.

"Get back to your bed. There's a hot-water bottle for you to cuddle." He helped her back through the screen door. She kissed him goodnight; although it had just gone four o'clock it was dark.

"Don't leave me alone," she said in a tired voice. "Be here when I wake up." He knelt by her bed and stroked her face gently.

"Goodnight, little sister."

"I'm not your little sister any more. We have three half-sisters, remember? You are still my big brother, though." She in turn stroked his face, then gave him a playful slap, before turning her face towards the wall. "Goodnight."

II

He woke before her, made a pot of tea and poured himself a cup. He had for some time been struggling with *Joseph Andrews*. He took the book from the shelf and began to flick through it. He was not in the mood for reading or writing. He was accustomed to doing both rapidly, but only when he was lonely. He had not been lonely these last six months, what with Winnie and then the sisters Puncie and Lurline. Now that Flowers had come up to join him he feared the time and the urge to do anything creative would be rare. He hoped he could keep abreast of his evening classes. He hoped Blossom too would go to evening classes until she was accepted by a hospital to do nursing.

However, at that moment he had found himself engrossed in Joseph's letter to his sister Pamela: "*London is a bad place, and there is so little good fellowship, that the next-door neighbours don't know one another.*"

In that case London had not changed since Henry Fielding wrote those words. He did not know his neighbours in the house in which he lived. Although the truth was he had not the slightest inclination to acquaint himself with their affairs. He knew fewer than thirty people in London that he could call friends. The day before there had been a funeral cortège starting out from three doors up the street. He stood and raised his hat, as was the custom, but he did not know the person who had died. Back home when anyone dies in a neighbouring district you could hear the women bawling across the valleys and hear the bells tolling at the Baptist Church high up at Bun Dutty Gap. You would eventually know the name of the deceased, for everyone in the hill districts above the Yallahs was related, however distantly. You might, if you wished, attend the funeral; in Jamaica only weddings require an invitation. Certainly *Joseph Andrews* would most likely die of fright should he be transported to the London of the second half of the twentieth century. How would he cope with the world of horseless carriages roaring along the streets, the bright lights, flying engines, the swirling, charging mass of humanity that included young girls in short skirts halfway between their ankles and their knees? However, he would soon find out that neighbours still don't know one another!

"Morning!" the voice, still half asleep, emanated from a figure swathed in bedclothes standing in the screen doorway. "Where did you say the bathroom is? Oh, my breath! Eeyak! My mouth taste like the stench of dead flesh." Eventually her head emerged. She continued to unwind from what could have passed for burial clothes. Then she stretched.

"We do not have a bathroom as such. A washing bowl and the pale in the privacy of your room will have to do," he saw the look of consternation on her face. "Oh, come, you must first have a cup of tea. No one in England is considered fully awake until they've had a cuppa. This blessed beverage gives us courage to face up to the rigours of the day." He handed her a mug of tea.

"I notice it's not best china. Don't look at me like that. I went to the cinema a lot, and in British films people are always drinking tea," she took a sip. "Nice, but I must go to the bathroom."

"Put your coat over your dressing-gown. It's like the Arctic once you leave this room. There is one outside and while you slept I lit a paraffin heater so it should he warm enough by now."

"This is barbaric."

"I agree and welcome to London. You have a choice... the pale or the walk across to the outside loo... You will soon get used to it."

"Why don't you people write home and tell the truth about *migrant* London?"

"We do not want to sound as if we are keeping you away from the streets which are paved with gold. What makes you think that migrant London as you call it is any better than working class London? I work on the bus and see families getting off at Walworth Bath for their weekly baths."

"Weekly baths?"

"Complete with towels rolled up and tucked under their armpits."

"Gosh, I have a lot to learn."

"You are in transition. If you get a hospital you will no doubt be living in the nurses residence which will be tolerable I guess..."

" Do I really have to go outside?"

"It is your choice."

"I did wonder why you did not enthuse about the basement flat you managed to get for us!" she said cautiously. She wrapped the dressing gown around body and struggled into his coat and stood in front of the door like a swimmer making up her mind before plunging into a deep and very cold pool. Suddenly she pulled the door open and walked towards the outside convenience.

III

It had just gone twelve o'clock when they started up the stairs from the basement to street level.

"You're right, I do need some gloves," she said. "Let me try on yours. They're warm," she said, slapping them together, "but they're too masculine," she gave them back. Walking beside him she managed to stuff both her hands deep into his left-hand coat pocket. He placed his left arm around her waist. There was bright sunlight, but it did not carry the promised warmth of moonlight.

"It will get warmer, right? Winter ends 21st of March, right? We are already halfway through March, right?"

"Three rights do not spring or summer make," he said, smiling. "Yes, it will get warmer. Eventually it might even reach into the nineties in June or July this summer, but for now there are many colder days ahead with sleet, snow, smog and rain."

"I want to go home. Please send me home. Right now the Yallahs Valley, even without you, my brother, is still is paradise!"

"Do you know why we stay in England?"

"Out of some weird sense of loyalty, helping to rebuild 'the Mother Country' after the war?"

"Not quite. We borrow from friends and relatives to get here. When we get here we have to work to repay our debts, then have to save our fare to return. By the time we save enough, it doesn't matter any more. Someone has fallen in love, another is buying his home, others studying to become nurses, lawyers, accountants, teachers, whatever. I tell you, Flowers, the first winter is always the worst; by the second and the third, there are other things to worry about. Babies, houses, courses."

"You sound so wise and so sad. I don't want to be sad. Have you no warm words for me?"

"There were pictures in the newspapers in early January of people in swimsuits walking into the sea clutching hot-water bottles. That's known as the bulldog spirit."

"What a great idea!"

"New Year's Day was freezing. I reckon those people have since died from hypothermia."

"Serves them right. What I had in mind was to have had my hot-water bottle under my coat. Am I original or is it a common practice?"

"I haven't looked under many coats lately," he said, chuckling. "Last winter an old bus driver told me I should put brown sugar-paper next to my skin under my vest to keep the cold off my chest. I tried it; he was right, but he never told me I'd rustle like someone eating celery."

When they reached the intersection with Coldharbour Lane they could see the blackened ground and first floor of the Colonial Club. There were about seven or eight people assessing how badly the fire had damaged the building. Alonso spotted Jimmy, Warren and Lincoln. He piloted his sibling towards the gutted club. As he got closer he saw that someone had daubed the initials *KBW* on the charred wall.

"The British Union of Fascists have been around to gloat. Their minions torched the place; now they've returned and left their calling card. *Keep Britain White!*" he explained to Rosita as they crossed the road to join the trio. "Hi, guys, this little frozen creature here is my sister Rosita."

"Hi ya, Blossom," said Lincoln, "you've grown since I last saw you. What is it? Four years?"

"Blossom? I thought you said her name was Rosita," said Warren.

"My sister has more aliases than a con artist. She is Rosita, to me she is Flowers, to others Rosie, and to many Blossom."

"I can speak," Blossom said testily.

"I was about to say we've got to be nice to you, Lonso, on account of you having such a lovely charge, but she's quite capable of speaking for herself," said Warren.

"You better believe it," said Alonso.

"You are beautiful," said Jimmy lifting one of her hands from Alonso's pocket and kissing it. "You're freezing, put it back in his pocket... Bad news, I was telling these two that Melbourne was asleep in the club office when the fire started. He inhaled a lot of smoke. He's still in hospital. He was also under-insured."

"It comes in threes," said Warren.

"Fire, hospitalisation and under insurance," suggested Lincoln.

"Could be," said Warren. "How about buying you fellows a drink in the Black Pepper, before I gotta take a delivery over to Hackney?"

"I thought the police raided that dump and closed it down a couple of months ago," said Lincoln. "I can't join in anyway," turning to Alonso and Blossom, "I really need to see you, Lonso. Are you dropping by your tonsorial artists later?"

"What's this about *'tonsorial artists'*? Back to the days of Dr Johnson and powdered wigs?" asked Warren.

"I might," Alonso addressed himself to Lincoln, "after I've taken she-who-clings-to-me on her first shopping expedition."

After shopping at Brixton's two largest department stores, Morley's and Bon Marché, Rosita expressed a wish to return to the flat. She had bought some warm gloves, which she wore home. She also bought a pair of slacks and her brother persuaded her to buy an umbrella and a mackintosh.

Later in the day Lincoln called at the flat. He had waited at Curl and Dye and when they did not show up he decided to visit them at the flat. He bought Blossom some flowers and a vase.

"I've been told often that my room is too masculine. I understand that to mean I don't have any flowers in it. I'm sure that brother of yours would never think of brightening up the place with flowers. I bought you a vase because if Lonso put these flowers in a milk bottle, I'd throttle him."

"How thoughtful," she said. "No one's ever given me flowers before. What are these called?"

"Daffodils."

"As in Wordsworth?"

"The very same."

Both Lincoln and Alonso had boarded with Myrtle Morgan. Although they had known each other nearly five years they were not close enough to be the keeper of one another's secrets. Alonso was the romantic, the idealistic, while the more serious Lincoln knew not just the price but the cost of everything. He read Paul Samuelson and John Kenneth Galbraith while Alonso read Hemingway and Fitzgerald. Both men had a healthy respect for each other but never traded confidences.

"I guess you guys want to talk men's talk, eh?"

"I want to talk business to your brother," Lincoln said. "To be truthful I wonder if you could help me to change his mind."

"He can be stubborn. People born in January usually are. Romantic, ambitious, kind, but not easily persuaded."

"Would anyone seriously accept a reference from a younger sister?" asked Alonso.

"Maybe not," said Lincoln, failing to recognise any humour in what Alonso said. "Let me hang what I have to say on the ambitious aspect. I spotted within a month of coming to England that there are opportunities for black migrants. We have to make the best of those opportunities. No one's going to offer us anything on a silver platter. Black people want houses. Even if the local council is liberal enough to place Coloured peoples' names on their housing waiting list, they tell them to expect a result in ten years. By then their babies will be ready to sit the eleven-plus exams. Do any of us know what's going to happen in 1968? I want to go into property. If I had property today I could rent rooms to ten people or more. Later on I'd convert some of these houses into flats so that people could have a bit more space and privacy. A big room rents for three pounds ten shillings a week. These days you can still get mortgage for less than twenty pounds a month. You can't lose...."

"Exploitation!" Alonso interjected.

"Call it what you may, but if you don't do it, others will. They won't have your scruples. Have you forgotten Drury Lane? Leave that aside. I came up to London before you and shared a room in Ladbroke Grove with eleven other guys. The landlord was Polish. He charged us thirty shillings each. There were four bunk beds and two single beds in the room. You couldn't find space to move once you get off your bed. Then there were the guys who brought in their girls..."

"Girls!" Rosita exclaimed.

"I'm sorry. I don't want to offend you, but the answer is yes. If they still teach good maths at Wilberforce you'd have noticed that not everyone had a bed to himself... I had to smell the sweat of those men, had to be careful they didn't steal my trousers. It was then I hit on the idea of buying my own house, providing some poor unfortunate with shelter at the same time as making a few bob in the bargain." He paused when he saw that he was not convincing Alonso. "Tell you what, you come in with me and be the conscience of the outfit. How's that?"

"I don't know if I have the steel to be a businessman."

"Rubbish," Lincoln said, but not harshly. "You could bring moderate doses of charm and good sense to counter any Scrooge-like excesses that you think I'm likely to have. People are coming up by boat and plane. Women and children are coming to join husbands, sweethearts, parents and..."

"Brothers!" suggested Blossom.

"Thank you, and they are standing at the back of a very long queue for council housing. Let us do our own thing. By helping them, we can help ourselves. Look at it in another light. We owe it to ourselves to convince everybody that we can accept responsibilities even before it's pointed out to us. We can think for ourselves and achieve by our own hard work and planning. There are laws governing landlords and tenants alike. We won't break any laws, Lonso."

"All of what you have said makes sense," said Alonso. "After all it's me who introduced Lurline and Puncie to you. Thank God our women don't have to sit on a chair at the top of the landing to have their hair done. There's now a properly run hairdressing salon for black women. I think I'm right in saying that the hairdressing business is like any other salon in the high street and it's going great guns. I can spot talent, don't you think?"

"And that is only the beginning. Women who work shifts now know they don't have to wait until Saturday or Sunday to get their hair done in somebody else's bedroom. They don't have to sit in corridors or on top of stairs while someone heats a comb on the cooker to press their hair. They can have it done in a spacious, clean salon before going to work or after work. I must say, though, that the weekends are still too crowded. We have to find two more good people who can work weekends, lifting the workload off Lurline and Puncie. We're looking at a place in Camberwell. If we go ahead, Puncie would manage that one. So you see we're providing a service. Would you accuse Gody Myrtle of exploiting our fellow immigrants?"

"You lost me," Alonso said puzzled.

"She has got Nello to fix up the basement, turning it into a nursery. She is planning to look after children when their mothers are out at work at two pounds each per week. Four moms leaving children with her and she will be earning more than London Transport is paying her per week."

"That's a good service, surely," said Blossom.

"Yeah, yeah. I guess I'm just not as keen about the profit motive as you."

"I know you have family back home. Send them the money you make. From my calculation we could pay ourselves about twenty pounds each per week."

"Are you serious? I'm doing well if I take home eleven pounds a week."

"I've never been more serious. You could take home seventeen pounds after National Insurance and income tax. The accountants will sort that out..."

"Accountants?"

"Lonso, do you think I intend to run a Mickey Mouse organisation? This will be a properly run business audited by a qualified accountant. Any money that goes into my pocket will come from what I'm paid. Creole Enterprises will be registered at the Board of Trade."

"The Board of Trade? You'll be selling shares next."

"Why not? It will be a registered company. I want it done right. We start in London, then on to Birmingham, Maudslay, Liverpool and so on. We're not going into business to exploit people but to provide a service that at the moment only racketeer landlords cater for, and they don't give a tu'penny damn about the people they're screwing. Of course we will make money; that's what a well-run business does. Money doesn't inevitably mean expensive cars, as with Jimmy and Melbourne. Neither does it follow that you must have an endless stream of dolly birds. You shouldn't be thinking of exploitation; as someone who frequented the Colonial Club now of blessed memory, you know there was nothing more exploitative than the prices in that place. You could blow a week's wages there in one night! There are two reasons why you won't come in with me."

"Yeah? I'm waiting." Alonso braced himself.

"You feel safe working on the buses. Regular wages. But the days of the prestige of the coloured bus conductor are gone. In 1955 there were a few coloured men working on the buses. It showed you had achieved a high educational standard. You were civil. You were the acceptable face of the new migrants. Nowadays anyone who can correctly subtract fifteen shillings and ten pence halfpenny from one pound can be a bus conductor. It doesn't suit you anymore. Take your case, for instance. You can't even attend evening classes regularly because of the shift-work you do. What time have you for any serious writing? None. Am I right?"

"So far. Now what about the second reason?" he asked, feeling a little uncomfortable.

"This one causes me great concern. I don't want it to ruin our friendship." His eyes appealed to Blossom. "You're probably thinking that you don't want to work for me. Look, before you say anything, can I reiterate that you wouldn't be working for me. You and I will be employed by Creole Enterprises. We would both be directors. At the moment I have all the shares, but if you join me there'd be a redistribution of the company's shares. I won't be your boss. Does this allay your fears?"

"Why me? I would have thought Melbourne Welch or Jimmy Fairfax would be more likely to be your partners. Weren't you talking to Melbourne about this?"

"Yes, I talked to Melbourne, but he's no businessman, even though he took a business course after his demobilisation. If I had his chances I would have made the Colonial into a popular jazz club. He could have had the top US performers visiting London queuing up to appear there. He was in at ground level. He wasted that opportunity. Who comes to the club these days? As Jimmy said, he was under-insured. That's a clear signal that he's going under the financial wave. By the way, Melbourne is out of hospital. He's OK physically, but I don't think he's OK financially."

"I'm not financially robust either. Anyway, there's still Jimmy Fairfax."

"How little you know your acquaintances. Jimmy is a good lieutenant. He would be just the man for the job if I wanted a deputy. He's not an up-front man. If he were he'd have left Melbourne long ago. Apart from that, he seems addicted to the club scene. He's already showing interest in the Black Cherry Club in Clapham. They belong to the age that is, thank God, dying the age which thinks the Coloured man can only succeed as an entertainer. Although he is the equal of any white performer, the best that he can get is a guest appearance. These guys just sit in the waiting room hoping they'll be offered a job. It's not about how patiently you sit in the anteroom. You have to get up and hammer on doors. You got to make a nuisance of yourself "

"Melbourne understands very well the role of men like C.L.R. James, George Padmore, Eric Williams and Kwame Nkrumah. Nation builders! Incidentally, I think he's met all of them."

"You offer Melbourne's knowing these eminent men as evidence of his importance."

"Precisely! Those blokes didn't sit around *Waiting for Godot.* They are shaking things up. They move things. In the last year or so there were openings when Melbourne could have thrown his hat in the ring for a seat in federal politics."

"Federal politics! You don't lower your sights, do you?"

"CLR is back in Port of Spain as party secretary."

"Hold on there. CLR is in a class by himself. Have you read *The Black Jacobins*?"

"No. I haven't read the *Decline and Fall of the Roman Empire,* either. What I mean is Melbourne is interested in politics. Instead of making use of the opportunities to launch himself as the leader of Britain's migrants he just shows up like a model at a photo call and leaves people floundering in a rudderless boat the rest of the time."

"You are mixing your metaphors. Do you guys ever come up for air?" Blossom asked.

"This is why I need your brother in at the start of Creole Enterprises. He can come out of his corner punching and he does not bear you any malice," said Lincoln. "I don't like people who seem to think that if you are not thirty at least then you have no understanding of anything. You are the historian, Lonso. How old was the Younger Pitt when he became Prime Minister?"

"Chancellor of the Exchequer at twenty-three and Prime Minister at the age of twenty-four."

"*'And as to my age I am doing something about that each day.'* I think he was supposed to have said that to someone who thought the country's affairs had been handed over to the care of a boy," Rosita interjected. "Don't look at me like that. Lemuel Reid is Head of History at Wilberforce High School. He's a good teacher. Lincoln, I like your schemes. I wish you well with them."

"Wait a minute," Lincoln said. "Am I looking in the wrong direction? I like a woman of vision."

"We're a team," said Rosita moving to stand by her brother. "I'm old-fashioned where loyalty is concerned. He leads, I follow!"

"I wouldn't dream of coming between you," he said. "However, let me bring you up to date about Creole Enterprises. It has two houses that have been rented out. We're planning to have five by the summer. It has 'Curl up and Dye ladies salon and gentlemen's barber shop'. We are agents for the *Jamaica Island Shield Insurance and Mutual Building Society.* Our vision is to have houses for renting in ever major town where there are Coloured migrants."

"I must hand it to you, Lincoln, you have a cinemascopic vision," laughed Alonso.

"High, wide and in glorious colour. Don't give me your answer today. Talk to your sister, and anybody you think is worth listening to, then talk to me at the Morgans' on Sunday. You know it's Prophet's birthday, don't you? Rosita, you must come and taste Miss Myrtle's chicken."

"I tasted it many times when Lonso boarded at her place. But since I can't cook and my brother's culinary exploits rarely go beyond bacon and beans or corn beef and cabbage, it will be a pleasure to have a square meal.

And Lonso has told me he'll be on late duty, which means I'll be on my lonesome all day. He's promised to take me to Gody Myrtle on Sunday, so I'll see you there."

V

Lincoln left shortly after six that evening. Alonso suspected he had gone to see Enid Swaby.

"He is very ambitious," said Rosita turning on the radio and desperately trying to find Radio Luxembourg. "There is a station here call Sotton. Where the hell might that be?"

"A little to your left of Radio Luxembourg. Steady. That's it. '*Suddenly there is a valley*' I could listen to Jo Stafford warble those notes all day. Back to real life. Yes, our Lincoln Franklin Delano Grant is an ambitious young man. He should be; his father named him after three US presidents."

"You don't like him much, do you?"

"I do. It's just that ever since I first met him, we've never been able to sit down and talk silly talk. He's always very circumspect, very serious. *No childish thought to him was ever pleasing*, if I may interpret Milton."

"Milton. Brother, *he* is serious stuff. What you mean is Lincoln doesn't sit around telling tales about girls. About their legs and their tits..."

"Whatever makes you think I do that sort of thing?" he pretended to be startled.

"Sorry to shock you, but I am of that age, size and shape that seems to entitle me to get a lot of compliments. Some remarks are very flattering, although mostly unwelcome. It's always: '*Hi pretty girl! Yes, look at that!*' They say that when you are walking towards them. '*Look at them jump!*' Their eyes fastened on your bosom, and when you pass them, it's '*Watch that gas tank, see how it shake and the shape of those legs, boy. The girl got a chassis!*' I know the routine by heart," she said and as she flopped into her chair.

"Which part of that routine don't you welcome?"

"There's so much in a person that has to be learnt. You can't feel the goodness in a person with your eyes," she shuffled herself into the chair like a nesting hen. "*Nino*, do you dissect girls like that when they walk past on the street?"

"Honest?"

"You do! *Nino!*" She flung a cushion at him. "I guess I must stop seeing you as my brother. *Nino*, you're just a man. Do you use the same tired routine? Go on tell me, what do you say?"

"I do not shout after girls. I do look. I do admire but I never shout...wait a moment, it happened sort of involuntarily once last summer. I was on a bus somewhere between Norbury and Thornton Heath when this well-groomed young woman got on my bus. She must have been coming from the hairdresser. Her red hair positively glistened like fine gold. She had her back to me, waiting to get off the bus. Suddenly I heard my own voice say 'Redhead.' I didn't intend to say it. It just got out. I think only she heard it. She spun around glared at me and said, 'Don't be personal.' I was embarrassed and ran upstairs."

"That could have got you mutilated in Georgia, USA," she said gravely. "So you like redheads, then?"

"I've never given the matter serious thought, though I have noticed they general have beautifully shaped bodies."

"You have given it serious thought. You admire their chassis! Would you like to go out with one... a white girl I mean, whatever her hair colour?"

"Are you tired of my company already?"

"Horses for courses," she said. "It wouldn't be the same as taking your sister to the pictures."

"I guess not," he said. "I don't think I could stand the stress..."

"Is life with me stressful, then?"

"Of course not! I mean, going out with white girls. I see the way the passengers on my bus look at coloured men and their white women. When I go out with a woman, I want all the men to envy me, all the women to envy her. I don't want both sides hurling insults at my companion. Flowers, you have to see it to believe it. While the atmosphere is 'I wish you would go back to your jungle' when a coloured couple boards the bus, it's charged with hatred at a mixed couple. Sometimes it's women who start the row: *'Slut! You disgrace all decent white women with your behaviour.'* That usually comes from middle-aged women. *'So our boys ain't good enough for you? Filthy whore.'* That's usually from the men. I must say, some of these women with coloured partners are quite spirited, or should I say bold? I once heard one answer the women, *'If decent women are disgraced, what's bothering you? You ain't one of them!'* On another occasion this coloured man's white woman fought back and upset the whole bus by retorting, *'Sure our boys are fair enough,'* she said, *'but not good enough. It's the extra thirty minutes that does it'*. Well, I thought there was going to be a fistfight. A Babel of protest exploded, obscenities most likely from those men who couldn't go the extra thirty minutes and those who were certain they could go the distance. One woman who had bought tickets for a longer journey got off at the next stop with her two young daughters."

Alonso thought it best not to tell his sister about the red-haired girl who had haunted his dream in Ostade Road, and certainly not about the girl in the shop window in Streatham. Those stories would have to wait for another time.

"I cannot believe white people can behave like that!"

"First lesson, little sister: the whites we meet in the colonies are fairly well-educated people who settle at the top of our society. Among other things they taught us cricket. The white people you're likely to meet in your work over here are working-class, who couldn't wait to leave school at fourteen to get a job and start courting, and their national game is football! Girls get married before they pass their mid-twenties or they're considered old maids! The young men all think they're going to be well-paid footballers! Forget the white people you may have met back home, you're not likely to meet any from their strata here. Over here we're appended to the white working class, whose native language is Cockney, so forget everything J.C. Nesfield so authoritatively laid out in *Outline of English Grammar*. I'm not being condescending, and not all migrants have Third-Year Local Examination Certificate or are graduates of good secondary schools. In fact, many are just coming to terms with flush toilets and soft tissue paper. But I'm talking about you and me. For instance, one driver I worked with couldn't understand why I should want to read *Tom Jones* when we don't have electricity in my country and the people still live in trees."

"You're making it up, *Nino!*"

"I am not. Another driver gave me a lesson in the difference of bone structure between coloured and white. Coloured can't swim because they have heavier bones; by the way, he weighed about eighteen stones. He claimed that although there have been black Olympic record-holders such as Jesse Jackson, Herb McKinley and Arthur Wint, there'll be no coloured swimming champions. He further suggested should we jump from the window of the first-floor canteen, head foremost. His skull would be fractured and his brains spattered all over concrete; I might suffer some minor bruises, but my skull is thick enough to withstand the impact on the concrete below."

"*Nino,* you're making it all up," she said.

"I think he was daring me to jump, but I decided to play chicken."

"You should write all this down, *Nino*. You tell a good story, but I'd still like to know about you and girls."

"What about me and girls?"

"Who'd be your favourite girl? What would she be like? Don't mention Dorothy Dandridge or Eartha Kitt again."

"Honest?"

"Honest. Tell me and I'll see if there's one like her among the girls I know."

"You're my favourite girl for now. I want a few more years of bachelordom before complications set in."

"If I'm your favourite girl," she said gravely, "then there'll be more than complications ahead, *Nino*. I mean, I'd have the task of selecting my replacement. That's where complications would set in. Has Lincoln got a girl?"

"A good question."

"Are you going to answer it?"

"Do you know Enid Swaby? Her relatives live at Pretty Tunning."

"I don't know her to speak to. You know us country people, we know about people who live ten... fifteen miles away, not like you Londoners who don't know the names of the people who live in the flat above them... I heard Enid is in London."

"And living at the Morgans', so you'll meet her on Sunday. She's a lovely young woman."

"*Nino!*"

"Shut up! I don't mean it that way. Lincoln got her a room at the Morgans' and is paying court to her. Funny thing, she's supposed to be his cousin Adlyn's best friend, but that cousin lives in Birmingham. Enid didn't go to Birmingham though, instead she asked Lincoln to find her a room in London. It's obvious to someone like me, who adds two and two and get four and a half, that there might have been lots of correspondence between Lincoln and Enid."

"You think he sent for her?"

"That's what is peculiar about our friendship; we don't confide in each other. He hasn't said a word to me."

"Wait a moment. I did meet her about two years ago. She came back to Wilberforce when Miss Wilson, the Headmaster's niece was leaving to study at McGill. They were batch mates, you know. Una Wilson and Enid, I mean. They paraded her around a bit. You know the routine. Old girl made good. She was legal secretary in the office of barrister Elkinson QC, Member of the Senate and who is bound to be a Member of the House of Representatives next time 'round and all that. She's not pretty, pretty, but attractive, and certainly very well dressed. So that is Lincoln's choice!"

"A few weeks ago all hell broke loose. Let me tell you the story. Apparently Enid had fallen for the QC's chauffeur, one Wellesley Young."

"A chauffeur? Couldn't be the same girl. She struck us girls as the young woman who heard that clarion-voice whispering Excelsior!"

"Your middle-class slip is showing, little sister! Anyway I hate that young man in that poem by Longfellow. Fancy ignoring that maiden who invited him to rest his weary head on her breast..."

"Alonsooo!" she said in amazement."

"This chauffeur in question," he said quickly, "was an ex-serviceman who was seriously thinking of coming back to England to continue his study of Law. What Enid did not know was that he already had a wife in England, a former ATS, now a senior nurse who was wondering what was keeping her husband out there in Jamaica. To cut a long story short Enid got pregnant and was naturally expecting marriage, when suddenly a bigger and equally fertile girlfriend turned up and beat the hell out of her. Enid miscarried. When she was better she went back to Pretty Tunning to lick her wounds. I think Lincoln made her an offer she could not very well refuse. She came to London and now has a room at the Morgans. Little did she know that the Morgans' home is a place where if you visit often enough, you are bound to meet everyone who has a passport signed by Hugh Mackintosh Foot! So one Sunday Lincoln and Enid walked in, and guess who the Morgans were entertaining? You have it, Mr and Mrs Young. Well, Enid, like every wronged woman, blew up."

"How awful. *Nino,* don't tell it in that voice. You're mocking and it's too serious for that."

"I don't mean to mock her. I like Enid. However, this episode has definitely brought her and Lincoln closer. I wouldn't be surprised if you're obliged to put by some of your first savings towards getting a nice dress for a summer wedding."

"Do you think that's part of the reason behind Lincoln's hurry to get you to join him in his enterprise? His wanting to have a steady hand at the helm while he is planning his wedding?"

"Could be, but whatever happens, Lincoln will never be far from the centre of things. Lincoln likes power."

"Are you going to say yes? Or does the thought of all that power frighten you?"

"I don't need to ask you what I ought to do. Your mind is made up. It's not that simple for me. I need a steady income. I need a job that gives me time to study. I have obligations, so it follows that I need the security of a sound organisation paying all the dues the government expects. Lincoln's schemes are OK, but it's not a matter of starting a business just like that. Companies must be registered with the Board of Trade. Oh, sister, I don't know if I want all those problems."

"From what he said earlier, I think Lincoln knows about these problems."

"Oh, he does."

"So why are you so unsure?" she asked. "Do you think I will get a job quickly?"

"I thought you were going to go straight into nursing."

"Over the last few weeks I've been thinking. Juanita is coming up fifteen. She's bright. If we could get her up here she could finish school, go to college, get a part-time job when she's old enough.... I don't have all the answers. I think that as you struggled to get me through Wilberforce and now to London, it's my turn to help Neeta. What is there for a girl to do at Guava Flat when she leaves school? I don't want her growing up too fast."

"We never talked about this before."

"No. Oh, God, how do I put this?" She sat up, but avoided his eyes. "You're the world's best brother and son. You did so much for me and Mama. Yet you ignore your five younger siblings."

"I do not," he was on the defensive.

"The money you send Mama does help take care of them, but you don't even know their birthdays. You don't write to them or ask after them. It's not their fault they have Bullah Cameron for a father. They are all our mother's children!"

"Oh, Blossom!"

"You haven't called me that in a long while. Are you angry with me?"

"Of course not. I never meant to hurt the children. I guess Bullah has hurt me in more ways than one. I've always seen the children as his children, but by supporting Mama I know I make it possible to buy them clothes and feed them, and I don't mind in the least. I guess I still haven't got over that beating Bullah gave me."

"Me too!" she said, moving closer to him. "All that is going to make what I have to say difficult and muddled."

"Say it, whatever it is," he encouraged with a squeeze of her hand.

"I don't like Bullah," she began. "I have a plan to help our mother get rid of him..."

"Flowers! That does sound drastic," he said in mock amazement.

"I was about to propose we send for him..."

"You got to be joking! Me stay in the same room with Bullah? I need more time to distance myself from him."

"Listen to my plan. Tell me what you think about it in a month's time. I know he'd jump at the chance of coming to England. With Lincoln's help we could find him a room. We don't even have to see him. Once he gets a job and is working, he might or might not support his family back home. Frankly, I don't care. He'd be out of our mother's life and stop giving her babies. Who knows, he might even find himself another woman over here and forget Guava Flat."

"Where have I heard this story before? Ah, yes, the two women who run Curl and Dye. Their mother was up here. Her husband is a terrible man, so she went back to Jamaica and is rejoicing in the fact that she hasn't got to see him in a hurry."

"So there is merit in my plan, then?"

"If it means I can be reconciled with my young sisters and brother, yes."

"Neeta has written to you. She told me not to give it to you if I thought you'd get vexed."

"Gosh, I don't stand tall in her eyes..."

"Rubbish! You're their hero, but like all heroes you are more than a bit distant from them."

"Does Mama ever talk to you about this?"

"Yes. She thinks you only acknowledge me, not the others. She thinks you're still unhappy about her having taken up with Bullah, that he's beneath us, you think she's a bad woman..."

"Gees! What have I done? It's not in my nature to hate. How could she think I would consider her a bad woman?" He got up and walked towards the door leading to the corridor. Rosita went after him and put her hands around his neck.

"I love you. Mama loves you. Everybody loves you. You've been working since you left school. It's because of you I was able to go to secondary school. You've been supporting your mother. Don't be hard on yourself."

"Neeta's letter, where is it?"

"You'll read it?"

"Do you think I'd tear it up?"

Her unpacked case was on top of the wardrobe. She climbed onto a chair and was about to lift it down when Alonso reached up and relieved her of it. Sitting on the bed beside the case, she opened it, searched in one of the pockets in the lid for the letter and handed it to her brother. He lifted the seal and pulled out a single piece of paper torn from an exercise book. He began reading:

Dear Brother Lonso,

This is from your sister Juanita. I will be fifteen years old in October, and this is the first time I am writing to you. When I knew for sure that Rosita was going to leave for England was the first time that I thought of writing. I felt scared. I guess I was never all that close to you. None of us other children are. Not like Seeta. You see I have a pet name for her too just as you call her Flowers. I am sure you know that there are five of us Camerons. Even I have come around to the idea that five is more than enough.

I was little at the time, but I remember how my father hurt you, and I guess that's what caused you to distance yourself from us. I don't think you knew it, but I was hurt too. Well you know what they say about blood thicker than water, so I am writing to say please take care of my big sister. I know you will continue to be good to our mother. I know that she misses you and now that Seeta is going to leave she is taking it to heart like she will never see you all again. I will try my best to look after her for all of us, so don't worry about her on that score.

I am sure you knew that I passed my First Year Examination last year and this year I will be working hard for my Second. I would like to be a teacher, but that is in the future.

One other reason for writing is for you to get use to my hand writing since it will be me who will be writing to you when Mama want to answer your letters.

God bless you both.
Your Sister Juanita

He finished reading the letter and stood staring at the piece of paper, as if he expected it to become a mirror whereby he could communicate with his sister. He had no idea how long he stood. He became conscious that Rosita had her arms around him.

"You're crying," she said, and she too began to cry.

"Lord, how I must have hurt Mama. She must think I blamed her. Perhaps I do blame her. Had she not taken up with Bullah Cameron the three of us would have been OK. We didn't want anybody else. We could have made it. What did she see in him, anyway?"

"Stop it," she kissed him softly on the cheek where the salty tears had left streaks. "If this is what you really think, then you're not alone. It's what everyone thinks, Gody Ivo, Head teacher Frazer, the Reverend Carr, people who don't dislike her. These are people who really like her, and even me who loves her nearly as much as I love you." She loosened her arms and walked away.

"You love me, your brother, more than you love your mother?" he asked.

"She's my mother, and for that I respect and love her. You are my brother and my best friend. For that I trust and love you. The worst time of my life was the years since you've been away here in England with me out there in Jamaica. I was so lost. You're at once my father, my brother and the great love of my life. Does that shock you?"

"Flattered."

"I said that once to a girlfriend of mine at Wilberforce. She was shocked. She thought I was confessing to incest. She said she could never put her arms around her brother. It sounds as if she was afraid of him. Anyway back to what I was saying. I never could understand what my mother saw in Bullah, but I love my sisters and my little brother. You will too once you get to know them."

"I've paid so little attention to Bullah's children that sometimes they could be distant relations. I can't even remember their birthdays."

"I'll remind you. The next one coming up will be Hector's in July. Look, you have a calendar; I'll write them on it. In descending order of age, not birthdays, first comes Juanita who's fifteen, call her Anita or Neeta. Next comes Hector, he'll be fourteen in July; next is Dona who is twelve and very pretty; and does she know it? Ana is ten and last of all, and I really mean it, is Teresa, who's three. I pray they're not thinking of making any more babies and that Teresa is what Jamaicans call the 'washbelly', for Mama gets thinner and thinner after every birth. Another one and she'll die. Poor Mama. She could have done better. Sometimes I thought he must have raped her and when she found she was pregnant, with that Catholic upbringing, she gave in to him."

"Don't you ever think there's a perverse god Cupid whose fickleness gives him great pleasure in shooting his darts hither and thither?"

"Like you and Winnie," she said.

"I wondered when you'd get around to that. As I explained in my letters to you, I gave her refuge. She was on the run from Lias. By the way, I've since learnt that she's married to an elder or someone important in her church. Good luck to her, I say. As far as our mother is concerned, we dare not take Juanita away from her. She couldn't manage on her own. It might be a blessing if Bullah would want to come to England but Juanita have to stay to help with that brood."

"You may be right. If we agree on sending for Bullah, we'll have to go through Gody Ivo. He has great respect for her. She'd probably tell him she was lending him the money to go to London. That it would be a good way for him to start supporting his family. She spoke to me about leaving our mother to the mercy of Bullah Cameron."

"What is more urgent is to convince Juanita that I don't dislike her and the others because they are Bullah's children. They are my mother's children that cannot be disputed. How do I set about repairing the damage my pride and pig headed behaviour has caused?"

"Just write to her acknowledging the awesome responsibility that has befallen her now that both of us are away. Tell her about the faith and the trust you have in her. How you depend on her to look after everybody, not only Mama. Tell her you love her and hope she loves you too. Promise her that after she passes her Third-Year Exams, you'll pay for her to go to Shortwoods or Mico to become a teacher," said Blossom, as if she was dictating.

"You think it will work?"

"Trust me. Write soon though."

VI

When Alonso called at Lilford Road to collect Blossom on her first Sunday in London, he found the Morgan's front room buzzing with friendly conversation. A smell of over-proof white rum pervaded the atmosphere. All eyes were focused on the television screen where there was a game show. Alonso's eyes were practised at taking in any group of people as if they were the passengers on his bus - those who had paid, those attempting to ride beyond their paid fare, however inadvertently - so now his eyes took in the hosts and visitors; the Morgans, Blossom, Lincoln and Enid, Nello, Miss Vie, Miss Nicey, two young men and a young woman. These last three he did not know.

"Lonso, you want some a this rum your sister brought?"

"Kept back a little flask just for medicinal purposes, you understand," he grinned, "but I could murder a cuppa. It's blowing up wicked out there."

"Well," said Myrtle, "you know where the kitchen is." Before anyone could move she got up and, taking Alonso by the hand, propelled him out of the door towards the kitchen.

"That means trouble," said Isaiah Morgan. "Somebody is going to have his ear bent. It reminds me of the Englishwoman teacher at our school when I was a boy. She would sit at her desk till she spy somebody misbehaving. She would go and grab him by the hand and lead him to the little cupboard by her desk. Everybody would be quiet, listening till we hear the whack, whack of the three-foot ruler she got leaning up beside the cupboard. Ssh, you all listen hard, see if you hear the rolling-pin 'pon Lonso head."

They listened dutifully and, hearing nothing, were about to start talking when Isaiah wrested their attention back. "There's a funny story about that woman, you know," He chuckled. "She took over our school, which was run by the old English parson and his wife. Parson Reverend Cole died at the wheel of their car, which careered off the road into a canefield. Mrs Cole was badly injured and went to hospital in Kingston and later returned home here to England. The new teacher, Miss Blake, came straight from England. Them must have advertised the headmistress post in the paper that English missionaries read. So she came to Chelsea Ridge. The name of the place must have interested her, sounding like Chelsea Bridge, because nothing else did. Cut a long story short. She would sit at her desk and watch the black teachers do all the work. As soon as she see a child doing something wrong she would get up and walk over, hold the culprit by the hand and lead him or her to the little cupboard I told you about. You never heard her voice, just someone bawling out and the whack, whack from that three-foot ruler. She stayed about four years, then her dog Crongy died and she buried him, with a headstone saying: '*Crongy, a terrier, beloved pet of Miss Hilda Blake of Granby in the county of Northampton, England. 1920 to 1924*'. She left money with the new black parson to make sure the grave was looked after. Them say that in 1941, when this country was at war, she did write to the parson and ask him to send her a photograph of the dog's grave."

"Prophet," said Enid laughing, "you tell a good story. Is that dog's grave still there?"

"More to the point, have they renamed the district Crongy's Grave?" asked Lincoln.

"You think is lie me a-tell? Would I lie to you all?" asked Isaiah, grinning into his rum. Anyway if you listen hard you'll hear Lonso getting his knuckles rapped." He looked at Blossom, "You got any idea what you brother been up to?"

"Me? No, sir." She was meeting Isaiah for the first time.

"You all hear that? The girl got good old Jamaican manners and respect. She said, 'No, sir.' Over here everybody is on first name. Once upon a time even the English kids would call you Uncle if you was a friend of their parents, now is Isaiah from the smallest one." He patted Blossom's hand. "It's nice to see that pretty face and good manners still go together. Anyway no fret 'bout you brother. If I know Myrtle she probably just cutting Lonso a piece of that nice black cake, and giving him the chicken leg I had me eye on for later." Almost on cue Alonso returned. He had a small plate in one hand with a piece of cake, in the other a cup of tea. "You see what I mean?" said Isaiah winking at Blossom. "Between these two boys we're being eaten out of house and home." He looked around as if for support. Finding none forthcoming, he said with feigned anxiety, "Oonu look here, you all hurry up and get married so I can come to you house for Sunday dinner." The entire party laughed politely and trailed off into silence with eyes resting on the three young women.

"Don't you all look at me," protested Enid, making to put distance between her and Lincoln.

"Well," said the young woman whose name Alonso had not yet learnt, "I'm getting married next month, and as soon as I settle down you all are invited to us for Sunday dinner."

"And we want to see you all at the wedding," said the older of the two men who were equally unknown to Alonso. "Old time people in Jamaica say that no invitation not needed for nothing apart form wedding. Well we inviting you all..."

"You all look like one family," interrupted the prospective bride, who on closer examination was four of five months pregnant. "So, yes, we'll be glad to see you there. I praise God for how things turn out. Is the Reverend Locksley Hood told us about you, Mrs Morgan. We so pleased you can bake the cake and do the food. We take up a lot of you time and you hospitality, and tomorrow is Monday, so we gwine leave you now." Her two companions rose, the older man assisting her to her feet. Hands were shaken all round before Isaiah Morgan accompanied them down to the front door.

"Lonso," said Nello, "you see me van parked outside, a Vauxhall?" He jangled the keys.

"I notice a blue van as I came along," Alonso said, moving towards the window and looking down at the street below. "What do you want a van for?"

"Feltham is long way from Brixton, man. There's a lot of us working out that way. Eight people me carry out there every day, you know? Don't worry, man, it will soon pay for itself."

"Colonel, don't you know Lonso is a socialist who doesn't believe in making a profit from the labour of fellow workers?" said Lincoln. "Do you know his Spanish surname means worker?"

"Peasant, actually," said Blossom, slightly annoyed, *"de Campesino."*

"What can I say about a man whose names are Lincoln Franklyn Delano Grant? I think his dad expected him to be the first black president of the United States."

"Dream on," said Blossom.

"Delano," said Enid, "you didn't tell me that was one of your names."

"I was born when FDR was waiting to be inaugurated. People were expecting a new era."

"Lucky for you your father wasn't interested in European politics or you could have been named Adolf Schicklgruber."

"What any of this got to do with me van?"

"Too much education," lamented Ziah, who had just returned. "Them all went to Wilberforce High School."

"Not me," interrupted Lonso. "Those three have the same *Alma Mater*. I'm just a poor country school boy like the rest of you."

It is usually easy to tell when a party is over. Old conversations suddenly become stale and new ones start with the slow determination of an opening batsman grimly hanging on for the drawing of stumps. Just as spectators start restlessly packing their hampers and gathering their things, so at a party one can detect the restlessness not only of the visitors but also of the host and hostess. Lincoln and Enid seemed the first to recognise this and left for the privacy of the latter's room. Colonel volunteered to take Alonso and Blossom as far as the corner of Barrington Road and Coldharbour Lane, after which he would turn left and take home Miss Vie and Miss Nicey to their house in Camberwell.

"What were you and Gody Myrtle talking about?" asked Blossom as they walked towards Geneva Road.

"She was encouraging me to show an interest in Lincoln's business. Apparently she's put money into it and would feel happier if I was minding the shop while Lincoln is away in Jamaica."

"What! Lincoln's going back home?"

"You know he worked for Island Shield after leaving school. He made some good contacts here for them. He wants to present them with a plan to represent the company over here. I have some holiday time due. I've agreed to take over till he comes back. Whatever happens, I'm not giving up my job yet."

"It's cold," she said, then as if one thing linked with another, "I got on very well with Enid. She's the sort of girl I would choose for you," she continued poking her elbow into his side.

"Why don't I do a deal with Lincoln? I'll have his girl in exchange for my sister."

She thumped him hard on the back. "You're not getting rid of me that easily. Anyway Lincoln is too full of himself. She can have him."

"The point is, never send a relative to choose a partner for you..."

"I don't know. All Abbey knew you were sweet on Anh Hosang that Chinee gal. Did you know that she's over here studying medicine, at Edinburgh I think."

"Tomorrow," he said trying to kill that conversation, "I take you to the Labour Exchange. A boring office job will take your mind off love and romance. But there again, you might find the man of your choice..." Thump! Another blow to his back.

"I want to get a job for a year before I go into nursing. I probably won't be a Sister before I'm twenty-eight or so. Only then will I think of getting married. Did you see that woman at Gody Myrtle? She was big, big pregnant. Her wedding dress is going to be very large."

"You get yourself into that state, don't expect me to walk down the aisle with you on my arm, even though that is part of giving you away." Thump! Another heavy blow to his back.

"I see we'll have to get to know each other all over again. Whatever gave you the idea that's my priority, a baby then a wedding? In the corner of the empire where we were brought up women have several children and consider themselves well rewarded if in middle age someone made them an offer of marriage. It doesn't follow that every girl from that backwater supports that agenda."

"Are you angry?"

"You guessed right."

"I wasn't accusing you..."

"Predicting is even worse. If sex is the result of going to the cinema with a bloke, then I'll go on my own, unless my brother accompanies me. Do you know that Enid and Lincoln will be keeping their separate rooms until after their wedding?"

"My friend is always one for making it clear that Caesar's wife is beyond suspicion."

"Brother, I love you very much but at times I don't *like* you at all. I'm retreating to my sanctuary and don't care much to hear your voice or snoring for the rest of the night."

20

The estate agent Cass and Cass arranged for Lincoln and Enid to visit 109 Fonthill Avenue, Streatham, at 7.30, a time when husband and wife would not only be home but would have finished their tea. It was at the end of March, and although it was dark enough for drivers to have their sidelights on, daylight had not completely disappeared. The estate agent on Lincoln's insistence told the vendors that he and his bride to be were coloured. It was therefore not surprising that they were met at the door with broad almost genuine smiles. They were ushered into a sitting-room furnished with old pieces that struck Enid as too short in years and quality to be classified as antiques, compared with the more expensive pieces she had been looking at in the furniture stores from Brixton to Peckham and Clapham. She was aware that Britain was moving out of the functional era of the Second World War and the immediate post-war years into a time of richer designs.

They spent the first ten to fifteen minutes in what Lincoln called sparring. Their hosts wanted to know where in the West Indies they were from. Were they married or about to get married? Were they students? Did they find much evidence of colour prejudice? Was it not dreadful what was happening in the United States of America and South Africa? The overture having set the mood for what was to follow, they moved from room to room. Occasionally the husband, who was handy with tools, pointed out some personal triumphs, such as the removal of a chimneybreast, the installation of heaters in every room, and there were the mere trifle of putting up shelves. In the garden, the lawn was about the length of a cricket pitch and had already had its first spring mowing. Shrubs and creepers were planted along all the fences in a deliberate attempt to keep the neighbours' prying eyes firmly on the tops of fast-growing fir trees.

Over the inevitable cups of tea, their hosts expressed a wish that Lincoln and Enid were front-runners among those who wish to buy the house. They allowed them a little time on their own. The vendor and his wife were pleased they wanted to proceed with the purchase of 109 Fonthill Avenue, SW4. The wife, a woman a little over five feet tall, with a build that could be considered plump, volunteered the information that she worked for a large building society and should they have any difficulties in obtaining a mortgage she was sure her firm would facilitate their application.

"What are they, some trendy white liberals?" asked Enid on the drive back to Lilford Road.

"You know what they say? Never look a gift horse in the mouth." During a subsequent visit on a Sunday afternoon, when all the neighbours were either washing their cars or mowing their lawns, the vendors confessed that they had never got on with their neighbours and were pleased to be going back to Ramsgate. They were small-town people who harboured a dislike for the great metropolis. The neighbours had no knowledge that their property was up for sale. They had asked Cass and Cass not to put up a For Sale sign outside the property. They were sure the neighbours would not miss them, neither would they miss their insular neighbours. They were looking forward to small-town life once again. They even promised to send the new owners of 109 Fonthill a card telling them how they settled in, and perhaps they might reply. They said their goodbyes, clasping each other firmly by the hand.

II

On the first Sunday after Lincoln received the keys for 109 Fonthill Avenue he and Enid decided it was time to show off what was to be their new home to their friends. He swung his maroon Rover 90 into the drive, allowing Colonel enough room to park his van in front of the gate. While Lincoln unlocked the front door, Alonso gallantly opened the rear passenger door of the Rover to let out Enid, Blossom and Myrtle Morgan. On the street Colonel, Isaiah Morgan, Miss Vie and Miss Nicey paused by the van to survey the street and nodded their approval. It was quiet; there were no small boys kicking football, the pavements were even and clean and apart from the suds produced as residents washed their cars there was nothing to disturb the most road-proud citizen.

"When the rubbish truck come to collect the garbage and any piece of paper is left behind, I bet somebody is bound to phone the council and complain," Myrtle whispered to Enid and Blossom.

The group from Colonel's vehicle was talking loudly as they brought up the rear of the party of nine. Alonso lingered by the door, so all went in ahead of him. He took another glance up and down the street. The car washing and the gardening on either side of 109 Fonthill and those houses in front of it were suspended, all eyes trained on number 109. He closed the door behind him, but said nothing to the rest of the party.

The visitors inspected the house, walking from room to room, their footsteps echoing on the carpetless floor. They voiced compliments to Enid and Lincoln. When they reached the upstairs front room Ziah Morgan suddenly pulled from his overcoat pocket a bottle of J. Wray and Nephew white rum and unscrewed the top. Viola Mackenzie stood on one leg, rested her very large handbag on her raised knee and extracted some glasses.

"To absent friends!" said Isaiah Morgan, tipping some of the rum onto the floorboards.

"Amen!" said Colonel "Nello" Walters.

"Oonu fool, fool, eh!" said Myrtle Morgan with a hiss of her teeth followed by laughter from the rest. "Oonu think that English duppy gwine pay any notice to all that superposition?"

"So all that dilly-dallying in the kitchen this morning was because you was stuffing glasses in you bag?" Eunice Mackenzie asked her sister. "But see me crosses! I bet is Colonel put you up to it."

There were only six glasses, but Miss Nicey, Myrtle, Blossom and Enid declined a drink. Alonso was standing by the window looking out of the curtainless window. He turned as Colonel nudged him and handed him a drink.

"To Lincoln and Enid, may you both be happy here," said Isaiah

"Lincoln and Enid," they all said in unison.

"Come look here," Alonso called to the party. "The natives are getting restless."

From the window they could see several groups of varying numbers of men and women and some children talking in an agitated manner. All eyes were trained on number 109. Across the road a short balding man with shirtsleeves rolled up above his elbows had to be physically restrained by two women and a young man.

"Dirty Nigger bastards. We're not having any of this!" the little bald man said, and those who sought to restrain him managed to pull, push and drag him into the house opposite. The council of war that had been convened further down the road seemed to have come to a decision. Two men, a stocky young man and a tall willowy middle-aged man, walked ahead of a delegation that was making its way towards number 109.

"Is what them want, war?" asked Colonel.

Lincoln and Alonso led the party downstairs. From the front room they could see that the main delegation had halted on the pavement outside while the stocky young man and the middle-aged man walked up to the front door.

"Come with me, Lonso," said Lincoln, "the rest of you stay back..."

"No, man," said Colonel, "you can't leave me out of this."

"You are in reserve," said Lincoln, "you'll know when to come in. Keep your eyes peeled."

There was a knock at the door. The two young men went forward and opened it.

"Can we help you?" asked Lincoln.

"We are representatives of the Residents Association," began the older man.

"Aah! an organisation I am looking forward to joining," Lincoln interrupted quickly.

This momentarily threw the delegates. Their recovery, however, was quick.

"The residents object in the strongest possible terms to you people moving into this street."

"We intend to make sure you don't move into this house," the stocky young man interrupted.

"May I ask how you're going to accomplish that?"

"If we have to drag you out of here kicking and screaming..."

"Any kicking and screaming not gwine come from we," said Colonel, elbowing his way between Lincoln and Alonso.

"Cool it!" said Lincoln, grabbing Colonel by the coat and pulling him back from the two delegates, who were retreating at the sudden emergence of the belligerent Colonel. "These two gentlemen are here under a flag of truce. We will accord them every courtesy..."

"So who talk about dragging out kicking and screaming?" demanded Colonel.

"An unfortunate slip of the tongue," said the older delegate. "What he meant is that we will use every means at our disposal to prevent you taking over this property."

"And what might those be?" asked Lincoln

"We will make an offer significantly higher than what the vendor is asking..."

"But there's no vendor," said Lincoln. "This is my property and I'm not selling. Now go back to the law-abiding residents of Fonthill Avenue with this message: I do not intend to be stoned out, burnt out, nor dragged out kicking and screaming, not by you or your organisation, the British Union of Fascists. I am a British subject or, as the 1948 Nationality Act puts it, *Civis Britannicus Sum*. This house is my castle and it's my right, nay, my duty as a British subject to defend it."

"It's in *your* interest to discourage your friends from coming on to this property," said Alonso pointing to two men who had ventured a yard or so into the drive. "One of the men behind me" he motioned to Nello, "was 'Jersey' Joe Walcott's sparing partner," he could see however, from the look on both their faces they had heard of the American heavyweight, although Alonso himself could not think why he had settled on 'Jersey' Joe. Metaphorically speaking, he decided to throw a powerful right jab, and it seemed to be working.

"Nello here knocked out and crippled a rising young contender, and he was just another sparring partner. You don't want to tangle with him."

The middle-aged man fell for it; he held up his arm as a signal for the intruders to halt. His reddened face showed signs of panic.

"Now I suggest you leave. We are within our rights, and you are standing on our property. It's you who are causing an affray. Now I ask you again to leave..."

Alonso was interrupted by the bells of a police car racing up the venue. Two policemen came out the vehicle and were immediately surrounded by yelling, angry citizens of Fonthill Avenue. It was a considerable time before one of the officers could enter the drive. Some of the demonstrators fell in behind. He turned around with both arms raised to chest level, palms turned towards the intruders, he moved towards them and they stepped back onto the pavement. Satisfied with his competence at crowd-control he continued up the drive to where Lincoln and Alonso were confronting the two men from the Residents' Association.

"What seems to be the problem?" asked the officer, looking at the two delegates.

"There was a knock at the door," said Lincoln, "so we came to answer it, only to find these two gentlemen standing here..."

"Perhaps you might ask them what is their mission..." Alonso intervened.

"One at a time," said the officer, dismissing Alonso but still looking at the white men. "I suppose you have permission to be in this house, sir?" he asked Lincoln, his eyes finally coming to rest on the owner of 109 Fonthill Avenue.

"Not mere permission, officer," said Lincoln. "I and my friends have a right to be here. This is my property, and I have a hefty mortgage to prove it."

"Officer," said Alonso impatiently, "we have caused no breach of the peace. The problem lies with these two and those at the gate."

"You have a lot to say for yourself, sir," he said to Alonso.

"I do," Alonso insisted, "that's my right as a British subject. *Civis Britannicus Sum...*"

"And a lawyer too, I bet..." the policeman began, still refusing to look at Alonso.

"He threatened us, that he did," one of the delegates said.

"What kind of threat might that be, sir?" the police officer asked the middle-aged delegate, switching his eyes back to the white men.

"A heavyweight boxer," was the reply.

"He threatened you with a boxer?"

"Yes. That one. The stocky one," he pointed to Colonel.

"Only after he threatened to drag us off our own property," said Lincoln.

"And why would you want to do that, sir?"

"We're English," said the younger delegate. "We're only trying to protect our interests, our wives and our kids. You let these kind of people into a nice quiet street like this and soon it's overrun with twenty of them living in the house. Look how many of them there are! The value of our property will go down. We'll be forced to sell. Other coloureds will move in and this lovely street will be a ghetto before you know it. It's happened in Brixton. We're English and we have rights."

"So have we!" insisted Alonso.

"Of course, you have, and we're here to see them enforced. However, if as this gentleman says the property is his, then it's you who are trespassing. If he has broken the law, then I'll take appropriate action. I suggest you go and talk to my colleague at the gate. I want to have a word with these folks," he motioned to Lincoln and Alonso to precede him into the house. Once inside he took the names and addresses of all nine, and satisfied himself that Lincoln was the new owner of number 109 Fonthill Avenue and was merely showing off his home to his friends.

"There was some practical jobs to be done like the measuring of floors for carpets and of windows for curtains. I hope to be in residence within a fortnight's time," Lincoln explained.

"All nine of you?"

"Yes," said Alonso haughtily.

"Of course not," said Lincoln, a bit too eager to please. "We," he said, his right hand extended towards Enid, "are getting married soon. This incident has thrown all of us all," he smiled at Enid then at the police officer.

"May I point out that you are not helping," the officer said to Alonso. After about ten minutes, assured there was nothing he could arrest any of the nine for, he left. His colleague appeared to have succeeded in getting the residents to return to their homes. From their vantage points the curtains were in constant motion as if a whirlwind was raging in every lounge along Fonthill Avenue.

As soon as the police officer left all nine began talking at the same time. They were shouting at each other, then they fell silent as Enid started to cry.

"Listen," said Alonso, "last September nine coloured teenagers in Little Rock, Arkansas, stood up to a whole city of hostile people. We're not going to back down. Tomorrow Lincoln and I will go and see Claudia Jones. She knows people. We have right on our side. We have to stand our ground or else we'll have to live only in the old houses vacated by the white man."

"I can't live here," pleaded Enid. "How can I, with all those hateful people out there? I don't want to live my life to prove a point..." she directed her anger at Alonso.

"But don't you see? We coloured people are forced to prove a point all the days of our life," insisted Alonso.

"Lonso, do you really think I could spend a night on my own in this house? Didn't you see the hate in those people's eyes?"

"Enid, I've had some rough times working on the buses, but there was never a time when there wasn't a passenger ready to stand up in my corner. Think about it. Someone telephoned the police. Whoever it was didn't do it because they thought we were in the wrong."

"That still not enough," said Myrtle Morgan. "You said this woman who run the paper could talk to people in high places. What sort of help can they offer?"

234

"Talk!" said Colonel, dismissing the idea. "Talking not going to put in a broken pane of glass."

"What you suggest?" asked Lincoln. "We start throwing bricks? That would be just what they expect. We're going to settle this because this is where I intend to live for the foreseeable future. Once they see we don't fit their stereotype, they'll back down."

"By which time half the avenue will have moved out," said Colonel.

"And more coloureds moving in. I remember that when my brother got his place in Maudslay, the neighbours push shit in a' envelope down the letter box..."

"Prophet, is lie you a tell!" exclaimed Blossom in her Jamaican accent, surprising everyone.

"No, me dear," said Myrtle Morgan, "but then he added to the problem by marrying a white woman. Is true that now they are settled in good, but time was when things was like a war. So let's go hear what this woman can do to help."

"Yes," said Lincoln, "the sooner the better."

"You putting you fate in this one woman?" said Colonel with great scepticism.

"Claudia Jones has been fighting racial bigotry from the 1930s when she graduated from Wadleigh High School, Harlem. When she became too hot to handle the mighty United States deported her to London," Alonso tried to impress his companions.

"She knows people like Paul Robeson, Learie Constantine, David Pitt and all the MPs who support coloureds like us," added Lincoln.

"Well," said Vi Mackenzie, "them say is not what you know, is who you know. Whatever you do, it got to be quick because like Enid me gone off this place."

"By the way, champ," said Lincoln said, trying to bring some levity to the situation, "how come you never spar with Joe Louis?"

"Ask me manager," Said Nello.

"A matter of credibility," said Alonso. "If I had said the Brown Bomber, they would guess I am lying, but come down a bit from the top and they think you might be telling the truth."

"Never mind all that," said Ziah Morgan, "we have more pressing business ahead."

III

This incident took place on a Sunday. The next day Lincoln tried to contact Claudia. In fact, they were unable to see her before the middle of the week, during which time three distinct events had occurred. On the Monday when Lincoln and Alonso returned to 109 Fonthill Avenue they found a "Keep

Britain White" sign painted on the wall outside the drive. When they opened the front door there was a card on the coconut doormat. It read simply: *"Welcome to your new home. We hope that in the colonies we taught strength of character. Best wishes from three of your new neighbours."*

"One thing is clear," said Alonso, "none of these three painted *'KBW'* sign on your wall. The old British desire to see fair play is alive and living somewhere in Fonthill Avenue. What did I say about someone being there to shout his disapproval?"

The third event was an article in the mid-week edition of the *South London Citizen*:

FONTHILL AVENUE PETITION TO MP
West Indians' take-over bid, say residents

Twenty residents of Fonthill Avenue, one of Streatham's 'quietest and most conservative avenues', by their own description, have delivered a petition to their MP seeking his help to prevent what they fear will be a take-over by West Indians of their avenue. The householders say the take-over is facilitated by the Rent Act, which frees many of the houses from control. West Indians by living in apparent unlimited numbers to a house are able to raise and repay the sum necessary to buy any house that becomes unoccupied, says the petition.

"In the near future, owing to the decontrol of many houses in this area, owners of single-tenant occupied houses will no doubt try to capitalise on their property, creating a situation in favour of the immigrants, many of whom are prepared to live in over-crowded and unhygienic conditions. The householders think the result will be to drive English owner-occupiers to sell at a loss to get away from the area. The only people likely to buy the houses will be further groups of West Indians," adds the petition.

The residents want to ask these questions of their MP:

> Why were immigrants allowed to enter this country in large numbers when housing is in short supply?
> Why were the working and professional classes not consulted when it was obvious they would be the people to suffer under this invasion?
> What has happened to the LCC's powers to ensure a minimum living space and decent sanitary conditions?

The petition adds: "Here it seems we may well have a repetition of what has happened in Brixton, and the Rent Act, contrary to intentions, will help those immigrants to create further slum areas.

The possibility of imminent eviction of the old-established population under the Rent Act, followed by the taking over of the property by colonial immigrants with resultant discomfort for those who remain, will cause serious disturbance. A source close to the Residents Action Committee commented on the frustration they are experiencing:

> "Legally there can be no control over entry of West Indians into this country. Nevertheless, they are seriously overcrowding many of the houses, which they somehow seem able to get possession of in this and neighbouring boroughs. The LCC has no power to intervene but the borough council has powers to prevent overcrowding beyond the limit of ten persons in a room. The trend nowadays among white citizens is to limit family size to three or four children. We agree with those who say there ought to be control over the entry of coloured immigrants. We acknowledge that some of our coloured colonials played a valuable part in helping us to win the war, but that is now history. However, the contribution of a few does not give the right to hordes of ignorant and socially backward people to enter our country unimpeded. They are crowding us out of the workplace, where they are prepared to undercut our decent standard of living with their willingness to work for less pay. They are ruining our streets by overcrowding into every room in a house. They are threatening the future of our children by the low standard of their lifestyle. The disgraceful behaviour of some of our lower-class women does not help the situation. The inability of the Parties in the House of Commons to see things from our point of view forces us to take things in our own hands and even to seek the help of more radical parties."

The *Citizen* has learnt that the British Union of Fascists is active in the area, and two evenings ago Fonthill Avenue residents had leaflets from that organisation dropped through their letterboxes. However, some residents agree with the *Citizen* that the ugliest side to this matter is the painting of the swastika and *Keep Britain White* (*KBW*) signs on the wall outside number 109 Fonthill Avenue.

IV

A delegation of Lincoln, Enid, Alonso and Blossom went to see Claudia Jones at her flat in Meadow Road, near Kennington Oval cricket ground. She had been ill and away from the *Gazette's* office at 250 Brixton Road when Lincoln and Alonso had called earlier in the week. They had spoken briefly to two young reporters. One was an East Indian, whose West Indian accent meant he was probably from Trinidad or British Guiana. He wore a tweed jacket with elbow patches, reminding Alonso of the caricature of an English schoolmaster. The other was a black Jamaican, his accent clearly identifiable. He wore a brown bomber-jacket. They assured Lincoln and Alonso that a message would be passed on to Claudia and if she was better she would surely want to see them. When Lincoln telephoned later that day the Jamaican reporter said Claudia would see them at her flat.

The door was opened by Bomber-Jacket, who flattened himself against the wall as they trooped past. "First room on the right," he said.

There was hardly any need for direction, as Claudia was standing at the entrance of the front room. She had a sunshine of a smile as she held out her right hand in welcome.

"Lincoln, it's always a pleasure to see you, my dear."

Lincoln introduced Enid as a friend, then turned to Alonso and Blossom. Claudia recognised Alonso as someone she had met but whose name she could not recall. They entered the room to the sound of Shostakovich's 'The Song of the Forests' issuing from a radiogram which was almost hidden by books and magazines. Alonso counted at least three titles by Joseph Stalin. The young man in the bomber-jacket who was working close by leaned over and reduced the volume, turning the sound into musical wallpaper. Claudia waved them all to seats. Bomber-Jacket twisted himself around and handed her the *Citizen*, then turned back to the typed pages he was proofreading. He became so engrossed in what he was doing that it was as if he had faded from their presence.

"I've already made some phone calls. All MPs on the Anglo-Caribbean Association are furious. Someone will ask a question in the House. I suggest we write to the chairman of this residents' association asking that we be allowed to address their next meeting. What do you think?"

"I've rejected the suggestion that we should march down Fonthill Avenue. I want the residents to know that I too want to be a proud house-owner."

"It hasn't escaped us that the previous owner used Lincoln to get back at his neighbours with whom he didn't get on. You could, if it wasn't so serious, have a good laugh," suggested Alonso.

"You haven't heard the most recent twist in this tale. A colleague of mine on a 'national' tried to trace this couple. They haven't moved to Ramsgate, Kent. Would you like to guess where they are?" she asked, still smiling. "They are living in Ramsgate, somewhere on the Indian Ocean coastline between Durban and East London..."

"But that's in South Africa!" said Blossom.

"You're pulling my leg," said Lincoln when the closed-mouthed silence was finally broken.

"My source is reliable," Claudia insisted. "'The *Chronicle-Recorder*' will have a story on it in a day or two. Of course, it might not be news then. It will depend how these people decide to play it."

"Incredible," said Alonso, shaking his head in disbelief.

"I wonder what their neighbours in their new exclusive white area would say if they knew that he had sold his property here in London to a coloured man?" asked Lincoln.

"Perhaps not much," said Claudia. "The Afrikaners might be in power, but it's the English ex-patriots who keep them there. This case is not unique. I propose we draft a letter; drop by the office tomorrow and see if you approve of its contents. I have a meeting with Marcus and Fenner at the House on Friday; would you like to come?" she addressed this to Lincoln. He looked around at his companions; Claudia explained that only one person could accompany her. It had to be Lincoln.

The delegation stayed for another hour or so, during which time while getting to know one another Blossom was able to explain that from next Monday she would start working for the British Caribbean Association. Of course, she had no idea what her duties would be, but she wondered if the Anglo-Caribbean Association was an allied organisation. Claudia told her that she had often spoken at meetings sponsored by the British Caribbean Association.

Next day Lincoln called to pick up the letter:

R.J. Vellensky,
Chairman Residents Association,
Fonthill Avenue, Streatham, S.W.2

Dear Mr Vellensky,

My legal advisers have instructed me that the criteria for joining the Residents' Association of Fonthill Avenue are that I should be a resident and that I should pay the annual subscription of half a crown.
I am sure you are in no doubt that I am the owner 109 Fonthill. I shall be in residence by the end of next week. I enclose my subscription as per postal order. I now expect to be invited to all future meetings, which of course, includes the one scheduled for next Tuesday, at which our Member of Parliament will address the residents. I shall be accompanied by an adviser.
My postal address is of course, 109 Fonthill Avenue, Streatham, but should you wish to contact me urgently you may ring either of these two numbers: my solicitors Wilkes, Wilkinson and Wilson of Brixton Road or the West Indian Gazette, also of Brixton Road.

Yours sincerely,
Lincoln F. D. Grant

Lincoln was not surprised that with the time available Claudia had been able to identify the Chairman of the Residents' Association to know of the proposed meeting at which the Member of Parliament would be in attendance. The solicitors, having moved from the razed building that housed the Colonial Club, had found temporary offices in Brixton Road at the corner of Burton Road. Lincoln signed the letter and hurried to the post office in Acre Lane determined to catch the last post. He was hoping to have a reply before the end of the week.

Lincoln spent most of Friday up to midday at 109 Fonthill with the workmen laying the carpet. He left shortly before one o'clock to accompany Claudia to the House of Commons to meet with sympathetic Members of Parliament. He returned to Fonthill Avenue with Colonel and Miss Nicey at about eight o'clock with the curtains and found an envelope that had been dropped through the letterbox. It was short and to the point:

Dear Mr Grant,

I regret to inform you that the Residents' Association has taken the democratic decision to disband itself at an extraordinary meeting held last night. It was called as a matter of urgency and every effort was made to notify you, but we could not obtain any reply from either of the numbers you gave us.
We are, therefore, returning your subscription fee.

Yours,
R. J. Vellensky

"Well, well, what do you know?" asked Lincoln.

"What happen?" asked Colonel. "A win we win?"

"It ain't necessarily so," Lincoln said. "This is just to stop me attending the meeting. As a fully paid-up member I couldn't be legally excluded from the meeting. They just couldn't cope with the tone of my letter. They know they weren't dealing with a lot of hotheads who were going to meet them stick for stick and stone for stone."

"Like me?" asked Colonel. "Man, some guys who work with me over Feltham way, when I tell them what a-gwon last Sunday, them was ready to come up here and bruk a few skull."

"What good would that do, apart from getting us in the papers? Like we is troublemakers. Tcho, some of you people think with you fists. Lincoln used his brain and them back down. Now them going to watch you good. Them will be listening out for loud music and whole pile of coloured people spilling out on the pavement swearing and chatting loud 'pon the top of them voice. But I tell them, they can wait till Satan wear him overcoat because hell turn cold. Is nearly two years Lincoln living with me and we never hear his radio," said Miss Nicey.

"I must get a telephone in this place," said Lincoln impatiently. "As soon as we finish here I have to go to see Claudia. I'd like her to help me get an appointment with my new MP. She was good enough to introduce me to some very understanding and influential Members of Parliament."

21

Winnie Price sat at the table reading:

> *Let him kiss me with the kisses of his mouth for*
> *Thy love is better than wine*
> *I am black, but comely.*
> *Look not upon me because I am black,*
> *Because the sun hath looked upon me...*

She wiped her cheeks. She had promised herself that she would not cry. She did not want him to return and see her with reddened eyes. He had been good to her ever since she came to Maudslay. But she had not forgotten Alonso. She could not. She remembered the night he read to her from the *Song of Solomon* in the little red-covered Bible he said he had bought for two shillings and six pence in the Brixton branch of Woolworth's. She could still hear his voice reciting the lines: "*Thy two breasts are like young roes that are twins, which feed among the lilies.."*

She remembered how hotly she contested that the Holy Bible would never have such lines. Now that she had read *Songs* she could not recall hearing a preacher refer to that book. She recalled that he had said that if it was left to modern Christians that book would be censored. Indeed she would not want Brother Brown, as she addressed her husband, to return and find her reading *Songs of Solomon*. Was it not the same King of Israel with hundreds of wives and concubines? She continued reading but was prepared to find a Psalm before anyone could get from the front door to the dining room. A loud knocking at the door interrupted her reading. She tried to ease her bulk out of the chair. It was not easy now that she was more than eight months pregnant. She called out, "I'm coming. Hold your horses." After a slow waddle, she opened the door to a tall middle-aged fair-skinned man. "Brother Brown, you forget you keys again? You back quick."

"Brother Ralph give me a lift. How you been?" Gladstone Brown asked with sincerity, as he took off his hat and began wiping his feet on the mat in one compulsive action.

"I think this baby going to grow up playing football, the way him kick. You know anything 'bout football? Wait! Give me you hand." She placed the stiffening reluctant hand against her belly. "You feel it? Wham! Bam!"

The man pulled his hand away, more embarrassed than excited, and began to disengage himself from his overcoat, hanging it up in a small alcove leading off the hallway. "I'm hungry, you see," he said, as he headed towards the bathroom first with quick steps.

"The food will be on the table in a minute," she said, laying a place for one. "I hope you don't mind but I had mine an hour ago. I just couldn't wait."

"I understand," the man said. "After all, is not you alone now. You can't control how you feel these days," said Gladstone, coming back downstairs from the first-floor bathroom. He sat at the dining-room table and begun to serve himself. Having piled his plate he began eating and kept his head down for five or six minutes. He took on the stance of an opening batsman, head held rigidly forward down the line, determined to play himself in. When he raised his head, his hands moved in a practised motion towards the glass of ice-cold carrot juice. He drank long. "Nice," he said. "You're a good woman. You look after a man just right."

She moved towards him. "You are the most kindly man I know," she said. "You're a good husband and going to be a good father."

He reached out and pulled her gently towards him. She was surprised when he leant his head against her belly. Suddenly he jerked his head away. "Eh! Him nearly split me eardrum with him kickin'." He laughed then resumed eating his meal.

"How did the meeting go?" she asked.

"Is why you don't ask what you mean? You mean to ask if *him* was there? The answer is yes. Lincoln Grant and Alonso Campbell, but them look like two little boys. Them hardly start to shave yet, but them can talk. Lincoln is the stocky one and Alonso is tall, slim and brown-skin, right? Anyway them talk good and them not 'fraid to answer question, and there was a lot of question. Them was straight with people, that is what I like. In the end I take one of the forms them were giving out. Tomorrow we read it again and sign it and send it off to Island Shield office in Jamaica."

"So you think it make sense..."

"It always make sense to save," he cut in quickly. "It's who a-mind your money that give me anxiety. I know something about Island Shield, because is only when I was coming up here two years ago that I draw the whole lot of me saving from them to pay my fare. I been meaning to start saving again, but with buying this house and paying compensation to that woman..." he broke off.

"I know," she said stroking his head and sighing. "And now you got me instead."

"The difference is that you no hurt me. I know about your situation," he said. "I talk to the Elder about you. I talk to your cousin. I know that in you the Lord is working his purpose out. Sometimes we have to face great hardships and perplexities before the Lord work his will. Nothing can compare with his dealings with Job and Hosea. His blessings will flow. Just give it time. I know the baby you is carrying is not my own seed, but I know what we have done is right. This child will be a blessing, you wait and see."

"I will honour my vows. There is no kinder man than you in all the universe," she said. Tears rolled down her cheeks.

"No start that. Tcho!" He pushed his plate away. "I get meself into big trouble with one woman who treat me like dirt. I tell you the story over and over. I spent three years in the States doing farm work and sent every cent I could spare to the woman I was planning to marry. When I came out she was already married for a year and they use my money to buy house in Kingston and furnish it. I get mad and smash up the place and them sue me. I was lucky I didn't go to prison. Is the church that rescue me. I pay them money for smashing up things that me money bought in the first place. But God never abandon me. He was harsh to Hosea in the beginning but in the end..."

Breaking off, he reached for the Bible, which Winnie had left on the table. He hurried through its pages with well-practised fingers. Holding it close to his face he read Hosea, chapter 14, verses 8 and 9:

> *I have heard him, and observed him. I am like a green fir tree. From me is thy fruit found. Who is wise, and he shall understand these things? Prudent, and he shall know them? For the ways of the Lord are right, and the just shall walk in them...*

He closed the Holy Book, got up and assisted his pregnant wife to her feet. They moved slowly up the stairs.

There was movement on the second floor and a man's voice boomed down, "Brother Brown, Sister Brown, me and Sister Vicky having a season of prayer in about ten minutes, you coming?"

"Yes, Elder Bogle," said Winnie, gripping her husband's arm tighter, as they climbed the stairs.

22

If e'er I tread the highways of the world,
'Twill be for thee, my country! For thy name
I am most zealous; unto thee I owe
All the imaginings of beauty sown
Deep in my soul, and unto thee I bring
What thou has given.

From *Daphne* by J.E.Clare Mc Farlane, 1929

"In a recent Private Member's Bill twelve Labour Party Members of Parliament, led by Mr Fenner Brockway had stood up to their convictions", began Alonso determined to lay down the topic for discussion..."

"What's that you are reading?" Asquith interrupted Alonso with a world weariness tone not because he was weary of yet another editorial on race, but because it was something he ought to have picked up on and he had missed it.

"*The West Indian Gazette or WIG* for short!" said Alonso," one of those fly by night rag as you often dismiss publications of the left." He hurled the paper at Asquith before he had finished wriggling to find the most comfortable position on his chair as a family pet would before selecting down in the most advantageous spot on the rug. The Bajan was well known for reading only the 'TIMES' and the FINANCIAL TIMES and should those august journals be struck from existence then he would condescend to buy a copy of the TELEGRAPH and should that mysterious bug continue in Fleet Street then it would not matter since life as Asquith understood it would have ceased to exist.

Asquith, Warren and Alonso left Kennington College of Law and Commerce discussing the recent effort by the nation's legislators to make illegal discrimination against anyone on the grounds of colour, race and religion in the United Kingdom of Great Britain and Northern Ireland.

"Fenner and his eleven, if nothing else, were prepared to stand up and be counted," said Alonso continued. Recalling the recent problem at 109 Fonthill Avenue he wondered if those Labour Members of Parliament had been influenced by Claudia Jones.

"Sometimes I wonder why we've become wards of the Labour Party, why that party alone accepts us as their responsibility. I bet the leadership regrets that. It's bound to cost them the next election."

"There was a time after the war when the Tories were almost paternalistic, speaking about the white man's burden while Labour was losing the decaying inner cities because of their sympathetic utterings towards us," said Warren.

"Of course, Labour will lose. We move into the decaying heartland of the towns and cities. These were the only places we could find accommodation and work. Coincidentally they were also Labour strongholds. The traditional Labour voters move out to the new towns, cutting Labour's majority. The stage is set for the Fascists to come in and scare those who didn't head for the landscaped green playing fields and modern leisure centres. They tell them they're going to have a nigger for a neighbour, and your party has a marginal seat. What then?" Asquith's Barbadian accent never lifted his speech to the Jamaican's level of excitability. "Anyway if the Bill has done anything, it's given us a working definition of what discrimination is. If I'm not mistaken it goes something like this: '... a person exercises discrimination where he refuses, withholds from or denies to any other person facilities or advantages on the grounds of colour, race or religion of that other person'."

"All this is about public places, not private dwellings with a room for rent," said Alonso.

"But of course," said Asquith. "That would bring the 'buck nigger', to quote an eminent MP, too close to the daughters of Shem. Remember the famous TV debate a few months ago?"

"Why is it when the subject of race is discussed we always reach the point where coloured men are lusting after white women?" asked Alonso.

"You blokes are trying your damnedest to depress me, but you won't. I'm in a good frame of mind... the joys of spring and all that. Come, I'll buy you both a couple of jars. Go find us a table." So saying, Warren headed towards the bar.

Minutes later Alonso watched as Warren, clasping three pints, expertly picked his way between tables to reach them. He lowered the glasses to the table without disturbing the foam that capped them he instructed the other two, "Raise your glasses to the absent friend, Wellesley!"

"I haven't seen that bastard since his wife threw him out," said Asquith.

"Where did you hear that?" asked Warren. "Listen to me and take heed. The differences between man and wife aren't the same as the Cold War, you know! Iris and Wellesley have been married for over ten years. Their emotions run deep. The long and the short of it is that they have up sticks and gone to Canada..."

"Canada!" spluttered Asquith. "Didn't anyone tell them it's north of the Promised Land and touches the North Pole? It's like the Children of Israel ending up in Afghanistan instead of Canaan."

"I take it you don't like Canada," said Alonso.

"Apparently Iris was investigating going there for some time and in a gesture of reconciliation Wellesley has joined her. She has a job in a hospital in Ottawa and he hopes to get into law school."

"Ottawa!" shrieked Asquith. "Who the hell goes to Ottawa apart from politicians and diplomats it being the capital? If you got to go to Canada, then go to Toronto, Montreal, Quebec City or even Halifax in Nova Scotia, but Ottawa... Jeeschrist, man!"

"You know what? For a bloke from a fucking small island, one hundred and sixty-six square miles, you're fast running out of countries to like," said Warren.

"Perhaps Asquith just don't like Canada and Afghanistan."

"Did I ever tell you blokes that when I was coming to England I overheard a quarrel between a Jamaican and a Bajan..."

"Was this the time you stowed away?" Asquith could not pass up the chance.

"I only came to England once from the West Indies. Well, these two were going hammer and tongs, the Jamaican getting the worst of the argument. He suddenly pulled himself up and said, 'Tcho, man, you from a small island. If I stand in the middle I could piss right round it.' That shut up the Bajan."

"Not this Bajan," said Asquith, opening a packet of cigarettes and offering one to Warren. "You still abstaining?" he asked Alonso, who nodded. He replaced the pack in his jacket pocket. "I recall that you said you're in a good mood."

"Yes," replied Warren, "and it has nothing to do with the migration of Wellesley and his family. Three things have gone well for me this week. I've landed a contract with Toilers Home Furnishing to deliver goods to their customers, and since coloured people are buying houses through the estate agent Cass and Cass and furnishing from Toilers I might have to buy another van and take on another driver. Then my little blond blue-eyed son has gone and passed his eleven-plus and has been accepted at Peckham Grammar. And, last but not least, I've got a place to do a part-time Law degree at Lewisham Poly. Life is good, don't you think?"

"Good for you," said Alonso. "Your blue-eyed son is your wife's son from her previous marriage, right?"

"Why ask when you know the answer? We were out the other day and he called me *Dad,* the little blighter. He did it on purpose, since from he was a toddler he call me *'Uncle When'*. You should see the looks everybody gave us. But things will change, it got to or we are doomed."

"My paternal grandfather's grandfather was a Scotsman from Glasgow. As an overseer of a slave estate, God knows how many children he fathered. On my maternal side we have Maya and Hidalgo blood. Mixed race is not a post-war phenomenon."

"I married a white woman not because of status; it's brought me none. I didn't marry her to prove any fucking point. I married my wife because I fell in love with her, plain and simple. I won't tell you the problems we've faced, the prejudices that would have ruined almost any alliance you care to mention. I'd recommend it only to those who are in love, and even then they'll need something else. Whatever that is, they've got to have it. Anything less and it's bound to fail. I hope you understand," said Warren in a serious tone.

"Come on, man, don't put on your undertaker's face," said Asquith. "Last year I live with a white woman. I tell you, man, the pressure got to me. I couldn't cope with the remarks people threw at us, and not white people alone. I don't know if some of the black people were jealous or just downright prejudice. They would suck their teeth; turn their heads to hide their smiles. Sometimes they were openly hostile. It comes a time I just could not walk down the street with her, so in the end we split up. Last time I saw her she was with a Jamaican. They seem to be happy enough."

"Well," said Warren, trying to regain a pleasant posture, "everybody to his own. I said I was buying tonight. Drink up. The same again?" He went off once again towards the bar.

"Warren is a nice guy. I like him. Did you have to go through that minefield?"

"Minefield my arse. Race is the big issue today. We were just talking about Fenner Brockway's bill." Asquith's nostrils became a twin exhaust for exhaling his cigarette smoke. He looked at Alonso with wry amusement. "Look, man, haven't you ever... how shall I put it? Yes, you Jamaicans say *rudeness*. You never *rudeness* a white woman?"

"What the hell!" Alonso was taken by surprise. "What that got to do with anything?"

"Well, have you?" he shook his head and laughed. "You haven't, have you?"

"You make it sound like the most desirable of outcomes," Alonso said, burning with an inner rage he could not quite explain. Was he outraged that he had allowed someone to peep through a chink in his armour, or was it because he lacked some sort of perverse ambition? "What, have I failed grade one of the black man's aspiration?"

"I think you should?"

"Should what?"

"Fuck a white woman."

"This is a big thing with you, isn't it?"

"You must do it, man. I tell you, the first time I did it, the next day was the first time I really looked a white man in the eyes."

"Amazing! You had settled the score of three hundred years of slavery, colonialism and being the hewers of wood and the drawers of water? Has any one woman really got that power? Did she scream in a moment of coital ecstasy, 'Yes, black boy, the debt is paid! You've been avenged!'"

"I didn't rationalise it, apart from the fact that everything *he* did to me, *he* said was to protect *his* women folk. Now the wolf had entered the fold."

"So honour has been satisfied! Hooray! I am naive! I've always thought the geography of all women is the same. Everything *is* where it ought to be, and during the sex act most people close their eyes, so I never thought of it as an act of vengeance or a vendetta. I once overheard an old woman back home warning her son, *'If you know what you woman look like, no light fire at night to see her face,'* or as the Middle Ages writer said, *"When the candles are out all cats are grey."*"

"That's deep, man. Very deep."

"So what you *are* saying *is* that*, 'It is a trend universally observed that a black man with some prospect must be in need of a white woman!'"*

"You bastard! How do you think up these things?" asked Asquith through clenched teeth? "I will get you for this, but at the moment let's lighten up a bit. Warren's coming back."

They watched Warren, hands held at shoulder height, pick his way through to their table and lower three frothing glasses in front of them.

"Will you be taking over Lincoln's Creole Enterprises next? Or will it be a merger?" Alonso asked, as if he and Asquith were discussing economics of the new black entrepreneur.

"I should have gone into the housing business years ago," he said, distributing the drinks. "No," he said. "Good luck to Creole. Live and let live, I say. I'll allow Lincoln to make his million. Strange how the prejudice of councillors and councils have given him a chance to make money. If only there wasn't this policy of not renting flats in high-rise property to black people. Drink up, guys. I promise myself that when I return to Jamaica it will be to be called to the Bar. Perhaps I'll be the first stowaway on a banana boat to return with such honour. From now on I want to settle down to some serious studying. I wonder how long before I can take silk?"

"One step at a time. It takes a patient man to ride a donkey," said Alonso, moving his hands up and down to indicate calm. "I too have a place at Lewisham Polytechnic. I'm going to do a Language degree course. So this is goodbye to the Horns. It's the dissolution of the Round Table. Wellesley has gone to Ottawa, Asquith going on to Holborn to do his LLB, and you and me going to Lewisham. Oh, by the way, do you know that the Morgan twins have got places at Peckham Grammar too?"

"No," said Warren. "However, you know that the girls' school is on a different site from the boys'? You want to know what's going to be fun? At the best of time teachers can't tell coloured pupils apart and the Morgan girls they are identical. I can't tell one from the other. Can you?"

"Well, I have known them for over five years, don't forget."

"Talking about getting coloured children into good schools, that's when you see racism at its most foul. There was a little Bajan boy at the same primary school as our James. This boy got top marks, the best for his class. He had his interview the week before James. The boy's father said the headmaster was amazed at how bright the boy was. *'You people don't usually get such high grades!'* But the father got a letter the day before James had his interview saying that the school had its full intake and there were no more places left. James went for his interview; his grades were nowhere as good as good as the little Bajan, yet he got in. How do you account for that?"

"Easy, my dear Watson. Your stepson is white!"

"Do you think I should have protested?"

"And ruin James's chances?"

"That's what I thought. How easy it is to feed into the system... don't rock the boat and all that shit."

"Did you go with James to the interview?"

"No, his mother did."

"She's white, beautiful and intelligent. Why are you surprised?"

"I'm not... just annoyed."

"What you think will happen to the little Bajan?" asked Asquith.

"He'll end up in one of these new Comprehensives. Their aim is equal standard of education for all, but they're just continuing the two-tier system: Grammar and Secondary Modern. You bet your last bob on it, the coloured kids will be in the Secondary Modern school! I'm worried about my little Lillie-Beth. She won't have it as easy as her brother James or blonde sister Helen."

II

"So you little sister let you out for good behaviour?" asked Lurline. She brought down the headpiece of the drier over the customer's head and patted her shoulder reassuringly. She turned to Alonso. "Puncie was cussing you stink all over the weekend."

"Where is she?" he looked around, thinking she might be in the next room ready to pounce.

"She not here," she said. "That's why she was so cheesed off with you. She miss you... we both miss you these days; since that sister of yours come, we ain't see you much. Anyway, Puncie in Jamaica now. She called me today. She gone to bring up the children, mine and hers. We got to act now because them going to close the door to England soon and people won't be able to come here any more. You know, like what America been doing from long, long time, well, it's England's turn now. So we getting them up before the door is slammed in we face." Lurline checked that the customer under the drier was comfortable, then turned back to Alonso. "Puncie was vexed, you see!"

"Why?" he inquired.

"Me no know. Perhaps she just wanted to give you a goodbye present."

"Good," he said. "Perhaps she left it with you to give me."

"Boy, you really facy y'know! You're really forward. And all this is because you sister gone to stay with Enid at the White House."

"White House?"

"Yes. Isn't that where the President live, and all those high-powered discussion take place? No look at me like that. I heard that last week there was a cocktail party and all sort of Very Important People were there. High Commissioner, MPs and yourself."

"Oh, that!"

"Me not jealous, you know. You ever hear any black people in Brixton or Camberwell giving cocktail reception? While you people was having cocktail me and Puncie was having oxtail," she laughed. "Anyway, I must watch me Ps and Qs in front of you these days. Don't stare at me like that. You playing fool to catch wise?" She had got her scissors out and started tidying around the side of his head. "Everybody know you supposed to be minding the shop while the boss man back in Jamaica," she ended her tonsorial duties and patted his cheeks with a bit more force than necessary.

"Just you remember that," he said in mock firmness. "I can come and have a nightcap with you, then. Of course, we could discuss the state of the business. Oh, by the way, that cocktail party was a *West Indian Gazette* reception. The editor wanted to impress politicians and businessmen that this paper is the voice of black migrants. I think it was a good move. I'm sure the curtains twitched and the Fonthill Avenue residents couldn't but be impressed when they saw the Commissioner's Armstrong-Siddeley with its CD badge and all those taxis dropping off important-looking guests at number 109. The waiters were in uniform, how do you beat that? I know for a fact that since then some people who used to be stone-faced have managed a smile at visitors to Lincoln's place."

"See what I mean? He has the name of a president, that make you Secretary of State Dulles."

"That's an insult! Me, as John Foster Dulles? You gwine pay for this! I'm coming to see you tonight."

"After you tuck your sister in? No bloody fear. I'll be cuddling my pillow and fast asleep."

"Can you lay off this sister business? It's beginning to bug me."

"Is tease me teasing. Still, when she and Enid come in here is like them is visiting royalty."

"Blossom and Enid?" he asked. "Surely not. I let you into a secret: they are scared of you both, especially Puncie. Don't let this high school stuff go to your head. Wilberforce High School is not even in the top twenty secondary schools in Jamaica. If they'd gone to Our Lady, The Virgin Mother, that would be a different thing."

"I don't think it make so much difference," she said looking anxiously at her customer, "Them still have that look of innocence, you know what I mean? That perpetual virgin look. Them still believe the white people story about don't give in till the honeymoon night. Knights on shining armour and all that shit."

"Oh, dear," he sighed. "This is getting into deep waters and I'm not a good swimmer. Let's change the subject. Anyway it's time for me to get back to the garage for the last part of my shift. I'll see you later. Before you say it, make me say it for you. I will be calling in at Fonthill Avenue after work. It's near the garage and I generally call in for something to eat. Not to tuck my sister in, or Enid for that matter, but as far as you are concerned I will be dropping in for a nightcap and if you want I might even tuck you in."

"Drop dead!" she said, pushing him towards the door. "Get out of here before I do you a mischief..." She waved a pair of scissors menacingly as the glass-panelled door closed behind him. He made a funny face from the pavement, and she with her back to the customer, cupped her hands around her mouth and moved her lips knowing that he could lip-read her reply. "Fuck off!"

III

By the time he reached Fonthill Avenue it was nearly ten o'clock and Lincoln had already telephoned. He was still in the United States at his father's home in New Jersey. He hoped to be in Jamaica early the following week to keep his appointment with Island Shield Insurance Company.

Both young women tried to persuade Alonso to spend the night. Blossom pointed out that since she was sleeping in the master bedroom with Enid there was a spare room available. In fact the house had four bedrooms, so he could have had his pick from three rooms. He said he was due to start work before nine o'clock the next morning and needed to change his clothes, though Blossom pointed out that there was enough time for him to get home, change and get to the garage on time. After all, she and Enid had to be in their respective offices in the centre of London by nine a.m.

"Let him be, Blossom," said Enid, "can't you see that he has a date!"

"But it's gone eleven at night!" she said.

"Blossom," admonished Enid, "I see I'll have to talk to you, seriously."

A frown came over Blossom's face. It was difficult to know whether she was a little put out for being naive or if it was the thought of being temporarily separated from her brother.

"It's well past our bedtime," she said. "Don't let us detain you."

They did not. Once he had turned off Fonthill Avenue, he broke into a sprint and caught a number 59A bus at the lights at the corner of Christchurch Road and Brixton Hill and hopped on. The old conductor recognised his uniform and nodded. The bus would accept passengers going as far as the Oval, then it would switch off the internal lights and turn into Camberwell New Road, which was off its assigned route. From there it would drive fast to Camberwell garage. As a member of staff Alonso realised that this was the quickest way he could get to Camberwell Green at that time of the night. From there it should take less that ten minutes to get to Lurline's place in Caspian Road.

"Go easy on that bell," said Lurline when she opened the door. "I have a frustrated old bitch on the first floor who complains if you turn over at night and the bedspring creak. I bet she see you coming in. I could swear she is a spy that me stepfather plant here."

"You still worried about you stepfather?" he asked, putting an arm around her waist. "And you have the nerve to tease me about my sister. At least I can say that as big brother I have to try and convince her that big brother is behaving himself as he expects her to behave herself."

"So," she said slapping his hand, "right now she is unbuttoning some guy shirt front and touching what no concern her." She allowed him to continue to unbutton her pyjama blouse.

"As we say in Jamaica, 'what the eye no see, the heart no le'p'."

"Wait till a see her," Lurline's voice was softer, almost nervous. "I gwine tell her how you come down to me yard and rudeness me."

"Rudeness you," his voice trailed off into her ear, her neck and between her breasts, all smelling of talc. "Rudeness you all night."

The spring dawn struggled through the curtains like a yawning child. There was the faint ghost-like tapping of rain on the windowpane. The lovers turned to each other, frightened by the intensity of their passion, and relaxed as if the rhythm of their movement was part of a vast orchestra. His mind wandered in the passion of an opera, voice against voice, voices against music. Who was listening? This was the tragic death scene and as the blood sang through his veins he felt heaving movements fade into a series of shudderings and then lifelessness. Then he felt the inescapable urge to plunge deeper and deeper until the darkness encompassed him.

"We won't be able to have times like last night when the children come up, you know," she said as they waited at the stop for the number 35 bus outside Keats House on the Walworth Road.

"I got to start behaving like a mother of three. I know Puncie is worried sick about her daughter Darlene. Mama write to say that she getting interested in boys; well, she going on fourteen, and at that age Puncie herself was very flighty. It's one thing that me and she can play with you, but when this pretty fourteen-year-old start to wet herself over you, things gwine get a lot complicated."

"Who says it's going to be me? It could be the guy upstairs or somebody she'll meet at the cinema. You are aware that the age of consent is sixteen. For the next two years she is prison bait to any man who try it on."

"It's the same in Jamaica. I tell you, Puncie started consenting from she was twelve. That was before me and I'm two years older than her. It's going to be difficult for her to start insisting that Darlene obeys the law."

"Are you saying Darlene is having sex?"

"That's what Mama thinks. She is worried that her breast quite suddenly gotten big. It's worrying to cope with a girl changing from child to woman. My own feeling is that Mama wants to get rid of the responsibility of looking after this young girl. It's best that she come to her mother."

"So both of you going to be model parents."

"What me is saying is that our threesome cannot go on. There's no way we could control Darlene if she knew what her mother and auntie getting up to. Come to think of it my first girl, Linda, is going on ten and I don't know if Darlene has been influencing her."

"I get the distinct feeling I'm being given the heave-oh."

"Me not saying never, but we got to be careful. It's not that you're living on your own and I could come over when I feel like it. Whether I like it or not I'll have three kids to look after. Believe me, Puncie's going to have her hands full with her one daughter. I got to be there for hers and mine. It going to be tough... Look, there's a thirty-five coming."

23

Lincoln returned to London at the end of April. He was extremely pleased with himself, with good reason. Island Shield Insurance and Building Society of Jamaica had appointed him their agent in Britain. His father, who had resided in New Jersey in the United States of America since the 1930s, had played the role of absentee parent with great style. His interest in his son had appeared like peaks on an otherwise flat land. Lincoln's life had been dotted with presents on rare occasions: a bicycle for his sixteenth birthday; a few dollars sent infrequently at Christmas, Easter and other birthdays, occasionally accompanied by a photograph of Grant Senior posing besides his latest motor car. This outward show of affluence confirmed that Grant Senior was doing very well as a senior employee of a Coloured People's Insurance Company in the United States. Now Lincoln's business acumen had renewed the father's interest in him. His confidence in Lincoln manifested itself in the eventual appointment of him as agent of his firm for Great Britain. He had even agreed with his son to jointly develop a housing project at Iron Mango Tree, some twelve miles east of Jamaica's capital city, close enough to Kingston for residents to commute. Lincoln returned to London to find that Creole Enterprises had exchanged contracts for a house in Peckham and another in the Birmingham district of Handsworth. He was satisfied with Alonso's work. Above all he had returned with just less than two months before his approaching marriage to Enid Swaby.

"He came back by plane," said Blossom to her brother, "or so he said. I think it was Cloud Nine." They were walking towards the Morgans' place in Lilford Road. "Things are going his way, and I wish him well. Enid said she wants a small wedding, but no woman ever really wants a small wedding. I think it's going to be a big event. I can't wait to see eyes pop along Fonthill Avenue," Blossom said with authoritative wisdom. "Eh, what's the matter?" Alonso had pulled up limping.

"It's that pain in my right ankle," he said, wincing. "Actually it's my heel. It's easing off now." She held his arm and pulled him up straight.

"Put your arm around my shoulder and lean on me. I think it's time you had that heel seen to. It used to bother you a great deal when we were kids. At the time we thought that a cricket ball might have given you a hairline fracture. Come on, lean on me."

"What will people say?"

"Anyone who knows us will say he has his arms around his sister's shoulder. You shy to put your arms around me in public?" She smiled. "Oh, I see!"

"What do you see?"

"Enid was saying the other day that brothers usually become shy of their sisters when they start getting involved with girls. They discover a woman's body and suddenly realise that their sisters are the same under that dress."

"Enid said that? You two should write a book."

"She said that fathers are the same with daughters too. As soon as their daughters approach puberty they withdraw from them. Some become terrified at even touching them. You're the nearest thing I've had to a father..."

"I'm only four years older than you..."

"Three, to be exact. You've never been scared of me. At least I never felt it before. However, of late I am feeling a draught, like a window is not quite closed. Have you got a girlfriend?"

"No. It could be that you have a boyfriend."

"If ever I am interested in a young man, you would be the first to know. That is even before he gets the message that I am interested. I have told you before, my mission for the next ten years is to help you take care of our mother and our younger siblings. You must make up your mind, of course, but for me love and romance definitely has been postponed. I have taken vows of chastity, poverty and obedience to my obligations." When he said nothing, she said, "We are almost there. Look! Your fan club is out to greet you. Now they'll want to know why you have your arm around my shoulder." She looked up to the top of the steps and shouted at the two girls, "Hi, Christine, hi, Catherine. He has a pain in his ankle. Can you two go get a stretcher?"

"Stretcher?" asked one of the Morgans' twin daughters, Blossom could not be certain which.

"Did he sprain it?" the other asked Blossom.

"You can talk to me, Catherine. It's my heel that's hurting not my brains," he said.

"You went to kick him in the shin and he got it in the ankle," Christine accused Blossom.

"I'm not the villain here," said Blossom. "I've been virtually lifting him since Loughborough Road. Here, come give a hand. One of you to his right, the other to his left. I better warn you that he is suddenly very shy of girls. Two thirteen–year-olds helping him might be too bad for his image."

The girls immediately pounced on Alonso and escorted him into the house, where their mother, who was halfway down the stairs hands akimbo, demanded if they had finished their chores.

"Yes, Mama," declared Catherine.

"Look, Mama," said Christine, "Alonso hurt his foot real bad, and Blossom had to carry him from way up the street."

"Lonso," said Myrtle Morgan, "I been nagging you to check out that foot. You know what Jamaican people say about hard-ears pickney."

"Aunty Myrtle," said Blossom, "no pay him any mind. It's sympathy he is looking and his devoted fans will see that he gets it." Blossom laughed.

Myrtle nodded her head in agreement. She turned and started up the stairs. They followed her to the front room where Enid and Lincoln were sitting close to each other talking. The twins looked at the couple on the sofa, looked at each other and started humming the wedding march.

"Shoo," said Myrtle Morgan to her daughters, "that is big people affair. Go and dry up the dishes and put them away. Move! Do it before Miss Nicey and Miss Vie get here with Irone." The girls walked towards the kitchen. "I hear that you and Irone were at school together," Myrtle continued, now looking at Blossom. "Guess you'll be happy to meet each other again."

"Guesso," said Blossom; she did not say that she had not told Irone she was coming to London. Likewise Irone must have known she was coming here to join her mother, grandmother and grand-aunt but neither had confided in the other; an indication of their trust in each other. She thought that she would greet her former classmate with the old classic, "Snap! Fancy meeting you here!" That would leave Irone with, "Fancy that! Small world indeed!" Blossom was roused from her reverie by her brother's voice.

"Don't be too hard on the girls, Gody Myrtle."

"Eh, eh, is who tell you that them paying me any mind? By the way, a watching you and me washbelly pickney, them. One of them having a crush on you is bad enough, but is the two of them that is after you."

"Gody Myrtle, they are babies!" protested Alonso. "What am I? A cradle snatcher?"

"Baby!" exclaimed Myrtle, "you look at them recently? The pickney them just pop up in the three years that I left them with their two bigger sisters. Lord me God, me and Ziah never sent for them a moment too soon."

"Well," began Blossom, "they not too tall, neither are they fat, so when you say that they pop up, you must be thinking of the size of their busts," said Blossom. "People always think that they can read young girls' character by looking at their breasts. It just isn't fair."

"All women pickney been through that, my dear. Nothing new in that. I'm not accusing my own children of any rudeness. Their sisters, Monica and Lou-Lou would wring their necks if they dared put a foot out of line, though neither of them have any children yet. They are very strict. Monica's husband, Cleveland is high up in the Civil Service. He was her boss when she first join' the Service," Myrtle could not avoid a dash of maternal pride. "As for Lou-Lou, well, she's a schoolteacher and has that look that can freeze you blood. No, sweetheart, I'm not accusing them of any bad doings. It is just that as I look 'pon these two I know it's time that they be with their mother and father. While we're talking about little girls, have you seen

Puncie's daughter Darlene? I don't like putting my mouth on people's children, but I can't wait to see how Puncie going to handle that little madam. Before you say it, Blossom, it got nothing to do with her breasts..."

"Good," said Blossom trying not to be too serious, "because somebody once say that if the idea was that there should be a lust-free world, then a woman is a major design fault."

"Come again?" said Lincoln, sitting bolt upright in his seat. "Which professor of human physiology did you get that from?"

"I don't know what you talked about when you were at Wilberforce, I rather think that the conversation topics have changed among the senior boys since your days."

"My class was only five years ahead of yours. You make me sound ancient."

"I'm glad we decided to take the twins from Wilberforce. It seems that a lot of big people talk take place at that school. I don't like how so many of you Wilberforce people all surround me. There are three of you in this room; two out in the kitchen and soon Miss Vie granddaughter will join us. I tell you, I get the feeling that we being over-run by people from that damn school," she laughed, as Alonso stood by her in an exaggerated show of solidarity.

"We will fight them on the beaches we will fight 'em in the streets. We will never surrender!" His attempt at imitating Sir Winston Churchill's famous exhortation to his country during the darkest days of the Second World War was hardly recognisable.

" Fun and joke aside, Puncie will have to be careful with *that one* Miss Darlene. Yes, missus, I tell you, *that one* has serious problem with her attitude," she went to the door; looked to make certain that the twins were still in the kitchen and not eavesdropping. "You-all see how she dress in those shorts that they call pedal-pushers? Well, it so tight that you can see every vein on her backside. I don't think Puncie can deal with her. Back home somebody, whether it be her mother, father, grandfather or grandmother, drop some licks on her backside to straighten her out but you can't do that over here. Like Ziah been saying all the time, this country is for animals and children. You don't see how dogs hold them head high when them trotting across the street in London? In Jamaica dog hold down them head. You shout 'bruck kitchen!' and them gone at top speed." She clapped her hands and pointed to show speed and direction. "Over here dogs look 'pon you as if them own you." Myrtle demonstrated the actions of English and Jamaican dogs, to the amusement of all. "As to children, well, a woman we know from back home, now living in Lewisham, was going to hit her daughter because she is so cheeky. Want to know what the pickney say? 'Go on, you lay a finger on me and I go straight to the police station, and they'll have you for abusing me. You'll end up in prison. This ain't Jamaica, you know?' I tell Ziah that if it was me I would box her teeth down her throat and make them put me in prison and see what would happen to her when they take her off to the children's home. Somebody tell me what them mean by abuse. I know people in Jamaica who drop licks on them children, but them would not abuse them flesh and blood."

"She threaten her own mother?" asked Enid. "Back home you accept licks as part of growing up. I was fifteen when I got my last beating from my grandmother. I was up from town for the summer holidays and was talking to a cousin; I didn't know she was pregnant, but my grandmother did and was furious that I was talking to this girl who had disgraced the family. Another girl said my grandmother went on as if she thought pregnancy was catching. She talked too loud and Mammy heard her. Well, she marched the girl out of her yard and start to beat me, just like that."

"You felt the pain," Myrtle consoled, "but it was you cheeky friend she was really beating."

"I didn't see it like that. I was too big to cry and was ashamed because I was humiliated before my companions. The next time I was up from Kingston my grandmother tell me, 'That facie one Miss Girlie a-breed. So it seem that it catching after all!' Malicious gossips have a saying that at Pretty Tunning if a girl reach seventeen and she isn't in the family way it's because she's a member of the Bible Church of God or there's something wrong with her tubes, or as they say it 'chubes'." They all laughed.

"I won't have you all talking about my two friends using these terrible examples. I'll have you know that Catherine is going to be an archaeologist and..."

"Where did she get the idea from?" asked the puzzled mother.

"From me," admitted Alonso. "It must have been about six years ago. They came into my room at your place in Penn Street. I was reading Agatha Christie's *Murder in Mesopotamia*. It's about an archaeological dig. I remember Catherine going to the dictionary and looking up the word."

"What I tell you, this man has been leading me pickney them astray from long time," said Myrtle laughing. "They must have been eight at the time."

"Nine, I think."

"Christine wants to be a doctor," said Enid. "Don't tell me she put a bandage on your finger and that gave her the idea to study medicine?"

"As a matter of fact..." Alonso got no further as his sister leapt on him.

"Enough!" she shouted, holding a cushion over his face. "You spend too much time with that friend of yours, Warren. You seem to have a story for every situation."

"Them say the children's homes are full of half-caste children. These black men them breeding one white woman and then move on to another one," said Myrtle, trying to bring the conversation back to young women and their behaviour.

"I think we'll have to change the lyrics from, 'brown-skin gal, stay home and mind baby' to 'white-skin gal, stay home and mind baby'," Enid said.

"'My father sowed the idea of me, it was my mother who fathered me','" quoted Blossom.

"Only that they are not staying home and minding their children. The Social putting these half-caste kids in children's homes," said Myrtle.

"Lincoln," began Alonso, "have you noticed that all of a sudden the finger is pointing at us?"

"Not at me, man," said Lincoln. "I have no skeletons in my cupboard. I'm soon to be a happily married man."

"I'm glad to hear it," said Enid, hooking her arm through his.

"The coloured men in this town are crazy, you know, Aunty Myrtle!" Blossom startled everyone, since all eyes were now on Enid and Lincoln. "Everywhere you turn there is one ready to chat you up. The other day I was coming from work when one came into the tube and plunked himself down next to where I was sitting and start to chat me up. Honestly, Aunty Myrtle, you should have seen him. He was well into his forties and his sweat was as strong as *Tacku ram,* as they say in Jamaica," she waved her hand in front of her nostrils as if the smell still offended her. "He started to tell me that he had a good job and the next time he got a throw of partner he was going to buy a house, he wanted to settle down. Miss Myrtle, this man was old enough to be my father, and he was getting ready to propose. I was vexed, you see. Suddenly an idea came into my head. *Que decias? ?De que habla vd?* It took him completely by surprise. He looked at me, then he sucked his teeth, 'Damn foreigner. I don't like Africans, you know. Always talking in their language. Got to admit it, though, this one not bad-looking.' I wanted to laugh but I couldn't let him know I understood what he was saying. 'Still, African is African and me can't stand them.' He got off at the next station. As he was about to leave the car, I said, *No puedo soporarte.* He turned and smiled at me as if to say, 'Sorry you're an African, it's not your fault.'"

"He smiled at you, although you told him that you could not *stand him*?" her brother explained to the non-Spanish speakers and at the same time rebuked his sister.

"What bothered me is how anybody could mistake you for an African," said Myrtle Morgan.

"Miss Myrtle, don't be like that. Not all light-skinned coloured people come from the West Indies and America, you know," rebuked Enid. "And not all Africans have tribal scars, either. Blossom could pass for a Cape Coloured or an Egyptian."

"I worked with a man in the post office for six months before I knew he was African," said Lincoln. "I couldn't place his accent, but then I can't place many Caribbean accents. I'm fairly confident of Jamaican and Barbadian accents, after that it's pure speculation. Anyway this guy turned out to be a Cape Coloured."

There was a polite knock at the door and two heads swung around the half-opened door.

"It's the front-door bell."

"I think Miss Nicey and her sister are here," said Christine.

"You think!" repeated Myrtle to both girls. "Stop thinking and go and open the door and see who it is."

"You go," said Catherine, coming fully into the room and closing the door on Christine.

"No!" said Christine, opening the door and pulling Catherine back into the corridor "You go, just in case there's a blackheart man at the door."

"You see my crosses?" said Myrtle Morgan leaping to her feet. "The two of you go and open the door. Then the blackheart man will get you both. Problem solved and put an end to me going grey before my time." There was a scream followed by a clattering of feet as the girls raced downstairs. "Talk to them, Lonso. They'll listen to you. Now tell me where they hear all this foolishness about blackheart men, because I haven't heard about it since I was a little girl living at Guinea Fowl Walk. Lord me God, we work our finger to the bone. We out in the snow and the cold to get money to send then to good school and they come up to England talking 'bout blackheart men. Is where they get it from though?"

"You know the saying Gody Myrtle, 'you can get them out of Jamaica, but you can't get Jamaica out of them'. All that is part of our culture, and they must not forget it."

"Lonso!" Myrtle shrieked, "Stop putting whole load a foolishness in me pickney them head."

"We were telling duppy stories the other day," said Enid, "when Blossom said that she was never afraid of duppies but she was afraid of blackheart men who drove around Jamaica kidnapping little children and cutting out their hearts and their livers. So now you know who to blame this time. It is hard for me to admit but it's the sister this time and not the brother."

"It may be a good thing that little girls should believe in such phenomena as black-hearted men" Blossom defended herself.

"It's true, Gody Myrtle," Enid explained. "If you read the papers there are a lot of black-hearted men living in this country only they don't call them that. To be truthful some of these men are not only black in their hearts, but black on the outside too. Did you read *The Citizen* last Friday? Well, it had a story on page five with the headline: *SCHOOLGIRLS WENT TO COLOURED MAN'S ROOM.* It was about two white girls who went to a coloured man's room. He claimed that they went to listen to his records but their parents and the police thought otherwise."

"You see what I mean about the law and children in this country! I bet he didn't drag them in his room. Back home their parents would beat their backside until they couldn't sit down. Then tell them that what go *sweet nanny goat gwine to run her belly*, but over here..." Myrtle shook her head in frustration.

"That guy faces twelve months in the slammer. Hope he thinks it was worth it," said Lincoln.

"Knocking off two white girls in an afternoon. I hear of guys who would go to the gallows for that," said Alonso.

"You know what, I hope when him get sentenced him hear that the girls are both up the spout," Myrtle Morgan's gesture was as if she was cracking a whip.

"Miss Myrtle!" exclaimed both Blossom and Enid in unison.

"Don't worry, things over here are not like back home. Look at Irone, she is twenty and her mother is about thirty-four. Over here young girls in the family way just stick them head into the gas oven and..." She never got to finish the sentence as Colonel knocked and pushed the door leading in Miss Nicey, Miss Vie, Irone with Catherine and Christine jostling not to be the last through the door.

"I know that you women just hitching to get down to wedding plans," said Colonel, "so what about us men removing ourselves to the Knatchbull Arms for a pint? Tell Ziah where we gone when he come from work."

"When he comes from work," said Myrtle squaring up to Nello Walters, her hands akimbo, "he is going to wash and change and sit down to his dinner. Him not going to any pub tonight. Him going to eat his dinner, you hear me? Not drink it."

"You sure you want to go through this?" Asked Nello, looking at Lincoln. "Boy, come with me. I buy you a drink because quite soon you free paper bu'n. Boy, it gwine harder than prison." They all laughed.

"But what a jailer," said Lincoln, stooping to kiss Enid on the cheek, to an accompanying barrage of embarrassing giggles from the twins. The men headed towards the door.

"Since them burnt down the Colonial, the Knatchbull has become their new church. I reckon both Ziah and Nello must be deacons there now," said Myrtle Morgan in resignation.

"In that case my brother will have found himself a niche as the devil's advocate," added Blossom.

"A man must have a local," said Nello leading Lincoln and Alonso out of the room. "It's no use going to the Rosemary Branch or the Prince of Denmark because they make it abundantly clear that they don't welcome coloured people there. I won't go as far as to say that the landlord of the Knatchbull would want me getting too close to his wife or his daughters, but at least he don't draw you a pint in a dirty glass like they do when black people go into the Admiral Nelson. I think the landlord of the Knatchbull was quick to notice that coloured drinkers don't nurse one pint all evening like some of his regular white customers. We don't like to linger till our beers go flat. We get through a few pints and that is the name of the game. Ennit."

"What about his wife and daughters?" asked Alonso mischievously.

"What about them?" Nello looked puzzled at Alonso. "No idea if he's married or has a daughter. What happen since you all come to England you all only interested in white women?"

"Oh, forget it," replied Alonso.

"I'm really getting to like the game of darts. When I go back home to Jamaica, I might just open a rum bar and model it on the English pub. I'd want lots of room for people to play dominoes and billiards and throw darts. In another room I'd put a jukebox and sell kids soft drinks. A man could make a fortune," he paused and looked at Lincoln.

"I tell you what, you could open your pub at our new development at Iron Mango Tree," said Lincoln.

"Is what kind of animal was the Knatchbull?" asked Nello, politely ignoring Lincoln's offer.

Lincoln shook his shoulders, "That's something you better ask of Warren." As an afterthought he turned to Alonso. "Do you know?"

"Well, it's not an animal in the sense Nello used it. Knatchbull was one of the Hugenots who came over from France at the end of the seventeenth century."

"Sorry I asked," said Nello. "The last thing I need is a history lesson when all I really want is to murder a pint of bitter."

"All this prove, Nello, is that other refugees have beaten us to Brixton. They got here nearly three hundred years before us lot. Although according to Warren there are documents showing that a parish in Lambeth gave two shillings to a black woman and her child, early in the eighteenth century. She could have been born here about the time the Hugenots came."

"Boy, how come you head hold all that amount of information?" Nello asked, as they entered the bar.

II

Adlyn Grant returned to Birmingham at the weekend. There had been many excursions to the shopping centres of South London, which provided the dressmakers with ideas for Enid's wedding dress. The elderly Mckenzie sisters were anxious for the bride to be satisfied with what they had in mind. During the last week they had visited the high streets of Brixton, Croydon, Wandsworth, Peckham, Lewisham and further afield to the Northwest to Tottenham and Dalston. It seemed as if they went to every department store that sold bridal dresses.

"If only we had patterns," began Blossom, who was acting as secretary to the group.

"Is what we need patterns for? Asked Miss Vie, sucking her teeth.

"It's the way nowadays," said Myrtle in a dismissive tone. "In this country musicians can't play a tune if they don't have the music sheet. You got to have City and Guilds in this and that. When I went to work at the London Transport garage canteen I had to go for training. Lord, they train me to collect dirty dishes and how to wash them. You ever hear such rubbish? Like you don't have to rinse the suds off plates before you stack them up for draining," she turned to her daughters. "Just make me catch any of you not rinsing off the plates when you do the washing-up." The party laughed.

"Make me see it," Miss Vie reassured Blossom, "and I will cut the cloth, and if I cut it then Nicey will sow it. I don't want no patterns."

"Miss Vie," Blossom said, resting a hand on the lady's wrist, "I have seen your work. It is you who cut Vicky's wedding dress and it better than anything we have seen in the shops. What I meant was that if we had the patterns here before us, then we could be looking at them all at once."

"Don't worry, girl. I just forget the ones that Enid didn't like. I think she have three that she making up her mind about. Me right or me wrong?" her last sentence addressed to prospective bride.

"You remember the one we saw in Cheiseman in Lewisham?" began Enid. "That is the one."

Myrtle clapped her hands to indicate the end of foot-slogging from one store to the next. "The Lord be praised," Myrtle said.

"I tell you what," said Miss Vie, "I gwine go back to the store to have another look. I think it's the number 36 bus that will put me off right outside the store."

"The sixty-nine will take you there too," said Myrtle.

Suddenly Miss Vie started to laugh.

"Is what the matter now?" asked Myrtle anxiously.

"Me just thinking, suppose me make the journey to Lewisham and them done sell the dress?" asked Miss Vie.

"Don't say things like that, Miss Vie," pleaded Enid.

"Don't worry you pretty little head, my dear. I got it up here," she said, tapping her head. "They did allow you to try it on so I did have a good look. I just want to have another look. It can't hurt. So you having your Chief that is Adlyn, and four bridesmaid, Irone and Blossom, and the two smaller ones, Catherine and Christine, right?"

"Nothing has changed," confirmed Enid.

"We start sowing next week, right, Miss Nicey?"

"Like you said, Vie, you cut it and I will sow it. I tell you, this wedding is going to stop traffic dead. You're going to look a picture. You got the photographer already? You have to be quick off the mark because June is the month for weddings."

"We have booked Jerome the photographer because both Harry Jacobs and Campbell are busy on the day."

"Jerome is good. Him was taking nice pictures of coloured people long before those other two come on the scene. He done a good job when Vicky got married."

"He seem to have contract to take pictures at every coloured people wedding," said Miss Vie.

"What about the men folk then?" asked Miss Nicey.

"Nicey, you getting water on you brain? You know that the groom and his mates hiring them suits from Moss Bros. Why you bringing it up now?"

"Is forget me forget," she said. "So them wearing those cut-away jacket things?"

"Morning suit," said Blossom

"Come to the dining-room and have something to eat," invited Myrtle, rising to lead the way.

"So," began Miss Nicey, standing beside the twins, "which of you gwine catch Enid bouquet when she throw it?" The two girls promptly ran from the room ahead of their mother.

"Lord, Miss Nicey," interrupted Myrtle, "please don't put you mouth 'pon me pickney them. No go full them head a nonsense, you hear?"

"No joke me a joke," replied Miss Nicey, then turning to face Enid, Irone and Blossom, she said, "I suppose is the bigger ones who'll be interested, Adlyn and Blossom," she laughed.

"Why me? What about Irone? She is older than me," explained Blossom.

"I'll be married to my studies from September," Irone assured the party. "I can tell you that I'll be otherwise engaged."

"Me too," said Blossom. "I have a sickly mother at home, a no-good stepfather who drinks every penny he can lay his hand on, together they have a whole heap of children that me a my brother have to take care of. Marriage is not on my agenda. It won't be for another ten years maybe."

"But wait a minute, what about you, Miss Nicey or Miss Vie? It's never too late, you know," said Myrtle.

"Girl, no make fun of me, you hear? Me and Miss Vie are old fowls, no cock no crow for us no more." She slapped her thighs and laughed. The two sisters followed Myrtle and Enid out of the room, leaving Blossom and Irone on their own.

III

"Has Lonso got a girlfriend?

"Why? Are you interested? Wasn't it you who said you'll be married to your nursing studies?"

"I'm not asking because I want to marry him. I'm just interested, that's all."

"Not to my knowledge."

"What kind of answer is that?"

"It means that I'm not his keeper. He's never mentioned anyone, but of course what he gets up to when I'm not around he has not got to report to me. You know what they say, 'what the eye has not seen the heart will not leap'."

"So would your heart leap if he was to have one? A girlfriend, I mean?"

"Irone," Blossom sighed, "I don't know what impression we give you, but believe me when I tell you that Alonso and I are very poor. I mean poor. Alonso has been supporting the family since he was seventeen. He is only four years older than I am, but he saw to it that I had a good education. He paid my school fees when I was at Wilberforce. If you don't understand our relationship, this will help you. He is my hero. Now I am in England we've decided that another couple of five-year plans are necessary to pull the family out of the poverty trap."

"What you telling me your family history for?"

"I want you to understand the debt I owe my brother and why my family think he's the most selfless person on earth. If you are interested in becoming his girl... that's what you'll be up against."

"So you are telling me to back off, because there is nowhere in your carefully laid out five-year plans for your precious brother to have a girlfriend?"

"Irone, perhaps Enid's wedding is getting to us. We all think of the big weddings, you know our day of fame, when all eyes are on us. Every woman who sees the bridal car and the party of bridesmaid will envy us. If that is what you want you will be disappointed. For instance, we are planning to send for our stepfather, that means scraping every penny we can put together to buy him a suit and pay his fare. Now you tell me where my brother is going to find money to take you out?"

"Girl, you need to let him go and then you must find yourself a man."

"I don't want a man," she said with mounting anger. "If my brother wants a girl, I couldn't stop him even if I was that stupid to try. If you are that girl, then so be it. Even if I were to tell him some of the stories that circulated about you around the Upper Sixth at Wilberforce... you know, about you and Hopeton Bull and the guy who used to drive that delivery truck... it would not stop him from having you. If you are his choice..."

"Don't tell me you believed those stories. I think it's time you realise that there are boys who will kiss and tell, and there are those who have a very lively and vivid imagination. Stories from the latter group are often born of the bitter experience of not being able to have their way with a girl."

"Sorry, Irone, but we all thought they were all kiss-and-tell stories. We never thought that boys like Hopeton and Linval had that great an imagination. After all, the story went that you had to see Miss Pringle. Girls were only sent to Miss Pringle when they were about to be kicked out. The rumour was that you were going to be expelled for bringing the school into disrepute."

"Do you think if I was behaving badly I would be allowed to stay? Some girls just happen to get talked about more than others."

"And Irone Simmonds is one of those girls."

"I like the attention men pay me. Look, Blossom, I'm not as attractive as you, but while guys fancy their chances to come and chat me up, they take one look at you and right away see that *'I am saving myself for Mr Right'* sign above your head, and that stop them dead in their tracks. I don't think that makes you a saint and me a tramp."

"You said it."

"Perhaps it's in my genes. After all, I am twenty and my birth mother is thirty-four. Do you know that she's expecting a baby? My God, when I'm twenty-one I'll be having a brother or a sister! Then there's the business of Colonel screwing either my grandmother or grand-aunty, or both."

"Irone have some respect! Don't talk about your relations like that."

"Drop dead! These people don't mean a shit to me."

"They are very nice people."

"I don't know any nice people! Aunty Maude took me from my birth mother when I was about nine months. She did give me a good life and sent me to Wilberforce and all that, with lots of promises that she would adopt me officially. Suddenly her son sent for her to live with him and his family in Chicago and she forgot all her promises. She will only be a skivvy to her rich daughter-in-law and that son of hers, who is after the life his wife's money can buy. That bastard took my virginity when I was fifteen. He was thirty. Come to think on it, my mother was only twenty-seven at the time. I could have made her a grandmother by the time she was twenty-eight."

"You could have said no."

"People who say that are people who have never been touched by a man in that special way in the special spot when you're floating above the clouds. To be held close, to smell that hypnotising effect of aftershave lotion, to feel his strong powerful arms around you, his muscles taut and hard."

"You've read too many romance stories from those American magazines we used to buy from Hidalgo Drug Store on West Parade."

"The bastard went back to the States soon after that and married the only child of a very rich coloured man who owns several pharmacies. I'm sure Aunt Maude guessed he was screwing me. We must have left some tell-tale signs. I'm sure that's why she changed her mind about adopting me."

"Why are you confessing to me? Anyway can you blame her? If she had adopted you, her son would have become your brother. What the hell did you expect her to do?"

"You and your brother are close."

"Not that close," she said with mounting anger. "Let's finish this girl-to-girl talk." She got up and moved towards the door.

"I've never told anybody this," Irone said, stepping quickly to block her progress. "And for your ears only."

The need to confess weighed heavily on her. "He is the only man I ever did it with."

"I have no secrets to share in exchange for the dark passionate side of your character."

"They say your brother is quite a ladies' man. Is that so?"

"Sisters are usually poor judges of their brothers' sex life."

"So he has one! Unlike his sister, who's saving it up for her honeymoon," she laughed, but the angry look on Blossom's face forced her to change her tone. "Tcho, man, your face look like when those black ugly clouds gather over the Blue Mountains before thunder and lightning signal the start of the rainy season."

"Never mind the rain, watch out for the thunder and lightning," Blossom put both hands on Irone's shoulder and pushed her away from the door.

"Blossom, don't go. We've known each other for the last three years. OK, we've never been really good friends, but we could be. Look around you. There are no girls our age. Soon Enid won't have any time for you. Anyway she must be nearly thirty. She's getting married and will soon be thinking about babies and all that crap. You and I could be what they call over here 'mates'."

"Drop dead, Irone. You're not interested in me. It's Alonso you're interested in. I can't stop you from going after him, but I won't set him up for you. The only advice I will give him is to wait long enough to make sure you haven't a baby inside of you before he frigs you."

"What have you got against me?"

"Nothing."

"London is a lonely place. When I leave here I'll have no one to talk to. I can't keep up a conversation with Aunty Nicey and Aunty Vie, and as to that Sister Vicky, who's supposed to be my mother! The only luck I have had in that quarter is she's leaving Willesden to live in Maudslay so I won't see her too often, thank God."

"You don't like your relatives, do you?"

"Blossom, don't be a hypocrite. These people are St Thomas bush people. You must speak the truth and shame the Devil."

"I'm from St Thomas bush too. We're so bush that we have two patios words in the name of a nearby district, Bun Dutty Gap. I suppose in the Queen's English it would have been something like Burnt Earth Gap."

"There's a saying that you can get some people out of a place, but you cannot get the place out of them," Irone said. "What the hell you expect from people who come from a place call Guinea Fowl Walk?"

"What about people like Myrtle Morgan and her family?"

"She had the good sense to get out of the place as soon as she left school, although she cleaned a lot of white people floors and wash their children behinds."

"All of which you'll have to do come September when you start training to be a nurse."

"Nurses have status. Maids have none. Would you believe that Aunty Vie wants me to come and work at the old people's home where she's working?"

"It could bring you some pocket money and a lot of experience, until September."

"Not on your life. I'm not cleaning up after any smelly old derelicts. It's all right for you, you're a civil servant."

"Apply to the Civil Service Commission, then."

"Can you talk to somebody for me?"

"Irone, this isn't Jamaica, where you can cut corners because of someone you know. Go the Labour Exchange and get then to send you to the Commission. Although I doubt they would take you on for such a short time."

"Oh, don't worry, I'll just lie around all day listening to *The Teenagers* and the *Everley Brothers*. Let me come and spend some time with you."

"You can't, Irone, for two reasons. My bed is just as wide as my pillow. The two of us couldn't sleep on it. Before you make the obvious remark, my brother's bed is the same size. Secondly, I leave at seven-thirty for work. Next week Alonso is starting work just after midday, I think. By the way our bedroom is partitioned. You have to come through his section to get to mine. It's a family thing. We can hear each other turn in bed."

"I can come around at the weekend, then?"

"Not this week. Alonso's working until two o'clock on Saturday, then he has to leave for Nottingham to attend a meeting about Island Shield Building Society. He'll be back late Sunday night. In the meantime I'll be at Enid's. You know I keep notes on what's been done and what's still to be done for this wedding. You have nothing to do but look pretty on the day. The guys will be fighting to get near you. I'll be so knackered, I'll look a wreck with my 'not for sale sign' over my head."

24

It was unusual to see Jimmy Fairfax behind the counter at the Theo's Record Shop at 250 Brixton Road. That could only mean that Theo had been called away as in an emergency. This music store specialised in swing, rhythm and blues, jazz and calypso. It had been the first coloured business to have been started in South London after the end of the war. The proprietor was a fellow ex-serviceman, who had an almost encyclopaedic knowledge of Jazz. He was a little below medium height, rotund, always impeccably dressed, with a pleasant smiling demeanour and a slight lisp. On the few occasions when he was not in the shop it would be attended by a couple of pretty young coloured girls who had spent their formative years in London. This day Jimmy Fairfax was minding the shop. The Fats Domino recent release of *"Blueberry Hill"* was playing in the background as musical wallpaper. It was clearly Jimmy's choice, since it was repeated again and again. Alonso knew that the repetition was for the benefit of Saturday night partygoers. Other tracks for the *smoochers* would come from Shirley and Lee and for the boppers there would be Lloyd Price's *Staggerlee.* Those were the staple diet of all Saturday night front room and basement parties and there were some prospective customers loitering in the entrance of the shop.

"It's true that Melbourne has never been the same since *that* fire destroyed the Colonial..." Jimmy was talking to a tall man who was wearing a postman's uniform. "He just couldn't believe they would do that to him in *his* town. He believes that Brixton is his town. You've heard his party joke over and over: Columbus discovered America, Balboa discovered the Pacific and Melbourne discovered Brixton."

Both men laughed.

"Let's face it, he's been living in Brixton since he was demobbed. He only ever spent seven months back in Jamaica when he was demobbed."

"You right. He was back by '47 and start concentrating on his music and his business and politics. They all took over his life."

"Rumour has it," said the postman in a conspiratorial voice, "that he's on the verge of bankruptcy, but this..." He paused.

"That," emphasised Jimmy, "has had nothing to do with the accident."

"You heard something?" the postman asked anxiously.

"No. I'm thinking aloud. All the same it's strange that after he went on TV with that fascist hack Birbeck Samms to discuss race relations his club should burn down. Then three weeks ago a letter arrived from the Ku Klux Klan. Is it all just coincidence?"

"Wait a minute," said the postman, "I never knew the KKK operated so far from Waco, Texas. I thought those Southern rednecks GI's took it back with them after the war. So you think it wasn't an accident, then?"

"I'm not saying it isn't," said Jimmy, "but Melbourne has been a marked man for quite some time. He received hate mail, including that pernicious diatribe from the Ku Klux Klan.

"All the way from Waco, Texas?" asked Alonso.

"They've internationalised their organisation, haven't you heard? That letter was from *'King Kleagle, Klavern No 1 Province of Londinium, Imperial Realm of Albion, Aryan Knights Ku Klux Klan of Great Britain.'*"

"Quite a mouthful," said Alonso.

"So what, you think that he was dragged from his car and beaten up?" asked the postman.

"You never saw James Cagney in the film *Each Dawn I Die?*"

"Isn't that the one in which an investigative journalist is framed for a hit-and-run fatality?" asked Alonso, who had recently seen the film at the Clifton, Brixton Hill.

"How can you frame someone for a hit-and-run accident?" asked the postman.

"Easy!" said Alonso. "Knock the man out, sit him down behind the wheel, douse the car with whisky, release the brake and set it rolling down the hill to slam into a crowd."

"That might be good enough for the make-believe world of cinema, but in real life things are a whole lot different." He turned to Jimmy and asked, "You been to see him? Is he receiving visitors? Is that where Theo is?"

"He's still unconscious... I mean Melbourne. The doctors say his injuries are consistent with injuries received in an automobile accident. Only families and close friends are being admitted. Dorrit is there and his sister is flying in from the States. I was there first thing this morning."

"Dorrit?" asked the postman sceptically.

"She's the mother of his children," said Jimmy shrugging his shoulders in a resigned fashion.

"Takes things like this to mend fences and pour balm on hurt," said the postman.

Alonso realised that it was not because they were of the generation before him, but the camaraderie of the armed forces was binding on all these ex-servicemen and women of the Empire. Sometimes he envied that time past but the war was over a few months after his eighth birthday.

"Is what you are thinking..."

"I don't even know what I'm thinking," said Jimmy. "What I know is that the driver's window was wound down, it was a balmy evening. The car doors were locked except for the driver's door. There've been incidents in the last few weeks where coloured men have been dragged from their cars at traffic lights and beaten up. In the climate of today's race relations I don't rule anything out."

"But you just said that the doctor says his injuries are consistent with him having had a motor accident," recalled the postman.

"What else could he say? His patient was brought in, having been found beside his wrecked motorcar. There's a meeting going on now upstairs in the *Gazette's* office, a discussion with the student leaders. Apparently some students want to hold a vigil outside the hospital. Melbourne was their warden for a while, you know. That invitation to debate with Birbeck Samms came to the students and they unanimously asked Melbourne to be their spokesman. They are his constituents."

"Of course, anything that happens in America in the morning is news to us five hours later," said the postman.

"Or less than that. Don't let the time difference between London and New York fool you. Reports of an incident will be burning up the wire as soon as the reporters get hold of a phone. But it's not just copycat reaction. Our race relation problems are real enough," said Alonso.

"And that bastard Samms is about to exploit it further. You know that he has a book due out soon? One evening paper has promised extracts starting next week."

"You' lying!" said the postman.

"Samms flew out to Jamaica and got on board a banana boat which picked up migrants from island to island down the spine of the Eastern Caribbean, as far as Barbados before heading out into the North Atlantic. The title is *The Auriga Crossing.*"

"It has been done before," said the postman.

"*They Seek a Living*", said Alonso. "But Joyce Edgington and Birbeck Samms are not from the same planet. The *Auriga* is the name of the ship I came up on," continued Alonso, with a curious mixture of romance and anger. "On the surface it sounds uncontroversial, but I doubt if Birbeck Samms is thinking of writing a book that will show migrants in any light but of the uneducated, misled country yokels coming here to live off the National Assistance."

"That man is a scoundrel. At the branch meeting of our Party the other night someone who has her ears close to the ground said that Samms will be in the contest for the bye-election in Maudslay," the postman said.

"But that has always been a safe Labour Party seat," said Alonso. " He has not got an earthly chance."

"Young man, spit on your finger hold it up and feel where the wind's blowing. Voters will put their cross beside the candidate of any mainstream party that comes out against more immigrants coming to the Mother Country. They know where Birbeck Samms stands on that. Labour will oppose him and will lose. Mark my words."

"Funny how things change," began Jimmy Fairfax. "It was the Conservatives during the War who used to talk about our brave and loyal colonial boys."

"They were saying it after the war too when the country needed labour," said the postman.

"Patronising bastards! In the 1950 election there were Labour Parliamentary candidates who were worried that too many coloured migrants were going into the inner cities while working class whites were moving out. You know what Labour feared would happen? The solid working-class voters which Labour used to depend on was ebbing away from its traditional heartland. How the hell did Labour manage to become our Godfather, anyway?"

"If you find the answer to that, don't forget to let me know," said the postman. "Well, James, my old son, I got to love you and leave you. I'm due at Mount Pleasant sorting office in less than fifty minutes and you know what the buses are like this time of day. I'll ring later to see when and where this student thing is taking place." he moved towards the door and added over his shoulder, " I guess that will be at Collingham Gardens.

"That's where the Students Centre is." Jimmy reminded the postman.

II

"I bet you all these young coloured people are going to the West Indian Students Centre," said Alonso to Enid and Blossom as they got out of Gloucester Road Underground station. They were swiftly swept into a stream of young people heading towards Collingham Gardens. They fell in behind two young women who spoke with Jamaican accents which their Kingston High School education and a few months in London had failed to eradicate.

"We'll be there soon. I tell you it's not far," one said reassuringly.

"I hope so, because I can't walk far in these shoes. My feet are swollen from all that tramping from store to store... and in the end you didn't buy anything." She aimed her accusation at her colleague, but loudly enough for others to hear.

"Tcho, girl, you complain too much. I got this Harrods bag, which I want to send to my sister in New York. Her friends going to drop dead from jealousy," replied her companion. "If your shoes still hurting you, then do what your uncle does in the bush country you're from. Take them off, tie the laces together and throw them over you shoulder."

"Don't mock my Uncle Arthur! He bought those shoes way back in 1938, and all he ever had done to them are new heels. Country road rough, you know." They turned, laughing, and saw that Alonso, Enid and Blossom were right behind them and could not conceal the fact that they had overheard the conversation and were laughing too.

"You know what they say about us St Thomas people; one foot longer than the other so we can keep our balance in that hill and gully country."

"Oh, no, don't tell me you're from St Thomas too. It looks like everybody from that parish is here in London," said Alonso.

"St Thomas people don't generally go further west than Kingston, but you can find plenty of us in New York, London and Toronto," said the young woman whose shoes were too tight.

"Yes," said her friend. "They stopped going west since they finished digging the Panama Canal and planting United Fruit Company banana, sugarcane and..."

"Ouch!" said Alonso, "you stepping 'pon me corn. My grandpappy was a labourer in Colon and Bocas."

In the crush they separated from the two young women as they hurried along Courtfield Gardens, overtaking other groups and themselves being overtaken. In the crowd they were churned up as in a huge stomach and regurgitated once again before being digested that is they had reached number one Collingham Gardens together.

It was already 8.30 and the meeting had not yet started. People were greeting each other, reacquainting themselves with old friends, perhaps even old adversaries. Colleagues were being introduced to new friends. Addresses and telephone numbers were being exchanged. Alonso pointed out the tall figure of the Federal Minister of External Affairs for the West Indian Federation he had met in the office of the *West Indian Gazette* the previous week.

"I suppose he's responsible for us since his portfolio covers Commonwealth Relations. Apart from that he rose to the rank of Wing Commander during the War. Strange how only the near-white ones got promoted to such dizzy heights."

"You find that strange?" asked Enid, missing the sarcasm in Alonso's voice.

He became aware of Blossom's elbow thumping into his ribs. "Look! That girl there, talking to that tall guy at the table. It's Anh Hosang. I heard she was over here studying medicine." Then to Enid, "She was Alonso's girlfriend. Go on, big brother, go over and renew acquaintances."

"Don't push! Anyway, look who she's chatting up... none other than Archie Islam."

"So what if his family owns half of downtown Kingston?" Blossom asked.

"It's the merchant class versus the plebs."

"But, brother, with all their newly acquired Marxist-Leninist revolutionary shit you can't lose. Go on, big brother. You're a genuine socialist!" she urged mockingly.

"That's him?" asked Enid. "There was a piece on him when he left to study engineering at Glasgow. His sister is married to my former boss. He's well connected and a good looker, too."

"Behave yourself, Enid, you'll be married in a fortnight," Alonso reminded her with a gentle slap on her wrist.

"What's wrong with looking? I'm not touching, just fattening my eyes," she replied in equally jocular vein.

In the continuing mêlée Anh and Archie were swallowed up and dispersed to somewhere out of sight. There seemed to be a certain amount of caucusing before a programme was arrived at. It was approaching 9 o'clock when the chairman rapped the table loudly and, assisted by colleagues who could stick their fingers in their mouths and whistle, the meeting was called to order under the chairmanship of Archie Islam. His antecedents were people from the Eastern Mediterranean whom Jamaicans called "Syrians", although his grandfather came originally from the Lebanon. He was solidly of the merchant class, as too was Anh Hosang, although somewhat down the social order since their business meant dealing with village people. The merchant class was wide, as there were room for social mobilisation if the entrepreneur were ruthless and charming in equal proportions. Because of the nature of the unwritten constitution of Jamaican racial hierarchy; first came the whites, then the near-whites, which included half-whites and those from the Mediterranean region, then the Chinese, then the Indians and finally the blacks.

Despite the visual presence of the clerical-collared Reverend Dr R. Locksley Hood, the meeting did not begin with the religious overtones of an American Civil Rights meeting. However, a young man who was identified by Alonso as Roy Henry sang "Go Down Moses" in a strong baritone voice before the Chairman began his address. Archie explained that the difficulty in arranging a programme for the evening was that it was decided that it should not be a valediction. Melbourne was alive, not yet out of danger, but alive. He mentioned the widening chasm between students and workers. That gap must be closed. Workers should not look on students as of the privileged class and as individuals here to obtain degrees and then return to be masters, perpetuating the aforementioned rift. It cannot be denied that some of the students come from the privileged backgrounds; people who were bred by the colonial masters to keep the masses in check. Education should not merely show that some people are capable of three or four years of academic study, but should bring workers and students closer in the project of societal and nation-building. Out on the streets the white man sees us as coloured; he doesn't see students as separate from bus conductors. The racists who attacked Melbourne did not see the full picture, of an eighteen-year-old with the courage to travel 5,000 miles to fight for his "mother country". Nor did they see a man with a good scholarly record. They did not see his musicianship, nor his exemplary public service. What they saw was, as always, a face that was not white. It could have been the face of a bus conductor, the face of a factory worker, the face of a man who sweeps the streets: a coloured man, a descendant of Ham, our Biblical antecedent.

"And nothing will change until we have blacks speaking for blacks," said an impatient young man. His accent identified him as either a Trinidadian or a British Guianese, Alonso could not distinguish which. This comment caused quite an uproar that took another ten minutes to subside.

"I am a Jamaican," said Archie proudly. "As such I'm within my rights to be a member of the West Indian Students Union. I have a right to be here. I have a right to be elected by my peers. Look at the West Indian cricket team. Which of you would deny the rights of such names and varying skin colour and racial origin as Rohan Kanhai, Sonny Ramadhin, Bruce Paraudeau, Bob Christiani, Garfield Sobers, Worrell, Weekes and Walcott, Stollmeyer et al?"

"Don't forget Achong, who gave the cricketing world the *Chinaman!*" Since E.E. Achong was a Trinidadian, Alonso was satisfied that the voice came from a Trinidadian and not a Guianese.

"You're missing the point. The powers that be still think that it's cricket to have a white man, or as near as damn it, as captain of the West Indies. Don't forget that they brought back Goddard as captain in '57. Now we got you chairing this meeting. You mentioned the streets; well, out there, you're one of them. My problem out there is not your problem," the speaker's accent was Jamaican.

"But it is!" shouted Archie in fighting mood. "When people walk on the other side, or look away because the problem isn't theirs, or act as if there is no problem, it serves only to perpetuate racism not to eradicate it. I'm willing to stand down if the feeling of this meeting is that I'm not black enough. First look around, then take the logical step and ask all those who you don't think of as having the correct hue to leave the room. Then carry on talking to the converted." He sat down amid catcalls, cheering, hooting and general pandemonium.

"Because of our unique experience we find ourselves in the mid-twentieth century not knowing whom we are or what we are." The speaker was a tall man, impressive and dignified, nut-brown in colour. He had the overwhelming presence of someone who demands to be heard. He was Jan Carew, the author of two novels, *The Wild Coast* and *Black Midas*. Alonso had seen him in the office of the *West Indian Gazette* a few days earlier asking probing questions of the Federal Minister. Alonso proudly communicated this in a whisper to his two companions.

When a man or woman says, 'I am a West Indian,' he or she knows that this envelope of life with a West Indian address is faceless, a cipher. And the West Indian will only cease to be this when through a creative representation of the smell of his earth and the dreams of this people, he can discover a true image of himself. The images by which our middle-class live today are borrowed and spurious. There is the carbon-

copy English type - the black, brown and high-yellow man in
search of a cultural hyssop with which to wash himself white.
Then there is the slave boy dressed up in a diplomat's clothes
image. And going down the scale of the pseudo-?' became
the quagmire in which the wheels of this meeting became stuck.
Above the Babel a voice sophistication, there is the 'Good
Negro', the cipher shaped by a mission-school philosophy that
equates respectable servility with being 'cultured'...

Carew's authoritative speech was interrupted by spontaneous applause. Whether it was that the majority of the students had recognised him or had understood what he was saying was not clear. When the applause subsided a single voice was heard to shout, "Carry on, man." This was agreed by acclamation.

The clock ticked past ten o'clock the question of *'why discrimination'* rang loud and clear.

" It's the myth of the sexuality of the coloured man," a voice from the multitude shouted.

"Who says it's a myth?" demanded a bass voice. "You ain't gonna sell my birthright, boy!"

After the pandemonium, calm rested over the hall like a bird of prey surveying the landscape for its next meal.

"God in His infinite wisdom made the English an inventive race. They were to become the first industrial nation and all that. Then there were great inventions such as the steam train. He gave them an Empire on which the sun never sets; the greatest naval force to defend that empire; but He did not intend the English to dance! All you have to do is to watch the English male drag arse across the floor, knees rigid, arms ramrod like walking sticks. The women are different, though; to start with they too were stiff, with their one, two, three steps and spin, and, by God, they could spin! Now they have learnt to inject some rhythm into their movements. They are swinging those hips and using their shoulders. This, ladies and gentlemen, is the root cause of the problem. The last time I was at the Lyceum you could see the white boys becoming red with rage as their girls accepted coloured men's invitation to dance. It's nothing new. That was the reason behind every dance hall *fracas* during the war. Now to stand and watch your woman wriggle her hips to the rhythm of the jive of a rock 'n' roll, or to see a man drop a mento, rubbing his belly on hers; wars in history have been fought for less. To add to all that, you have these black guys with their *blue spot* radiograms busting out the latest discs in their basement rooms, while most working-class English homes only have a wireless. I say the situation is fraught with danger. That, ladies and gentlemen, is what lies behind racial prejudice. Good old-fashioned sexual jealousy," said Caleb Zebulon Morgan, barrister at law with chambers in London and Maudslay. He was the brother of Ziah Morgan, husband of Myrtle of Lilford Road, Brixton. It had not been easy to follow what the speaker was saying after the first three sentences, so great was the hilarity. But a public meeting by its every nature is a wild beast, which only feigned to be tamed while looking for the opportunity to leap to its feet and wreak vengeance on its tormentors. Someone shouted from the floor that the meeting ought to remember the lynching of Emmett Till; another reminded the audience of the Nationalist Party of South Africa and its Apartheid policies. Yet another recalled the words of the Honourable Elijah Mohammed, that the White man is the Devil incarnate. Suddenly the enemy had been identified.

"Kill the man," someone shouted.

"This is not the purpose of this meeting," the chairman said. "We are not a lynch mob. That's the way of the Ku Klux Klan. The Students Union does not copy the KKK. Our course is integration. We must rise above the morass of hate and bigotry to the level of love and dignity."

"Besides if you kill all the white men, who'll be there to father white girls?" Enid whispered to Alonso and Blossom. "Just look at the amount of white girls in the audience. How do they take all this crap and go back to their flats and make love to their black lovers? Have you ever considered that while the white man is the sole father of his race the black man isn't the sole father of his race? Come to think of it, the black woman hasn't got sole rights as mother of the coloured race either. For all his pious uttering Caleb Zebulon Morgan's coloured children have a white mother."

"I often wondered how Helen felt during the ten-year siege of Troy and the ensuing slaughter," said Alonso.

"It must have been kinda nice to stand on the topless towers of Ilium and watch all those godlike heroes giving up their lives so you and your lover can be happy," said Blossom.

"You think that's how these white girls feel, even if their lovers get castrated by their fathers tomorrow?" asked Enid.

"These aren't working-class girls. There are a few coronets among the plebs here tonight," said Alonso. "For them this is the mid-twentieth-century equivalent of the Grand Tour. It's all very exotic. In a few years they'll be married to some dull merchant banker or the like, quietly reminiscing about their misspent youth. In middle age they'll sign petitions to send the blacks home. They'll hold dinner parties where the guests talk about the sexuality and morality of coloured people being closer to the apes. Having become more like their mothers, they'll be terrified of their own daughters being bedded by a coloured man. Their secrets of been bedded in a single room in Appach Road, Brixton, won't be passed on from mother to daughter, well, not directly anyway."

"Did you just think that up?" asked Enid. "Don't answer that, coloured men spend too much time thinking about white women without any encouragement. Tell me, where is this meeting taking us?"

"Mr Chairman, with respect, some of us spent last night outside St John's Hospital where Melbourne is in intensive care. The police pushed us around and moved us on. We moved, then we came back when they thought we had left for good. Some of us have to appear at the Magistrate Court for causing an obstruction. Can you tell me what we're achieving at this meeting?" Once again it was the young woman with the lisp, who had been identified as Beaulah Burke, a nurse working in a hospital in Maudslay or perhaps it was in Congreve. She was with Zebulon Morgan's party from the East Midland's contingent.

Meanwhile chaos ensued. The warden intervened and threatened to close the meeting unless order was restored. Calm was restored and the chairman announced that a group of people had been working on a proposal. It was now ready to be placed before the meeting. Four people emerged from a committee room. One was Warren Hall, the young woman was Anh Hosang; the other two members of the committee were unknown to Alonso.

"The proposal is this," said Chairman Islam, "That this house votes into being an organisation to be called Students and Workers Against Racial Discrimination, STUWARD for short. Its purpose will be to unite workers and students in the fight against racial discrimination and to create an atmosphere of harmony between migrant and host community. It can begin by providing help, financial or legal, to the brothers and sisters who have to appear at the Magistrates' Court next week. If you approve the proposal, we would ask everyone here to start tomorrow by organising groups at your workplaces. Students must take the message back to their institutions and recruit members. We can meet here, or at some venue in the Midlands, or at Lambeth Town Hall, Brixton, or Kensington Town Hall or St Pancras Town Hall, whichever is available in four or six weeks' time. At that meeting we'll elect national officers and draft a constitution. In the meantime I further propose that Melbourne Welch be approved as our Honorary President." His voice was drowned by a roar, taken to be appointment by acclamation; Melbourne was approved as leader. "Obviously it will be some time before he can come and address you. Someone must hold the fort until we meet again to formalise our organisation. The committee would like to bring you the name of a man who has worked with Melbourne since the end of the War, as it were content to stand in his shadow. Tonight we ask that man to step forward and to take on the onerous task of interim Organising Secretary. Ladies and gentlemen, please show your approval by welcoming Jimmy Fairfax."

Jimmy's appointment was duly approved. The meeting set about forming a committee to work with him until the formal election in a month's time. Anh Hosang from the Students Union, Claudia Jones, editor of the *West Indian Gazette,* and Warren Hall, representing ordinary migrants, were among those appointed. The meeting asked the Federal Minister to take back to the Parliament in Port of Spain the hopes, fears and the anxieties of the migrants. A lone voice suggested financial support. There was irony in the peal of laughter that suggested most people were aware that the penurious Federal Government of the West Indies had come to London to ask the Commonwealth Office for more funds. Finally it was decided that for a minimum of five shillings annual subscription members would be able to vote and stand for election. The Chairman asked that everyone write his or her name and address in order to be informed of the next meeting. A collection of sixteen pounds four shillings and ten pence halfpenny was taken up.

III

"We could wait and get a lift from Warren or Jimmy, but both are going to be busy for the next hour or so," said Alonso. "Anyway, I bet the committee will end up at someone's flat and the talking will go on all night."

"Anh might be there," teased Blossom.

"Old-time people say," said Enid dropping into Jamaican accent, "two old fire-stick easy to catch alight again."

"Not if rain fall 'pon them," was Alonso's reply. "Five years absence after what was a strictly platonic and epistolary affair, at that, can dampen the ardour."

"For an elementary-school boy, he uses a lot of big words," Enid complained to Blossom.

"It means that there was no rudeness between them," explained Blossom.

They both said "Ahh" and "tut tut," in mock sympathy.

"Rudeness a Chinese girl, you a black boy? Your light complexion wouldn't save you ass. Them Chinese would hire a back-a-yard bad man fi chop you up. You wouldn't live to tell the tale," said Enid, looking at Alonso.

"The same thing would happen if you had fool round with East Indian girls or those high-colour girls from St Andrew," added Blossom.

"Is that why they go wild about white girls once they get to London?" asked Enid.

"Well, it was the white man who started it with captive slave women... Tell me why you black women allow them to get away with it for so long?" Alonso began.

"So it's payback time to all those White, Chinese, Indian and high-colour boys that make free with black women. Sister Enid, do you think they are doing it for us then?" asked Blossom.

"Listen, girl, they'll tell you that this is revenge for what the slave owners did to our ancestors. It's not a nice job but someone has to do it." They laughed, clutching each other like drunken revellers.

"You two confessing to something?" Alonso placed a hand on his sister's shoulder and spoke directly to her. "Ever since you told me about that letter from Panji I been hoping to meet one of his sisters. I heard that Mina is a nurse at a hospital in Leicester. Come to think of it, Lincoln asked me if I was available to go with him to Leicester," he looked at his companions. "I never did like Panji Pechey. I notice he waited until I left Jamaica to make his move... well, he's not in Leicester to protect *his* sister."

"He wrote me just one letter," confessed Blossom. "He started by complementing me on my brown eyes, good looks and brains. It was sweet. It's when he started on my breasts that I got angry."

"He started on your breasts?" asked her brother.

"It was a letter, for God sake," Blossom was embarrassed.

"What did he say... I mean, what did you do?"

"Never mind what he said," she said. "I did what all decent, shy and well brought up Jamaican schoolgirls do. I burnt the four corners of his letter and returned it to him."

"You didn't?" he asked, proud that his sister was capable of rejecting the unwanted attention of a boy he did not like. "How did he take it?"

"He never spoke to me again. So you don't have to make that trip to Leicester. I doubt if Mina's that easy anyway. She's six months younger than me and I know you prefer far older women."

"Ouch!" he said. "Going for the jugular, little sister?"

"I have nothing to say," Enid said and moved ahead of Blossom. Alonso stretched his strides to over take them both.

They started down towards the platform at Gloucester Road Underground Station.

25

When Alonso got home it was almost eleven o'clock. Blossom was sitting on her bed, Buddha-like, surrounded by bits of paper.

"And here I was being as quiet as I could, thinking that you might be asleep."

"How did it go?" she asked wearily.

"As usual. People trying to go further than the fares they paid."

"Not that." She sounded disappointed. "Oh, don't tell me you didn't go to see Dr Kalra about that pain in your heel? You got to go to the doctor, preferably before you're taken there in an ambulance. You're not scared, are you?"

"Oh, that! I went to see Dr Kalra. He said I have a cyst. He's writing to the Trade Union Hospital in Golders Green, you know the Trades Union Hospital that is, for me to see a consultant."

"Why so far away? Suppose they keep you in, how do I get to visit you?"

"Golders Green isn't the end of the world. It's on the Northern Line. The tube from Stockwell will get you there. Apparently as I'm a fully paid-up member of my trade union, I contribute to the running of that hospital. It will be like going to a private hospital. I've been told that many top consultants work there."

"Are you scared?"

"Scared what of?"

"They'll probably have to operate. You could be laid up for weeks, even months," she said.

"A week or two, maybe. I will be paid full wages while I'm off work."

"So we'll manage," but she looked anxiously at the letters and a crowded notebook beside her.

"What gives with all those pieces of paper?"

"Letters from home... and have you forgotten that I'm a bridesmaid with responsibilities for keeping notes on all there is to be done?"

"I didn't know that bridesmaids have any duties besides looking pretty and attending to the bride on her big day."

"This is going to be the coloured wedding of the decade."

"Weddings ought to be *white* not *coloured*."

"Aha!" she said humourlessly. "This has nothing to do with the bride's sexual experience or lack of it. Have you any idea what the total cost of this wedding is going to be?"

"Near a thousand pounds, I shouldn't wonder."

"Don't wonder, *mi hermano*. It will be more than two years' salary for me. Now you believe me when I say that I'm putting off romance for at least ten years. You won't be able to pay for my trousseau before then," she laughed.

He liked to hear her laugh. He wanted her to be happy. He had been responsible for her happiness all his life. He remembered the little girl hiding behind him as the children taunted them because neither he nor their mother, and certainly not his little sister could understand the *patois* spoken in the country. They could hardly understand the English spoken in Kingston, which was nearer to the Standard English on official documents. He recalled shielding her as the children, frustrated in their efforts to communicate, hurled stones at them, shouting "*Panya pickney* dem no know English." Sometimes they were called "Cuban pickney". Whichever term, it hurt. Much later, when he was accepted as a member of the cricket team, he would tell them that the great George Headley too was born in Panama. He and Blossom were born in the north-eastern town of Bocas del Toro. He wondered if the West Indies greatest batsman was ever called a *Panya pickney*.

"It's fathers who pay for daughters' weddings, not brothers," recalling their earlier conversation.

"I know, Dad," she laughed. "Can you recall our father at all?"

"Not clearly. I have blurred images in my mind's eye of a tall, thin light-complexioned man picking you up and throwing you in the air and catching you before you hit the ground. I cannot remember much of his features. Oh, one thing more, I have a hazy picture of someone shaving under a tree. Maybe it was a mango tree and the mirror was hanging from a nail driven into the tree. He was using one of those cut-throat razors. I once told Mama and she thought I was making it up. Perhaps I did. My mind could be playing tricks. It was such a long time ago. Eighteen years ago."

"Since then you've been my protector. Come here. I want to hug you," she knelt on the bed as he came closer, and then she threw her arms around his neck. "I love you, Alonso Alfredo de Campesino. Do you think we should revert to our Spanish names? The Black Muslims in America are dropping their English surnames. Their slave names, as they say."

"What good would it do? It's still a European name. Don't forget it was the Spaniards who introduced African slavery to the Americas. The English were the traders but the Spaniards created the demand. Getting rid of our slave names isn't as easy as the Honourable Elijah Muhammad would have his followers believe. "

He accepted her caresses as a father would, but he was not her father and there were only four years between their births. Now as a young woman of nineteen, she was nearly as tall as he was. It was not easy to tell the difference in their ages. He reached up and pulled her hands, which were clasped behind his neck, and gently pushed her into a sitting position.

"Now tell me the bad news," he said.

"We need to pay the rest of Bullah's fare by the end of the month if he is to come up by the end of September. The other thing is Reverend Hood want us to come to a rehearsal at the church on Tuesday. The rest are letters from home, Mama and Aunty Ivorine. You can read them later. Gody Ivo said the headmaster would like you to send him a copy of Trevor Huddleston's book."

"Naught for our Comfort?"

"I guesso."

"It won't break the bank. I think it costs twelve shillings and sixpence. We should be able to meet the payment on Bullah's fare from my moonlighting at Creole Enterprises. Also Gody Myrtle had promised us a draw of partner."

"But that is to pay down on our new maisonette. You promised that we'd never share accommodation with Bullah. We can't use that money to send for him."

"Flowers, take it easy. Not only do I not want to share a flat with Bullah, I think the time has come for us to leave Geneva Road. At the moment both Somerleyton and Geneva Roads are synonyms for slum accommodation." He reached for her hands again, "I meant to tell you; I've been holding out on you," he paused, then spoke rapidly as if to get it out before he changed his mind. "I joined up with Colonel to throw an extra hand of partner. Half of it is mine, sixty pounds!"

She pulled her hands away, folded them below her breast and pushed herself against the wall. "What other secrets you are keeping from me?" she had become serious.

"Only that I have a wife and three kids, and I'm having an affair with Irone; our baby's due next month." He thought that would bring some degree of humour back to their conversation.

"You have been busy," she said. "Don't say I didn't warn you about Irone. Are you sure it's yours? I hope she keeps this one." Realising she had divulged too much too quickly, she covered her mouth, too late.

"Now who has been keeping secrets?" he asked. "So she had an abortion. When was that?"

"I don't think her folks know about it. In any case she swears it's a lie, but the rumour was rife at Wilberforce and the Head called in her aunt. True or false, she had a terrible reputation, and I don't want you getting involved with her, you hear?"

"Yes, Ma'am. I still think she's kinda cute."

"Men! Idiots all of them," she scolded. "Come here," she held out her arms as if to receive a child who needed reassurance. "I was worried about you being broke so often lately. Now I know you've been saving for the extra hand of partner. You did it so we'd have a reserve should we need it, and we do. In future please tell me everything. I'm a big girl."

"It seems you alone have the right to use the phrase *big girl.*"

"I use it correctly."

"Anyway now we can afford to buy Lincoln and Enid a really nice present. Tell me about the rehearsal. Tuesday, you said. That's good; I'll be at Chiswick learning how to drive a big red bus."

"Do you really want to be a bus driver?"

"No, but it's an easy way to get a licence. Since I wasn't brought up anywhere near trains I've always wanted to drive a big articulated truck." He realised she had lost interest. "Each day for the next fortnight I'll be home in the early evening. I'll have dinner ready by the time you get home. Tell me about the rehearsal."

"I've it written down. Groom and best man (that's you, Alonso de Campesino Campbell) will leave Fonthill Avenue to be in the church by the latest 2.15. Meanwhile at the Morgans' house in Lilford Road the chief bridesmaid Adlyn and the other bridesmaids, Irone, Blossom, Catherine and Christine and stand-in mother Myrtle Morgan, will leave to arrive at the church by 2.20. The bride Enid Swaby (she won't be using Swaby after the wedding) will leave in a 1934 Rolls Royce car with her stand-in father Isaiah Morgan to arrive at the church by 2.30. The proceedings will start at 2.45. After the ceremony, allow half an hour for taking photographs. The wedding party will proceed to 109 Fonthill Avenue for the reception. There'll be a marquee for the eighty invited guests with their lively Master of Ceremonies Mr Alonso de Campesino Campbell. The bride has requested that there should be funny stories but no rude jokes, please."

"Convey the MC's respect to lovely bride and tell her tradition demands that there be funny and downright rude stories at the expense of the groom, but obscenities will be vigorously expurgated."

"Don't interrupt! Now, where was I? Out of respect for the sensitivities of the good neighbours of Fonthill Avenue the wedding dance won't be held there but at the Pimento Club, with Mr Jimmy Fairfax as host. The traditional bridal dance, with the bride and groom attempting to waltz and succeeding in tripping up each other, will be danced in the ground-floor front room, where D.J. Warren Hall will preside. The Pimento Club will be taken over for the night. Mr Nello Walters will be behind the bar keeping a watchful eye on the white rum. Miss Rosita Maria de Campesino Campbell, secretary extraordinaire to the wedding party, will collect all cards from gifts so that thank-you notes can be sent in due course. The bride and groom and their American guests will depart from Heathrow Airport at 11.30 for their flight to New York. Miss Campbell and her brother have agreed to stay at 109 Fonthill Avenue until the newly-weds return from honeymoon. I think that covers all." She dropped her notebook, head bowed in an attitude of absolute exhaustion.

"Girl, you are ready to take over the United Nations. My advice to Dr Ralph Bunche and Dag Hammarskjold is that you're on your way to take over their jobs. But all that won't be rehearsed at St James' on Tuesday, I bet?"

"Oh, that!" she said, downgrading what she had begun to say. "Mr Hood just want to talk us through the services and warn Enid not to be too late.

"I bet you'll be the prettiest of the attends."

"You are prejudiced, but thank you all the same."

"Am I being too corny if I say I'm not ready to give you away yet?"

"I'm not ready to go yet. So there," she threw a pillow at him.

"Talking of father figures, why do I find the relationship between Lincoln and his father a sort of game? Lincoln first saw his father on his sixteenth birthday, when he was presented with a bicycle; then nothing apart from the occasional letter with a few dollars until a year or so ago. Yet Lincoln has tried to imitate his father by going into business and somehow managed to get the old man to lend him money to start Creole Enterprises. Now it has taken off, the father needs no arm-twisting to invest. I wonder about this need to be like one's father, to want to please, to be a clone."

"His mother is in the States too, but married to someone else."

"At least she paid his school fees and provided the money for his fare to London. He has a good relationship with his mother, but his relationship with this man who absented himself for so long and is now by his elbow interests me. Am I too cynical or is it because he's rich?"

"That's a terrible thing to say, *hijo*."

"Don't get me wrong, I'm only trying to understand. I think Lincoln has a good idea that will succeed and may make him rich, so why does he want to please his father so much? Is it a kind of rivalry? Further, are these loans a way of saying you owe me and this is how I'm going to collect?"

"They are our friends. Never try to put your friends under the microscope. It's going to be fun for them visiting Lincoln's father, then on to his mother in Chicago and back to Enid's mother in New York. Some honeymoon. In the meantime, guess who'll be minding the shop?" He had lapsed into silence and she felt this was not the time to be morose. "I think you'll be a super father. You said you have only hazy images of our father. I don't think you have to have a father influencing your formative years. George Lamming, our greatest wordsmith, was spot-on when he wrote, 'My father sowed the idea of me. It was my mother who fathered me.' "

"Our mother did the best she could. Mama's instinct was to save her children, that's why we ended up in Jamaica. That was a brave move for a young woman who wasn't much older than I am now. She had no English. She had only the little money the company paid in compensation after her husband, our father, was murdered. Thanks to her relationship with Goody Ivorine, whom she had last seen ten years previously, we were refugees..."

"Panya pickney dem," she said gravely. "I can't remember any of it."

"I can't remember going to our father's funeral, but I have this hazy picture of sitting between two strong arms on the crossbar of a bicycle going at speed. Another thing I recall was drifting off to sleep and this person tucking me in and whistling softly."

"Those are good memories," she said. "I have none of him. I've always had Mama and, of course, you. I couldn't have had a better mentor than you." She tried to stifle a yawn, flung her arms wide in a stretch. "I'm tired. Go to your bed. Go, go," she waved her arms, dismissing him. She watched him stoop to go through the partition. She pulled back the sheets of her bed and wriggled down in the warm cocoon of bedclothes.

"Buenas noches, hijo."

26

It was an unusually hot evening in early June when Alonso, Blossom and Enid set off for the inaugural meeting of STUWARD, which was being held at Lambeth Town Hall, Brixton. Present was the entire London-based Morgan family consisting of Isaiah, Myrtle his wife and twin daughters Catherine and Christine. Nello Walters made up the contingent from Lilford Road.

"Girl," said Myrtle to Enid as they met outside the Brixton Hill entrance, "You getting married in a fortnight's time. Is what you doing here? You no have time for all this foolishness!"

"Tcho, Gody Myrtle, the collywobbles won't set in till I start down the aisle on the arms of your husband who'll be giving me away. Anyway, my fiancé is right now talking to the Committee. They want to put him forward as one of the advisers for the meeting with the Minister for Migrant Affairs."

"Ah don't like politics," Myrtle said, closing the conversation.

"At the beginning of this year there was a widely viewed debate on television. I personally think it was television at its best," began Warren Hall. "Two men debated the meaning of racism. I thought that Melbourne Welch came over the more credible, the more sincere. He had clarity and was completely without malice. Isn't it strange how things turn out? Not only is Melbourne's life hanging in the balance in the intensive-care ward at St John's Hospital from the injuries he received in *that* accident, then, as we were thinking there was light at the end of the tunnel, he had his first heart attack. Meanwhile Birbeck Samms, who displayed such barefaced racism, has moved from strength to strength. His career was flagging; 'journalistic driftwood', 'journalistic flotsam and jetsam' were two of the more polite terms he was called by his erstwhile peers. Today he's the most sought-after journalist in Fleet Street, hailed as the man who can't be gagged! Politicians of the centre and of the far right, the clergy who are still hung up on a drunken Biblical patriarch; members of right-wing groups, who are all hungry for words from Birbeck Samms. The latest is that he's been accepted as the Nationalist & Unionist Party candidate for Maudslay, an old industrial town that grew with the Industrial Revolution. This is a town that's been loyal to the Liberals from the Great Reform to the end of the century. A town that has been a safe Labour Party seat for over fifty years. In six weeks' time Maudslay's representative at the Palace of Westminster could very well be Birbeck Samms. There seems no stopping this man."

"Old-time people have a saying, *the higher monkey climb, the more he expose himself.*" The woman who interrupted Warren wore a very stylish hat and led the laughter that followed the apt reminder that pride comes before a fall.

"We're told he's to be the principal speaker at the Trafalgar Square anti-immigration rally," said a man with a Barbadian accent.

"I was at the corner of Effra Road and Rushcroft Road, Brixton," continued Warren, "when the speaker from the Union of Fascists (they actually call themselves that!) suggested that people consider marching to Trafalgar Square and having a monster rally so that the country's policy-makers could see that ordinary people wanted an end to black immigration. A couple of weeks later we were being told stories about marches from all the town halls of the London boroughs with any sizeable black population joining in. That meant marches from Kensington, from Paddington, from Lambeth, from Willesden, from Hackney, from Southwark, from Lewisham, and from Greenwich."

"You forgetting Wandsworth and Bermondsey," a man shouted.

"Thank you," said Warren. "There are even stories that coaches are expected from many Midland cities and towns. Maudslay South-East is on everyone's mind these days, I suppose the town will be empty on that day as all its inhabitants head south for London."

"The marches won't now take place," said Jimmy Fairfax soberly. "Not because it would be one of the most provocative acts imaginable, but because the Head of the Metropolitan Police said his force couldn't adequately supervise these marches and still provide the capital with the protection it deserves. Be it as it may, we will not be sidelined or silenced, for while the fascists are peddling their hate at Trafalgar Square we'll be having a peaceful protest at Speakers' Corner, Hyde Park. I sincerely hope you'll attend and bring as many friends and relations as you can. Convince them that this is important. We have an impressive list of speakers. Each day the mail brings letters and cards from people supporting us. I urge you to keep the faith brothers and sisters, keep the faith."

"All this thing with Birbeck Samms is because of what Fleet Street calls the silly season," said a white man who had been making notes on a copy of *The Worker*. "Samms will slip. Things are going too well for him. He's bound to stumble, and great will be his fall. Give him enough time."

"We don't have time," shouted a young woman with a lisp that in other circumstances could be considered sensual. "Why are we always told we're moving too fast? What are we *to wait* for?"

The audience erupted and it took Jimmy Fairfax at least ten minutes to wrest control of the meeting back from a very vocal audience. Having succeeded, he recognised a man who had been waving his hand to catch the chairman's eye. He was a very black man with a thin moustache and eyes that were red, possibly from lack of sleep. He wore a well tailored suit, a shirt without a tie, and an expensive-looking watch that was visible as he brandished a piece of paper in his raised hand. At last the chairman Jimmy Fairfax recognised Caleb Zebulon Morgan, Isaiah Morgan's brother. As Zebulon Morgan spoke he displayed gold teeth. He had not lost his Jamaican accent despite having left his homeland seventeen or eighteen years previously.

"This piece of filth was in the letter-box of a client of mine when he got home one night last week." Zebulon was incandescent with rage, his voice shaking as he read from a handbill. "'*Look out! Has a foreigner taken your job yet? Is a foreigner your employer? Does a foreigner represent you in Parliament? If not, then you are fortunate, for your country is steadily being taken over by the triumphant alien.*'"

He paused for breath. "I arrived on a troop ship in 1941. No one told me then that I was an alien. No one told me I was taking away somebody's job. The most hated people then were the fascists. We were the 'good, loyal colonial boys'. Women came out of their houses offering us cups of tea. We knew the sacrifice they were making in giving us their tea, but it shows there was a degree of solidarity. I helped to win the war and went home. I came back just over a year later to find that the Germans and the Italians were welcomed and I had been demoted to being an alien. In 1948, I learnt another Latin tag: *Civis Britannicus Sum,* I am a British citizen. It's the law. How do we get this country to live up to its obligations? Don't blame the Teddy boys. Show me one national newspaper that admits to a racial problem. As far as they are concerned the bad feeling between the races is caused by black men making prostitutes out of white women. Black landlords cause problems by overcrowding. Young coloured people have noisy late-night parties. *We* have been labelled criminals. On the other hand white men who roam the streets looking for coloured men to attack are not criminals but hooligans. Racism isn't a crime if the perpetrator is white, it's hooliganism! Look at their suggestions for easing the tension: first stop coloured people migrating to Britain. The 1948 Nationality Act was a sham. Colonial peoples are no longer British citizens. Any coloured person found guilty of an offence must be deported. In the meantime the hooligans will grow out of their racism and take their rightful place as upstanding members of society."

"OK, Caleb," said Jimmy, recognising a fellow ex-serviceman. He seized the opportunity when the speaker paused for breath. "As you know, we have a petition that we'll be presenting to the Home Office. We hope everyone in this hall will sign. You, of course, are one of the delegates who'll be meeting the Colonial Secretary next week. Your contribution is as usual invaluable."

"My generation remembers the Mosley fascists before the war," began a middle-aged white woman. "We opposed them then," she continued, "and during the war we were told never again will we allow blind hatred to turn one group against another. The previous speaker was right. We welcomed you during the war. We appreciated the splendid contribution you made and there are people like me ready to apologise for the behaviour of those *fascist criminals* in Notting Hill. I call them *criminals,* not hooligans. I appeal to your better judgement not to retaliate. Before the war the objects of their hatred were the Jews in the East End, then there were the Irish in Liverpool. In fact, as someone who is proud of her Irish roots, I say this: until you people started coming over here, I mean since the war, it was the Irish who were the scapegoats. Prejudice is latent in most people and I'm not trying to excuse it. We've got to learn to live together."

"Permission to speak, sir." He was a stocky black man with a bald patch in the middle of his head. The fringe had thick growth of salt and pepper colour hair in need of trimming. He wore a suit of a greyish colour that hung loosely, giving the distinct impression that he had lost weight. "I am not used to public speaking. It seems to me that some of you are here because you were here during the war and the rest of you come up to study. I've not heard anything from the likes of me, the people who save and scrape, borrow and even steal to find the seventy pounds to pay our fare to London. I don't speak for anyone but myself, but perhaps some of you in this hall know about what I am going to say. I come to London because it is the capital of the Mother Country. I got that drummed into me from I was at school. I tell you the truth, don't laugh. You know how some things you can't forget, even if you try hard? When I think about my school days, I always remember two photographs. One was on the wall behind where the headmaster sat. The man in the photograph had a beard and looked like he was in some sort of uniform. The headmaster said that was King George the Fifth. The other picture was on the wall just inside the school front door. It was a woman with a sash, sitting up straight like somebody just pinch her backside. That they tell me was Queen Mary. Everywhere you turn in the schoolroom the two of them their eyes follow you. I tell you I was 'fraid to break wind in case they heard. Miss Watson our teacher used to tell us that they were looking down on us their children. So every 24th May we marched to Nelson Fort to meet other schools. We would sing songs like '*Rule Britannia*' and '*Land of Hope and Glory*'. I left school the year after the war started. I was fourteen years old. A few years after that, when I went with my brother to enrol him in school, by that time England was at war. The headmaster put up other pictures. This time there was Churchill, Roosevelt and Stalin. The headmaster divided the school into two Houses and put my brother in Roosevelt House. My father went to see him and tell him that Jamaica was in the Empire and his son was to be put into Churchill House. I tell you this because it didn't matter how backward the mountain district you was from, you know that England is the Mother Country. You learn it as you suck your mother's milk. They tell us that England is the mother hen and we like chickens hiding under her wings. Well, it did'n teck me long in this country to find out that that was a whole lot of shit."

He waited for the laughter to subside, but, still not ready to yield the floor, he raised his right hand. "You know, there are two types of immigrants in this county. One type is like me. I come to work and save money so when I go back home, I can better meself. The other type is like most of you. The first thing you do is to find youself a white woman. That means you not going back home. What happen, you not laughing any more? I can't see you taking your white women back to you little wattle-and-daub hut up at Cabbage Hill? It is you that make white people turn against us. The white man don't worry do much when black people get jobs because we only get the shitty jobs anyway. When you tell him you going back home he feel good. He'll laugh and then ask you, 'Now you see what real house look like, you going to come down out of them trees when you go back home?' You see, he never was told anything about us being children of the Empire. He will tell you he'd invite you to his house, but not into his family..."

At last the speaker was forced to yield. While his audience found much to cheer in the earlier part, the latter part of his speech had enough barbs under the saddle to make the rider uncomfortable.

"I'd like to ask the last speaker," said a very large woman, "why our brothers cannot take their white women back to their wattle-and-daub thatched huts up in the Jamaican mountains? It seems to me that is where a lot of us black women are coming from." She sat down amid laughter, although only a few might have got the irony.

"This isn't the time to be trying to score points," said Jimmy. "The choice of one's partner is not the issue here."

"You think not?" asked the man from near Nelson Fort. "I stand up a street corner and watch people pass. I watch how white people look at black men arm in arm with white women and I see the disapproval on them face but when him is with a black woman, white people dem smile. But you people not living in the real world, you all living in the world of 'if things was as right as it should be'. Well, things ain't as they should be. Look at the nice building you have at that place over at Collingham Gardens. That is for students, but it is we the ordinary migrants who a pay for't. Yet we don't have nothing like that. You form your organisation and elect one another as leaders and claim you are representing us the workers. The day will come when all those white people gather in Trafalgar Square, and you all gather at Speakers' Corner, and people like me won't give a damn. We will get up in the morning and run to catch the early morning bus, or the train or the tube, or perhaps one of our mates will pick us up in his mini-bus and we will go to work. We will come back with our pay packet. We will write back home, go to the post office, put in a postal order and register it to our people back home. That's what we come here for. I wonder what you people come here for?" The man from near Nelson Fort, having said his piece, walked with disciplined fury from the main auditorium of the Town

Hall to a generous round of applause, which he steadfastly refuse to acknowledge.

"If anyone knows that, brother, I do wish they'd try and persuade him that this organisation needs him," said Warren Hall. "I mean this most sincerely, folks, if you happen to know anything about him let me know. I'd like to get to know him better. Personally I feel that some of what he had to say shows up the weaknesses of this organisation which we proudly boast is the STUWARD of Coloured People's welfare in this country."

27

A few days before Alonso was due to go into hospital to have the cyst removed from his heel Dr Kalra certified that he would be off work for at least a month. Alonso was advised to do as little standing and walking as possible. A month before, he had passed the test for a Public Service Vehicle licence and had changed from being a bus conductor to a bus driver. He hoped that the change in position, from standing throughout his shift to sitting behind the wheel of a bus with pre-selected gear, would facilitate his speedy recovery.

"I'm not happy about you staying in this basement slum while I'm away," he told his sister.

"I'll be all right. You fuss too much," she said, sitting in her usual position with one leg folded under her, the other stretched out in front. She looked over the brim of her cup of Horlicks.

"Oh, no, I don't believe it," she said, placing her cup on the little table beside her.

"You don't believe what?" he asked.

"You don't trust me. You think fellows will be knocking at the door and I won't be able to resist them."

"Don't talk daft," he said, aware that he did not sound convincing. "You are here most nights on your own when I'm working late shifts."

"That's different."

"How so?"

"Only our friends know that you're my brother. The guys at the corner of Somerleyton Road and Coldharbour Lane have seen us together. I'm sure they think you're my bloke. If you disappear for two weeks they might think you've run out on me, so they may come calling."

"I see what you mean. What I have to do is to be in and out of hospital in a couple of days."

"I'm a big girl now. I have to fight some of my own battles."

"I have no problem on that score. However, this is a dreadful area; we ought to get out of it. Rumour has it that the council will be knocking down our street, Geneva Road soon. "

"That will be after we leave here. Our flat in Kennington will be ready in less than a month and Kenilworth Gardens is really nice, overlooking the park. Lucky for you that your involvement with Creole Enterprises allows you special rates, otherwise we couldn't afford it."

"I have a brainwave. Why didn't I think of it before? What about asking Irone to come and stay with you?"

She growled, baring her teeth, then she leapt on him. He flung his arms wide to avoid spilling the hot beverage over them both. That they were not scalded was because the force of her attack had knocked the mug out of his hand, spilling the drink about a yard away.

"See what you made me do?" she accused. "Now who's going to clean that up? It had better be you. Anyway this is your side of the partition," so saying, she walked on through to her side of the *flimsy* curtain, as they had nicknamed it. She stuck her tongue out at him and said, "Sanctuary!"

"In that case," he said, "I'll have yours." He picked up her mug of Horlicks and began to drink. "We should renegotiate the Treaty. My part of the room is an open thoroughfare, a free port, while yours is a sanctuary!"

"Don't you remember your history? Danzig. The Polish Corridor and all that!" The taunting continued with a change from daring to astonishment. "You're drinking my mouth water," she said in the best Jamaican accent she could muster. "I dribbled spit in it!"

"Nice," he said in a matter of fact voice. "And here's me thinking it was the extra spoon of sugar you put in it."

"Yuk!" she said with mock disgust. "How can you bear to drink someone else's mouth water?"

"With absolute confidence. We say in Jamaica, *what no kill you will fatten you*. It's your loss, my sister. You see, *when horse dead cow get fat*, as they say."

"Stop, man. I got one for you. When you finish drinking my drink, you call *'Horlicks?'* and see if it answer you, then call *'Flowers?'* See out of the drink and me which will answer you."

"You've given me an idea. I'm going to start making notes on Jamaican witticisms. Perhaps there are enough for a book. But I'm still determined you should stay somewhere else when I'm in hospital. The rumours that the council is considering demolishing the houses along these roads to build a new estate could turn out to be true. Until then, people have to run the gauntlet with men and women waiting outside the Employment Exchange. Some say they hang around the offices hoping to be picked up. It's a sort of lonely-hearts market. Then again it being so close to Brixton Market doesn't help."

"Let me see if I understand you correctly. You think I'd fall for one of those guys?"

"Of course, not. But why put yourself through all the cat-calls and the like?"

"I'm going to tell you something, although I'm sure you're as guilty as any other man. A girl is never safe from cat-calls anywhere, even if she has a bag over her head."

"In Jamaica we say 'even if she has a *crocus* bag over her head'".

"Here you go again! *Mi estimado hermano*, men are divided into one or more of three categories, tits, bum and pins."

"Hey, you've grown up while I weren't looking."

"What the hell do you expect? I'm pushing twenty years of age. I travel by bus and crowded underground trains to get to and from work every working day. I can look after myself. It's been some time since I turned to a boy and said, 'I gwine tell me brother and make him bus-up your mouth.' Tell me, you ever beat up anyone on my account?"

"I warned Copeland not to bother you."

"What did he say?"

"That I can't protect you all the time. He also said that if I look at other boys' sisters he had the right to look at mine."

"Sounds fair enough. Now whose sister were you looking at? It couldn't be his sister Essie, she's younger than me and you like older women. "

"Ouch!"

"Did I step on your corn? Sorry but that was deliberate. Well, who was it?"

"I can't remember."

"Liar! Was it Miss Love? All tits and bum she was. Miss Love with no bra and the thin cotton dress. You blokes had quite an eyeful..."

"No!" he shouted.

"Ouch! That touched a nerve," she said. "She's a nurse in a hospital in Birmingham; would you like to get in touch?"

"Tell me more about your theory of tits, bum and pins."

"It's all very boring, but, for the record, I think you're a tits man."

"Me! What's led you to that conclusion? Who do we know who fit the other two categories? Even more intriguing, which category men give you the most wolf whistles?"

"Boring! I'm tired. I'm off to bed. By the way, I've made up my mind. Miss Myrtle had the same fears you have so she invited me to take over Enid's old room. She's apparently saving it for a friend's daughter who is due up shortly. Guess what? She's going to study nursing."

"If you're going to Lilford Road why were you acting up for?"

"I like to provoke you," she said. "Oh, hell!" she shouted, locking her head between the palm of her hands. "I completely forgot that a letter came for you today." She went to her dressing table and returned with a brown envelope but did not hand it over immediately.

"It's nearly eleven o'clock."

"Yes, but you only got in about an hour ago," she looked at the envelope again. "I know where it's from. I thought of chucking it in the dustbin but that would only cause more trouble."

"Come on, hand it over."

"I hate these people. Can't somebody tell them that the war has been over for a long time?"

"Hand it here. Conscription is still the law, Flowers. To tell you the truth I've been expecting my call-up papers since about January."

"Can't you just tell them you're going into hospital and might have to lose a leg?"

"I won't be losing my leg. Honestly, what's the matter with you?"

"Well, it's better than being shot to pieces by the EOKA guerrillas in Cyprus. What is there in Cyprus that concerns you?"

"You wouldn't ask that if you'd been to Stamford Hill and seen those Cypriot girls, dark with long black hair."

"You think that would interest me? I work with a girl call Katerina who's from Limassol. I'll tell her my brother wants to go to her country to shoot her brothers," she flung the letter at him and went back to her side of the partition. "Anyway, I thought you fancied European girls with red hair."

He read the letter and went in after her and sat next to her on her bed. He put his arm around her shoulders. "This isn't going to be a huge problem. I'm going into hospital next Tuesday. I'll show the letter to the doctor in charge of my case. I'll leave it up to them to tell the War Office Medics whether in light of what they have to do to my heel I'll be fit to do any *square bashing?*"

"What's square bashing?" she tilted her head slightly.

"Having to wear those heavy boots and drill in the square, that sort of thing."

"You think it will work?"

"I'm not making it up. After all, this country isn't at war, although there are trouble spots all over the world, they still want men who can stand for hours on their two feet. I won't be able to do that for a couple of months and it's anyone's guess what the outcome of the operation will mean even for my job as a bus driver."

"You're leaving the buses, anyway."

"Yes. Thank God with the help of our chaplain Locksley Hood I'll be starting as an assistant school keeper at the new comprehensive school Barrett-Browning. Did you know that Browning had West Indian connections? That was why Elizabeth Barrett's father was so uptight about Robert marrying his English rose of a daughter."

"English rose she might have been but she was left estates in Jamaica by a relative. So said our history master at Wilberforce. I still think the old man was brimming over with too much paternal love. You know what I mean? The male of the family can be so smothering at times."

"You have experience of that, of course." He rose abruptly.

She grabbed his hand. "Nino!" She pulled him down beside her. "That was way out of line. Our relationship isn't like that. You're not that sort of brother, and if you were I wouldn't stand for it. By the way, a couple of us girls went to see the film *The Barretts of Wimpole Street* when it was showing at the Carib Theatre in Kingston. That was the one with Sir John Gielgud.

Our teacher told us that the 1934 version with Charles Laughton was better."
When he did not respond, she pushed her elbow into his ribs. "Don't sulk.
You don't smother, it is I who cling." She picked up a pillow and held it
high above his head. "Smile or I'll do some smothering myself." He tried to
wrestle the pillow from her. The next moment they were laughing.

"I don't like your choice of jobs. They have no status and aren't well
paid."

"That's what I like about them. I won't be in any of them for long. This
one shouldn't be too hard on my feet and I'll have evenings to go to my
course at Lewisham Poly. I'll also have time to finish rewriting my novel."

"Stella Clarke has been waiting on that for ages. Apart from that, I'm
pleased you'll still be able to do some work for Lincoln and his Creole
Enterprises, won't you?"

"We'll certainly need the money to pay for the furniture we will need
for the flat, which, may I remind you, does belong to Creole Enterprise."

"The last thing we need is the government turning you into a soldier and
paying you two pounds a week."

"I really can't see Mr Strong the surgeon recommending me for military
service after operating on my heel. Whatever Britain's international
obligations might be."

"Your obligation is to your family. You and I can't begin to live our
lives until Bullah comes over, gets a job and starts to support his family
back home. You've been doing it for him, supporting our mother and the
never-ending stream of children that he's given her."

"He's due up in three weeks. Nello said he'd take him to see the foreman
on the building site where he works. He's bound to get a job. How he treats
his family... well, we can't interfere. It was planned a month ago. If he
accepts his responsibilities, it will lift some weight off our shoulders,
although we'll still have obligations to our mother and our siblings." He
rose slowly and she noticed that he dragged his right leg as he went back
through the partition.

"Buenas noches Rosita Maria de Campesino."

"Am I too grown-up for a goodnight kiss?"

"What? With all that smothering, clinging I better..." the pillow hit him
in the back as he pulled himself through the partition.

II

"I'm surprised that Blossom has deserted you the weekend before you are
due to go into hospital," Lincoln said as they drove towards Fonthill Avenue
for Sunday lunch.

"I'm due in hospital on Tuesday afternoon. She'll be home tomorrow.
This weekend with her new friend was planned a month ago, well before

the date of my hospitalisation was known," replied Alonso. "And she hasn't deserted me. She's nearly twenty. She's a big girl now, as she's quick to remind me. I think it's a good thing that she has friends who have no connections with the family."

"I recall that she has strong views on the term 'big girl' now. I hope you mean she's capable of making her own decisions. What do you know about the girl she's spending the weekend with?"

"Didn't Enid have lunch with them last week? I think you know as much as I do. She is white; I think mid-twenty perhaps thirty years old. Her family farms in Essex. She works with Blossom in the same office having started on the same day. So they tend to talk to each other a lot."

"Enid tells me that she is very pretty and has worked as a model and even appeared in a film as part of a prize for winning a local beauty contest."

"Did Enid tell you this young woman's brother is the leader of a pop band? You know that type of stuff, a couple of electric guitars, drum and clarinet. The brother's wife, who's their lead singer, is heavily pregnant, and they discovered that Blossom can sing a bit. This weekend they'll be performing at a youth club. That will be hardly rhythm-and-blues stuff."

"Do you see a career change?"

"For Blossom? Nah, she still wants to be a nurse, though she's quite taken with being a clerk in the civil service."

"So does Enid. She tells me that if she's still with them in two years' time she'll be due to go before a board to be interviewed for promotion. Those are the rules, but will they be the same for a coloured woman when the time comes?"

"They need a token, so they can say we are not prejudice. Look at Ralph Bunche, UN Under Secretary in New York, but if he had a daughter in Little Rock Arkansas, she wouldn't be able to get into Central High School."

"Did you know that guy got the Noble Peace Prize back in 1950? Went to Harvard, and London School of Economics..."

"Howard wasn't it."

"He became Professor of Political Science at Howard University Washington, before he was twenty-four but he did study at Harvard. Eh, man I know more American history than you. Come on, give me a break," he glanced at Alonso and smiled, elbowing him as he did so.

"Lurline says you're going into the hair products business; a very important business," said Alonso, feeling that Lincoln was enjoying this tiny victory and expecting to be accompanied by the *Stars and Stripes.*

"I mentioned it to you sometime back, but it was like you had no interest. Do you realise that all cosmetics and hair products in this country are manufactured with the white woman in mind?"

"I never gave it much thought. I never examine Blossom's dressing-table."

"I hate it when you adopt that tone."

"What tone?"

"'I don't give a shit' attitude."

"Sorry. I'm not a businessman at heart, but I'm proud of you and what you are doing."

"Really? Then pack in all this rubbish about becoming an assistant school keeper and come and work full time in the business. You won't have to limp around the length and breadth of a school yard watching little scallywags writing 'Keep Britain white' on walls."

"You know I haven't got money to buy into the business."

"Forget that shit, man. I don't look on it as if I own the business. Rather it employs me. Pays me a salary. It can afford another person. If you don't accept, I'll have to find someone else. I'd prefer it to be you. We've come a long way since we were teenagers boarding at the Morgans' place in Jones Town, Kingston."

"Not to mention that terrible basement in Drury Lane. How many of us were living there?"

"Eight. How could you forget? Although in that talk you gave on the Caribbean Programme for the BBC it became nine. You remember that night when Jide, *I am the son of a Chief,* brought that prostitute back?"

"Don't remind me. She said we all could fuck her for a pound each."

"Stop it."

"She had a fifty per cent take-up. That was the worst time of my life since the 1951 hurricane ripped through Jamaica and brought down the Baptist church at Grass Piece Gap on twenty of us."

"You realise that it was from those days in Drury Lane that I got the idea about buying houses and renting them out? Talk about renting. Guess who came into the office a couple of days ago with his pregnant white woman wanting accommodation?"

"Surprise me!"

"'Lias Carter!"

"You don't say!"

"You don't mind talking about it?"

"Of course not. I bear him no ill will. As far as I'm concerned he treated Winnie badly. She ran away. I gave her shelter. He thought I took his woman from him. He threatened me. Winnie went back to more bad treatment. She finally left to go and live with her church colleagues in Maudslay. End of story."

"By the way, when I was in Maudslay a month ago I did see her. Of course she doesn't know me that well. Her husband is an Elder in their church, I think... Anyway I promised 'Lias a big room on the ground floor in the new house in Treherne Road."

"Does he know that I have any connection with Creole?"

"Do I have to remind you I don't know the man personally? What struck me about 'Lias was how he was attentive to this woman. She had very pale skin but jet-black hair. I'm sure it was dyed."

"I'm not surprised... not about the dyed hair, I mean. Black men always seem to treat their white women better than they treat black women. I bet he's sent photographs back home to show the folks a happy couple hugging and kissing."

"It wouldn't surprise me. I remember this guy talking on top of his voice in Coolieman's barbershop above the old Colonial Club, that one of the first things he did when he came to London was to screw a white woman on Clapham Common. She gave him the clap, but as he put it he tasted a white woman. He laughed. I thought, 'you bugger. I wonder what you would have done if a black woman down by the wharf in Kingston had given you the pox? You would have sort her out and perhaps slapped all her teeth down her throat.'"

They drove into the drive at 109 Fonthill Avenue. Alonso grinned at the three neighbours who were busily cleaning their cars. They paused long enough to acknowledge Lincoln. Enid opened the door and kissed both of them. She stuffed a piece of paper in her husband's hand.

"Go call that number right away, a Mrs Ismenius. She called three times already."

"She has a couple of big stalls in Ladbroke Grove and Brixton markets respectively. We're planning a joint venture importing foodstuff from back home for the Asian, African and West Indians migrants. In America they call it *soul food*." Having explained the reason for Mrs Ismenius calling, he looked at his wife and friend and said. "*I call her 'Is many of us'*. Behind her back, of course." He went into the sitting room where the telephone was. Enid led Alonso into the kitchen.

"Take the weight off your feet and sit on the stool; your sister ask me to keep an eye on you."

"Fuss, fuss, fuss. Everyone is fussing so much. Catherine and Christine are tossing for the privilege of pushing me in my bath chair. You would think that I'm going in for a major operation."

"But they are in love with you."

"Please!"

"Don't knock it. When I think of them and their relations with you I cannot help thinking of a forward boy three years my junior annoying me with his letters."

"And we all know where that lead to. Any way they are nine years my junior..."

"They won't he thirteen forever."

"Nor will I be twenty-four for much longer... Unless I don't make it back from the anaesthetic."

"Rubbish. They'll probably give you a local. Stop depressing me," she waved her hands about as if to dismiss the whole thing. "I want to ask a favour, and you mustn't give me an answer until you're ready to start thinking of working again. I'm worried sick about Lincoln. He has more irons in the fire than a team of blacksmiths. He'd better watch it or he's going to burn himself out. The way he's going he'll have a heart attack before he's thirty. He's a dreamer. Hard-working, but a dreamer all the same. You're a thinker. You can see the positive and the negative. I think it was Ziah Morgan who said the two of you are like opening batsmen. You're the sheet anchor and Lincoln the impetus chance-taker at the other end. I don't know much about cricket, but I understand what he's driving at. Don't give me an answer now, but think about joining him in Creole Enterprises?"

She heard Lincoln coming and raised an index finger to her lips. Alonso nodded.

III

The operation was scheduled for Thursday morning. Alonso wondered why they asked him to put on the white gown over his underclothes when the object of the operation was only to remove a cyst from his right heel. Had he been given the choice he would have walked to the operating theatre, but he was lying flat on his back on the trolley as they pushed him gently along the white corridors. He was finding it difficult to concentrate. Would it have impeded the surgeon Mr Strong, in this most technical of task had he Alonso been wearing a three-piece suit with the turn-ups above his ankles? He was too groggy to articulate all this. He remembered being put under lights. He heard voices. One sentence was clear.

"So they want to make a soldier out of you, do they?"

He woke as from a dream. He was sitting under a large tree on the brow of a hill. The land dropped away sharply and the valley stretched for miles. His knowledge of amphitheatres was gained from pictures in books and the current spate of Roman and Biblical themed films that Hollywood was turning out. Half awake he thought he was sitting high up on a tier of the vastest amphitheatre ever. He thought of what might have happened millions of years ago. A small inland sea swirling as if a giant plug had been pulled out, as it swirled pushing the hills asunder and then finding a crack between the rocks it gurgled its way to some distant shore. To his right and to his left he saw the giant trees standing like sentinels, motionless like the mounted guards in Whitehall. There was no wind. The heat of the sun shimmered from the valley floor like a haunted mind.

Slowly a figure emerged from the shimmering heat. It was clothed in white and was riding a black horse. At first he thought that it was a desert warrior. He had reconciled himself to Sir Walter Scott's Tory politics and had begun to read the author again. He had finished *Kenilworth* and was halfway through *The Talisman*. Neither book matched the excitement of *Ivanhoe*, but he had first read that ten years ago. Here on this hillside he thought, as he watched the white-robed figure, this was a valiant Desert

Warrior to be dispatched by the brave Sir Kenneth. Then he saw the cross was in flame and he heard a voice said, *"This is King Kleagle, Klavern No.1 from the Province of Londinium Realm of Albion... Who will challenge me?"*

He felt ashamed and sad that there was no challenger. The white-robed figure galloped around the vast amphitheatre unchallenged, arrogant and undefeated. Alonso wanted to ride out and challenge *the Kleagle*, but he did not have a horse. He rose to his feet and started to run down the slope, waving his arms and shouting. He fell and the speed with which his body hit the ground sent him spinning and rolling down the hill like a barrel. At the bottom, he fell into a pool. He clambered out and looked around him, but *the Kleagle* had disappeared. Alonso was now standing at a bus stop on an unfamiliar London street. However, he knew he had to get to Notting Hill. He seemed to have been waiting for ages. When the bus did come, the conductor stood on the platform holding on to the pole that linked the lower deck to the upper and would not let him board. When he asked why not, the conductor said, "Wait for the bridegroom!" The conductor stroked his waxed moustache, smiled, rang the bell and the bus moved off.

As in a movie the scene changed and Alonso was playing the part of Ivanhoe. He was mounted on his powerful steed with its snow-white mane, riding with his lance held high for his lady to place her token. He saw faces, oh, so many faces, but none of them was familiar. A masked lady beckoned him. He approached, his lance a few inches from her masked face. "Take this, valiant knight." And she placed a wig of copper-coloured hair at the sharp point of his lance. "Wear it with honour, Sir Knight. Attend the bridegroom." There was a ribbon pinned to the wig. On it was written in bold letters one word: *UXORIOUS!*

With his visor still raised he glanced at his shield, hoping to read his motto *"Desdichado"*, but once again he saw the word *uxorious*. Then the crowd took up the chant: *uxorious, uxorious!* The most recent reference of that word, as he recalled, was when Melbourne Welch offered his congratulations to Lincoln and Enid, Melbourne doing his usual playing with words. Having had a failed marriage himself, he dared to lecture others on the union between a man and a woman.

> *... Enid, Yniol's only child,*
> *... And Enid, but to please her husband's eye,*
> *Who first had found and loved her...*

Immediately Alonso recalled the Penguin selection of poems by Alfred Tennyson, which was a prescribed book for the Jamaica Local Examination (Third-Year). That had sent him back to the book given to him by a departing head teacher. It was now dog-eared, the spine torn and pages falling out; he searched for a line or two for his best man's speech. He realised that as with all selections from verse he would have to be very cautious.

He knew he could not dare to wear that wig in public. Perhaps this was for the bridegroom. Who was he? And how would he recognise him? Easy, he thought, he would be the one with the bride by his side. But where did Melbourne Welch come into this? From what he had gathered, Melbourne's relationship with his wife was anything but uxorious. He rode on past where they were tilting and jousting. There were knights in pain and there were knights victorious.

He ignored them and rode on until he reached the chapel with high cathedral doors. A man stood with bowed head. As he approached and the bowed figure pointed and mumbled as if in distress. "The bridegroom awaits!" He dismounted and entered the sanctuary, walked slowly up the aisle past pews of people wearing sad and mourning faces. He approached the bier. The guards clashed their lances and blocked his way. An attendant reached for the wig but he would not let it go. The attendant pulled and he held firm. He wanted to get past the guards' lances to see who the corpse was. Could it be Melbourne? The attendant jerked the wig from his hands, falling backwards, knocking down the guards and the bier, and the scene faded like a tropical twilight.

"I was beginning to get worried," said Blossom, holding his hand. "I've been sitting here for half an hour. How do you feel?" She had managed to get her arms around his neck and had him in a crushing hug.

"As one woken from unpleasant dreams," he said, taking in everything and remembering more and more. He smiled at her. "You smell gorgeous. Great after-shave." He pushed her gently.

She relaxed her embrace. "It would be a pity to wake up from silly dreams only to be suffocated."

She called the nurse, who began checking pulses and eyes and asking questions, then she turned to Blossom and asked her to wait outside. When she came back the nurse told her that the patient was doing fine. Mr Strong would see him in two days and a decision would be made when he could go home. The nurse told Blossom that she could stay for another twenty minutes. Then the nurse left.

"How do you really feel?"

"Stupid, lying here with my right foot under a dome. Go on, have a look and tell me how much of my foot they cut off."

"Silly boy. It's all there," she said, feeling under the dome. "I'm sure it's not the operation that's bothering you. What is it?"

"I had a silly mixed-up dream. The word *uxorious* that Melbourne used in his strange pedantic way to congratulate Lincoln when he was told of his forthcoming marriage to Enid featured in my dream. It is bothering me. Any news of Melbourne?"

"To tell you the truth I haven't been thinking about him. It's you we've been thinking of. Look at your table. There are flowers from me, seven cards from your friends, and the fruit's from Catherine and Christine. By the way, the Morgans are coming to see you tomorrow. The twins said they are coming to eat the fruits so you mustn't eat them all."

"They are funny. Tell my friends not to fuss. I'll be home in a few days. Are you being smothered at the Morgans?"

"No more that usual. I know I've only a few minutes left but I must introduce you to someone."

"Boyfriend? That was quick work!"

She paused at the screen and mouthed something quite obscene before disappearing into the ward. When she returned she found him reading one of the cards and chuckling. The card was from Warren Hall. He looked up and saw the young woman standing beside Blossom. She was white and her hair was exactly like the wig at the end of his lance in his dream. He wondered if he was still under the drowsy numbness of the anaesthetic. Was he still dreaming?

"Good Lord!" Blossom's companion said.

"Do you two know each other?" asked Blossom looking from her brother to her friend.

"I'll say," said the young woman.

"So no introductions are necessary?"

"I'm Sheila Cox," she said. "The window dresser in Sue's Boutique, Streatham. Remember? Your bus used to stop outside the boutique. I think we got as far as waving to each other."

"I remember. What I'm not sure of is if I'm still under the influence of the anaesthetic."

"The anaesthetic wore off a while ago. The nurse said so," Blossom continued to look from Sheila to her brother. She settled her gaze on her friend and spoke directly to her. "My brother has the most vivid dreams from as far back as I can remember. Sometime ago he dreamt there was a *duppy* girl in his room. Duppy is Jamaican for ghost. He never saw her face but from her size, colour and hairstyle he's absolutely certain she was the same girl he saw in the shop window in Streatham."

"My God! It's frightening," she said as her recollection of moments of innocent flirting returned to haunt her. "Would it help if I was to say that I've never been dead, and as to haunting someone..." Although she smiled she could not hide her uneasiness.

"Oh, I don't think the apparition in his room haunted him. What can please a man more than watching a woman getting dressed?"

"I never said anything about her being undress." Alonso protested.

"I suppose if she was dressing then she must have been undressed at some stage. This young woman is the real flesh and blood person you saw in the window of that boutique in Streatham and that haunted you. Eh, *Nino?*"

"Can you see me? I was listening to you both and thought I was still under the anaesthetic or having another dream," he said wearily.

"Shouldn't you have said *hermano?*"

"*Nino* was what I heard my mother called him and I followed." Turning to her brother she said, "Sheila's learning Spanish. She went to Spain for her holiday and plans to go back next year."

"We went to Valencia for our honeymoon three years ago," she deliberately moved her hand so that he could see her rings.

Blossom's eyes darted from the rings to her brother's face. She was annoyed that she could not detect disappointment. Was it because of the anaesthetic? Looking at Sheila she thought that she was using her rings as a batsman uses his bat to kill the spin.

IV

Anyone who had spent a convivial hour or two in company of Alonso or any of his close friends would have heard the story of the ghostly apparition in his room in Ostade Road SW2. In fact Alonso himself had heard the story re-told with a North London setting. Lincoln was told by one of Adlyn's friends that the story was being told in Handsworth from as far back as 1950. There are many versions of the story. One introduced a carpet with dark red stains, which became brighter when cleaned. By this addition we are to understand that suicide or murder might have brought about the end of the young woman's life. Scenarios abound as fertile minds long practised in storytelling create a myth of a provincial teenager who ran away to London. She was pregnant and alone and ended her life with two sharp and deep slashes of a razor blade to the wrist. Did she scream in the tomb-like silence of the empty house in the middle of the day as her lifeblood drained away, cold and silent, to be found on rent-collection day?

So intrigued was Alonso by the proliferation of these stories that he began reading back copies of the *South London Citizen* searching for a report of a suicide or murder to fit the legend. There were certainly many suicides by young women. In some cases the coroner admitted they were unmarried women who were pregnant. The preferred way of ending their lives was by gas. Nearly all the cases ended with the coroner's explanation that '*she took her own life while the balance of her mind was disturbed*'. There was no mention of any of this happening at any address in Ostade Road. He reflected on the bloodstained carpet, which had definitely not been in his room. He thought of young girls who were knocked down by vehicles on their way to work. Some were murdered. Perhaps this tragedy happened more than a decade ago and this poor girl was killed by a V2, Hitler's final solution to obliterate London. However, the greatest mystery of all was the resemblance of the ghostly apparition and the window dresser in the store in Streatham. This part of the puzzle was known to only a few. When he told Lincoln about the girl in the window, Lincoln pointed out that since he had not seen the face of the apparition he could not be certain they looked alike except for the abundance of red hair. The two instances were separate. Lincoln's preference was the apparition in the attic room in Ostade Road, a girl getting dressed. He told Alonso that he was turning the dream and the girl in the shop window into something as silly as the plot of an opera.

28

Sheila Cox was told that she should turn left on leaving the underground station. After about one hundred yards or so she was to cross right and turn into Prince Albert Road, first right would bring her into Kenilworth Gardens. It should be easy to distinguish Consort Court with its ornate features. It was only four floors high and was dwarfed by the newer London County Council residential tower blocks. It stood back from the pavement separated by an apron of well-kept flower gardens, a crescent drive with IN and OUT at respective ends. This showed off the residents' affluence by the cars they owned, Daimler, Lanchester, Jaguar and a Humber Super Snipe. By contrast the LCC buildings began at the edge of the pavement and were divided into blocks, each with an archway leading to the start of a spiral staircase. There was a distinct smell of bleach and or urine at the entrances, depending on how recently they had been cleaned.

There was a young woman standing two rungs ahead of Sheila on the escalator at Kennington Underground Station. Outside in the bright autumn evening she turned left on leaving the station and Sheila fell in behind her. Five minutes later they turned into Prince Albert Road, then right into Kenilworth Gardens. A few yards into Kenilworth and Sheila could see the crescent drive that led to the entrance to Consort Court. The young woman became conscious of Sheila following her turned and smiled. Sheila took two quick steps to lessen the distance between them. They were almost walking beside one another as they reached the entrance to Consort Court. The young woman raised her right knee so she could rest her bag as she rummaged for her latchkey. She turned the key and the door swung open grudgingly. She was about to close the door when Sheila lifted a hand to prevent the closure. "Please may I come in? I'm going to the second floor."

"I live on the second floor, I can't recall seeing you before, you visiting?" Suspiciously, she positioned herself so that Sheila could not slip through if she was up to no good. Did she not see the sign "No hawkers"? But she did not look the type.

"My friends have only just moved in..."

"On the second floor? You sure?"

"Perhaps not so recently. Oh, you can't have missed them. They are black..."

Sheila was taken aback by the speed and vehemence of the agility of the young woman as the door was pushed shut. It was as if a sudden force of hurricane strength had ripped the door from her hands. Sheila intuitively swayed from the explosion of lock clicking firmly into place and in her panic her handbag slid from her shoulder and the contents spilled on the ground. She stooped to retrieve them. A storm raged in her mind. Should she flee back to the station and home? She did not recall that Blossom had given her precise instructions about gaining entry.

"Tut tut! How many times has a woman spilled the contents of her handbag looking for her keys? Well, I don't know!" said a male voice from a great height.

She looked up and through her tears saw a tall man with silver hair and moustache, his hand outstretched to assist her to her feet.

"Why the tears? Nothing's missing or broken, I hope?" he asked. He leaned forward to place his key in the latch, opened the door. "There you are. In you get."

Sheila thanked him and walked up the stairs to the second floor, dreading that she would once again come face to face with the angry young woman.

II

"You did warn her about being precise in ringing the right bell?" asked Alonso.

"I'm sure Sheila understands the technology of the intercom..."

"That's our flat door bell," said Alonso. "How did she get into the building? Some kind folk must have opened the door for her."

"What the hell!" he could hear Blossom. "Sheila, what's the matter?" Then he heard the sobs.

"Fi... fi... first she slammed the door in my fa... fa... face and just now she ca... ca... called me a ni... ni... nigger-loving whore." She was holding on to Blossom. The sobs were pulling at her chest like some strange and powerful suction machine. Blossom held her tightly until she calmed down. "I must go... My make-up is running... I'm a mess... I must go... so sorry."

"You're not going anywhere," said Blossom, "'cept to sit in that chair... Who let you in? Why didn't you ring the intercom?"

Alonso had limped over to the cabinet to pour a brandy for Sheila. "You may prefer tea but this is quicker to dispense and kicks in rapidly. Here, take a good swig," he instructed.

It was more than an hour before they could piece together the story of Sheila's experience.

"I've heard countless conversations about black men and white women. I've heard the whispered remarks when a white girl and her black man friend get on the bus or the tube. At times I grinned back at the whisperer who was sitting next to me, just to be polite... I mean, to challenge outright would be to get embroiled in something very ugly. I'd found I couldn't look

309

the couple in the eye. I would tell myself it was none of my business. I had never been out with a coloured man, never lived next to one, so what business was it of mine? Then I met Blossom and we became friends," she touched Blossom's hand. "I'm very proud to walk down the street with you, as with any of my white girlfriends. We've been into so many places and I never once felt apologetic, yet... it would be different if I was out with Lonso... I'm really sorry but that's how I feel. Am I a white racist?"

"You were born into a racial group that thinks it's the greatest and is in the majority here. Culturally you were born into a racialist society. It would be odd if you weren't a bit racist..."

"Thanks a lot... So why did that woman call me a Nigger lover? Why does she think I've betrayed her?"

"She thinks you've betrayed what society expects of you. That means you've moved away from all that crap you were told as a child. You've joined the many people who've succeeded in educating themselves out of the *status quo*, and I don't mean at college or university. People from any class can educate themselves out this institutional racism crap. You haven't got to walk down the street with me to prove that you don't belong to the race-hate brigade. Many people seem to think that the races getting on together in harmony means that their daughters will marry a black man..."

"Look, Sheila," Blossom interrupted her brother's lecture, "I've told so many black guys that I'm not interested in them... come to think of it I've told a couple of white guys the same thing."

"John Kingsley," said Sheila brushing away her tears and laughing, as she recalled the clerical officer with the crush on Blossom

"Precisely," agreed Blossom. "I think you should have the same rights. To tell you the truth I sometimes feel embarrassed walking down the street with Lonso. Everyone thinks he's my boyfriend." They all laughed together.

"What does colour really tell us about anyone? Look at Tom..."

"Your husband?"

"Yes. He's tall, fair-haired, blue-eyed and very handsome. He's an assistant cameraman in the film industry. My parents worship him. My three younger sisters adore him. My two brothers envy him. Yet what a bastard he turned out to be. Not only is he unfaithful, but he loves boasting about his so-called conquests. Apparently his greatest triumph was to have bedded three sisters who were his childhood neighbours..."

"At the same time?"

"Lonso!" screamed Blossom, "don't be so coarse."

"It does happen, my dear sister." He thought of Lurline and Puncie.

"I don't think he'd be against that either," Sheila said. "He boasted about going all the way to Sydney, Australia, to bed the oldest sister. She had migrated, you see. There she was married with three children and not doing so well. He took her out, wined and dined her, then bedded her and came back to talk about it as if it was merely a class reunion."

"Did he tell you about it?"

"No, but he told someone who was bound to tell me," she said. "Now I worry about him and my three sisters. What a coup – four sisters!" tears welled up in her eyes again.

"Come on," Blossom intervened, "Jaime is only ten. Tom will be past fifty by the time she's of the age of consent!"

" Age of consent! What is that when it is at home? Jaime once told him that he should have waited until she had grown up, because I was too old. Strange how the seventeen years between us make me old, but the thirty-four years between her and Tom makes him attractive to her. He is old enough to have had a child my age, and a grandchild at school with Jaime."

"What that says is that you and your sisters can't resist his charms either. In a way it's a compliment to your excellent choice. "

"Obviously, big brother! That's why she married him." Blossom wanted to shut up her brother and had not quite digested his comments.

"What puzzles me about your next-door neighbour is that she'd probably never spoken to either of you, yet she seemed to think I was coming to see Lonso. How did she know you two weren't a couple? Or is she just against all whites mingling with coloureds? She saw sex in it somewhere or else why would she call me a whore?"

"Oh, I think the grapevine in Consort Court is as good as anywhere else. I'm sure she knows that we're brother and sister. She probably belongs to that group who thinks that whites who bother to mix with coloureds are part of the great unwashed, trying to end civilisation, as she knows it. Seeing a gorgeous creature like you asking for the address of coloured people, she just exploded."

"Stop embarrassing the girl?"

"If Sheila doesn't know that she *is* gorgeous, then it's high time she was told. Or do you want me to be very Jamaican? Sheila, in Jamaica we never say babies are pretty, otherwise duppies or ghosts would haunt them, so we say the baby is ugly. I think it works for women too."

"Blossom, you must teach me some of your Jamaican sayings. I'll tell you this, white men see all coloured women as the rhythm section of the entertainment industry. They go wild about their sensuality. Every pretty coloured woman is either a singer or a cabaret dancer. My two brothers and my dad go wild about Dorothy Dandridge, Eartha Kitt, Pearl Bailey, Shirley Bassey... come to think of it, they're wild about you, Blossom. But coloured men are different. They're seen as unacceptable rivals. When I mention Harry Belafonte, who I think is simply gorgeous, they give me a funny look, as if to say 'We'll turn you out with a curse if you bring a coloured man in this family.' When I say I'm coming to see Blossom, someone usually asks, 'And what's her brother's name again?' By the way, anybody ever tell you that you could pass for Belafonte's younger brother?"

"Do you think they've twigged that it's not Blossom you're seeing, but it *is* really me?"

"Alonso!" Blossom screamed.

"I think they'd carry out their threat and emigrate to South Africa."

"You ain't kidding!"

"We have an Aunt Ethel who married into big money and is living in Johannesburg. All the family worships Aunt Ethel... for her vast wealth. Well, I can tell you she would let out a roar in her best Lady Bracknell's voice: '*A black man! A Kaffir!*' With every relative jostling to be her favourite and heir apparent, my dad would commit murder... yours!"

"You better believe it, brother!" said Blossom. "She did drop in on a rehearsal at the church hall once. I was never so unsettled in anybody's presence."

"So we won't be announcing our engagement, then?" asked Alonso with mock innocence.

"If you don't behave yourself, you'll be back in hospital, this time with a couple of cracked ribs," threatened Blossom.

"So," said Alonso, ignoring his sister's threat, "how did a nice girl like you end up marrying Tom the assistant cameraman, if one may be so bold to ask?"

"I won a beauty contest. Tom was one of the judges. As he was used to photographing film stars the other judges went with his choice. Part of the prize was a bit-part in a comedy, *Girls' Academy....*"

"I saw that film!" Alonso threw his hands in the air and leaned forward.

"But I bet you didn't see me... even if you didn't sneeze," Sheila continued. "After that I modelled for a couple of West End stores. I didn't have the talent to make it either as an actress or a model. Then I married Tom; all I wanted was to have three or four kids! All he wanted was to prove he could take my virginity and if it meant giving up his bachelor status for a while to satisfy his desire then so be it. He made it plain that parenthood had to wait. Much later he revealed that his ex-wife had custody of their three children, he didn't want to be a father again. When it became clear to me what he really was like, I walked out. Look," she held out her hand, "I'm still wearing his ring. To ward off unwanted attention. Tom will find another hard-to-get girl, who's determined to keep her virginity for the marriage bed... In which case he'll ask me for a divorce so he can marry another pretty girl who keeps annoying him by saying no, as I did."

"That," said Blossom, slapping her knees, "is enough! Sheila, come with me to the kitchen and help me finish making the dinner. I'm cooking chicken, as Gody Myrtle, Gody Ivo and all Jamaican kitchen supremos used to and still do, bless 'em all. Brother dear, consider yourself 'unwanted attention', courtesy of Aunt Ethel, and set the table."

29

About half an hour after Melbourne Welch's death, Jimmy Fairfax and Melbourne's widow, Dorrit, addressed the small but tenacious group of students who had kept vigil since he was admitted to St John's Hospital. There was nothing else to do now but go home. There were funeral arrangements to be made. Later there would be time for tributes. Some of the students wept unashamedly. Many were comforted by their peers and began their sad journey home. Jimmy Fairfax and his party drove away. The two policemen who had watched over the students' vigil exchanged words with the rump of the students who seemed too grief-stricken to even contemplate their next move. From that moment on no one was certain what happened. *The Kensington Coronet* reported a dialogue between students and police that went some away to explain what might have happened.

> *Officer*: Your friend is dead. There's nothing more that you or anyone else can do. My advice to you is to go home.
> *Student*: What's happening, officer, you anxious to have a cup of tea?
> *Officer*: There's no call for that. We've been patient with you lot for a long time. Now, move!
> *Student*: You've already arrested some of us. Can't you leave us alone?
> *Officer*: Right, I've had enough of you, move!"

He pushed one of the male students, who lost his balance and knocked over a female student. In the ensuing mêlée two students (several, said the police) broke away and ran into the hospital shouting, "They killed him. They killed Melbourne."

Police reinforcements came in black Wolsley cars, their bells clanging. Many arrests were made. They were taken to Ladbroke Grove Police Station. Before long a large hostile crowd had gathered on the pavement outside the station, shouting and hurling abuses at passers-by. Black and white community leaders took some time to pacify the protesters. The students who were arrested were bailed and an uneasy calm seemed to settle over Notting Hill.

As evening fell a small but noisy group of white protesters trickled out of Lansdowne Crescent into St John's Gardens. It marched under a poorly written banner declaring an end to Black Immigration. Turning right into Clarendon Road it began to gather strength. A hail of milk bottles which were hurled at them by some coloureds and their white radical supporters impeded the marchers' progress. Most of these missiles whether by design or poor marksmanship fell in the street or on the pavement. The result was to send the protesters into a whirlpool of angry chanting, "Nigger! Nigger! Nigger! Out! Out! Out!" It whirled like a stream in full spate lashing at its banks. It had re-formed by the time it reached Elgin Crescent this time under the banner of the British Union of Fascists. There was a banner proclaiming: *Ku Klux Klan of Britain, No 1 Province of Londinium.* There was another stating *Keep Britain White!* As they swept right into Blenheim Crescent it was like a tropical torrent swollen by myriads of smaller streams fed by the summer rains. It carried all before it.

Two coloured men who had minutes before left Ladbroke Grove Underground station were now turning into the opposite end of Blenheim Crescent. They heard the chanting and could see in the distance the crowd hot with lava like anger flowing towards them.

"You no see that there's a whole pile a bangerangs a-gwon?" someone shouted from the second balcony of flats on the right.

The men stopped. A coloured man ran past them. He shouted as he came close. "Get you bloodclawt self off the street! You no see riot start?"

"Kiss me rarse!" said one man, nervously gripping his mate's shoulder.

"Foot," said his companion, *"Foot nyam no gie me none."* He was beseeching his own feet to extract every ounce of energy his body could produce and take him fast and far from this scene.

The men turned and started to run. The crowd was now mindlessly angry. "Niggers!"

"Don't let them get away."

The men were running faster. They hoped to evade their pursuers once they had turned back into Ladbroke Grove. There was no plan. They only knew that they must run! As they turned left into Ladbroke Grove an old white woman called out to them. "Hey! This way." They ran down towards the basement. She closed the door behind them and continued to put out her milk bottles nonchalantly. As a young woman in the 1930s she had manned the barricades in Sidney Street, East London. She had survived the bombing of London in the dark days of the early 1940s. She was standing with her hands on her wide hips as the scouts and outriders of the crowd came around the corner from Blenheim Crescent. They shouted, "Keep Britain white", as they passed her. They might have been telling her that what they were doing was in her name and for the greater good of her children and grandchildren. She stood as if on a reviewing stand as the crowd swaggered on down the street. The crowd had mistaken her silence for compliance.

From their sanctuary the two men could hear the crashing of milk and beer bottles and the exploding of petrol bombs. The Notting Hill racial disturbances of 1958 were on its way.

III

"Will the riots come to Brixton?" asked Christine.

"What?" asked Nello, "You want to see blood flow in the street?"

"Don't frighten me pickney dem," Myrtle was angry at Colonel's intemperate reply.

"What do you think, Lonso?" Christine persisted as she squatted close to where Alonso was sitting. She looked up at him as if she valued his reply.

"I hope not," he replied, then he continued as if rehearsing a speech. "I think there's a marked difference between North Londoners and South Londoners. There are ethnic groups in all parts of London, but in the North that's what they really are. Many racial groups hanging on to their cultural ethnicity. In the South we're more integrated."

"What's that word again?" asked Myrtle.

"Ethnicity? Surprising the terms the American civil rights have turned up. It's Greek and it means nationality."

"Well, well," said Myrtle, "you live and learn." She paused as Lincoln followed by Enid and Isaiah Morgan burst into the room.

"Quick, man, quick! Turn the radio to the Home Service. Claudia was interviewed last night. It's on now. We might just catch it," said Lincoln. After what seemed an age, they heard the now familiar voice:

> "British citizens from Jamaica and the rest of the West Indies, Ghana and other countries, who live in North Kensington, are not the reasons (for overcrowding) because the population now is lower than it has ever been since 1946. These people have not taken your homes, because the homes were never there to be taken. Everybody in North Kensington, everybody in the badly housed areas, whatever their colour, is equally badly housed. Those who want to exploit this situation will use it to spread hatred and bad feelings. Do not be deceived into hating your neighbours when they are suffering the same misfortunes as yourselves."

Claudia's reply was cut short as the announcer brought in a reporter who was interviewing some white residents of Notting Hill.

Interviewer: You've all lived in Notting Hill for some years. What do you think is happening here?

Man's voice: Ordinary white people, the working people, the salt of the earth, are saying enough is enough... we want them out... back to their own country.

Interviewer: But this is not national. These disturbances are localised to Nottingham and Notting Hill, not all over the country.

Man's voice: It ain't yet. This is only the beginning... Is this what the war was about? Stop Hitler killing the Jews so the government can bring the Niggers in?

Interviewer: It's all a Jewish plot, then? Are the Jews responsible?

Woman's voice: Well, they're the ones making profit from it. They rent them rooms... pack them in like sardines... selling them flats and houses that should have gone to honest white working people.

Second woman's voice: You go down to Aldgate... the Jews got them there working in the garment industry... cheap labour. They won't employ white people there any more.

Interviewer: These people are our own colonial peoples. They fought for us during the war...

Man: We don't need them no more... If we don't watch it we'll become like Portugal... with black blood flowing in our grandchildren's veins... Give 'em their independence... we don't need them.

1st woman: Yeah... mongrelising the white race... send them back to their jungle, I say... A white woman and a darkie... it's sickening. It ain't natural.

2nd woman: 'Course it ain't natural. Blackbirds and sparrow don't mix...

Man: Mind you, I'm not saying we ain't got some responsibilities, but let us look after our own first. After all, charity begins at home.

1st woman: Damn right. Tell me this, why have we got to bleedin' have them over here? Why can't we help them to build up their own country? Send them some money, machinery and what have you. Just get them out of our country. We don't want to mix with them. Think of us for a change... Too much mixing... White girls having their babies... I'm sorry for the children... half-castes...

Interviewer: So in Notting Hill you are protecting the white...

2nd man: White values... the white race... we ain't the same as them, you know. As a kid my mother used to take me to Brixton... good shopping centre, it was... Bon Marche,

Morley's, lots of other shops... Do y'know that Brixton was so important, it was there that the first street in this country to be lit by electricity? Now that area's run down since they started coming over... just ten or so years... I wouldn't go there if you paid me... the darkies are all over the place...

Interviewer: There are no riots in Brixton...

2nd man: 'Cos all decent white people are clearing out... their town's a slum thanks to the darkies. Send them back to live with the monkeys. That's what they're used to...

Interviewer: Miss Jones who speaks for coloured people said that working-class whites and black migrants face the same problems: bad housing and poor job prospects; they should work together...

All voices together, then 1st man: We don't need help from the Niggers. Send them home and there'll be more houses... jobs... that's obvious, ennit?

2nd man: If the government don't act, we will...

1st man: We've made a start.

Interviewer: So you don't feel this is a shame on Britain, which is the head of a great empire?

All together, but distinctly, 2nd woman: Shame on the likes of you and the BBC. What're we paying our licences for? You stand here giving us the third degree. I bet you don't live near them! You can be all nice and liberal because your penthouse flat is far from their Saturday-night parties..."

"You and your kind can afford to like them. They ain't your neighbours.

Interviewer: Now back to Broadcasting House.

"Something for you to remember," Blossom said, looking at Lincoln, "when you join the committee to advise the Home Office minister in charge of immigration..."

"If indeed it goes ahead. Don't forget the creation of such a committee was a recommendation. Don't hold out much hope. I fear the Migration Department will want only to hear what the government is comfortable with, which is that migration from the non-white Empire and Dominion ought to be stopped."

"Indeed," sighed Enid. She had her arms around Blossom and Catherine. "These Kingdoms are no longer at ease... Britain is like a hen rejecting all her black chickens, as that man said at the meeting the other day."

"This is my passport. Today I went for my call-up interview with my heel still strapped up. Cut a long story short, I was considered to be medically unfit for military service." He opened the document and read: " *'Request and require in the Name of Her Majesty all those whom it may concern to allow the bearer to Pass Freely without let or hindrance, and to afford every assistance and protection of which he may stand in need*'. I say it doesn't matter a damn whether the words *pass* and *freely* are written with initial capital letters. We're witnessing and exposing the end of the myth of Pax Britannia. The dissolution of the Empire. I daren't say the Mother Country ever again?"

The radio was silent. Someone had turned it off as if as a mark of respect at the passing of an elderly relative. No one spoke for perhaps two minutes. Then the engine of a taxi sounded reveille.

"That will be my friend my friend Sheila Cox. I'd forgotten about her... In case you didn't know it, this is the redheaded girl my brother dreamed into existence..."

"The one that reminded him of the duppy girl that was in his room?" asked Nello.

"The same," said Blossom heading for the door.

"So is she coming to see him or you?" Nello wanted to know.

"Her," shouted Alonso. "I bet she's here to talk business. They're trying to form a band, *The Icenis.*"

"So what happening, Miss Blossom? I never knew you could sing," Nello said and was cut short by Lincoln.

"I thought your were at our wedding! Don't you remember Blossom singing solo the first three verses of 'Love divine, all loves excelling'? "

"Colonel started very early on the white rum, you know," the prophet reminded the party.

"Who me? I wasn't drunk, man. It wasn't me who was getting married, man," Nello said in mock indignation. "Anyway that was church singing, but this business *is rock 'n' roll,*" he made a few dancing steps. Blossom pushed him playfully as she passed him with a grin. She knew that her new interest was no longer hot news to anyone who frequented the Morgan's household. They all knew about her weekends in Danetree, Sheila's hometown. The rumour was either she had found herself a boyfriend, or something extraordinary was happening on those weekends. If it was not a man why was her only visitor this redhead, Sheila? They already knew that they happen to work in the same government department.

"Another visitor, and I haven't prepared anything," announced Myrtle Morgan, throwing her hands in the air and bringing them down with a slap on her knees. "Girls, let us go see what we can wheel up. Let's see what there is in the kitchen."

"I for one can't imagine Gody Myrtle with empty cupboards," said Alonso. They all chortled as the two daughters and Enid followed Miss Myrtle into the kitchen. Blossom had gone down to the front door to meet her friend.

"Nothing has changed," said Lincoln, accepting a glass from Ziah Morgan. Then, turning, he said spitefully to Alonso, "You're still on antibiotics. Have some tonic water." The men cackled as they looked at each other, waved their glasses at poor Alonso and drank without giving a toast.

"You know," began Isaiah Morgan, "you all have short memories. Well, I been listening to you all and I even look at the papers and everybody been saying how what happened in Notting Hill was the worst thing that happen to black people in this country. Well, make me tell you something, this no bad like what happened in Deptford in 1949."

"What happened in Deptford in 1949?" asked Lincoln and Alonso in unison.

"Only one rarseclawt of a race riot," said Ziah Morgan taking a gulp of white rum. "Pardon my French," he said and they all chortled. "I can't believe you guys never heard about the Deptford Riots of 1949. It was all over the papers and Melbourne Welch, God rest his soul, was there in court all through the trial and the conference that followed at Goldsmith's College." He paused for effect, enjoying the fact that he knew something that neither Lincoln nor Alonso knew. He savoured the moment, knowing that in a day or two one or the other would research into the Deptford riots and become more expert than he could ever be. "I was sharing a room with three other guys in a back street off the Old Kent Road. I tell you boys, you never see just a run-down place. There was this African guy who seemed to run the whole show. The landlady was a big Englishwoman; she had a husband who was a cripple. 'War wounds', that was what they told those who didn't know the whole truth. This African did everything for the old man. Lifted him out of bed, give him his bath and..."

"Prophet!" shouted Lincoln, "this have anything to do with the riots?"

Isaiah waved the protest away and continued. "They said that a building collapsed on him when he was fire-watching during the Battle of Britain. Even then the man was too old to join the army and his wife..."

"Prophet..." interrupted Alonso, "I know that there's one hell of a story coming up about the African, the wife and the crippled husband and I really want to hear it but for the moment can we hear about the Deptford riots?"

"And the little half-caste girl," said Isaiah.

"How did she get into the picture? And who the hell was she?" asked Lincoln.

"Tcho, man, don't interrupt the man," Colonel, remonstrated with the two younger men "make the man tell it his way, nuh."

"Thank you," said Isaiah. "We used to drink in a pub called The Pilgrims Way. It was in that pub that we first heard how that half-caste girl came to be living in the house. She must be the same age as my twin girls. The story went like this, the woman went away for three months and come back with this baby which she said that she adopted."

"Baby in three months?" questioned Lincoln.

"I tell you, the woman was so big and fat nobody would guess she was pregnant. She never told anybody. I don't think anybody was fooled though, not even her old man. Everybody knew it was the African that knock her up."

The wife, the African, the crippled husband, infidelity, the half-caste girl and a pub called The Pilgrims Way," grumbled Lincoln leaning forward impatiently, his posture urging Prophet to get on with the story.

"Why can't I come up with a plot like that? I guess that was the route the Pilgrims in Chaucer's *The Canterbury Tales* took..." suggested Alonso.

"Alonso!" Lincoln barked, dismissing his friend with a "Ssh!" and a wave of his hand.

"Any of you know Brookmill Road in Deptford?" asked Isaiah, not waiting for an answer. "Well, that's where Carrington House is. I guess it's still there to this day. In those days it was a hostel for black seamen, mainly West Africans. You know the age-old story of white women and black men. I tell you, guys, all these stories about black colonies getting independence don't mean a damn thing because the white woman will still be mistress, calling all the shots."

It was Blossom's coughing that drew the men's attention to a white woman, Sheila Cox, standing beside her in the half-opened door.

"It just isn't fair," said Sheila. "You got rid of my white brother with his plumed hat and all that ridiculous get up, then his daughter married the young fire-brand politician and became first lady. It ain't fair..." Blossom tugged at her hand and they went towards the kitchen before any further digression of the story of the Deptford riots of 1949.

"I tell you, Lonso, you better do something quick about that redhead before some guy do it for you," said Colonel.

"Someone already has," said Alonso, "didn't you see the rings she is wearing? She's a married woman." He felt no need to tell them she had been separated from Tom Cox for over a year.

"Well, like I was saying", Prophet said, regaining his subject, "these guys used to sneak white girls into the hostel and when it became common knowledge, groups of white men gathered to show their disapproval. One newspaper said that about a thousand white men besieged the hostel, which had about fifty or so coloured men. The *brothers* retaliated by throwing out of the window lumps of concrete from the fireplace, broken bottles, bed linen, chinaware, and even red-hot coals on the protesters below. When the white blokes tried to rush the door the *brothers* came down and, boy, there was one hell of a fight. The police was called and was caught in the middle. Remember what I said, there were about fifty to sixty coloureds and about a thousand white men, but you know what? The police them could only remember that it was the coloured men that attacked the white men. There was the testimony from one officer who said that from New Cross he saw the whole thing. What a lie! If you know where New Cross station is, even if you got a binocular you couldn't see the entrance to Carrington House. Well, this officer said he saw a black man run into the hostel and came out with a sword. (That is a machete for those of you who don't know weapons.) So this coloured man waded into the crowd brandishing this sword."

"Did you see any of this, Prophet?" asked Alonso.

"That was why I mention that African right at the beginning. We, the four of us who was sharing, was all going to go down to Deptford Broadway to a pub there called the *Marlowe Arms*."

"That would be Christopher Marlowe. He was murdered somewhere in Deptford in fifteen ninety-something..."

"Lonso, we don't want a history lesson now," remonstrated Lincoln. "Go on, Prophet."

"As I was saying, this riot went on for three, four nights. I think it was the second night we was getting ready to go and see what was happening when that big ugly black bastard intervened. He told us that if we go out, when we come back we would find our things outside on the sidewalk. The man put his foot down, treating us as if we was his pickney boys. We was forbidden to go out, as if we was little boys. We had to obey. We had no choice. In those days a room, however smelly and dirty and overcrowded, was home sweet home! If the man put your things out on the street, who was going to help you? Not the boys in blue. Where would they put you, in a cell? The council would tell you that the queue for housing was seven years long. So where you going to live between then and 1955 before a council flat come through? Them was tough days, tough days!" He paused for a drink. "You know who could have back me up if he was alive?" He spat out the name, as he would have slammed down a winning card in a game of dominoes: "Melbourne Welsh! God rest his soul. He was at the big conference they held at Goldsmith College later that year, in December, I think. He was there every day, all the time arguing, asking questions, generally laying down the law. You know the sort of bloke he was. It was all over the papers. Ask Jimmy Fairfax, he was around at that time, too; wherever Melbourne went, Jimmy wasn't too far behind. We thought then that it was the end, that they were going to round us up and ship us back. And there were those in Parliament asking for us to be sent back. But decent men in Parliament like Marcus Lipton and Fenner Brockway were on our side. So it never happened, they never put us on the boat back to the islands. Still we was nervous like hell. If you was coming home late one night and two or three white blokes started to walk behind you, you get frighten. Somebody told me about a Jamaican guy who carried a machete down him trousers leg all through the winter of 1949. You know how these stories go, somebody always know a bloke whose friend know bloke who did that. Then one morning we wake up and things calm down. The newspapers was not writing any more about us. It was if nothing never happened. Things change, I tell you."

"So is what change things?" asked Nello.

"Well, not change exactly... things just carry on as before, then come the summer and the Lord's Test Match at the end of June 1950 and, boy, did we whup them arse on the green field at the very home of cricket!"

They burst out laughing, whether at the sound of Colonel's rendition of the famous calypso or just the sheer joy of reliving the coming of age of West Indian cricket, no one could be certain.

"The truth is that Rae and Walcott, the two centurions at Lord's, and those two little pals of mine Ramadhin and Valentine, probably never heard of Deptford," said Lincoln soberly.

"Don't spoil it, man!" said Alonso. "All that summer everybody was talking about the all-conquering team. What a pity they let us down last year..."

"They coming good now, man. Boys like Sobers, Kanhai and Hunte start shining. It not going to be easy for England who is due there in the next two years," Colonel intervened.

"What a meanta say half an hour ago is," said Prophet Ziah, "give things a little time and it will simmer down. You think the rioting in Notting Hill going to stop people having parties, getting married? You think people going to be running back to Jamaica with them tail between them legs? You think this going to stop black guys going out with white girls?" he paused long enough to look at Alonso. "If you will forgive me saying so."

"I'm not going out with Sheila, Prophet. She's a married woman," Alonso said.

"You might be right about things simmering down if you give time and some sort of distraction," said Lincoln. "*The Gazette* is planning a carnival at St Pancras Town Hall in January."

"Carnival in winter!" Ziah wanted to laugh.

"It will be held in St Pancras Town Hall. There will be beauty queen contest, jump-up; as the Trinidadians would say, we going to *play mas*..."

"Mama said will you please come into the dining-room," said Catherine, entering the room. "Can I be a beauty queen?"

"Girl, you been listening at the door?" her father scolded at the same time pulling her ear playfully. "Anyway you're only fourteen..."

"I think you'll find she's still thirteen..." Catherine interrupted Alonso with a thump to his back.

"Catherine, you have assaulted an invalid."

"I just did, didn't I?" then pulling away from her father she dropped back and placed Alonso's hand on her shoulder. "Lean on me," she said. In the dining-room, she shouted, "Guess what... there going to be a carnival and we going to be beauty queens..."

"What!" interrupted Myrtle Morgan. "*But see mi dying trial*! Girls, you just thirteen. You got nothing worth showing off yet." At this attack on their aspiring womanhood, however motherly and well meant, the twins bolted from the room.

322

"Gody Myrtle," said Blossom going after them, "you may have to revise that in a year's time. You know what they say? Today lemons and tomorrow grapefruits!"

"What!" a chorus of voices went up, then Lincoln's voice was distinct: "... Anyway they have to be between seventeen and twenty-six to be contestants."

"That rule me out," said Enid placing both hands on her growing belly.

"Lawd, missis, you wouldn't be able to find a swimsuit to fit that bulge," Myrtle added and got another round of laughter.

"You know we have an audition next Tuesday at the Black Cherry Club for the Carnival?" asked Sheila. "We're going to do a little number written by and to be sung by our own lead singer, Miss Blossom herself. You all should come and listen."

"I still think that pretty ladies like you and Blossom would be better off in the beauty parade..." suggested Ziah. "Good figure... what they call it? *Hourglass figure*. Give up this foolishness about being in a band and get in you swimsuit."

"Anyway they wouldn't let me. All the girls must have a Caribbean connection. Blossom, yes, but me they wouldn't have. This is where you all should say *Ah!* showing you feel sorry for me with me sickly pale skin. If Blossom changed her mind and was a contestant, I doubt if our band would get a chance to play in the carnival jump-up. This could be a big break for us."

"So exactly what *you* do in the band?" asked Colonel.

"I'm the drummer," said Sheila Cox.

"That's not a lady's instrument. Is what the band call again?"

"Nello, come on Tuesday and if I don't pass your test as a good drummer I'll buy you a bottle of Jamaican rum. If I do pass, then you'll have to wear *mas* costume in the jump-up contest," Sheila threw down a challenge. "Our group is called the *Icinis*. You know the statue of that woman driving her chariot opposite Big Ben on Westminster Bridge? Well, that's Boadicea. She was queen of the Icini tribe. If someone can prove that my people have been living in Danetree since Roman times, then that would be my tribe. I might be her descendant. A princess, no less."

"Girl," he said, "you on. But is where you gwine to get Jamaican rum from?"

"Never you mind," she said. "I might have to get J. Wray and Nephew to fly a crate over. I know that our record is going to get into the charts. Trust the *Icinis*."

"I never heard of white people belonging to tribes..." said Ziah.

"Well," interrupted Sheila, "I guess you've just met your first *Icini.*" She held out her hands mimicking the ancient queen driving her war chariot.

"Well, I never. I thought it was only black people and Red Indians who belonged to tribes. What tribe Jamaicans belong to again, Alonso?" persisted Ziah Morgan.

"I said there's enough evidence that the Ashantis had a significant impact on Jamaican history, but not all Jamaicans were taken from the Gold Coast. By the way, Sheila, based on where your family has lived for generations I'd think you're more likely to belong to the *Trinovantes* rather than the *Icinis,* who were more in the Norwich area..."

"Don't argue with him, Sheila, or he might decide to give us a guided tour of his own ancestry, the *Hidalgos*, the *Maya,* the *Spanish Conquistadors* and the *Peons.* God help us," said Enid to a peal of laughter.

"So give us a taste of this hit song you talking about," encouraged Nello.

"I'm not the singer, but I'll let you into a secret. Did you see the film *Carmen Jones?* "

"If it is not a cowboy film show, me not going," said Colonel.

"Films hurt my eyes," said Ziah Morgan.

"Liar," accused his wife. "It put him to sleep most likely. A whole group of us went to see *Carmen Jones* and my husband snored all the way through it!"

"Sorry to have to say this, guys, but that film had the most handsome Jamaican male I have ever seen, Harry Belafonte. All he has to do is to snap his fingers... I am his."

"You've come on a bit," Alonso could not conceal the surprise in his voice as memories of previous conversation flashed through his mind.

"Ssh!" cautioned Sheila, a flash of embarrassment on her face.

"This one," said Enid, elbowing Lincoln, "had a framed picture of Dorothy Dandridge cut out of a newspaper with the headline announcing *'Carmen Jones comes to town'.* I was going to dash it whey. The man was almost in tears. I felt sorry for him. If he ever was to meet her, I would have to pack my grip and go back to Pretty Tunning. How could I compete?"

"The song is called 'Carmencita'. Well, if Otto Preminger could take such liberties with Bizet's opera, then we can jolly well take liberties with *Carmen Jones.*"

IV

Warren Hall looked around the crowded church hall of St James', Loughborough Junction and whispered loud enough, "Ask around and I'll bet you'll find ten would-be writers busily engaged on writing the great West Indian novel. Our keynote speaker tonight is working on his third..."

The audience began to cheer. Carew had brought the hall to its feet with thundering applause. He had come to the end of his thoughtful yet somewhat polemic essay, 'What is a West Indian?'

> *... an obstacle in the way of our recognising and appreciating what is ours culturally, is our persistent habit of servility. There are those of us who need telling over and over again:*

'look man you don't have to bow and scrape anymore, we
are living in a new age in which the coloured man as already
won the right to stand up to his full height'. But the trouble is
that most of us don't realise that we are bowing and scraping
for this has become an instinctive reflex.
Besides the servility is more subtle these days. There are some
West Indians who will show how emancipated they are by
appointing a European to a post under them. This adds to
their prestige and puts a greater distance between themselves
and their countrymen. There are many other refined
variations, but they all add up to the same thing, that we're
still seeing ourselves and the world through the eyes of our
former rulers.
At a time when we boast about our 'independence' it might
be well to look into these things. Artists and writers are
making their contribution, holding up a mirror for the West
Indian man to see his image, but the mirror needs to be
gigantic, for it's being held up four thousand miles away.

There was a brisk questions-and-answers session. Carew, standing well over
six feet and powerfully built, intimidated his audience by his mere stature
and the power of his argument, expanding on the topic 'What is a West Indian?'

That question must concern every thinking person from the
Caribbean. Artists and writers must be even more profoundly
involved in the quest for their own identity and that of the
West Indian peoples who stand at the cultural crossroads,
for the directions taken by the writer and the artist affect the
people's future and destiny.

The evening at St James' ended with cheese and biscuits and soft drinks,
and Canon Hood, chaplain from the Anglican diocese of the Caribbean,
who had been sent to minister to West Indian migrants, thanked Carew for
coming to speak to the Brixton Anglo-Caribbean Association. He promised
the membership that he was hoping to get Dr Pitt or Learie Constantine to
give a keynote speech to the association in the near future. The applause
was like heavy tropical downpour on zinc roof and thereafter the audience
broke up into groups. One man, obviously part of the Anglo section,
confessed that he was confused that the speaker had said *What* is a West
Indian? rather than *Who* is a West Indian? and was hoping to get close
enough to the speaker to have him explain it.

Warren pointed out to Blossom and Irone some of the people he knew,
mainly young men under thirty busily writing the great Caribbean novel.
"There's Ken Khalhi with his trade-mark patched sleeves and pipe. He's

from Trinidad..." he said, as if that explained everything. He made room for the woman with short-cropped brown hair to join them. "Of course, Stella Clarke is well known in these circles. She's built a following among West Indians for single-handedly for bringing Caribbean literature to the wider public. Who can forget her production of *My Father Sowed the Idea of Me?* which was a dramatisation of the sociological study by Philys Melrose, an Englishwoman who taught in Jamaica? Stella transcribed it for the stage as a humorous attempt to explain West Indian fatherhood. You know the theme, *Brown-skin gal, stay home and mind baby...*"

"Thank you, Warren, if ever I have need of an agent I'll bear you in mind. Never mind the great Caribbean novel, which I know someone not three feet from me is writing. I'm waiting on *your own story,* Warren." Stella had been eavesdropping. "After all, you were at various times a Kingston handcart boy, longshoreman, stowaway, London coalman, a soldier, now businessman and law student. Wow, what a story! I told you I could have three publishing houses fighting to sign you up."

"It won't help my case if the Lord Chancellor knows I was a stowaway," replied Warren. "Go after young radicals like Alonso here. Dangle the carrot before him so he get a move on and finish his novel. I think the working title is *Hold Tight*. I told him that Miss Rhodes our old English Language teacher would go nuts. 'Mr Campbell! It requires an adverb not an adjective to modify the verb hold... *Hold Tightly!*' He's been very lazy since that story about that basement in Drury Lane."

"I can't get him to re-write his first novel, which has possibilities. He pours out one hundred and fifty thousand words and thinks the publishing business must accept it. I'm yet to convince him that in today's world when a writer thinks he's finished a book, the real work has just begun. The working title is *Without Lets and Hindrances*; well, in the present climate, that title is redundant. The drawbridge is about to be pulled up." Stella Clarke had her arms around Alonso as if to comfort him.

"The gods are *agin* me," said Alonso, feeling sorry for himself. "First god, Somerset Maugham said that anyone can write one book, but it takes a real writer to write a second book; and then the god Hemmingway tells me that it took him six weeks to write *The Sun Also Rises* and five months to complete the rewriting. So I spend three years writing a novel, and another nine years re-writing it. Wow! I'm on schedule! I have six novels swirling around in my head. I'd like to write them one after the other then I could spend my middle age rewriting them, howzat?"

"It doesn't work like that. You must trust your literary adviser as you would your doctor," Stella had not been pleased with him for some time. How different from when they first met in 1957.

"He's been writing a novel long before I came up," said Blossom. "One of his letters was full of it. His problem is not having the discipline to refine what he has roughly hewn."

"I've seen the manuscript and have discussed it with him whole areas that need rewriting," Stella said. "Oh, don't misunderstand me. Your brother can write; what's more, I know he can deliver the Caribbean's first international bestseller."

"That good? I bet you've said that to all the writers and wanabees in this room," said Warren.

"Stella's laying it on thick," said Blossom. "He'll believe you, and I'm sharing a flat with him. Are there any instructions on living with an international best-selling author?"

"I'm so lucky! I have a sister who thinks I'm a big-head, a legal adviser who was a stowaway and now a literary adviser who thinks I won't become a proper writer unless I give up my day job!"

It had seemed easier when they first met.

In fact, Stella had been at university with Alonso's English Literature teacher at the evening school he attended. He had hesitated for two terms before plucking up the courage to show his teacher his poems and stories. The story about nine migrants living in a basement flat caught Miss Hine's attention and she showed it to her old friend. At first it sounded like the beginning of a fairy story. The whole procedure had taken five weeks. Alonso met Stella Buick and they had lengthy discussions on his being black and living in London and wanting to be a writer. He had to explain some incidents that happened during his and Lincoln's tenure in the basement in Drury Lane. Stella's emotions ran the gamut from disbelief to absolute outrage. As the weeks went by she could laugh at some of the incidents. Eventually she decided there was merit in the story and that a script had to be prepared for the BBC's Caribbean Service. She was sure of an acceptance of his short essay for the *Letter from London* slot. It was about two months later that Alonso recorded it. Then things started to happen. Andrew Salkey interviewed him for the BBC Caribbean Programme. After that the BBC Home Service broadcast the story of a colonial migrant in London. The day of the broadcast Alonso made sure he was on late shift so he could listen to his own voice recalling moments from his early experiences in London. While he was still basking in the warm glow of success, Stella insisted he attend a workshop for aspiring playwrights in East London, followed by a master class by a distinguished playwright. This rekindled his interest in writing a play. He had begun a verbose sketch with characters pouring out eight hundred words of dialogue page after page. Stella threw her hands up in disbelief and took him to see his first play on the stage of the Old Vic. That was *A Woman Killed with Kindness,* a set book for the English literature course he was taking at evening school. Stella had talked him out of wanting to be a playwright and got him to concentrate on dramatising his short story. When at last she was satisfied that it had some merit, she offered it to a television producer, who thought that it was worthy of an hour of television time. Shortly after that *Nine in a Basement* was put on in a small dilapidated theatre in East London and ran for six weeks before disappearing in the box where he kept his literary efforts. In more ways than one 1957 was his *annus mirabilis.* Alonso's acquaintances were disappointed that no calls came from any West End theatre producers nor from a film studio! But Alonso had been infected with that aggressive and fatal disease: the urge to write. He knew he could not expect to recover from what was to become a prolonged and debilitating malady.

30

Thousands came out of the tropical heat of the Carnival at St Pancras Town Hall on the last day of January 1959. It was a cold and bleak London night. The Lilford Road group's spirits warmed to the rhythm of the Stanley Jack's band and his mastery in general as music director of the carnival, entertaining the large crowd of West Indians and their friends.

They were pleased to see that *the Icinis* had appeared, but were equally disappointed that they were only allowed to play before the carnival properly got under way. After the carnival queen was crowned the audience wanted to dance to the traditional calypso tunes. They wanted rumba, rhythm and blues, so extravagant in every movement, those London dailies that were brave and liberal enough to review the Carnival jump-up saw only "a seething mass of gyrating black bodies". The Icinis could offer none of that. They all agreed that, personal connections aside, the Icinis, and Blossom in particular, acquitted themselves with honour.

Catherine wanted to know if she would be permitted to enter the carnival queen contest the following year. Myrtle told her daughter that it was about time she knew how old she really was. If she calculated that she would be seventeen by the time of the next carnival, then of course she could be a contestant. Christine wondered why any woman in her right mind would want to show-off so much of their body in public on a cold January night.

Nello had left the van in Russell Square so the party consisting of the Morgans and their twin daughters, Miss Vie and Miss Nicey, and of course their driver, Colonel Walters, walked on.

"So, Nello," asked Ziah, "did you win?"

"Win what, Daddy?" asked Catherine.

"If Sheila was a good drummer, Nello had to wear a mask during the road march. If she was no good then Sheila would have to buy him a bottle of Jamaican rum."

"I think him lose the bet. She was good. Nearly as good as Warren," said Miss Nicey.

"Wha'appen? You lot didn't see me when I borrowed that Red Indian outfit from somebody and join in the road march? Alvin, the man I borrowed the costume from, is Trinidadian. He's in my team at work. These blokes live for carnival back home. Yes, Miss Sheila played the drums really well. So I paid me forfeit. Wonder where she learnt to play so well?"

"At school, Uncle Nello," said Christine. "They teach us music, you know. We're learning the recorder."

"What's that?"

"It shaped like a clarinet. It's a very old instrument," Catherine explained. "Next year I want to begin learning the saxophone," she added.

"You joking," said Colonel. "That definitely not an instrument for a lady."

"My sister is a lot of things, but she ain't no lady," Christine said.

"I'm going to start my own jazz band when I'm old enough."

"Your own jazz band! The role of a woman in those big bands, my dear twin sister, is to warble notes and look..." Christine thought of *sexy*, but conscious of the presence of grown-ups, she decided on... "pretty, like Lady Day, but as I've said you definitely ain't no lady," said Christine.

"Drop dead! So when the *Icinis* becomes famous and Blossom is rich and have her pictures in all the magazines and on television, you'll tell her to her face, that she ain't no lady?"

"You think Blossom wants to be a singer? She's just helping out until the lead singer have her baby..."

"An unexpected break is the main ingredient in showbiz, my darling sister. If their record reach the top twenty they'll be fighting to give her a contract. Watch this space."

"Blossom is not the show business type," insisted Christine. "If she decides to give up her job in the Civil Service, I bet she will become a teacher or a nurse."

"Have it your own way. I wouldn't give up a life of glamour and adoration for a smelly old classroom," Catherine hastened her steps to catch up with her mother.

"You ain't Blossom," said Christine, hanging on to her father.

The party finally reached Russell Square and everyone was glad at the prospect of sitting down and under cover again.

"I bet Warren, Lonso, Lincoln and all that lot will end up at somebody's place and haul and pull apart how the carnival went. They will be at it until daylight tomorrow," Myrtle said.

"Well, Warren just bought a house in Dulwich which could hold half of the crowd at carnival..." said Nello.

"That big?" asked Miss Nicey.

"You better believe it. I tell you, some of our people beginnin' to make good here in London town," Ziah Morgan said.

The warmth generated by nearly a thousand bodies wet with sweat, yet in a state of combustion caused by their closeness and vibration, wore off as the party turned into Bedford Street.

"Say what you want," said Nello, "but I think colour is everything, even when coloured people put on a show."

"I don't know what you mean, man," interjected Ziah. "Tonight I see a whole lot of black beauties. Boy, is where them been hiding?"

"Me not contradicting that, is not only those on the stage alone. I shake my leg against a few of them during the jump-up..."

"I bear witness that I see you dropping mento on some of them. But I still don't get your meaning," said Miss Nicey.

"Well," began Nello, "For my money the wrong girl was crowned queen tonight. She was too much of a St Andrew high-colour woman..."

"So is you," said Miss Vie, "come to think of it."

"What?" asked Ziah of Nello, turning to block his path. "You need new glasses, man. They crown the prettiest girl in the contest. I not seen such a pretty coloured girl in many a year."

"For my money gie me the girl who came number two. What a body!"

"Nello!" shouted Miss Myrtle. "You two grey-back men should be ashamed of you'selves. Both of you have daughters older than any of the contestants." She was restrained in her admonition on account of the presence of Christine and Catherine.

"I think she got it because she's a cabaret dancer in the West End club and is very light-complexioned," Nello repeated almost in a sulk.

"Well, number two is an actress. She played the part of one of Cleopatra's attendants in that big film everybody is talking about."

"How come you know so much about them?" asked Miss Nicey.

"Well, Miss Nicey, it all boil down to who you know in this town," boasted Ziah.

"Lonso and Lincoln were on the committee that interviewed the contestants at rehearsal last week," said Catherine. "Number two was Lonso's favourite. He was quite smitten by her..."

"He wasn't," interrupted Christine.

"Shut up, both of you!" their mother, said sharply.

"So Lonso was talking to you about this sort of thing? I must have a word or two with that young man," said their father severely.

"I bet Lonso and Lincoln was not talking to these two. They just happen to have the biggest ears in the whole world," said their mother.

"Say what you like, tonight was the best jollification I been to for a long, long time. I like to watch young people enjoy themselves. I never spend a better five shillings," said Miss Vie.

"What does she mean 'a better five shillings'?" Christine whispered to Catherine. "Are all the rest forgeries?"

"You know how these old folks talk. If you must be pedantic: 'this was the best value she ever had for five shillings'," Catherine whispered.

"Now who is the spoiler of jokes?" Christine said.

"Nello, you lost the van?" asked Miss Vie.

"No, no, man, it in the square..."

"Expect that the police might have towed it away," said Ziah Morgan.

"No say so," pleaded Miss Vie. "I jus' beginnin' to feel the cold reachin' me bones and this pair of shoes is killin' me".

"We haven't far to go," said Christine. "The square is at the end of this street.

31

In the summer of 1960 Isaiah Morgan was summoned by the Lord Chancellor's Office to jury service at Clapham Crown Court. One particular case stood out for him, and despite any admonition the learned Judge might have given members of the jury the Prophet Ziah Morgan continued to regale many an audience with the proceedings. What became known to visitors to the Morgans' home at Lilford Road as Ziah's most famous case was not his case at all. In fact, during the selection of the jury for the Crown versus Bulford Cameron of Geneva Road, Ziah Morgan was obliged to admit that he knew the defendant, so was excused. It being one of the last cases scheduled for that afternoon, Ziah was free to go home, but his curiosity got the better of him and he sat in the public gallery.

A police officer explained that he and a colleague had Cameron under surveillance since he left the Admiral Nelson in Acre Lane. It was late November 1959. They saw the accused approach another coloured man, now known to the police as Nahum Shepherd, but known among the black community as Backra Man. The men talked for a while, then Cameron took a small dark packet from his overcoat pocket and passed it to Shepherd, who hurriedly stuffed it into an inner pocket of his overcoat. The two men parted. One officer followed Shepherd while the other followed Cameron along Atlantic Road, across the lights into Railton Road. The accused stopped and talked to several coloured men, but did not pass on any other packets.

At last the accused turned right into Marvell Road and descended the steps of the Bunch of Bananas nightclub. The officer followed and as he entered the dimly lit corridor saw Cameron approach another coloured man had handed him a packet. The recipient who was facing the entrance must have seen the officer and tried to return the packet to Cameron. The officer suspected that Cameron had by this time realised that he was under surveillance and refused to accept the packet, which his companion let slip to the floor as he turned sharply and went back into the club. The police did not know this third coloured man. The customers in the club were uncooperative and it was easy enough for a coloured man to make good his escape in that atmosphere. The officer picked up the packet that had been dropped in the corridor and Cameron was arrested. Police tests revealed that the packet contained marijuana, known in the immigrant community as *ganja* or *weed*.

The Prosecutor told the Court that the accused was extremely hostile to the police and had accused them of 'planting' the illegal substance on him. He declared that the arresting officer was well known in the Brixton area for supplying marijuana to coloured people. Indeed he had been approached on occasions by the said officer offering "weed" and as a law-abiding citizen had refused and on one occasion had threatened to report the officer to his superiors. Cameron gave his threat of reporting the officer as a possible reason why the officer had decided to frame him.

Because of this attack on the character of this detective, His Honour agreed that the jurors should know the character of the man who dared to besmirch the good name of an officer of the law.

"You are Bulford Cameron, also known as Bullah Cameron, of Geneva Road, Brixton?"

"Yessir."

"Good. I take you back, if I may to March of last year 1959. Do you recall the police had reason to search your flat on Monday 2nd?"

"Them search it, but that no say that they had no right to do it."

"Be that as it may, you were at the time cohabiting with one Helga Schwarz, a German citizen, were you not?"

"No, me kick her out long, long time. She have bad mind, that is why she called the police. Is vengeance she after."

"Your Honour, *kicked out* are the operative words. Since in an altercation with the defendant Frau Schwarz received cuts and bruises. She claimed they were inflicted by the accused, although she later withdrew the charges."

"Because she knew that nothing no go so. Your Honour, the woman like her drink, but she can't hold it. I tell you she was drunk coming back from the pub and it was fall she fall downstairs to the basement. She even bumped she head on the fridge door one time. That woman! She too damn lie," said Bullah with an air of dismissal.

"You Honour, the weals and bruises on Frau Schwarz body, face and hands were consistent with being made by a belt, and not by someone falling down steps."

"But wait she ain't no chile. Why should I want to beat she with a belt?" asked Bullah Cameron with great astonishment at this alleged cruelty.

The Prosecutor could not hide his annoyance at Bullah's denials and outright lies. He moved on to something for which he had solid proof. "A search of your flat revealed three pots with marijuana growing in them. Isn't that a fact?"

"You Honour," Bullah Cameron appealed to the judge, "this German woman say that she had *green fingers*. She was always growing things in pots on the windowsill and in the kitchen. I no know what she was growing."

"Mr Cameron, the Court will not have failed to observe that you are a native of Jamaica, where it is said that marijuana grows unattended like any other type of grass. Are you asking the Court to accept that you could not identify this plant, which was growing in your kitchen?"

"That's right."

"One great conspiracy! The entire establishment is out to get you. I cannot wait to hear your response to the charge of attempting to steal a bike in front of the *Drunk and Disorderly* second-hand shop on Railton Road."

"Your Honour," Bullah appealed to the Judge once more, "I am a law-biding citizen. I was walking along Railton Road. I reached the second-hand shop; I almost tripped over a bicycle that was lying on the pavement. I thought that if I have good eyesight and nearly fall over this bike, then what would happen if a blind person should come along? So I picked up the bike and was just about to wheel it to the other side of the doorway where I was going I was going to lean it up. As soon as I pick' up the bike the shopkeeper come running out of the shop shouting 'Thief' and carrying on as if I was going to ride away on his bike. Your Honour, people nowadays, them no grateful, you know."

"Are you denying that on 7th November 1959 you met Nahum Shepherd at the corner of Atlantic and Brixton Roads, where you proceeded to pass to him a packet containing the illegal substance known as marijuana?"

"I did meet Nahum, Your Honour, he is me cousin from back home. We call him Backra Man, because of his light complexion."

"I'm obliged to you for that piece of information," the Judge acknowledged, with what looked like a frown.

"I did pass him something, but it did not have marijuana in it."

"May we inquire what was in that packet you passed to Shepherd?"

"Yes... but you see it's a bit embarrassing."

"However, the Court will want to hear it."

"Well... well, all right then... You see, Your Honour, my cousin is seeing this woman, but him is afraid of catching *the clap* so him ask me to buy him some protection, because him is too shy fi go in to a barber shop and ask for it. I'm telling the truth. That is why when the police catch up with him and search him they did not find any marijuana."

"Neither did they find a packet of condoms, for that was what Mr Cameron is alluding to, your Honour." Turning back to Bullah, he asked, "Are you also going to deny that the packet retrieved from the passage of the Bunch of Bananas club and which did contain marijuana came from you? You were seen in conversation with another coloured man, to whom you handed a packet. Was that another piece of police fabrication?"

"Your Honour, the policeman said that the corridor was dark, me hand is black as me face, I was wearing a darkish coat, and the packet he said was dark. Your Honour, I say that policeman must have better eyesight than a pussycat. When you think that it was a dark, wet November evening, and there was no light in the corridor, I don't believe him could see anything. I swear I did not have anything to pass to nobody, except the packet of rubbers

I passed to me cousin Nahum. If the officer pick up anything off the floor in that dark corridor, all I can say he either dropped it there himself or somebody else dropped it, but that somebody was not me."

His Honour sent the jurors to their room to consider their verdict, asking them to take into account the police character study of the accused against the veracity of the officer, who had served the public with great honesty and dedication over a number of years.

The jury took less that two hours to return a verdict of not guilty.

Alonso and his sister were amused more at Prophet's art at storytelling than the behaviour of their stepfather. They were pleased that Bullah had not been sent to prison; how long he would escape being a guest of Her Majesty was anyone's guess. They knew that he grew and sold ganja back home in Guava Flat. Everybody in the Upper Yallahs knew that Bullah was in the habit of disappearing in those most inaccessible hills above a rocky place known as Quatty Wo't. (A quatty was the colloquial term for a penny-halfpenny, or a quarter of a sixpence, the local people's calculation of the total worth of the property.) Up in those hills Bullah and his cousin Nahum Shepherd (more widely know as Backra Man) cultivated patches of marijuana. Shepherd was bequeathed the land by his grandfather who never bought more than quatty worth of tobacco, sugar or salt. The cultivation of ganja was Backra Man's business. The rumour was that when he left for Britain after the storm year of 1951 it was the proceeds from the sale of marijuana that provided the money for his fare. From then on people expected that Bullah his lieutenant, who after the departure of Backra Man became the sole purveyor of ganja in the area, would in the fullness to time follow his cousin to England.

Blossom and her brother thought the gossips at Guava Flat were convinced it was money from selling ganja that paid Bullah's passage. As a matter of pride he would rather people say that than knew the truth: that his wife's children, whom he despised, had paid his fare. Did he realise that their plot was to remove him from their mother? It certainly was not an attempt on their part to help him to improve himself; they had left him in no doubt that they did not intend to show any interest in his affairs beyond turning over to him their old basement flat in Geneva Road and asking Colonel to find him a labouring job on a building site. They had not seen him for over a year, and Anita had written to say his letters were infrequent and those with money were even less frequent.

II

The police were in the habit of raiding the Bunch of Bananas nightclub. So frequently did this happen many people were surprised it had a clientele at all. It had a reputation for being a club where marijuana and white prostitutes were easily obtainable, a combination the police used as good enough reason to raid the club. The anti-immigration groups also used these reasons in their continuous petitioning to the Council to close down the club. The residents of Marvell Road were ever watchful of those who entered the basement premises. They complained of the volume of noise from the music. They complained about the crowd issuing from the premises in the early hours of the morning. They were outraged by the *carryings-on* with white girls in full view of any insomniac child who happened to be standing at a bedroom window at three o'clock in the morning. The possibility that a white child might witness all that was too dreadful to contemplate. It was never commented on, that black men might also be seen "carrying on" with black women. That an insomniac black child might witness these carryings-on was never commented on.

Alonso had long considered it incongruous that in this insalubrious corner of Brixton, heading towards Herne Hill, five of the language's great architects – Chaucer, Spencer, Shakespeare, Milton and Marvell - should have roads named after them. He could trace no Brixton connection to these poets. He wondered what Brixton might have looked like towards the end of the seventeenth century when Milton and Marvell died. Alonso imagined a countryside of tall trees and murmuring brooks. That might have been so, but in reality tall grey Victorian buildings were the scenery of the mid-twentieth century, a sober reminder of change and decay and Marvell's poignant words:

> *Fair trees! Where'er your barks I wound,*
> *No name shall but your own be found.*

Not so, Andrew Marvell! The walls along the road that bears your name are wounded by knives whose blades had carved deep instructions. *"Keep Britain White! Send the Niggers back! White Trash! Black Bastard! Jungle Bunny! Golliwog! Karen is a White Slag! Nigger Lovers!"*

Nearer the Railton Road end, a sign above a ground-floor window with an arrow pointing towards the basement bore the legend "*Bunch of Bananas*", as well as a poster of some tropical scene, depicting a smiling black woman with a bunch of bananas on her head.

32

"What are you giving those girls?" asked Myrtle Morgan of her husband rather anxiously.

"A drop of rum and coke to toast me birthday," Ziah, the Prophet replied as he busied himself behind the cabinet bar.

"Lawd me Gawd," Myrtle said in broad Jamaican dialect. "You gone mad? You may be fifty-five, but that no mean you take leave of your senses," she rose from her seat and walked over to the bar where her husband was presiding. "I will allow a little wine or some sort of fizzy drinks, even a drop of champagne to toast you' birthday, but not rum."

"Where I come from we don't know nothing about fizzy drinks. I'm giving me daughters a drink that their father and grandfathers before them know about. Don't worry, woman, I water it down. Come, my daughters," He held the drinks high and managed to out-manoeuvre his wife who was determined to confiscate the drinks. The girls colluded with their father, snatching the glasses and disappearing among the flaying limbs and gyrating backsides of the dancers.

"You going to turn the pickney them head," she squared up to her husband. "I bet you don't even know how old they be."

"Sweet sixteen."

"Shet you mouth. Them's not fifteen till August. You don't even know you children's age. What about them two in Jamaica? How old is Monica, your first daughter?"

"Woman lef' me alone. It's me fifty-fifth birthday!" he said defensively as he did his mental arithmetic. "They are women now. Never reveal a woman's age..."

"You don't know, do you?"

"What is this? Twenty questions? Anyway Moni is half my age. She's twenty-seven and a half and Lou-Lou is getting on for twenty-six." He reached out, pulled his wife towards him. "In those days I was bad, you see. I didn't make the woman recover before she was 'specting again..."

Myrtle struggled free and said, embarrassingly, "You not that drunk, so you better stop that sort of talk right now, you hear me."

"After that it was off to America to do farm work..."

"I say, enough," Myrtle admonished. "Look like the rum gone to your head."

Ziah saw his twin daughters by the window and waved his glass at them before lifting it to his lips for a long sip. Catherine imitated her father and with her free hand grabbed her throat as if to prevent the rum reaching her stomach. She coughed and spluttered, looking at him accusingly. "Dad! This is poison, man." She held the glass as far from her lips as her left hand could be extended. She began to fan her opened mouth with her right hand. "Fire!" she croaked. "My mouth, my throat are on fire and my eyes are spinning and watering like I am peeling onion."

"This one no fi me," he said denouncing his daughter's action.

In the meantime Christine took two good sips and pulled air into her mouth with a long, "Ah. This is wild! It packs a kick like an old mule." She rocked back on her heels then onto her toes. "Wow and double wow!"

"Ah warned you, Isaiah Morgan. See what you gone and done to me pickney them?"

"Tcho, man, me grandfather was dipping his finger in rum and rubbing it on me lips before I started to crawl, and it ain't done me no harm."

"That's a matter of opinion. Well, I have to find a new hiding place for the drinks cabinet keys. Until today I could hide them in the girls' room; that's one place he never go into. As from tonight I got to hide it from all three of them. The rum a-turn their heads look, look no!"

"I don't know that much, Gody Myrtle," said Enid. "Catherine has put down her glass... wait it look like she has given it to that *one* Darlene and as to Christine, I think is just sipping it to please her dad. She is going through the motions.

"Darlene, that *one*, she turned up here in that pedal-pusher trousers. Me take one look at her and march her upstairs to the girl's room to find a skirt. I told her I didn't care whether her mother is here or not, she not parading round my house with everybody seeing the outlines of her panty as plain as an A to Z. map of her backside."

The older women nodded in approval, the younger ones found it hard to contain the laughter.

"Gody Myrtle, you have a good turn of phrase. You should write a book," said Enid.

"Me leave that up to Lonso. I hearsay him just finish his new book," Myrtle said. "So it going to be a long time before we... what do they call it? Collaborate."

"Oh, don't worry about that," said Enid. "I don't care what the song say, the second time around is more difficult, for everything. I recall that one of the critics say that Lonso had given his audience a promissory note, and that promissory notes had to be redeemed. Going one better is always more difficult," she looked down on her swelling belly.

"Miss Enid, is what you mean?" Miss Vie sounded alarmed.

"Expecting the first baby was exciting. This time round it's not so easy, I can tell you. I keep fainting and experiencing what they back home would call 'bad feelings'. We're just praying for a healthy baby with all the bits there. We wondering if it going to be a girl again... and all this blackout I am having."

"It going to be a boy," said Miss Nicey, as if it was for her to authorise the sex of the unborn child.

"You bet," said Miss Vie concurring, "with all that kicking you said you getting."

"I tell you what," said Enid, "he's not going to play cricket. He's rough, tough and ready to play rugby."

Alonso and Irone had just stopped dancing and were heading in the direction of where the women were sitting, when Irone broke away from Alonso.

"I'm going to rescue John from that little bitch Darlene," she said.

"Come'on, John is a GI. He has seen action in Viet Nam. He can take care of himself. Over here! Over paid! And Over... "

"That is it," she interrupted, "that little prick-teaser is hoping that the Second World War saying about GIs is right. I'm going to pour an ice-cold drink down her knickers."

"Irone!"

"Don't tell me that she hasn't tried it on with you?"

"Nearly as often as you used to until GI John came on the scene."

"I only did it to tease your sister. She had the cheek to tell me her perfect brother would have nothing to do with me. That's when I told her that I could do things with you and for you that she couldn't legally do. It's the truth, ain't it? She saw red. 'Sorry, Rosi,' I said; we didn't know her as Blossom then. 'Short of you getting the law on incest changed, I am one ahead of you,' I told her."

"That's why she wants me to adopt you as a sister," he joked.

"You've missed your chances," she said, "John has the makings of a good husband."

"Thanks to GI John. Come let's dance this. It's a nice slow one. The Platters' *'Smoke Gets In Your Eyes'.*"

"And leave little Miss hot-knickers Darlene to fasten herself on my man? No fear. Come let's go and cut in. If you were upright enough to escape my advances in what was my green and salad days you should be able to take care of yourself from the leech-like embraces of a fifteen-year-old. Com'n!" she started across the floor.

"Somehow, I don't think so," he wriggled free. "I'll just go over there and talk to the women and have a drink."

He went and perched on the arm of the deep chair Myrtle Morgan was sitting in and stretched his arm along the back of the chair.

"Did you see Ziah giving the girls rum?" Her fingers dug into Alonso's knees, "Lawd me King, look at Christine. It looks as if Blossom is holding her up. The chile is drunk!"

Christine and Blossom approached, whispering and laughing. Soon the entourage included Sue, Betty, Lincoln, Warren, Puncie and Catherine. Christine, leaning heavily on Blossom, led her party right up to where Alonso was sitting next to her mother.

"This is a leap year, right?" said Christine, somewhat unsure of herself.

"It's 1960. So it's a leap year," Alonso feared the worst.

"And it's the 29th of February," Betty said with a wicked grin.

Alonso was near panic.

"That being so, girls are allowed to do things they can't do three out of four years, right?"

"You've lost me," he said, fearing he was been set up for a prank.

"In that case," she said, "I'm going to do the asking. Will you marry me?"

A well-rehearsed applause broke out, but it stopped as everybody saw the surprise that hit Myrtle, causing her jaw to fall. Her fingers dug deep into Alonso's knees. He rose awkwardly as she was still pinching him.

"This is the most romantic thing that's ever happened to me. However, seeing that you're under age I must ask you to let me withhold my answer for one of those three out of four years when guys are allowed to pop the question."

"No," said Warren's wife Sue, "a leap-year proposal can't be left like that!"

"A refusal must be accompanied with a white handkerchief," said Betty.

"But..." Alonso was about to say *this is not a refusal* but not wanting to call forth the *kracken* of Myrtle's anger, he said, "there are things like school to finish. O-level and A-levels you know..."

"What about the age of consent?" asked Puncie.

"That's something completely different," said Betty. "You can get engaged at any age."

"Izaiaah Morgan!" shouted Myrtle. "Come see what you foolishness done to me pickney."

Ziah, who had been dancing with Sheila Cox, came to see what the commotion was about.

"Them don't stay pickney for long," commented Miss Nicey.

"But this is big people business," added Miss Vie.

"Is drunk she drunk?" said Myrtle defensively. "I wonder who put her up to this?" She gave Blossom a withering look.

"Is what happen, now?" asked Ziah

"You make Christine drunk. She just this moment propose marriage to Lonso."

"Me rawted!" said Christine's father in broad Jamaican dialect. "You know," continued Ziah, "I always think that Catherine was out there in front. She was the one always saying Lonso is this and Lonso is that..."

"Dad!" Catherine's voice was almost a scream as she scrambled for the door.

"She's still not sixteen."

"Is what all this magic about sixteen?" Ziah wanted to know. "I tell you, to my mind it was going to be Catherine. I never see Christine coming up on the inside to pip her at the post."

"My children ain't no race horses," said Myrtle, becoming serious.

"I'm still waiting for Lonso's reply," said Betty, now joined by her GI boyfriend Leroy.

Suddenly Christine looked at Alonso, then her mother with the look of someone who had just woken up to find the world and his wife staring at her nakedness. She twisted herself free from both Blossom and Alonso and raced for the door as if to catch up with her twin sister.

"When she sober up," asked Myrtle, still looking at Blossom with distrust, "who going to tell her what happened here tonight?"

"That should be Lonso with the customary bunch of red roses or a box of white handkerchief," said Betty.

"Him better no break my baby's heart," warned Ziah, with a tinge of fatherly disapproval.

"Who would think that you Britishers would be so romantic?" said GI John, who had now been rescued from the adolescent clutches of Darlene. Then looking at Irone Simmonds, he said, "We got engaged in the Mess hall. Didn't we, hon?"

"Yes, love, and it was you who proposed." Irone gave him the assurance he needed. "It was so embarrassing, with all those crazy guys urging you to get down on your knees. 'Do it right, John! Do it the American way!' It was embarrassing. I just wanted to die."

"Did he? Go down on his knees?"

"That I did, Ma'am," said the proud soldier.

As spontaneous applause broke out, they all gathered to see Irone's engagement ring.

"I wonder how Catherine going to take it?" Ziah wondered aloud.

"Prophet, don't worry," consoled Warren with a hand on his shoulder. "This sort of thing happens at parties and no one thinks anything of it in the cold light of day."

"This different. These two have had crushes on Lonso for more than half their lives," said Lincoln, enjoying Alonso's obvious unease.

"Boy," said Warren, "who do you think you are, Jacob? Who is Leah and who is Rachel?"

"Music!" shouted Myrtle still quite flustered, but determined to take charge of the situation.

"Somebody put the music back on. Play *Staggerlee*," she ordered. She knew that no one would want to sit out Harold Price's hit record.

II

It was Blossom who first mentioned that she had about five calls over the last two weeks and when she answered the phone there was no one at the other end and certainly no heavy breathing. The telephone would go dead. It happened to Alonso twice in a few days. Blossom jokingly said that since there was no heavy breathing it probably was not meant for her anyway. There were no such calls during that week. Blossom had spent the weekend at Fonthill Road as Lincoln had gone off somewhere on business. This time the telephone rang just before he was about to leave the flat and on Monday morning of all days. He thought it was his sister calling to remind him of something or other.

"Hello, dear, what is it now?" the line went dead. He swore under his breath and was going towards the door when it rang again. "I'm listening," he said into the silent instrument, then for no reason he could give, he said, "Chrissie, it's you, isn't it? Chrissie, please talk to me."

"I miss you!"

"Well, I've been to your parents' house about four times since your father's birthday and every time you've taken refuge in your bedroom. Why are you avoiding me? Why the sulks?"

"I'm not sulking. Not avoiding you either."

"So why are you behind the barricades?"

"I'm embarrassed."

"What about?"

"You know..."

"No, I don't."

"I'm just a silly teenager, embarrassing you before everyone; I want to die. You must hate me."

"Why do you want to die? Please don't do anything silly. I certainly don't hate you..."

"Don't you, really?"

"Why should I hate you?"

"Silly teenage girl having a crush... saying what I did before all those people. You must hate me. I am pathetic..."

"Chrissie, I don't hate you. Look, I think we ought to have this conversation face to face, don't you?"

"I couldn't. Can't, just can't. I gotta go. Bye..." Just before the telephone clicked into silence he thought he heard a kiss. He smiled at the instrument before hanging up.

When Alonso next paid a visit to the Morgans' in Lilford Road it was Catherine who opened the door and led the way up to the families living room. She continued further down the corridor and knocked at the door of the room she shared with her twin; then, turning to face

Alonso so he could see the mischief on her lips, she shouted, "Chrissie, your fiancé is here."

"Ah, ah, ah" Christine replied, then the door opened a crack. "Give it a rest, you juvenile. That joke is wearing thin... Hi, Lonso. Long time no see. I'll be out soon." With that the door closed again.

"Go easy on the perfume, and keep your paws off my new top. He knows what you look like, already. A paper bag over your head might be an improvement..."

The door was dramatically flung wide open. "I heard that! I tried the paper bag business and you know what? Everybody thought I was you." She stuck out her tongue at her sister, before stepping back and banging the door shut.

"Christine!" shouted her mother, "do that again and that door goin' fall off its hinges. Look, I've been warning you girls, I want this foolishness stop. Y'hear me? It gone on long enough. You hear me, Catherine?"

"Yes, Mama, but..."

"But me no buts. Christine, c'mon out of that room or I'm coming to get you. Stop all this foolishness right now!"

"Yes, Mama."

"I have a solution to the problem," said Isaiah from behind the *News of the World*. "You all remember the story from the Bible about the two women who was fighting over the baby? King Solomon said, 'Bring me a sword so I can cut this baby in two and give half to each woman.' Well, all we have to do is to cut Lonso in two..."

"So how you gwine do it?" asked Nello, lowering the *Sunday Pictorial* and peering over the top. "Cut him top and bottom or split him from him forehead straight down the middle?"

"How macabre!" said Catherine.

"Stop your foolishness!" Myrtle said to the men, but to her husband in particular. "Is your doing that start all this."

Prophet rustled the newspaper as if to block out his wife's voice and as a bird would rearrange twigs and straws to provide comfort he rustled the paper again and shuffled himself into the softness of the chair.

"Pardon me for breathing... Don't bite me head off."

"Where's Blossom?" asked Christine, suddenly materialising in the doorway. "Don't tell me she's spending another weekend with Sheila Cox. They can't be still using the band as an excuse. They're no longer in it. You think she's found herself a boyfriend this time?"

"I have my suspicions too." Alonso looked towards her briefly then to the back page of her father's paper. It seemed there was a scandal brewing in a football club; he was not interested.

"Perhaps Blossom is just giving you two a bit of space, seeing you are engaged," said Catherine in *sotto voce*.

"Me is not deaf, girl," her mother interjected. "Catherine, you not too big to be sent to your room. You better watch it! You asking for a good old-fashion slap."

"Eh-eh," sniggered Prophet from behind his paper, "that no goin' to solve nothing, because when Lonso come next time, it will be Catherine who will be hiding in her room..."

"Isaiah Morgan!" Myrtle hit a note of menace.

"Tell you what," said Prophet folding the paper haphazardly. "You said that Courtland and his friend challenging us to a game of dominoes? Well, make we go see how good they really are."

"Now you talking, man." Nello wrapped rather than folded his *Sunday Pictorial* and dropped it on top of Prophet's *News of the World* on the coffee table. He stood up and stretched lazily. Looking at his hostess he offered a mixture of praise and apology. "Miss Myrtle, after your Sunday dinner all I want to do is doze off."

Both men headed for the door. Courtland was a tenant of six months who had rented the big bay room on the first floor, where he lived with his girlfriend, whose brother had just come to London and was staying until he found a room of his own.

"If you going to slam down dominoes and give your Red Indian whoopee like you in the Coolieman rum bar at the corner of Baker Street and Penn Street, back in Jones Town, Kingston, then go down to the basement..."

"Yes, Gody Morgan!" said her husband. "Anything you say, Gody Morgan! It's back to school. We going to the nursery."

The girls began to giggle, then their mother turned her withering gaze on them. "I thought you two promised to clear up the kitchen after lunch," she pointed dramatically towards the kitchen.

"We're on it Mamma," said Catherine, grabbing Christine and towing her out of the room. "Phew! Poor Alonso."

"What has he done?" asked Christine wrenching her hand free.

"Nothing that I know of, but to Mamma we're growing up and having someone near our age like Darlene, everybody knows what she is up to, and she does come around. That's what is sending shivers through Mum and Dad's collective spines..."

"We're nothing like Darlene, for God sake! For a start she has left school and is working at that dreadful peanut factory in Walworth. We're still grammar-school girls who'll sit O-Levels this summer.*"*

"Of course we're not like poor Darlene. We weren't brought up in some back-of-beyond Jamaican village by a grandmother who was young when Queen Victoria was on the throne."

"But she was up here in London, wasn't she? She can't be all that bushyfied."

"You can take people out of the Jamaican bush, but some people you can not take the Jamaican bush out of them. We are always surrounded by people who wanted to improve themselves and us. We owe it to our family to achieve. But try telling concerned parents that. They think given the chance every girl would misbehave."

"No way. You cut it out, right now! I don't like the assertion that all girls are like little well trained pets at the beck and call of any man who crooks his finger and beckon them..."

"Everybody thinks we're in love with Lonso..."

"He's like a brother to us. If you listen to people they all think we're both waiting to run off with him. He's a friend and he's definitely not like Darlene's DJ *The Soundman,* as far as I know."

"No, he isn't. Mamma puzzles me though, she seems happy that we want Lonso to escort us to the school party because he can be trusted, and we both take it in turns to chaperone each other."

"Safety in numbers, eh?"

"Something like that, yet she'd be happier if he was married like Lincoln and busily giving his wife a baby every year..."

"Up to his elbows in nappies. No time for roving eyes and even less for roving hands..."

"Christine, sometimes you sound quite grown up... Don't tell me you've been listen to Darlene's X-rated stories..."

Christine interrupted her twin with a push that sent her stumbling along the corridor. "I'm not that depraved. I'm quite capable of controlling my rebellious teenage body, thank you very much."

III

"Lonso, I'm glad we're alone. I want to talk to you."

"I guess you might," he said now that he was alone with Myrtle Morgan.

"Something has been perplexing me," she started to re-arrange the ruffles on the coffee table, from which she had removed the Sunday papers to a magazine rack against the wall. "For the first time since I met you back in 1953, I feel embarrass..."

"That is unlike you, Gody Myrtle," he put his hand on hers. "Anyway, let me help you out. It was about the girls, isn't it?"

"Yes," She turned to face him.

"You're about to ask me not to come around..."

"What? No, man. Anyway what good would that do? They know where you live and now Blossom doesn't seem to be home at weekends..."

"You think the opportunity is there for one or the other to come calling on me. Gody Myrtle, either you don't really know me or you don't understand your girls. I respect you and Prophet and I trust your daughters, all four of them..."

"I feel shame to start all this. I know that you would not... would not..." she broke off and wiped tears from her eyes.

"No, Gody Myrtle, I would not, but if you want me to stop coming around," he paused, "it's done."

"Don't you dare," she said, once more in command. "It's just that I heard things about that one Darlene and she is just about six months older that them."

"Gody Myrtle, the situations are different. It's not fair that you should compare these girls with someone like Darlene. I know you don't boast about it, but after all your daughters are grammar-school students looking forward to sitting their O-levels and then going on to their Advanced Levels and, who knows, even on to university. I know you are aware of the circumstances of Darlene's upbringing and leaving school at fourteen, and working with those loud-mouth women at that peanut factory in Walworth can't help her self-esteem. Poor Puncie is trying, but the time for playing loving mother has passed. Darlene is what the Americans call street-wise. Puncie can only hope that DJ 'the Soundman' looks after her..."

"Look after her!" Myrtle rose to her feet, hands akimbo, towering over Alonso, who was trying to get to his feet. Myrtle pushed him back into the chair. "That no-good man has been having his way with Darlene for over a year now. Did you know she has had an abortion?"

Alonso dropped back into the chair and shook his head; "I didn't know that."

"So much for all this rubbish 'bout the age of consent. You know that she pulled a knife on a white woman she found in her man's room? You shaking your head, and here was I thinking that you, Puncie and Lurline are friends..."

"Gody Myrtle, I've been so busy preparing for exams and working on my book, I haven't got time to socialise."

"You got some socialising to do because my two want you to escort them to the school end-of-term dance."

"Me?"

"Yes, you. I'd be worried if it was one of them, but it's the two of them. They might look alike but, take it from me, they are different in their like and dislikes. When the time comes their taste in boyfriends could be different..."

"So you agreeing with me that they see me as the brother they never had?"

"Never doubted it."

IV

Towards the end of 1960, three years after living with the Morgans, Colonel 'Nello' Walters gave up his room with the Morgans in Lilford Road and went to live in the ground floor flat of a house in Milkwood Road. This was a new acquisition of Lincoln's Creole Enterprises. The flat had two bedrooms; part of the dinning room was converted into a third bedroom for the oldest child. There was a much smaller dining room leading to the kitchen, the floor of which was a foot lower than the dining room. This area had a very small bathroom containing a toilet and a hipbath; at the other end was a gas stove and a sink with draining board. A man on his own demanding so much space would immediately become the subject of much speculation. Myrtle Morgan came to the conclusion that Nello was getting ready to send for his wife, Miss Imo. Although there were thousands of couples who shared single rooms, she did not object to him wanting to accommodate his wife in more spacious surroundings. From what she had heard and learnt from Nello himself, the Walters family were Jamaican brown-skinned people who were kept on the periphery of the lower middle class; had they good connections and education they would be at the outer edge of the privileged classes. Myrtle had listened to tales of commodious houses in Port Antonio and some other rural district that she could not recall. So as far as she was concerned, moving out to more spacious accommodation here in London was a step in the right direction. That in itself should not have prevented Nello from visiting regularly, and particularly should not have prevented him dropping in for his Sunday helping of rice and peas and chicken, until Miss Imo arrived, of course. Myrtle had heard of West Indians who were buying houses and not taking in tenants. Good luck to them. It would be some time before she and Ziah could do without lodgers. Already two nurses had taken the room that Nello had vacated. She was quite pleased with them, although one had said that she was considering emigrating to Canada. When Myrtle told Lincoln of the young lady's intention, he explained that many people saw going to Canada as a way of getting into the United States.

Five Sundays slipped by and Nello had not shown up. Myrtle imagined the worst. She had at least expected he would bring his wife around for a meal and an introductory chat.

"Ziah, what happened between you and Nello?" she asked.

"Is what you mean, woman?" Ziah's reply was shifty.

"You know exactly what I mean. You and Nello used to be thick as thieves; you must have fallen out. It's five Sundays and he not even drop by to say, '*Dog, how you do?*' He has been having Sunday dinner with us since 1957. He has been living in that room on the ground floor since January 1958. Suddenly he moved out. OK, the place he gone to is bigger than the room here. If he's going to send for his wife and children then he needs more space, I accept that. All that I understand well enough, but what I don't know is why suddenly him forget 'bout us, as if we done him some 'arm. It's bothering me a lot. He was always such a talkative man, yet all I could get outa him was that this new flat was part of the deal he did with Lincoln for being in charge of repairs and all that. Of course, he could have fallen sick. I heard a story the other day; it was in the Sunday papers, about a man who went missing for five months. Apparently he had gone up to the attic where he must have had a heart attack and died. No one knew where he was for five months. Lawd, loneliness is a bad thing. Make me feel better... go round to his new address and see what's happening," she pleaded.

"I don't think Nello is living alone..." her husband said, still being shifty.

"Well, he's a big man and hasn't got to report to anyone. Are you telling me *you* didn't know that Nello has had his women in the room downstairs? So why living with somebody cause him to stay away?"

"He probably thought you wouldn't approve. You know how it is. All these people think highly of you. What you think mean a lot to them..."

"I am not his mother... not his sister... Tell me, what is going on?"

"You going to know sooner than later anyway," Ziah sighed. "Nello sent for one of his other women from Jamaica... and their three children. The little one was born after he left Jamaica."

"But Lawd, hear me trial! So how many women and children he left in Jamaica?"

"I never thought of asking. But *any* man who had the sort of job he had and living away from home is bound to have whole pile of women..."

"That count in England too? You were in England since 1948 and me only come up in early 1955... I wondering now if you got another family somewhere in Kilburn or in Maudslay where you stayed with your ex-serviceman brother."

"As my granny would say: *cock mouth kill cock.* Or, what the English say? ... *hoist by my own petard.*"

If living away from one's wife was a licence to have affairs, then indeed he had been nearly eight years in England before Myrtle joined him. He did not like the direction this conversation was heading. He hurriedly swung the rudder.

"Nello' woman is a really pretty coolie woman. That surprise me because Indian women them don't go with black men..."

"But Nello not black. Well, not black, black. You know what I mean. Didn't he say his father was white?"

"You right. It funny how many *coolie royal* people you see in Jamaica, but none of them have coolie mother. Is always the coolie man dem sowing wild oats."

"So is what you would call these pickney them? Quarter-white and half-Indian? I bet them is really good-looking. I bet them have good colour..."

"But wait, is what you mean about 'good colour'? The man has a lawful wife and he is breeding a young woman younger than his own lawful daughter and all you can say that the children must be good-looking?"

"Well, the next time you see Nello, you tell him that all this is none ah my business," she said, ignoring her husband's statement. "Tell him to come round."

Ziah knew that Myrtle's curiosity had got the better of her. She just had to see those children. After all she did not know Miss Imo and owed her no loyalty. She did not believe there was an association of legally married women.

One evening a week later, Nello Walters stopped by on his way from work. He brought Myrtle Morgan a large bunch of flowers and a bottle of rum for his old drinking partner Ziah.

"This is Edwin Charley over-proof," enthused Prophet Isaiah Morgan. He kissed the bottle as a priest would a rosary. Then his wife wrenched it from his grasp.

"You not going to see this again until you do all those little jobs I've been going on about," She turned to face Nello Walters. "Hi, stranger," she greeted. "I was telling Ziah I must have done you something I was not aware of. It nearly two months since you been around."

"No, man, you no do me anything. There is this situation and I didn't know how you would take it. I know this other woman now for nearly ten years and I got to see her right. She is young and wants to do things like studying accountancy. She's a kind of outcast from her family because of our relationship, so she only have me..."

"And your children..." Myrtle intervened.

"Miss Myrtle, say what you want about me, but I'm not a man to shirk my responsibilities. I'm not gwine to turn my back on my children. I know it sounds like foolishness but Miss Imo and me know where we stand. We have the biggest house in Cedar Tree. It's the first house in that area with flush toilet at the back of the house because she would not have it in the house. I build the house on enough land to grow banana and ground provisions. We have people working for us. I tell you, if I don't send Miss Imo any more money, she still make a good living off the land. There's just one thing, I couldn't get her to shift from her house in Cedar Tree. I bought another house in Port Antonio and beg her to leave Cedar Tree, mainly 'cause it no got electricity. Cedar Tree is really bush country at the back of beyond. I wanted her to go and live in town. You know what the woman said? She is not going anywhere that she can't find privacy to *dash 'way the contents of her chamber pot*. I told her that in Port Antonio you don't need a chamber pot, that the house have flush toilet inside the house unlike the one I built her in Cedar Tree. She suck her teeth and say that she want more than fence between her and the neighbours. I'm not telling you a lie."

"Well, I suppose she's happy in Cedar Tree among her relations and friends."

"Precisely," sighed Nello. "She's the queen in her neck of the woods. Our daughter Glenda said, 'Well, Daddy, the one-eyed man is the king in the country of the blind.' Miss Imo is set in her ways. Even though I modernise the house at Cedar Tree she still have her chamber pot. Can you imagine that? So the house in Port Antonio is rented out. The rent pay regularly in the bank, and she has access to it. She no poor."

"So she... Glenda, I mean, know all about you other children? Tell me if me too fast," Myrtle slipped in.

"Me never hide Meena. She's a lovely person. When I first saw her she was sixteen, but we never talk until three years later,"

He seemed to shake himself from his romantic reverie. "Yes, man, Glenda met her little brother and sisters before she left for the States. Miss Myrtle, I got one big fault: I couldn't keep myself loyal to one woman! I never tell lies about that and Miss Imo knows I was along with somebody else when she come on the scene. Imo wanted the ring on her finger, the *Norah Bobb*, as she call it, though she knew no wedding ring was ever going to tie me down."

"So what about Meena?"

"She's young and England is a funny place. She want to study. It might be that is she going to give me the push. After all, I'm nearly thirty years older that her..."

"Who is thirty?" Catherine pushed the door and entered the sitting room.

"Girl, you ever heard about knocking at doors?" asked Ziah.

"Oh, Dad, it's just you, Mom and Uncle Nello... Hi, Uncle Nello, you back from your ho... holidays?" She deftly substituted holiday when with monumental cheek and sarcasm she was thinking honeymoon. She had worked out that with Nello, not having seen his woman for number of years his absence from Lilford Road, must be to enjoy his reunion, call it what you may.

"Catherine, what you want?" her mother demanded. "Big people talking..."

"Mum, I'm nearly sixteen. With your permission I can get engaged..." Catherine was about to lower herself into a chair when she noticed that her mother was lifting herself out of her chair with the sternest of maternal looks that would brook no nonsense.

"I'll give you married," the mother pulled herself up to full height and was bearing down on her daughter like a malevolent battleship on a frigate that was listing and in serious trouble. The daughter fleet of foot was through the door before the mother could reach the recently vacated chair.

V

The following Sunday, Nello brought his new family to Lilford Road for Sunday dinner. When the exhaustive introductions were over, Christine and Catherine took the children down to the basement, which three years ago Nello their erstwhile lodger had helped to convert into a playroom for the children that Myrtle now a registered child minder was looking after while their parents were at work.

"It could be dad, daughter and grandchildren," Catherine said to Christine when the older children were out of earshot."

"You can say that again," Christine said, "and it's disgusting. She must be about Enid's age and he must be pushing sixty!"

"Don't exaggerate," counselled Catherine, "he's about fifty-five, same as Dad, I suppose, give or take a year."

"That's ancient. Would you go out with a forty-six-year-old man?"

"Well, let's see... Sidney Poitier is thirty-six and Harry Belafonte is only thirty-three..."

"Ah, shut up... In Jamaica anyone ten years older that you is called Miss or Mister. So how could a nice woman like Miss Meena get involved with Uncle Nello?"

"We're twins and you're looking to me for answers? Anyway Lonso's nearly ten years older..."

"Drop dead!"

"That ain't nice. I bet that if we were Siamese you wouldn't say that. I wonder how it works; if one dies, what would happen to the other one?"

"For God's sake, Catherine, do you have to talk like that?"

"I'm sorry, I get these thoughts and I just have to articulate them!"

"I know and they always get you into trouble. Or people just shrug and say, 'Well, it's Catherine being funny again. Or as Mamma would say, '*she giving laugh for peas soup!*'"

"If you want to discuss why young girls have sex with older men, why don't you ask Darlene? Her DJ boyfriend 'The Sound Man' must be pushing forty. He has a string of pickneys from Hackney to Walthamstow and I bet he has sons and daughters older than Darlene back home. From what I've overheard, according to how the conversation ran when we were coming back from Maudslay the other day, it seems that back home there are two reasons why young girls go for older men. One is his economic standing and the other is his colour. In a Jamaican context Uncle Nello had both. Lincoln and Lonso were chatting to Daddy the other day..."

"And your big ears just happened to be near the key hole again..."

"As a matter of fact we were in Lincoln's car and me and Daddy were in the back. They were talking about Uncle Nello and his women. Girl it seems he's a real ram-goat...."

"I bet if I was there they would not..."

"Before you start your routine about everybody treating you like my younger sister, which incidentally you are by ten minutes, Daddy told me to close my ears, as if it was possible to close one's ears as easily as one's eyes."

"In Nigerian Yoruba culture I would be considered the elder, because I ordered you to go out of the womb and report what the outside world is like. I would be called Tiawo and you would be Kehinde. Why do they always treat you as if you're more grown-up than me? After all, I started my period before you."

"Tell them that," said Catherine.

"What?"

"You heard me," replied Catherine. "Anyway the secret of hearing things is to be in the wrong place at the right time," she continued. "You're too damn serious. They all think I'm too scatterbrained. 'Oh, can't tell the twins apart?' they say. 'Catherine is the scatterbrain and Christine the serious one.' I bet I could pass myself off as you, but I doubt if you can play me," she challenged.

"We must try it sometime. Finish telling what Lincoln and Lonso were saying while Daddy stuck two fingers in your lugholes."

"Not much except that there's a woman in Maudslay asking Uncle Nello for money to send for their son who's about to leave high school. Apparently Uncle Nello has sent registered letters to other women in several places, from Montego Bay to Port Antonio. It seems he was a North Coast operator. I bet those envelopes contained child maintenance money. Daddy confirmed the first day they met he noticed that Uncle Nello was sending registered letters to different addresses in Jamaica. "

"So instead of singing *'Brown-skin gal, stay home and mind baby,* it is brown-skin man, go 'way and find work to mind you' babies."

They laughed at Christine's attempt to sing the old calypso, for the new line did not work.

"Anyway, imagine Uncle Nello, brown-skinned, well dressed, having a good job and driving an American car. I don't think teenage Meena had a chance, do you? If Mum and Dad didn't send for us we could have been facing that problem in three years' time, if not before. Think of poor Darlene. Men are so primitive..."

"That, my darling sister, is called power, and from time immemorial men have had it over women in more ways than one. When God asked Adam where he was, his excuse was, '*The woman whom You gave to be me with, she gave me of the tree, and I ate.'* Adam's power was in his excuse. He had someone to blame."

"Wow!" said Catherine. "Have you been sneaking off to see Lonso? That sounds like him."

"Piss off."

"Hang on a bit... 'Drop dead' and now 'Piss off'. Am I getting too close, sister dear? Let's see, when did you have the opportunity? You went to the optician a fortnight back. Oh, my God!"

"Drop it!"

"Hmm."

"What you mean by 'hmm'?"

"Ssh, I'm thinking; that optician is near the Oval, which isn't far from Consort Road. Hmm."

"Hmm!" mocked Christine, sticking out her tongue at her twin.

"Now who's the sly one?"

There was a knock at the door and the girls switched their conversation.

"I reckon Suzy and Courtland are old enough for primary school. I bet Mamma will be asked to look after Ike."

"Most likely."

The door swung open for Myrtle Morgan and Meena Mahabihar entered the room.

"This is where you look after the children?" Meena asked.

"I got four at the moment," Myrtle said, stooping to collect toys from the floor; she was sure they were not there when she had left the room. She did not mind the litter of toys when the children were in her care, but now they were back in their own homes she expected *her* home to be tidy.

"It would be nice if you could look after Ike, especially if Suzy and Courtland manage to get a school nearby. They could come here and wait till I get home from work. I got a job working in an old people's home, you know."

"It seems as if Nello been busy planning my life for me!"

Myrtle said it as a joke. She even smiled, but her daughters got the message clearly. Meena, pretty as she was, light complexion Indian as she was, she was not going to be one of their mother's closest friends after all she was younger than their older sisters Monica and Louise.

33

When Lurline had finished trimming and shaving the back and sides of Alonso head, she sprayed a pungent smelling liquid over the areas where she had passed the razor.

"What was that?" Alonso asked.

"*Kalanga Water!*" she said and then she whipped the towel she had used to cover his jacket with the action of a bullfighter. "What you *no* like? You never protested before."

"This one, in the immortal words of Jane Russell, smells like a *friendly skunk.*"

Lurline pushed him from the chair. "Have a bit of respect for, for... what is it you call me, again?"

"My tonsorial artist. That is from the Latin *tondere* which means to shave."

"See, ladies, I am a tonsorial artist," she announced to the two ladies who were patiently waiting their turn.

"Me no want any shaving," said a large lady. "Me going to me niece wedding in Birmingham. Just straighten and style it because me after a certain young man."

"This one," said Lurline pushing Lonso, "is free, single and disengaged and him is a writer. Have a book coming out soon."

"He's good looking enough but a little too free. And he sound as if he just swallow the dictionary."

"You right, you know," said Lurline, spreading a gown over the woman's ample chest and pulling it across her shoulders and pushing it down between her back and the chair. "He swallowed three dictionaries, French, Spanish and English."

The customer burst out laughing, her eyes creasing and tears running down her cheeks.

"Mentionin' French and all that, well, somethin' happened at my work place yesterday, I must tell you about. This African woman was late again. I think it was three times since last week. Boy, this white forelady start on the woman. 'You people are lazy, you don't want to work. You come to this country expectin' everythin' to fall in your lap. It is either too cold or it is rainin' or you are sick. All this doesn't stop you havin' a baby every nine months. If I have my way I would ship you all back to where you come from.' And all that time this African woman bowin' her head and jabberin' in her language and, 'Yes, Mrs Gwen' and jabber, jabber in her language,

354

'Sorry, Mrs Gwen. It won't happen again, Mrs Gwen.' When it was over, I go over and said to this African woman. Is why you bowin' and scrapin' to this white woman for? The African woman put her hand on my shoulder. 'Hilda,' she said, 'if you only knew what I was sayin' to that *motherfucker* in my language you would have to give me a bucket of disinfectant to wash out my mouth. Sorry to repeat that word before you, but motherfucker is mild.'"

The woman ended her story laughing and using the gown to wipe her eyes. It was difficult to decipher if the other customers in the salon were laughing at the humour or at the method of delivery.

"Why don't you go and see Puncie? She is round the back."

"What is she doing there? Who is minding the shop in Camberwell?"

"Why don't you go and ask her?"

"Whisper sweet words to her in Spanish," said a slim young woman dragging fiercely on a cigarette. "I heard that Spanish is a real romantic language, *amour, armour...*"

They all laughed and Lurline waved her hand with the hot comb in the direction of the closed door beyond which was the rest room

The rest room had two doors on the far side, one leading to a small kitchen, the other to the toilet. There was red sofa capable of seating three and a couple more chairs. There was a cooker and a refrigerator, a sink with cups on the draining board. Above the sink was a notice urging all users to wash up after themselves; but it was the door beyond with a plaque of a little boy urinating in a chamber pot and the legend below it which usually forced a smile from Alonso:

> *Gentlemen, please stand closer,*
> *It is shorter than you think!*
>
> *Ladies, please sit throughout the whole event!*

As he entered the room he could see Puncie sitting at one end of the sofa and Darlene, her daughter sitting as far from her as she could without leaving the sofa. At a glance the situation reminded Alonso of No-man's Land of the First World War tensions between the trenches and the current Cold War tension between the Western and Eastern Bloc countries.

"Which of you is Dulles and who is Gromyko?"

"I'm not up to your jokes today, Lonso. Can't you see how vex me be and me eyes red from bawling?" Puncie said, waving him further into the room.

"What's up? You are smoking! It was you who had a bet that I couldn't give up smoking..."

"No mind that now. I am upset and vex." She turned her tear-stained face towards Darlene. "Stand up! Darlene, stand up, no?"

"What for?" came the defiant reply.

"Stand up so Lonso can have a look at you?"

"What for?" came the reply again, this time accompanied with a powerful intake of air through clenched teeth. Her stare swept contemptuously from Lonso to her mother, then to the toilet door. "Don't treat me like how they sell goat back home. Stand up, turn round. Any moment now you goin' to tell me to show him me teeth," she dropped her voice, "or something else."

"Lawd, girl you fresh, eh! You is what in Jamaica we call facy! You don't have any manners, you know. You givin' me a whole lota grief and botheration, you know! I tell you if this was back home in Jamaica I would gie you one thump in your head..."

"Bad luck," she intervened, "this ain't Jamaica. You touch me hard and I call the police. Anyway is what you call him in here for? Him not old enough to be my father, whoever that was. I wonder is whose boyfriend he is? He ain't fi me." The smirk disappeared from Darlene's lips as her mother leapt to her feet, towering ever her with rage and clenched fists. Darlene cowered, both hands protecting her head and her knees pressed tightly together. Alonso held Puncie by the shoulders and pulled her away.

"That won't solve anything," he said, holding her firmly. Puncie wrenched herself from his grasp, just as Darlene escaped from the sofa and ran towards the door of the toilet.

"I gwine kill her. See God dey," she swore.

"Look," said Alonso, "whatever this is, it is family business and Darlene is right, you should not get me involved..."

"Look at her, no. You no see she a breed," Puncie interjected.

"What!" exclaimed Alonso.

"Is what you telling him me business for? It's not his, you know! Him long and *magher* like, you think him could gie woman baby? Me catch him once or twice looking at me, him eyes roving all over me tits and me legs, over and over, you know..." Darlene having strategically arranged her retreat escaped into the toilet and slammed and bolted the door from within, as Puncie made a dash for her. Having failed to catch the recalcitrant progeny, Puncie returned to the sofa.

"She just turned sixteen and this is the second time that no-good bastard breed her," she waved her hand at Alonso, silencing him. "The first time he took her somewhere and she had an abortion. She was off school for two weeks claiming that she had heavy periods. I never heard of a girl having periods for two weeks. I had my suspicions. I threaten to call the doctor and she told me the truth, up to a point. She did not know the man who drove her to the place where the woman did what she did. Did not know the place, did not know the woman's name, did not know the other man who brought her home. I should have gone to the police then. By now that no-good bastard would be in prison. I thought of the grief and botheration it would cause, and thought that out of bad there would come good. She would learn her lesson and settle down and make something of herself. But no, oh, no! That fuckin' little bitch had a' itch that a man has to scratch. Wham, she breeding again. OK, so she feel like givin' her pussy to some guy, why couldn't she get him to use a French letter?"

"Suppose I don't like it that way?" Puncie and Alonso turned at the same moment to see Darlene leaning against the toilet door.

Moments like this one occur from time to time. A moment of pathos, of humour, a defining moment, when to be strong is a sign of weakness and one's weakness becomes the soil from which strength can grow. Alonso watched Puncie as she rose from the sofa. He did not attempt to restrain her. Darlene saw her coming and did not retreat.

The door from the salon half-opened and Lurline squeezed in.

"You all makin' a lot of noise. I don't think they can hear what you sayin', but they beginnin' to put two and two together and makin' six! There is a lot of whisperin' going on. Well, look at it from their point of view, mother and daughter in a room shoutin' at each other, then in walked a young man; you all catch me drift? Sorry, Lonso, *you* name gawn abroad..."

"My name? Oh no! Don't make jokes like that."

"Oh, boy, Lonso you should see your face. It's a picture! I don't think that they heard anythin' specific, but they know that there is somethin' goin' on. So me advice to you is to keep it down," Lurline squeezed herself back through the half-opened door.

"Don't fret," said Darlene. "I don't think he could gie a woman a baby. Tell him that you have a' *itchy fanny* and I bet him would think that you tellin' him about a' Italian bike," she looked Alonso up and down and up again, then slowly she looked away.

"You little bitch," Puncie reeled as if struck suddenly and fiercely across her face. She leaned against the sofa, one hand pressed hard against her belly. "Is this really the chile I gave birth to?"

"Me bad, but me no that bad to take wey my mother's sweet man," she knew she had the power to hurt and she was going to enjoy watching Puncie crumble.

"I'm not your mother's man," Alonso felt he was being inextricably drawn into a family problem in which he had no right as neither participant nor arbiter. "And, by the way, I think I know more about motorbikes than you do, Italian or Japanese." At another time he would have even smiled at the rude humour of her rejoinder, but she was enjoying the hurt she was causing her mother. "Like you, Darlene, I don't know why I am here, apart from the fact that your Aunt Lurline sent me in to see your mother. I had no idea that you would be here too. I sure as hell didn't have any knowledge of your condition..."

"Condition!" she said scornfully. "You know why me spirit just can't take you and your *virgin* sister?" She might know that her voice conveyed sarcasm, but she wanted Alonso to understand that she did not believe in the virginity of any woman of more than twenty years old, by which time she calculated they should already have had a baby or several boyfriends. "You all too high and mighty an' *dawg nyam dawg...*"

"That old chestnut!" He was no longer surprised or angered when people implied that the relationship between him and Blossom was incestuous.

"Jeezas!" shouted her mother. "Shet up your mouth. Don't interfere in things you don't know nuthin' 'bout... She didn't mean it, Lonso. She's just a silly little girl. She's pretending she is big and can handle her problems, but deep down she is scared. Tell Lonso, not me... tell him."

"Sorry," she said.

"Wait! You mean he have to put his ears down your throat to hear what you sayin'? Talk up no!"

"I'm sorry Lonso. I guess it would be nice to have somebody to look after me. Somebody to tell me right from wrong," Darlene directed at Alonso, then she turned to her mother with venom. "You lef' me with Gody Lovey in that back-of-beyond place call Red Wattle Gap. She too old to be bringin' up a child. When I was near twelve years old she look 'pon me and say, 'Gal, you must write to you mother in England... You mus' tell her say you need a pair of bra.' Another time she tell me that I gwine see blood, that I was not to be frighten'. At the same time boys was tellin' us girls that blood gwine fly to our head if we didn't make them *rudeness* we. There was nobody to ask if the blood Gody Lovey say was goin' to come, was the same blood that the boys was sayin' would fly to our brain. Well, one day the blood did come and I was sittin' down in class, me head splittin' and back a pain me. I don't know what would have happen if Miss Barrett the teacher did not see how distress I was. She send the class out to recess and come and put she arm around me. Nobody never done that before. 'Don't fret,' she tell me, 'this means you are a woman now. All us women have to go through this misery every month.' She put a towel around my waist and took me down to her house. She cleaned me up. That was a job for my mother. Miss Barrett take me home to Gody Lovey. It is then she write that you should come for me. All the time me wondering why my mother always leavin' me with people while I growin' up..."

Puncie moved towards her daughter. Darlene tensed up, raising her hands to shield her face.

"I not goin' to hit you. I promise I will never raise my hands to you again. I just want to hug you and say that I am sorry." Suddenly they were holding on to each other and crying. Alonso began to creep towards the door.

"Don't go!" it was a command. He turned around thinking the voice was Puncie's. He realised that from the position in which the two women were standing, it was Puncie who had her back to him and it was the tear-stained face of Darlene that was pleading with him to stay.

"I don't dislike you. I got no cause. You never treat me like dirt. True, me not in the same circle like Catherine and Christine who I see hug and kiss you whenever I am at their parents' place and you come there. Blossom never say anythin' bad 'bout me that I ever hear either. So I have no cause to say the things I was sayin' earlier. Where I come from when a boy put his hand round a girl shoulder, you know what he is after and what that hand is headin' for. Ah swear that boys them have more than two hands..."

"You shouldn't be talkin' like that," interrupted her mother. "You was only thirteen when I came out to get you! You was still a chile..."

"Ah, ah. Well, that half-Chinee girl, Miss Pretty from Manhem Corner, did have a baby when she was only thirteen..."

"Ssh Ssh," her mother remonstrated. "Babies having babies..."

"We have feeling too, you know!"

"I don't need you to tell me about growin' up in Jamaica..."

"Yeah, I know, I hear' a lot a things 'bout you when you was growing' up. I wonder sometimes if they was true. I hear, people say to my face, that I was goin' to be just like you!"

"I was nineteen when I had you," said Puncie defensively and with a dash of virtuousness. "I was not just givin' my body to every boy who ask me for *rudeness*."

"Who said I did? The baby I making is for the only man I been with in this country, and we did'n do it in the back of his car either."

"And he is about three times your age. He could go to prison for havin' sex with you, you know that?"

"I never call no man's name," she said.

"We all know who he is, right?"

"I wonder how you know that! I was sure there was nobody under the bed..."

"I am tryin' to make amends. I want you to feel ashamed. Just get down off that high horse. Look, girl, in fifteen years you might be standing where I am now. Don't leave it till then to feel what I feel now. If I turn me back on you, you know what will happen? The authorities will take you into a home. The baby will be put up for adoption. You will soon find your little arse back on the street. I don't want this to happen to my flesh and blood. So start talkin' humble like you sorry for what happen and let us see how we can get through this mess. You' body might be capable of givin' birth, but you is still a chile. You not all that mature and your childhood finish. It done. From now on every time you think of doin' somethin', buyin' somethin', goin' somewhere, you'll have to think if you stoppin' your child from getting' somethin' it really could do with."

"Child!" she said, steering at her mother and resenting the reclassification. "If I am a child and bein' immature, as you say, why I been havin' *feelings* for a long time? I wonder how some people get to be twenty and more and manage the *nature* that God put in their body?"

"God also give you brains to think, and somethin' called shame. That tell you when somethin' is wrong. That is why we don't do it out in the open like dogs."

"We didn't do it in the open or in the back of his car either..."

"Darlene, you' tryin' me patience." Puncie turned to Alonso. "Talk some sense in her head."

"It is not my place. Whatever I say will be like a red rag to a bull," he said.

"Say you piece," said Darlene moving away from her mother. "Suppose it happen to Blossom..."

"Blossom is past twenty-one. She's a woman fully grown. If she chooses to have a child at least she will have done it with the experience of an adult. She has known poverty and sacrifice. If she hasn't suffered the fate of some of the kids we grew up with it was because we were determined to make something of ourselves. In your case someone has had sex with you while you were under sixteen. You may say that was your business, but in the eyes of the law you were raped. Soon you'll have to go to pre-natal clinic. They'll find out things about you. You will have to give your age. When it is established you conceived under the age for lawful intercourse, you'll be under pressure to name the father. Your mother will be accused of not being a fit and proper guardian and you may have to go into a home..."

She made as if to shut him up.

"You gave me permission to speak, so my advice to you is to talk it out with your mother and arrive at a situation where you will have your baby and with your mother's help care for the baby. At the same time grab any chance to make something of your life. Perhaps go to evening classes..."

"Study, books and more books, I hate them. You mean if I was a bookworm like Catherine and her sister you would treat me like you treat them, all hugs and kisses? Tell me something, when you put your arms around them you don't think that they feel anything?"

"Darlene!" screamed her mother.

"Maybe they do, maybe they don't, either way neither of them is having under-aged sex with me. If either of them is pregnant it is not for me. I think you ought to meet your mother halfway. She is really trying. Darlene, let me tell you a little of my history. At seventeen I passed the Jamaica Local Third-Year Examination and went to Kingston to work, sending back money for Blossom and my mother and the children she had for her no-good husband, who never earned a week's wages while he was in Jamaica. Oh, he planted my mother's land, made money from bananas and so forth, but I was the real breadwinner. An old cousin lent me part of the fare to England when I was nineteen. I started working in Lyons Corner shop, washing up dirty dishes so my sister Blossom could go to secondary school. Now both of us are working to support our mother and the five children that Bullah Cameron gave her. It's like bringing up a family since I was seventeen. I don't think I'm going to be in a position to have a family of my own until I'm in my mid-thirties. You, young lady, have taken on quite a commitment. You just don't have a child and expect your life to get back to normal as if you've woken up from a bad dream. Before you reach thirty it will be your turn to worry about what your daughter is up to. Even when you are forty and your child is an adult you won't stop worrying. Having a child is a commitment for life. You won't be able to do it on your own. You're going to need your mother. You'll have to grow up fast."

"Darlene," Puncie went towards her daughter, held her shoulder and turned her around. "I hope you was listenin'. I know you didn't like me bringin' Lonso into what is our family problem, but I find him to be a sensible young man. He talked some good sense and it's goin' to be me and you from now on. We goin' to manage this thin'. If you let me stand by you, I'm sure we can work things out. You'll see," she was pushing back the hair from Darlene's forehead. "You'll see."

Alonso moved silently towards the door opened it and left quickly.

34

He woke from a deep, deep sleep. The dream had been a pleasant one and he felt satisfied and excited. He experienced a feeling of expectancy as if waiting on the starting block to be energised, waiting as that warm feeling began to course through his veins like a stimulant. Without moving his head he could see her. She was sitting in front of the mirror, her copper-coloured hair tumbling over her shoulders, swinging gently to the movement of her head as she applied her make-up.

"You are awake at last," she said. "Yes, I believe you are fully awake!"

"How can you be so sure?"

"First, you're not back at Ostade Road, Brixton Hill in the year of our Lord 1957..." and she paused as she swung around so that he could admire her, from the fringe above her brow with the neatly shaped eyebrows down to where the dressing-gown had fallen away, revealing long beautiful legs. She caught the look of excitement on his face and wrapped the gown around her lower half. "I have a face which some think t'is worth looking at, and if you raise your head a little to the right you should be able to see my reflection in the mirror. I'm not a ghost, or a duppy, as you would say. Now are you awake?"

"I'm awake and ar..."

"Down, boy, down," she said with a grin. "May I recommend a cold shower?" She sat back in front of the mirror. In a deliberate act to excite him further, her head swayed from left to right and back, so that her hair swung like a pendulum. She watched him as he pushed back the covers and dropped his feet to the floor.

"I'm your *Nicodemus* girl," she said.

"My *Nicodemus* girl? Wow," he said spinning around. "Now I know I'm dreaming." He had both hands held out and with high measured steps changed direction away from the bathroom towards her. "So you're not my duppy girl, but my *Nicodemus* girl! Come here!"

"Ye gods! What if that frustrated, racist bitch down the corridor should knock at the door for some sugar?" She covered her eyes, then shouted at him, "Modesty! Modesty! Please!"

"She might consider me sweet enough as I am! Who needs sugar when you have honey? Anyway it would only be brown sugar... and she no like that!"

"Stop boasting and cover up yourself. Get in the bathroom."

"I ain't gonna have another bath."

"What? You dirty man!" She threw a towel at him, which he caught and wrapped about his waist.

"*Nicodemus* redhead goes to Coloured man's room,' said neighbour. Can I borrow your title? This could be what Stella my agent says my novel is lacking."

"Wasn't there a story about one of the Greek mortals of ancient times marrying a god who only came to her at night and without any light on in their chamber?" she asked, ignoring his last statement. "How did she know it was the same man?"

"I had the lights on. I saw your face. You are the one."

"We didn't have the lights on. Everybody knows that the lights must be turned off, thanks to the ancient Greeks."

"Cupid and Psyche, the Roman counterpart of the Greeks," he said, wrapping the towel around his waist even firmer. "I read it in *The Golden Ass of Lucius Apulius.* That was supposed to be the first novel ever written over three thousand years ago."

"You colonials bemoan colonisation, but it seems Old Britannia looked after your education. I never heard of *The Golden Ass*, and I went to a grammar school."

"It wasn't on the curriculum. The headmaster had a bookcase on the wall behind his desk. He let some of us borrow books. I suppose I felt what Keats experienced when he first opened Chapman's Homer. There are no more original jokes. I didn't have to wonder what they were up to in the dark. I read lines like 'fearing for her virginity' and 'Cupid making a perfect consummation of the marriage."

"Ahem!' she interrupted. 'Didn't she light a lamp to see his face and some of the hot oil fell on him at which point he fled into the night?"

"We're in a role-reversal situation here, are we? Shall we have a quick demonstration of what they were up to?"

"The shower!" she said firmly. She stood up and held him off at arms' length. "The shower is the best remedy for your condition my lad". She spun him around and slapped his backside and pushed him towards the bathroom. "Now get!"

"Spoilsport! There's a rumour that the English consider certain activities to be strictly nocturnal. So tell me about your nocturnal visitations. Are these to be regular occurrences?"

"You know my feelings. I like you... no, that's not true. I do love you, but that has to remain our secret. I'm not confident enough to walk down the street hanging on to your arms. My heart goes out to the girls who can, like Sue Hall and her sister Betty. Yet when you think of it she'll have done well, for a coalman's daughter, when Warren is called to the Bar, and that will be soon, won't it?"

"Yes. Warren was a coalman himself, you know."

"You know what I mean. I don't know of any white coalmen becoming barristers, do you? We're still tied up in this class thing as you are in the race thing, whatever the prime minister may say about the class war being over and that we've never had it so good. I was born into a class-ridden and racist society. I can't help how I feel." She looked as if she regretted those feelings, then she continued. "A girl got on the tube the other day holding on to her black man. She wasn't very attractive in dress or manner, but she was so proud of her man she was completely oblivious to the malicious looks she was getting. It made me think. Was he a student of medicine, law or engineering? Such a man would be a good catch for any woman, let alone a working-class woman. I smiled, for at that moment I was thinking of you research for your PhD, and with a novel published. My smile was intended to give her support. I meant to be encouraging but she probably thought I was smiling at her man and held on to him all the more. I wish I could do that while travelling on the tube with you, but I can't and I don't think you'd be confident to kiss me while waiting at the bus queue. Would you?"

"Sheila Cox, you are both a racist and a snob!"

"Guilty!" she said. "So are you, if you were honest enough. If I was black would we be in this long-distance and secret love affair? I don't think so. If you were white you'd be a terrific catch for a girl like me. You have a degree and you're a writer. Perhaps in ten, fifteen years you may become one of the few black professors in British universities. My mum would hang out a banner saying: 'My daughter is married to a university lecturer.' Honestly, I'm not afraid of your blackness. I quite like it, as a matter of fact, but this is 1962. I grew up dreaming of a fair-haired blue-eyed husband. Despite the war years with coloured GIs and colonial troops, you were the *blacky* who would take me away if I was bad..."

"You have been bad..."

"Shut up! Stop embarrassing me, for heaven's sake. Think of all that shit down south in Alabama. Some time ago there was a story about a white rabbit marrying a black rabbit. It caused one hell of a row. It was in a children's book, for heaven's sake! In reality a rabbit on heat doesn't give a damn what colour buck mounts her, nor does a dog. The family of dogs is a lot more diverse than the human race, yet they seem able to recognise all branches of the species. Do you agree that our ability to think has robbed us of the sense of recognising and celebrating our own diversity?"

He did not answer. The bathroom door was still open and he had not turned on the shower yet.

"You see!" she said triumphantly. "You wouldn't be able to, would you? I mean have a smooch in the cinema. We're two of a kind."

"I heard of a story about a Southern white girl and a black man, the family's handyman, whose courtship took place in a public park. They sat back to back on the park bench pretending to be reading their respective paper and magazine while plotting to flee to Canada."

"Well?" she shouted above the sound of the shower. "Isn't that what Betty and her boyfriend are planning? He's leaving the US army and they're going to get married and live in Toronto." She finished dressing while he showered. "Well, did the Southern couple get to Canada and live happily ever after? Is Canada the refuge of black and white couples? You think we ought to try it?"

"No one knows."

"You see... You couldn't do it, could you? Neither could I."

"Hold your horses, I was thinking about the Southern couple. They apparently changed their names and got themselves lost in order to find their love. All we can do is to wish them well."

"The problem with you writers is one can never tell where facts stop and fiction begins. I think you made this up. By the way, when is Rosita due back?"

"Six o'clock tomorrow morning."

"We must make sure I don't leave any incriminating evidence. You must hoover the bed! Tom said hairs on the pillow and bedclothes are dead give-aways, and he ought to know. I caught him out enough times. I will make every effort not to leave any of my ginger hair as incriminating evidence. You must double check."

"I promise. Although I do not think that my sister will want to inspect my bed linen."

35

Alonso had been standing at the window for over fifteen minutes. From the window of the sitting room, two floors up, there was a good view of the lawn of Consort House and the rose beds at the borders. The farthest border of the lawn had two apple trees and a peach tree. Beyond the fruit trees were the fences of the back gardens of the houses of the street which ran parallel. Alonso had been standing looking out on the brown autumnal scene. It had been raining since early morning. The rain had nagged away like a medium-pace blower, who having struck the perfect line and length kept wheeling away until the game was in danger of grinding to a draw. He did not expect the rain to stop until it dragged darkness behind it, as the groundsmen would drag the covers across the wicket.

Blossom came up behind him and put her right arm around his waist; in her left hand was a mug of tea a foot in front of her brother's face.

"Penny for them," she said.

"They're not worth more than a farthing," he said in a depressed mood. "I'm not selling today. I have a hefty dose of homesickness just you telling stories about the old place back home has filled me with nostalgia. It's seven years since I left; I should have gone back..."

"To do what? You're not Superman. You've done enough. I didn't pay my own fares for this trip. You know that. It was Enid who asked me to come with her. She had three children to look after. I jumped at the idea because her grandmother lives so close to where our mother is living..."

"Three miles over some very rugged country road..."

"Don't interrupt. Lincoln arranged the whole thing. The proverbial one stone killed two birds. It's nice having a rich friend, especially when you're not too proud to accept charity." He knew that was meant for him. "Lincoln built his grandmother-in-law a three-bedroom house with *en suite* bathroom a little way from the old house, but the old lady refused to live there and stayed in the old house. If you ask me I think he built the house so he could feel comfortable when he and his family went to the country for a visit. Well, Hurricane Gladys didn't see things the old lady's way and ripped off the roof of the old house and sent it clashing into Ma'Jilly Gully!"

"Who was living in the new house?"

"One of the teachers, but it being end of the school year she had returned home to somewhere near Mandeville. The house had been fully furnished, so it wasn't difficult for Enid to take full possession. The people from the village, who had been given hospitality by the old lady because their own houses had been flattened or damaged, quietly slipped away when Enid arrived. I stayed there the first night, then went on to Guava Flat the next day. Our house was battered and it lost some of its roof, but the rest was good enough not only for Mama and the kids to stay put, but they were able to offer shelter to others. I know I already told you this when we spoke on the phone from Kingston, but I'll say it again. I drove all the way up the hill to Guava Flat. Of course, by then the worst part of the roads were repaired. Mama and the kids were so impressed to see me behind the wheel of Lincoln's Morris Traveller. Hector wouldn't believe I was a qualified driver until I showed him my International Drivers' licence..."

"I would have thought that your manoeuvring such places as Big Hill and Elbow Bend would convince anyone you can drive. How old is he now?"

"Hector? Eighteen. He's quite tall and not bad looking. Anita said all the girls are after him, and he knows it, and is quite a playboy. That's putting it mildly. He was so protective of me. When I was out with him I couldn't stop to talk to anybody, especially young men I went to school with. I don't think he was worried about me being swept off my feet by Clevie or Godson, rather that I might be moved to hand out a few pound notes."

"I must go back. Hopefully I'll be able to do it next year... I have an extension for my thesis."

"Who knows, by then *Scribe-Inc* will have published your new novel. Then *voila* fame and fortune. Hi, your tea is getting cold," She stepped back and picked up her mug from the coffee table. "Let's not have any more long faces. After all, it's not that you can't afford to go back home now. You want to go back a successful and rich author. Some of the guys from the Caribbean Services of the BBC are radio and television presenters out there now."

"Oh, Flowers, am I that vain? That transparent?"

"Only to those who really know you."

"Such as?"

"Mama and me. 'Is he only going to come back when he is rich and famous?' she asked me. She misses you so much, Nino."

"Put this down to the artist temperament. I've been reviewing my life and I'm not sure where I'm going. Should I have stuck it out with Lincoln?" He did not want to tell her that more and more he had been thinking of Sheila Cox.

"Lincoln has done well. The first three years were bonanza years. In those days black people had to depend on the few black house-owners renting them a room. Or there were the exploitative white landlords who under the guise of liberalism were prepared to rent to anyone who didn't mind paying through the nose. Times are changing; now more and more black people are buying their own homes. There's a tailing-off of migration; that apart, the newcomers seem to be coming up and going to people who have room to put them up. So Lincoln has to be thinking up new projects to keep his business afloat. He's now heavily into importing of African and Caribbean foodstuff; black hair products; getting involved in new housing projects in Jamaica. He's far from broke, but I know Enid is worried about how stretched he is financially. She's scared that the bottom will fall out..."

"Women folks worry too much."

"We have to, especially when our men folk start feeling sorry for themselves." They both laughed and touched cups has they saluted each other. "I don't know anyone who thinks you're a failure," she said. "You're of the age when men get seriously involved with the opposite sex. So many people asked me if you're married or involved with a woman..."

"What was your reply?"

"Oh, something like: 'Sisters are the last to know what's going on in their brother's life'."

"That works both ways."

"Sometimes I'd say something like, 'He's in love with his writing and his studies.'"

"Did anybody believe you?"

"I don't believe it myself. Here you are, a twenty-six-year-old part-time teacher at Myatt Fields Comprehensive. OK, it's not the most glamorous of schools in South London, but you're one of the rare breed, a black teacher. Your second novel is due out soon. Maybe I shouldn't say it, but you're not bad-looking, so young women should be queuing up round the block, and it ain't happening, or are you being so devious that I'm in the dark..."

"I could say the same about you, seeing you're one *bunununus*, as Louise Bennett would say; so why aren't you attached to a young man? You're in the Civil Service with a good job at the Migrants Service Department. They say women mature quicker than men, so the three or so years between us should make you more mature than your bachelor brother. Am I missing something, or are you too devious for me to fathom? Did I hear mention of Ransford Carr?

"You might have. He is in London preparing the High Commission for when the Federation is finally dead and buried. By the way he is ahead of you. He is hoping that his thesis will be published early next year..."

"He had ahead start with High School in Jamaica and university in Canada, and always seem to be crossing your path..."

"I'm glad you said that; he wants me to meet him at the Students Centre at Collingham Gardens this evening."

"I thought we were going to Gody Myrtle."

"Gody Myrtle will be the first to clap her hands and stamp her feet and shout alleluia when she finds out that I have a another bloke who was a teacher and is an author and he is not a relative..."

"Of course I have not seen him for at least six years, but we have always got on!" he said, putting a hand on her shoulder and then pushed her gently away. "I cannot wait to give you away."

"*Play* it softly he is just a friend... a good friend and neither of us have any attachments but don't get too serious just yet." she said shaking his hand from her shoulder. "Now when are you going to tell me about the birds which have been fluttering in and out of this flat while I was a away?"

"Birds?"

"It was I who introduced you to the woman of your dreams..."

"You mean Sheila Cox?"

"The same, my friend, my colleague at work, ex band member..."

"She did drop by for a drink, but as you know neither of us has the courage to be involved in a mixed-race relationship in the full glare of a public which can be so offensive."

"Racist! Anyway I did say in and out of the flat. A lot can happen here away from public glaze."

"Flowers!" he shouted feigning a mocked surprise. "What a picture you have of your brother!"

"Perish the thought. Anyway I can get it out of Sheila. Oh not the details I will just watch her face getting redder and redder."

"Never saw you as a Grand Inquisitor. I wonder if I would be fair exchange for the possibility of her inheritance... remember the South African aunt?"

"Ah'm."

"What do you mean by 'Ah'm'?"

"Ah'm... There are enough women around. You could have had your pick, but that woman has to be custom-made. Of course, you could be waiting for either Christine or will it be Catherine?"

"Let's change the subject."

"Yeah, let's. However, I want to tell you again that there are many people who are so proud of you! Do you want a list? Mama and the kids, Gody Ivo and everybody at Guava Flat for starters. At last things are beginning to come together. I think you could do a lot better than being Head of House at Myatts Field. Just think of the number of coloured families who are sending their boys to your school! You could be very important among the coloured communities in South London. That's why people want to teach. They help to shape lives. That has to be your guiding star, because neither teaching nor writing guarantees great financial security. You're beginning to make progress in both. Of course, you don't have projects in Jamaica, England and USA, like our friend Lincoln. You're both doing what you want to do. I'm not embarrassed to say I'm proud of you both. Let me see," she said, "you've been supporting your family since you were seventeen. You helped support them by going to Kingston to find work. At nineteen you borrowed money from Gody Ivo to pay your passage to England. God knows how you managed to repay her, but you did it, and still managed to put your sister through secondary school. Of course what you earned from your literary endeavours helped. At the same time you managed to improve your own education and finish a degree course. You're almost at the end of a higher degree course. I don't think that's bad going, especially since what you've achieved academically is through part-time study. What's wrong with that?"

"You're prejudiced. Be warned, a sister who advertises such a record of achievement before any future sister-in-law would be accused of vetting."

"But I'm proud of you! I'd hate to see you hitched to a woman who's all tits and pouting lips. Have you considered how lucky we've been? Oh, yes, lucky. I've had a brief flirtation as a lead singer in one of the thousands of bands which were not going anywhere. Why did I do it anyway? OK, I earned a couple of hundred pounds extra over a six-month period. That meant Mama and the kids were better off than they've ever been. I've just come back from Guava Flat and there's not one of those girls who were in my class at government school with me who wouldn't change places with me." She paused and gently dug her elbow into his side. "Of course, coming to live with you for them would be different in the circumstances, but you know what I mean. All the females under thirty in Bun Dutty Gap, Guava Flat and environs were in love with you, did you know that?"

"Ah, if only I didn't have a little sister dogging my footsteps..."

Her punch was harder than she intended and he spilt some of his tea. "You are going to clean that up," she said. "I was only looking after number one at that time and that was little me. If I'd allowed any of those girls to get their hooks into you, you'd now probably be working still as a salesman in a Kingston store to support their babies and I'd be selling women's underwear in a neighbouring store. Look at us now! If I'm successful in my civil service exams and pass my board next year I could be an Executive Officer. That will put me on the road to a worthwhile career. When I was home I talked to the girls who were at school with me, and I wanted to cry. Remember Janey? Well, she's expecting her fourth child at twenty-two. Mind you, she was expecting her second when I left five years ago. Bibbie Marshall has had so many scandals about her with other women's men and is expecting her second child, Two older women who are themselves very prolific child bearers cursing poor Bibbie because they suspect their boyfriends got her pregnant. It seems neither Bibbie nor anyone else can be sure whose child she is carrying. Now I ask you... Poor Bibbie looks twice her age. That could have been me if I didn't have a brother like you. What's astonishing is that you're just three years and a bit older than me. You are my hero."

"Don't heap praises on me. Have you ever thought that if you weren't the person you are, no amount of lecturing from me could have made it work? Lots of brothers and sisters don't get on. Perhaps those days when we *three*, you, Mama and me were planted in an alien environment helped to shape our relationships and our destinies. We were so dependent on each other. Look what happened when our mother broke ranks and took up with Bullah Cameron."

"He's almost out of our lives. Do you know he hasn't written home in the last six months? Although Mama won't admit it, lest the children's feeling get hurt, she's relieved to be rid of him. I don't think he'll ever go back. Soon his children will forget him. It's embarrassing, but it's us, Brother Lonso and Sister Rosie, that they idolise. By the way they call me Blossom now. We're their sole support. Every morsel they eat, every stitch they wear comes from the money we send Mama. Another couple of years and Anita will graduate from Shortwoods Teacher Training College and I know she'll contribute to the support of her siblings. Do you realise that from the impoverished family we once were Mama and the kids are fairly well off? You've carried the heavy responsibility of this family since you were seventeen. We are grateful. We love you for being so selfless."

"You're doing your bit too. As you said a while ago, the extra you earned when you were with the band prevented the old house from falling apart."

"And now Hurricane Gladys wreaked its havoc and tore off most of the roof. I wished it were you who had gone out and not me. A decision had to be made whether to repair the damage or build a new house. I didn't think we could afford a new house, so I decided on repairing it. The builders are people Lincoln uses. We mustn't make him pay the bill. That's the sort of thing he would do."

"I can deal with Lincoln. You did well on your own. I support your decision to repair and modernise the old house. I love that old place although I have not slept in it for about thirteen years."

"Well, it's yours."

"Ours," he said quickly.

"Yours," she insisted. "The price of Gody Ivo agreeing to the marriage of Mama and Bullah was that the deeds were transferred to your name. As a mere girl I was expected to depend on a husband to provide me with a roof over my head. How old was I then? Five or six?"

"Ah," he drew her closer. "As Ruth said to Naomi, 'Wherever I am so shall you be also...'"

"Stop it! Anyway, Ruth said no such thing. What she said was, 'Wherever you go, I will go; and where you lodge, I will lodge."

"That's it. You said it so well..."

"That wasn't fair," she interrupted by driving her elbow into his ribs. "Well, Ruth might have been prepared to live with her mother-in-law and her sister-in law Oprah. I haven't got the slightest intention of sharing a house with my sister-in law and or mother-in-law. Of course, there'll always be a place in my house for my bachelor brother. Especially if he turned out to be as half as good an uncle as he is a brother," she rested her head on his shoulder.

"Do I need to have words with Dr Ransford Carr?"

"Eh?"

"The bloke you will be wining and dining you this evening..."

She pushed him away. " Ransford is a lovely guy. I guess every inch like you, and don't you think I don't know things..."

"What things?"

"Oh Winnie, Puncie and Lurline for starters," she said. "I heard a lot of things which Nello and Prophet inadvertently let slip..."

"They did! Did they?"

"I guess they said it to see how I would react, Nino. On the other hand, if I was having affairs after affairs I would expect you to feel that I have let you down. Instead all I have to worry about are the innuendoes about our relationship and since I am on as good relationship with those two sisters as any other I think they at least know I am not an interfering, frustrated old maid."

"Then came along Ransford?"

"He has always been there," She said with a guilty look.

"Why do I get the feeling that you are going to surprise me?

"I did tell you that we sat in neighbouring seats from Palisadoes Airport to New York when I was coming up five years ago. Well we have been in correspondence. He sent my letters to Enid and Lincoln's address."

"But why?"

"Don't be angry. I never expected it to last and that being the case I would not have to explain anything."

"Do you think I would be jealous?"

"No! but it has saved a few years of teasing."

"I am disappointed..."

"So have I. Do you know that I left Enid's house on occasions and went to collect some clothes from Geneva Road only to find that you were not there? I had my suspicions that you might have been warned."

"This is heavy stuff, Flowers..."

"Heavier than using a friends address for a letter or two..."

"We must not quarrel. Let's talk about those girls who were lodging at Gody Ivo."

"What do you want to know?"

"The three 'states' as we used to call them. Anyway, the girls used to be away in Kingston Monday to Friday at school. Weekends were for homework. That's if they didn't stay on in town for concerts, cinemas and visiting their posh friends. Don't forget we were the poor relations. Remember how one of Gody Ivo's iron rules was that all bedroom doors must be kept open?"

"And I haven't forgotten that she was an insomniac who walked about the house all hours of the night. Well, she had three nieces in her house: Georgia, Virginia and Atlanta. Would you credit it? Georgia is a brother's daughter and Atlanta and Virginia are her sister's daughters. Did they want to show Uncle Sam how patriotic they were by choosing these place names?"

"None of them was born in the States. I think the brother went to the States as a musician. He must have toured the Black clubs in the South and he struck up a relation with a young woman, who eventually came out to Jamaica. After Georgia was born her parents went to the States, this time to New York. That was a novel way for a black woman to get out of the South, don't you think? At that time everybody was talking about the Scottsboro Boys."

"Not another history lesson, brother dearest? I know the rest of the story. Miss Elsie after having two daughters worked for an American evangelist and his wife who spent some time in Jamaica. When their tour of duty was finished they took Miss Elsie with them back to the States where she has been ever since. Of course Miss Ivo took in her sister's children, and now both Virginia and Atlanta are married and living in the States but are safely above the Mason Dixon line. I bet you didn't know that Virginia's other name was Elizabeth, as in the virgin queen?"

"No, I didn't know that, but I can tell you that the original Atlanta was equally zealous of her virginity. She killed two *centaurs* to emphasise that point..."

"Nino! I hate it when you insist on trumping other people's argument. We started out amazed that a family should want to name their children after places in the United States. Weird!"

"Of course, there were boys at our school called Kent, Stafford, Ashford, Walton and Bromley."

"OK, OK! There you go again! Anyway I don't think Gody Ivo's insomnia was to prevent the girls having assignation with any young man from Guava Flat and environs. They were all going to the High School of Our Lady, The Virgin Mother."

"So it could have been you then!"

"Me?"

"Yes. Aunt Ivo moved you in with Georgia when you and Perro crashed in on me that first night."

"I would hardly have attracted any admirers then. Have you forgotten what I looked like? A stick insect, I was. I didn't have any breasts until I was fourteen going on fifteen, remember?"

"I didn't pay much attention."

"Like hell you didn't. No man, whether he happens to be father, brother, cousin, parson or priest, ever looks at a woman without noticing her breasts."

"Flowers! Take that back."

"*Nino,* I've made a life-long study of you. Men are either 'headlights' or 'gas tank' lovers or both and you are definitely a headlights man!"

"I think you've said that before. Now, my sister, be careful. Walls have ears," he warned. "There are some who view us with suspicion because neither of us is married and as far as they know haven't got a love life. We discussed that earlier."

"Tell me something new. The other day Enid asked if I'd never met a guy I fancied. Another time she asked me if you have a girlfriend. This is the age of romance and folks won't believe that a clever and good-looking guy like you isn't fighting off the girls. Bibbi shook her head in disbelief that we're sharing a flat and neither of us is romantically involved with anyone. 'A pretty, well educated girl like you can't find a man in all England? What happenin', you brother still think him is you father? Girl, me would have to strike out on me own. Tell him is time him leggo.' I could see her little country-bush mind working overtime..."

"Believe me, when you encounter love there's no Canute that will be able to rebuke that tidal force. Not me or anyone else will be able to stand in its way without being crushed and swept out of the way..."

"Wow! I must tell Ransford about this for when I fall in love I want to be fully in charge of my faculties. I don't want to walk senselessly into that night..."

"Don't think of it as night, I think of it as a revelation both of your own vulnerability and your power and strength. A loving relationship doesn't mean you've been conquered and colonised."

"Hi, hi! Stop! This is really too heavy. Anyway, you're not in a relationship that I know of. How comes you're such an authority? Is it the writer or the lover speaking? I need to see Sheila."

"I just don't want to be accused of being over-protective brother. That's what people like Bibbi think."

"So what? There are those who think I'm preventing you from having a girlfriend," she said with a dismissive wave. "I willingly put up my hands to scaring the likes of Irone Simmonds from getting her hooks into you... By the way it's nearly three years since Christine proposed..."

"Stop it, right there..."

"She's nearly eighteen. Have you seen how those two have grown? And Christine is a bookworm. I like her."

"Yes, I've noticed how all parts of them have grown, but they are still my friends' daughters who are preparing for their A-levels." He turned the conversation to their own family. "You were saying how Dona is sixteen, we ought to consider sending for her before the new immigration law pulls up the drawbridge? Hector you said wants to join the police..."

"I get the message."

"Which is?"

"Neither you nor I are ready to let a significant person into our lives at this juncture. It's the two *panya pickney* still sticking together, eh? We cover much ground and there's still some way to go. We can't start thinking of ourselves until all the family are grown-up and independent. Nino, we are bringing up a family. I guess, Juanita, Dona and little Ana will all have started their own families before we start our own... separately, of course." They laughed.

"So it's settled then? We start the ball rolling by getting Donita up to London when she is old enough to enrol as a student nurse. Who knows, she may be the one who becomes a nurse. Of course Hector might change his mind about joining the police force and choose to come to London. In the meanwhile, Anita will be closer to starting her teaching career, that will only leave Ana Teresa. We can cope. The family will almost be taken care of, so there'll be time to concentrate on ourselves... That is separately."

"What will be your next big project? To find me a husband?"

"Me? I thought Ransford is on the inside tract to becoming your significant other. You'll be meeting him later. Make sure you leave with plenty of time, particularly since you're going to find Collingham Gardens on your own. It can be tricky."

"I will find my way. If true love can only be attained by an irrevocable wrench from those whom one has loved all one's life then one will take Hamlet's advice and get oneself to a nunnery," she said in queenly tones. He followed her into the kitchen and she took the mugs from his hand.

"I hate dirty dishes," she pulled a horrible face.

"All right, I'll wash and you dry up," he said. "I had meant to wash up last night's dishes but I was so tired. You weren't meant to see them all plied up in this unsightly mess."

"I don't know, though, I could inspect them and see if there's any lipstick on the cups. Not that I object to you bringing your women around when I'm not here, but I just want to know which side of the cup to drink from."

"Whoops," he said, "I'd forgotten about that," he said with mock surprise. "Anyway you came back yesterday; any lipstick detected today would be yours, so there." She splashed suds in his face and dried her wet hand by pushing it down the back of his neck.

"Mummy," she said imitating the child in the famous television advertisement, "you have soft hands."

"I'll get you for this," he promised, staggering blindly, wiping his eyes with his shirt tail.

When he was able to see again Blossom was sitting serenely on the sofa reading the *Manchester Guardian* "Who blinded you, my dear Cyclops?"

"Nobody," he roared. "Nobody blinded me," he threw himself on the space next to her. She shielded her upper half with the broadsheet, ready for any retaliation. "I did have a few visitors while you were away. Let's see: Catherine and Christine, Irone and John. By the way, John isn't leaving the US army. He's extended his stay and will be going to Vietnam with another group of US advisers..."

"Vietnam? What for, to stop Ike's dominoes from falling over?"

"JFK said they are only advisers, but then some of us are old enough to remember that the soldiers in Korea were going to be home by Christmas

1950. They were not. Irone wanted to show off John Jnr and the fact that she is heavily pregnant again. She was sorry that you were not around."

"I wonder why?"

"Perhaps she is perverse enough to want to show off that again she has done something that you have not done or can not do."

"Ah Ah, flipping Ah Ah! With my mother's fertility record her daughters are set fair to populate this planet and as to her sons, let's pass over them in silence. Who else came calling?"

"Darlene..."

"Who?"

"Darlene with her baby and her mother."

"What did they want?"

"To invite us to the baby's christening reception. Also they want me to be godfather."

"You agree to be Darlene's baby godfather? I suppose it's better than being *the* father," she said coldly.

"Flowers! It started with me being cranky, now it's you who have the blues. Darlene's baby is innocent," he said putting his arm around her. She rallied first with a smile and then a quick kiss on the cheek. "We were suppose to be popping round to see the Morgans later, but you have a date. They'll want to know what Jamaica looks like after Hurricane Gladys. You know that Prophet's father died after the hurricane and was buried before they could send a telegram. He's very low in spirits, wondering if he'll get out there before his old mother dies. It sometimes happens, you know. One dies and the partner follows quickly."

"I have a bottle of rum to cheer up Prophet. What have you got to cheer me up?"

"If you were not meeting Ransford I could take you to the Taj Mahal in Vining Street. They do the best curry in South London."

"Now you're talking," she paused. "No I have not got a telephone number for Ransford so we can't invite him."

"That sounds very very final."

"What with Ransford on one hand and you on the other I need to sound half intelligent. You must go to the Morgans and tell them that I have found a bloke who is taking me out. Myrtle Morgan knows the Reverend Carr and his family. Please tell her it ain't time for her to start soaking fruits in white rum for a wedding cake yet. Tell her that because I know how her mind works."

"You are right at that," he said, moving once again to the window. It was still raining. "The white rum might not be a good idea. It will serve to torture poor Prophet."

"Eh?" she pulled her legs on to the sofa, rearranging her skirt to cover from knees to ankles.

"Don't you know that Prophet is diabetic?"

"Of course, but since when would the state of his health stop Isaiah Morgan from knocking back a drop of white rum? In any case Gody Myrtle will confiscate it for use in her Christmas cake. Mentioning diabetes, the latest in Jamaica is the old people have two types of illnesses. You said, 'Good morning, Sabee, how you do?' and back comes the answer, 'Me ah blow fe life. Me *pressure* is under control but the doctor man say that the *sugar* no so good.' It is always the *pressure* and the *sugar*. Now you are telling me that Prophet's *sugar* is not so good."

"I guess I am. Another piece of news is that Betty has settled in Toronto, but her GI has gone back to his old sweetheart."

" I was only away for three weeks. Betty was already in Canada before I left for Jamaica. I am not surprised I never thought that Jordan was right for her. But if it is a black man she wants there are plenty of Jamaicans in Toronto."

"That's wicked," facing her from the window.

"Oh, come on, I don't think Betty's ever looked at a white boy since she first saw Warren."

"He is married to her sister. You know somebody said that quite recently..."

"Who said what?"

"I can't remember," he lied. He did not want to bring Sheila Cox into the conversation. "Whoever said it intimated that Betty's ideal man has to be black..."

"I wonder what the story is. It is plain that she is potty about Warren. If ever I get married and any of my sisters were to be so attached to my husband as Betty is to Warren, I'd be worried."

"I overheard someone say that they wouldn't be interested in me because we are too close."

"Who said that? Or have you just made this up?"

"Not this time. I overheard Miss Nicey saying how nice it was to see a brother and sister so close and Miss Vie said if she was young she wouldn't be interested in me because I am *too* close to you."

"Are you worried?"

"I'm not. People have been teasing us since we were knee-high to grasshoppers. As I've said before, when I find my ideal woman and when you find your ideal man we'll know, and we'll be happy for each other..."

"These persons will have to be custom made," she said.

"Until then we remain best of mates, brother and sister," he said.

"Brother and sister," she said as if it was a toast.

"Another piece of news is that Asquith has gone Dutch."

"I thought you said he never buys a round of drinks."

"He still doesn't. He has met this Dutch-speaking woman from Suriname. He's going to marry her and they hope to practise law in Paramaribo. He's learning Dutch. Her family is political. They also have lots of money."

"Now that you're a committee member of STUWARD there's a chance you could re-kindle your relationship with Anh Hosang. She's well connected, in wealth and politics. She must be near graduating now."

"If I didn't know better I'd think you were in a hurry to get rid of me. Have you forgotten that we've pledged our lives to the family until they are old enough to manage on their own? Especially now that our step-father has started a second brood in Brixton..."

"I heard he had a couple of children with other women before he started working for Mama," she said as if it did not matter.

"I heard the same story."

"You did," she said, leaping from the sofa and stamping over to where he was leaning against the window. "Why didn't you tell me? I'm a woman fully grown."

He reached out and pulled her towards him. "I didn't think it was true at first because I thought if it was Mama would send him packing; when she didn't I dismissed it from my mind and really didn't think of it again. I hardly ever think of Bullah Cameron these days. I can't see him going back to Guava Flat. I'm hoping that shortly Mama will divorce him on grounds of desertion."

"You forget that Mama was brought up a Catholic. Come to think of it, we were both baptised in the faith. I've been thinking of reaffirming my faith."

"You? Ransford is the second son of a Baptist parson."

"Yes, but it is Burchell who is at the Seminary in Boston. I might even consider taking the veil if I am not married by the time I am thirty. Does that surprise you?"

"Something happened to you in Jamaica. Do you want to talk about it?"

"Nothing happened. Those three weeks were carefully documented. Between Mama and Enid they could tell you everything I did and everyone I saw." She held him by his shirt collar and shook him. "I'm not a frustrated spinster yet. I have no intention of hiding myself away in a nunnery. You haven't got rid of me yet, brother."

"Thank God for that. Just in case, I'll start putting together that composite picture of the brother-in-law I could live with."

"Don't you dare! I want to surprise you," she said pulling away. "Are you going to Lilford Road as you are? Please don't wear that ridiculous jacket with the patched sleeves. That is the British cinema's interpretation of what a poor teacher ought to wear."

"Yes, miss. By the way should I put the night latch on?"

Her lips moved but the sound was inaudible as she swore at him so she emphasised it's meaning with an appropriately rude gesture.

36

The industrial town of Maudslay in the Midlands was not alone in playing its part during the dark days of the Battle of Britain. However, to the grateful nation in its greatest hour of need it seemed that at that vital moment the citizenry of this old mill town was capable of an act of unified defiance, which encouraged the country in its duty.

Maudslay had been involved in providing arms for the British army and navy since the Crimean War and for the Royal Air Force too since the First World War. But like a true hero it had gone that extra mile. Although regularly bombed, its production of guns, engines for the war effort, remained high. Defiant to the last, the town proudly displayed what could be considered the war spirit on its *Monument to the Glorious Dead* in the town centre, known as Arsenal Square. There is a sculpture of the Bishop of Maudslay the morning after the most serious aerial bombing of 1940. He is standing on the rubble of his bomb-damaged cathedral blessing the workers of the massive Arsenal plant as they turned out to resume their jobs making guns, bombs and engines of all sorts to repel the might of Hitler's war machine. So inspirational was the collective action that the national newspapers campaigned for the town to be given the George Cross for valour. The town was held in such high esteem that its long-serving Member of Parliament from 1920 refused to be ennobled as Baron Maudslay. He deemed it a sobriquet of the ruggedness of the spirit of the George Cross town's people themselves and not something to be appropriated by any one man, even one who had worked his way through the unions before being elected to represent the town at Westminster.

From the earliest days of the war men and women ammunitions workers were recruited from the empire to its factories, and the post-war sculptor did not forget that. It was not unusual that black workers settled in the town and that their families joined them later in the post-war years. Its record of racial tolerance was second to none in the United Kingdom until the by-election of 1962. In fact this by-election was generally considered to be a foregone conclusion, the Labour Party was expected to win by at least 15,000 votes. Were it a general election the expectation would have been nearer 25,000. The 1962 prospective candidate was a man of impeccable working-class pedigree, the very first of his family to have gone to university, after an apprenticeship in Maudslay famous engineering factories and later to be mentioned in despatches from the front during his war service. He was a safe bet to win. The intervention of Birkbeck Samms as a nationally known journalists and television personality was not expected to upset the results. Then two weeks before the election there was an outbreak of fly-posters all over the town. The most audacious act of the perpetrators was to cover the outside of the wide windows of the Maudslay Labour Party headquarters with a banner that changed the mood of the election by announcing:

If you want a Nigger For a Neighbour, Vote Labour

It was obvious that opponents were trying to sabotage the Labour Party's campaign. That was the beginning of what was known as a media feeding-frenzy. Once again the wounds on the body politic were ripped opened. Within days every journalist who had a by-line had filed a copy from Maudslay. Documentaries with scenes of Maudslay in the hungry thirties and the valiant war years; there were interviews with former Munitions Workers both black and white; from the war years. There were interviews with the *Newcomers* to Maudslay since the post-war years; there were discussion groups in public houses, in clubs in families' front rooms; among the employed and the unemployed. There was something in these articles and documentaries for everyone. One elderly lady in aprons outside her front door recalled: "I boarded three *darkies* who worked at the Arsenal during the war. Bill, me husband was a foreman in them days and he swore there were no more willing workers anywhere. Good lads they were. Two went back to Jamaica after the war and one married one of our girls, a white girl, I meant ta say, and moved to Birmingham. I won't have a bad word said about them."

"I don't want them living next to me," said one young woman. "Their cooking smells disgusting... they crowd into rooms like wasp on a rotten apple."

"It's a scientific fact," said a well dressed young man, "proven to all men of intelligence, that the white man is over a thousand years in advance to the black man on the evolutionary scale."

"Send them back to their jungle... bleeding jungle bunnies," said a pear-shaped middle-aged man.

The week before the polls the tabloids came into their own. The Labour candidate's son who was the Student Leader at Maudslay Polytechnic was photographed dancing with a Staff Nurse from the nearby hospital. Her family came from Jamaica; her brother was a law student at the Poly. It did not improve the student leader's father's chances of winning the election when he was reported having declared nonchalantly, "Beaulah was the most attractive female on the dance floor, and by far the best dancer. She kept telling me to unlock my knees and to bogey on down. Whatever that meant."

When Beaulah was interviewed about a possible romance she replied that she had danced "with quite a few guys at that social and did not have the slightest inclination of having a relationship with any of them".

The candidate himself was asked what he thought of the prospect of having a black daughter-in-law. His reply was honest but did not win him many votes.

"I'm not the head of a dynasty. There are no restrictions on my part on my children's partners. We are halfway through the twentieth century. Which parent would dare chose a partner for his or her offspring?"

One paper ran the headline: "My Children can marry blacks if that is their choice!"

"But isn't that the same paper that carried the story on the Sharpeville massacre?" asked Christine. "I remember their correspondent in South Africa interviewed an African cook or housekeeper about life in the land of apartheid and the poor woman saying that life was fine but the bad black people were causing all the trouble. Doesn't anyone remember?" she pleaded.

"Christine, you ought to see Lonso's scrapbook. It's the only thing he keeps tidy," said Blossom. "Look how they twisted things around. Anyone reading that article can't fail to get the question. *What would you do if your blue-eyed blonde daughter comes home with a buck nigger and say she was going to marry him?*"

"Blossom!" Myrtle Morgan was upset.

"Sorry, Gody Myrtle, but *it has already been said,*" Blossom reminded her. "The question is not aimed at what you would do if Christine comes home with a white boyfriend."

"Me! Why me?" asked Christine.

"He would have to pass the rice and peas and cowfoot test," said Ziah Morgan.

"Listen to yourselves," said Catherine. "Versions of this conversation are taking place in many English homes and if you were to eavesdrop, you'd call it racial prejudice. Are you all certain you are not just as prejudiced?"

"Have you noticed that when those reporters are interviewing people about their daughters marrying someone of another race they never ask black parents?" said Enid. "I was testing Lincoln the other day, daring him to name a black show-business female of any international fame who wasn't married to a white man and he couldn't think of one."

"What about Ruby Dee?" asked Blossom. "She's married to Ossie Davis and they are a formidable couple among the Civil Rights activists.

"It did cross my mind if Blossom had not given up her show-business career she might have married a real go-head manager? Of course he would have to be white..." Ziah was interrupted by a withering look from his wife and an interjection from his daughter.

"Would you, Blossom?" asked Christine. "Have married a white man, your manager?"

"In the first place I never thought that I had a show-business career. As to the rest, I must plead the Fifth Amendment. I will say this, though, when I get married you all can rest assured that I will love the man uxoriously..."

"What is that when it's alive?" asked Ziah Morgan, pulling himself halfway out of his chair.

"Dad!" Christine looked at her father with a mixture of surprise and disappointment. "It means excessive devotion to someone."

"Thank you, my daughter. They didn't teach us those things at Chelsea Ridge Elementary School. I'm proud that the money I am spending on you is not being wasted."

II

The days leading up to the by-election saw the opinion-formers once again out on the streets, microphones pointing in the faces of passers-by, pencil scribbling on writing pads: "Would you be happy if your daughter was to marry a black man? The Labour candidate said he would not object."

In all this war of words the opposing candidate Birbeck Samms remained aloof. In a TV interview he insisted that the offensive leaflets and banners did not originate from his campaign Headquarters. The sentiments expressed were not his, but were obviously those of people who were opposed to having blacks living near them. He himself was against mass immigration, but feel that the colonials now living in Britain ought to have the opportunity to be properly housed and should find jobs for which they are qualified. If they were willing to emulate the British in all things, then they should be allowed to live in dignity. It was the British way!

Despite the fact that Labour showed signs of closing the gap in the public opinion polls during the days leading up to the by-election, Birbeck Samms won Maudslay parliamentary seat after three re-counts.

The Home Secretary spoke for the government, but probably not for the country as a whole when it placed great hope in the hurriedly resuscitated Commission for Migrants. The new chairman was an old colonial Governor who had been greatly admired in his day. The Commission had an advisory board made up of people appointed from organisations, which considered the task of supporting migrants' welfare to include their settling and integration into the 'host community'.

Since 1961, Alonso had been a committee member of STUWARD, which had now re-modelled itself on Student Non-violent Coordinating Committee (SNCC) of the American Civil Rights. His friend Lincoln had resigned after a year on the Commission's Advisory Group pleading the pressure of his growing business. Alonso had by now attracted some notice as a writer following the publication of his novel 'Hold Tight' and was considered the ideal person to replace Lincoln.

The meeting at Maudslay's Civic Hall was well attended. Conspicuous by his absence was the newly elected MP for Maudslay, Mr Birkbeck Samms. Although there was a small group of bad-tempered protesters outside the

Civil Suite it was heavily protected by a cordon of police officers. Meanwhile inside the crowded auditorium some said Samms had been invited but dared not attend. Others said he was not invited but might attend anyway since it was a public meeting. As the evening waned it was clear that he was not coming. Simultaneously the protesters disheartened by a cold nagging rain and the absence of their Member of Parliament, Samms' supporters disappeared in the gathering gloom of the night. The absence of Maudslay's parliamentary representative might have contributed to the good nature of the party, from the buffet and on into the two hours allocated to the speeches.

The Junior Minister whose portfolio was Commonwealth Immigration was also the Member of Parliament for the neighbouring constituency of Congreve. He had at a very short notice agreed to chair the meeting as the Chairman of the Advisory Commission on Migrants had taken ill suddenly and had been admitted to a London Hospital. However, because of a long-standing engagement the Junior Minister had to leave immediately after introducing the team of advisers. He emphasised their duties. He regretted not being able to stay for the rest of the meeting. However, he assured the audience that he had already had an advanced copy of Alonso's paper. He promised the audience a speech of great historical and human struggle, which would incite much debate, and would doubtless be delivered without rancour. He then left for his appointment in his constituency.

The meeting then had as its chairman Hopeton Zebulon Morgan, younger brother of Isaiah Morgan. After Zebulon had been demobilised from the RAF he returned to Jamaica but in 1947. He returned to Britain on the *S.S. Almanzora*, a year before the more famous *S.S. Windrush* voyage on which his elder brother was a passenger. He took up residence in Maudslay because he had been attached to the Office of Procurement during his days in the RAF and had dealt with manufacturing firms in Maudslay. He thought that at least one Manager of the Manufacturing Industries of that town would remember him. However, in 1947 he was no longer an officer in His Majesty's Armed Forces. He was now a black immigrant considered to be over here for a life on the newly installed Welfare State, or to be after the white man's job, his house and his woman. Morgan accepted work as a night watchman. However, with almost dictatorial direction from his feisty English wife he persevered with his legal studies and was now a successful lawyer.

Hopeton Zebulon Morgan, who preferred to be called Zebulon, had met Alonso on numerous occasions. Today he introduced Alonso as one of the shining examples of the hard-working and industrious immigrants who asked for no favours apart from fair play, which is the English way. He inevitably made reference to *Nine in a Basement,* that *classic* of West Indian migrants' historiography and *Hold Tight* his recently published novel.

Alonso spoke for about fifteen minutes and estimated that he had left about the same amount of time for questions and answers. It had been a long day and Alonso was relieved that the end was in sight. He still had not decided whether to try to catch the last train back to London or to take up the option of going to the flat that Lincoln had made available to him, which he had used on many occasions as an associate of Creole Enterprises.

"The title of your talk is in a foreign language," a man asked quite unimpressed. "What's its meaning? And why do you people always show off like that?"

"*Civis Britannicus Sum?* The title is not mine so I was not showing off," Alonso began testily. "That was the actual title of the Act on British Citizenship in 1948. It merely means 'I am a British subject.' I think one can gather from that how Britain felt towards its Dominion and Colonies for the loyalty shown during the war. Look into your old passports signed by the governor from whichever colony you came from and see how the implied threat was supposed to protect you: *Request and require in the name of His Majesty all those whom it may concern to allow the bearer to pass freely without let or hindrance..."*

"Them days were the days of *gunboat diplomacy*," a voice from the back interrupted. "If you know your history you will recall what the Battle of Jenkins' Ears was about..."

"Well, I don't know no history," said a woman in a high-pitched voice. "Just tell me this, if you can: will we have to fight like our brothers and sisters in the US of A? It seems to me the only country that won't make you pass freely without *let and hindrance* is right here in Britain..." the rest of her statement was lost in loud applause. It gave Alonso time to collect his thoughts.

"Segregation is supported by the governments and constitutions of the Southern States. We gave heard statements from State Senators and Governors saying that segregation will remain in *Dixie* and unless the Federal Government intervened segregation will continue to thrive below the *Mason-Dixon Line.* You know that it's illegal to drink from water fountains not designated to your race *etcetera, etcetera.* Over here there are no such laws. It is difficult... I would say that it is almost impossible to find a British person who will admit that he is a racist! *They* tell you that *they* don't hate blacks. *They* are protecting *their* jobs *their* women and *their* way of life. If the government would stop immigration and send us all back home, then *they* would support increased taxation to develop whichever or all the colonies that we are from. Of course this is a lie. The truth is *they* whoever *they* are would fit in comfortably in any of the segregationist groups in Alabama or the Carolinas. However, the British racist with a high profile is impossible to find... even this constituency's high profile Member of Parliament declares he is not one of them."

"If you believe that, then perhaps you too believe that the moon is made of green cheese," said a small white woman, whose glasses were resting on her large bosom suspended from a ribbon around her neck.

After the laughter and many voices competing were heard, a female voice said, "But they do exist."

"Of course, they exist," Alonso raised his voice. He was not going to be considered and apologist for British racism. "In 1948 President Truman's Executive Order desegregated the US Armed Forces. Black GIs will tell you that segregation is still rife in the military, yet there are senior black officers in all branches of the US Armed Forces. On the other hand the British will tell you that there's been no need to desegregate the British Armed Forces because colour bar does not exist. Yet where are the senior officers in the RAF? ... in the Navy?... in the Army? Where are the black police officers on our streets?"

"Ah hope you people... Ah mean those of you who supposed to be advising the Minister is asking them these same questions and getting good answers," said a man in a wide-rimmed hat, "because my children ain't going to be patient. You hear what Ah sayin'?"

"People are asking for integration, others asking for equality; are they the same thing?" asked a young woman.

"No," Alonso said.

"I was expecting an explanation," the young woman said.

"OK," said Alonso. "You could say that what we have here in Britain is integration, and that is intolerable. Equality as I see it gives to every man, woman and child the personal dignity and freedom to express himself and achieve his potential without let or hindrance. In Britain today no black person has that freedom and the dignity that goes with it. What they see is your blackness and by that you are judged. No white person standing at a bus stop has to prove that he is literate, honest, moral or that he belongs to this country. In fact there's more chance that a white person at a bus stop isn't a citizen of this country. The black person because of his Dominion and Colonial status has a right to be here. On the other hand if that person is a European his whiteness absolves him from any burden of proof. In the meantime my blackness to the average white person is evidence of all things that are negative. However, I don't think we'll be hiring coaches and driving down to London in our own version of Freedom Rides. I know you have black crews working on most Midland buses. Of course, there is Bristol and a few small towns on the south coast, which are holding out against employing black drivers and conductors. On the south coast, the operators say that they haven't had any inquiries from black applicants. We are investigating and a report will be published."

"My experience of a few days ago might support your statement. The other day I was in Woolworth's store," said the young man sitting next to the last questioner. "I was fairly well dressed. My trouser was well creased, blazer well brushed and matching the rest of what I was wearing. My shirt and tie were elegant (though I say so myself)," his hands moved in expression of his sartorial elegance. "Across from me there was a tramp. His face and most likely the rest of his body hadn't been washed for weeks; his clothes probably hadn't been changed for months. In short he stank! Yet this man shouted across the crowded store, his eyes fixed on me, 'You dirty, stinking black bastard...'"

The audience interrupted with a collective groan. "What?"

"You better believe it," the young man carried on. "People looked at me, then they looked at him. I didn't detect an ironic smile nor did anybody say, 'look who's talking!' The tramp's *right* to say what he did was because of his whiteness, although his whiteness was buried under weeks of dirt. Dirty as he was the customers acknowledged his whiteness as above my blackness, yet he was not responsible for his being white anymore than I was for being born black."

The audience threatened to drift into snippets of personal experiences when Zebulon Morgan wound up the session with a call for tolerance. He reminded the audience that the Biblical origin of *his* name was Leah's hope that her husband would honour and tolerate her after the birth of their sixth son Zebulon.

"Not a chance!" someone shouted back. "You forgetting that Jacob had another wife who was Leah's own sister Rachel and two other mistresses as bonuses. Why should he worry about honour and tolerance when every night he was the master of four bedrooms?"

"Young Mr Bogle," said the chairman contritely, having recognised a younger member of a well known evangelical family, "I am not going to argue the Bible with you, even though you are the *black sheep*, oh, I should not have said that... um, unbeliever of the family."

"Amen," sang a chorus of voices.

"Amen, it is," said the chairman. He had spotted the caretaker of the hall with an enormous bunch of keys hanging from his waist. He directed Zebulon's eyes to the clock and then drew his right hand across his throat which meant that the guillotine was poised for the fatal slide.

The crowd was in fact beginning to melt away. Like almost all meetings largely made up of delegates from numerous organisations there was a hard core that stayed to debate various issues only some of which were raised. Others wanted to test the mettle of the people who had the job of advising the Minister for Immigration. Naturally Alonso as the keynote speaker for that night had a large group around him, but the others had their followers too. In fact, delegates wandered off catching snippets of conversations which they thought would grow into something interesting which they could take back to their respective organisations.

The Duty Officer at the Civic Suite made several attempts at clearing the hall, when these failed he locked the doors. He would open the door to allow people to go out and then as politely and quickly as he could he would lock the doors again. At last it dawned on the twenty or so who still lingered on that it was time to go. As they spilled out onto the elaborate stone steps of the Civic Suite Alonso's following had dwindled to the two young questioners from earlier in the discussion. Tonight was not the first time they had met as they too were both well-known activists in what was fast becoming the race relations industry, according to some conservative commentators. In fact Alonso was well acquainted with Everton and Beaulah Burke. They were brother and sister as Beaulah was usually quick to explain as if she was anxious that people should not misunderstand their relationship. Once someone had referred to Everton as her boyfriend.

"Having him as my brother is one of those crosses our parents have laid on me, as to him being a husband, that must be some other unfortunate girl's burden to bear."

A situation Alonso understood well enough for when he told Blossom, she immediately expressed a wish to compare notes with Beaulah.

Everton was a part-time student at Maudslay Polytechnic studying law. He was also a committee member of the Maudslay Anglo-Caribbean Association. Beaulah was a Nursing Sister at the Victoria Hospital in nearby Congreve. They offered to give Alonso a lift to the station, but the last train to London had already left. Instead they offered to drop him off at the Arsenal from there he could easily get a bus to Bowes the part of town where Lincoln had a flat. Alonso had spent many nights there after meetings involving Lincoln's Creole Enterprises and its Midlands' interests. When Lincoln knew that Alonso was to be in Maudslay he insisted that Alonso took a key. Lincoln was well aware of how long and drawn-out these meetings could be when those who would not speak to a crowded meeting would wish to have a quiet authoritative word in smaller groups.

The Arsenal is one of the famous landmarks in Maudslay. This imposing structure incorporated the marble War Memorial to the glorious dead, with a frieze depicting weapons of war, for which the town's factories were internationally renown for neigh on one hundred and fifty years. The frieze did not only illustrate the changes in the uniforms of the various branches of the military since the early nineteenth century, but also the weapons which Maudslay had produced in all the wars since then.

Everton drove past the Arsenal Square with its wide pavements, which accommodated the streets traders, which was another attraction the town offered to its neighbouring towns seven days per week. He was about to stop the car then decided to carry on for another quarter of a mile to the bus stop before the Congreve roundabout by so doing he had overtaken some buses in an effort to make sure that Alonso would not have to wait long for a bus going to Bowes. On their way from the Civic Suite Beaulah Burke had said quite openly that the principal reason why she wanted to meet Alonso this time was that she wanted to talk to a real life writer. She was a poet and had never met anyone who is a published author.

Alonso was flattered. He liked Beaulah, especially her lisp as she spoke. He considered her very attractive but not pretty. He wondered if she was telepathic and could read his thoughts. He was sure Everton did. He thought of his sister Blossom and told himself quietly that brothers always do.

To Beaulah he hastened to explain that although *Nine in a Basement* had gone from a talk to a radio to a dramatised version, then translated to television and eventually to a play at an experimental theatre, he has had very little success with any of his other literary endeavours. Of course his recently published novel he is hoping will attract the attention of both critics and readers. If it doesn't do well he will resign himself to the thought that *Nine in a Basement* was what they call a flash in the pan. Beaulah had ordered her copy and at some time would like him to autograph her copy. Now she would like him to read some of her poetry. She had been writing since she was a schoolgirl in Jamaica and had even sent some of her poems to Una Marson at the Pioneer Press. She had returned them with a letter saying that although she did not think they were good enough for publication she would urge her to continue writing. That was the only contact she had had with a writer until she met Alonso.

"When her poems were returned she cried for a month. Boy, was she vexed!" Everton interjected.

"It was a rejection!" she explained. "Just as when you went into a big, big sulk when that Coolie-royal girl sent back your love letter", she hit back at her brother.

"What have you brought that up for?"

"Tell me," Alonso intervened, "did she burn the envelope at the four corners?"

"She spared him that final indignity. He was just a little boy in short trousers and she was about seventeen or eighteen. She was my friend," the sister laughed.

"If I promise not to interfere in your literary discussion, will you get out of my early love-life?"

"'Even the sacred moments when we played
All innocent of passion, uncorrupt...'"

Beaulah recited as she continued to tease her brother, at the same time showing off to Alonso, who joined her for the next line so it became a duet.

"Claude McKay!" said Alonso, "from his *Flame Heart*. I read it at least once every fortnight. I can't explain to you the feeling that swept over me when I first opened *A Treasury of Jamaican Poetry* and discovered Claude McKay..."

"I had a copy. Guess what? My lovesick brother gave it to another one of his girlfriends, who took it with her to the States. What hurts me is the book is now out of print!"

"I didn't give it to her, she borrowed it. I expected her to return it," Everton said in his defence.

"I wished you wouldn't impress your women with my things," she said feistily. "Have you got a brother, Alonso? Oh, but it wouldn't work that way, and sisters are different."

"How would you like to walk all the way to Congreve?" her brother asked.

"I don't think the last bus has gone yet," she said challengingly. Then, turning to face Alonso in the back seat, she handed him a folder. "I have a present for you. Here are some of my poems. My address is in there somewhere. Tell me about them sometime, no rush. For God's sake don't you dare say, 'they are good. I like them'."

"I see you've trodden the writer's road. That's the standard reply from friends when they read your stuff!"

"Eh, eh," her brother grinned into the rear view mirror, "I know it's not the first time you meet this young man, still I think you rushing things a bit by giving him your address and phone number. You sure you haven't included a love letter?" he swung the car into the curb near the bus stop sending a sheet of water like a wave onto the pavement.

"All my poems are love letters," she said, as she dropped the folder onto Alonso's lap before he could open the car door.

III

Alonso watched and waved as the car swung away from the kerb and crossed into the right-hand lane. In anticipation of the Congreve turn-off she had the window down with her head poking out, whatever she said was lost in the roar of the traffic. She drew in her head like a turtle. A huge articulated lorry, also anticipating the Congreve turn-off, settled in the lane beside Everton's car shielding the car from view. As Alonso looked to his right towards the Arsenal he could see the bus for Bowes. It would terminate at the *Miller and Wheatsheaf* public house. Its indicator was already flashing as an acknowledgement to people at the stop. Two young men hanging off the platform hit the ground running as they jumped off the bus.

As soon as he got on to the bus he pushed Beaulah's folder into his briefcase. He felt the need to get her out of his mind. He was completely mesmerised by her lisp. He thought of the young man who had bandied words with Zebulon Morgan in the Civic Suite. He was a member of the well-known Jamaican family of evangelists, the Bogles. He recalled that Vicky had married a Bogle, brother of the more famous Easton Bogle of the Church of God of Prophecy. Irone, who was Vicky's daughter, was incensed.

"I'm twenty-four years of age and my first child is older than my mother's third child. Most mothers of a twenty-four-year-old woman are blissfully looking forward to grandmother status. Oh, shit! I can't even ask my brother and sister to babysit my child. Two are blooming toddlers and my sister is three months younger than my son Manley. Now you all know why John and I are going the settle in Philadelphia permanently. How bloody embarrassing that my mother is only thirty-eight years old. Fourteen years my senior. That woman could be producing babies for another ten years! She has got a new lease of life. People might think her children are mine. I don't want my children calling kids who will be at school with them uncles and aunties."

On the other hand Eunice and Violet (better known as Miss Nicey and Miss Vie) revelled in their roles of grandmother and grand-aunt. They sold their house in Lothian Road, Camberwell, removed themselves to Maudslay and accepted their responsibilities with Naomi-like pleasure.

He could not help thinking of Winnie, whom he had not seen since the late autumn of 1957. She too had married into the Bogle church, one of the fastest growing businesses in the Midlands. Through the sisters Vie and Nicey he had learned that Winnie had since had two children, a girl then a boy. The thought of dropping in to see both families was brief and compelling like a flash of lightning. On second thoughts he did not think it would be during this visit to Maudslay. He was aware of the strict moral code demanded by the Bible Church of God of Prophecy. Winnie's husband was now an elder and was deeply religious. Alonso wondered how much of an embarrassment it would be if he were to present himself at Winnie's home. How much did Mr Brown know about Winnie and Alonso in the autumn of 1957? And how would he introduce himself to her husband? As an old friend who happened to have slept with her in the same bed for nearly two months? What would that mean to a husband who wore religiosity as a badge of honour? He mused that all religious men are jealous, because to them there is no greater sin than sex. If she had not already told her husband about the relationship they had during late autumn of 1957, it could now be to poor Winnie as if a wound was being re-opened, with all the pain and distress that would entail. Any pain on his part would be the realisation that she was hurt again and that this time it was he who would wield the scalpel on the scab of a partially healed wound. He had never considered himself to be in love with Winnie, but it had been an episode in his life to be treasured. After all, she had loomed large in the fantasies of his youth. He was not sure that he was ready to see her again. He did not think she was ready to see him either. What he had heard of her husband was that he had forgiven her the sins of her past life. Any remembrance of things past deserved the fate of Lot's wife. He earnestly wished Winnie a happy life.

"*Miller and Wheatsheaf*! All change here," the conductor shouted. "All change, all change!"

He stood up, allowing an old lady from further down the bus to pass. She paused and picked up a London newspaper someone had left behind on the seat, a copy of the *Sketch*. She folded it carefully and stuffed it into her bag, then shuffled on in front of an impatient young woman. The young passenger was dressed for the weather, her mackintosh belt knotted around her waist. Alonso fell in behind her. They were the only passengers on the lower saloon. Many young men had rushed down the stairs of the upper saloon, jumped off and sprinted for the bus behind which was going further to Grange Parade. The old lady joined two other elderly ladies who might have just got off another bus because they started to sing:

I take the low road
and yer take the high road
and I'll be in Scotland
before yer...

The young woman in the mackintosh crossed the busy road and turned left. Alonso walked towards the traffic lights, crossed and fell in about five yards behind the young woman. A further ten yards and she turned into Granary Lane, which was the way Alonso was heading to reach the flat in Mill Road. It was about eleven-thirty and there were still lights on in some front rooms. Unusually there were no other pedestrians; the nagging drizzle might have tipped the balance in favour of staying in. He made no effort to catch up with the young woman or to overtake her though she glanced over her shoulder and then quickened her steps. He liked walking along Granary Road in the summer for it was well known for its well-kept front gardens, but this typical autumn night was cold for him. He was thinking of reaching the flat and switching on the electric heater. Next he would ring Blossom to tell her that he was staying overnight and would get a mid-morning train the next day. He was feeling hungry and hoped that Lincoln had maintained a good stock in the larder. After he had eaten he would look at Beaulah's poems. He had already made up his mind that if they had any merit he would hand them over to Stella Clarke his agent suggesting that she gave a professional assessment. The young woman quickened her steps into a jog. Alonso did not try to close the gap. About ten yards ahead she was wrestling with the latch on a gate and by the time Alonso reached the gate she had given up fumbling in her handbag and was hammering on the front door. Alonso continued towards Mill Road at the same pace since entering Granary Road. He was feeling hungry. Those daintily cut sandwiches and cups of tea were eaten some four hours since. Once again his expectation grew that Lincoln had remembered to replenish the larder, then he detected a noise. At first it sounded like heavy drops of rain on a zinc roof, then as it got closer it was unmistakably the sound of hard shoe leather on the pavement moving towards him at a very fast pace.

"Hi, you! Nigger bastard!"

He turned and the first blow caught him on the right side of his mouth, then another and other. He raised his briefcase to shield his face, then a knee collided with his stomach. He wanted to scream but could not. He felt a lump in his throat and vomit exploded from his mouth like a bursting dam. He staggered to the edge and tried to hold on but everything was slipping from his grasp. His whole body was one jellied mass of pain. He was slipping again, falling, and falling, spinning, down, down... falling... spinning... down... the dark unfathomable hole... down and forever spinning...

IV

He woke up in a darkened room. He could not see anything. Slowly and painfully he arrived at the truth. He could not open his swollen eyes lids; hence the darkness. There was a smell of disinfectant. His first conscious thoughts were of how stiff he was and how the pain zigzagged across his body like flashes of lightning. His neck was restricted. He could hear voices, but his swollen eyelids prevented him from seeing anything. His throat was on fire and his swollen lips meant he could not speak.

"You're awake? Good! You're in the Congreve Victoria Hospital," the voice was familiar, but he could not recall where he had heard that sensuous lisp before. "It seems you're currently our 'top of the pops', a celebrity, no less, Mr Alonso Campbell, you really are! We've had a veritable fan club outside, including the Minister for Migrant Affairs (though he didn't stay long). You have many friends, colleagues who've telephoned. Some visited, but were turned away. Others are hanging around in the waiting room and still others are on their way from London. Oh, the police are here too. Well, let's see how you really are... hmm... your left side is bruised but nothing's broken. Let's see... can you squeeze my hand?" She touched his hand and held it. "That's not much of a squeeze! Is that the best you can do? We'll have one squeeze for 'yes' and two for 'no'. It's always harder to say no, you already know that, don't you? OK? Can you see me? That's a 'no'. Do you know my voice? Not to worry! It is a very recent one... and so quickly forgotten. Your eyelids are badly bruised; when the swelling goes down and you can open them you'll be able to see. Now then, do you know what happened to you? That's a 'yes'. Were you in a fight? That's a 'no' so you were attacked? That's a 'Yes'. The police will want to hear that. Oh, by the way, they have priority over the rest of your fan club, especially since close relatives and friends are still in transit from London. I'll tell your friends outside that you're in no shape to hold court but that you're on the mend. OK? All except for the police, they'll want to talk to you but you won't be able to answer unless you squeeze one of them and there's not a WPC among them! I bet you're disappointed."

Later that day his left eyelid opened just a crack and objects became blurred shapes. The voice that had spoken to him earlier belonged to the ward sister Beaulah Burke. He had become used to her touch. She told him about an hour ago that his sister Rosita and some friends were leaving the motorway and would soon be in Maudslay. Was ever an hour so long? How many minutes now?

She read him some of the many telegrams of good wishes he had been sent. Among the telegrams was one from Birbeck Samms, the Member of Parliament for Maudslay South-east. Then there was the presence of Everton Burke who, swingeing with rage to blinding fury, had taken up residence in the visitors' lounge since early morning, hoping to see Alonso.

"You were attacked last night," he recognised Everton's voice. "Them mash you up bad, bad, man. You're going to be all right, though. I feel guilty, man. You could have come with me to drop off Beaulah at the nurses' home in Congreve, then I could have dropped you off next at Bowes. Beaulah blames me. She's professional in her duties, but she is blaming me all the same. The good news is the police have arrested the two blokes responsible. They claimed they were protecting their sister; well, one of them is her boyfriend, actually. She had come home hammering on the door in a distressed sort of way. They said she told them a coloured man had followed her all the way from the Arsenal. She claimed she didn't expect them to go Nigger-hunting. Those were her words. Well, they did. Apparently many good citizens live on Granary Road and heard the commotion and rushed out to see what was happening. The police and ambulance were called; the two couldn't deny their involvement. I promised my sergeant major of a sister I'd be out of here in less than five minutes and she's just come back in. You know I'm secretary of the Maudslay and Congreve United Communities; we're having our Annual General Meeting in a fortnight's time. Promise that you'll come. You could say a few words; perhaps answer a question or two. Nothing too..."

"Out!" boomed the authoritative voice of Sister Beaulah Burke. "I want you out of here. His sister and his London friends will be here in less than ten minutes. I am sure he'd rather talk to them than with you. Out, I say!"

"Damned spot!" her brother quipped, as he headed for the door.

V

Three weeks after Alonso was attacked, the *Maudslay Mercury* carried the following story:

Maudslay, the George Cross town, has had a rough autumn. These past three months have seen events unfolding that have shaken this old Midland town to its foundations. It has appropriated the headlines of the national dailies. Events in this town have pushed the activities of USA Federal troops in Ole Miss from the front pages. In nigh on a thousand years of history not even the medieval civil war nor the nineteenth-

century Luddites have brought the town such notoriety.

Its beginning was firmly rooted in medieval times. Historians have said they first found mention of it in the twelfth century, when as a Saxon village it was the probable site of a battle during the anarchy presided over by King Stephen and the Empress Matilda. The battle seemed to have gone in favour of the Empress, for the village emerged as Matilda Crossing on the River Slay. In the late Middle Ages it somehow acquired its present name of Maudslay. Its mills ground the grains from the farms of the fertile Slay Valley. When the age of water power arrived it was well situated to be in the vanguard of the Industrial Age. Maudslay has a claim as good as any Midland town to be called the cradle of the Industrial Revolution, if not acknowledged as its true birthplace, then at least it was an important corner of its nursery.

Although the motor vehicles produced in the factories of Maudslay have been on our roads since the first decade of the century, it has been just twenty years since the nation took this Black Country town to its heart. Much has being written about the picture of the Michael, Bishop of Maudslay, together with other religious leaders, in a spontaneous show of ecumenical unity and national pride standing on the bombed wreckage of the Anglican cathedral. The churchmen, arms outstretched, blessed the munitions workers, who stood heads bowed before going to their factories to produce what the armed forces needed to repel the Nazi enemy. That act of solidarity portrayed the national bulldog spirit and inspired this country to steel its back to the task ahead. A grateful nation urged the government to grant the town and its citizens the George Cross for gallantry. All that is immortalised on the frieze at the base of that imposing structure inscribed to the glorious dead in the centre of town.

However, these last three months have shown the nation and the world that there is another side of this town, which many would like to forget. While the heroism of twenty years ago with spontaneous actions supported by the majority, the racism for which this town now stands accused is the work of a tiny minority. Some would say that racists from other Midland towns some say that from as far south as London invaded Maudslay during the last week of the election. Newspapers had in fact published pictures of coaches roaring up the Motorway with political agitators heading for Maudslay. There was certainly a banner draped from a coach: English Freedom Riders. This was obviously an attempt to mock the Civil Rights Freedom Riders of America. The contrast was that they had the freedom of the highways. They were never stopped. Their passengers were never beaten, arrested, neither were their vehicles burnt out and protesters killed. However, the fear of being swamped by black immigrants from the colonies with all the attending horrors real or imagined whipped up an emotional tidal wave which swept a well-known anti-immigration candidate Birbeck Samms, into the Palace of Westminster.

Forgotten in all this was the incontrovertible fact the ammunition workers from the Empire worked in Maudslay during the war and many chose to make their homes in the town. We must not forget that Empire and Commonwealth service men and women were stationed here. So too were Coloured troops from our ally the United States of America. It was inevitable that after the war, which their contributions helped to win, that some would decide to make their homes in the town. They were soon hosts to their friends and relatives who after the war came over to help rebuild war-torn Britain and at the same time make a life for themselves, better than they have experienced in the colonies burdened with high unemployment and uncertain future.

What this town has endured in the weeks leading up to the election of Mr Samms can be seen in various degrees in districts of bigger towns and cities throughout our nation. This tide had hardly receded when the government insisted on launching in Maudslay its new advisory team on Migration. There were those, including this paper, who thought that a wiser course would have been to choose another town, perhaps Birmingham or Liverpool, or Bristol or even London. Some have argued that was the opinion of the former Colonial governor who was appointed to chair this board. We hope had he not taken ill that he would have pressed his point. After all he was chosen for his clarity of vision and his customary vigour of putting over a point. In the colonies he has served in there are politicians of every shade of political thought who would testify to his nerves of steel under fire. Just like our town. It seemed the government was hell bent on meeting racism, wherever it raised its ugly presence head on. But racism cannot be crushed any more than apartheid and segregation can deal a final blow to human dignity and triumph by building a state to last a thousand years on the shoulders of the oppressed. I hasten to agree with those living under those systems in South Africa and the United States of America that they have been forced to stand with shoulders bent and downcast eyes for what seems a thousand years. To them I will not caution patience. Neither do I forgive the thousands of Maudslay South-east voters who were overwhelmed by the emotive slogan: If you want a nigger for a neighbour vote Labour. Nor do I forgive the incumbent Member, who while saying that the slogan did not come from his campaign headquarters was only too quick to point out that it was the desperate cry of people who believe that in a generation they would lose their identity. His statement ensured that those who held that assumption would think that they had found a representative to champion their cause. Indeed the three times he spoke in the House were on immigration. He prophesied decades of racial strife towards the end of this half-century. I daresay it's beginning to dawn on those voters who supported him that it's easier to predict Armageddon than to produce the blueprints for avoiding it. The meeting of the reconstituted Migrants Advisory Board at the Civic Centre was after all not as heavy-handed as some of us had expected. The fifteen members were drawn from as wide a cross-section of the community as is possible. There were representatives from migrant communities, representatives from the host communities, representatives from the trades union movement, from the Employers Association and activists from major political parties. The Minister proudly showed off his team to the audience and asked the representatives to spend no more than three minutes in introducing themselves. Fifteen minutes were reserved for what was called the "keynote speaker", an American term that seemed to be gaining credence over here. This was Mr Alonso Alfredo de Campesino Campbell, a rather athletic young man who could pass easily as a member of the West Indian cricket team or a runner in the mould of Arthur Wint and Herb McKinley. Paradoxically while he is a Jamaican citizen, he was in fact born in Panama in one of the most descriptive names a town could have, Bocas del Toro (the Head of the Bull). His paternal grandfather left Jamaica as a young man to seek his fortune during the building of the Panama Canal in the early years of this century. British Caribbean islanders have had a history of exporting their labour since emancipation of 1838. For three hundred years Europeans imported slave labour from Africa to create the wealth which shaped our continent. Atlantic slavery brought us wealth, which gave us the power to build empires and armies to protect them. We became strong and leaders of the world. West Indians coming to our shores since the end of the Second World War are following a trend ever since 1493 when the Pinto, the only one of Christopher Columbus' three caravels, limped back to Palos. It brought back among its cargo the first natives of those regions ever seen in Europe. Alonso Campbell proved himself an effective speaker, as one would expect from a writer whose ten-minute talk on the BBC Caribbean Service on the lives of migrants in Britain about five years ago had been anthologised, dramatised and televised. His talk was entitled Civis Britannicus Sum. It ranged from Sir John Hawkins, a pioneer of the awful slave trade in the middle of the sixteenth century, to Arthur Davidson of the Cato Street Conspiracy of 1820. From John Archer the black Mayor of the London Borough of Battersea during the First World War to the call to arms in both World Wars and finally, the call to rebuild a shattered Mother Country. There was nothing controversial as such in his speech but it was a history lesson unfamiliar to most of us since we prefer our history masculine, heroic and rather shame-facedly White Anglo Saxon Protestant or as the Americans say WASP. We don't like to hear what we did to the natives, but rather what we did for them. So there was nothing in that speech to warrant an attack on the speaker either verbally or physically. Indeed both incidents were unconnected save for the fact that the speaker was cowardly attacked scarcely ninety minutes after his talk.

The attackers claimed they did so in defence of a female family member whom they had considered to be in danger, in that she was followed by a black man for nearly ten minutes. During this time he had not closed the distance between them, neither did he call to her nor try to attract her attention in any way. She had arrived home safely, but quite agitated from a situation she considered threatening. Her brother and her fiancé acted on impulse. What roused them? Was it because she said the man who followed her was a black man? Three weeks later, and much recovered from his ordeal, Alonso Campbell was again speaking to an audience, this time in neighbouring Congreve. Again I detected nothing controversial in his speech and, above all, an absence of rancour. The essence of it was that the consequence of having an empire was the genesis of a multi-cultured society; it is rare indeed that a society will emerge the poorer for it. We report part of his talk below:

'I grew up in a corner of the world that was part of the British Empire. I was not sure if I ever knew what that really was. In that case I was no better off than any small child who was my contemporary in a small town in Georgia or Alabama. What could that child know of the United States of America? In our small schoolhouse I glazed on the picture of King George VI and Her Majesty the Queen. My American counterpart perhaps looked at F.D. Roosevelt and Mrs Roosevelt. I'm sure he would get the same omnipotent stare that pictures seem to have as they follow you around, taking in your every thought. There was also that feeling that, however small and insignificant you were, you belonged to a greater whole. Mine was a Jamaican childhood and Jamaica was part of the British Empire. Britain was at war, so Jamaica was at war. Our school was one of four others that descended on the little township of Abbey Look Out to see soldiers of the Canadian army give an impromptu drill to the sound of bagpipes. We might not have known it at the time, but there was something more happening to the fabric in the tapestry of the British Empire. It was a network of interlinking blood vessels so if the wound was serious enough we could all bleed to death. That was what we understood the loss of freedom would have meant during those terrible years between 1939 and 1945. At the end of the War I was in my tenth year.

'You asked me to speak to you tonight because of what happened to me just over a fortnight ago. What happened was not unique and it was not an occasional occurrence either. I may in passing mentioned two... Melbourne Welch and Kelso Cochrane cases which made the nation sat up and took notice, even if it were just for a while. Were I to ask this audience of about three hundred or so, about racial attacks, I bet many of you would confess to knowing someone who has been attacked as I have been attacked... I can see heads nodding... I flatter myself that you are here tonight because you want to know how I am and to show your solidarity. Perhaps you are moved by the same spirit that has embued our American cousins in their fight for justice, for equality with dignity, heads unbowed.

'So I speak of my right to be here, a right bound up in over 300 years of British history. I am not a cost upon the British Exchequer. As a 19-year-old I came to Britain where I have washed dishes in the famous teashops at corners of busy London streets. I have packed boxes and loaded lorries in factories and in the evenings I have dragged my tired body

to evening school to satisfy my hunger for learning. I had exhausted what the colonial government had provided for my education between the ages of seven and fourteen. (May I remind you that Britain has had a stake in the West Indies since the 1620s and the first university in the part of that region where Britain ruled, is still only about fourteen years old. The Spaniards established their first university in 1530, a little matter of over 430 years. Thirty-eight years after Columbus landed on Watling Island.) Contrary to what the anti-immigration lobby would have you think, no one provided for us immigrants. If we found a place to sleep it was hardly out of the kindness of the landlord's heart or because he was cajoled by government agencies to do so. It made sound economic sense to him. So with my friend Lincoln Grant shared a basement room with seven other men. It cost each of us thirty shillings per week. A room for thirteen pounds ten shillings per week. At that time some of my fellow white workers were paying twelve shillings a week for their council flat. Incredible as it might sound we began attending evening classes. Not only did it promise us some sort of future, which we dared not speculate on, but it kept us out of that black hole of Drury Lane for a few hours. If there was not a class that night we went to the cinema. Neither Lincoln nor I would recommend studying under a forty-watt bulb with nine men plus sometimes a couple of prostitutes in the same room with you. We used to joke to ourselves that the situation brought a new perspective to the meaning to Free Trade which neither Adam Smith nor William Pitt, The Younger ever envisaged. 'So here I am before you, aged 26, a colonial in London. That is a well-trodden path, by millions of colonials since the eighteenth century. I came not to set the world right, but because of the inner hunger which had gnawed at my soul since I was a boy. It was not all romance it was also a way of surviving. I echoed what thousands have said, that is, I wanted to make something on myself. I have worked not just to keep body and soul together, but to maintain my mother, my sister and other younger siblings. I have studied hard and now hold a BA gained at Lewisham Polytechnic. I am a part-time teacher in the Modern Languages department of a comprehensive school for boys. I am also a published author. My achievement is not unique. I was never the only colonial at any of my classes I ever attended. Indeed our English Language lecturer went out of her way to compliment 'her colonial students' for our hard work. Patronising? Yes, but at times that was more acceptable than having the door slammed in your face. God forbid that she should pretend we were not sitting in her class to become the invisible students. But then, who would know? There are many whose experiences and achievements make mine pale into insignificance. I was never a drain on the system. I found work within three days of coming to London and have been paying taxes ever since. Let us turn to the reason for my being attacked three weeks ago.

'What is the story? My attackers said they were protecting a sister and a girlfriend from a fate worse than death. The attempt at chivalry is as old as time itself. A young woman was walking ahead of me. I did not call to her, there was no wolf-whistle, nor effort made to catch up with her. When she turned into her gate I continued at much the same pace. I must confess that I could not have identified her until her pictures appeared in the press. My recollection was that she was about five feet five or six inches tall. I can't recall whether she wore high heels or not. I reckon that apart from my not being white, she did not really see me. This is an important point, for when most white people say they saw a Coloured man it may mean that they looked at you. They haven't seen you well enough to be to assured of the honesty, integrity, the humour, the suffering or the beauty of the person they say they have seen. What they saw is a face that was not white. If in those fleeting moments she had seen a white face, then she would have taken for granted that all the above-mentioned attributes were intact. Was it the face, seen darkly, that caused her to drop her keys, then be too nervous to look for them? Would she have told her brother and boyfriend: 'A white man has been following me since the Miller and Wheatsheaf'? Would that have been enough to arouse their anger so that they raced out of the house and took to the streets to go man-hunting, even though it meant abandoning the television programme they were watching? If they did, I think they would have engaged him in some sort of dialogue first. I think it was the mention of colour that incensed those two. It's strange what colour means to these men. In a way it's the most precious possession they have. Yet they did not earn it. They did not set out to achieve it any more than I had set out to achieve my blackness. Once they become aware that whiteness had been bestowed on them they are the equals and heir to greatness. For with the realisation of their colour, a thing that could not be achieved through hard labour or

serious scholarship, they have arrived at a position far in excess of any achievement by a man like me. This philosophy that being white equals being superior was the rationale that emboldened those nine young men in Notting Hill in 1958. Across the Atlantic it was this supposed mantle of superiority that closeted Carolyn Bryant in so much anger that four days later, still in shock, she told her husband Roy, that a "Nigger boy", Emmett Till had said "bye, baby" to her. We know the result. This fourteen-year-old was beaten to a pulp shot and tied to a cotton gin and thrown into a river. To the racist the arrogance of colour is worth more than nationality. Witness those who migrate to countries like South Africa, Australia and I daresay the USA, they pass almost unnoticed into the ruling elite because of their whiteness. They are exalted above non-whites.

'So on that night coloured meant villainy and their whiteness promoted them to be judge and executioner. Whether or not they had heard of Mr Justice Salmon and his 1958 judgment, nothing seemed capable of making them think rationally. May I remind you of the learned Judge's conclusion: 'I am determined that you and anyone anywhere who may be tempted to follow your example shall clearly understand that crimes such as this will not be tolerated in this country, but will inevitably meet in these courts with the stern punishment which they so justly deserve.'

The speaker sat down to prolonged applause, a complex mixture of anger at what had happened to Alonso, relief that he was well enough to deliver a vigorous speech and approval of the court's attitude to racial violence, albeit four years ago.

The chairman announced that he would take a few questions. The first question came from the *Maudslay Mercury* colleague. "If you were to meet Carol Blackburn, what would you say to her?"

"What made you think I fancied you?" the voice of a young coloured woman pre-empted Campbell.

The audience laughed uproariously and the Chairman had a difficult time restoring order.

"I asked the question", the *Mercury* reporter said, brushing aside the speaker's interjection and the audience's response, "because you quoted Mr Justice Salmon. I'm sure you're familiar with Fenner Brockway's plea that those youths were as much the victims of the hysteria that swept over Notting Hill in the late summer of 1958. There was something approaching hysteria in Maudslay during the recent by-election..."

"I'm sure Alonso has thought of it; notwithstanding, I caution him not to answer, bearing in mind there may be a court case," the Chairman intervened and quickly moved to another questioner.

The speaker looked at the Chairman. "I'd like to answer the reporter's question. I too have no pleasure in seeing people sent to jail. Indeed the recent election has chalked up another shameful episode in our country's history. My answer to the first part of your question would be close to Miss Burke's (identifying the young coloured woman who had spoken earlier), responding to another question. What were her reasons for thinking I was stalking her? I touched on this already, but it's worth repeating; had she seen a white face rather than a black man coming off the bus and crossing the road behind her would she have behaved as she did?"

"To sum up," said the chairman, "before I move a vote of thanks how do you see the future?"

"Drawing, I suppose from the speeches of Fidel Castro, Che Guevara, the African National Congress and, not least, the anthem of the American Civil Rights movement, I shall be brief and to the point, using the first language I learnt: '*Venceremos! We shall overcome!*'"

37

It was Monday and Alonso would not have finished his duties at Myatt Fields Comprehensive School until midday. The arrangement he had with Catherine Morgan was that she would visit her parents' before mid-day.

He had trusted Catherine and had succeeded in convincing himself that she trusted him.

Catherine Morgan now aged nearly twenty had not seen her parents for over a year and a half and the last communication had been a postcard depicting the energetic nightlife of the Turkish port of Bodrum and that was nearly a year ago. Both her parents were frantic and expected Alonso to explain their daughter's irrational behaviour. To Myrtle the behaviour of her daughter was part of the complex phenomenon which has been known to metamorphose those aged between years thirteen and twenty otherwise known as the *teenage years*, which had not been a part of her upbringing and most certainly not the experience of her first two daughters who were still living in Jamaica, one a teacher and the other a civil servant. They had succeeded in making the transition from a firm foundation which led upwardly from childhood to happy adulthood. Alonso hoped he too had succeeded in convincing everybody that he had safely crossed the border into his third decade before American psychologists had worked out that the last seven years of the second decade of human existence was fraught with problems and these were as confusing to those who added teens to their years as they were perplexing to their parents or guardians.

Nevertheless he half expected to hear anxiously raised voices as he bounded up the steps to the Morgan's Lilford Road residence. It was in the nature of things that the returning prodigal should be received with a joyous party. Neighbours and relatives would have gathered around to welcome the one that was lost and was now found. In the original story there were new clothes instead of the tattered rags of a traveller returning from a far off country; rings signalling a new beginning would be placed on her fingers and of course there would be a great feast!

As he climbed to the top of the steps he had a full view of the Morgan's well laid out front room, dominated by new and expensive sitting room furniture and the low tables and their croquet decorations all of which the Morgans were planning to take with them when they eventually made their move back to Jamaica. He could see Isaiah Morgan stretched to his full length in his chair. He had now retired and the deteriorating health had placed him, as his wife complained to anyone who would listen now that he was nowadays just under her feet. Ziah Morgan must have fallen asleep for the newspaper he had been reading had dropped onto his face and his hands fell limply against the arms of the chair.

There was no revelry!

Alonso pressed the bell lightly and could see Isaiah's sudden movements as if he was electrified. Then he heard light steps racing down the stairs; undoubtedly that would have been Christine performing her version of tripping it lightly as she raced her mother to the front door.

"I'll get it Mama!"

The Morgans had recently reorganised their house to suit their upwardly mobile working class life; which meant that their former tenants had given up their single rooms so the Morgans could expand. So Christine who was approaching her twentieth year now had her own room and in the spirit of parental fairness her twin was granted a room in absentia; a place to store what Catherine had accumulated in nearly eighteen or so years of her life spent under her parents roof.

"You know Mama very well," Christine reminded Alonso. "She is scrupulous to the extent that she changes the bed clothes weekly which had never been slept in and she is careful in displaying the toys and tattered teddy bears on which Catherine used to lavish much tenderness in her younger years. Oh I must not joke about it. It is a loss and if the truth be told I miss her terribly."

Christine pulled the door wider to let the visitor in. Alonso had guessed she had probably seen him from her first floor room window.

"How did you know that Mama is cooking your favourite nosh, stew peas and rice? Boy have you got food foot." She pulled him into the hall and collided backwards onto her mother.

"Lonso," said Myrtle bracing herself for the impact, "long time no see! It seems you deserting us. If Ah did not know any better Ah would say that since Catherine gone and left we, there is no further attraction for you at our humble abode..."

"Mama!" the daughter's exclamation was almost a scream. "Mother, I think I will have to have a quiet word with you. Especially since there are some people who have said that I drove Catherine away so that I can have Lonso all to my self... Eh Dad?"

"Pickney, you far too brazen!" her father remonstrated from his chair.

They had reached the door of the front room and Isaiah Morgan was once again sitting upright and pretending to be reading the sports pages.

"If what you say is true Honey, then it not working 'cause him not buzzing around," said Myrtle pushing her daughter into the room and towing Alonso after her. She directed him to a chair and was about to sit down when

Christine still a little uneasy when outnumbered by her elders moved towards the door.

"Tea and cake, anyone?"

"Your Dad must not have any more of that cake".

"Mama he is not driving. No one is going to breathalyse him! Although you did over do it with the overproof rum."

"I did'n know that it is the Metropolitan Police you want to join. Here me thinking that you want to be a doctor... Your father is a diabetic. Give him half a chance and he would knock back a glass of white rum."

"Go on and torture me. Me old man died last year well into his nineties and never been to the doctors and here I be not quite out of me sixties and taking pills after pills. Anyway what bring you to these parts... an' what you do to Blossom? Ah notice that since she find herself that new boy friend Ransford she seem to forget about us?"

"Don't blame me. My role as big brother is over. Their engagement present is a tour of Andalucía, Spain. You cannot do that on a part time teacher's salary..."

"Not even with a part time director's salary from Creole Enterprises and royalties from your books? If it is a travelling companion you are after, I will come with you?" said Christine with one foot in the room and the other in the corridor.

"Not as long as you are under our roof," the mother said. "And another thing how come a Baptist parson's son is travelling alone with his fiancée before they are married?"

"Mama this is the nineteen sixties, the twentieth century is coming up for retirement and both Ransford and Blossom are adults. Anyway they might have visited Gretna Green first."

"Well you would know as you and Blossom are as thick as thieves. Now where is that tea?" Myrtle shoved her daughter into the corridor and pointed her in the direction of the kitchen. "Get!"

A well-laden quietness fell over the trio. They had passed small and introductory talks. There was a message in the air and it was oppressive.

"Well?" asked Alonso who was still convinced that Catherine had carried out her part of the bargain by coming to see her family.

"Well what?" grunted Isaiah.

"Catherine! I saw her this morning and she promised that she would be coming to see you. I promised to drop by later just to catch up on the news."

"Catherine!" both parents exclaimed in unison.

"You mean that you know where she is?" It was difficult to decide if it was a solo from either parent or a duet from mother and father.

"You mean that you know where she is?" Once again it was difficult to decide if it was a solo from either parent of the duo from mother and father.

"Well not exactly, I saw her in Maudslay yesterday and convinced her to come to see you..."

"She's been with you since yesterday?" asked Isaiah with rising anger, disappointment and distrust.

"We drove down last night. It was late when we got to London. I did try to persuade her to let me take her to you, but she said that she was not ready; she was tired. She promised that she would be okay by the morning after a good night's sleep... Look I could not force her to come and even if I had locked the door after we got into the flat and then phoned you can you imagine the raucous that she could have kicked up? She had been through quite a lot and I had to reason with her and the best I could get was that after a good night's rest and bath and all the rest of it she would come and see you. She promised and there was no reason not to believe her..."

"That is my twin alright! She is the consummate actress. She can be convincing," said Christine who had picked up on the conversation from the corridor.

"What Ah want to know," said Isaiah "is why she get in touch with you? We are her parents; her family and as far as I know we never did her any harm. Wherever I turn you are always there, I want to know what is goin' on!" demanded the father, the husband and the head of the family, Isaiah Morgan.

"I want to know everything Lonso, and don't spare my feeling for I know that something is wrong and I can feel it in my bones," said Myrtle Morgan as she moved to tower over the sitting Alonso. "I don't care what others may say but I trust you. I know you a long time. You better begin at the beginning," she encouraged.

Alonso regained his composure and took a sip of his tea.

"As you know I am usually in Maudslay on Creole Enterprise business from Thursday to Saturday and sometimes even until Sunday. I guess the telephone number is well known as both Lincoln and I stay at that address when we are on business. Catherine rang at midday on Saturday. She wanted to see me, but would not come to the flat. She sounded so desperate I volunteered to meet her at the station. She said she did not want to meet anyone else. That did not worry me since it could equally have been Lincoln who was in the flat and picked up the telephone, but of course it was me. She did not speak long, despite the desperate tone in her voice. Believe me she did not show herself for about three hours. I was worried and was thinking of returning to the flat when she suddenly appeared. I can only guess that she was making sure that I was alone.

"You mean she did not want to see us... her family?"

"I did not say that," said Alonso defensively, "and neither did I get that from my conversations with her..."

"So why did'n she just come home. We no rich but we could pay her fare," Isaiah shouted. "What is bothering me is why you always seem to be there! Catherine know that this is her home. She know the address... she have the telephone number... and as sick as I am I would drag myself to where ever she is... but no it got to be you. What is going on between you two?"

"Dad!" Christine's interjection was brushed aside.

"Alonso start again, I want the whole story from start to finish, then ah will make up me mind," said Myrtle Morgan who continued to tower over Alonso.

"Oh Gody Myrtle she looked so haggard and bedraggled you would not have recognised her..."

"Me own child!"

"Well you know what I mean. It seemed that she had been living in a squat..."

"Catherine living in a squat?" Myrtle folded her arms around her middle and began to groan until her knees buckled and she swayed against the arm of Alonso's chair. "But that is when those no-good troublemakers take over people's property and barricade themselves to prevent the police from clearing them out. How did she get herself in this sort of a trouble?"

Alonso looked from father to mother and sister. He was nervous and it showed. Eventually he lifted his head and blurted out, "She had broken up with her boyfriend..."

"Her what?" asked Isaiah.

"Catherine was living with a man?"

Christine sat with her hands hugging her knees on which she had dropped her head.

"How come you know all of this?" demanded Isaiah.

"She told me," said Alonso. "It seemed that they became friends while they were in the cabaret on that cruise liner and when their tour ended they moved in together..."

"You know about this all along did'n you?"

"How could I? I was never on that cruise ship and she never sent me so much as a postcard. Look, you are putting me in the dock although I am as much in the dark as you were. To tell you the truth, I did not think that she would want to meet you Gody Myrtle in the state that she was in. I think she wanted me to help her to straighten out herself before she got in touch with her parents."

"Who is this boy?" Isaiah shot at Alonso. "Who is this boy?"

Alonso who had over the years imposed himself on his family or was it the boy who had mistreated his daughter? Alonso took it to mean the second option.

"I never met him. It seemed that the relationship was good and she was considering bringing him to meet you, then he tested for a part in a new serial which a television company is making. Suddenly he saw fame and fortune and decided to dump her. She said that he said that she had no part in his future plans. From then on the relationship started to get worse. One night she came back from a 'gig' that is a dance engagement and found all her things piled up outside the flat door. The lock had been changed and she could not get in. With what money she had she called a cab and took her things to a lock-up at the station and then began to stay nights with friends, but that did not last. That was when she went to the squat. Of course there is no honour among thieves and they began to steal her stuff, so she took what was left and went back to the station lock-up," he paused.

"Lonso," Myrtle Morgan, looked at her young friend, and lifted his chin with a crooked finger, "no try to hide shame from me... I want to know."

He glanced from father to mother and twin sister whose face was awash with tears. Like her mother Christine had feared the worst.

"She had not been eating regularly as you can guess and she fainted on the street and the ambulance was called. She was hungry all right but they discovered that she was about three months pregnant..."

All three rose to their feet and descended on Alonso as if he was an improbable trap door through which they could enter to reach the errant daughter and sister.

"Catherine pregnant!"

"But she need me. I... I got go find her."

"Tell me this is one of Catherine's outrageous jokes."

"From what she tells me she must be four months pregnant and she has not been successful in contacting the father..."

"Bastard!"

"How comes you know so much about my daughter?"

"Dad!"

"There is more than meet the eye. You know too much of me family business. This is something we as a family should know about and for you to come here and start telling us 'bout me own daughter..."

"I consider myself a family friend and I know that your daughter is in distress. I could have come and have tea and chat with you and once I realise that Catherine had not come to see you I could have left and you would be no wiser. However, I decided that you must know and how you handle it is up to you. I do not know if she has gone back to Maudslay or if she is in London, so I am going to see if any of my contacts have heard any news of her..."

"What about the agent that got her the job on the cruise ship?" asked Christine.

"That was a one-off booking, I do not know her current agent."

"My daughter is pregnant, she is hungry, homeless and she needs me... I am her mother. Give me your best guess. Where do you think she is in London? Or is Maudslay?"

"That is a hard call. I think they were trying get jobs or 'gigs' in the working men's clubs in the East Midlands. I would'n think that she would get a dancing job in her present condition."

"But what is left of her things? Them at the Creole Enterprise flat or them at the station lock-up?"

"She did bring some things with her to London and the rest is in the flat, but she does not have a key for either flat."

"No matter," said Myrtle. "I will go to Maudslay and stay with Miss Vie and Miss Nicey. The church to which they are members have lots of people and that is plenty eyes and ears. They also do good works like running soup kitchens. Ah going to find me pickney. A pregnant woman must go to the doctor..."

"Mama, Catherine is passed seventeen. Even if you were to stake out every surgery in Maudslay and you found her you cannot force her to come..."

"Sez who?"

"The law, Dad."

"Animals and small children that is all this friggin' country worry about," Isaiah ended his sentence with a loud sucking of air through his clinched teeth. Isaiah eased himself back into his chair. He was still angry with Alonso. "You drove her to London. Why did'n you bring her here to her home?"

"She told me not to..."

"She told you that?"

"Yes sir. She said that she wanted to get in the right frame of mind to meet you. Secondly she told me that if I was to drive her to Lilford I would have to hold her down because she would be screaming her head off. I believed she would. I thought she was being reasonable when she said that she would think it through and that she would come and see you on her own. I left early before she woke up. I wrote her a note and left her some money for her to have breakfast at the café at the corner and to take a cab if she did not feel like walking. It must be three miles from Kennington and there is no direct bus route."

"I am going to Maudslay. Christine you look up British Railway in the phone book and find out how the trains run to Maudslay. After you finish I'll ring Miss Nicey and tell them to expect me and put me up for a couple of days..."

"Mama you can't..."

"Me can't do what?"

"Mum, I am still at College and Dad needs seen to."

"No talk 'bout me as if me isn't here. If it was not the damn blood pressure going up and down Ah would be out through that door looking for me pickney. Ah will be all right. Ah will take my medicine and behave meself. Any way somebody got to be here just in case she change her mind and come home. All I ask of you Lonso is that in case she turn up at your flat in London or when you get to Maudslay just ring and make me speak to her. You suppose to be a man of great intelligence you will find away of getting in touch with me with out raising her suspicion."

"There is one possibility I have not taken into consideration and that is that she could be still at the flat in Kennington. I had a lot to do after I finished teaching this morning so I have not been back to the flat. Can I use your phone."

"You 'ave fi ask that?" said Myrtle.

Alonso froze. The thought flashed across his mind; Catherine would only be in the flat if she was ill. Once she had let herself out of the Consort Court there would be no way back in since she did not have a key.

"What am I doing?" He explained the dilemma. They encouraged him to ring.

"No one is there," he said. "Still I am going perhaps she has left a note."

"Wait for me," said Myrtle Ah just get me bag and me coat. "Christine you stay with your dad," she bustled out of the room, turning at the door to see if Alonso had risen from his chair. "We must move fast. Lawd children are nothing but trouble... whole lot of trouble."

"And all this cause from that damn performance at your school. Catherine and Christine were not even pupils at your school."

"Prophet the school allows the youth club to use the gym for their meetings. It is really nothing to do with the school. It is true that the young woman who developed the sketch was our writer in residence attached to the Drama Department at Myatt Fields but the school cannot be blamed... as a matter of fact some people were excited about the opportunity which presented itself and apart from the obvious parental reservation it was good to see Catherine on national television and later to hear that she was accepted by a respectable agency."

The outline of the sketch was simple. An inexperience teacher was left in charge of a class of disruptive pupils. After ten minutes of chaos she left her class to find a senior teacher who could restore order. By the time she returned with reinforcement the class had created a dance routine based on the Jamaican dance hall craze, *the ska.* Both Catherine and Christine had spent three weeks of their summer holidays in Jamaica and had promoted themselves as experts of this genre. It was about eight minutes of vibrant dance routine with rhythmic movements of shoulders, hips and display of fancy foot works. The reinforcement which included the Head teacher and her deputy were so excited by what they saw the rhythmic vitality of the dancers and the excitement of the audience that the group was allowed to carry on uninterrupted. The youth group was asked to perform their dance to the school's morning assembly where they were filmed and as things sometimes happen an early evening television programme anxious to broadcast items local to its area showed a clip of the dance which led to it being shown in a national programme dedicated to music of the young. Before long everybody was doing the *ska.* It was little wonder that Catherine who was identified as the British Ska champion was offered a short contract by an agent who was recruiting dancers for part of the cabaret on a cruise ship escaping the hurricane season of the Caribbean by rerouting its cruises to the Eastern Mediterranean.

"If only she had not gone that night to that confounded Youth Club. I knew that nothing good would come of it."

"Oh dad you were as proud as a lord when Alonso brought home the tape and everybody gathered around to watch it... and I mean everybody."

"And do not forget that it was a matter of choice, for Christine could have gone too, but it was her choice not to." Myrtle reminded her husband.

"Yeah ah guess so," he conceded. "Ah wonder why she did'n go too, Them say that twins look a like, them think alike and act alike..."

"Dad you know that I do not want to be a professional entertainer and Catherine does," she said testily. "Look Lonso, Mama is ready." She saw her mother and Alonso to the door, watched as they went down the stairs to Alonso's white Ford Consul. As he drove off Christine could see his right hand waving above the roof of the car then he lowered it to signal that he was about to turn right into Ackerman road. She waved and muttered "Bye, bye" then stepping back into the passage, she closed the door and started to cry.

Isaiah heard his daughter's footsteps as she ran upstairs.

"H'mnm h'mn," he muttered to himself. "Now she gwine throw herself 'pon her bed and bawl floods of tears. Is so it go." Isaiah heard the slamming of his daughter's room door. "Mind the hinges," he said, but no one heard him.

He pulled himself out of his chair and went into the kitchen and with practised covertness opened the grocery cupboard at the bottom of which at floor level was his toolbox with an assortment of tools which never interested his wife and which he himself hardly ever used. About ten inches below the hardly ever used products of Stanley the toolmakers, he pulled out a small flat bottle of white rum which Nello had smuggled passed the ever watchful Myrtle. Isaiah's movements had lost much of its vigour, but he managed his errand well including restoring the camouflage. All will be safe when he returned Mass Charley to his hiding place. He moved to the kitchen table, got a glass into which he poured a generous portion of rum, held it up to the window, smacked his lips and said, "Howdy Mass Charley! Come keep mi company." He returned with his ever faithful comrade to the sitting room.

II

When Alonso and a very worried Myrtle Morgan arrived at Consort Court the flat was empty. Myrtle collapsed into a chair and wept copiously.

"It must be my fault... I tried so hard bringing them up in this country where pickney them have so such rights and protection. You think I was too hard on them, Lonso?"

"Course not! It was not your fault Gody Myrtle. You've done your best for them."

"I sometimes listen to them talking about their classmates who got a boyfriends. Was we too strick?"

"Did either of your girls ask permission to bring a young man home?"

"No!" she said. " They sometimes go out in groups to parties and the cinemas, I guess boys must have been in the parties. I just did not think them was ready to get serious..."

"Wait!" he said, "there is a note on the newspaper over there." He went over to the coffee table and picked up the note. "It is from Catherine alright." He read aloud:

Lonso I just couldn't do it. I've hurt them enough. You have been great. You should not have to get involve any further. I was afraid that you had gone to fetch my parents to their prodigal daughter. I got to do this on my own. I am going back to Maudslay. Thanks for the money. I raided your kitchen and that will have to keep me going for a while. I think this money will buy me a one-way ticket back to where all this started. Can't write any more.

Kate

PS. Tell Kitty to look after you and you look after Mom and Dad for me. Love to all of yer. I miss you all loads.

K

Her signing herself as Kate and addressing her twin sister as Kitty touched him deeply. He had not been prepared for that.

For the next hour he watched as Myrtle Morgan wrapped herself in grief with her hands folded around her knees rocking backwards and forwards uttering unintelligent sounds.

Alonso brought her a hot face towel which she took and dabbed her red eyes and her tear stained face.

"Is who she know in Maudslay?" she asked. "No, no she would'n go to her Uncle Zebulon and she certainly would not go to Miss Vie and Miss Nicey... Lawd me God she gwine go kill herself..."

"No! don't think like that Gody Myrtle. I do not think Catherine is the suicidal type. She needs time to think and then she will come back to you."

"So what all this tell Kitty to look after you and you to look after Mum and Dad, all about if it not goodbye she saying?"

"Oh that doesn't matter now. Those are what we in Jamaica would call nicknames. You know that Gody Myrtle."

"You know I think all along that my pickney them was safe with you. I never think no harm would come to them by you. You like a brother to them and they watch how you look after your own sister Blossom..."

"Gody Myrtle!" he called to her, "I know that Prophet doesn't trust me, but I always think you know how I respect you and your family. I have known these two since they were eight years old!"

I know, I know. Come drive me back to Lilford Road. I got to make plans about going to Maudslay."

"Miss Myrtle as you very well know Maudslay is a large industrial town." He knew she was no longer listening.

Myrtle Morgan left for Maudslay the next day and spent more than a week searching for her pregnant daughter. She visited the halls where the Bogles' churches took the commandments to feed the hungry, clothe the naked and to shelter the homeless as the essential pillars of their Christian faith; but there were no sightings, nor rumours of Catherine.

The mother returned home to London, firm in the belief that her daughter was alive; that somehow, somewhere a kindly person had taken Catherine in her care. Myrtle hoped it was a woman for if it was a man... she raised her eyes to heaven and slapped her thighs in agony as she could foresee a future laden with many problems.

Further to the distress of having all but lost a daughter she brought the news that Miss Vie had a stroke and was now stricken unto death.

III

The building, which housed the Congreve Victoria Hospital, had not changed since it was built to honour the monarch's fifty years on the throne. It seemed to emphasise the popular feeling of the time when it was built that to be well, the body of a person or inanimate object must be outwardly robust and strong. Apart from that there is the old maxim which said that if it was not broken, then there is no point in attempting to make it better. Another line of thought was that if the might of Germany could not destroy this building then it ought to be given cathedral like longevity.

Such was the building which Catherine Morgan faced on that evening late in November. It took her sometime before she felt able to walk up to a uniformed woman whose desk did not have a queue.

"What can I do for you?"

"My cousin, Beaulah Burke is a staff nurse on Rosebery Ward. Could I give you this note to pass to her telling her that I am waiting to see her. Please?" She summoned up a smile which could not be easily resisted.

"Alright, but it will be sometime.

"I'm in no hurry," she said pleasantly. "I'll go over there and read a magazine. Thank you ever so much."

She returned to a chair near the exit and reached absent-mindedly for a magazine without taking her eyes off the clerk at the desk. She saw the clerk beckon a nurse but could not hear their conversation. It did not matter as the nurse took the note and glanced over at Catherine to see the young woman who had given the note in the first place. The nurse moved towards Catherine who dropped the magazine and standing up took a step towards the approaching nurse.

"It will be ages before Staff gets a break. Who should I tell her is waiting?"

"Catherine Morgan, a friend of Alonso Campbell," in case she did not get it she repeated "Catherine... Catherine Morgan. We came up to see Alonso Campbell when he was attacked and beaten up in Maudslay a year or so ago. She had talked to me then..."

"Okay! I'll give her your note." She turned and walked away.

Catherine dropped back onto the chair and without looking she picked up the magazine she had dropped a minute ago. The title of the magazine said pointedly, "*Expecting A Baby.*"

Catherine dropped the magazine as if it had burnt her fingers. She had been waiting nearly two hours before Beaulah's brother Everton arrived. She half hid her head in *Gardening World* trying to think whether she ought to go over to him. At that moment a woman leaned across to get a magazine and *Gardening World* slipped from Catherine's hands unto the magazine table. There were mumbled apologises enough for Everton to spin around.

"Miss Twinkle Toes herself!" he said loud enough for several eyes to turn towards where the magazines were. "What brings you to this neck of the woods?"

Catherine rose to meet him and found that they were the centre of attention. Catherine placed a cautious finger on her lips. Everton grinned as if that was enough for an apology and both walked to the further corner of the room as if that provided a place of invisibility.

"I am homeless in Maudslay," she heard herself say.

"Is that all? The only problem is we do not live in Maudslay GC. We live in Congreve. If you are not particular I'm sure we could put you up for the night".

"And whom might my brother the valiant Sir Galahad be rescuing... It is the Princess of *the Ska!*" Beaulah said in one breath, as she threw her arms around Catherine.

When they got to the Burke's house Beaulah told Catherine that had she come to find her the following day she would have been out of luck since she is now on leave and was booked on a flight to Canada at the weekend. She was pleased to see Catherine again and wondered what had brought her to Maudslay. She wanted to know how her dancing career was progressing.

"Give the girl a break," said Everton.

"Brothers! You don't have a brother, do you Catherine?"

"No, the nearest I suppose is Alonso."

"How is that charming sister of his?"

"Blossom? Still pretty and charming?" said Catherine.

"I wonder if Alonso would do a trade? His sister for mine?" asked Everton.

"Have you ever heard anything like this? After me having brought him up by hand as it is said he is getting ready to trade me off for a younger sister."

"You are only three years older than me... but sometimes going on twenty." Everton said.

Beaulah threw a cushion at her brother who temporarily sought refuge in the kitchen.

"Alonso read some of your poems to us; they are good."

"Stop!" said Beaulah holding both hands as if to shield the unsolicited praise, but Catherine could see that she was pleased. She jumped up and having caught her brother stepping back into the sitting room she pushed him towards the steps. "Go and set a bath for me. Catherine and I want to talk... girl talk." She looked at Catherine the anxiousness had crept back in her demeanour. "Let's go to my room."

Once started Catherine could not stop until she had brought Beaulah up to date. She hugged Catherine wiped her eyes and assured her that all would be well and that she and her brother would help, but although she did not know the Morgans all that well, she did not want to deceive them. Her parents have a right to know where she is. She told Catherine that she could stay at their home but she would like to hear on her return from Canada that Catherine had informed her parents of her whereabouts.

Everton agreed with his sister, but after she left at the weekend he changed his tune and found a distant cousin who was willing to take in Catherine. This cousin was of the opinion, which Everton did not correct, that Catherine's expected child was Everton's and he needed time for his domineering sister to get use to the idea.

When Beaulah returned from Canada Everton showed her the note Catherine had left the previous week.

You both have been fantastic. I thought it over and know that you Beaulah is right I ought to go home, but I cannot at this moment.
I have a last dice to throw.

Love you lots.
Catherine

PS. Who knows I might be back

The final illness and death of Miss Vie, Aunt Vie, Gody Vie or plain Violet McKenzie affected her friends and relatives not only in Maudslay but also in London and other parts of the United Kingdom. Within a few days it was obvious that Colonel's minibus would not be big enough to transport mourners from London, so a fifty-seater coach was hired. The organisers in London advanced the time of the funeral by two hours so no one would be late for the service. Many people had remembered that Miss Vie had insisted that above all what she wanted from mourners at her burial was beautiful singing loud and clear as she was being laid to her eternal rest. The mourners accepted their responsibility and to do it right they had to be there on time.

Miss Nicey sat beside the open coffin of her sister Miss Vie below the platform of the church at Slay Cross as the eulogies from a long and impressive list of senior members of the Good News Church of God. The church was crowded with members' relatives and acquaintances all dressed in black.

Beside Miss Nicey were her immediate family. There was Vicky her only child and the latter's daughter Irone whom she had when she was fourteen or fifteen. Vicky's second group of three children were considerably younger than Irone. In fact they were between nine and three in descending order. Irone who was now the wife of an America GI looked somewhat embarrassed at being on display, grasped her little son as he buried his head into her bosom; she gazed blankly at the mourners in their crow black funereal clothes sitting impassively in a service which had already lasted more than an hour.

The death of Miss Vie had not only put an end to a life which had no visions and had produced no heirs, but had robbed the sisters of their dream of returning to Jones Town, Kingston Jamaica where they had planned to open a shop selling fried fish, dumplings fritters, coconut cakes and iced drinks. This kind of an establishment was colloquially known as a *cold supper shop*.

Between the eulogies was the singing of mournful hymns in very slow metre:

Oh Beulah Land! Sweet Beulah Land!
As on the highest mount I stand
I look away across the sea,
Where mansions are prepared for me.
And view the shining glory shore,
My heaven, my home for evermore.

The cortege stretched for nearly three quarters of a mile on its way to Slay Cross cemetery; and despite her grief Miss Nicey felt impressed that so many people had come to give her sister a 'proper' send off. She had told the chief elder that her sister had always express her disapproval of a congregation which did not sing at a funeral. Her sister had heard the phrase 'thousands of angels sing thee to your rest!' she had no idea who said it, but she had liked the idea of a thousand voices singing their reply to her prayer.

Shall we gather at the river
Where bright angel feet have trod
With its crystal tide forever
Flowing from the throne of God?

Violet had told her sister that although she will not hear the voices from her coffin she will be with the angels and from that vantage position, she will hear every note:

Yes we'll gather at the river
The beautiful, the beautiful river
Gather with the saints at the river
That flows from the throne of God.

It took the Marshalls nearly half an hour to get the cortege on its way. Eunice was supported on one side by her niece Vicky, daughter of the dearly departed Sister Violet McKenzie, and on the other by her old friend Myrtle Morgan. Progress behind the bier towards the front of the church where the Daimler funeral limousines with their directors in their pin striped trousers and black jackets ushered close family and friends in their time of grief. Once on its way the cortege stretched now for more three quarters of a mile towards Slay Cross Cemetery. The grave attendants were impatient as Violet Mackenzie was the last burial of the day. They were ready to bring their diggers determined to fill in the grave when Nello stepped forward.

"You blokes better stop right there. This is a funeral and not a building site. We goin' to bury our dearly departed with the respect which is our custom. Right fellows?"

"It is part of our culture," said Lincoln taking off his jacket and handing it to Enid as he accepted a shovel from one of the gravediggers. Alonso took the third shovel as the mourners began to sing through their tears:

Nearer, my God to thee
Nearer to thee...
Though like the wanderer...
There let the way appear...
Then with my waking thoughts
Bright with thy praise...

The official grave attendants watched from a distance with a curious mixture of anger and admiration as the grave was filled in and eventually crowned with a mound on which the mourners laid their wreathes as the final song was sung:

Sleep on beloved
Sleep and take your rest
Lay down your head
On the saviour's breast!
Good night! Goodnight!
Sister Goodnight!

V

"So is why she have to gone and leave me for? Me is the older sister," said Miss Nicey as she sat back in the deep comfort of the limousine with her head leaning against Myrtle Morgan's left shoulder. They had just left the cemetery for the church hall where the goodly women of the church had prepared a meal for the mourners.

"Miss Vie was a good person," Myrtle consoled her old friend by putting an arm around her shoulder. "She has gone home... to her rest... no more pain, no more sorrow not even hurricane, snow, cold or drought can bother her now. She is at eternal rest..."

"Miss Myrtle, you know that me was the older one and I always think that I would be the first to go and that I would be buried beside our Mammy and Pappy at our district at Guinea Fowl Walk and when her time come Vie would be put beside me. Well all that plan gone out of the window for we just put her in a grave at Slay Cross Cemetery. Well I can't leave her there on her own. I don't think that them have much black people buried at that cemetery. There might be a lot of black people buried at Mill House Cemetery in East Maudslay, so to make sure that we lay side by side when my time come I already pay for the plot next to her."

Myrtle squeezed her friend's hand.

The death of Violet McKenzie was not the beginning of the fracturing of the circle which had seen such happy times at Lilford Road, London. It was a progression. Just as one does not notice that an extra day adds intrinsically to the maturity of one's stature or to one's age so no one seemed to have noticed that the old order was changing. But changes were taking place. Two years ago the McKenzie sisters had moved to Maudslay to be close to Vicky's new family; Nello had moved out to a flat to accommodate his girl friend and their growing family and hardest of all Lincoln and Alonso were so deep in their business adventures and their studies that they were not as frequent in their visits as they used to be. Now that Isaiah had retired and with the onset of rheumatoid arthritis, high blood pressure and diabetes his wife was beginning to fear the worst, especially since Isaiah was so careless in obeying the doctor's advice. On top of all these was the absence of Catherine. Why does not she ring? Why doesn't she call? She has now passed her twentieth year and cannot be dragged back home kicking and screaming but this is still her home and she is still her child. The last one she gave birth to.

Myrtle suddenly became aware that tears were running down her cheeks. It took her a long time to retrieve her handkerchief from her handbag without disturbing Miss Nicey. Although the tears were not particularly for Miss Vie, she consoled herself that she was at a funeral and that there should be tears at a funeral.

Myrtle was not against changes. She was not afraid of death. Perhaps like most people she had some apprehension about the actual process of dying. Her faith was not as simple as Miss Nicey's who seemed to think that the physical task of being buried next to her sister was like being in the next bed and that they would be able to chat long into the eternal night. Yet at the same time she did not want to die in England. This she had discussed with Isaiah along time ago and it so perplexed him that he had promised her that should she be the one to die first he would take out a second mortgage on the house and send her body to Jamaica for interment. She squeezed his hand and said thank you. These days she watched her husband and longed for the days of long ago when he would pretend that he did not feel the cold and that he had no need of doctors apart from the annual medical test for the over sixties which London Transport Executive insisted he took at the Medical Centre upstairs Peckham Bus Garage. What if Isaiah was to die first? He had shrugged off the suggestion with his customary nonchalant, "Won't bother me none," he said "jes' stick me in a hole and cover me up. The next time you see me will be judgement day," and he would pull the blanket over his head as an act of finality and either by pretending or did he possess the good fortune of being able to fall a sleep as soon as he closes his eyes; either way Myrtle would hear his snoring slow and measured leading to the more grasping struggle like a carpenter pulling his saw through a knotted piece of timber.

But Myrtle would lie beside him thinking of that cemetery on a hillside six miles east of Kingston with an unrestricted view of the waves rolling in towards the shore line where it either rained or the sun shone all day long. It is a good place to await eternity. This could be her purgatory.

VI

"You sound' so hot and bothered," said Lurline throwing her bag in the first available chair. "What's up? Don't let your new title of Director of Cosmetics fly to your head. Although I understand that you will be required, that's Lincoln's words not mine, you will be required to visit the States and sort out the products that black manufacturers puttin' on the market."

"He has been even-handed," Puncie said defensively, "you are to be Director of Hair and Styling and it means a lot of travelling and people to hire and train. We are doing well and I have no complaints on those fronts."

"So what is up? Tell big sister after you pour me a glass of wine."

"There is always one thing that is always up and it is always up with that no good daughter of mine, Darlene," replied Puncie in some distress. "Just make me take these aspirin. Where is the water?"

"Don't tell me that she has gone out again and left you to look after her baby? My lot should be at the Library. They won't be back before eight and I have a hot date with this bloke who drives a red Jaguar. So if it is baby sitting you are after sister dear your are stuck!"

"Worst than that! Darlene gone and get herself pregnant, knocked up again!"

"Again?"

"Again. Marcus is just beginning to take his first steps."

"But Puncie, I thought she had broken up with baby' father..."

"Ah who tell you that? That no good man was interested in her once he had banged her up? Anyway you don't have to be in a relationship to get pregnant."

"And here is me thinking that she was making an effort to put her life together. I mean that things looked like they were working out since you took her into the shop as an apprentice. You even fix up that little box room at the shop as a playroom for little Marcus. She was becoming a good stylist and I know that some women were asking for her to do their hair. What is wrong with these young girls nowadays? She must be the third girl of around her age I heard of who is pregnant. Ah wonder what them thinking about? That sex is like Christmas and that is Santa Claus bringing them a toy?"

"If that is so then Santa not taking them back. He just show' his generosity each year by bringing another one. Lurline she is only seventeen. Want to know what she said to me when Ah hook her up when I found out that she pregnant again? 'Ah want to have me children when Ah young so Ah can grow up with them. Ah did'n want to grow up with her when I gave birth to her. I was nineteen I gave her to our grandmother to look after and Ah coul'n leave quick enough for Kingston to try and put me life together. Thanks to you starting out as a hairdresser I was able to learn the trade and can now earn a living. The other thing Ah tried to talk to her about contraceptive, and you would never guess what she said to me! She said that there is no fun in that."

"Fun?"

"Yes missus! To her it is like children playing chicken. You know what I mean? You see it in films when children run across road daring drivers to knock them down. Chicken!"

"Well the little bitch get caught. I did'n know about any of this, but there was some thing that had been playing on my mind, so I better say it. You have done your best for Darlene; taking her in and teaching her the trade and providing a home here for her. But she still keep pushing the boundaries. Quite a few time ah got home before you and found my lot looking after Marcus. The reason has always been that Darlene just stepped out and would be back soon and sometimes she would roll in when Marlene and Tyrone should be in bed and Lorna doing her 'O' level homework. She is just two years behind Darlene and I am beginning to have panic attack. Darlene is taking liberties. Apart from being my sister you are my best friend and I don't want any aggravation between us. Lincoln said that he would not mind which of us take over the new shop in Clapham. As you know it as a flat on the first floor..."

"Ah would like that," Puncie said in a panic. "I was hoping that we could afford to get rid of the tenants here and turn this place into a real family house..."

"Ah would like that too since you and me don't seem like getting married."

"Married! The last man in my life came to the shop and started counting my customers and was offering his services as my manger. I just told him that I was an employee so he was not to get his hopes up. I have not seen him since then..."

"Who was that? Not that Ola Somebody! His father is a big chief in Nigeria?"

"And when he said big chief he means big," and she flung her arms wide. He probably have a bus load of wives." The sisters both dissolved in laughter.

"Girl," said Lurline "we have to find ourselves a couple of blokes. Perhaps we ought to get Darlene to introduce us to her boy friends' dads..."

"I don't think my niece and I have the same taste bearing in mind the old saying that the fruit never fall far from the tree, their old men would be just after what they can get. You think we will end up like Miss Vie and Miss Nicey?"

"Heaven forbid. We both in our forties, own a house have good jobs. The right guys ought to be somewhere."

"Don't forget that we have four children between us. As for me I want to avoid men until Lorna leaves home on account of how some blokes like to fool around young girls..."

"Stop it Lurline."

"But on the other hand some of them choose their own course. Look at Miss Myrtle's Catherine. Who would have thought that she would be behaving as she is doing and causing so much grief to her parents? You know that her dad is suspicious of Lonso..."

"What about that he knocked her up and have her hidden up north in Maudslay? That is not his style..."

"So you know his style then?"

"I did once upon a time. Come to think of it so did you."

"I hope Darlene never hear about those days, because we had fun and Ah suppose there was a' element of chicken in it."

"Good ole Folly Castle." Puncie sighed. "The last thing which Darlene said to me before she left was that she might move in with her boy friend."

"But you said that she did not have a regular boy friend?"

"That was the one she was with yesterday... what the hell do I know? Ah watched her going to the gate and even walking down the street with this bloke, but I don't know what his face looks like. But when you think of it which young boy is goin' to take on a seventeen year old girl with a baby on the hip and one in the belly?"

"You remember when we first came up to this country, how we used to join queues, go and sit down next to another black person rather than push up on white people? Well the new generation said that we was weak and let the white people walked all over we and now them not taking it. Them standing up for their rights. You know what I think? It is what is going on in America and South Africa that is rubbing off on our young ones. Them see police dogs and policemen with guns chasing black people and they are re-acting..."

"And getting their backsides thrown into police cells, because the police over here seeing the same pictures and thinking that they have to toughen up their laws. Even the teachers in schools are saying that our kids are educationally backwards... that we the parents are too ambitious for our kids."

"What is wrong with ambition? Look at Alonso. When he came up he worked in factories and warehouses sweeping and cleaning up. It is just over ten years since he came up and already he has a degree and got a part time job teaching, him publishing books and before long you will have to call him Dr Campbell."

"You got to have drive. Things are too easy for this new generation. You read the local papers and it is full of pictures of our kids getting into fights and mugging people. That was not our style."

"May be not, but our kids are heading for trouble. I think we got'to call a council of war and discuss this with them. Lay it on the line that Darlene has to mend her ways or she will be out on the street. After all the law said that when they are seventeen you cannot force them to come home so it must be that when they are that age they have not got the right to ruin your home life. Right?"

"I agree, but I would'n hold me breath as far as Darlene is concerned."

VII

"Blossom was telling me the other day that you thought you saw our daughter Catherine dancing in a club in Manchester," Myrtle Morgan said as she shook Ransford Carr by the hand.

"That might have been a year ago. You know how these thinks are. We get invitations from groups all over Britain trying to convince us that they are well behaved and doing superbly well. They want us to join them in flying the flag. That sounds so patronising; I did not mean it that way. Anyway Catherine's group did not stay for drinks as they had another engagement." He quickly changed the subject. "I hear that you know my dad."

"Of course, I know your dad, Reverend Carr. T'was he who baptised me, you know? By the time I left for Kingston you were only a toddler," Myrtle explained as she shook hands with the young man who seemed to be unable to disentangle himself from Blossom. "So what this I am hearing 'bout you running off to Spain with our Blossom?"

"Oh Mrs Morgan, can I call you Gody Myrtle like everybody else?"

"Might as well."

"Where did you hear this story?"

"From an unimpeachable source, as they say in the papers."

"From where? Un... im... peach... able," Ziah stuttered, "woman mind you don' break your jawbone," warned her husband who had come closer to Ransford Carr.

"I hope these rumours do not reach the manse at Grasspiece for with a father, an uncle a grandfather and brother being men of the Cloth I am under heavy manners. Gody Myrtle, this is a well-chaperoned trip organised by a Hispanic Catholic group that my brother the Reverend Burchell in the name of Christian unity or ecumenical togetherness got involved with while studying at Boston USA. Blossom only was invited to come along when one of the women had to withdraw. I think that unimpeachable source of yours was only jealous that he was unable to come with us."

"Why is everybody looking at me?" protested Alonso.

"Yes why is everybody picking on Lonso?" asked Christine.

"I wonder why?" asked Enid.

"Now Miss Blossom," Ziah looked towards her, "I hear say form the same kinda source as me wife that Ransford should be properly addressed as Dr Carr and your brother soon to be Dr Campbell..."

"Don't forget me," interrupted Christine.

"But see me dying trouble," exclaimed Myrtle Morgan, "but that will be long time to come in the future.

"True, but you know what they say about these PhDs? They are men in a black-out room trying to catch a black cat."

"You know when we West Indians came up and started to mix with the Africans they used to insult us by saying you people from the West Indies are here to work! We Africans are here to study and go back to liberate our country and you blokes will still be here working and copying the English working class. Now it seems that every West Indian you stumble across got a degree or is studying. The last conductor they gave me told me he was studying zoology. What is he planning to do run the Kingston Zoo?"

"That could be part of it," Alonso and Ransford began to speak at the same time, and the party burst out into laughter.

"See what Ah mean?" asked Ziah. "Blossom how you gwine cope when these two lock horns discussing the price of salt fish?"

"Prophet, I will always have a mug of ice cold water to dash over them..."

"That could be quite invigorating on a very hot London day like some we had last year."

"I concur..." Alonso did not get to finish his statement as he saw Enid and Lincoln with their glasses raised approaching both Lonso and Ransford with menacing grins on their lips.

"Prophet," began Ransford, "don't want you to go on thinking that migrants have struck the academic gold mine here in this country because a few of us have degrees. As a son of the Manse I was sent off to Calabar by the time I was ten years old. That was because of a special perk of my father's job. By the time I was twenty-one I was a graduate of the new University College. That was not the way open to boys of my age like Alonso and hundreds of thousands of people my age. In other words not every migrant has a nice house like yours. We get a wider picture at the High Commission. I know of a man who was a head teacher in Jamaica and came over here hoping to teach and had to work as a bus conductor while he enrolled on a degree course because teaching is on its way to coming a degree profession..."

"A former headmaster accepting a job on the buses?" asked Christine.

"He had to pay his rent and send something for the folks back home," Ransford explained.

They had been eating Jamaican black cake and drinking red wine in the dining room, when suddenly too loud raps sounded at the door followed by a sharp harsh ringing of the bell.

"Now who can that be? Don't tell me that fool fool man on the top floor forget his key again. Christine see who that is."

"Yes Mama." She walked determinedly towards the door thinking what she would say to their only tenant who was always forgetting to take his key with him. She pulled the door towards her then stopped as if she had been stunned by a comic book ray gun. Then she let out a scream so high pitched that it might have been meant for a hound or a creature blessed with a preternatural sense of hearing!

"Kiss me raw-ted! Who-yoo! Catherine! Oonu come quick," she broke out unusually for her in Jamaican patios, but ever so good for emphasis.

Suddenly there was a scrum as everybody moved at once to get into the corridor.

"Lawd-a-mercy oh!" said Myrtle "Meck me see nuh!" as she pushed her way to the front. "Lawd-a-mercy me heart gwine jump outa me chest!"

Catherine Morgan stepped into the corridor holding a bundle which was her baby. The infant having been startled by the exuberant greeting was seized with panic as the party surged forward and the chorus of voices intensified; began a strong masculine solo. Myrtle spread her arms wide to encompass her errant daughter and her grandchild. "Ziah! Ziah come quick, quick I tell you."

The scrum parted to make way so that the grandfather and the grandmother who were also parents of the prodigal daughter could advance and they could place their arms around the newcomers and with an amalgamated effort somehow managed to drag, push and otherwise made it possible for the party to return to the dinning room. The baby continued to advertise the power of its lungs by a continuation of its bass-baritone solo.

"You are a Morgan from Chelsea Ridge in the Parish of Portland, Jamaica. That is how noisy they are!" said Christine as her twin stepped forward towards Isaiah and Myrtle Morgan and presented her son. "Mama and Dad! I am back, and this is here is your grandson Kwame Isaiah Morgan."

Myrtle stretched out her hand and lifted the scream child out of her daughter's arms and began a rhythmic march around the room followed by cooing sounds and funny faces which together somehow managed to quieten the child so through it's tear laden eyes it saw its next source of interest which was his grandmother's rather large earrings which were bobbing to the rhythm of her movements.

"Come here Ziah, this here is your first grandson. You are always complaining that with your four daughters and three grand daughters you are surrounded by women. Well here is a man child."

Ziah inched forward and made awkward attempts at lifting the baby from his grandmother's arms. The operation was comic in its execution but was in time successful. He began a gentle swinging movement of his arms where the baby was cradled. Ziah examined the child's face as intently as he himself was being observed.

"This child is half caste," announced the grandfather.

"Dad!" screamed Christine, who perhaps as aunt to the infant felt that she was next to have possession of Baby Morgan.

"Mixed race," corrected the baby's mother as she moved ahead of her sister as if her intention was to remove her child from the grandfather's arms.

"Mixed race! Half-caste! Say what you like and the result is the same: This is a white man's baby, and that is the truth," announced Ziah with the authority of one who has seem it before. The rest of the party surged forward to get a better view of the child.

"Dad you're a racist!" accused Catherine as she moved towards her father with a look of great disappointment and a determination to relieve him of her child. "

"Me not criticising," Ziah explained and at the same time he swung away from his daughter in order to retain possession of his grandson.

"What ah stating is fact and you and your baby better get used to that. Wha' you say that his name is again?"

"Kwame Isaiah Morgan," the young mother said defiantly. "

"So why you have to give him African name for?" queried Isaiah Morgan. "

"Mr Morgan there are two other names, one is Jewish and the other sounds like Welsh to me," said Ransford.

"Dear God," intervened Myrtle the proud grandmother almost penitently. "This is a life. I thank God that all this time of worrying... times when I was so frightened that the worst would happen; that the police was going to knock at the door and tell me that them found a body and... and..." she broke off as three perhaps four mighty sobs exploded in her chest.

"Mama! Mama! I'm sorry. Forgive me," pleaded Catherine turning to embrace her mother. Suddenly the other women in the room, led by Christine, had joined in one giant hug and tears were cascading down their cheeks. The men, not wanting to be excluded, formed an outer cordon as if to preserve the solemnity of the reunion. With Isaiah and the baby excluded temporarily from the group, he was able to detect that there was another person in the room he did not know and was not aware of.

"And who might you be, sir?" he directed his question to the young man who was standing next to Alonso. The young man was shorter than either Alonso or Ransford and was thick-set and darker in complexion than Lincoln.

"Me sir?" the stranger queried.

"Yessir, you. I know everybody in this room but you", explained Isaiah with authority.

"I'm Everton, sir ... that is, Everton Burke."

"I'm asking because I want to know what part you playing in all this," said Isaiah shifting his gaze from the light-skinned Alonso to the darker Everton as if he was assuring himself that neither man could have fathered Catherine's pale-skinned son.

"I'm the driver who was asked to deliver your daughter and child to this address, sir."

"Somebody pay the driver."

"I'm not a taxi, sir. Some people here will remember my sister Beulah who was the nurse who attended to Lonso when he was in hospital in Congreve Victoria Hospital. It's she who asked me to deliver your daughter and grandson to you, sir."

"Beg pardon... so much been happening and all at once," said Isaiah who must have thought that it was the father's role to maintain a stern visage. "At least you manage to bring her home, unlike some people who I won't bother to name. Ah still don't get it how your sister who is not known to me got to meet my daughter. Is that where you been all this time Catherine?"

"I am sure that the full picture will come out in time, sir, but let me just say that Beulah is a Staff Nurse in Congreve and she recognised Catherine in the line of her duties. Beyond that others will have to tell," Everton looked from Catherine to Alonso.

"Figures!" exclaimed Isaiah, "somehow it always come back to Alonso... Some times Ah think that the only way I gwine get rid of this man is to marry him off to one of me daughters. The problem is which one."

"Ziah stop playing the rum bar lawyer. For one I would like to say it like it say in the Bible... this is my daughter who was dead and she has come back to me. Lawd all those night when I woke up in cold sweat after dreaming about me child... that maybe she is murdered and her body thrown under some bush in some woods. Now she is here alive and with a child in arms. Lord Ah thank you for miracles."

"We all will say Amen to that!" said Isaiah with some reverence, then as quickly he moved on.

"Ah don't know if this baby is christened or not, but I think we ought to wet the baby head. Grandmother Myrtle you better go and bring out the Wray and Nephew over proof rum from wherever you been hiding it and make us welcome the little one into the family."

"Isaiah Morgan, you blow hot and you blow cold. I got to watch you like a hawk, because you' drinking days are over. It not like when you and Colonel used to sit down and knock off half a bottle..."

"Yes, yes," agreed her husband, "But it is time like this that Ah remember Mass Sol, my uncle saying that just like him never want to be the healthiest corpse in the grave yard him did not want to be the saddest. What Ah meanta say go get the rum."

Myrtle shuffled free of the circle and took Christine aside and whispered instructions to her. Christine nodded and as she passed Alonso she caught his hand and led him out of the room towards the rooms on the first floor.

"You want me to know the secret hiding place?"

"Here I was hoping that you would seize the chance of getting me alone in my bedroom!" she whispered conspiratorially as they started up the stairs ."Your bedroom?"

"Where else could Mama be sure dad would never go? My dad is of the old school who stopped hugging their daughters on the onset of puberty and would never enter their rooms unless accompanied and that is when they are changing the light bulb."

"Do you approve?"

"Approve or not that is how things are. I like to think he respect my privacy," they reached her bedroom door and she swivelled around so that their bodies touched.

"I've never taken a man into my room before," then as quickly she turned around and opened the door and dragged him inside with comic sauciness. She stooped and pulled a suitcase from under her bed and deposited it on the counterpane. "Now can you imagine dad riffling through my slips, bras and knickers to investigate why this case is so heavy? Look!" she encouraged him to come closer to see at least six bottles."

"So now I can be in Prophet's good book by revealing the hiding place," said Alonso. She replaced the suitcase and stood up facing him,

"Think about it! You are going to tell my dad you were in my room and you know where I keep my old bras and knickers!" She stared at him, then the old conspiratorial smile came back to her lips.

"I know he is getting shaky on his pins, but you tell me what would your chances be?"

"I see what you mean," he said and getting hold of her he embraced her quickly and tightly before turning her towards the door.

"They will be wondering what we are up to..."

"Don't worry. This is me Christine the good one, butter would not melt in her mouth..."

"I know, she is the one who proposed to me five years ago..." She stopped suddenly and pushed her elbow hard into his stomach.

"I thought you had forgotten. Although there have been times when I thought that my actions might have changed Catherine for she knew then that she would have to fight me for you. I pretended that I was shedding my ever such a good girl image..."

"Pretend! I was taken in. I almost accepted."

"Liar. I was just fifteen or there abouts. You would have been banned from the house and I would have a curfew put on me. This is where I am not like my twin sister. She dropped out of this family when she was just passed eighteen. We have not heard from her for nearly a year. Oh, the worries she put us through. My father's sister would say she put us through hell and Quatty worth, then *voila* she turned up unexpectedly with a mix-race baby and suddenly she is once again the centre of all attention!"

"You sound jealous."

"Jealous? She went off on what was to have been a three-month gig on a cruise ship entertaining passengers in the Mediterranean. We got a few postcards from her. She must have fallen for a white passenger or fellow entertainer who knocked her up and then abandoned her. Eventually she turned up playing the prodigal daughter, but ignoring the part about playing the hired hand. She shed a few tears and there she is at the centre of it all and everybody is lapping it up. I am so tired of being the good girl Christine. I wonder what would have happened if I had got knocked up? I know you would all say silent rivers run deep. What reception would I get?"

"I don't know, but I probably would be prime suspect..."

"You have missed your chances."

"That is what everybody would say, but we know differently."

"Stop hitting yourself. Your family needed you more than ever during these couple of years and you have been a brick. You kept this family together by being just you. They needed that. They depended on it. They may not have told you, but they were grateful to you for being the person you are: Christine Morgan."

"You know what at times I consider myself the dull but necessary prose leading up to that last dramatic paragraph which is my sister, the only puzzle to be solved is this; is it the end of the chapter? Or is it the beginning of a new book?"

"Christine! What keeping you up there so long?"

"Coming Mama." She said griping the bottle of rum in one hand and towing Alonso with the other she took two steps at a time down the stairs like children jumping puddles they hurried down to the waiting guests. "You took your own sweet time," accused Myrtle.

"It is the rush hour, they had to wait a long time for a bus," said Lincoln.

Christine stuck her tongue out at him as she handed the bottle to her mother who began to pour small quantities into the glasses she had arranged on the low table during her daughter's absence. Isaiah Morgan cradled his grandson in the crook of his powerful left hand and cleared his throat giving notice to all that he was about to speak. "This here is my first grandson and he was born in this the Mother Country, and we welcome him. In these your first few months," he said speaking directly to the child, " I guess that you must have faced many hardships, but I can tell from your big bright eyes and the way you grasp my finger that you are strong and you ain't going to put up with no foolishness. Dam right you won't because the years ahead ain't going to be easy. This is your Mother Country and you will have to take your rightful place and I say God bless you all who will be sailing in her."

"Amen and amen," they all said. Isaiah then dipped his right fore finger into his rum and pronounced a benediction by drawing a cross on the baby's forehead and then wiped his finger on Kwame's lips.

" Isaiah Morgan!" shouted his wife, "what are you doing to the poor infant? Give him to me," and she reached over and lifted her grandson from her husband's arms.

The baby burped loudly just as his face was parallel to his grandmother's.

"There!" said Isaiah, "you got your answer."

The party laughed as all gathered around the new addition to the Morgans at Lilford Road in the capital city of the Mother Country.